PRAISE FOR *HIDDEN*

"A rich, massive tale. A fine first effort for Victoria Lustbader."   —Anne Rivers Siddons,
New York Times bestselling author

"A luscious melodrama . . . chockful of passion, romance, and hidden desires."   —*Booklist*

"With characters ranging from robber barons to spiritualists, and settings as seemingly disparate as the trenches of World War I and the concrete canyons of Manhattan, *Hidden* explores the impact that a world in flux has upon its citizenry. Deftly, masterfully, and with the utmost compassion, Lustbader writes of families— and a world—suffering the pangs of growth while searching for grace. *Hidden* is a truly spirited debut."
—James Reese, author of
The Book of Shadows and *The Book of Spirits*

"Lustbader's debut novel, set in roaring '20s New York, updates the *Rich Man, Poor Man* plot with a *Brokeback Mountain* twist."   —*Publishers Weekly*

"The fully dimensional and deftly drawn characters keep the reader entranced with their conniving and duplicity. This [book is] hard to put down . . . and entertaining."   —*Library Journal*

"The story of these two families comes to life as the marriages, deaths, births, desires, and ambitions of the different characters jump off the page and into readers' imaginations. The characters are vibrant and full-bodied. This is a gripping story."

—*Romantic Times BOOKreviews* (4 ½ stars)

"A sprawling, character-packed, emotionally spiraling saga joining the fates of two families."

—*Kirkus Reviews*

A captivating debut novel, *Hidden* marvelously re-creates New York in the 1920s, from the hustle and bustle of the Lower East Side to the hushed hallways of the homes of the rich and powerful. In graceful, eloquent prose, Victoria Lustbader presents a fierce, compelling story of loyalty, forbidden desire, and the end of innocence.

The battlefield traumas of The Great War cement an improbable friendship between Jed Gates, scion of the wealthy Gates family, and David Warshinsky, first-generation American from New York's poverty-ridden Lower East Side. David sacrifices his family and his Jewish heritage in pursuit of his untamable ambition while, in eerie parallel, Jed sacrifices his private desires to assume the burdens of familial expectations.

David's young sister, Sarah, suffers the torments of a sweatshop and hardens her heart to the brother she once adored. Jed's rebellious sister, Lucy, becomes a nurse in Margaret Sanger's revolutionary birth control clinic. Sarah finds a tender love in sensitive Reuben Winokur, an immigrant tailor destined to prosper in his new country, but Lucy falls hard for David, who belongs to another.

Brilliantly evoking time, place, and person, *Hidden* draws readers deep into the past to illuminate the present. For nothing is more eternal than human feeling, and nothing more important to the human heart.

HIDDEN

Victoria Lustbader

A TOM DOHERTY ASSOCIATES BOOK
NEW YORK

This is a work of fiction. All the characters, organizations, and events portrayed in this novel are either products of the author's imagination or are used fictitiously.

HIDDEN

Copyright © 2006 by Victoria Lustbader

A Forge Book
Published by Tom Doherty Associates, LLC
175 Fifth Avenue
New York, NY 10010

www.tor-forge.com

Forge® is a registered trademark of Tom Doherty Associates, LLC.

ISBN-13: 978-0-7653-5463-1
ISBN-10: 0-7653-5463-2

First Edition: June 2006
First Mass Market Edition: August 2007

Printed in the United States of America

0 9 8 7 6 5 4 3 2 1

*This book is dedicated to the vibrant memory of
Rubin and Michael Schochet*

*and to my husband, Eric, and my mother, Dorothy Schochet,
my greatest fans.*

Acknowledgments

The author gratefully acknowledges the following sources of information used in the writing of *Hidden*:

America in the Twenties by Geoffrey Perrett
Gay New York by George Chauncey
The Other Side of Silence by John Loughery
The Jewish Catalog (in three volumes), edited by Sharon Strassfeld, Michael Strassfeld, and Richard Siegel
The American Heritage History of World War I by Brigadier General S. L. A. Marshall
"My First Job," by Rose Cohen, from *Out of the Sweat-shop,* edited by Leon Stein
Five Sisters: The Langhornes of Virginia by James Fox
"We Saw Him Land!" letter written by Julia Richards in 1927, from *Smithsonian Magazine,* May 2002

And last but not least, Google.com and more than a hundred invaluable sites on the Internet, for information about everything from clothing and culture, to politics and economics, to cirrhosis and contraception, historical buildings and the New York subway system, Christian Science . . . well, you get the point. Everything.

Also, a tremendous thank-you to the following people, who, directly or indirectly, through their love, generosity, talent, fearless self-expression, or force of personality, provided me with the support, inspiration, and motivation to find my own voice: Marc Strauss; Julie Sigler-Baum; David Gray; Nicholas de Fleury and his creator, Dorothy Dunnett; Greg Lichtenberg; Viggo Mortensen; the Dorph-Lowrie family; Fay and Frank Panico; Bonnie Smolen; and Nancy Lerner.

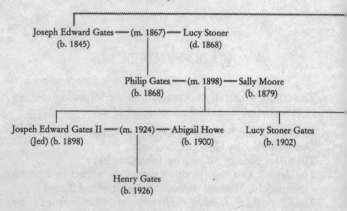

The Gates Family

Joseph Edward Gates ～～～ (m. 1867) ～～～ Lucy Stoner
(b. 1845)   (d. 1868)

Philip Gates ～～～ (m. 1898) ～～～ Sally Moore
(b. 1868)   (b. 1879)

Jospeh Edward Gates II ～～～ (m. 1924) ～～～ Abigail Howe   Lucy Stoner Gates
(Jed) (b. 1898)   (b. 1900)   (b. 1902)

Henry Gates
(b. 1926)

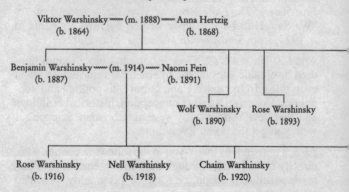

The Warshinsky Family

Viktor Warshinsky ～～～ (m. 1888) ～～～ Anna Hertzig
(b. 1864)   (b. 1868)

Benjamin Warshinsky ～～～ (m. 1914) ～～～ Naomi Fein
(b. 1887)   (b. 1891)

Wolf Warshinsky   Rose Warshinsky
(b. 1890)   (b. 1893)

Rose Warshinsky   Nell Warshinsky   Chaim Warshinsky
(b. 1916)   (b. 1918)   (b. 1920)

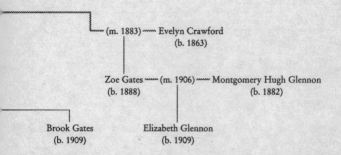

———— (m. 1883) ~~~~ Evelyn Crawford
(b. 1863)

Zoe Gates ~~~~ (m. 1906) ~~~~ Montgomery Hugh Glennon
(b. 1888)   (b. 1882)

Brook Gates   Elizabeth Glennon
(b. 1909)   (b. 1909)

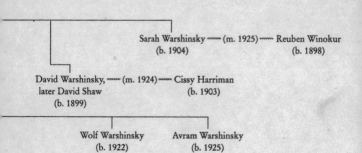

Sarah Warshinsky ~~~~ (m. 1925) ~~~~ Reuben Winokur
(b. 1904)   (b. 1898)

David Warshinsky, ~~~~ (m. 1924) ~~~~ Cissy Harriman
later David Shaw   (b. 1903)
(b. 1899)

Wolf Warshinsky   Avram Warshinsky
(b. 1922)   (b. 1925)

HIDDEN

Prologue

NOVEMBER 1927

"Joe? Are you awake?" Evelyn pushed open the door of her husband's study. Her hand, the skin still smooth and unblemished, rested on the gold-plated knob as she cautiously leaned through the doorway and peered into the dim recesses of the shadowed, overwarm room.

A still life. Joseph in his wheelchair, his back to the windows, a thick wool blanket wrapped tightly around his legs. He was always cold now. Behind him, the partially open shutters fractured the rays of the afternoon sun; a chill early-winter sun, good for decoration only. Alternating stripes of darkness and light fell across his still, thin figure. Evelyn was disconcerted by the sight of him. The stripes looked to her like the bars of a cage, imprisoning someone long used to freedom. Steam hissed from the radiators and a fire burned in the fireplace. On Joseph's lap lay the day's *Wall Street Journal,* crumpled under the weight of his limp, heavy hands. His chin rested on his bony chest, and his bifocals had slipped down to the very tip of his nose.

Evelyn walked quietly to the sitting area by the fireplace and placed the envelope that had just arrived by messenger on the low table there. She made her way to the window, relieved to see the slow rise and fall of Joe's shoulders. Breath. Life. Lately, every time she left him, even for no more than a minute, she grew anxious that she would return to find him dead. She knew it would happen soon; he was nearly eighty-three, after all, and growing frail. She knew, too, that she would never be prepared for it. After forty-five years of marriage, life without him was unimaginable.

She touched his shoulder, shook him gently. Joseph woke with a start and a grunt. His left hand flew up; the newspaper slipped to the floor. "What, what . . . ?"

"Joe, wake up," Evelyn said softly.

Joseph's head whipped up, and he was instantly alert, his blue eyes impaling Evelyn with a glare of anger. "Pick up the paper, goddamn it, and where the hell is that nurse?"

Evelyn sighed. He was very much alive and well. "She's in the kitchen preparing tea." She bent down and retrieved the *Journal,* neatened it, and replaced it on Joseph's lap. "Joe, you have a—"

"Did you see this?" he blurted, pointing to a front-page article about economic instability in Germany. "Didn't I tell that idiot Wilson that we should either wipe Germany off the face of the earth or put them back on their feet after their defeat in the Great War? I can't believe I helped the man get elected. What the hell was the matter with him, shoving that hideous treaty down Europe's throat? Everyone knew it was a mistake. Our own Congress didn't even ratify it! We crippled Germany and left them ripe for this nationalist bigot, this Hitler. He's crazy, but like a fox. That book he wrote, *Mein Kampf,* it's enough to give you nightmares, and no one is taking him seriously. I'm telling you, he's going to undermine Hindenburg and the Weimar. And the Communists—any minute now Trotsky will be out and another idiot, that Stalin, will be in. Mussolini in Italy. The whole goddamned continent is falling into chaos. And that pitiful League of Nations . . . no teeth without America's participation. The world economy is going to collapse and we're going to have another war. Why doesn't anyone see it? Why?" Joseph's rant ceased abruptly. His hands, balled into angry fists, dropped onto the paper in his lap. His eyes squeezed shut and he turned his face up to the ceiling, his head wagging quickly back and forth in frustration.

Evelyn petted his hands and waited. She said nothing. That second, debilitating stroke on New Year's Eve had left his mind as sharp as ever. He had learned to speak clearly around the droop of his mouth. He had become adept at relying on his left hand to feed himself, to read, even to button his shirt. Yet Evelyn knew what immeasurable, irrevocable damage that stroke had done. It had made everyone suddenly realize that Joseph Edward Gates was old and thus, in the next heartbeat, conclude that he was irrelevant. A lifetime of brilliance, success, influence: over. He was a relic now, treated with solicitous respect, remembered and visited, kept informed. But no longer pulled into the center of important economic or political events, his advice rarely sought, not even in matters of his own myriad businesses. He had adjusted to life in a wheelchair, to paralyzed legs, a shaking right hand that was useful for very little, speech that slurred when he was fatigued, spittle that occasionally escaped from the side of his mouth and crept down his chin. He would never adjust to being a man without power.

Joseph pushed her hands away. "Is it time for my pills? Where is that stupid nurse! Four months and she is still a moron!"

"No, no pills yet. You—"

"Then why did you barge in here while I'm trying to read? Can't I have any peace in my own house?" Joseph gave the newspaper a one-handed flap, clutched at it with the other hand, putting it up like a shaky wall between them.

Evelyn paid him no mind. The angry outburst, the sudden surrender, the soothing touch—it had become a familiar ritual to them. Since the summer, he'd begun having little seizures, and with every successive tremor that wracked him, Joseph had become more emotional. It was as though the tiny, internal rattlings had cracked open a door held tightly shut for the whole of his long, confidently lived life. Eruptions of anger and frustration, piteous bouts of weeping, came bursting out of him without provocation. Though these episodes were not frequent and he was fully himself at all other times, Evelyn had been at first terrified, not only by the emotions themselves, so foreign in their relationship, but also by the fear that Joseph was losing his mind. But Dr. Barre had assured her that this leaking out of pent-up emotion and uncensored verbiage was not uncommon among elderly people who had suffered bodily trauma. Patience and detachment were called for. After a time, Evelyn came almost to relish Joe's episodes, would have hungered for them were it not for the obvious pain they caused him. They revealed his hidden core, in incomplete, hurried glimpses—something urgent caught in the weak lens of an amusement-park penny telescope, its time about to expire, blackness coming down.

Now she sighed and allowed his harsh words to blow by her like a sudden swirl of wind. He wasn't angry at her, didn't mean to be rude to her, although he occasionally snapped at her like a mad dog. It was that he was too weak to do battle with the losses in his life, with the unhappiness and grief in his family. He couldn't fix things anymore. She bent down to tuck the blanket more securely around his useless legs.

"Stop that!" he yelled, pushing her away with surprising strength. "I can't stand it when you hover over me like some demented old hag. What do you want, anyway?"

"A messenger has delivered an envelope for you. From Leonard Hillman," she said. "He said it was important. I've been trying to tell you."

Evelyn saw the stab of fear in Joseph's eyes and felt cold despite the heat of the room. "I left it on the table by the fire. Shall I bring it to you?" She laid her hand on his shoulder and, rather than brushing it off, he covered it briefly with his own and stroked her fingers.

"No, leave it where it is." Slowly and with effort, Joseph folded the newspaper and placed it on the round lamp table next to his chair. "Please, Evelyn, open the shutters and then leave me alone."

He knew her so well, as she knew him. With that small touch they shared his agitation, her desire to know its cause, his need for privacy, the love and patience they had always had for each other. Evelyn didn't say a word, although now she was sure there had been something more than debility causing his terrible moodiness of the past month. She cast a curious glance at the plain-looking envelope as she left the room, as though she might divine its contents.

As the door closed behind her, Joseph ran his fingers through hair the color of old, yellowed snow. It was amazingly thick still but had long since faded from its former golden glory. His hands wandered over the breast of his lounging robe, smoothing the midnight-blue silk. He tried to empty his mind of expectations. In total secrecy, he had hired Hillman to investigate Jed's accident. Rejecting the obvious, Joseph sought confirmation of what he believed must be a more satisfying truth. A month ago, he thought that would quell his rage and helplessness. But what if he was wrong? Or what if he was right? Would one truth be more acceptable than another? Would any truth change what had happened?

He wheeled himself around to face the window and looked out at the fairyland of frost-glazed Central Park, serene and majestic beyond the bustle of Fifth Avenue. From here on the ninth floor the life below seemed doll-like and unreal. Figures in long coats leaned into the ferocious wind as they pushed their way up and down the avenue. A shiny yellow LaSalle, Cadillac's newest model, with curves as graceful as a young girl's, was parked in front of a building down the block. The doorman was helping a woman, bundled in fur coat and hat, into the backseat. Strangers, going about their trivial lives. For the first time in Joseph's own life, he envied another human being. What more did that woman have on her mind than staying warm on an unseasonably frigid November day in New York?

He took a deep breath and straightened his back so that he sat high in his chair, like a dog on point. He swiveled away from the window and maneuvered himself to the sitting area. The wing chair nearest the fireplace had been removed to make room for his bulky wheelchair. He inched close to the granite hearth. The heat felt good on his skin but did nothing to dispel the chill that had taken up permanent residence inside him. Maybe he should just throw the envelope into the fire unopened. Stop imagining possibilities that even Hillman, a man equal to himself in his distrust of humanity, had discouraged him from entertaining. But no. It would go against his deepest nature to let lie any situation that nagged at him; Joseph hadn't become one of the wealthiest and most successful men in the country by leaving business unfinished.

He reached for the envelope, opened it, and withdrew a surprisingly puny report. As Joseph unfolded the single sheet of paper, he remembered something Hillman had said during their last conversation. That his clients fell into one of two types: those who thought they knew all the answers before the questions were ever asked and those who were hopelessly, stubbornly confused and wanted him to discover the things they already knew but could not bear to believe. Hillman admitted that he usually preferred the latter sort—they were better prepared for the truth. At the time, the comment had seemed amusing, the gentle chiding of a client with whom he had a special rapport. Joseph realized now that Hillman had been warning him to not invest too richly in his preconceptions.

Joseph read. He was firm of resolve, determined to treat this like any business situation—get the facts, act on them, come out on top. He read the terse report and thought only, *How concise and well presented this is.* He was aware that his mind had gone quite blank. It was an odd and unsettling feeling. He gazed into the fire for a moment, blinking furiously, trying to clear his head of the numbness that had crawled over his scalp and seeped into his brain. He had understood every word and yet the meaning seemed to have eluded him. And so he slowly read again, dragging his consciousness through the chilling reality like a blizzard-blind man struggling through dense, high snow. Such a strong desire to lie down and go to sleep, only the instinct to survive pushing him on.

He leaned forward, placed the paper on the table, and found that he had no strength to straighten up. He rested his forehead in his good left hand, and when a hot tear fell onto his arm realized that he was crying. His tears pooled in his glasses and dripped onto the table, onto the cold facts lying exposed on an innocent piece of paper. He felt sick to his stomach as clashing waves of revulsion, anger, disbelief, and love swept through him. This was beyond unexpected; it was inconceivable. And yet he knew it was true, with all its implications; knew it surely and profoundly.

He remained hunched over the table until his muscles stiffened and began to ache. Until his tears stopped, his breathing slowed, his head began to clear. He became aware once again of the snap and crackle of seasoned wood transformed into light and warmth, and he grew calmer. He whispered into the hot, dry air, "I am too old; I cannot deal with this." He heard his own words as though spoken by another, by some cowardly pup telling him that he was too fragile and could no longer act. But he was only playing with himself, throwing out a challenge so that he could rise to it and prove what he was still capable of.

He sat up, took his handkerchief from his gown pocket, dried his tears, and blew his nose. He had decisions to make. Who would he love and who would he condemn? Who would he forgive and who would he destroy? Who would he tell and who would he protect? He had only to formulate the questions in his mind to begin to know the answers. Of one decision there was no doubt.

He folded the paper and replaced it in its envelope. He wheeled himself to the side of the room opposite the windows and slid the envelope under the mattress of the daybed that, since the summer, occupied the space against the wall where once stood a massive mahogany bookcase and where he now spent his mostly sleepless nights. He turned and wheeled himself to the bedroom door, swung it open, and called out into the hallway. "Evelyn? Evelyn!"

He heard the clink of a teacup against its saucer, then her quick, light footsteps moving toward him from the drawing room. "Coming, Joe." Her voice sailing through the air like a lifeline.

Evelyn had been waiting patiently, drinking cup after cup of aromatic Earl Grey tea without tasting it. When she heard him call her name, she immediately marked that his voice held none of the querulousness of the past month. In his room there was a noticeable absence of the disquiet that had filled the space like a penetrating fog. Joe sat by the fire, gazing into the flames, still but not tense. She settled herself onto the love seat across from him. As she did, she glanced discreetly around the room, but there was no sign of the envelope she had brought to him earlier. When he turned to her, she spontaneously smiled to see how clear his eyes were, how serene his countenance.

Joseph returned Evelyn's smile. "Looking for that envelope, were you?"

Her smile broadened and she tilted her head questioningly. "Why do I not believe this was about Leonard taking a position with the company?"

"Because you are a smart woman," he said tenderly, admitting that he had lied to her a month ago about why Leonard Hillman had come to see him. "It was about something potentially serious with a senior employee. Happily, it turned out to be nothing," he lied again.

They sat for a moment, content to simply look at each other. Finally, Joseph took a deep breath, let it out with an audible sigh. "You look very beautiful today. I love that dress on you."

She made a little noise of surprise. It seemed such an odd moment to say such a thing; Joseph's way of apologizing for a month of barking. "Thank you. I'm glad. It's still one of my favorites."

"Evelyn. Come sit next to me." He patted the arm of a second wing chair that had been left in its place. "And pour us some brandy, why don't you?"

"Ignoring Dr. Barre's advice again, are we?"

"I consider it my obligation to do so from time to time, as you know."

"Good for you."

She went to the granite-topped sideboard that stood opposite the fireplace. She brushed her hand over the cool green stone, absorbing its elemental solidity, its reassuring durability. She poured generous amounts of brandy into two Baccarat snifters, settled herself in the chair, and handed the slightly fuller snifter to Joseph.

He raised the glass toward her, holding it steady as a rock in his left hand. Illuminated by the fire, the amber liquid seemed infused with a magical, life-giving energy that glowed in the air between them.

"Evelyn. My love. My one and only love. I think it's

time finally to talk about Zoe. I want us to talk about her."

Evelyn drew in a sharp, quaking breath. Oh so carefully, her hand shaking just a little, she placed her glass on the table and turned her eyes to him. Her mouth began to tremble. "Yes. Oh please, yes. Can we do that now?" she whispered.

"We can. We can tell one another how much we miss her. How much we love her."

Silent tears crept down Evelyn's face. She nodded mutely.

With difficulty, he leaned over the arms of their abutting chairs and kissed her wet cheek. "Even your tears are beautiful to me. Evelyn, what would I be without you?" He smiled, forcing a small one from her in return. "We'll spend the afternoon drinking brandy and talking. About Zoe, and about Jed. And about other things as well. We've had such a life together and there's so much that needs to be said before it's too late. I'm running out of time, Evie, and you know how I hate to leave business unfinished."

Late in the night, Evelyn gave up trying to sleep. Her heart was calm, but she was wide awake and vibrating with emotion. There was, of course, some small speck of sadness for a past that could have been different, but Evelyn was not one to dwell on the past. What she felt most strongly was joy for what she and Joseph had the chance to share now, in the present and for as long into the future as he might still be with her.

She got out of bed and pulled on her satin robe. She tiptoed past his room on her way to the kitchen and heard the gurgling of soft snores coming from behind his partially opened door. It made her heart lighter yet to know that he slept, that their talk had calmed him, too, enough to overcome the sleeplessness that had beset him for months.

Working quietly by the meager illumination of a nightlight, not wishing to wake any of the staff, she made a pot of camomile tea. She poured a cupful, sweetened it with loosestrife honey, and took it into the drawing room. She sat on the deep-red leather sofa, turned on the reading lamp. Through the Tiffany shade, the lamplight glowed with vibrant jewel tones, spreading over her like a rainbow. After a few sips, she put down her cup and picked up the family photo album that lay on the glass coffee table. She began leafing through it, the long history of the Gates family revealed in a series of frozen images. She wondered if everyone and everything would look different to her now.

Evelyn turned the pages, lingering on the photographs she loved best. A spotted, brown tintype of Joseph's long-dead parents. One stained and creased photo of Lucy, his first wife, who had died giving birth to Joseph's son, Philip. Evelyn and Joseph's wedding at her parents' home in Hyde Park. Dear lost Zoe, perched like a queen atop Sirocco, her gallant horse; Evelyn stopped and traced her daughter's youthful face with her fingertip, over and over. After a while, she went on. Philip and Sally's wedding. Countless baby pictures of Jed, Lucy, Brook. And little Elizabeth. She came then to one of her most favorite of all, the one of the two beautiful boys: Jed and David on a clear spring day in France in 1918, before the war found them, their uniforms new and crisp, their arms around each other's shoulders, light head leaning against dark, grinning into the camera like a pair of baby baboons.

Such unlikely friends, from opposite worlds. Such different people, David quick hungry fearless, Jed languid and quiescent. So many friendships forged in the hardships of war cooled and disintegrated with the resumption of normal life. But theirs had flourished. Was that it? Was it David, the unexpected guest who came and never left, who had somehow directed the course of their family's fate? Would anything have turned out differently if he'd been left to slip back into the life he'd been born to? But he was so determined to leave it and Jed was so insistently eager to help him, to keep him close. Foolish thoughts. David was part of their family, essential and beloved. Hadn't she and Joe spoken of him, too, today, as much as of anyone else?

Evelyn closed the album. No, she wasn't one to dwell on the past. And yet she couldn't help herself from wondering, just for the space of this private, quiet moment, what all their lives might have been like if she and Joseph had been able to share their tears and their anger and their fear and all their love, everything in them, as they had this afternoon, from the beginning of their marriage and not merely at its end. Her heart grew suddenly heavy again. She wanted more of this than she was going to get. She reached for her cup, for one last warming sip, but the tea was pale and cold as ice.

～ PART ONE ～

June 1917–January 1919

1

Jed was fidgeting uncontrollably. After torturous hours of waiting, he was nearly to the long row of tables manned by army officials registering the endless line of men who had come to the 69th Regiment Armory to enlist. Men between the ages of twenty-one and thirty-one were required to register. Jed was only eighteen, but the decision to join up had come upon him like a thunderbolt on the very day in April that war had been declared. It had come to him with the undeniability of a sign from God. He did not question it and for two months had refused to consider the consequences of having made a major life decision on his own when all previous decisions had been made for him by his mother and grandfather. Rather, he had told no one, not even his sister, Lucy. He had kept his plan a secret so that his mother would have no chance to subvert his will and take his choice away from him. But during these past four hours amidst a restless crowd of rough and determined-looking men, Jed had grown increasingly confused as to just what he imagined he was doing. A sudden urge to turn and flee, to save himself— although he couldn't say from what—took hold of him. Now, the deed about to be done, he struggled to maintain his faith in the face of his dread of his mother's reaction. His stomach clenched into a fist as he pictured himself telling her what he had done. His equilibrium teetered and his body torqued. With one graceless lurch his elbow landed firmly in the back of the man in front of him. The fellow whirled around faster than a guard dog, jaw set with menace.

"I'm so sorry. Nerves, you know. Having trouble standing still."

Jed's apologetic blue gaze collided with a pair of feral light brown eyes shot through with golden specks. He felt as though something had slammed into his chest. The eyes bored through him, taking his measure and dismissing him in the few seconds it took to look him up and down. Without responding to Jed's apology, the other man turned away. Although Jed had been the one rudely treated, he knew that it was he who must have somehow done something inappropriate, shown himself to be dismissable. He was instantly embarrassed by his beautifully tailored silk gabardine suit, his elegant hat pushed back on his thick dark-blond hair, by the fact that he was comfortably cool in the clotted June heat. The man in front of him was sweating into his well-worn, coarse cotton clothing; his brown hair was damp and unruly, inexpertly cut. Yet despite his obvious low-class origins and the fact that he couldn't have been much older than Jed himself, once seen full-on he was impossible to ignore. He exuded a spiking, confident energy, even now, with his back turned. It washed over Jed like a balm and subdued his cowardly urge. He squared his own jaw as his confidence returned.

David turned his back on the man behind him, aware that he was being rude and not caring. There was no point in talking to someone like that, a wealthy *goy*, the undoubtedly pampered son of a long line of pampered sons who had gotten rich exploiting poor immigrant families like his own. People with sleek golden hair and long elegant limbs encased in suits of fine material, people who looked like they owned the world and knew they deserved it, didn't want to know people like David. What right did golden boy have to look at him with friendly eyes? He didn't mean it. David had met plenty of people like him before. If they were to speak, he'd be unfailingly polite and leave David feeling like a servant.

The last man between him and the registration table was finally finished being processed and David stepped up quickly, eager to get this ordeal over with and leave. As he held out his papers, an older, larger man rushed forward and tried to elbow him aside. The jockeying had been going on all day, as hot, weary men took advantage of the loosely monitored lines; the soldiers had broken up several fights already. David pushed back and barked, "Hey, I got here first. Wait your turn."

The man grabbed David's arm and shoved him away from the table. "Get outta my way, you little snot. I been waitin' here six hours. Go back to your mommy for a diaper change."

With the finely honed instincts of the eternally persecuted and perpetually defensive, David chopped down on the man's wrist with his free hand and kicked viciously at an exposed ankle. *"Putz! Kush meer in tokhes!"*

The man yelped in pain. "Fuck you, kike!" He lunged at David, his greater weight bringing them both crashing to the floor. David flailed at the man's sides and face, trying to land at least one good punch. Before either man had a chance to do any damage, they were pulled apart and yanked to their feet, voices of authority telling them to cut it out, now.

Mesmerized, Jed watched the altercation unfold in front of him. He heard every ugly word, could almost feel each increasingly violent contact. He saw rage suffuse the exotic features of the boy pinned to the ground, his dusky olive skin now redly undertinged with his racing blood. Jed's own blood rose and his heart beat wildly. Before he knew what he was doing, he had thrown a hold—perfected during years as captain of the wrestling team at Browning—around the bull neck of the older man, dragging him off his slighter prey, hissing at him, "We don't use such language in civil society."

Soldiers materialized around the tussling threesome. One of them pulled Jed off the big man and began leading him toward the tables at the far end of the hall. He patted Jed's back. "Nice work there, son. Wish more like you were signing up." But Jed wasn't interested in the soldier's approbation. He wrenched around, his eyes searching for the boy on the ground. He was on his feet now, being herded in the opposite direction. His mouth was slightly open as though he wanted to speak, and he was staring directly at Jed. Their eyes locked and Jed's head swam as he read the boy's thoughts in his piercing, distrustful gaze. *Who are you? Why did you help me? What do you want?* Jed didn't know the answers.

David emerged into the early-afternoon furnace of 26th Street and Lexington Avenue, the air only barely cooler on the street than it had been inside the Armory building. He knew he should catch the Second Avenue El downtown and get back to work as quickly as possible, but he needed to move, to shake out his pent-up energy. Before exiting the still-mobbed hall, he had taken a second to look for the blond boy who had pulled that miserable bigoted piece of shit off him; it wouldn't kill him to say thank you. He hadn't seen him, nor did he see him in the crowd of men milling around the Armory's entrance. It was impossible to find anyone. David gave up and began walking.

Lexington Avenue ended at 21st Street, at small, lush Gramercy Park. David stopped and leaned into the tall wrought-iron fence, breathed in the tree-cooled air. He rattled at the locked gate, meant to keep out intruders like himself; only residents of the elegant buildings around the park had keys to this private green oasis. David's gaze swept across the park's interior and then took in the brownstones, town houses, and low apartment buildings bordering it on all four sides. This was where he would live someday, he promised himself for the thousandth time. He would have a key and the right to breathe its perfumed air any time he chose.

David walked on, around the park's perimeter and down Irving Place, unaware that a blond boy, cool in ecru silk gabardine, a key to the park in his pocket, walked carefully half a block behind him.

Jed waited outside the Armory entrance until he saw the dark-haired boy come out. He saw the yellow-flecked eyes scan the crowd and he shrank back against the red stone wall. He thought the boy might be looking for him. He didn't know what he would say. He watched the mop of dark hair, long and curling against the collar of a faded blue shirt, bob down Lexington Avenue, and he followed at a safe distance. He stopped across 21st Street while the boy leaned on the park fence, then followed him again, past his own front door at 21 Gramercy Park South, down Irving Place, into the hubbub of 14th Street, west two blocks to Broadway, turning downtown again to 13th Street, where the boy disappeared into the ornate entrance of the Horn & Hardart Automat. Jed stood outside, his heart pounding. What was he doing? Why was he so intrigued by this angry, disheveled Jew in shabby clothing? Jed came from a world far above his; they couldn't possibly have anything in common. And yet Jed wanted to look into those eyes again, see the unwavering conviction in them that he'd seen this morning.

He'd never been inside an Automat. Mother said it was for the hoi polloi. But he'd heard that they had delicious coffee and he was fascinated by the idea of depositing nickels into a slot, opening a little door, and finding food waiting there for you. And today was certainly the day for disobeying his mother. He slipped into the hungry human stream and let himself be swept away.

"Mind if I join you?"

David looked up from his dish of macaroni and cheese to see the blond boy standing at the table, a cup of coffee in one hand and a small plate with two chocolate-frosted cupcakes in the other. A hopeful smile on his handsome Gentile face. David covered his surprise by waving carelessly at the chair across from him and muttering, "Suit yourself."

Jed put his coffee and cake on the table, lowered himself into the surprisingly comfortable chair. In an agitated rush that revealed a nervousness he could not control, he proceeded to lie, as he knew he must. "What a coincidence! I was coming for a cup of this great coffee when I saw you through the window. Thought I'd come over and make sure you were all right."

"I'm fine," David said, blunt and ungenerous. He stared impolitely at the smooth, pale face until the genial smile froze in confusion. He retreated, tilted his head in a gesture of acknowledgment. "I appreciate what you did. Thank you."

"Forget it," Jed said. Faint pink stains bloomed on the ivory skin of his cheeks. "That fellow was an animal. I was afraid he'd bash your head in. What did you say to him, anyway?"

"I called him a dick and told him he could kiss my ass. I doubt if he understood Yiddish, but he sure as hell knew I'd insulted him."

David stared into eyes the color of those little flowers on the climbing vine some optimist had planted in a stingy patch of earth by the back porch of the settlement house on Henry Street: not quite blue, not quite lavender, not pale, but not dark, either. He waited to see their innocent curiosity turn to revulsion now that he'd revealed himself as a Jew and paraded his crudeness and lack of self-discipline. When he saw the eyes filling with genuine amusement, he grinned despite himself, and suddenly they were both laughing, at the lunacy of what had happened, at the unlikelihood of having managed to start a conversation.

Jed wiped his eyes and held out his hand. "I'm Jed Gates. Well, Joseph Edward really, but everyone calls me Jed."

The slightest delay, just a heartbeat, before David offered his hand in return. "David Warshinsky."

Warshinsky shook hands warmly enough, but Jed had noted his hesitation. "I won't hit you in the back again; I promise," he joked.

"I wouldn't let you." David scrutinized Jed thoroughly, his gaze lingering on the expensive suit, the swell hat, the gleaming hair, the friendly face. Men like Jed rarely offered to shake David's hand. His wariness returned. Still, there was something in the clear blue eyes, something honest and ingratiating, that softened David's reflexive distrust and dislike. Softened but did not eradicate. He stretched his legs out in front of him and crossed his arms over his chest. "You don't look like someone who'd be comfortable shaking hands with a low-class Jew."

Jed was taken aback, but only momentarily. He had met Jews; he'd even recognized that David had cursed that man in Yiddish. Jews were all around Wall Street, all around Hanover Square where the Gates Building was. He worked with a few during his summers at J. Gates, his grandfather's department store, and never thought twice about what they were. His grandfather had Jewish business colleagues. His father, too, knew fellow artists who were Jews, emigrants from Eastern Europe. But Jed had never known his family to socialize with a Jew, let alone one so obviously from the lowest working class. Jed wasn't stupid; he knew that no Jew, not even a wealthy, successful one, was truly welcome in the world he inhabited. He thought it best to simply ignore David's challenge.

"That man who jumped on you, he thinks we're too young to be in the army." Jed put a swagger of unconcern into his voice to hide his fear that the man might be right.

"Yeah, well, he's just full of shit," David said unhesitatingly. "An eighteen-year-old can fight as well as anyone. Believe me, I know."

"You're eighteen? So am I. You seem older."

"Poverty has a way of aging you quickly," David said flatly. "What the hell are you staring at?"

Jed was staring at David's face, a perfectly young, imperfectly arresting eighteen-year-old face, now that Jed looked carefully. He was staring specifically at the five-inch white filament of an obviously old scar that ran from just in front of David's left ear down along his jawline and disappeared under his chin.

"Did you get that in a fight?" Jed knew he should drop his eyes, but he couldn't.

"No. I got it when someone who looked a lot like you took serious offense at my trying to kiss his sister."

He held Jed's eyes, his look bold and invasive. Jed felt himself squirm inside. He understood how someone might want to hit David. Then David smiled and his eyes warmed. Jed felt as though the sun had emerged from behind a cloud to shine just on him.

"Jed. Go on, drink your coffee before it gets cold."

Jed tore his eyes from David's face and took a cautious sip. "Oh my God! This *is* really good coffee!" He looked down at the heavy porcelain cup as though it had mutated to gold in his hands.

"Haven't you had it before? It's the best coffee in the city."

"Yes, well, no, well actually . . . I've never been in here before at all. My mother most definitely would not approve."

David smirked. "And do you do everything your mother tells you?"

"Oh no. She certainly didn't tell me to enlist, I can assure you." Jed didn't see David's face or catch the baiting edge in his voice. In delighted shock over the deliciousness of the coffee, Jed had turned his attention to one of his cupcakes. He took an exploratory bite and all but moaned in pleasure. "I can't believe this! These are as fabulous as anything my grandmother's cook makes! Who would think something so cheap could be so good!"

He looked up to share his discovery and found himself impaled by a hot, stony glare. He blanched. He held out the plate. "Here, please, have one. I can't possibly eat both."

"Mommy wouldn't approve?" David said sarcastically. He stared at Jed's ashen face, at the unspoken apology in his eyes. He noticed that the slim-fingered hand with its neatly clipped nails shook slightly as it held the plate in the air. David slowly reached out and took the cake.

"Thanks. So, if Mommy didn't tell you to enlist, why did you? Why would you want to join the army when you have everything you could possibly want handed to you on a silver platter at home?"

Caught off guard again by David's hostile directness, Jed blurted out the truth. "I wanted to do something that my mother didn't think of for me." A deep blush rose quickly in his paled skin. "Something she wouldn't approve of."

David let out a little grunt and coughed, pretended to choke on a cupcake crumb. Jed's reason for enlisting wasn't all that far from his own.

"What about you, David? Why are you enlisting? Does your family know? Mine doesn't. I'm supposed to be starting at Columbia in the fall, not reporting to training camp. I can't imagine what I'm going to tell my mother." Jed licked chocolate frosting off his fingers.

"No. My family doesn't know. And I'm enlisting because if I'm going to have the life sucked out of me, I at least want to get to choose who does it and why." David looked down at his macaroni and cheese, gone cold and congealed into an unappetizing yellow mass. "Also because I think it's the right thing to do."

"Yes, exactly! It *is* the right thing to do!"

"Well, if we get killed, it will have been a very stupid thing to do," David said wryly. "But it was the quickest and best way I could think of to get the hell out of the Lower East Side and away from the nothing life everyone wants me to be happy with."

"I didn't even think of it. It just sort of came to me," Jed said simply, and then grinned as though to show that he wasn't ashamed of his lack of initiative. "And anyway, I don't intend to get killed."

David made a little snorting sound. "Actually, neither do I. But then I don't imagine anyone does."

"No, really. I was . . . I was . . . called to enlist; it was like a vision. I can't believe God means me to die. I know He'll keep me safe."

"I thought it was a vision of your mother having a fit that called to you."

Deaf to David's taunting, Jed said earnestly, "No, I think it's God's way of leading me where I need to go. A way to show my mother that I'm a man now, that she can let go of me."

David was rendered speechless by the intimate revelation Jed had unknowingly given up. He laughed a little, busied himself with a healthy bite of cupcake. He pushed down on the tendril of affection that wanted to rise inside him.

"You think I'm a fool, don't you?" Jed said, misinterpreting David's reaction.

"No, no. I don't. It's just . . . I don't believe in God."

"How can you not believe in God?"

"It's easy. You should try it. Just look around you."

"No. I don't understand. How can you do this if you don't believe that God will protect you?" Jed had never had a conversation even remotely like this in his entire life. David was so different from anyone he had ever met. In Jed's world, reserve and decorousness were revered. It was hideously bad manners to burden others with disquieting emotion or opinion. Jed had known this even before he knew how to speak, the knowledge embedded like nourishment in the formula his nurse had fed him. No one had ever had to tell him how to behave. Grandfather and Mother were certainly intense enough. But their intensity was cold, focused and purposeful. David's was hot and unruly; it flared in his eyes like an eruption of sunspots. Without thinking, Jed started to reach across the table to touch him, to feel his heat, and immediately pulled back his hand.

David made no sign that he'd noticed Jed's motion. "I think probably we're both fools. You think God will protect you and I think I can protect myself. The truth is, we'll just have to be lucky." He pushed his plate away. "I've got to get back to work. Stay; enjoy your virgin visit to the Automat." He stood up. "Thanks for the cupcake." This time, he was first to hold out his hand. "You're a nice guy, Jed. I'm sorry if I was rude. But if you're going to survive the war, you'd better learn how to get angry and defend yourself." He was teasing. If Jed had been someone from his own world, he would have said, *See you at the baths,* or, *How about a game of handball on Saturday?* Those were not things he could say to someone like Jed.

Jed jumped to his feet, took David's hand. "Well, maybe you can teach me." If David had been a fellow met at school or during an evening at the Club, Jed would have said, *Say, give me your number,* or, *Lunch at Delmonico's next week?* But not to this person.

David laughed. "If we were together, I wouldn't have to teach you. I'm angry enough for the both of us." He let go of Jed's hand and started to walk away. "Take care of yourself."

"You, too." Jed stood stiffly by the table, his hand slowly

falling back to his side. "Maybe we'll see each other again."

David turned back and shrugged. "Sure. Who knows."

Jed watched David thread his way through the big room and onto the street. He caught one last glimpse of him through the plate-glass window, working his way up Broadway, undoubtedly heading for the 14th Street El stop. Jed had planned to spend the afternoon on a shady bench in Gramercy Park with his sketch pad and charcoals. But that was before. Now he would hail a taxicab and go downtown. He could no longer keep his enlistment a secret, at least not from everyone. Nauseating as was the prospect of defending his decision to his grandfather, Jed had to convince Joseph, who had fought in the Civil War, to understand, to conspire with him, and to help him. Jed needed Joseph to dip into his vast ocean of influence and arrange for a certain David Warshinsky to be assigned to the same training camp as fellow enlistee Joseph Edward Gates II. He couldn't leave it to chance. Maybe wasn't good enough. He had to know that he would see David again.

2

"Rachel, it's almost sundown. I have to get to Gershon's before they close. We both have to get home." David gently untangled her arms from around his neck.

They were alone in the alley behind Levy's, the men's and women's clothing store where David had worked, six days a week, from the time he was twelve years old until today. The perpetual din of the Lower East Side was a muffled backdrop to their parting.

"You'll write to me every week?" Rachel resisted his strong hands, tried and failed to keep her hold on him.

"Of course I'll write to you."

"And you'll come back." Her voice was steady, but there

were tears in her dark brown eyes. "Tell me you'll come back, because I'm going to wait for you."

David glanced impatiently down the alleyway. "Rachel, don't. Don't do that. This past year was great, but I don't know what's going to happen in the future."

"I'm going to wait for you!" she said fiercely. "I love you."

He smiled and kissed her. "Thank you for keeping my secret all summer. Come on. I'll walk you home." He took her hand and led her out of the alley, to the soot grey tenement on Eldridge Street where the Cohens lived. There, he held her and kissed her again, and left her.

David quickly retraced his steps, past Levy's, its door now locked. A block farther on, he slipped through Gershon's closing door and, with a charming smile of apology, picked up the two loaves of challah that Mrs. Gershon saved for him every week. He exited the bakery and continued pushing his way through the discourteous crowds. It was Friday evening, an hour before sundown. Everyone was in a rush to get home. It was Shabbos eve and tomorrow was the day of rest. Tonight, in every apartment on the Lower East Side, Jews were preparing Shabbos dinner, grand or sparse as their means allowed. At the Warshinskys', dinner would be fine: Anna's incredible chicken soup, then the boiled bird served with roasted potatoes and carrots, a noodle kugel sweetened with sugar, cinnamon, and raisins, homemade applesauce, sweet wine, and challah.

He clutched the two shiny-crusted loaves of egg bread under his arm, salivating as the yeasty aroma wafted toward his face. The delicious smell of the warm bread, carrying with it centuries of tradition, mingled in his nose with the crisp evening air of early autumn. Only a week past Labor Day and already, as abruptly as though a great celestial switch had been thrown, the stifling humid air of August was gone, replaced by September's poignant yet invigorating clarity. David felt himself a blood-and-bone manifestation of the changing season. Over the three long months since he'd enlisted, his initial guilt and melancholy had slowly been supplanted by a sharp, resentfully suppressed excitement. Today had been his last day at Levy's; tonight would be his last Shabbos with his family. Tonight he would tell them that he was leaving tomorrow to become a soldier, an action that constituted the greatest possible execration imaginable for their beliefs and their history. An entire sweltering city summer had not managed to sweat out of him the explanation that would make his decision acceptable to them. As he shouldered his way home, he tried in vain to picture how this evening could end in anything but disaster.

The teeming streets did nothing to calm him. A lifetime of familiarity with the mass of immigrant humanity had not made the constant activity and unrelenting noise any less of an irritant to his senses. Shrewd women with shrill voices haggling loudly over prices, pushcart merchants singing out like auctioneers as they hawked their merchandise, unsupervised children yelling as they scurried like little animals around adult legs, shop owners standing in their doorways importuning passersby to examine their wares, pious men mumbling prayers as they shuffled along or swayed on street corners, oblivious to the hordes. This daily tumult assaulted David's American ears in a jumbled cacophony of languages: Yiddish, Italian, German, Hebrew, Polish, Russian, Lithuanian . . . a veritable Tower of Babel. He was fluent in three of those languages and conversant in the others but for years had refused to speak anything but English, except when commerce or mischief absolutely demanded it.

The evening cooled and darkened quickly as the sun fell behind the buildings beyond the Bowery, the broad avenue that marked the western edge of the Jewish ghetto. Some Italians still lived there, but the neighborhood had been overrun by an influx of mostly Russian Jews who had arrived in the past two decades, adding to the existing Jewish population in this warren of streets south of Houston and east of the Bowery. A soothing peacefulness began to settle over the strictly bordered universe. It happened every week, as the daily struggle for survival was set aside from sundown Friday to sundown Saturday, twenty-four hours to rest, to thank God for His blessings.

David was late. He knew he shouldn't dawdle. But as the world around him grew still and dim, he became more and more reluctant to go home. He suddenly realized that he might never walk these streets again, that he might die in the war, that if he lived he would never want to come back. But he was here now and there was a little piece of his life on every block. That was the butcher from whom he'd stolen a chicken when he was eight years old and not in the mood for fish for dinner. Innumerable pickles from those barrels had disappeared into his mouth when no one was looking. On that corner he'd had his arm broken by a gang of Italian boys. Across the street was where he'd broken one of their noses with his cast the next week. He'd kissed some girl in almost every doorway. There was the elementary school, inside whose dirty brick walls David had been an angel, his ravenous desire to learn taming the little devil in him. Once out the doors his wings and halo had vanished. He never graduated; he'd been pulled out of sixth grade and sent to work after Rose died and Anna was injured.

And the synagogue. The spiritual heart of his community, the holy place where his father spent most of his waking hours, where Ben prayed every week, where David had not set foot since the day of the factory fire that had killed his sister and crippled his mother. No matter how much Viktor wailed and Anna pleaded and Ben hit and Sarah cried, David had had enough of twitching through services to a God he'd never believed in, Ben cuffing him to be still every five minutes. Enough of listening to the hypocritical whispers of supposedly devout men as they sat in their sour-smelling grubby black clothes and did their grubby little business deals in the back of the room while the rabbi read Torah.

By the time David reached their building on the corner of Ludlow and Broome, the narrow streets were filled with nothing but long shadows. Warm yellow light, broken by the silhouette of a burly moving body—Ben, pacing—shone from the windows of the larger of the apartment's two rooms. How on earth was he going to do this? How was he going to tell them that he was abandoning them, that they would have to get by without his income? That he was going to be taught to kill, that he was going to go where he could die. He unrooted his feet from the sidewalk and dragged himself upstairs.

"You're late."

Ben grabbed the *challah* from under David's arm as soon as he walked through the door. Everyone else was seated at the table, waiting for him. Mama, Papa, Sarah, Ben's wife, Naomi, holding Rosie, their baby girl.

"Sorry. I walked Rachel home."

"What, is more important you make to kiss your girlfriend than you should be to Shabbos dinner on time?" Ben had been seven when the family arrived in America. After twenty-two years, his English was still awkward and heavily accented. "Why always you do like this?"

"All right, Ben. He's here now. David, wash your hands, and both of you come sit down." Anna the peacemaker, her cane hooked on the back of her chair, her golden eyes fixed on the face of her favorite son as he stood unmoving just inside the front door. "Duvidel. Next week you will be on time." Her voice was low and her gentle smile pleaded with him to be good.

David met his mother's gaze. He felt as though his heart had wedged itself in his throat. He looked away, but there was no better place to rest his eyes. Viktor was rocking in his chair, *davening* over the prayer book open in his hands, his head down; it had been years since David had allowed his father to place his lips on his forehead and bless him, as fathers were meant to bless their children on *Shabbat*. Sarah was staring at him with wide-open, round eyes. Naomi quickly glanced away and shifted Rosie on her lap.

Less than a minute home and already the tension in the apartment was thick as smoke. He had planned to say nothing until after dinner, but now he knew he couldn't wait. He couldn't sit with them and try to push soup past the constriction in his throat. He couldn't pretend that he would be here next week at all. He went to Naomi and with a questioning nod reached for his niece. Naomi smiled her myopic smile and handed the baby up to him. Rosie nestled happily in his arms. He bent his head and inhaled the Lux soap scent of her hair. She, at least, wouldn't think ill of him for what he was about to say.

"I have something to tell you." He moved away from the table.

"Enough, David. Is sundown. Time to pray. Sit, be silent, and respect." Ben, standing at his place, looked up from slicing the bread.

"You can all pray in peace when I'm gone."

"What do you mean? Where are you going?" Sarah jumped up, her eyes filled with fear.

Anna put a hand on her daughter's arm. "Sit down. He's not going anywhere. David. Don't say things like that; you frighten your sister. You don't have to pray and you don't have to leave. Just come to the table."

"Mama. Please. Listen to me. I am leaving. Tomorrow. I've joined the army."

Stillness heavy as a shroud smothered the room. Viktor stopped *davening*. Rosie began to fuss. David and Anna stared at each other.

"Mama. Say something."

Anna didn't move. She said nothing. It was the sound of the knife falling onto the *challah* plate and Ben's heavy footsteps coming rapidly toward him that filled David's ears. The sound of Rosie howling as she was wrested from his arms and thrust at Naomi. The sound of Ben's big, open hand making violent contact with the side of his face.

"No! This you do not do!" Ben hollered.

David's head throbbed with pain. Tears sprang to his eyes. He backed toward the door. "Goddamn it! Keep your hands off me! I did it! I enlisted in June. I'm going. You can't tell me what to do."

"Stupid, stupid boy! Selfish boy! How you can do this to your mama and papa? After Wolf. After Rose. What, I did so wrong with you?"

Ben tried to get a grip on David's arm, but David wrenched away from him.

"You are needed here, David," Ben yelled. "This is your family! From where will come enough money for the rent, for food, for Mama's medicine?"

"Why is that my responsibility?" David yelled back, his face mottled red from Ben's blow. Blind anger, spawned by ambition and nurtured by frustration, burned away his guilt and hardened his heart. "Tell Papa to get a job! Get a back-bone and ask Rothstein, your fat slob of a boss, for a raise! I don't want this; can't you understand?"

"You talk more like that, I will close your *pisk* for you!" Ben came at him again, his hand raised, but David ducked away from him.

"Let him go."

Ben and David froze. As one, they turned toward the sound of Anna's raspy voice. Sarah hid her face in her hands and began to sob.

"Mama, no. What are you saying?"

"Let him go, Ben. He doesn't belong here. He never belonged here." Slowly, Anna levered herself up, leaning on the table for support. She took her cane and limped to the corner of the room where she and Viktor slept, to a small space given a semblance of separateness by a hanging sheet. She pushed the sheet aside, and before letting it fall like a curtain behind her she turned to David. "Go find what you're looking for."

David stared into her eyes, his mouth open, his breath turned solid in his lungs. He strained to read her expression. He saw no judgment, only love and misery. His head swam and he swayed unsteadily on his feet. Then the curtain fell and she was gone.

Ben grabbed the collar of David's shirt. "You don't belong here! You are no Jew. You are not my brother! You are rotten, *paskudne!*" Ben yanked David toward the door. "You go, and you don't come back! My hands are washed of you! I don't know you!" He pulled the door open with his other hand and shoved David out onto the landing.

Sarah screamed as Ben slammed the door and threw the bolts.

David stumbled, reached for the stair railing to steady himself. He hovered there for a moment, stunned and para-lyzed. The sounds of crying and yelling came to him through the thin wood of the locked apartment door. A dish dropped, bounced; his father's voice admonished, "Sarah!" Their good china, Viktor's dead mother's china. David righted himself and galloped down the four flights of stairs, eyes filled with tears. He missed a step and tumbled down the last half a flight, moving so fast that he fell limply, like a cat, and came to a stop in the building's entry, dazed but un-injured. He scrabbled under the staircase and retrieved the small bag he had packed and hidden there earlier in the week. He burst through the heavy glass and iron doors. At the corner, his mindless forward motion hit an invisible wall. He didn't know where to go. The train to the army camp in Massachusetts didn't leave until tomorrow morning.

"David! David!" Sarah came rushing out of the building and hurled herself at him, nearly knocking them both into the gutter. She wrapped her thin arms around his waist. "Don't go!" she cried. "Don't go!"

David's furious energy collapsed. He dropped his bag and hugged her, trying desperately not to cry. "Sarah, I'm sorry, I have to do this."

Her tears had left streaks on her delicate skin. "What do you mean, you have to? Some general marched into Levy's and put a pistol to your head?"

"Sarah, please."

"Please what? Ben is right! How could you be so selfish?"

David pushed her away from him and picked up his bag.

"Oh God. The hell with you, too. What should I do, Sarah, work at Levy's all my life? Marry Rachel and have a half-dozen kids before I'm thirty? You can live in the past if you want, but I can't and I can't live in this present, either. I want a different future."

"You are an idiot! You don't like this life so you're going to go to war? What do you think, they're throwing *latkes* at one another over there?"

David couldn't suppress a snigger.

"Don't laugh at me!" she yelled. "What are we going to do for money? How could you do this to us?" She began to cry again through her childish rage.

David clenched his jaw. He was through being the one to comfort her. "There's a hundred dollars in an envelope under my mattress. It's everything I could put together since June. With Mama's piecework and the money Ben gives us, you'll be all right for at least five months. After that, if Papa and Ben live up to their past uselessness, you may just have to get a job."

Sarah stared at him in horror. He felt like a monster, but he couldn't stop. "It's a tough life, isn't it? I was already working two years by the time I was your age. Rose started when she was eleven. You're not so special, Sarah. You're spoiled. Now it's time for you to grow up. Go back upstairs. I'm leaving. And don't you dare judge me."

He spun away from her, striding quickly west on Broome Street. Light, rapid footfalls came after him. When she caught up to him, her small hand dipped in and out of his pants pocket. She shoved him hard in the back and through a sobbing breath whispered, "I hate you." He began to run.

The glaring lights and nonstop bustle of the Pennsylvania Station waiting room were not conducive to sleep. David put his bag under his head and tried to get comfortable on the hard bench. His stomach was growling. He was hungry, but he couldn't think of eating. He was trembling with shame. Shame at being curled up like a child, missing his mama, feeling alone and afraid, wanting to crawl back to Ludlow Street and beg their forgiveness. Shame at the comfort he took in clutching in his hand the Star of David that Sarah had slipped into his pocket. It had been Anna's mother's, a fragile silver-filigree star with a garnet center, meant to keep its possessor safe from harm. He swiped at his eyes and then closed them, wrapped his arms around himself and tried to shut out the intrusive sounds of the world and of his own traitorous thoughts.

"Are you all right, son?"

He looked up into the kindly, concerned face of an older man, well dressed, neatly groomed. David immediately recognized the avid sexual interest in the man's light eyes. He sat up and hugged his bag to his chest.

"I'm fine."

"You look upset. Do you need a place to sleep? Something to eat?"

"No. Absolutely not." David stood up and began to walk away.

"Wait." The man reached out a tentative hand. The look in his eyes had changed; nothing but sympathy could now be seen in them. "I have a sofa. It's a lot softer than this bench." He glanced around and lowered his voice. "I promise I won't touch you. You shouldn't have to sleep here."

"I told you, no. Just go away and leave me alone."

Even if David could trust the man to let him sleep unmolested, he wouldn't spend the last night of this hateful life in the presence of yet someone else who wanted something from him that he wasn't going to give. He found another bench to lie awake on. Early in the morning, as soon as the train was ready for boarding, he made his way to the back end of a middle car, stowed his bag on the overhead rack, and sank into the leather seat. He was exhausted, but he knew he wouldn't sleep. For the first time in his life, he was all alone. His past was gone, and what lay ahead was unknowable. He leaned his head into the seat and fought against the urge to cry like a baby. Long minutes later, still caught in that limbo, he saw Jed's sunny face beneath its cap of golden hair coming toward him down the narrow aisle. For just a second, his eyes filled with tears of relief.

Philip put Jed in a taxi at seven that Saturday morning. He offered to come to the station with him, stay until the train left, but Jed demurred. Lucy and Brook came out to say good-bye to him one last time. Sally stayed in her room.

I would never have believed that you could do this to me. I thought I could trust you. You have been disobedient and totally uncaring of my feelings or my wishes. I am only permitting you to do this because your grandfather has convinced me to do so. He believes it will be a good experience for you. He has assured me that your tour of duty will not be hazardous or overlong. You will respect the efforts he has made on your behalf and not succumb to some ill-advised, manly urge to be brave and put yourself in harm's way. If you get yourself killed, Jed, I will never forgive you. And when you get back, I am warning you, you will never do anything like this again. Do you understand me?

That was what she had said to him when she'd found

out. Not as bad as he'd expected, and he had his grandfather to thank for it. His farewell dinner at Delmonico's had been wonderful, everyone anticipating his great success and quick return. It had been hard for him to enjoy it fully, however. Despite his mother's orders and his grandfather's maneuverings, Jed had every intention of going wherever he was needed; how else could he truly prove himself, prove that his decision had been a good one? Now that the time had come, all he could think about was how and when he was going to find David and make him his friend. He still believed that God would protect him, but if it should happen that He got busy elsewhere and had to look away, Jed knew he'd still be safe if he was near David.

He made his way slowly down the platform, looking in the windows of every car. Midway, he saw David, alone at the rear of a car, looking sad and tired, staring off into space. Jed gave his bags and a five-dollar bill to a porter, pointed to the rack above David's head. He hurried back to the terminal, bought two cups of coffee and some pastries. Then, breakfast in hand, his heart beating fast, he entered the car from its forward end and walked the aisle to where David sat.

3

It was only six o'clock in the morning, too early for the appearance of the winter sun with its cruel reminder that warmth would not return to the world for many months. Although the window was shut tight to the February chill, the air inside the apartment was frigid. Sarah could hear her father moving in the large room that served as kitchen, dining room, and living room as well as her parents' bedroom. He was lighting a fire in the coal stove. She would be gone, running errands for Mama, before its heat could warm her.

She lay awake on her narrow bed in the small room, two

clean but threadbare blankets covering her small frame. The family had moved into this New Law tenement apartment in 1910 when Anna, Ben, and Rose were together finally earning enough. After fourteen years in a squalid, airless tomb on Stanton Street, these two light, clean rooms were paradise, with windows looking out over the intersection of Ludlow and Broome Streets and a toilet in the hall that they had to share with only one other family. Then the big room had slept all four children and Viktor and Anna had the small room for themselves. The family's happiness lasted one year. In the spring of 1911, the fire at the Triangle Shirtwaist Factory left Rose dead, two weeks shy of her eighteenth birthday, and Anna a nightmare-plagued invalid. In 1914, Ben married Naomi and moved out. Now David was gone.

Sarah felt the once joyful, protective space pressing in on her. There was a sound in her ears, like ocean waves. It almost drowned out the noise from the streets below, the dawn-to-dusk frenzy of the Lower East Side, a clamor unaffected by the changing of the seasons. It was Sunday; Shabbos was over; there was no more rest for her. She was too frightened to move. At two o'clock, she had to present herself at the shop on Hester Street where Ben had cajoled the owner, one of Levy's suppliers of men's and women's coats, to give Sarah a trial as a feller hand. Today she would work for six hours for no pay, but if she was good enough she would have a job as a finisher of sleeve linings starting tomorrow. She didn't want a job. She wanted to stay home and take care of Mama, like she always did on Sundays.

Stop being a baby. Get up! Sarah turned her head and looked across the room, at David's bed, stripped and bare. As she did every morning, she felt a sickening jolt of disbelief that he wasn't there. And as she did every morning, his horrible parting words resounding in her head as she told herself it was because he wasn't there that she had to do this thing she so fearfully did not want to do. She had watched this moment come closer and closer as the money he'd left got spent for new medicine for Mama's lungs, as Naomi became pregnant again and her eyes worsened and she had to stop her piecework, as Ben's pittance of a raise went to support his own growing family.

Sarah pulled herself up, swung her legs off the bed, planted her stockinged feet on the cold floor. David had called her spoiled and useless. But it was he who had run away, not her. She would show him who was useless. The fear in the pit of her stomach eased a little. The sounds of Papa firing the stove had stopped. Sarah rose and padded into the big room. The curtain wall was down, only silence from behind it. She quickly washed herself in the kitchen sink with icy water. Shivering, she scurried back to her room and slipped out of her flannel nightgown into a long, worn wool dress that had been Rose's. Sarah pulled her boots over her stockings and laced them up with numb fingers. She brushed her tangled hair and gathered it into a bun at the nape of her neck, and, praying that Mr. Krinski was not already there, she hurried out into the hall to the toilet. When she returned to the apartment, Papa was at the table, methodically spreading chicken fat on two pieces of coarse rye bread.

"For your dinner, for later," Viktor said quietly, speaking, as always, in Yiddish.

Sarah watched him wrap the bread in a piece of newspaper. The care he took in preparing her food seemed suddenly a terrible cruelty. Despite her resolve to be strong, she heard herself whimper, "Papa, please, I don't want to go. I want to stay home with Mama. I want to go to school tomorrow."

Viktor didn't look at her. "You can go nights to the Alliance, like the others."

She stared at her father's bowed head and was hit by a nauseating wave of hatred. Why wasn't he telling her that she didn't have to go? Why wasn't *he* going in her place? For an ugly instant, she saw him as David had: a weak man who, after over two decades in this country, still did not speak the language, could not keep a job, could do nothing but study and pray all day long and leave the squalid realities of life for his woman and children to deal with. The feeling fled Sarah as quickly as it had come, replaced immediately by guilt. She couldn't hate her father for what he could not do; it wasn't as though he hadn't tried.

In a bright, strong voice she said, "Of course, Papa. I'm sorry. I'm just nervous."

Viktor raised his head and smiled. "I'll go to *shul* now. Here is the list of Mama's pieces to pick up for today and here's the shopping list for groceries. When you come home tonight, I will have dinner waiting for you."

"You're going to cook? Maybe I might as well work all night then; what do you think?"

Viktor looked at her, his love sweet like honey in his warm dark eyes. "My precious Sarah. You are such a good girl." He kissed her softly on both cheeks and left to go pray.

The wall of sheets was pulled back for the day. Anna was propped up in bed, her dark hair fanning out behind her on the white pillowcases.

"You slept well last night, Mama; you look beautiful today." Sarah bent over and kissed her mother's cheek. "Did you enjoy lunch? I'm getting good at the barley soup, aren't I?"

Sarah had run all her errands, made a small lunch for herself and Mama, and cleaned up the kitchen. It was one thirty.

Anna lifted a hand and smoothed an errant strand of hair on her daughter's temple. She smiled up into Sarah's face. Sarah and David, her two youngest, they looked so much like her. The same thick hair, rich dark brown shot with red, glowing like polished wood; the same eyes, amber with flecks of gold in the centers; the same skin, smooth and dusky. Even the bones of their faces were like hers: finely chiseled, with high slanting cheekbones revealing an undeniable Mongol ancestry. After years of sickness, Anna no longer felt beautiful except when she looked at her daughter. Only then did Anna remember that she had been thought one of the most beautiful girls in Smolensk, a prized maiden whose hand had been won by the most unlikely contender.

"Mama," Sarah said sharply, seeing the unfocused look in her mother's eyes, "I have to leave in a few minutes. Do you need anything before I go? Who is going to take your finished pieces back to Mr. Corelli and Mr. Leyrowitz?"

"Papa will do it."

Anna's heart constricted. What good was Sarah's beauty in this miserable life she and Viktor had bequeathed her? Anna felt a torpor come over her, heavier even than the constant fatigue she suffered from being unable to draw enough oxygen into her damaged lungs, and knew that she would sleep again as soon as she finished the last of her work. She pointed to her sewing box on the corner table.

"I wrapped up my extra thimble and scissors and two needles for you, there, on the top of my box. Take them. And don't lose them."

Sarah held the small package to her breast, her head bent, her slim shoulders slumped.

"Sarahle. Come here," Anna said. Her voice was unnaturally soft and husky. It was a beautiful, sensual voice, a gift of scarred larynx and seared lungs.

Sarah hurried back to the bed and sat on the edge, carefully so as not to jostle her mother.

Anna took her daughter's hand in hers, stroking it lightly as she spoke. "I won't lie to you, darling. It will be hard, and although Ben says this Pankin is a decent man, he is already taking advantage of you because you are a child. He wouldn't ask a woman over sixteen to work for free to show her ability. He will hire you—there is no one better with a needle—and you insist that he pay you for today, do you hear?"

Ben had promised her that Pankin, the foreman, wasn't a bad sort. But still Anna worried. Nonunion shops were harsh and only a nonunion shop would hire someone as young as Sarah.

"Just do your stitches. Others there may try to make you feel bad because you are so young and taking work from their hands. Pay them no mind. We need the money as badly as anyone. And at eight o'clock you get up and leave, no matter what. Don't worry about me. Sadie is next door and Papa will be home by six."

"And you don't worry about me, Mama. I'll be the best

feller hand they ever saw!" Her words were brave, but fright glittered in her eyes.

Anna squeezed Sarah's hand. "Go now, darling. And don't forget your bread."

In a minute, Anna heard the front door open and close. Her head fell back against the pillows and she stared up at the ceiling in despair. If Sarah couldn't handle this job, there wouldn't be enough money. One daughter had never had a childhood. Now Sarah's was over before her fourteenth birthday. This wasn't what was supposed to have happened; it wasn't for this that she had dragged her family to America.

"Monty, you can't go out now! We're expected at my parents' for my father's birthday dinner at three o'clock. Mother is sending Ralph to pick us up in half an hour." Zoe put her hands on her hips and glared at her husband as he made for the front door.

"Don't worry, love. I'm all dressed and ready. Thought I'd leave for a short bit, let you make yourself and Libby beautiful without me distracting you."

Zoe's mouth twisted. "Don't give me that big Irish smile, you liar. It's thirty degrees out; what are you going to do, take a nice bracing walk through the park to Fifth Avenue?"

Monty put his hand on the doorknob and said, "I need a little bracing to deal with a Sunday afternoon with your family."

"If you could ever stay sober in their presence the experience would be more pleasant for everyone. You promised me you wouldn't drink today, Monty, please. You're already half-drunk. Don't go out."

Monty stood for a moment without moving. Then he turned and looked at his wife with such coldness that she involuntarily retreated a step and clutched her satin robe tight to her throat. "I've put up with a dozen years of your parents and your stick-up-her-ass sister-in-law sniffing their disapproval of me every time I enjoy myself a little. I've had enough. I'm going to Shannon's to drink as much whiskey as I can in the next thirty minutes so that perhaps I can live up to their expectations and puke all over your mother's precious goddamned heirloom tablecloth. And if you don't like it I'll be happy to have my dinner at the saloon with my friends. You decide, love." The false smile was back on his angelic face, a frightening exposure of white teeth below his straight nose and expressionless matinee-idol blue eyes. The ugliness of his words was magnified by hearing them cushioned in the musical lilt of his faint Irish brogue.

"Nothing to say, eh? That's a smart girl." Monty's eyes narrowed and he took a menacing step toward her. He laughed sharply as she drew back, then yanked open the apartment door and left, slamming it behind him.

Zoe stood in the gloomy entryway and stared at the still-vibrating door. Monty had never behaved quite so horribly before. It was her fault. She should not have sniped at him. He was always uncomfortable around her father; he wanted Joseph to like him, to give him a chance, but Joseph never saw the good in him.

"Mommy?"

Elizabeth's timid voice came from behind her.

"Mommy, where's Daddy? Aren't we going to Grandmother's?"

"Yes, darling. He just went out for a few minutes. Come; we have to wrap Grandfather's gift and then make ourselves beautiful. Don't we want Daddy to be proud of his girls?"

She smiled, took her daughter's hand, and led her through the empty apartment.

An hour had passed and Monty had not returned. Zoe and Elizabeth sat in silence in the living room, waiting. The doorman had rung up twice to say that Ralph was downstairs with the car. Zoe didn't know what to do. She couldn't believe that Monty meant not to come to Joseph's birthday celebration with them. He had never done anything like that. She couldn't march down to Shannon's and get him. Neither could she send Ralph to fetch him. She couldn't go without him. It would be too humiliating; no matter what excuse she gave, her parents would suspect the worst of him. She would wait another fifteen minutes.

Ten agonizing minutes later there came the sound of keys scraping ineffectively at the lock, followed by a rhythmic pounding on the door.

"Go to your room, Elizabeth." Zoe rose quickly and moved toward the entry. The girl sat, owl eyed with uncertainty. "Now! Do as I say!" Elizabeth let out a whimper and scurried from the room.

Zoe steeled herself before opening the door. Monty staggered across the threshold. He reeked of liquor; his face was red and his dress clothes disheveled. He had been this drunk more times than she cared to remember. She had learned how to handle him. He would swagger and posture, but in the end he would do what she asked of him.

"Monty, go into the bathroom and clean yourself up. I'll bring you a cup of coffee."

"Make me, you stupid bitch." He planted himself in front of her, blocking her access to the hallway.

Zoe's breath caught in her throat. The awful coldness was still in his eyes, but now there was something else in their beautiful blue depths, something she'd never seen before. Loathing. Her husband, whom she loved, was looking at her as though he hated her. Zoe felt herself go numb with incomprehension. She forced herself to think, to stay calm. "All right. All right. You don't have to go. Libby and I will—"

"Oh, so now you don't want me to come. Don't want me in your parents' fancy house. I'm not good enough, hey? I'll contaminate your daddy's special day." He reached out and grabbed her arms, shoved her back against the entryway wall.

She turned her head away from the sour whiskey stench of his breath. No matter how drunk he'd ever gotten, he'd always remained lucid. She just needed to speak reasonably, to keep him thinking clearly. She swallowed hard and then met his eyes, keeping her expression neutral. "Monty, darling, you're hurting me."

He dug his fingers more deeply into her flesh. "Say it, Zoe. I'm not good enough for you and your damned family."

"You know I don't think that," she said as calmly as she could.

"That's what you say," he said slyly. "But you're your daddy's girl, aren't you? And your daddy doesn't give a damn about me and neither do you, you bitch." He began to shake her, jerking her like a puppet.

"Monty, stop it!" The shrill quaver in her voice gave away her terror.

"That's right; be afraid, you useless cow." Monty pushed her away.

Zoe was frozen to the spot. "Monty, just tell me what you want to do. You don't have to come with us if you'd really rather not; that's all I meant."

"I'll tell you what I want. I want you to stop nagging me. 'Monty, tell me what you want.' 'Monty, get a job.' 'Monty, stop drinking.' Monty do this and Monty do that." His voice grew louder with every word, his face contorted with rage. "What the fuck do you ever do for me? You can't even get your son of a bitch of a father to give me a decent job!"

Zoe responded without thinking. "My father did get you a decent job, after I begged him. What's wrong with being the manager of the Club dining room; you should be grateful! You should thank me! Now we're late and you're a drunken mess! Stop whining and get cleaned up! I want to go!"

Monty's eyes bored into her. He lurched toward her, maliciously mimicking her. " 'I want to go. I want to go.' Zoe wants to go to her mommy and daddy." His head wagged back and forth like that of some mindless, threatening beast. His speech began to slur. "Why the hell did I ever marry you, you nagging, controlling slut!"

Zoe burst into tears. "Monty!"

"Is Daddy's girl crying? You want to know why I married you? For your lovely money. You were so easy, all I had to do was this. . . ." He put a rough, clumsy hand on her breast.

Hurt and fury surged through her. She pushed his hand away and slapped him hard across the face. Before she had time to feel the sting of the blow on her own palm, she saw, in a blur of furious movement, Monty's balled fist coming at her face. She felt a dull impact on her left cheekbone, heard a sound like a slab of meat being thrown onto a butcher's counter. She was driven backward. Her right hip smashed into the corner of the entryway table and a flower-filled vase crashed to the floor. Zoe hit the wall and slid down into a puddle of broken glass, water, and scattered daylilies. Through a haze of shock, she saw Monty's glossy patent-leather shoes pass by her head as he stumbled down the hall. She heard the light patter of small feet on the polished wood floor, Elizabeth's voice screaming, *"Mommy! Mommy! Mommy!"*

And then came the pain. Hot, searing hammer blows of pain in her face and her hip. She lay on the floor, trying to understand what had happened. She caught at Elizabeth's ankle, trying to still the awful sounds the girl was making. Zoe pushed herself to a sitting position and pulled Libby into her arms. She sat and rocked them both until the blood cleared from her eyes and she could see and think again. She stood up. The right sleeve of her dress was soaked with blood; a sharp shard of the vase had cut through the fabric.

"Libby, stay here. I'll be right back."

The girl clutched at Zoe's skirt. "Daddy hit you. I saw him."

"He didn't mean it. Everything's all right. Stay here." She kissed her daughter's cheek and disengaged the desperate little fingers.

Cautiously, Zoe walked through the apartment. Monty was passed out under the dining room table, faceup, snoring. The marks of her splayed fingers still showed white against the alcohol flush of his naturally pale skin. She put a trembling hand to her own cheek as she stared down at him, at his shining, matted blue-black hair, his perfect features. What she told Elizabeth had to be true. He hadn't meant to hit her. He had never done it before; he certainly would never do it again. She had provoked him. She had hit him first. And she *was* a nag. She and Libby should have just left when Ralph came for them. Monty could have joined them later. Or not if that was what he truly wanted. She needed to be a better wife, more supportive, more understanding, less demanding.

She returned to where Elizabeth obediently awaited her. "Libby, put on your coat and go down to the car. Tell Ralph I will be a few more minutes. Wait for me there. Take the present."

The girl nodded and didn't ask about her father. As soon as she was safely out of the apartment, Zoe limped into her bedroom. Swiftly and efficiently, she cleaned and bandaged the cut, struggled into a new dress, and artfully reapplied her makeup to conceal the bruise that was already developing under her eye. She put the jar of foundation into her purse, grabbed her coat and shawl. On the way to the front door, she walked through the dining room, stepping deliberately over Monty's feet where they emerged from under the table. She poured herself a stiff shot of Scotch and drank it in one swallow. She heard the telephone ring in the parlor but did not move to answer it. Without a look down or back, she left to join her family on the occasion of her father's seventy-third birthday.

Sarah worked her way through the jostling crowds. Every space not filled by a cart was packed with people. Children and adults alike scurried by with heavy bundles of cloth or other goods strapped to their backs or balanced on their heads. Shoppers haggled with vendors eager to sell their dwindling wares before they became too manhandled to fetch a price. Years ago, before the fire, Sarah would come to shop with Anna in the early mornings and give her mother childish advice on what looked good that day. While Anna poked and prodded Aronson's Fresh Fruits, old man Aronson would slip a treat into Sarah's waiting hand—a smooth orange, a crisp apple, a sweet banana. Sarah would giggle and hide the fruit behind her back while Anna paid for her careful selections. Back upstairs, Anna would pretend to be shocked and amazed at Sarah's prize, mother and daughter would discuss whether they should return it, and then they would share it for breakfast before Anna went off to Triangle with Rose.

It had been seven long years since Sarah had shared a piece of Aronson's forbidden fruit with Anna. In any case, old Aronson had died four years ago and his son gave nothing away to anyone. Now, Sarah thought she would do anything to be able to go back in time, to stand with Anna again in front of that cart, wondering hungrily what Aronson's gift would be that day.

Sarah arrived at the address Ben had provided, on Hester just off Forsythe. It wasn't quite two. Ben had said not to go in before or Pankin would expect her early every day. So she waited an endless five minutes on the stoop, until she thought she might faint from anxiety. Then, not caring what time it was, she put her hand on the well-worn porcelain knob, took the deepest breath she could, and opened the heavy door. It swung closed behind her, leaving her in darkness. Above the pounding of her heart, she heard the clattering of sewing machines. She followed the sound, slowly groped her way to the top floor. Twelve people, all of whom, she knew, had been there since seven that morning, were hard at work in the shop's one room, bent over long tables laden with piles of coats. Some worked at machines, others with needle and thread. The air was cold and filled with fabric dust. A grime-covered window faced out onto the adjacent building and let in a small amount of depressing grey light. No one looked up.

A heavyset man stood alone at a small table, inspecting the stitching on a finished garment. He raised his eyes and scowled at her as though she were a roach that had crawled in under the doorjamb.

Tears clogged her throat. She fought them back and said in a small voice, "Are you Mr. Pankin?"

"Yes; who are you?" His voice was not unkind, but his gaze was hard and Sarah felt her face flush under his scrutiny.

"I am Sarah Warshinsky. I'm here for the feller hand job. My brother Ben—"

Pankin waved a hand. "Yes, yes." He considered her without sympathy. "You don't look as though you can fell a sleeve lining, little girl. They have to be perfect in this shop—flat to the cloth!"

"I can, too!" she retorted, but inside she began to quake, terrified that she wouldn't remember how to take even a simple stitch.

"We'll see." Pankin picked up a coat and threw it at her. "Take it over there"—he pointed to a table where the other finishers sat—"and go to work." He turned his back.

No one moved to help her. She hurriedly took off her coat, stuffed her bread in a pocket, and put it down without paying attention to where it landed. There was no free chair at the work table; nor did there seem to be room for one. She frantically looked around for a place to sit.

"Move!" Pankin's voice boomed at her back. "The day is half-gone. If you can't work I don't need you here."

Sarah whirled around, her eyes rolling with fear. Pankin grabbed a chair with a broken back from behind him and shoved it toward the table. "Reuben, Ida, don't sit there like dead things; make room for the new feller hand!"

Sarah heard tittering from across the room. Her heart beat so hard her body shook. She positioned her chair between the two workers and squeezed herself into it. They were so close to her she could feel the warmth of their bodies. She tried to take up as little space as she could. She looked to her right, thinking to smile at the woman Pankin had called Ida. But Ida turned a cold shoulder to her. Sarah quickly looked away. It was just as her mother had said— these people would hate her just because she was here, trying to earn money they wanted for themselves.

She bent her head over the coat. She understood that if she didn't sew the lining on these sleeves perfectly and quickly, Pankin would throw her out. With trembling hands, she unwrapped the package Anna had given her, donned her thimble, threaded her needle and began to work. *Don't twist the lining; take small stitches; work quickly.* Anna's years of instruction repeated themselves in Sarah's head. The coat seemed to move under her agitated gaze. She couldn't tell if she was stitching well or terribly.

Finally, she was done. She took the coat to Pankin's table. Without so much as a glance at her, he inspected it, pulling at every stitch with his needle. Sarah waited, not daring to breathe, wondering how she would survive when he said her work was no good. But he said nothing, just put down the finished coat and handed her another. Her heart leaped. Her work was good.

Sarah stretched her stiff back, then hurried back to her place. Now she stitched quickly and more confidently, although her hands still shook. The man on her left was sneaking peeks at her. With a sinking in the pit of her stomach, she turned toward him, expecting another hostile face. She was surprised by a smile.

"You did well, yes?" Reuben said quietly, looking away when their eyes met. "I see you have good sewing. Use your hands, not your head, you will be fine." He spoke good English, with only a slight accent. He kept his voice low, his words meant only for her, although everyone at the table could surely hear.

"She shouldn't be here taking food from our mouths," Ida hissed, pushing her needle into the cloth. "She's just a snip of a girl; she has no right!"

"Ida, leave her alone," came another voice from across the table. "Pankin said he was hiring someone else. You can't work twenty-four hours a day."

"I could take more home! We don't need a child here!"

"Sarah, is it?" Reuben's voice came softly from her left. "Don't mind Ida; no one does she like, not even Reuben. Can you believe that?" When Sarah didn't look up, he poked lightly at her hand. "That was a joke, I thought. Not funny?"

"Reuben, you're a fool," Ida said, but her voice was no longer angry.

Sarah looked at Reuben then and had to smile. His face was completely transformed as he beamed back at her. He was younger than she had thought and would have been good-looking if he hadn't been so painfully thin.

"You should eat more." Sarah blurted out the first thought to come into her head. She blushed bright red. "I'm sorry," she whispered. "That was so rude."

"No," Reuben said, "that is true. Always I am too thin. That is why I work here, so I can eat more and become a fat American." He laughed. No one could become fat feeding himself on sweatshop wages.

"Another joke, right?" Sarah smiled at him again. "My family won't be able to eat, either, if I don't earn money now. So don't say I don't belong here!" Her little girl's voice rose in pitch, and she looked directly at Ida.

"Quiet, all of you! This isn't a social club; you're here to work! I'll send you home, little girl, if you cause trouble!" Pankin, reducing everyone to busy silence and Sarah to tears again.

Evelyn was growing more tense by the minute. Seeking diversion, she wandered with determined aimlessness into the kitchen and, in an uncharacteristic paroxysm of nosiness, peered into the oven, lifted lids on pots, rearranged the placement of canapés on an antique Chinese porcelain platter.

"Miz Gates, please." Angelina spun from the marble counter where she was rolling out a piecrust and took a wooden spoon from her employer's hand before she could do any damage.

"Do I smell something burning? Don't you overcook that goose, Angelina!"

The cook shot Evelyn an incredulous look—as if such a thing were even possible!—and Julie laughed.

"What is that look? You're not Escoffier, you know. And just what are you laughing at, Julie? Do you think it's funny, what you are doing with those apples? I hope they are not for the pie; you are slicing them too thin."

Evelyn was instantly mortified at her unjustified outburst. "I'm sorry; I'm so sorry. I know I'm driving you all mad today. I just can't seem to relax. I want this party to be perfect. What with everyone worrying about the war, and about Jed . . ."

Angelina and Julie both clucked in sympathy, but Evelyn felt unworthy of their easy forgiveness. Even as the words had emerged from her mouth, Evelyn knew them for a lie. She was not concerned about the war; it was far away and did not affect her life. Jed was still on American soil, finishing his training, already a first lieutenant; he'd be coming home for a visit next month before shipping out. With Joseph quietly pulling strings, Jed would see no danger.

Zoe was the cause of her tension. Zoe and Monty, that embarrassment of a son-in-law. As always, they were late. Just how long would dinner have to wait for them this time? How drunk would Monty be when he arrived? What fluttering, feeble excuses would Zoe offer for their tardiness and her husband's irritating, mock-ingratiating behavior? Evelyn hated the agitation she felt every time they were to see one another, hated anticipating the disruptive nonsense the Glennons unfailingly brought into her well-ordered and well-behaved world.

Joseph had been right, as always: Monty was as charming and clever as they came, but beneath the seductive facade, he was nothing but a lying, lazy, grasping drunk. It had taken Evelyn longer to see it; Zoe was eighteen when she had fallen under Montgomery Hugh Glennon's spell, the same age as Evelyn when she'd fallen in love with Joseph and as sure of her feelings as Evelyn remembered being of her own. For the first time, she had sided with Zoe against Joseph, abetting the girl's rebellion against her father's judgment and wishes. It was a mistake Evelyn would never make again.

Zoe had been a fool to marry Monty and perhaps a bigger fool to have stayed married to him when Evelyn had suggested a quiet divorce a year later. But then Elizabeth had come, and the years had passed and, remarkably, the marriage had endured. Evelyn had to give Zoe credit, in a backhand sort of way. The girl had learned to handle the difficulties of her marriage very well. And Evelyn was aware of the sexual bond that existed between Zoe and Monty even after all these years, something whose power and comfort Evelyn understood quite well. She had to admit that Monty was an attractive man, despite everything. It was beyond annoying, however, that because of Zoe's rebellious, willful foolishness, and adolescent lust the whole family had to suffer the man's appalling antics in polite silence.

"Ma'am, there you are; I've been looking everywhere!" Mary, Evelyn's personal maid and housekeeper of fifteen years, popped her head into the kitchen. "Mr. Joseph is asking for you. He's in the drawing room. Mr. Philip's family has been announced."

"Ah, good. Let's get this celebration started, shall we?" She brushed a dusting of flour off her sleeve, straightened her lace bodice.

"Yes, ma'am. If I may say, that dress still looks beautiful on you."

"Thank you, Mary. I've gotten good use of it, haven't I?" It was a *Callot Sœurs* that she had had made for her in Paris four years earlier, a gossamer silk-and-cotton gown of a deep ivory color, the fabric light yet opulent, artfully studded with gold sequins. It set off her full figure and her ebony hair perfectly and was one of Joseph's favorites.

"The day will be lovely, ma'am," Mary said reassuringly, before disappearing into the servants' wing.

Evelyn watched her go with a feeling of satisfaction. She and Joseph were truly fortunate with their help. Evelyn had never believed in having an ostentatious staff. Let the Guggenheims have their dozen; four live-in staff were quite sufficient for her and Joseph's needs. When, in 1911, they had taken possession of this sixteen-room apartment on the ninth floor of the brand-new McKim, Mead & White–designed apartment house at 998 Fifth Avenue, with its sweeping views across Central Park, she had decided then and there that she would never fill the six rooms of the servants' quarters. The two largest rooms were given to Mary and her husband, Walter, their butler, and Angelina and her husband, Ralph, their chauffeur and Joe's valet. A third room was kept as a bedroom for the occasions when Julie, who came five days a week to clean and help cook, needed to stay over. A fourth was used for storage, and the staff were given the use of the last two rooms for themselves. Evelyn was happy to furnish two sitting rooms at their request, one with a radio and one without, for moments of complete quiet.

Evelyn paused at the wide arched entry to the octagonal drawing room as she heard Walter at the front door, admitting Philip, Sally, Lucy, and Brook. A slanting beam of midwinter sunlight caught her in its watery illumination as it poured through the drawing room's south- and west-facing windows, shot across its twenty-foot expanse, and spilled through the arch into the hall.

"Grandmother! Look at you! You're an angel!" Brook made as if to run to her, his arms outstretched. His joyous forward motion was abruptly halted as Sally grabbed him by the collar of his jacket and yanked him back.

"Brook, we do not fling ourselves at people. Now approach your grandmother properly."

Evelyn smiled broadly at the boy and held out her arms. But it was too late; the delight had gone out of his eyes and his body was stiff and formal in her embrace. She accepted Lucy's sweet kiss and Philip's modest peck.

"Walter said we were the first to arrive. I thought surely Zoe and Monty would be here by now, as we were kept by Philip's extraordinary Sunday appointment." Sally managed to skewer Philip with an accusatory glower while decorously passing her cheek near Evelyn's.

"Ralph is crosstown fetching them now. Children, why don't you go see Cook in the kitchen." Angelina always set aside a special treat for them. Evelyn was gratified to see Brook's eyes regain their animation as he anticipated the savory tidbit.

"Actually, I'm glad they aren't here yet." Sally laid a conspiratorial hand on Evelyn's arm. "Evelyn dear, forgive my preoccupation, but I must speak with Joseph about Jed, just for a moment. Is he in the drawing room?"

Evelyn nodded and Sally swept into the great room without even a backward glance at Philip; his presence was clearly not needed or desired for a conversation concerning the fate of his elder son. Philip looked after his wife with such naked yearning that Evelyn fairly squirmed with discomfort.

"So, Philip, what was this mysterious Sunday meeting?"

Philip slowly turned his gaze to her. "Yes, well. Not so mysterious." He cleared his throat. "It was about a possible commission. A portrait of the wife as a gift for her approaching fiftieth birthday. The husband wanted to see more of my work, and today was the only opportunity for him, as he leaves for Europe tomorrow. You probably know the family. Edgar and Dorothy Woolbright?"

Evelyn's eyes grew large. "Woolbright! Yes, of course I know them. Old money on both sides. Very influential people, great philanthropists. Tremendous collectors of art and antiquities. This is wonderful, Philip! You must be very proud!"

"I don't have the job yet, Evie. I'm amazed that they came to me at all."

"You shouldn't be, Philip. Your talent is more and more recognized among the people who matter. Dorothy! My, it's been ages. She's a Baines, you know. She came out a few years after I did. They spend so much time on the Continent, I've hardly seen them in recent years. They are both very genuine, very likable. And she is a lovely-looking woman."

"I didn't meet her. Woolbright said he would decide when he returns in the spring." With nothing more to say on the subject, his gaze threatened to again travel in the direction of the drawing room.

"You are all looking well," Evelyn said brightly.

"Yes, we're all well." He sighed deeply. "Although I'm a bit worried about Sally's infatuation with this Christian Science nonsense."

"It is quite the rage in society now, here and in England. Not that I can imagine why. It's just a fad, Philip; I wouldn't be too concerned about it. Perhaps it gives her comfort. I'm sure she's worried about Jed, your father's protective powers notwithstanding."

"Yes, she is. We all are. Once he sails next month . . . And Sally of course won't let me—"

Evelyn fluttered her hands to stop him. "Jed will be fine. Sally will be fine. Just take a breath and wait it out, Philip. Everything will be fine."

Philip gave Evelyn a wan smile. He had never been able to think of her as his stepmother. It was ludicrous, really; she was only five years older than he. She had been a mature, vivacious twenty-year-old when she had married his father, a thirty-eight-year-old widower, and Philip had been a somber, quiet young man of fifteen. After his mother died giving birth to him, he had been raised by his maternal grandparents in a small town in the Hudson Valley. His father came to visit occasionally, but Philip hardly knew him. Yet when Philip came to Evelyn and Joseph's wedding, *the* event of the 1883 season, he decided to stay and live with them in New York City. It was because of Evelyn. Though perfectly well matched to her husband despite the difference in their ages, she enjoyed Philip's company and he hers. She became his friend, his protector, helped him forge a relationship, albeit superficial, with his father. She turned Philip into a man of the city and supported his ambition to become a painter. He had believed then that he and Evelyn would always be able to talk to each other. He'd been wrong. She remained warm and supportive, always loving and generous, but before long she'd become as emotionally inaccessible as the man she'd married. But Philip needed to talk to someone. He tried again.

"Evelyn. How are things going to be fine? Sally is so unhappy. And you know why. It's me. I don't know how to make her happy."

"It is not for us to speak of these things, Philip," Evelyn said quietly. "They are between you and your wife." She played with the silk-covered buttons on the sleeve of her dress. "What advice could I give you, in any case? That you might try to be more the kind of man Sally believes she needs, more forceful and ambitious? That you should stand up to her when it comes to the way she treats the children, the way she treats you, this religious foolishness?" She looked directly at him and her look put an end to the conversation. "You have a lovely streak of paint in your hair, you know."

He'd gotten more than he'd hoped for. In the same breath that she refused to discuss his marriage, Evelyn had shared her astute perception of its problems. Philip wasn't sure if that made him feel less or more alone with them.

"Don't I always. It drives Sally crazy."

Joseph looked up from his reading as he heard his daughter-in-law approach. He watched her stride across the room, admiring her long, shapely body encased in an elegant cut-velvet gown the color of a semiprecious aquamarine. Her platinum hair was swept up in an elaborate arrangement, with several alluring tendrils deliberately left to brush at the skin of her neck and cheeks. Her piercing eyes were the same gemlike hue as her dress. Diamond and emerald earrings sparkled on her fleshy lobes. A matching necklace encircled her pale throat. She was every bit as beautiful and chic as Evelyn, yet for all her beauty and her subtle flirting she stirred no heat in him. She was at her core icy and reserved. Some men, his poor son as a prime example, were titillated by the quest for a passion they imagined lay dormant beneath such an exterior. Joseph had always preferred to trust what he could see. Evelyn's dark earthiness, the smolder in her nearly black eyes, had never abandoned him to the workings of his imagination since the day they had first met. He wouldn't have chosen Sally as a lover or wife, but he admired her almost masculine ambition and determination.

"What's on your mind, my dear?" Joseph said as Sally settled herself on the settee across from his chair. He didn't need to ask; he knew perfectly well what was on her mind: Jed, her firstborn child, the love of her life. Close up, she no longer looked unchanged from the accommodating nineteen-year-old debutante Philip had married nearly twenty years before; she was a magnificent-looking woman approaching forty with steel in her eyes and heart.

"My son, your grandson, what else," she said bluntly. "I don't like the letters I'm getting from him; he is enjoying himself altogether too much." She leaned over, giving him a generous view of her lovely bosom, and tapped him on the knee. "You know, Joseph," she pouted, "I've never quite forgiven you for not immediately telling me he'd enlisted."

Joseph's gaze drifted toward the soft swell of Sally's breasts and lingered for a good look. He couldn't deny that he enjoyed the way she presented herself to him, always with that little sexual edge. A man didn't have to wish to bed a woman to appreciate that kind of attention. "The boy did ask for my confidence. I believe he's entitled to trust me not to betray him. Besides, I had no doubt that you would find out on your own."

"Well, of course." She had discovered the conscription papers in August, along with a letter from Columbia University agreeing to hold his acceptance, stuffed between the pages of an old sketchbook collecting dust on the cluttered top shelf of his armoire.

"Not a chance in hell of him having a secret from you, is there?"

Sally made a slight moue of disapproval at his blasphemous language. "What does he need with secrets? What he needs is for me to know precisely what he's doing."

Jed had never been successful at keeping things from Sally, although she occasionally allowed him the fancy of a private life. She saw nothing wrong in this. She was his mother and he was her firstborn, destined for great things. He had charm, looks, and brains; he'd graduated at the top of his class at Browning and was a natural leader in the Knickerbocker Greys Cadet Corps, rising to the rank of major, looking marvelous in his white duck pants and grey cap. And he was the elder grandson of Joseph Gates, the heir to Joseph's business empire, his vast wealth and influence, his prominent social status. The path of her son's life was as clear as crystal to Sally, and it was her job to keep him on it.

"Joseph, I want to know exactly what you have in mind for him when he returns from this adventure of his."

Sally had a wonderfully focused ability to ignore the potential danger in Jed's immediate future and set her sights only on the future that mattered to her. Joseph was quite charmed by it, but he couldn't resist sticking her just a bit.

"Aren't you even a little concerned that he might not return from this . . . adventure . . . at all? Or has Christian Science convinced you that even death is an illusion of the flesh, so there is no need to worry?" Joseph's tone was deliberately bland, explicitly underscoring his derision.

She stared at him, unblinking, with an expression that dismissed his comment as beneath contempt. She would not give him the satisfaction of admitting to the peace of mind she found in her new religious beliefs. After a long silence, she struck back. "You assured me in August that you would protect him. That he would become an officer and be assigned to desk duty in Paris. Should I not have believed you, Joseph? Are you not capable of doing that?"

Joseph grunted. "Touché."

Joseph would not admit to Sally that he could protect Jed only so far. This war was every day a more and more serious matter. Once the boy's regiment sailed for France, there would be greater pressure on Jed to stay with them wherever they went. And if he chose to do that, there wouldn't be much that Joseph could do to keep him in Paris. He wanted Jed to come home safe and sound, but privately Joseph thought Jed could use some toughening up. It would be good for him to see some fighting.

All things considered, it was safer for him and Sally to build a bridge of silence over the coming months and plant their feet firmly on the shore of Jed's return.

"You know what I have in mind for Jed. I didn't think we needed to discuss it. He will attend Columbia University and study economics and business. When he graduates, he will come downtown. He has considerable intellect, a capable head on his shoulders. My intention is for him to succeed me in running the company. You do realize, of course, that I intend to stay at the helm until I keel over, but I am seventy-three. . . ."

"Yes, Happy Birthday. You are healthy as a horse and will live forever, Joseph," Sally said dourly.

Joseph chuckled. "Thank you for that lovely, if disingenuous, blessing. The only unknown ingredient in your son's future is the extent of his own ambition."

"Don't concern yourself with Jed's ambition. He wants whatever you and I want." Satisfied, Sally fondly patted Joseph's knee again, then gestured with her sleek head toward the door. "Come; let's join the others. They are eating up all of Angelina's delicious hors d'oeuvres." She rose and crossed the lush Aubusson carpet. "Darlings! I hope you left some smoked salmon for me!"

Zoe, Monty, and Elizabeth should absolutely have arrived by now, and Evelyn's insides were beginning to churn. Ralph had driven the Packard across the park to pick them up a good hour ago; they should all have been back long since. Evelyn had tried telephoning the apartment but had received no answer. Of course, with that family, one never knew what to expect. They would undoubtedly arrive any moment in their customary swirl of motion, Zoe flustered, Monty jocular, and little Elizabeth silent. Finally, just as Evelyn was deciding to phone again, she heard the doorbell ring. Evelyn hurried out into the hall, curtly brushing past Walter.

"I'll let them in, Walter, thank you."

"Ma'am."

Annoyed and already impatient with her undoubtedly inebriated son-in-law and apologetic daughter, Evelyn flung open the door. Only two people. Zoe, standing rigidly and wearing too much makeup, and in front of her Elizabeth, eyes to the ground, stoically bearing her mother's fingers digging into her shoulders.

"Where's Monty? Why are you so late, Zoe, honestly!" Evelyn peered around Zoe into the vestibule as though Monty might be hiding somewhere in the square, open space between the elevator and apartment door.

"Hello, Mother. Monty wasn't feeling well; we left him home. But we're here, aren't we?" Zoe said cheerfully, and pushed Elizabeth before her into the oak-paneled entry. She kept her face averted as she shrugged out of her coat and laid it, along with Elizabeth's, on the hall bench.

"Have the courtesy to look at me when you make your excuses! It's your father's birthday, for God's sake, and you're over an hour late." Fed up, Evelyn reached out and grabbed Zoe's arm.

Zoe pulled herself from her mother's grasp, kept her face turned away as she made a show of smoothing her hair. She continued her vapid chatter. "I am sorry we're late, Mother, truly. But poor Monty, I couldn't leave him without some tea and toast. Oh, and doesn't something smell delicious! I'm starving."

Zoe had always been a terrible dissembler. Even as a child, her bright eyes and tumbled words would give her away every time. Monty must have been particularly difficult; Evelyn's anger began to ebb. "Libby, darling, go on into the drawing room. Brook and Lucy are there and they'll gobble up all those mushroom pastries you like so much if you don't hurry." Evelyn kissed her granddaughter's cheek and gave her a gentle push down the hall. "Now, Zoe. Turn around and look at me or I will be very cross with you."

Zoe stood with her back to Evelyn, staring at the wall as though fascinated by the fine grain of the wood.

"Zoe, turn around."

Slowly, she turned and presented her face to her mother, defiance radiating from her deep-set dark eyes. She had done an excellent job with her makeup, but Evelyn nonetheless was able to discern the shadowy purple smear beginning now to puff beneath her left eye.

"What happened to your face?"

Zoe gave a quick, light laugh. "I'm so clumsy. I was rushing to get ready and knocked the box with my heavy winter boots right off the closet shelf. It hit me in the cheek. I was lucky; it could have taken my eye out!"

She was lying. Evelyn knew it. "A box fell on you? Or was it your husband, falling down drunk and dragging you down with him?"

"No, Mother! I told you, it was a shoe box. And Monty is not drunk; he is ill. Why must you always suspect the worst of him?"

She was so proud and stubborn, she would defend herself and her rotten husband to the end. Evelyn looked into her daughter's pleading eyes, silently asking Evelyn to believe her. The least Evelyn could do, she admitted to herself, was not make these moments harder for Zoe than they were. The girl was saddled with an unpredictable drunkard for a mate; she didn't need to be reminded of it at every turn.

"Yes, you were lucky. Be more careful next time, or better yet, don't be rushing around late."

Zoe gave Evelyn a hug. "You look beautiful, Mother. Give me a moment to fix my hair."

Zoe stepped into the marble-and-gilt powder room off

the entry. She locked the door behind her and waited until the sound of her mother's footsteps faded away down the hall, leaving her alone with the deadly, ticking silence inside her head. Then she carefully lowered herself onto the closed toilet seat, covered her face in her hands, and began to cry, muffled whimpering sounds coming from her throat as tears leaked through her fingers. She felt the silence in her head begin to fill with a familiar litany of self-loathing. She was no good; she never did anything right. She was a disappointment to everyone. It was no wonder that Monty was always angry with her. She deserved whatever she got. How dare she hope that Mother would say, *Zoe, darling! Did Monty hit you? Tell me; I will protect you.* Mother had told her to divorce him. Father had told her not to marry him in the first place. He'd wanted her to go to college, but she'd refused. She was in love and determined to make her own decision for once. They were wrong about Monty; she would prove it. She just had to stop making Monty mad. She had to think before she opened her mouth.

Shakily she rose to her feet and examined her face in the mirror. Tears had striped the custom-blended foundation. She fumbled in her purse for the cosmetic jar and set about repainting a mask of normalcy. As she fingered the discoloration on her bruised cheekbone, a wave of panic washed over her. In an unwanted flash of memory, she saw again Monty's face, livid with rage, looming in front of her as he called her a bitch and a cow and told her he hadn't married her for love. She felt again his fist collide with her cheek. She knew he didn't mean to hurt her, so why did her cheek throb and her back ache? She knew he loved her, so why were her heart and soul shriveled by his ugly, hateful words? She was so confused. What was real? Monty's love or her aching flesh? What was it that Sally had tried so often to tell her about this religion, this Christian Science she was so devoted to? Wasn't it to do precisely with this very question of what was real and what wasn't? What had Sally said . . . that the material world was just an illusion, illness and pain did not exist, evil and death did not exist. Only God existed, and through understanding one's relationship to Him one could be healed and could heal others. Could that be true? Wouldn't God say, *Tell me; I will protect you*? How wonderful if Monty's anger and his viciousness and his fists and his drink and her pain did not really exist and all she needed to do to make him happy and keep her safe was learn how to pray to God truly and properly and understand His Divine Mind. Certainly she could do that. Zoe felt hopeful. She would talk to Sally and find out more. Perhaps, finally, this was a path she could walk without fear of failure.

At four o'clock, the gas jets over the tables were lit against the darkness. By five, Sarah felt as though she'd been trapped for an eternity in a dim, wordless world of hunched backs and flying fingers. Another three hours to go and this was only a half day! Pankin gave Sarah only one coat at a time, thrusting it at her and telling her to hurry, as though expecting the next coat, or the next, to be the one she did poorly, revealing her unfitness for the job. He seemed disappointed when each one she brought back was perfectly finished. At six, a peddler came by the shop selling the last of his day's rolls. Everyone bought one except Sarah. The rolls looked and smelled so good, but she had no money. She would eat what she had brought.

She had been too agitated earlier to eat much of the soup she had made, and now she was starving, her stomach hollow and aching. Starving and so tired she could barely see. She laid another finished coat on Pankin's table and went to find her food, her mouth watering in anticipation of the thick bread and creamy fat. She couldn't remember where she had dropped her coat. She began looking everywhere, underneath the tables, on the backs of chairs. Pankin was watching her; she became anxious and clumsy. She knocked over a pile of finished coats, and when she reached to pick them up Pankin shoved her hard against his table.

"Stupid girl!" he yelled. "What are you doing?"

Sarah wanted to die. She wanted her mother. Oh God, how would she ever be able to do this! She thought suddenly of David and began to mewl. Why wasn't he here to protect her? Pankin loomed over her, waiting for her answer. She opened her mouth to explain that she was just looking for her coat, for her food, but she couldn't speak.

A gentle hand on her arm, and her coat appeared in front of her eyes. She clutched it to her, looked up to see Reuben staring down at her. He kept his eyes locked with hers, calming her, while he spoke to Pankin. "She was finding her coat, is all, Isaac."

"Well, she found it! Now I should send her home in it!" Pankin bent to retrieve the fallen clothes. His face was red.

Sarah cried with fear. Reuben made a face, shook his head silently: *Don't pay any attention to him.* Reuben led her back to their table, switched chairs with her, and sat her down. Then he went back to Pankin. "Give me her next piece."

"You have a big nose, Winokur. You should keep it out of other people's business."

"Isaac, in Lithuania I know soldiers more nice than you."

Pankin glared at Reuben but got only a smile in return. "They didn't have to put up with the foolishness of little girls."

"No, they killed them," Reuben said, holding out his hands for a coat.

For a moment, it seemed Pankin would leap across the table at him. Instead, he threw two coats at Reuben. "Tell your girlfriend to do these quickly, or I'll send you both home."

"Oh, absolutely, yes," Reuben said mockingly. "Send home your best finisher and your best feller hand. . . ." He lowered his voice. "Sarah, she is faster and neater than Ida, no?"

Pankin's scowl told Reuben he was right.

"So, she is young. Give her a chance. She will be good. So, Isaac?"

Unwillingly, Pankin nodded, then shooed Reuben away. "Fah. Go to work." But his voice had lost its edge. "And no more talking," he called out testily. "Anyone!"

Reuben sat down in the broken chair. Sarah was slowly chewing on her bread, savoring the last bite, tears still sliding down her cheeks. He wiped her tears with the sleeve of his shirt and put her work in front of her, two coats this time, a sign of Pankin's approval of her sewing skills. She looked over to thank Reuben, but his head was already bent over his needle.

Lucy sat next to her little brother and watched as he rapidly gorged himself on oyster stuffing and little onions in sweet, creamy sauce. He always ate Angelina's wonderful food the way he would read an H. G. Wells story, with total concentration and urgency, as though it might be the last pleasure he'd ever have. A far cry from the way he ate Edna's cooking at home, solemnly and carefully, the way he'd read a boring schoolbook. Of course, here there was more to distract Sally and he believed he was safe. Lucy knew better.

Brook hungrily shoved an entire half a biscuit into his mouth, and a hail of crumbs fell onto his tweed jacket. With dread, Lucy looked across the table at her mother. Sally, deep in conversation with Aunt Zoe, nonetheless managed to notice Brook's sloppiness. Her icy gaze locked on him. Her delicate nostrils flared. Lucy nudged him. He looked up and his eyes popped opened in alarm. Pointedly Sally lowered her gaze until it came to rest below his chin. He brushed the crumbs off in quick nervous strokes, sending them onto his lap and the carpet beneath his chair. When he glanced up again, Sally was looking at him with detached, impersonal disgust. He turned pale and his eyes dropped to his plate. He looked at his food as though it had all turned to poison.

"Lucy, dear, pass that remaining biscuit to Brook; he loves them so and his last one ended up on his jacket." Sally turned her attention once again to Zoe.

Lucy wanted to throw her own biscuit at her mother's head. Biting down on her lip, Lucy slid the last biscuit onto her brother's plate. He looked up at her, an awful spidery confusion crawling in his eyes.

"Lucy, what did I do?" he whispered.

She made a funny face. "Oooh, a terrible thing!" she

hooted quietly. "You dribbled crumbs on your jacket and then brushed them onto the floor! You should be whipped!" She grinned at him. "Forget it. Just eat this one over your plate, okay? No crumbs?"

Lucy took Brook's hand in hers and tried to grab Libby's with her other, but the little girl pulled away and ran to her mother.

Everyone had been shooed out of the dining room so the debris of dinner could be cleared and the table prepared for coffee and dessert. The men, tonight only Joseph and Philip, went to the library for brandy and cigars, and the women and children headed back to the drawing room. As Sally and Zoe brushed past Lucy, arm in arm, heads together, still talking, Lucy overheard her mother saying "*. . . get the literature to you and you'll come to our meeting next week.*"

"Oh my God," Lucy moaned. "Has Mother been badgering Aunt Zoe about this Christian Science idiocy all this time?"

"Lucy!" Brook hissed. "Be nice!"

"Oh, please." She rolled her eyes. "Libby's strange tonight," she mused. "She didn't say a word all during dinner. I can't believe you two are the same age. She seems so much older than nine sometimes."

"What does that mean? You think I act like a baby?"

Lucy laughed and kissed his forehead. "No, silly. Just that she acts like a little adult. But you know, you really can't fall apart every time Mother looks at you cockeyed."

Brook looked down at his shoes. "I know I shouldn't, but I can't help it. I just get so . . . so mixed up. I never know what I've done wrong!"

"But that's the point, Brook: you don't ever really do anything wrong."

"What?" he said incredulously. "I'm always doing something wrong. Why would she be so angry with me otherwise?"

"Because she's mean," Lucy said matter-of-factly.

"She's not! Lucy, you're terrible!"

"Well, she's angry all the time, for no reason, and you can't take it personally. It doesn't matter what you do or don't do; she's just looking for a convenient target. Sometimes it's Father; sometimes it's me; sometimes it's you. I don't let it bother me," she said flippantly.

"Oh yes, you do!" Brook accused her. "You fight with her all the time! You're horrible to her. And she has a reason. She's worried about Jed. I don't want to fight with her, Lucy. I want to make her happy!"

"What are you two doing standing in the hall," Evelyn called out. "Come in here with us, darlings. I don't get to see you often enough."

As Lucy and Brook entered the drawing room, there suddenly came a commotion and the sound of a hearty male voice at the door. Lucy saw Aunt Zoe glance at Sally, saw Sally nod forcefully. Elizabeth, with a look that blurred the fine line between terror and ecstasy, cried, "Daddy!" and flew from the room.

"Uncle Monty, you're here!" Brook ran to the hall as Monty appeared, carrying Elizabeth easily in one strong arm as she clung to him with her arms and legs.

Monty roughly tousled Brook's hair and then caught Lucy up in a one-armed twirling hug. "Hello, you little pests," Monty roared. "Did I miss anything?" He lavished his attentions on the children, evading the eyes of the women.

The children, Jed included, had always adored Uncle Monty. He had never-ending patience for them. He told jokes and he sang songs they weren't meant to hear. He was invariably in a good mood, and he could do magic tricks with coins and cards. He never said no to any of their childish requests. When they were little, he used to get down on all fours and let them ride him around like a pony for hours.

"You missed Angelina's goose and oyster stuffing!" Brook cried.

"Ah, but I didn't miss dessert, did I." Monty eased Libby down to the floor, kissed the top of her head, and turned to the women, three birds on a wire, staring at him.

"You're looking stunning, as always, Sally." The compliment was given with absolute familial propriety, but he turned a private look on her that was just a shade too bold. He noted with satisfaction the pretty little blush that colored her ivory cheeks beneath her censorious grimace. "And Evelyn. I'm sorry I wasn't feeling well enough to come earlier. I'm sure dinner was wonderful."

Evelyn didn't reply immediately. Monty's eyes were clear, his color fine; he was well-groomed and thoroughly steady on his feet. If he had been stinking blotto three hours earlier, there was no evidence of it now.

"I'm glad you're feeling better, Monty. Perhaps you'd like to join Joe and Philip in the library? We'll be having dessert soon." Her voice was cool.

"Of course, I have to wish Joe a happy birthday. But first . . ."

Finally, he looked at Zoe. He could tell from the haughty way she held herself that she hadn't told Evelyn he'd hit her. As their eyes locked he thought, *That's my girl*. He saw the bruise on her cheek, proof of a new intimacy, more revealing even than the love bites he often left on her neck. But only they knew its true meaning. Their secret, thrillingly worn in the open. Of course, in the future it would be smarter to leave no observable marks. When he'd woken up staring at the underside of the table, he'd actually missed her.

"Zoe, come give me a kiss." His voice was all tenderness. There was a momentary flicker of reluctance in her eyes, but then she smiled, came to him, and kissed him firmly on the cheek.

"I'm so glad you are recovered. I was worried about you."

"Excuse us a moment, won't you?" Monty put a hand on Zoe's elbow and steered her out of the drawing room, into one of the guest bedrooms. He closed the door behind them and moved to take her in his arms. She flinched, oh so minutely, but he noticed and felt a strange elation well up in him, a pleasure in the power he knew he held, literally, in his hands. Then she cautiously wound her arms around his neck and pressed herself against him. He stroked her slim back with long, languorous sweeps of his big hands and licked at the tang of perfume that clung to the satiny skin of her neck. Her breath came faster and he began to harden against the soft pressure of her belly.

"Zoe, I'm so sorry." His voice was a thick caress. A sob caught in her throat and he held her tightly. "I don't know what came over me, girl. I don't know. I'm sorry." He pulled back and took her face in his hands, stared deep into her tear-filled eyes. "You know I love you, Zoe, don't you?"

She nodded mutely and again he felt that lovely thrill travel through him, all the way to his groin, adding a new element to his arousal. He had punched her in the face, called her a bitch, told he only wanted her father's money, and this was his reward: Zoe limp with need in his arms, a weeping rag doll eager to spread her legs for him.

"You didn't tell anyone what happened, did you?" he said quietly, holding her face still. "Because it won't happen again, so no one needs to know, don't you see?"

Zoe didn't hesitate. "No, Monty. I didn't say anything. My mother noticed the bruise, but I told her a box dropped on me. Please, just tell me you won't do that again." She was crying openly now, her hands clutching at him.

"I already said that, didn't I? You be good, Zoe, and it won't ever happen again." He kissed her hard on the mouth, slid his tongue between her lips, savored the way she opened herself to him so hungrily, matching his own need.

He broke off the kiss and abruptly took her arms from around his neck. "Now I want a brandy. Go back to your mother, but remember this"—and he grabbed at her ass with both hands and pulled her hard against his hips—"for when we get home." Then he turned and walked out the door.

The evening wore on. Sarah stitched and stitched, two coats done, two more to do, again and again. Everyone was too tired to talk, and the only sounds were of the sewing machines at the piecers' table, the click of needles against thimbles, the scraping of chairs against the hard floor, the hiss of the jets. Sarah lost all track of time; it seemed she had always existed in this lonely place. She got up to hand Pankin her pieces for inspection and saw the clock on his table read 8:00. Elation filled her and she made ready to grab her coat and escape. But Pankin was shoving more work at her. Confused, Sarah looked around, expecting to see everyone tidying up. But the machines clacked on; heads were still bent over now-stiff fingers. Sarah felt all hope drain out of her. She couldn't possibly be the only one to leave, no matter what her mother had told her. She knew she didn't have the courage.

Sarah sewed on, her fingers moving mechanically. Finally, she sensed a change in the sounds around her and looked up to see that the workday was over. Though stupid with fatigue, she carefully wrapped the precious thimble, scissors, and needles and put them into her coat pocket. She wasn't sure what she should do next. Did she have the job or not? She walked over to Pankin's table and stood there waiting for him to say something. When, after several minutes, he hadn't so much as looked up at her, she knew she had failed. Humiliated and dejected, she turned to go. As she reached the door, his voice boomed at her back.

"You be here on time tomorrow, little girl. Seven sharp. I don't hold with laziness! You'll get six dollars a week, flat, and you're lucky to have it. Nothing for today."

She stumbled down the stairs into the darkened entryway. She didn't have the strength to pull open the heavy door. She leaned against the wall, determined not to cry again. Someone came behind her, opened the door, took her arm, and led her out onto the street. The cold air slapped at her face; big, light snowflakes fell onto the scarf that covered her head. It felt wonderful. She wrapped her coat around her and took a deep breath.

"So, little Sarah, you have a job," Reuben said. "You know he is taking advantage that you are so young. If he had to pay you by the piece you'd make more than Ida; you are faster. But for now . . ." He shrugged. "Where do you live? I'll walk you home."

"It's not far. You don't have to." But she wanted him to. "Ludlow and Broome." On the street, he appeared taller and more graceful than he had in the cramped shop. A thin layer of snow already covered his ash-brown hair. She realized she hadn't thanked him. "Reuben," she said, timidly using his name, "thank you for everything you did for me today."

He dismissed her gratitude with a wave of his hand. "Pankin, he is not so hard, really. But you are like a little mouse coming there today, and he is like a cat wanting to swat. You are so young. You should not be there."

"I don't want to be there," she blurted out. "It was awful. How do you do it every day?"

"Because I must. And I think you must, too. Yes?"

"Yes." Sarah sniffled. "Does it get easier?"

"Not really. I have been six months there and still a day is too long and hard."

That wasn't what Sarah had wanted to hear. "Where were you before?"

"Lithuania." He laughed.

Sarah gaped at him in amazement. "You've only been in America six months? But you speak English so well!" She couldn't help thinking of her father.

"I study hard, very hard. Even tonight, I go to English class. Without good English, I can't go nowhere. Six months more, no Pankin. In two year, I have my own shop, a good shop."

He sounded a little like Ben, with his accent and imperfect grammar, but he reminded her more of David, independent, ambitious, and unafraid. He couldn't be much older than David, either. And he wasn't running off to the war. He was staying here and making something of himself. Like David should have done. Tears of exhaustion and resentment welled in her eyes.

"Sarah, no. It won't be so bad. Don't listen to what I say." Reuben put a reassuring hand on her shoulder.

It was too much. She burst out crying. "I don't want to do this! It's all because of my stupid brother!"

"What? Ben I thought is just trying—"

"Not Ben," she bawled. "David. My stupid brother David who ran away to join the army, and now I have to work!"

"Ah." Reuben grew quiet. "That is brave, I think, no? If I was a citizen, I might to do that, too."

"No! You wouldn't. Not if you had a family that needed

you! And it's not brave; it's selfish! And irresponsible!" She parroted what she had heard Ben say repeatedly, for weeks after David left, until Anna had insisted he stop.

"You miss him, I think," Reuben said softly.

"No, I don't! I don't care if he never comes back!"

"Hmm." He nodded. "Well. I have a deal we should make, maybe? I had a sister in Lithuania: Ada. You I'm thinking are her age. How old is David?"

She was intrigued. "Your sister didn't come with you?"

"No. I came alone," he said quickly, then smiled. "So, how old your stupid brother?"

"He would have been nineteen last month," Sarah said, referring to David as though he were already dead, no hint in her voice of how monstrously strange the day of his birthday had felt to her, with no one mentioning him at all.

"Okay, good. I am nineteen since August. So how is this? You don't miss David, and I don't miss Ada, and instead we come to be friends for each other."

His hazel eyes were serious and his smile was sweet. Sarah giggled and held out her hand. "It's a deal." She felt calmer. "Reuben. You're funny."

They walked without speaking the last block up Ludlow Street. It was late and bitter cold. Without conversation to rouse her, Sarah sank into a pit of fatigue. She was so disoriented, she almost walked right by her building. She stared dumbly at the door and moaned at the prospect of climbing the four flights to the apartment.

Reuben took her by the elbow. "So. Good night, little one. Get a good night of sleep and I will see you tomorrow. Bring something more to eat. It will feel a very long day." He opened the door for her, gave her one last smile, then turned and disappeared around the corner.

Sarah slowly mounted the stairs, feeling her way in the darkness. Her head. swam. Pankin, coats, Ida, Reuben. Reuben. The apartment door opened as she reached their landing and her father stood in the lit doorway.

"Sarah, you are so late."

She stumbled into the room. Anna sat at the sewing machine at the kitchen table, a shirtwaist in her lap. Sarah felt her mother's eyes on her, her father's presence behind her. Everything looked so incomprehensibly normal, so warm and bright. She was afraid to speak, afraid to look at either of them. She felt a torrent of tears and bitterness waiting to pour out of her. It wasn't fair. She was going to have to go to that dreadful place every morning in the dark and come home every night in the dark. When was she ever going to see the light? When was she going to eat or read or study or play? She didn't want to do this. Why couldn't her father do something? Where was David? She was paralyzed by a terrifying fury at everyone.

"Sarah, was it so bad?" Anna's voice was gentle, full of empathy and love. She held out a hand and Sarah crumbled. She could not be angry at Mama and Papa or she would have nothing. She threw herself into her mother's arms and began to sob. Anna held her, rocked her slowly. "There, there. The worst is over. Tell me everything, darling."

Sarah poured her heart out along with her tears. She told Anna about Pankin and Reuben and Ida. She told her, with an almost grown-up pride, that she'd gotten the job. She apologized for not having had the courage to ask to be paid for today's work.

Anna told her it was all right. She stroked her daughter's hair. Sarah was such a good girl; she would always do what was asked of her. They needed the money desperately, but Anna's relief was bitter. When Sarah had been born, Anna had sworn to herself that she would not have to go to work like the other children. Another promise broken, like so many others. She couldn't prevent Ben and Sarah blaming David if that was what they chose to do. But Anna knew whose fault it was, and it wasn't that of her discontented son.

"Sarah." Viktor placed a plate on the table like a peace offering. "You must be starving. Here, like I told you, I kept dinner warm for you. I even got a nice piece of fish. . . ."

Sarah thought herself to be beyond hunger, but her mouth filled with saliva as she smelled the baked fish and potatoes. She stared at the plate like she'd never seen real food before. "Oh, Papa. It looks wonderful. Let me just go take off my boots. Is there any bread? I'll be right back." She dragged herself from her mother's embrace and staggered into her room. When after five minutes she hadn't returned, Viktor went quietly to her door.

"Anna, she is asleep, in her dress," he whispered as he walked back to the table. "Should I wake her? She should eat."

"No, leave her. She needs rest more." Anna bent over the sewing machine.

Viktor tiptoed again to Sarah's door and looked down at her. She lay on her side, her blankets folded neatly at her feet, sleeping heavily like a baby. He carefully pulled the blankets free and draped them over her. It would get cold in the apartment during the night. For the remainder of the evening, until nearly midnight, Anna sewed and Viktor sat in his corner reading Talmud and praying.

Everyone had gone home; the apartment was cleaned and restored to its pristine state, the staff disappeared into their quarters, the maze of rooms still. Evelyn and Joseph were in their bedroom preparing to retire. She fluffed the down pillows and perched on her side of the bed. She watched Joe slip out of his new robe, a custom-made Turnbull & Asser midnight-blue silk brocade with braided gold trim that had been her present to him, and admired his still-lithe, strong body. Evelyn was in a strange mood. The party had been lovely and yet she felt dissatisfied. Had she been capable of realizing it, she might have admitted that she was sad.

"You're unusually quiet tonight, Evie. Are you feeling well? Did the party tire you?"

"No, dear. It's always nice having everyone here."

Joseph carefully hung his robe on his valet, turned to her with a smile. "I love my robe. Thank you, darling. You take such good care of me."

Evelyn's breast filled with emotion. A swell of love for Joseph and something unfamiliar that very nearly brought her to tears. She smiled back at him. "You're welcome, my love. Who else should I take such care of if not you?" *My children. My unhappy stepson and my bruised daughter.* She let out a small, involuntary, "Ah!"

"What's the matter? Is it your stomach again? Maybe you should see Dr. Barre."

"No, no. I'm fine; it was just a, a hiccough. Joe . . ."

"What?"

Evelyn couldn't think of what she wanted to say.

"What, Evelyn? You're acting very odd."

"Maybe I am tired." She shook her head to clear it. "Philip told me he might have a significant new commission in the spring—Dorothy Woolbright."

Joe grunted as he switched off the overhead chandelier. "I suppose that's good news. What do I know. I have one son and he's an 'artist,' pandering to the self-indulgent whims of the rich. God forbid he should have gone to law school as I suggested, or come into the business."

"You'll have Jed for that. Philip is very good at what he does, Joe. And he loves it."

"Yes, yes," he said begrudgingly. "I hear he is good. Well, that's nice to know. Ahh, what's the point. And as long as we're speaking of my disappointing offspring, what the devil happened to Zoe's face? Did Monty finally hit her?"

Joseph's sarcastic question was just a horrid, unfunny joke, but Evelyn's blood went cold. *Is that possible? Should I have asked her? But no, it was clear, she didn't want me to ask. And he was sober, and they were so affectionate when he arrived. No, that can't be what happened.* "She said a box fell on her."

"God, that girl is clumsy." Joseph turned off his bedside lamp and slid beneath the smooth sheets. "Turn off your light and come to bed, Evie. I know the perfect way to end my birthday and make you feel better all at once." He reached out and ran his hand lightly over her silk-covered hip.

Joseph's touch calmed her. She put out her light and nestled her body into his, fitting her back to his front. "Just hold me for a moment." His arms came around her, his warm lips pressed against the back of her neck. "How fortunate we are, Joe," she whispered. "That we are so happy with one another."

Although she was not looking at his face, Evelyn could almost see him raise his eyebrows, his signature dismissive gesture. "We came together with our eyes open. We weren't besotted fools." His words were simple and declarative, inviting no discussion. As expected from a man as blithely uninterested in his own psychology as he was in everyone else's.

Evelyn had always found his lack of introspection or sympathy for the weaknesses of others to be one of Joseph's greatest attractions. Being thus unencumbered made him a very powerful man, able to make decisions and take risks that other, more timid souls never could. It made her feel safe down to her very core to know that he would never fall prey to doubt, would always be sure of what needed to be done. *Our children are so unhappy; what should we do, Joe?* She could not talk to him of such things; neither should she be thinking them. Perhaps Philip and Zoe hadn't chosen well, weren't as content as she and Joseph, but they would survive. They were adults, responsible for their own lives.

She emptied her mind and in one fluid motion turned onto her back, snaked her arms and legs around her husband, and drew him on top of her, arching up with urgent desire to meet the reassuring pressure of his rock-solid body.

Late in the night, Sarah awoke. The apartment was cold and silent. She fumbled her way down the hall to the toilet, sat on the freezing seat, and peed a river. Returning to the apartment, she saw the plate of fish and potatoes that Viktor had left on the table. Like a rat crawled out of hiding, she gobbled down the cold food with her bare hands and scurried back to her hole. She slithered out of her dress and burrowed quickly under the blankets before the sheets could lose the warmth from her body. Just before she fell asleep, she thrust her arm out from under the covers and grabbed for something on the crooked shelf above the head of her bed. She rejected the first item she touched, pushed it roughly to the shelf's far end. Her fingers closed on the thing she was looking for, and, with it hugged to her chest, she passed into oblivion.

Anna is bent close over her sewing machine, working carefully on yet another shirtwaist. The deafening clatter of hundreds of machines is borne on air thick with years of accumulated dust and fabric particles. Her needle flies through the cotton. Suddenly a cocoon of silence envelops her. She strains but cannot hear even the smallest sound. Her machine begins sewing madly, stitching crazed lines across the thin material. She cannot stop it. Confused, she looks up. She is alone. Unattended machines chomp through cloth like little dybbuks, silent and malevolent. She is frightened. She stands up and puts her hands over her ears. A curtain of grotesque orange smoke hangs in the air. Through the haze she sees a herd of women and girls running frantically in all directions, their arms stretched out before them, their eyes and mouths open in identical circles of terror. Sound returns in a monumental wave, assaulting her. Piercing, inhuman screams of panic and agony ride like sirens above the sheeting, whipping noise of the fire that is tearing through the huge closed room. Giant demons of flame devour the air and reach huge limbs out the burst windows to feed on the oxygen outside. Heat rises around her legs. Anna cannot move. She twirls in place like a doomed figure atop a broken music box. She is looking for her Rose, her flower. There, by the window! She tries to reach her, but a torrent of flailing arms and wailing faces carries her away. She opens her mouth to scream her name, Rose. No sound emerges; fire rushes in to silence her. She is helpless, paralyzed and mute, but not blind. She sees Rose climb up onto the window ledge, her skirt a halo of flames around her legs. Sees Rose slowly turn her head, smile at Anna, and walk out the window on a carpet of crimson. And fall nine stories, a tender young comet, to take her place among her friends. Then, Anna screams.

Anna's eyes opened into darkness, the scream that always ended the dream stifled in her scarred throat. She had begun having the nightmare again after David left; dreaming of one dead child, anticipating the death of another. Carefully, so as not to wake Viktor, she slid out of bed and, using strategically placed pieces of furniture for support, hobbled through the sheet wall to the dining table. She was glad to see that the plate of food Viktor had left for Sarah was empty, nothing remaining but a slick of cold fish oil shining in the wan illumination from the streetlights outside. She pulled her robe tight around her and sat in the dark, cold room, her back straight, her hands calmly folded in her lap, her eyes closed. Dimly, she heard the rustle of sheets as Sarah tossed in her sleep, the breathy rattle of Viktor's snores. The small sounds filled Anna with guilt and sorrow. As she had done on countless nights like this, she sent her mind spinning backward, trying in vain to find the road she should have taken, the choice she should have made, the offense she should not have given God, anything so that she could emerge into a better life. But no matter how many nights she sat shivering in the darkness rethinking her life, dawn always found her in the same room with two of her children dead, nothing to offer the three who still lived, a spectral husband, and no hope.

She had had hope once, as much as she thought she would ever need. As a young girl in Smolensk, a rare beauty with flashing gold eyes, a quick mind, and a wicked tongue, she'd had enough hope to choose a shy, sensitive Talmudic scholar for her husband. She believed then that Viktor's goodness, his devotion to her and to God, was all she needed in a partner. She knew and loved her own strength, didn't want it taken from her by one of those handsome, cocky young men who swarmed around her parents' grocery store, bragging of their ambitions. When the store was burned to the ground by neighbors who were encouraged to blame their own misfortunes on the evil Jews, she had enough hope to move her entire family to the strange town of Yartsevo, to live with Viktor's parents, though they had little left themselves. Hope grew as she gave birth to Ben, and then to Wolf and Rose; as the

Warshinskys and the Hertzigs together worked hard and made a new store; as Viktor was left in peace to fill his senses with his beautiful family, bury his nose in his books, and offer his soul to God.

Hope nearly deserted her the day Wolf disappeared. After three hours he had not returned from delivering a small bag of groceries to Widow Voldinskaya—the proud, grown-up errand he had begged to do. They found his six-year-old body tossed into the tall grass by the side of a dusty road, his head beaten in, a bloody rock by his torn ear, *Die Jew* viciously scratched into the pale, perfect skin of his hollow belly. His outflung hand rested on an apple, crushed under an angry boot, its sweet juices staining the lifeless little fingers. Anna thought all hope went with Wolf into his small grave, but she retained just enough to propel herself, Viktor, Ben, and Rose to America. She didn't look back, didn't allow herself to consider the lonely and impoverished fate of their parents. Viktor may have been expelled from his Eden forever, becoming a ghost haunting the ruins of his life, but Anna believed her Eden lay across the ocean.

For fifteen years it seemed she was right. They struggled, and Viktor failed at one small job after another until Anna lovingly told him to stop trying, that she could earn enough for them both. And she did, working days at the Triangle Shirtwaist Factory and nights at home while Viktor spent his mornings studying and praying at the Eldridge Street Synagogue and his afternoons at the Smolensk *landsmanshaft,* the benevolent society, in the company of familiar men also desperate to regain their lost past. But though she struggled and they lived in squalor, hope somehow grew again. They were safe; they were healthy; Ben, Rose, and then David and Sarah lightened the dark shadow of Wolf's short life and pitiful death. The years passed slowly, but at last came the day when Anna's hopes were realized: they were living in a beautiful, bright, clean apartment; Ben was engaged to a lovely, devout girl; Rose was working by Anna's side; David and Sarah were in school. They had plenty to eat, and everyone, even Viktor, was content.

It was the fire that finally undid Anna. It flayed her raw with the realization that her hopes had been nothing but foolish illusions. A child could die as horribly, as needlessly, here as in Russia. America didn't care if men treated their workers like vermin, locked them inside their factory rooms for fear that they would steal scraps of cloth, let them die like panicked animals in those rooms, and then swore it was not their fault. The blaze that ended 146 innocent lives, took her daughter, burned Anna's legs, and scarred her throat left a puny pile of cinders where her lofty dreams had been. She retreated into an invalid's world where she strived for nothing more than to keep what hadn't yet been taken away from her.

And there she remained. As the predawn chill solidified around her like a shawl woven of ice crystals, Anna shook herself out of her reverie. She flexed her fingers, stretched her neck and shoulders, got up, and stoked the stove to put up water for their morning tea. Life would have taken her here no matter whom she'd married, where she'd taken a job. It was her Fate, *beshert*. And while she knew that she and Viktor could do nothing to help their children, she didn't want this to be their Fate as well. Didn't want it so fiercely that she thought sometimes the worry over their future would squeeze the very beat out of her heart. Thank God for Ben; he was all right. But David . . . It was meant to be that he would leave like that. She was right to have let him go. He was the chosen of God, and God would keep him safe. She believed it, and yet the mere thought of him conjured a vivid image of him slaughtered, his broken and bloodied body left to rot in tall grass under a foreign sky. She became so terrified thinking about him that soon after he left she willed herself to stop. As long as he was gone she would not think about him, would not talk about him. Now, no one spoke of him. It was better that way. Only when he walked back in the door would he live again for them.

That left Sarah. Anna turned from the stove toward Sarah's room. Though it was still dark as the deepest night outside, Anna knew it was time to wake her. She went to the closed door and, without knocking, opened it. Sarah was sound asleep, one arm thrown over her eyes, the other wrapped around a frayed stuffed bear that Rose had bequeathed to her on her sixth birthday. Hanging precipitously off the end of the shelf was the fragile, expensive bisque doll that David had brought Sarah soon after Rose died, to comfort her. David had sworn he hadn't stolen it, but to this day Anna didn't know where a twelve-year-old boy had gotten the money to buy it. Anna righted the doll and stared down at her youngest, her little girl. A flood of new shame washed through her. As she reached out to shake Sarah awake, Anna felt a faint stirring deep inside her, a long-forgotten emotion struggling to rise through a mountain of misery.

4

*David sat up on his narrow metal bunk. His unerring inter*nal clock told him that the first light of morning was lifting over the horizon. Here belowdecks there was only the murky semidarkness created by the bare bulbs in the corridor outside the enlisted men's hold. In another hour, all the lights would come on and the artificial twilight would be replaced with glaring artificial daylight. David hated it. He hated almost everything about where he was except that it wasn't where he'd come from. Every day he reminded himself that he was moving farther and farther away from home. To be doing that was worth even going to war. It had to be. He had to believe that something good awaited him as a reward for his boldness, his recklessness, for having such confidence in his own destiny to justify alienating and abandoning his family.

Physically at least, being in the army was so far surprisingly similar to the existence he had left behind. It was all so familiar, the suffocating, overcrowded quarters, the lack of privacy, the long grueling days, the impossibility of independent thought or action. The food was worse, incredibly bland. *Goyim* didn't know how to flavor anything. After five months of army cooking, David had begun dreaming of Anna's Shabbat dinners, waking with the taste of rich chicken soup in his dry mouth.

He groped in the dimness for his shirt, pants, shoes, dressed quickly. He draped his long overcoat over his shoulders and picked his way through the cramped hold, weaving a careful path around the metal bunks filled with fidgety men. In the shadows cast by the weak light David saw tense faces turning toward him as he passed, questioning eyes following his solitary progress. He didn't pause. He could feel the great ship's prow reaching out to close the distance between itself and the rising sun. Soon France. Soon the war. He needed to be up on deck.

"Warshinsky? Where you goin' in such a hurry? You see some Krauts in the hall?" A self-amused snicker, a heavy hand on his shoulder.

David glanced back into Vernon Cooper's homely face. David was starting to feel as if he couldn't go to the bathroom without Cooper popping up beside him. As always, the needy, hopeful look in Cooper's eyes made David think briefly of Sarah. "Come up on deck with me, Vern. I can't stand it down here anymore. I can't sleep."

David was tolerant of Cooper. It would be unjust to dislike him. Beneath his crude exterior, Vern was sweet and loyal. Being treated like utter crap by most of their fellow trainees early on had resulted in the forging of a self-protective alliance between the clever young Jew boy from New York City and the dull farm boy from Minnesota. David was well used to being judged and rejected on the basis of his name, his coloring, his clothing, but Cooper, raised in a gentler environment than David, was not. It hurt him that the men didn't like him.

David didn't give a rat's ass whether anyone liked him, except Jed. Privately he cared a great deal about that. As for everyone else, he knew he was better than them. Smarter and quicker. Cannier and hungrier. After two months of ignoring the insults and taunts, offering no retaliation of any kind—uncharacteristic behavior requiring a tremendous application of will on his part—he had earned their respect. It wasn't surprising. Most of them had never so much as seen a Jew before, and David, their first live specimen and the only one in camp, quickly became an exotic attraction rather than an alien threat. His dark good looks and strong, wiry body belied the common view of the Jew as a weak, bookish, subhuman species. He trained with a fervor and skill that promised a fearless determination to emerge the victor from any battle. That and his at times alarming mental quickness made the men near him feel safe, even men a decade older than he. He'd been promoted to corporal almost immediately and made sergeant just before they'd shipped out. And the fact that the dazzling Jed Gates, the camp's fastest-rising leader despite his similar youthfulness, obviously liked him enhanced his standing even further. Through it all, David let Cooper stay close to him. Small wonder that Vern adored him, clinging to him like moss to a rock.

Emerging on deck, they were hit by a freezing March wind. The ship was moving at a good pace. David quickly shrugged into his coat and flipped the collar up to protect his neck.

"Christ Almighty, David, it's cold up here." Cooper folded his arms across his chest and started jumping up and down.

"Is that how you stay warm in Minnesota? You look like a deranged chicken."

"Very funny," Vern said sourly, but he stopped jumping, shoved his hands in his pockets. "It gets colder than this on the farm, but you work so hard you don't even notice it mostly. Actually, this ain't so bad, sorta like a Minnesota summer." He smirked.

David took a deep breath of the sharp air. "I like it. I can't smell anything."

"I can smell the sea; can't you?"

"Of course, but it's so clean. It's not the smell of open pickle barrels, ashcan fires, unwashed people."

"No, I'd guess not."

David had no expectation that Vern would understand what he was talking about. They were on the sea, so Vern would smell the sea, just as at home on the farm he would smell the earth and the animals and the rain and the sun. He was lucky. His world was a simple place.

"Let's walk," David ordered, his impatient body already three steps ahead.

"Hey, wait for me!" Vern scurried to keep up. "Why are you in such a hurry? You act like you actually want to get to France, for Christ's sake."

"I do."

Vern shook his head. "Man. I wish I was back on the farm. Ain't you scared?"

"Yeah, of course I'm scared. So what?"

"You sure don't show it."

"Showing fear makes you vulnerable. But we're all scared, Vern. You'd have to be nuts not to be."

"I think we're nuts to be up here in this weather!"

"Then go back down."

"No, no, I didn't mean that. It's just so different from yesterday, you know. So quiet."

Yesterday. The mad crush of men on deck, shouting good-bye to America, waving wildly to the relatives and strangers who had come to see them off. Ears and cheeks bright red in the wind, but no one had felt the cold. Hot with excitement, their months of training over, they were going to find the war. By nightfall, home felt a lifetime away and nervous anticipation had transformed their excitement into a steady buzz of tension. It ran through the ship like a sharp electric charge, rendering the men edgy, restless, and subdued all at once. It was that palpable uneasiness that had driven David from the hold this morning as much as the letter that was buried, unopened and unread, in his coat pocket.

The dawn quiet on the nearly deserted deck did nothing to soothe David. He glanced over at Vern struggling to keep up with him, shoulders bunched against the cold and head pulled into his coat like a startled turtle. David felt like an animal himself, running on survival instinct, immune to the cold. He walked with his head up, inhaling and exhaling in long, luxurious breaths. The chill air was purifying, but not enough to cool the old fever of anger and guilt that had burned in him for the past three days, since the letter from Anna arrived. After five months of mutual silence, Anna's letter was the first he'd received from anyone but Rachel. He'd answered several of her frequent letters, but he hadn't written home. He had nothing to say.

As they reached the aft deck, David saw a tall, slim figure standing downwind, sheltered in the lee of the ship. A familiar blond head was bent in concentration over something held tightly in gloved hands. Jed. The tension inside David began to lose its murderous grip. He stopped before Jed became aware of his presence. Jed wanted to be his friend, but David still didn't know why any more than he knew why he found Jed soothing to be around. It wasn't altogether possible for David to accept that they simply liked each other despite being from two different worlds, that Jed was simply one of the nicest, most decent fellows he'd ever met. In David's experience, nothing was that pure or innocent. This hesitant friendship was too easy, and he had a massive distrust of anything that came easily. He was used to fighting for the things he wanted. Nothing worthwhile had ever just been given to him before.

"Oh hell, it's *Lieutenant* Gates," Vern muttered.

As if on cue, Jed turned his head. His gaze slid uninterestedly past Cooper. "David." He smiled with pleasure at the sight of him. "I've missed you. I would have come down to the hold, but I thought you would be asleep. Why are you up so early?"

They hadn't had much opportunity to see each other since Jed had been separated from the enlisted ranks for officer training. They hadn't seen each other at all during the past week, while Jed was back home for a farewell visit.

David didn't have a chance to answer Jed's greeting. Before he could even open his mouth, Vern jumped in with one of the oafish things he always managed to come up with when in Jed's presence.

"What brings *you* up here, Lieutenant? Did one of the real officers kick you out of your posh quarters?"

Jed's happy smile froze. "Do you have a problem with me being an officer, Cooper?"

"Hey. I was jokin'. *I* don't think your big-shot grandfather is pullin' strings for you, not me! No, sir!"

"Okay. That's enough." David grabbed Cooper's arm. "Vern, go down to the mess and find us something that might have been alive once. McDermott said they loaded crates of oranges. We'll be down in a little while."

"How can you stand him?" Jed's eyes filled with dislike as he watched Cooper hustle away. "He's a moronic toad. And how dare he imply that I didn't earn my commission!" Joseph had had nothing to do with it. Jed had asked his grandfather directly last week and Joseph had reassured him, *Now, why would I have to interfere, Jed? You're eminently qualified for leadership.* "You don't think the other men believe that, do you?"

"I have no idea, Jed, but what do you care what they believe? Everyone thinks you're a great officer, however you got there. So, at ease, Lieutenant," David joked. "Listen, do you think you could please find a way to get along with Vern? I swear, sometimes the two of you make me feel like a piece of meat being fought over by a pack of wolves. It's really annoying."

"I'm sorry, David," Jed was instantly contrite. He didn't want David to be annoyed with him. "He just really irritates me."

"He's a total boor around you, I know. But you intimidate the hell out of him. He has no other friends but me, and anyway, what am I supposed to do while you're off with the big boys?" David smiled.

A familiar bubble of childish satisfaction burst in Jed's brain. There he was, four years old again and delirious with relief that his mother wasn't interested in this horrid helpless Lucy creature whose arrival had disturbed his perfect world. He could try to be nicer to Cooper.

"So, how was the visit with your family? Was everyone weeping all over you?" David's tone was teasing but hardened by an almost jealous edge. David dropped his eyes from Jed's sympathetic look and gave a small, harsh laugh.

Jed had been looking forward to going home, but as soon as he got to Gramercy Park he wished he were back in camp. He hadn't realized how much he had come to like the physically disciplined army life until he was separated from it. Going home also meant leaving David alone with

Vern Cooper, the little leech. Jed had thought about asking David to come with him, but he knew David was fighting the natural rapport that had sprung up so quickly between them. Jed could feel him struggling against it as clearly as he'd seen him struggling with the man who'd attacked him on the enlistment line, as though Jed's interest in him were an offense to his self-reliance. But David didn't ever pull away too far, and Jed knew how to be patient.

He had heard enough about what had happened on Ludlow Street the night David left to know not to boast about how his mother expected him to become a four-star general. "No. It was a nice visit," Jed said. "David, I'm sorry. I'm sorry you didn't feel you could go home."

"Oh, screw that. I don't care." David looked at Jed again, his eyes vacant of expression. "What's that?" He gestured toward the papers in Jed's hand.

Jed let the conversation go where David wanted to take it. "A letter from my sister, Lucy."

"Already? You just saw her."

"Yes, but she sent me something to take to France. Her Chapin junior class photograph. Honestly, I think she sent it for you. She was intrigued by what I told her about you. Furious I hadn't brought you home."

"Why? What did you tell her?" David sounded both flattered and apprehensive.

"I told her you were smart and good-looking. She's fifteen and a half, so you can imagine what effect that had. And that you were Jewish, and . . . let's say . . . had grown up without the advantages we took for granted. So you would not be my mother's choice for her as a suitor, which was an absolute guaranteed thrill!" He laughed. David was smiling. "And . . . now David, don't be mad. I told her a little about your family, about how you parted with them. Lucy's a real pip; she drives my mother wild, but she's got a great heart. So, she really did send this for you, so you'd have someone . . . She meant well; don't be angry." Jed held out a small rectangle of shiny paper. "Here, take it if you want. I know what she looks like."

David hesitated a moment; his smile disappeared. He took the photograph from Jed's hand. A formal school photograph, a pretty young girl, poised and proper, beautifully dressed, long bright hair piled on top of her head. Light eyes blazed out from the glossy paper and were filled with the expectation of happiness. No fear or want marred the lovely features. So different from Sarah. David swallowed around the lump in his throat.

"What a sweet thing to do; she doesn't even know me." He stared at Lucy's face again, trying to see down into her. Reluctantly he offered the photo back to Jed. "But I can't keep it. She's your sister; you should have it."

"I already have one. I know she sent this for you. She'd be upset if you didn't keep it." He shrugged. "Just put it in your pocket. It would make her happy."

David looked away. "Thank her for me, okay?" He slipped the photo into his pocket. His hand found Anna's letter. The lump in his throat threatened to choke him. "Jed?"

"What is it? What's wrong?"

David withdrew the letter. "I got this a few days ago. It's from my mother." He tried to smile but failed. "I haven't been able to read it."

Jed held his breath. David's resistance was weakening; even for him, it was too hard to be alone all the time. He needed a friend, and not someone like Cooper—a real friend. "You have to read it, David."

David's mouth twisted. He stared out over the empty ocean.

"I'll stay here." Jed took a step away from him. "I won't look at you. I don't want to know what she says. I'll just be here. So you're not alone. All right?"

David looked at Jed with dispirited eyes and nodded. Jed turned and David was looking at his back, long and straight and strong looking under his heavy coat, offering itself to be leaned on, to be trusted.

My darling son,

I ask you to forgive me for being silent for so long, and also for if I cannot bring myself to write to you again. You have to know how painful for me is your absence, and how terribly I worry about you, even though I know

I was right to say to let you go. Adonai has marked you for greatness and He will keep you from harm. It doesn't matter to Him that you don't have faith, David. Ours is not a petulant or selfish G-d. You are His child as much as mine, and it is through you that He will redeem my choice to bring us to America. I believe this as surely as I believe the sun will rise tomorrow, but it doesn't stop me from fearing for your safety every minute of the day. I am your mother, after all.

I want you to keep what I've said always in your heart and never falter on your journey because of worry about us. We will be all right. Your leaving has changed me. When the money you left us was gone, we had to send Sarah to work. Since six weeks now, she is working in a shop like the first one you found after Rose died. She will do it, she is such a good girl, but she cries every night in her bed. She is not strong like you and Rose; she is still so young. But she is not your responsibility. She is mine, and I will take care of her.

David, I am going to get better. I am going to get better and get a good job. I even know who will give me one when I ask. It will take some time. I have let myself become so weak. Yesterday, after Papa left for shul, I walked in the apartment. Five minutes and I had to go back to bed. But every day I will do another minute and another minute and by the summer I will be strong again. No one knows but you. I don't want to say anything until I am nearly there.

This would never have happened for me if you had stayed and taken care of us. It wouldn't have happened if I hadn't had to wake Sarah in the dark and cold to send her to that shop. Something has broken loose inside me and it is good.

Papa misses you. I hear him pray for you. But we don't talk about you. You understand. We can't. Sarah and Ben, they are so angry and hurt, and anything I would do right now would only make it worse. But when I am better, and when you come back to see us, I will make us a peace that will last forever. For now, we leave things as they are and look to the future.

You don't have to answer this letter. I will know that

you are alive as long as I don't hear that you are not, and that is all that matters. You can tell me everything later. We will sit at the kitchen table, with tea and babka, and you will tell your mama everything, like you did after school when you were a little boy.

I love you so much I cannot hold my pen steady anymore to write, and so I say good-bye.

David returned the letter to his pocket, next to the picture of Lucy. Jed had not moved. David watched the wind ripple the back of Jed's coat and willed himself not to see, scrolling across the blank screen of thick wool, images of his little sister crying in the dark and his mother dragging her injured body across the apartment floor. For fifteen minutes David pulled apart his mother's words, picking out the ones that were dangerous and casting them aside so that they could not pierce him and reduce him to tears. In all that time, Jed did not move.

"Jed. You can turn around now."

Jed did, careful not to react to the bruised look in David's eyes, careful to keep his curiosity from showing.

David tried again to smile. This time he succeeded. "I'm fine. Thank you for staying here with me like that. It was . . . a very generous thing to do. Lucy's not the only one in your family with a good heart."

Jed smiled back at him. "You're welcome."

"Yeah." David's gaze traveled across the horizon. He inhaled deeply, slowly let the vapory air out of his lungs. "What do you say we find Vern and get some of those oranges? My mouth is awfully dry."

Late that night, David lay awake, contemplating his mother's unwavering faith in him. She had told him to find what he was looking for and that when he found it she would be redeemed. When he'd left home, he hadn't known what form his desires might take. But now, sleepless in his bunk with Lucy's picture in his hand, he did. He wanted to make his mark in the world that Jed lived in, populated by men like Jed's masterful grandfather, men who mattered, whose actions had influence far beyond the confines of their own tiny, personal universe; by men like Jed's father, men who had the freedom to exult in their abilities and talents, no matter what they were, and not have to destroy their own souls in order to eat. David knew what his talents and abilities were, and he wanted to use them to become rich, the kind of rich that the ghetto could not contain. And he wanted his success and his wealth to be recognized and to have meaning. He wanted to meet refined women, women who were educated and elegant, graceful and respectful; he lifted the photograph, studied Lucy's face in the sparse light. And in order to do all that, he wanted to be like Jed, calm and confident of his place, so that he could fit into such a world with such natural ease that no one would ever know he hadn't been born to it.

5

Philip swung open the ornately carved wrought-iron gate at Number 21 Gramercy Park South. The gas street lamps glowed with an ethereal light, casting ovals of creamy yellow into the purple dusk. Across 20th Street, behind the great iron fence, the trees inside the small perfection that was Gramercy Park were still, their majestic forms blending into the gathering shadows. In the fading light of a perfect May evening, the profusion of azaleas that filled Number 21's small courtyard radiated waves of color, incandescent shades of pink and purple. White-lacquered window boxes held masses of pansies and petunias, their velvety deep blue flowers leaking inky color into the darkening air. Philip stood quietly, wrapped in joy, his painterly eye drinking in the wondrous harmony between the work of man and the work of nature here in this quiet, peaceful square of the city. Sally would have liked to move uptown as his parents had, to a modern, aerie apartment in an opulent building, but Philip could not imagine living so far above the earth.

He was late coming home and hadn't telephoned Sally to warn her. She would be angry. He imagined he could feel her wrath seeping through the front door like smoke off a block of dry ice. He knew he should go in, but he was loath to leave the tranquillity of his garden for the disquiet he was sure to find inside. He turned away from the door and let his gaze wander aimlessly through the park's leafy shadows.

Philip missed Jed. He accepted that Jed belonged to Sally, as Lucy belonged to him. Never had he dared breach the territorial walls that enclosed mother and son. They had been in place too long, already standing by the time Philip was allowed into the bedroom to see his firstborn child lying peacefully in the unyielding arms of his beautiful, exhausted nineteen-year-old bride. Philip made do with adoring Jed from afar. He adored his beauty, his goodness, his eager disposition, his ability to make and keep peace in their often turbulent household. Philip yearned for Jed to know how much he loved him but had never found a way to tell him. Now he was afraid that there might never be an opportunity, that his son might die far from home, never really knowing his father, never really being known. Philip turned back and stared intently into the quietest, darkest corner of his courtyard. In the safety of the tangle of flowers growing there he buried his feelings like hidden treasure, for certainly he could not take them inside. Then he unlocked the front door and slipped into the vestibule.

"You seriously think I'm going to allow you to go to college?" Sally yelled. "You can put those grand ideas right out of your head! Your brother is going to college, but not you!"

"Why not?!" Lucy shrieked, all composure gone. "I have as good a brain as Jed and I want to use it! Women go to college now. You may be happy being ignorant and useless, but I'm not! All you know is how to be mean and selfish!"

Sally's palm cracked against Lucy's cheek. "How dare you talk to me like that! How dare you! You are spoiled and willful. Your father lets you get away with too much. You will go to Miss Foster's School after you graduate and learn to be a proper young lady and maybe, just maybe, some unfortunate man will take you off my hands! We will *not* talk about this again!"

"No, no, no! I will *not* marry one of your stupid friends' stupid sons—"

The sound of a key in the front door cut Lucy off and she ran toward the entryway. As Philip stepped into the vestibule, both women bore down on him with grim, flushed faces. Sally, one step behind Lucy, reached out and grabbed the girl's arm.

"Don't you run to your father with this! I have said *no* and that's the end of it."

Lucy shook off her mother's hand and planted herself in front of Philip. "You have to tell her to let me go to college! She is being horrid. Tell her, Father!"

He was trapped. No matter what he did, it would be no good. He took his time leaning his portfolio against the wall. "Let me take off my coat and hat. Now, what is this all about?"

"I want to go to college! All my teachers say I must! I'm going to apply to Barnard next year and—"

"She is not!" Sally interrupted. "There is no earthly justification for her to waste your money and her time on such nonsense when all she needs is a good finishing school. It is more than enough that you insisted she attend Chapin. Look at the ideas it's put in her head."

"Father!" Lucy wailed.

As far as Philip was concerned, Lucy could do whatever she wished and if it was a college education she wanted, so be it. He wanted his daughter to find something of her own that she loved before the crushing weight of adulthood fell on her. He had had the chance to do so and now, no matter what else was disappointing in his life, he loved his work.

Sally always got what she wanted for Jed; Philip owed it to Lucy to do the same for her. "If she wants to go to college, let her go, Sally. We have more than enough money to waste and you know she'll just make us both miserable if we refuse."

Lucy gave a victorious yelp and threw her arms around her father. "Thank you! Thank you! Thank you!"

Philip looked at Sally over Lucy's shoulder. Her eyes had lost their angry glare. Her expression was without emotion of any kind. She shook her head slightly back and forth. He could all but hear her thoughts. *Once again, Philip, you let me down. Why do I even bother to hope for anything useful from you?*

"Lucy, take my portfolio case up to my study, please." Philip disentangled himself from her embrace and gently pushed her away. "Let me talk with your mother."

Sally did not watch as Lucy bounded up the stairs. She kept her eyes on Philip and said, "What is there to talk about? You don't care what I think or what I feel. You say yes to whatever foolishness that girl puts to you. In a thoughtless moment, you undo all the good I try so hard to do. Why not continue, Philip? Why not go upstairs and tell Brook it's fine with you if he subverts his mind reading those horrid pulp magazines, that Tarzan trash, which I found him doing again today. Why should the children have any respect for what I tell them?"

"Sally, you are making yourself upset about insignificant things. Let's not stand in the hallway and argue."

"Where would you prefer?" she said caustically.

Philip sighed. "I am going to have a drink."

He took her by the elbow. She stiffened at his touch but let him guide her into the parlor. He settled her onto the sofa and poured himself a generous shot of cognac. He did not offer her anything. She used to relish a fine sherry or a good glass of claret, but since taking up with Christian Science she had rejected alcohol in any form.

"I don't know why you have to drink. And how many times must I ask you to call when you are going to be late? Why do we have a telephone?"

"I know; I know; I'm sorry. But perhaps you'll forgive me when I explain that I lost track of time for a very exciting reason. I met with Edgar Woolbright again. He has made his decision. His wife will begin sitting for me when she returns from London in the fall."

"How wonderful! Another foolish piece of work that all

of a dozen people will ever see!" She got up from the sofa and stalked toward the doorway.

"Sally!" He left his glass on the mantle and took a step toward her. "Can't you at least pretend to show the slightest respect for what I do! The Woolbrights had their choice of portraitists—Cecilia Beaux, Ernest Proctor, Clausen, even Sargent—and they chose me. That kind of recognition means a great deal. Aren't you even a little proud?" He hated himself for begging, but her belittling of his work was sometimes harder to bear than her overall disdain. He doubted much about himself, but he knew that he was a fine painter. All he wanted was to share his accomplishment with her, just for a brief moment.

Sally waved a conciliatory hand as she turned back to him. "Yes, all right, Philip, but really, I don't need another ill-behaved child in this house. Congratulations, your news is lovely. But you are selfish to come in here full of it and nothing else! Thinking only of yourself when I am so distraught and your children are out of control—"

"They are not out of control, Sally; they are merely beyond *your* control. Sometimes I think it is you who is out of control!"

Sally was still as a statue. "Remove your glass from the mantle; it will leave a stain on the marble. I will see to dinner." She stepped into the hall. "And kindly change your clothing before we eat. You look like a tradesperson in that horrid suit."

Philip took up his snifter and wiped at the spot where it had been, although there was nothing there. He returned the undrunk cognac to the decanter and placed the glass on the tray for Edna to remove. His momentary audacity was assailed by doubt and remorse. It was cruel of him to cause Sally distress. Since Jed had sailed for France, the very air that filled the house seemed to swirl and burn with her fear. She would not speak of it, though it stalked her like a malevolent ghost and rendered her incapable of anything but hostility toward Philip, Lucy, and Brook, who offended her merely by being in no danger themselves.

More than ever before, Philip did not know how to behave around her. Standing up for Lucy was not only the right thing to do but also the sort of thing Evelyn had hinted he should do. Yet Sally had grown even angrier and accused him of betraying her. There was one perverse benefit of disagreeing with her, however: it forced her to pay attention to him. Argument seemed his only remaining tool for sustaining contact with her at all. And occasionally, after she had viciously ground him to rubble, when her disregard for him could not be any more obvious, she took pity on him and allowed him into her bed. It shamed him, but there it was. He hoped that he had gotten her angry enough tonight to earn him the humiliating, obliteratingly pleasurable right to lose himself in his love for her.

He turned from the fireplace and went upstairs to change his clothes.

"Brook! Brook, can you hear me?" Lucy paused outside her brother's room on her way to her father's study. "Father's home. Dinner soon. I'll be right back. I've got to tell you what happened!" She banged twice on the closed door for emphasis and then scurried down the hall.

One more year at Chapin and then Barnard College! She was going to be free! Her next campaign would be to persuade Father to let her live uptown, near the college and out of this house. She hoisted Philip's portfolio case onto his drawing desk and bent down to kiss the expensive, worn leather. She loved her father. She straightened up and went to fetch Brook.

From his hiding place inside his armoire Brook heard Lucy call to him. He had crawled into his lair to shut out the sound of his mother's and sister's angry voices. Now he emerged and stood by the door. He loved Lucy the way he loved the feel of the sun on his face, the way he loved the song of the robins that nested in the locust tree outside his bedroom window. He loved his mother, father, and brother, too, but his love for them was a terrifying, bottomless well of hurt and doubt. If there were handholds somewhere, he'd never found them.

Lucy's footsteps were in the hall and he opened his door, the long afternoon's loneliness dispelled by the sight of her. He grabbed her hand, pulled her inside, and sat beside her on his bed.

"What were you and Mother fighting about?"

"College. She doesn't want me to go."

"Why not?"

"Because she's stupid and jealous."

"Lucy! She's not! She must have a good reason."

"Really? Give me one possibility."

The mouth of the well gaped beneath him. "I don't know. How could I know? But she must. She wouldn't just say no. Maybe it's dangerous! Maybe you'll become a, a, a fallen woman or something!"

Lucy burst out laughing. "Good God, do you even know what a fallen woman is? Where do you get your ideas? And if you are so sure she must have good reason, what is her good reason why you can't read *Tarzan*?"

"She says it will fill my head with nonsense, I'll become coarse and vulgar."

"You don't sound very convinced. What do you think?"

Brook looked down at his hands. "I think it's nifty," he whispered. "It's so clever and exotic, it makes me imagine all sorts of stories. I think it's all right if I read it. But then I think that liking it must be a sin. It means my thoughts aren't pure, I'm not close to God. I just wish I knew if it was really all right."

"It *is* all right. What does *Tarzan* have to do with God?" Lucy said impatiently. "This is all about Mother, and Mother is not God! Read the damn stories, and don't let her find out. You can do that."

"I don't know." His voice barely carried to Lucy's ear.

Lucy put a hand under his chin and turned his face toward her. "Brook, listen to me. The sooner you understand the way things are, the better off you'll be. You will never win Mother's affection by doing whatever unfair things she tells you to. She has a tiny heart and there's no room in it for anyone but Jed. She'd be happiest if you, Father, and I just disappeared. Of course, he never will. He *loves* her," she mooed, batting her lashes. "God knows why."

"Lucy!" Brook giggled nervously.

"Be selfish, Brook! She is. Do what you want. Don't go to those ridiculous CS meetings with her. Stay home and read *Tarzan*! She can't treat you any worse than she already does."

Brook pitched right over the lip of the well and went tumbling down. Maybe Mother didn't love Lucy, but Lucy was disobedient and hateful to her. And of course Mother loved Jed best; but that was because Jed was perfect and Brook wasn't, yet. But he could be if he tried harder. Lucy was wrong. He couldn't just do what he wanted; that was thoughtless and Mother would never love him. He had to do what Mother wanted of him.

Lucy gave his chin a shake. "Did you hear me? You're not a baby anymore. You have to learn to stand up for yourself. I'm not going to be here much longer. I *am* going to college, Father made sure of that, and as soon as I get there, I'm leaving this house."

Brook looked mutely into his sister's eyes and nodded like a little puppet. Without Lucy, there would be no one to pull him out of the well; he'd spend his entire life trying to claw his way up, and time after time he would slip on the slimy walls and fall farther down.

Sally let the door of the dining room swing closed behind her. She glided across the hallway toward the parlor, the brush of her unfashionably-long skirt against the polished marble floor the only audible proof of her passage. She loved the sound, loved the feel of the swirl of fine material around her feet, cared not a bit that forward-looking women were wearing their hems at midcalf. She found the new styles unattractive and unfeminine, another indication of how the world was changing for the worse, allowing— no, embracing—the steady erosion of the values that upheld all that was decent in society. At the base of the staircase, she slowed to a whisper and glanced up. Philip and the children were tucked into their rooms, finished with their daily assault of messy demands and desires.

They had no thought for her feelings, for her desires. No appreciation for how unfailingly hard it was to sustain herself as a proper mother and wife in the face of their disobedience and disrespect, her constant disappointment in them. They knew how upset she was, but would one of them think to venture downstairs to keep her company in her loneliness? No.

She sat for a time at her desk, pretending to read through literature she had brought home from her last Christian Science meeting. Her ladies' group had decided to work with the Women's Liberty Loan Committee of New York to help sell Liberty Loan Bonds to finance the war. She had committed to buying some herself, in Jed's name. They would be an excellent investment for him, paying 3.5 percent in semiannual tax-free interest, more than a savings account. And he could sell them any time he wished. Or hold them for the full thirty-year term and then—Her stomach gave a violent lurch as she realized how ridiculous she was being. Jed didn't need the paltry sum Liberty Bonds would yield him; he came from one of the wealthiest families in New York. Buying bonds for him, planning how he might sell or hold them, was an unworthy means of distracting herself from her constant dread of the phone call, the telegram, the knock on the door, that would inform her of the death of the one person in this world she truly loved. It was only through proper prayer that Jed would be kept safe. War and death were not God-created and so had no eternal reality; she had to stay focused on the constant correction of her belief and all would be well.

She stuffed the papers into the desk drawer and reached for her well-worn copy of *Science and Health with Key to the Scriptures*. Repetitive reading of the words of Mary Baker Eddy or the Bible, Christian Science's other sacred text, often calmed her. It would have been nice if anyone in the family had ever given her the slightest support in this—and Philip had the nerve to fault her for not respecting his work!—but all she ever got was patronizing disinterest or outright derision. Oh, Brook let himself be dragged along to her meetings, but he was as close to understanding the

Divine Mind as he was to understanding why every time she looked at him and saw a replica of Philip—the same sandy-brown hair, the same green eyes, the same unsullied goodness—she wanted to scream. For the past several months, at least, she had been able to share her greatest source of strength and truth with Zoe. Sally had never felt particularly close to her sister-in-law before, but it seemed they might have more in common than either one had ever considered. Clearly, Zoe was in need of spiritual guidance, and Sally was gratified that it was her, not Evelyn or Philip, to whom Zoe had turned.

Fifteen minutes of reading was all Sally could manage. The ice in her stomach would not melt. Her mind would not stop, despite how achingly tired she was, how heavily the stillness of the house weighed on her. She closed her book and turned off her desk lamp, folded the *New York Tribune* that Philip had left on his chair, and placed it on the side table next to her *Christian Science Monitor*. Her hands shook slightly. Philip's pipe, a beautiful Dunhill that Evelyn had given him many years before, lay in a crystal ashtray. The bowl's lustrous wood was still warm from his after-dinner smoke; the pleasing smell of slightly sweet tobacco hung in the air. She trailed her fingers over the pipe's smooth surface. The warmth moved from the wood to her hand, flowed gently up her arm. Lingering sweetness drifted into her lungs. She suddenly recalled the afternoon of her coming out and the moment she first smelled this very aroma and turned to see a pair of sea-green eyes staring at her in awe through a haze of smoke. Philip Gates, thirty-year-old bachelor heir to Joseph Gates's self-made fortune. Philip, love-struck in an instant.

In the course of a single dance Sally made her decision. His family's wealth and social standing were essential, certainly; the premature death of her adored father and the humiliating incompetence of her widowed mother now required that Sally rescue the Moore family from their slide into genteel poverty. But wealth and social standing were common commodities among the dozens of men begging to be allowed to dominate her dance card. Five minutes with Philip was all she needed to choose him, his gentleness, his lack of greed, his obvious intention to love her without condition. How could she know that she would come to despise him for the very qualities that drew her to him when she was eighteen and blind and deaf to her own anxious, insistent nature? How could she know how cruelly she would come to take for granted what she admired most in him, what made her feel safe and loved, and berate him for all the things he wasn't? This evening, she had wounded Philip deeply, as had been her intent. It gave her a terrible, righteous satisfaction, though undermined by her awareness that Philip did not deserve to be hurt.

Did she have to be so tirelessly vigilant? Mightn't she consider sharing her burdens with her husband? How easy it would be to let go, just a little—Quickly she caught herself. Devilish thoughts, evil seduction with its false promises. Nothing but disappointment awaited down that path. The sweet smell caught in her throat, and she jerked her hand away from the pipe.

Leaving only the light in the entry vestibule burning, Sally went upstairs. She stepped past Brook's closed door as though stepping over a chastened dog lying in the hallway, punished for having peed on the carpet and now ignored. She passed by Lucy's closed door. Her daughter was succumbing to the epidemic sweeping through the female population like plague these last decades. An epidemic of women who pushed themselves into a world rightly meant for men, went to college, took on careers that destroyed their femininity, never married. Sally had tried, but it was too late to save her. Let her go to college; let her vote, end up a sharp, withered spinster.

The door to Jed's room stood open. Beyond was only darkness and his absence. He should have been safe in Paris, but he wasn't. Sally still could not believe that he had disobeyed her direct order and followed his regiment to the front. Anxiety gripped her anew. The three live bodies in the house did her no good; they only reminded her that without Jed she was alone and nothing but desolation awaited her if he did not return. Her focus was straying again. Tomorrow she would go to the church and ask Lorena to pray with her.

Sally moved on, intending to go to her own room, lock the door, and lie awake staring at the ceiling until her heart's pounding eased sufficiently to allow sleep to overcome her. But there was a strip of yellow light across the hall floor, like a path laid out for her to follow, coming from Philip's room. He was still awake. She stopped. Without conscious will, her feet followed the path until she found herself at his partly open door. She went inside, closed the door behind her. Philip was propped up in bed, reading. He glanced up from his book, startled, and they looked at each other without speaking.

Sally came toward the bed, her eyes showing no change of expression as his grew muddled with longing and uncertainty. She turned her back to him, giving permission for him to undo the long line of buttons that snaked down the spine of her dress. His hands worked their way from her neck to her waist. She felt the occasional brush of his trembling fingers on her skin. He slid the dress off her shoulders. Yards of peach-colored silk pooled around her feet, and, without seeming to move at all, she stepped out of its confining circle, leaving her shoes stranded inside. She stood in her chemise and let him kiss the back of her neck as he pulled at the pins holding her chignon in place. In a gush, her heavy hair fell down her back.

"Turn off the lights."

Philip did as she ordered. Sally slid into his bed and lay on her back, unmoving, as her husband's hands, loving artist's hands, fluttered and stroked and traveled over her body. Her pulse quickened and she was taken by the desire to put her arms around his back, let the weight of him anchor her to the bed, protect her from every bad thing. Her hands lifted without her permission, and with them arose within her a panic so acute she could see it, black spots careening in front of her face in the semidarkness. She dropped her hands onto the bed, brought herself under control, and filled her mind with prayer and thoughts of what she might get Evelyn for her upcoming birthday. Thus distracted, Sally was able to hold herself intact while Philip panted and groaned and rocked above her, while he shuddered and cried out and lost all control of himself.

Before Philip's breathing had lost its ragged edge, Sally pushed urgently at his shoulders and made to leave the bed.

"Sally. Stay. Stay with me tonight."

She pulled free. "Don't be foolish. You know I can't sleep in the same bed with you." She didn't look at him. She gathered her clothes and walked to the door, growing colder and more lonely with each step. She paused facing the hallway, spoke without turning even her head. "I won't fight you about Lucy; I don't care what she does. But you won't corrupt the boys, Philip. I won't have it. You will defer to my judgment about what is right for them." She opened the door and stood in her clinging chemise, silhouetted against the dim hallway light, feeling Philip's eyes on her, allowing him one brief glimpse of her shadowed body. "I'll see you at breakfast. And Philip, congratulations on the Woolbright portrait. I'm sure you'll do a fine job for them."

Philip buried his face in his hands as the door closed behind her. His heart hammered in his chest and his breath came fast, his nerves firing with aftershocks of pleasure. Every part of him craved a part of her; his tongue craved the texture of her skin; his hands craved each exposed cool expanse, each secret warm place. Every inch of him wanted every inch of her. He wanted to believe that when he entered her, his penis engulfed by her heat, his hands tangled in her hair, his face smothered in the scented hollow of her throat—when he lost his mind from the rapture of it—she felt something. Although she had never given him any reason to believe it.

At that moment, he thought he would do almost anything to get her into his bed, to feel this way again and again, and he thought he would do almost anything not to want her anymore, not to be shown her eagerness to walk away from him when he longed to hold her all through the night. Nothing could be better between them while Jed was away. That was clear. He knew Jed would hate him for it, but Philip determined to call his father first thing in the morning. Maybe Joseph could find a way to bring Jed home before it was too late for them all.

6

*For three exhilarating months Anna had been living a dou*ble life under the unsuspecting eyes of her family. While in their presence she remained the Anna she had been for the past seven years, debilitated and despondent, unable to venture any farther than the hallway toilet or the Krinskis' apartment next door, taking to her bed in constant exhaustion. Everyone was so accustomed to her infirmities, had adapted their lives to her needs so skillfully, that not even Viktor or Ben could truly remember another Anna. And so if Anna had been a little careless now and again these past months, allowed a hint of something changing in her, probably no one would have noticed. But she wasn't careless. She had a plan.

It was a beautiful June day. It was Shabbat. Viktor was in *shul*, Sarah had gone to the Henry Street Settlement to play and to read. But she would be home in an hour, because Anna had told her to come back by noon. Today, Anna was going to share her secret with Sarah. She had wanted to wait until July Fourth—it tickled her to think of revealing her own coming independence on that most American of days—but this morning she had decided not to wait. Last night she had heard Sarah crying again, and this morning there were dark hollows under Sarah's eyes. Anna had to give some of her newfound hope to her daughter. She had to let Sarah know that soon she could go back to school, back to the childhood that should never have been so violently interrupted. Once she knew, the time she would have to continue working until Anna was fully ready would go quickly, and every morning mother and daughter could share their secret, the way they used to share Aronson's gift of fruit.

Anna swung her legs to the floor and reached for her cane. She walked slowly but steadily around the big room, barely limping, not needing to hold on to anything for support. She had been doing this every day since the end of March. At first, she had to exhort herself to ignore the agony of her stiff and atrophied muscles, the choking tightness of her unwilling, laboring lungs, the inner demon that tried to convince her that she would fail. She told herself to remember what she had written to David about destiny and to remember that she had one, too, now. She fought off the fear and humiliation that engulfed her when her weak legs gave out and she fell repeatedly and had to crawl to the table, a chair, the bed, anything she could use to haul herself back up. She lied to Viktor about the black-and-blue marks she couldn't hide. And then came a day when she fell only once. And then came a day when her chest opened and every breath was a gift of energy rather than a punishment for overreaching. And then came a day when her legs felt long and strong beneath the pull of the scar tissue and her knees and ankles flexed and straightened and her muscles bunched under her skin. She never fell again and every day she walked a little longer and a little faster. Then she began walking up and down the hall during the hours when she knew Sadie was out, her cane tip-tapping on the hard floor.

Now, it was time to master going up and down the stairs and she was going to let Sarah help her. One flight today, and for the next week. Two flights after that, then three, then four, and by August she would be ready to fly out the door. She would extract from Sarah her promise that she would tell no one, a hard thing to ask a little girl to do. But that wasn't the hardest thing Anna was going to ask of her. She was going to show Sarah the three letters she had received from David since she'd written him in March, just one line each but comprising all she needed to know—*Mama, I'm still alive. Love, David*—and she was going to make Sarah swear that on the very day Anna walked out of the apartment and came back with the job that Sol Leyrowitz was going to give her, the day Sarah left Pankin's, she would forgive her brother and would write to him and tell him she loved him.

7

Jed awoke just past dawn to the sound of birds. He lay with his eyes closed, breathing slowly, savoring the sweetness of the French spring air. He loved being up so early, when the light was delicate and the air was clear, not yet full of the dust of the division's activities. A new day stretched before him, rife with possibilities. Jed was happy. As he had every morning since the first days of training camp, he woke feeling free, unhampered by confusion as to what was required of him. How unlike mornings in his comfortable bedroom, where the burden of his mother's and grandfather's expectations lay on him like a heavy blanket. The expectations the army had of him were crystal clear, and he knew he would not disappoint either his superior officers or the men under his command.

Their time in France had been easy so far. The regiment had been attached to the U.S. 2nd Division, hunkered down and waiting, just southeast of Verdun. They were in a *bon secteur,* where the lines had remained stable for three long years and the 2nd had dug out a very domesticated existence for themselves. Conditions in the trenches were more than livable: beds with mattresses, tables and chairs, stoves, electricity, even some wooden floors. And no fighting.

There had been one brief period after they'd arrived during which Jed's unadulterated happiness had faltered. The couple of months of training with live grenades and sharp bayonets had put a metallic taste of fear into his mouth. After handling nothing but dummy wooden rifles through all his years in the Knickerbocker Greys and during training camp, Jed was panic-stricken by the stink of the explosives and the evil gleam of the deadly blades. In a shocking second, the simplicity of the army's physical expectations became a horrendously complex matter of life and death. His fear may have been normal, but he had not expected to be frightened.

The other men talked about their fear, joked about it, used it to feel close to one another. Even David, whom everyone had believed fearless, had thrown up in sheer terror the first time he felt the concussion of a grenade explosion. Jed said nothing. He pushed himself harder and harder in an effort to deny his own panic. He became the most zealous trainee in the regiment. Any lingering, unspoken suspicion that Jed's swift rise to officer status was driven by his influential grandfather was forever abandoned; it no longer mattered how Jed got there. He was a soldier everyone could count on.

When the special training ended and the regiment returned to their trenches and their waiting, Jed's fear slowly dissipated. The war became again a distant thrill of danger, a shadow that would never reach him. Daily the men heard news of skirmishes to the north and east, battles fought by the British and French troops they were here to support. They even began hearing of other American divisions becoming involved in raids and line holding. But it didn't seem real. When Jed thought of the war at all, it was with a vague sense of nostalgia, an image of playing hide-and-seek with Uncle Monty. If he tried to add to that the bayonets and grenades they had trained with, the image scrolled quickly ahead to one of him standing heroically over the fallen bodies of the enemy. What happened in between was a no-man's-land.

Jed stretched and opened his eyes. Sunlight moved like water on the ceiling of the tent. This morning, he would take a sketch pad and wander through camp until he found something that caught his interest. It might be the way the light fell on a distant hill or the density of concentration among a group of soldiers or the frivolity of the Dough-girls rehearsing one of their outrageous skits. Jed's caricatures had achieved campwide renown; everyone wanted to be lampooned by Lieutenant Gates's deft strokes with the charcoal. Today he thought he might sketch new costumes for the Doughgirls' next show. Over the months, Jed had filled six pads with his drawings, and every month, without fail or additional message, a new pad arrived from home, from his father.

"Ah, you're finally awake."

Jed turned his head. David was dressed and sitting on the bed next to him, one leg bouncing up and down, looking restless in that explosive way that only David could. Jed knew what that meant. David was going into town, without him.

Jed quickly sat up. "Give me a minute to get my clothes on and we'll go get some breakfast. Then how about we play some cards? You look like you need some diversion."

"I don't think cards will do the trick. I'm going into town."

"Don't you want to eat something first?"

"They've got food there, better than what we have." David gave him a mischievous look. "I'm sure Delphine will be happy to feed me."

Jed looked away. "I'm sure she will."

David laughed. "Come on, Jed. Come with me, for once. I mean, we haven't talked about it, but Jesus, you know why I go into town." The one leg stopped bouncing, and the other started up. "Listen to me. I woke up feeling really weird this morning. I think something's about to happen. We might die tomorrow. What are you saving yourself for? Delphine's friend Sylvie really likes you."

"We're not going to die tomorrow, and no, I'm not going with you! You know I don't do that. It's not the way I was raised. It's fine for you, but honestly, I don't want to."

David laughed again, this time in amazement. "More power to you, I guess. I haven't been able to not *do that* since I was fourteen. I figured if I was man enough to work, I was man enough to do everything else."

"Fourteen!?"

The bouncing leg stilled. "Yeah. With a young prostitute on the Bowery. There were tons of them all along there and Allen Street, always waving at me, offering to teach me for free." He chewed at his lip. "She was pretty, and really nice." He paused, a bit of a pained look on his face. "I haven't thought about her for years. I don't know what she was doing, being a prostitute. But it was a good thing for me. A great way to start when you don't know what the hell you're doing."

"Weren't you worried about getting a disease?" Jed wrinkled his nose and retracted his head as though someone were at that moment waving a pustular, germ-riddled piece of flesh under his nose.

David snorted. "Jed, I was fourteen. I had a permanent hard-on. I wasn't thinking about diseases."

Jed couldn't have been any more uncomfortable, talking about sex with David, and yet couldn't stop asking questions. "And after her?"

"There were some older girls in my neighborhood. Then there was Rachel."

"Rachel. The one who writes to you. Do you love her? Are you going to go back to her when we get home?"

"No." David stared off through the tent's open flap.

A tension he hadn't even been aware of suddenly drained out of Jed. He let his gaze follow David's and saw a pair of soldiers walking, arm in arm, laughing, heading off down the road. "Well, don't Foster and McBride look gay today," he said innocently. "I guess they're going to town for something decent to eat."

David gave Jed a knowing look. "Oh, I don't think they're going to make it farther than that abandoned barn down the road."

Jed looked confused; then his face tightened into a prissy mask. "Oh! That's disgusting! It's . . . it's unnatural!"

"Well, for being unnatural there sure is a lot of it around. I couldn't walk past Paresis Hall on Fifth Street without getting propositioned by some fairy. Here . . . those guys just find one another. You're such a choirboy, I guess you never notice. Which is kind of sweet. But you must have had your share of attention back home. You're a pretty young thing," David teased, "and you don't live that far from Billy's Hotel—on Twentieth and Third?—it's a notorious fairy haunt."

Jed turned bright red and gaped at David. "No! Never! How do you even know that? You're not . . ."

"No," David said indifferently. "Never appealed to me. But it's none of my business what anybody else does." He looked off into the distance again and sighed. "Me, I like women. Ahh, God, I love women." His voice had gone soft and vulnerable and his eyes had lost their focus. "They're so beautiful. That spot, where the back of the thigh curves up into the ass . . ." He tilted his head back and opened his mouth. "And they taste so good." He exhaled. "Oh fuck, that's it. I've got to find the lovely and willing Mademoiselle Delphine before I bust a gut."

David jumped up and grinned at Jed. "I'm a bad role model. There's nothing wrong with sticking with your moral convictions. You stay here and be good for the both of us. I'll go find Vern. He's probably at the mess by now."

Jed felt a pain like a hot poker in his stomach. Cooper was still attached to David like a fifth limb, even though he'd made other friends and earned a good amount of admiration for his hilarious performances as a blue-eyed, hairy-legged Doughgirl, high-kicking in one of Jed's outfits. But Jed still couldn't stand him, although no one would ever know it from his behavior. And he couldn't stand the thought of Cooper going into town with David.

Jed pulled on his scratchy uniform, laced up his hobnailed boots, and left the tent, headed for the latrine and then mess. As soon as he stepped out of the dugout, he felt it. David was right; something had changed. The war had found them. There were too many men up and out too early. A voice filled with exuberance carried on the tender morning air. "Lieutenant! Hey! We're moving out! We're moving out!"

Jed didn't turn to see who was calling to him. A sudden knot of panic constricted his chest. In an unbidden flash of memory, he heard his mother telling him how he had been three weeks late being born. *You hadn't wanted to come out. You must have liked it inside of me, and when you did come, you fought and fought, I was in labor with you for three days.* Ridiculously, it flashed through his head that he'd been in the army for nine months. Nine happy months. And he wanted to stay exactly where he was. He was not ready to be born into a world of blood and death.

He hurried to the mess. David was there, sitting with the core group of their infantry regiment, including Cooper, his hands wrapped around a metal cup full of steaming black coffee. Jed slipped in beside him. A chorus of "Hey, Lieutenants" greeted him.

"What's happening?" Jed asked, pleased at how authoritative his voice sounded.

David turned to him, eyes filled with excitement of a different sort, no longing for Miss Delphine visible in them anymore. "It looks like we're finally getting into it, Jed. No one seems to know exactly what's going on, but we've gotten orders to move out. Peterson here heard rumors from Captain Hummel that the Germans broke through the line of the French Sixth somewhere north of Paris."

"Yeah, and I heard that about two hundred guys from the First were killed in some town up near there—Cantigny; I don't know how the hell you pronounce it," Private Peterson added, mangling the lyrical name of the French town. "I think they're sending us up there."

Jed felt a balloon expanding inside his head. The table in front of him was receding at a rapid pace. "Aren't your hands burning, David?" he said.

David glanced at Jed's averted face. "Yeah, maybe a little," he said softly, and pushed the cup in Jed's direction. "Here, have some. I'm jumpy enough."

Jed reached for the coffee with an unnatural slowness. David looked at him carefully. Jed's face was expressionless, his blue eyes like clear pools of undisturbed water. David leaned closer and spoke so quietly that only Jed could hear him. "Jed, are you all right?"

Jed turned, putting a smile on his face. "Sure; this is what we've been waiting for." The golden lights flickering in the depths of David's eyes steadied him, burned away the eerie distance that had sprung up between him and the rest of the world. Looking into David's eyes was like staring into a banked fire. Jed could feel the power and the warmth waiting there. When he needed it, David would light that fire and let Jed draw strength from it. He sipped at the coffee. "God. This is strong enough to float a tank in."

"Yeah, it's our new secret weapon," Vern whispered, and everyone burst out laughing. It wasn't so funny, but it broke the tension.

Jed laughed along with the others. Everyone was scared. They'd all be fine once they got started. It was not knowing what to expect that was so hard. The image of himself standing triumphant over the fallen enemy rose in his mind again, and he thought of his grandfather's parting words to him; *Make me proud, Jed. Lead well. Don't show your fear; set an example for your men to follow.*

"Listen," he said, his voice strong. "We have to watch out for each other from now on."

"Don't worry, Lieutenant; I'm sticking close to you," Peterson replied. "You were the coolest thing I ever saw in training. If I'm near you, I'm gonna be okay."

Jed smiled at the score of faces turned toward him. "We're going to be the best infantry regiment in the whole damned American Expeditionary Forces!"

"I'm glad to hear that, Lieutenant." Captain Hummel materialized behind Jed and clapped a hand on his shoulder. Amusement tinged his voice. "Now I can sit back and relax."

"What's the word, Captain?"

"All I know is that there's a caravan of trucks coming in here to take us out. Even General Harbord doesn't know where we're going. But we've got to break camp, get ready to load up. So . . ."—Hummel rubbed his hands together—"let's get to it. Gates, you seem to be the voice of authority among this motley crew. See if you can get them ready for the real world." The captain was always easy with his men, and they responded well to him. He stood quietly with them for a moment, then said simply, "Good luck, all of you," and left.

The men sat in silence, not looking at one another. Suddenly Vern leaped up. "Hey, I got an idea!" He ran off, leaving everyone staring after him. In a minute he was back, holding Captain Hummel's precious camera aloft as though it were a war prize. "Pictures!" he shouted. "I'm takin' pictures of everybody!"

"Yeah! The Gates Brigade!" Peterson yelled.

The men scrambled out onto the dusty ground, oblivious of the rushing activity around them, pushing for position in the photo that would immortalize them.

"Wait; wait. David, you and Jed first. Come on; I want one of just the two of you, for me," Vern pleaded.

David grabbed Jed's arm and pulled him aside. They grinned at each other, infected with the excitement racing all around them. They threw their arms around each other's shoulders.

"Look at me!" Vern ordered.

The sun warmed their skin; the slight warm breeze ruffled their hair. They leaned their heads together. They smiled into the camera.

To allay their nervousness, the men were singing the bawdiest version of "The Fusiliers" he'd heard yet. Jed sat cramped between David and Vern, his eyes closed, rocking gently against one and then the other. They were in one of the lead trucks bumping slowly along the road north toward Paris. He pictured the U.S. 2nd Division caravan, fourteen miles long, stretched out behind them like a snake rattling its way toward dangerous prey. He felt Vern jab him in the ribs.

"Come on, Lieutenant; sing along!"

"My mother taught me not to use such words," Jed said with mock primness.

Everyone laughed. "Leave Gates alone!" someone joked. "He's saving his energy for the Germans!"

The Germans. The snake's target. Jed's eyes opened and he stared at the roof of the truck. He turned his head and looked out the open back. How sad. The beauty of the French spring was lost to him forever. All he saw was dust and the seemingly endless stream of refugees fleeing south. This afternoon a group of ragged, spiritless French soldiers were mixed in with the civilians. One of them cried vehemently, "La guerre finie," as he rushed away from the front.

"If only the war were over," David said quietly. After three months in France, David spoke the language like a native, better than Jed after his years of schooling.

Yes, then I could go home, Jed thought. He looked down at David's hands, his slim fingers beautifully bronzed from the spring sun. They were crawling up and down his legs. "Are you scared, David?"

David grunted. "Of course I'm scared. I want my bones to rest in some rich man's cemetery in New York, years from now, not in a battlefield in France." He squirmed on the hard bench until he was facing Jed. "Jed," he whispered urgently, "let's stick together. Let's make sure that we get out of here alive."

"Sounds good to me."

"God, how can you act so calm?" Getting no response, David shook his head and turned back to the other men. He knew Jed didn't like to show his feelings, but this was ridiculous. He left his hand on Jed's knee.

"David? Did some overprotective brother really give you that scar?" Jed's eyes were glued to David's face.

"Yes. That's exactly what happened."

"You wouldn't lie to me?"

David stared into Jed's eyes. He saw the fear there. "No. I wouldn't lie to you." David pressed his knee. "Jed, we're going to be okay."

Jed nodded. He couldn't say anything. He could not begin to express what he felt. *I'm floating,* he thought, *nothing to hold me down.* Nothing but the feel of David's hot hand on his leg. He scrabbled in his mind for his self-assurance. Everyone always told him he had it in abundance; where was it hiding? Strangely, what he found was an image of his father looking at him with calm green eyes, seeing him with utter clarity. *"What do you see?"*

"What? Where?"

At the sound of David's concerned voice, Jed realized he had spoken aloud. "Nothing. Nothing. I'm just thinking aloud."

The Germans had taken the town of Vaux; they were

pouring through Belleau Wood west of the Aisne River. The French army was being decimated. The 2nd was to relieve them and stem the German flood.

They marched east along the Paris-Metz road, through country unscarred by the war, gorgeous in full spring splendor. The greenery reminded Jed of his grandparents' estate in Oyster Bay, on the north shore of Long Island. He and Lucy and Brook spent wonderful times there, swimming and riding horses along the beach. Jed turned to David, plodding next to him. "Do you still have that picture of Lucy I gave you?"

David roused himself. "Yes, of course." He kept it with him all the time, in one pocket or another. Since they'd broken camp, he had also taken to wearing his grandmother's Star of David around his neck, carefully hidden beneath his shirt. He took the photo from his pants pocket and handed it to Jed.

"She rides beautifully," Jed said wistfully. He studied his sister's face for a moment, then gave the photo back to David.

David put it back in his pocket, but not before stealing his own intense glance. He had given up trying to make sense of Jed's recent bits of verbal nonsense. He had his own nonsense running in his head. *I'm going to marry her.* Everyone was dealing with the stress in their own way. Jed lost himself in thoughts of the past while David fantasized about the future. What difference, as long as they survived the present? *I'm going to marry a girl I've never met, a* shiksa *to boot.* He laughed aloud at the insanity of thinking such a delusional thing while German cannons were booming in the distance.

"What's so funny?" Jed asked, smiling.

David grabbed Jed's cap off his head and threw it in the air. "How would you feel if I married your sister who rides so beautifully?" he joked.

Jed's smile froze on his face. A voice inside him screamed, *Mine*, like a little baby. *You're mine!* Who did he mean, David or Lucy? He closed his mind to the thought. "Great," he said, grinning. "But you'll have to change your clothes first."

They both started to laugh hysterically. David didn't know what the hell either of them was talking about, but it was all funny.

They crept through the fields in a heavy early-morning fog. Retreating French soldiers slid through their advancing ranks, appearing suddenly like creatures formed out of the damp mist itself. No words were spoken; the gratitude on the faces of the *poilus* was more eloquent than anything they could have said. It was an eerie dream, silent and smoky. The dense mist swirled around the men's faces and blanketed all sound. Jed heard a muffled tittering from behind him, someone—Cooper—saying spookily "Hey, fellas, we've risen from our graves!"

Their graves. He'd dug his yesterday, a shallow body-length trench scraped out of the dry, dusty ground with his bayonet and mess-kit lid. They'd been told to dig in, to hold the line. He'd finished his before anyone else, jabbing at the ground with savage speed. He'd flopped into his grave and prepared to shoot anything that came within his fifteen yards of territory. He'd lain there rigidly all night with his eyes wide open, staring into the darkness in the direction of the front. He'd heard the pounding of German boots coming nearer and nearer, but no soldiers ever appeared. After an eternity he'd realized it was the beating of his heart. There had been no attack. They were ordered to move on, to find and engage the enemy.

Now it was morning again, although time had lost all meaning in the dull grey haze that was neither light nor dark. Jed groped his way blindly, dimly aware of his regiment around him, foliage brushing at his legs. He bumped into someone in front of him. "Listen!" David hissed. Jed listened. Distant booms and crackings. "This is it!" David was gone.

Jed followed. The fog was burning off. A brilliant shaft of sunlight hit his face and suddenly he was moving through a dazzling emerald sea of waving buckwheat, rippling sweetly in the June breeze. God, it was gorgeous! He stood up tall and looked around him in wonder.

"Put your head down, Jed!"

But David, it's so beautiful.

"Don't stand up like that; you're a target! Jed, get down!"

He lowered his head. The rippling became wilder, uneven. There were explosions, men screaming. Jed fell to the ground, his heart beating madly. He got up again and ran. Jesus, men were dropping, but where were the Germans? He heard Captain Hummel's voice echoing all around him, "Drop and fire! They're using machine guns! Stay down; crawl and fire!" Jed ran, shooting, falling, up, shoot, down. Tears were leaking from his eyes. Did Grandfather grow buckwheat in Oyster Bay? The clear air was filled with fog again, not the cool wet morning mist but hot, stinking smoke. Jed ran, feeling the wheat slap at his legs. He tripped and fell on top of something. He looked down and saw Peterson, half his head blown away. Jed shrieked and clawed at the ground. He stood up screaming and ran, firing into the blue smoke ahead of him.

It was so quiet. Where was everyone? He was lying on the ground on his back, looking up through the green shafts of wheat at a darkening sky the color of those deep-blue violets his father grew in little pots in early spring. Ah, there was the evening star! A face appeared in the twilight above him. *David! Looking so sad.*

David fell to his knees next to Jed's supine body. His eyes glistened with angry tears. He grabbed Jed's shoulders and hugged him to his chest. "I've been looking all over for you, goddamn it! I thought for sure you were dead, the way you ran right toward them. You must have shot a million Germans. What are you doing just lying here?"

"Look at that sky, David. Beautiful, isn't it?" He was croaking. Why was his throat so raw? Why was he shaking like that? He grabbed onto David and they held each other so tightly they could scarcely breathe.

"Come on. We're retreating for the night; we have to get back." David dragged Jed to his feet.

Jed staggered after him. "Peterson is dead, you know. I fell over him."

David shivered so hard he almost stumbled. "I know.

Vern and I buried him. We buried a lot of guys since the firing stopped." His voice fell to a choked whisper. "I can't believe they're making us do that!"

Jed saw David's shoulders shake; he was sobbing. An unbearable panic rose up from Jed's guts and spread through his chest. He opened his mouth to let it out. It floated away. "David, don't cry." He reached out and took David's hand.

They half-crawled, half-ran back toward safety in the wan light of a newly risen crescent moon. As they scrambled across the battlefield, Jed wrinkled up his nose. "What's that smell?"

"Oh, Jed," David moaned, "what do you think it is?"

Jed was about to say he didn't know, but then he realized it was the stench of death.

The major at the American General Headquarters at Chaumont stared at the telegram in disbelief. "Are you kidding? The second is fighting up at Château-Thierry. It's hell up there; I can't go find one lousy doughboy and get him out! I have a thousand more important mistakes to take care of."

"Look, just pretend to try, all right? This telegram came straight from the office of Senator Wadsworth of New York. His buddy Gates seems to be a personal friend of Bundy, Wilson, and God. This is the third telegram he's sent already. Poke around. See if you can at least find out if the kid is still alive, okay?" The colonel saluted, winked, and left.

"Jesus. Fuck that." The major threw the telegram in the garbage and turned back to his piled-high desk.

Jed wandered through the hastily erected encampment, stepping around the bodies of the wounded waiting to be taken out to the advance dressing stations and hospitals. In the week they hadn't been fighting, he did what the others did. He ate and slept and joked and waited. No one seemed to notice that he wasn't really there. He wondered if everyone felt like he did inside, foggy and detached, a constant hum in his head.

"Gates, go get something to eat and some rest." Captain Hummel appeared beside him and gently took Jed by the arm, led him toward the mess tent. Rich kid, he didn't have to be here at all, but look at him. He'd fought like a machine for a month. He'd dug his buddies' graves and dragged the wounded back in from the field. No wonder he seemed a little dazed. Well, shit, everyone was so tired even Cooper's frantic attempts to get a baseball game going had met with total indifference.

Jed nodded. "It's hot," he said, tugging at his jacket collar.

"It's the end of July, Jed," Hummel said lightly. "It's supposed to be hot."

July, Jed thought vaguely. *What happened to June? Wasn't it just June?*

"Come on, Jed. Go find your buddies and get some sleep. We're moving into place during the night. Tomorrow's the big offensive along the Marne."

Jed woke to rain falling on his upturned face. Up and moving. No fires, no coffee. Cold bully beef, inedible. Not hot anymore, cold, cold rain. Marching silently along roads so dark they seemed like tunnels. Into the woods, feet sinking into thick mud. Slogging endless hours through the murky muck. Legs aching, shoulders aching, David on one side, Vern on the other. Like sacks of wet flour, thudding onto the ground, three bundles of exhaustion lying inert until dawn.

Dawn, clear glorious rain-washed sky, light rays coming up over the eastern horizon like a chorus of angels. Sudden puffs of smoke dirtied the air; the morning quiet was broken by the rolling thunder of cannons and artillery up ahead. Tanks were rumbling in front of them. The earth trembled beneath their feet. *Up! Up and out! Here we go!* The hum in Jed's brain turned into a roar. He shook his head hard and it subsided. They ran across the broken ground, following their tanks. Cannon fire burst all around them. Everyone dropped; everyone minus someone got up again. Musical chairs. Over and over. How many were left?

"Gates, take your group, get through that trench. Knock out those damned cannons!" Hummel's voice boomed in his ear.

The Gates Brigade, what was left of it. Running full tilt, zigzagging across the field, dropping, waiting, up again. Pouring over the lip of a trench, shocked German faces staring up at the gleaming tips of their poised bayonets. Jed opened his mouth and screamed. He looked into the blue eyes of a baby-faced boy, staring up at him in horror. He screamed louder and plunged his bayonet into the boy's chest. Blood sprayed everywhere. The blue eyes grew grey and filmy, but the horror remained. Jed whirled, blue eyes all around him! He jabbed in all directions.

"Jed, that's enough! The cannons, let's go!"

David's hand on his back, pushing him up. Jed scrambled out of the trench, feeling his boots slipping on wetness as he pushed off against flesh. Someone threw a grenade and through the smoke they leaped onto the cannon crew.

"We got one!" Cooper's coarse voice.

Where the hell was the sun? Jed tried to find it on the horizon through the yellow-brown smoke. What was it doing way overhead? He started wandering back the way they'd come.

"Jed, where are you going?"

It's late, David; we have to get back home. He started trotting toward the trenches.

David ran after Jed, Vern close behind, struggling to see through the thick, acrid smoke. He fell into the German trench. There were bodies everywhere. He scrabbled up the far side and vomited without breaking stride. "Jed, you bastard, where are you!" There. Running off to the left. Suddenly the earth under David's feet disappeared and he flew up into the haze. He clutched at the Star around his neck. His father was laughing into his face, throwing him up in the air and catching him. He smiled as he sailed in the sky. He was smiling when he slammed into the ground.

His fist opened and the Star of David fell into the blood-soaked dirt.

Something hit Jed's back and kicked him over, knocked the breath out of him. He lay for a moment with his face in the muck. *I'm not supposed to get dirty! I'll say Lucy pushed me!* He got up and headed for a line of trees off to his left. He leaned his back against one and slid down to sit in the shade of its branches. He brushed the dirt off his clothes. He looked up and saw a strange shape lurching toward him through the smoke. Something moving, hunched over something on the ground . . . He got up and walked slowly toward it. Oh no! Someone was dragging David across the field, cruelly bouncing his limp body on the rough terrain. *Stop; stop! Leave him alone!* Jed grabbed his rifle and ran at full pitch. *Get away from him!*

Blue Eyes standing over David's body. No more! No more Blue Eyes! Jed ran with his bayonet at the ready, his mouth open wide, his tortured throat spewing out an unrecognizable inhuman screeching that filled the sky. In the deadly silence beneath the blanketing sound he stabbed with all his strength. *Get away from him; get away; get away!* Blue Eyes tumbled back and fell, pouring blood all over David. Jed threw his rifle aside and dropped to the ground. He pushed Blue Eyes away, his hand covered in hot blood, and put his head to David's chest. Alive!

Dead eyes were fixed on him from across David's body. Not Blue Eyes; blue eyes. Minnesota sky blue eyes set into Vernon Cooper's stupid, ugly, loyal, hated, dead face. Panic burned through Jed. He crept backward, shaking his head. He coughed furiously, trying to dislodge the panic. It wouldn't move. It filled every space in his body. He was going to die. He couldn't get any air. He scuttled like a crab under the trees, groping for his rifle. Why couldn't he see anything? He wiped at his eyes and face with a sleeve and it came away soaking wet. Sweat, blood, salty tears. His arm hit the rifle. He grabbed it in both hands, turning the bayonet point toward himself. He raised up onto his knees and blindly jabbed down, again and again, twisting and stabbing. He didn't feel anything and yet he heard himself screaming as though with pain. He flung the rifle away and started crawling. It took forever, but he got there. He curled up next to David and closed his eyes. Where their bodies touched, he could feel the beating of David's heart. Now, finally, he could have some peace.

8

The butterfly's time had come.

Anna waited until twenty minutes had passed from when Viktor left the apartment. There could be only one possible variation in his circumscribed routine, and it would occur only within the first ten minutes that he was out the door. If he didn't suddenly find himself gasping for breath, overwhelmed by anxiety and the need to see her face, or realize he'd forgotten a book, or decide that his wool *tallit* was too warm for August and he should wear the linen, he would safely reach the synagogue and stay there for morning services and beyond, no matter what strangeness might come over him later on.

As soon as she was absolutely confident that she would be alone for at least the next four hours, Anna threw back the sheet covering her thin, scarred legs and with hardly any difficulty rose from her bed. She hadn't told Sarah that this was the day. She wanted the ultimate moment to be a wonderful surprise to everyone. Today, in secret, she would carry out the final step of her plan and begin to rebuild everything that had gone up in smoke on March 25, 1911. Enough of her strength had returned, and enough of her hope.

Taking her time, Anna donned the better of the two good dresses she normally reserved for Friday evenings. She applied a small amount of rouge to her pale cheeks and rubbed a little into her lips. She arranged her hair in an elaborate twist. Each mundane movement executed on her own was a triumph and a liberation; it had been years since she'd had the strength to hold up her arms and lift and pin her thick hair. When she was done, she stepped away and looked at her reflection in the mirror. For the first time in seven years she recognized the beautiful woman looking back at her.

As she emerged onto Ludlow Street, the reality of life outside the apartment rushed up to greet her. It had been so long since she'd been on the streets. She'd forgotten how chockablock they were all day long with people and carts, and now so many cars, adding their noise and stink and danger. She'd forgotten how ugly it was, how inhuman, how frightening. She closed her eyes for a second's respite from the din and from the painful realization of just how cruel it had been to force her sweet Viktor to come to such a place. There was no comfort in knowing that she had had no choice. She hesitated at the curb, wondering if she should have let Sarah walk her around the block a few times before venturing out on her own. No. It was too late for that and, in any case, she knew in her heart that she could do this. She may have been out of practice, but she still remembered how to negotiate the labyrinth of perpetual motion that lay between her and Sol Leyrowitz's shop. It wasn't far by normal standards and she had visualized every step every day for six months: two blocks north on Ludlow, then two blocks west on Rivington to Allen. She would go slowly, carefully. It didn't matter how long it took; Leyrowitz would be there and she had plenty of time before Viktor would be home.

She started walking, crossed Broome Street with her heart in her mouth. Before she had gone even half a block, the sights and sounds had jarred loose a jumble of happy memories. How could she have thought, even for a moment, that the tumultuous life around her was ugly! It was beautiful; it was wonderful! She had been so foolish to cut herself off from it for so long. She was forced to stop; she was breathless from happiness.

"Oh my God! Is that you? Anna? Anna Warshinsky?"

Anna looked around and saw a tiny, wiry woman running toward her from the door of Gottbaum's Bakery. "Fay? Fayele? Is that *you?*"

The women embraced, and when they pulled apart Fay could not stop stroking Anna's cheek. "Oh, Anna. I never thought I would see you again. I tried, after the fire, but your family turned me away. They said you were too ill to have visitors. It was so painful, I stopped coming. I'm sorry. I should have tried harder; I—"

"No, no, Fay, it's all right." Anna reached up and clutched at her old friend's hand, holding it tightly between both of her own. "I couldn't see anyone. I might as well have been dead. It is I who should apologize, I who should have tried harder."

"But look at you now! It's never too late, is it, Anna? You are still so beautiful, and you look so strong! Where are you going? Can you come in? Business will be slow until sundown. I'll make some tea."

"What, are you working here at the bakery?" Fay Zizkin had been Anna's table mate at the Triangle Shirtwaist Factory. She had been one of the few lucky women who had pushed her way into the elevators with the men and executives, riding to safety while Anna had been forced up onto the roof.

"Well," Fay said shyly, "actually, I own it now. Two years. After the fire I couldn't stand the thought of sewing again. The Gottbaums, they had no children you know. Anna, they were so good to me. They hired me, taught me everything, left me to run the shop. Who knew I had flour, yeast, and sugar in my veins?" She laughed. "You know, we make the best *babka* in town. And, God bless him for all eternity, old Gottbaum left it all to me when he died."

"That is so wonderful. No one deserves happiness more than you."

"Oh, Anna. It is just like you to say that. What, don't you deserve happiness just as much? I was lucky. It's hard work, but I love it. So, you'll come in for tea or are you in a hurry to meet your boyfriend, all dressed up with rouge on your cheeks?" Fay teased her. They were so immediately easy together, it was as though no time had passed since they'd last spoken.

Anna flushed. "Fay, really! Yes, I'm going to see my boyfriend—Sol Leyrowitz."

Fay's eyebrows shot up. "Aha! You blush because you know he was always sweet on you, fat old Sollie. If you ever wanted a rich boyfriend, he'd be yours in a wink."

"Fay! You are impossible; stop it!" But Anna laughed and hugged her friend in spontaneous delight. "Well, I hope he's still sweet on me, because I'm going to ask him to give me a real job and pay me a lot of money. He's been very kind all these years, sending me work at home. Now I hear that his store has grown and that he is always needing someone to manage all the alterations."

Fay clapped her hands together. "Anna, how perfect! It must be Fate! He just this week fired the woman in charge of his tailoring staff. Some bigmouthed Italian who lasted all of four months before telling him what he could do with his thimble! He'll hire you before you even ask—and not only because he is still sweet on you. Because everybody in the neighborhood knows that Anna Warshinsky is an angel and the best seamstress to ever step off the boat! Oh, the business you'll bring in!"

Anna could barely speak. She was overcome to think of how much of her life she had thrown away. She must have been insane for the past seven years. What other possible explanation was there for so perversely denying herself the love of friends like Fay, for turning her back on life and all its opportunities and choosing instead to dwell in a ghost world full of misery and death?

She kissed Fay quickly on the cheek. "I hope you're right, Fay. I'm ready to work; I need the money. I need to take care of my family again."

"I'm right, Anna. No doubt whatsoever. And you hold out for at least twenty-five dollars a week—to start! Times have changed and Sol can well afford to pay you twice that. I'll wait right here and I'll have our biggest cinnamon *babka* all wrapped up for you. Oh, my friend, I am so happy to have you back!"

Most definitely still smitten, Sol Leyrowitz all but fainted with pleasure at the sight of Anna Warshinsky. As passionate an eater as he was a businessman, Sol was nearly as round as he was tall, yet because he saw himself as an attractive, charming man that was exactly how most people saw him, too. Today, however, his usual grace gave way to a schoolboy's awkwardness. When Anna asked if she might work merely nine-hour days, six days a week, and if he might possibly, if it wasn't too much to ask, consider giving her twenty-five dollars a week since she would be the sole wage earner in the family now, he insisted on eight-hour days, five days a week, reminding her that she would always be a touch fragile, and demanded to pay her thirty-five dollars a week for the privilege of having her in his store. He would never say a word to her, never do anything to make her uncomfortable, but Sol Leyrowitz, with more money than he knew what to do with, a cold, shrewish wife and two spoiled, ungrateful children, knew that he had been given his reward for a life properly lived. He had been given the opportunity to help Anna Warshinsky, the woman he had loved, chastely and from afar, since the day she had walked into his first small store looking for a job for her befogged husband. He, Sol, now could do for her what no other man had been able to: ensure her security and thus her happiness. And, as a bonus, he would get to see her eight hours a day, five days every week. God was truly generous.

An hour and a half after she'd left the apartment, Anna began retracing her steps, hardly aware of the unforgiving cement beneath her feet. Everything she had heard about Leyrowitz's store was true; everything Fay had said about Leyrowitz himself was true. Anna walked in a state of euphoric shock. Saturdays and Wednesdays off, thirty-five dollars a week, a clean well-ventilated workplace, busy happy people all around her! It was a dream beyond anything she had dared hope for. Her head swirled with wonderful, chaotic thoughts. Maybe she should march right over to Pankin's shop and drag Sarah out, now, this very minute. Maybe she should go to Kosar's Kosher Meats and splurge on a nice brisket and make Viktor's favorite *kasha varneshkes*. Her mouth watered as she imagined the taste of the smoky grain and noodles soaked with the meat's delicious juices. Her heart soared as she realized that they could now afford to eat brisket whenever they wanted. Yes, that's what she would do. But first she would change course and go down Orchard Street rather than Ludlow. She would *kvell* at the look on Ben's face when she walked into Rothstein's. She would tell him to bring the family for dinner, and then she would tell him why. He would hug her and they would weep and laugh together, just as they had so many years ago when they'd walked off the boat onto American soil. Then, for the first time in seven years, she would go to the synagogue. She would not disturb Viktor at his prayers; it would be too confusing for him to see her there, easier to explain later, at dinner. She would sit in the women's balcony and pray for her other son, from whom she had heard nothing for over two months, and give thanks to God for not abandoning her.

The store had been unusually busy all morning long. What was it about a hot sunny day in August that made women want to buy new towels, sheets, linens? Ben thought it was the light—the piercing, fiery, life-giving light of summer, that made everything old look yellow and shabby. One after another they came, women themselves suddenly bursting with life, looking to rejuvenate their homes, their tables, their beds. Ben loved to help them find what they were looking for. He had a knack for knowing what his customers liked, what would make their eyes light up with approval, their hands involuntarily reach out to stroke the fine material or soft nap. He knew what would convince them to buy and go home happy.

Now it was midday and for the moment the store was empty. The other men had gone to take lunch, but Ben stayed to count up the morning's income. The store was doing better and better every month, and he thought maybe he might ask Meyer Rothstein for another small raise. The baby would come in six weeks, and Ben didn't know if Naomi would be able to sew again after, if her eyes would tire less easily then. Without a little more money, he might not have enough to give Mama and Papa anything. He couldn't find a better job in a union shop for Sarah until she was sixteen. Six months at Pankin's had already made her skinny and sullen; he couldn't imagine what two more years would do to her.

As he refolded the towels and tablecloths that his customers had rejected, Ben gazed out the big plate-glass window facing onto Orchard Street, watching the stream of activity on the street without really seeing it. Feeling pessimistic, he wondered if he and his Naomi might have to take his parents and sister in with them. The Warshinskys might have to take a giant step back to living in too small a space, with no privacy. All because David had turned his back on them, run away from a life he found too hard, as though life was meant to be easy.

Suddenly Ben's eye was caught by the sight of a woman walking slowly and deliberately on the other side of the street. She seemed so familiar and yet his mind refused to believe what his eyes were telling him.

He dropped the towel he'd been folding onto the long wooden counter and ran to the door. As he reached the sidewalk, he stopped, immobilized by amazement and by the woman's gesture: an elegant hand raised, palm out, ordering him to stay and wait for her to come to him. She was beaming and her eyes were locked with his as she stepped off the curb. Out of the corner of his eye Ben saw the car come seemingly out of nowhere, moving too fast down the crowded street. He raised his own hands and screamed, "Mama! Stop! Stop! Comes a car!" He saw her head whip to the side in terror and, to his relief, saw her quickly take a step back as the driver leaned on his horn. People scurried away in all directions and Ben lost sight of her as the car passed between them.

In the aftermath of fear, he shook a raised fist at the retreating vehicle and then turned back to watch the miracle of Anna walking across the street. She wasn't there. Confounded, his eyes quickly searched the thick crowds at the curb and in the now-clear street. Had he imagined her? The crowd at the curb was growing larger, and he realized that they weren't moving; they were standing, surrounding something, murmuring over something, wailing over something. Blackness swam up behind his eyes. He ran across the street, pushed his way through the crowd. He heard someone call out, "Let him through; I think it's his mother."

The pack parted for him, gentle hands pushing him forward and supporting him all at once. He stood in the center of the hushed crowd, strangers' hands on him, looking down at his mama, the beautiful Anna, lying still and lifeless on the sidewalk. He collapsed to the ground.

"She tripped on the curb as she stepped back. She hit her head." Someone whispered in his ear. "It happened so fast. I'm sorry."

Thick dark blood had seeped into her hair and was still coming, puddling on the deadly cement. Her golden eyes were open and staring into the bright summer sky. Ben thought he would lose his mind. This couldn't be happening. He picked up her hand and pressed it to his lips. She could not be dead. Her hand was still so warm. And so limp. He began to sob. He rocked back and forth, moaning, holding her hand against his breast. After an unknowable time, he felt an arm slip around his shoulders, saw a plump white hand reach out and close Anna's eyes. He turned his head to see Naomi next to him, tears streaming down her round face. Ben would not let go of Anna's hand and for a little while, in the safety of his wife's embrace, he did lose his mind. For long enough to decide that if his saint of a mother was dead, so then to him was his sinner of a brother.

Two blocks away, Fay repeatedly darted to the door of the bakery, peering up and down and across the street, impatiently looking for Anna. Waiting on the counter was a white box tied with red string. Inside lay a perfect cinnamon *babka*.

Emptiness. Emptiness more terrible than death. Nothing left now but the shadow of a life. Viktor was beyond grief. His mind could find no way to make sense of what had happened or what might happen next. Numb to his very essence, he was vaguely aware of Ben making arrangements for Anna's funeral, respecting all the proper rituals and traditions. Anna's body was washed; she was never left alone, her face never allowed to look downward. The funeral took place within twenty-four hours of her death. Earth was thrown onto her coffin; an unidentified mourner blessed her passage, intoning, *"May she come to her place in peace."*

There were so many people, too many unfamiliar faces. Who were all these people coming to mourn his Anna? He recognized their neighbors, the men from his *shul*, his *landsmanshaft*. But the others. How did they come to be there? Why did they weep for her? At least the hands helping him and Ben lift and carry her coffin to the hearse and then to the grave site belonged to men he knew. There was young Reuben, who had become like family since Sarah began bringing him home for Shabbat dinner every week; Sol Leyrowitz, fat and red eyed; Yoshi Krinski, Meyer Rothstein, Sam Levy, even Frankie Corelli and young Aronson, the fruit peddler. Someone was missing, Viktor was sure of it, but every time he tried to think of who, he grew helplessly confused. He was sure he had heard Ben say *kaddish* for him, mourning his death in the same breath he mourned Anna's, but Viktor did not remember burying David. He remembered burying Wolf and Rose and Anna, yes, but not David. But then, where was David? Where was his son? If they hadn't buried him, why wasn't he there, helping to carry his mother's body to her grave? And if they had buried him, why did Viktor not remember? How was it possible that he would forget such a thing? When he asked, when he tried to say his son's name, no one looked at him. Was he not really speaking? Had he only dreamed that he had another son, beautiful and quick like his Anna?

Now it was over. The funeral, the week of sitting *shivah* when friends and relatives had come to the apartment to offer condolences. Now the candle was extinguished and the mirrors uncovered. There was nothing left to do but try to live. Viktor didn't see how he could. He sat in the corner on a low stool, where he had been for the past seven days, a glass of sweet tea and a plate with cake set on the windowsill near him, untouched. He watched ghostly hands dismantling his life and packing it into rough cardboard boxes.

Like a dreamer waking into a deeper dream, Viktor looked up into the shattered space of the apartment's large room. He was alone. No one there, only cold cartons stacked on the floor, dusty furniture pushed into a shape-less heap near the door. Raised voices came from behind the wall. Crying and screaming. Someone burst through the door from the other room. Anna! Viktor gasped and leaped to his feet. It wasn't her. So like her, but not her, too small, too angry. It was Sarah, carrying her precious doll. Such a sweet child, so good. Viktor smiled at her, but she paid him no attention. She threw the doll onto a pile of garbage in the corner and disappeared again. He retreated to his stool. Ben would come for him when it was time to go. He didn't care if he left this place. Without Anna, there was no reason to stay. No reason at all.

9

"Go on; don't be shy. Say thank you to your aunt Sally." Zoe bent down and whispered as she gently pushed Eliza-beth ahead of her across the vestibule's sleek black-and-white marble floor. "Isn't it nice of her to invite you to play with Brook?"

"Thank you Aunt Sally."

"You're very welcome, Elizabeth. Go on upstairs. Brook is waiting for you in his room. Edna will bring up some milk and cake in a little while."

The women settled themselves in the parlor, in comfort-able chairs by the window that looked out on Philip's gar-den, already beginning its melancholy autumnal descent now that another September had arrived. Tea and finger sandwiches waited on the small, round table.

"So, Zoe," said Sally, pouring out two cups, "it's just

thrilling how quickly you've taken to Miss Eddy's teachings. The ladies in our group quite adore you. Sugar? Cream?"

"Yes, both, thank you. Her ideas make wonderful sense to me. But it's hard, isn't it, to truly accept that all the harsh manifestations of matter—sin, evil, illness, even death— are not created or caused by God and so cannot exist? They continue to seem so real to me. I'm glad you think I'm do- ing well with it, Sally, but believe me, I struggle."

"It is hard, sometimes, yes. Especially as we are sur- rounded by nonbelievers. Our family is quite the tribe of pagans. But you don't see me getting discouraged, do you? Belief in the reality of matter is a very powerful lie. One must hold fast to the Divine truth, that God is all that exists and He is spirit, not matter, and so everything God-created is wholly spirit." Sally bit crisply into a cucumber sand- wich. "My son is spirit, God's spirit. We have heard noth- ing from Jed for three months now, but do you see me quake and tremble with fear? No. I know that he will come back to us. His essence cannot be touched by this war, which is itself but another falsity."

Zoe looked into Sally's cold blue eyes. "You are stronger than I am, I think."

"Nonsense, my dear. This is still new to you. And your false beliefs have created great discord in your life." Abruptly Sally put her half-eaten sandwich down and leaned across the table. She tapped Zoe's hand conspirato- rially. "But you have reason to be heartened. Everyone has seen the change in Monty, if I may dare say it. Even Joseph. He seems happier; he is drinking less. Philip tells me he is in charge of some grand project at the Club? The presence of the Divine touches everyone."

Zoe suddenly felt sick to her stomach. She put her cup down with a startling clatter.

"Zoe, what is it? You don't look at all good. You're not getting ill, are you? One hears about that dreadful Spanish influenza."

"No, no. It's just . . ."

The Divine had not touched Monty. He drank as much as ever. He just showed it less. From time to time, he hit her. After six months of devoting herself to Christian Science, contemplating her pure and indestructible relationship with God, Monty's unpredictable cruelty felt as real to her as before. He didn't even seem angry anymore, just cold and determined to remind her of how little he thought of her, how paltry and powerless she was. The more virtuous he became in public, the more base he allowed himself to be in private, as though he had chosen her to be the repository for his sins and his villainy and was thus free to be good everywhere else in the world. It was her doubt that was to blame. She was creating the ugliness in her life. It was because she still believed herself sinful that she drew Monty's sins to her. Until she truly and profoundly understood the transcendent nature of God and man's spiritual relationship, she would remain unworthy of drawing goodness from Monty instead.

"Zoe, are you sure you're all right?"

"I don't know. I have such a long way to go, Sally. Sometimes I think I will never get there. Life sometimes feels like such a lonely burden."

A hint of some nameless, soft emotion flickered to life in Sally's eyes. "You will. And remember this, Zoe. You can only bring others along with you so far. It is for yourself you do this, as I do it for myself." She reached out and put her hand over Zoe's. "Tell me, do the teachings bring you hope?"

Zoe looked down in shock from Sally's suddenly warm eyes to the warm hand touching hers. A simple gesture, but one of an intimacy that Sally had never shown her before. "Yes. They do," she whispered.

"Then stick with it. Do it for yourself. Don't you care what anyone thinks. I don't care what Joseph, Philip, or my oh-so-modern daughter think. My son is on a battlefield and I will be damned if I'll believe for one second that he is going to die. You know what you need, Zoe. Don't let anyone tell you it's wrong."

Sally released Zoe's hand and sat back. "More tea?" she asked, cool and composed again. "And please, have a watercress sandwich. They are one of Edna's specialties."

Brook was in envious awe of his cousin Elizabeth. Though he huffed to hear anyone say it, often even he couldn't believe they were the same age. She acted more grown-up than Lucy sometimes, as smart and correct as a little adult. Aunt Zoe let Elizabeth do whatever she wanted, yet she never got into trouble. He didn't understand how that was possible, since just about everything he wanted to do got him into trouble. Obviously, Elizabeth wanted only proper things. She was good and he was not.

"Shall we read?" Libby reached for the bag that Zoe had packed for her visit.

"All right." Brook plopped down near her on the floor. "You're allowed to read that?" he asked incredulously. She had pulled a copy of *The All-Story* with its new installment of *Tarzan, the Ape Man,* from her bag.

"Of course, aren't you? The stories are great fun. My father says they're swell. He loves them and he reads them to me when I can't understand all the words."

She grew quiet and stared at the magazine. Mother said that Libby was plain and too thin and that Aunt Zoe didn't know how to arrange her hair or dress her nicely, but Brook thought she was beautiful, the way a baby bird was beautiful.

"Mother says they're trash. I can't read them or bring them into the house. I really like them, but—I mean, Libby, when your mother says to do something, don't you have to obey?"

Libby's head came up and she looked at Brook intently. "Of course!" She quickly put the magazine back into her bag. "Then I won't read it, either. Let's do something else. Let's build something with your blocks. You always make the best things with them."

Brook's heart swelled as he dumped his box of wooden blocks onto the floor between them. Without a word, they went to work creating a wonderful house, building on each other's moves as though following a blueprint that had sprung from their shared vision of what a house should be. They worked feverishly, looking up for only a brief second to thank Edna for the slices of chocolate cake and glasses of milk she carefully put on the floor next to them.

"This is your room," Elizabeth said, indicating the largest space on the second floor, "and this is mine, this one with the big windows. And this could be Lucy's, and here is where Angelina stays when she comes to cook, and Grandmother can sleep here when she visits."

"There are no rooms for our parents. Where will they sleep?"

"They don't live here. They have to stay in their own houses."

Brook stretched over the top of their magic house and planted a childish yet impassioned kiss on Libby's sallow cheek. "Your skin feels so hot. You didn't even touch your cake."

"Brook, I don't feel good." She put down the block she'd been about to place. "My head hurts and I feel strange, like something is pressing on me, here." She put her hand on her chest.

Brook was frightened. Libby had grown sickly pale. A light sweat had broken out on her forehead. "Come on; we have to tell your mother."

"No! I want to stay here with you!"

"Libby, yes! Don't be a ninny. You're sick and you have to go home and to bed."

Zoe put Libby to bed with a hot water bottle as soon as they reached home. She spoon-fed her warmed consommé and wrapped her in blankets, but the girl still shook from a deep chill while her skin felt like it was on fire. Zoe settled herself into a chair next to Libby's bed, her Christian Science texts on her lap, and began to read and pray, struggling to align her mind with the Divine Mind, striving to convince herself that Libby's relationship to God was undisturbed and that therefore her illness was not real and would leave her. She considered calling Dr. Barre, their longtime family doctor, but rejected the idea as representing nothing more than another seductive temptation to abandon her confidence in her own beliefs. After her talk with Sally, she was determined not to let that happen. Libby's illness was a phantom of disbelief; material medicine could have no effect on something that didn't exist. As Zoe watched her daughter shake with fever, however, she decided that a small dose of aspirin probably couldn't hurt. She melted a tablet in a teaspoon of consommé and made Libby swallow the bitter broth. The guilt Zoe felt at that small betrayal of her new faith propelled her to read and pray all the harder. Before long, Libby had fallen into a peaceful sleep and her forehead felt cooler.

Relieved that Libby was recovering, Zoe made herself some dinner and called Monty at the inn in Newport where he was staying. The Club had put him in charge of the renovation of the dining room, and he'd gone to Newport in search of inspiration in the posh club and hotel dining rooms there. He'd been gone for three days and she hadn't heard from him once. She was afraid he'd be angry that she'd called, accuse her of checking up on him and interfering with his work. She knew that he was punishing her by not calling, leaving her alone in the formless void created by the absence of even his voice. Some part of her understood that she should have felt free with him gone, but she didn't. She felt frighteningly alone. She wanted to tell him that his daughter was sick, so that he'd worry, and then reassure him that she was taking good care of Libby, so that he'd be proud of her. The phone rang and rang in his empty room. She didn't leave a message.

Libby was still asleep and still cool, so Zoe gathered her books and went to her own bedroom for the night. She fell into a deep sleep unlike any she'd enjoyed in recent months, for while she believed herself to be missing Monty, a deeper part of her mind understood that tonight she was safe and must take advantage of danger's absence to regenerate her energies. She slept without moving until nearly dawn, when she was awakened by a strange, repetitive sound. As she came fully awake, she realized that the sound was emanating from Elizabeth's room, but surely not from the girl herself. Her little body could not possibly be the source of such an enormous sound: a rasping, heaving moan that punctuated, over and over, seconds of intervening, menacing silence.

Zoe leaped out of her bed and ran down the hall. At the sight of her daughter she nearly fell down in terror. Libby was pouring sweat and thrashing under the burden of her bedclothes, which she had pushed down to her waist. Her long brown hair was a tangled, sweat-soaked mass of darkness next to the sickly pallor of her skin. She was semiconscious, her eyes closed and her upper body arching off the bed with the monumental effort of each gasping breath. Zoe put her hand on Libby's forehead and recoiled instantly from the unnatural heat.

Calm down, Zoe; calm down. You know what to do; just stay calm. Zoe forced herself to think clearly, to make a plan and move through it one step at a time. She needed help; of that there was no doubt. Her parents were close, just across the park, and with Ralph to drive them could be here in no time. But she did not call them. They couldn't help her now; they would only confuse her and try to take control of Libby's fate. What she had to do, quickly quickly, was call Sally, ask her to come. Ask her to bring a healer. Though it was ungodly early, she knew Sally wouldn't mind. Zoe ran into the parlor, picked up the receiver, and rang through to the brownstone, far away downtown and on the other side of the city.

It would be almost an hour before Sally would arrive with the practitioner, the gifted healer Lorena, who would lead them in prayer for spiritual treatment and make Libby better. But there were useful things Zoe could do in the meantime. She stripped off Libby's sopping nightgown, pushed aside the sheets and blankets, and gently wiped Libby down from head to toe, again and again, with a towel soaked in cool water. Zoe wrung cool water out of a small clean cloth directly into Libby's mouth and laid a cool compress on her forehead and another across her throat. After a little while, the girl responded; her body grew still and her breathing seemed not quite so labored. Zoe dressed her in a new nightgown, put dry sheets on the bed. She was still hot to the touch, but Zoe thought she looked better. One more aspirin, just to be safe until Lorena came.

"Libby, I want you to swallow this now."

Libby's head turned toward Zoe and her eyes opened. They were glazed and unfocused, but she nodded and opened her mouth.

"You're going to be fine. You have a fever, but you'll be all right. Try to sleep. I'll stay right here."

Libby reached out and took Zoe's hand. "I'm sorry, Mommy, but don't worry," she whispered. "I'm trying really hard to get better. I won't leave you alone with Daddy."

Zoe felt herself turn to stone. Libby could not have intended anything but the most innocent reassurance. It was too hideous to contemplate that her little girl knew what went on in the tortured intimacy of her parents' relationship. Worse, even, to think that Libby felt responsible for protecting Zoe.

Zoe smiled. "Of course you're not going to leave us alone." She patted the little hand that clutched at hers, frightened all over again by the wrongness of the child's hot, papery skin. Zoe's thoughts now began to chase themselves in frantic circles. Christian Science taught her that illness was but a sign, a fleshly demonstration of spiritual disharmony, but it was as clear as day that Libby had influenza. People, even young people, were dying from it in terrifying numbers all across the country. Should she call Dr. Barre? She certainly knew what her parents and husband would do. But she also knew that they weren't always right, no matter how forcefully they tried to convince the world otherwise. Besides, doctors more often than not could do nothing for their patients once the symptoms of flu appeared. Despite all ministrations, victim after victim succumbed to pneumonia and died within mere days. In her heart, Zoe believed that someone who had found true unity with God could indeed call on the infinite powers of His spiritual being to work miracles in life. Sally's piety was perhaps lacking in the necessary degree of selflessness, but Lorena was the most spiritual and generous woman Zoe had ever met. In the past eight months, she'd heard many testaments to the longtime practitioner's healing abilities. Zoe made up her mind. She would follow the path she had begun walking and use the power of prayer to save her daughter. Her decision was confirmed by the doorman ringing up to announce the arrival of Sally and Lorena.

The practitioner sat in a chair pulled up close to Elizabeth's bed. Zoe and Sally's fretful presence had made it difficult for Lorena to concentrate during their hours of prayer, and so she had sent them into the kitchen to make tea, to occupy them while she worked and to calm them so that they could be helpful when they would be truly needed. Alone with her patient, Lorena placed both her hands gently on the girl's arm, bowed her head, and opened her mind to the highest way of knowing, looking for God's love to help cure this tender young creature who was so ill from her own belief in the evils of the world. The girl had floated in and out of sleep all morning and she startled Lorena now as she opened her eyes and looked around the room, making sure they were alone before she spoke.

"Lorena, am I going to die?"

The poignancy of such a question coming from one so young touched her heart, the more so because she was certain she already knew the answer. Lorena had sat at enough deathbeds to recognize a soul ready to fly free. "I don't know, darling. But I will share a wonderful truth with you. You must have no fear of death. You are eternal spirit, like Christ himself. This is the secret of life, that you will not die but will have eternal life with God."

Libby stared into Lorena's eyes. "But I won't be here anymore."

"No, not the way you are now."

Libby thought seriously about what Lorena had said. "Can I share my secret with you? And you'll promise not to tell?"

The practitioner smiled. The girl's voice was weak. Just to say those few sentences wore her out and left her gasping for breath, but her mind was for the moment clear. "Of course. You can tell me anything."

"My father hits my mother, hard, with his fists. She begs

him not to, but he does it anyway and she cries for hours. They think I don't know, but I do. I hear them at night when they think I'm asleep."

Lorena's smile froze to a rictus. The room filled with the sound of Libby's panting, rattling breath. This was not the secret Lorena had expected to hear. A child should not have such secrets as this. "Are you sure, Elizabeth? Grownups do fight sometimes, you know."

"Oh yes, I'm sure. I saw him once. He punched her in the face and she fell down. But you have to promise me you won't tell. My mother would be angry with me. No one knows. It's important that no one knows because we love him and he . . ." Libby's voice trailed off to the merest whisper. "Lorena, I'm so tired. I'm going to close my eyes now." Almost immediately she fell into a restless sleep.

"Yes, Elizabeth, close your eyes." Lorena stroked the girl's forehead. She continued to pray, but it was no longer with a mind to recovery into the material world. Libby's time here was over; she was destined to rest eternally with Christ, with God. As for the secret: Lorena would respect the girl's wishes and say nothing. If the monstrous thing was true, Lorena had faith that Christian Science would be Zoe's salvation. She liked Zoe very much; whatever spiritual guidance Zoe needed now, Lorena would be happy to provide. She prayed over Elizabeth for a last moment and then went into the kitchen to bring Zoe to sit with her daughter and sent Sally to the phone to gather the rest of the family.

Zoe walked forward into the musty apartment. She heard Monty close the door, heard an ominous *snick* as he turned the lock. She felt his presence behind her as a looming shadow, waiting impatiently to shroud her in its vengeful gloom. It was the first time they'd been alone since Elizabeth's death. During the intervening days and nights, they had stayed at her parents' apartment, surrounded by family, supported in their grief. Numbing shock and sorrow rendered everyone kind; not a word had been uttered about what Zoe had done or not done. Nonetheless, Zoe knew without doubt that at the very least her father and husband held her responsible. No matter that Dr. Barre himself had consoled her, saying he could not have done anything to save Libby. She knew the way those men's minds worked. They were never satisfied; there was always something more you could do. There was always something more she, in particular, should have done.

Throughout the ordeal, Monty had been an unexpected tower of strength to the family that had long since written him off as a useless, embarrassing nuisance. He was the soul of propriety, stone sober, clearheaded, and decisive. He did not hide his anguish yet was able to comfort his bereaved wife and show his gratitude to the family for their solicitousness. But in every loving embrace, every tender glance, Zoe read a different message from the one seen by the others. It was a message meant for her only, and its full impact was about to be delivered. Perhaps she deserved it, perhaps not. She didn't know anymore. But she was ready for it. She didn't bother to turn on a light. She simply stopped and turned to face him, inviting the blow she had been waiting for, yearning for. It didn't come. Standing silently in the murky light, Zoe felt herself begin to disappear.

Monty snapped on the hall light. "I could kill you and no one would ever know. I could push you out the window and say you'd jumped, you were so deranged by guilt and grief, and even your mother would believe me. Should I do that? Should I put you out of your misery?"

Zoe looked at him in horror. She wanted to beg him to hit her, to give her the beating he thought she merited for her mistakes, but she knew as she stared into his beautiful eyes that he was not interested in that. She understood nothing except that this new torment was not because of what happened to Libby. "Why, Monty? Why do you despise me so?"

He shrugged. "I don't despise you, Zoe. I just don't really care about you one way or another. Haven't you figured that out yet? That I don't really care about anyone one way or another? You shouldn't take it personally. It's not as though I would prefer some other woman, although I'm sure you realize I've had plenty. All things considered, since I have to be with someone to seem acceptable in the world, I'd sooner be with you. I've gotten very used to you. You're satisfying in bed, you're completely without backbone, and, best of all, you're an obscenely rich little brat with obscenely rich parents and I had my share secured through our daughter."

Zoe began backing away from him, groping behind her for the security of the wall.

He took a step toward her. "Oh no," he commanded. "Don't try to get away from me. You can never get away from me now, Zoe. You owe me for what you just did to me. You murdered my daughter. I was actually very fond of her."

Zoe shook her head. "No, Monty, I didn't. Even Dr. Barre said—"

"You murdered her!" he screamed. "You stupid abortion of a mother! Why didn't you know she was sick? If you had gotten her to a real doctor, not that quack healer, she'd be alive!"

Zoe turned, leaned her forehead against the wall, and covered her ears with her hands. Monty was quickly behind her, pulling her hands down, holding them to her sides while he pressed the weight of his body into her back, mashing her into the wall.

"She'd be alive!" he hissed into her ear. "My daughter, my heir, my guarantee of a hefty slice of your father's money. Did you let her die on purpose, Zoe? To try to cut me off?"

Zoe cried out and struggled to get free of his grip.

"No, of course you didn't. You could never conceive of something so wonderfully evil and clever. Well, it doesn't matter. I just have to work a little harder. I see how easily your father can be swayed. He's getting old and soft. A few months of playing the proper part and already he wonders if perhaps he's misjudged me. I can play that game as long as it takes. And I still have you, my loving wife, to help convince him."

Zoe moaned. She was trapped in a cage she had created from her own illusions. Her mind worked furiously to find something she could say to redeem herself in his eyes. "What do you want me to do, Monty? You know I love you. I believe in you, I believe you *do* love me, and you loved Libby; you just think you don't because—"

"Because why? Because I was never shown how to love?" Monty simpered, making cruel mockery of the ubiquitous talk of love and truth that had spewed from Zoe's mouth in recent months. "I think I don't love you because I don't. And as for what I want you to do, it's quite simple. I want you to be my adoring wife, my helpmate, my defender and champion. I want you to let your family know how happy we are together, despite our terrible loss. I want access to your parents' money. And I want you to do all that knowing that I don't love you and that I may never touch you again, in any way"—he twisted her arm up against her shoulder blade until she winced in pain, and at the same time sank a vampiric kiss into the crook of her neck—"unless I get an occasional urge."

He released her and backed toward the door. "I know you can do all that, Zoe, because I know you'll never stop believing that one day I will wake up and realize that I love you. And who knows, maybe I will." He laughed without humor. "I'm going to Shannon's to get drunk. When I get back, I want your things out of our room. You can sleep in Libby's room from now on. You can sleep with your memories of what you did to her."

The sound of the door closing released Zoe from the wall. Her head felt invaded by a seething tangle of snakes, hissing black, wordless thoughts. She found herself at the living room window, staring down at the building's inner courtyard four floors below. She slowly opened the heavy casement and let the cool air wash over her. She could jump. It would be so easy. She had nothing left; why not end it? Monty was right; no one would be surprised to hear that her grief had overcome her. Everyone always said she was overly emotional. She imagined herself climbing onto the ledge, tilting her body into the void, hitting the concrete paving, and being no more. Almost ruefully, she knew she could never do it. She was weak, she was stupid, she was wasting her own life and had been accused of giving away her daughter's, but for better or worse she was cursed with an endless supply of optimism. It lay quietly inside her while she dragged herself through her days, then rose up to save her at her darkest moments.

She turned from the window to make her way to the bedroom, turning on the lights as she went. As she started down the hall, the hissing in her head became a shriek. The open door to Libby's room stood between Zoe and the bedroom she had shared with Monty. Suddenly she thought she heard the contented humming of a little child engrossed in solitary play. It was a glorious sound that drew Zoe into the room, where she had been unable to go since her daughter had taken her last breath.

Zoe half-expected to see Libby sitting on her embroidered rug, bent over her favorite doll, singing softly to herself as she had so often in life. But, of course, the room was empty. And yet it wasn't. Distantly Zoe remembered that Lorena and a group of churchwomen had come to cleanse the room of the aftermath of death. They had restored it to a place of beauty and light. And Libby was there. Zoe could feel her everywhere, could feel her love and her intention to stay as long as she was needed. Gingerly, Zoe sat on the bed. Serenity settled over her like a holy balm. Light from the hallway spilled into the darkening room. She slowly laid herself down, her head on Libby's pillow, her body stretched full on Libby's bed, and cried. She wept until the pillow was soaked with her tears and the otherwise silent rooms were filled with the sounds of her pain and her joy. She would do as Monty ordered. He didn't need to know that forcing her to sleep in Libby's room was no punishment. And tomorrow she would go to a Christian Science meeting and ask Lorena to guide her to deliverance.

Evelyn walked forward into the comforting warmth of the apartment. Lights had been left burning in the hall and the drawing room, and the air smelled of lemon oil and cut flowers. She heard the reassuring sound of the door closing behind Joseph, forming a protective barrier between them and the events of these terrible last days. She felt his presence behind her as solidly as a sheltering wall. She turned to him and they reached for each other. They held each other tightly, wordlessly consoling themselves with the sharing of sorrow, the feel of each other's heat, and the joy of being alone together again.

"Come. We could both use a drink." Joseph took Evelyn's hand and led her down the hall to the drawing room.

The staff had discreetly retired to their quarters but had left a low fire burning in the fireplace. On a table rested a decanter and two glasses on a tray, along with a bowl of nuts and some chocolates. Evelyn kicked off her shoes, Joe loosened his tie, and they fell onto the sofa, exhausted.

"She should have called Barre. She should have called him right away."

"Joe, Dr. Barre said he couldn't have done anything."

"That doesn't mean it was right not to call him. How fortunate for Zoe that the girl's illness was fatal," he said, his voice full of irony. "What if it *had* been something Barre could have cured? How would you feel about her choice then?"

"I don't know. I don't know what to make of this belief of hers. It seems ridiculous to me, but many intelligent people subscribe to it and it does seem to be helping her and Monty. I really don't know. I just don't want you to hate her, to punish her, for this. She's just lost her only child, our little granddaughter." Evelyn's voice broke. "She needs our love now, not our criticism."

Joseph took a long pull of cognac. "I don't hate her," he said quietly. "She's my daughter, I love her. I won't punish her. I'll do something nice for her. She's asked me so many times to give Monty a better job. I'm going to do it. I'll give the bastard a chance. Maybe after this he'll straighten himself out." He paused, then said, "I just don't understand what's in her head half the time."

"Truly I don't, either. But you don't seem to have a problem with Sally and this Christian Science."

"Sally. She's a different story all together. She does what's good for Sally. She's convinced herself this crap will get her something she wants: social connections, Jed coming home safely, God knows what. She's probably hoping she'll become best friends with Lady Astor, as though Nancy would have any interest in a conservative house mouse like Sally." He drained his glass and put it down on the chased silver tray. He popped some cashews in his mouth. "You know perfectly well that Sally would hardly let a little thing like principle stand in her way— she'd be the first to call the doctor if she thought one of her children needed care. Believe me, she'll drop the charade once it's of no use to her anymore. But Zoe . . . Zoe is so susceptible to the influences of others. Why? Coming from this family, how could she have ended up so weak willed? That's what I have never understood."

Evelyn smiled. "She was strong enough to defy you and marry Monty."

"Don't remind me." He stared into the fire, thinking. "Besides, I don't know if that was defiance or just a cowardly trading of my influence for one she thought would be less demanding."

Evelyn sighed. "Oh, Joe. I wish you wouldn't judge her so harshly. She was young. She fell in love. It may all work out well in the end. She is still young enough to have another child, if they want to."

Joseph took Evelyn's hand and pressed it to his lips. "What a woman I married. Now give me one of those chocolates, lean your head right here"—he patted his own shoulder—"and stop talking."

No sooner had Evelyn made herself comfortable than Walter appeared to inform Joseph that there was an urgent call for him from the office of Senator Wadsworth.

"Tea, Edna, please, and hot chocolate for the children." Philip herded his family into the parlor and arranged them in a depleted huddle around the empty fireplace. Such a grueling few days; such a sad and poignant funeral, such an unnaturally small coffin.

Sally had not been herself since Elizabeth died. None of them had been, certainly, but Sally had withdrawn into an unfamiliar numbed silence. They had heard nothing from or about Jed for three intolerable months.

And poor Brook. He had cried piteously all through his cousin's funeral. He was still sniveling, his eyes were red and swollen, and he could hardly breathe. From out of nowhere, Sally produced a handkerchief and slid it into his hand. She put her arms around him and held him tight against her. Brook looked up at her for a startled second, then leaned against her breast and started crying again, quietly and steadily. Sally rested her chin on his head and stared catlike into space. Lucy got up from her chair and insinuated herself onto the small couch next to her mother. She placed a hand on Sally's arm. "Jed is going to come home safely, Mother. He is. We must believe it." Sally turned her head toward her daughter and kissed her softly on her forehead.

Philip, ever the artist, was achingly aware of the beauty of the family tableau before him. If only it were as easy to capture and keep in real life what he was so good at capturing on canvas. His family, reduced by tragedy to a state of love and caring that in normal times they abandoned in favor of anger and selfishness. He could have sat watching them forever, but Edna informed him, as she set down their tea and chocolate, that his father was on the phone. Philip was aware of Sally's eyes on him as he left the room, eyes full of fear she could no longer hide. Philip told himself that there were a thousand reasons why Joseph might be calling so soon after they'd parted; it wasn't necessarily to do with Jed.

"Philip?"

"Yes, Father, what is it? Is everything all right?"

"My boy, everything is better than all right. I just got off the phone with Wadsworth's office. They've finally gotten news of Jed! He's fine, Philip. He's wounded, but not too badly; he's recovering in an army hospital outside of Paris. They don't know when they'll be able to ship him home, it may be months, but at least he's not going back into battle. From what I understand, he's something of a hero. Philip, do you hear me? Philip? Your boy is alive, well, and coming home!" Joseph fairly shouted his relief, but with an unmistakable quaver in his proud voice.

Philip's legs turned to jelly and he slumped against the

wall. The telephone receiver fell to his shoulder and he heard his father worriedly calling his name. With a monumental effort, he brought the phone back to his ear and managed to mumble into the ether, "Thank you, thank you. Father, thank you."

"What a day to get such news, hey, Philip? We bury one child and get back another. Go; go tell Sally. Tomorrow we'll take you all out to Delmonico's to celebrate."

"That's a generous thought, Father, but why don't we wait a little while, just until Libby's loss isn't quite so raw." There would be no call for Zoe and Monty redeeming the terrible thing that had happened; there was no bringing Libby home.

Joseph cleared his throat in embarrassment. "Yes, yes, of course. I was just so . . . well, you know. Why don't you come over here then and we'll have a quiet celebration?"

"That sounds fine. Hold the line, will you? I'm sure Sally will want details."

Philip walked back into the parlor and knelt in front of the couch. He smiled up at this woman, this girl, this boy whom he loved so tenderly, and then looked only at Sally. "Sally, my love, Jed is coming home. It's over. He's all right." He saw a fluttering in the depths of her heart-stopping blue eyes; a collapsing of something adamantine inside her. "My father is still on the phone. I thought you'd want to know all the details."

Sally began to rise, then fell back. "I'll call him later. Tell us what he said."

As Philip spoke, tears began to trickle down Sally's cheeks. They had waited through an endless, surreal year for this news. For himself, Philip believed that life, or Fate—not God; Philip didn't believe in God—was offering him a second chance with his son. Now, Philip dared hope for even more: that Jed's safe return might help heal his family's many rifts, might make real for all time this loving portrait.

Sally bowed her head and pulled Brook and Lucy closer to her. She pressed her lips to Lucy's forehead again, then to Brook's. Her eyes closed and Philip saw a shiver run through her. She turned to him, her eyes still damp, and said in a calm voice, "Philip. Call Dr. Barre. Brook has a fever."

Out in the hallway, Joseph's frustrated voice came through the receiver lying unattended on the entryway table. "Philip? Philip? Sally? Where the hell is anyone? Aah!" And the phone went dead.

10

Jed drifted in and out of consciousness during the first weeks in the hospital. Every time he awoke, he prayed to fall asleep and never wake again. Wakefulness brought with it the horrific memory of Cooper's eyes, lifeless and yet staring straight at him as though they could see, for all eternity, the face of the man who had murdered him. The nurses, naturally assuming that Jed's terrible agitation was from the pain of his mangled leg, gave him morphine and he'd pass into oblivion again. He spent weeks licked by the flames of an internal hell, awaiting his worldly punishment, before he realized that no one knew what had happened. Rather, they thought him a hero: grievously wounded himself, he had risked his very life to go back onto the battlefield and drag his closest friend to safety. He had even tried to save poor Vern. Once Jed was awake, the adulation and congratulations from the other wounded men never stopped. Several times, while Captain Hummel was still on the ward with them, Jed played with the idea of telling him the truth, batting it about in his confused mind the way a cat plays with a mouse whose life it is about to extinguish.

Little by little, Jed became able to accept the congratulations without flinching. He accepted that to a host of worthy men who had known him for over a year he was a hero. He began to wonder if perhaps his own interpretation of events was somehow faulty. He reexamined his memories with that in mind, but they refused to reconfigure themselves; he knew himself for what he truly was: a murdering coward. His only remedy was to not think about what he had done. With a steely determination he hadn't known he possessed, he dug another grave, a shallow depression in a quiet corner of his mind, and there he buried the images, the guilt, the shame.

"I can't wait to get out of here." Jed sat on the edge of his bed. The five interminable months in the hospital had been made bearable only by the fact that David was there, too. In another week, they would finally rejoin their regiment. "Bad enough we weren't with our guys when the Germans surrendered, I don't want to spend Christmas cooped up in this hospital." His hands moved restlessly on his right leg. Hidden beneath the coarse material of his hospital-issue pants was a still-raw network of scars that alternately itched, burned, and ached down to the bone. The bayonet had made an ugly-looking mess, but he'd been lucky and the doctors skillful. Aside from the scars, the only permanent result of his wound would be a weakness in the leg and a recurring numbness in his right foot.

David nodded as he looked around the gaily decorated ward. "Neither do I, even though the hospital staff has really gone all out to make it feel like Christmas, haven't they? Look at the size of that tree!" He sighed. "I'll bet our guys are playing football all day and drinking champagne all night."

Although neither had wounds that were life threatening, Jed's bouts of depression and David's debilitating headaches had kept them from being released sooner. There was no cause for haste, in any case. Others of their regiment were recovering from wounds worse than theirs, and until all were released the regiment could not be shipped home. Even then, it might take weeks or even months before they were on their way; there simply weren't enough troopships to transport the nearly two million Yanks who had been stranded in Europe by the war's end in November.

"I wonder if they've resurrected the Doughgirls." Jed laughed, picturing the men outfitted in his clever simulations of women's clothes, dancing and mincing, singing in falsetto, making everyone howl.

David grinned. "I'll bet they have, but I don't know who they'd get to replace Vern. He was so funny, with that stupid hat, and the pearls, and his hairy legs." His grin faded. He looked down at his hands and shook his head. "Poor Vern. All he wanted was to get back to his farm."

Jed's hands stilled. He lifted his head and gazed off into the distance, his eyes unfocused, until the wave of nausea peaked and then disappeared into that place in his mind. It was automatic now, the shuttling of those feverish feelings into the safety of oblivion. True, there was always that tiny panic-blinding moment before the horror relinquished its grip on him, but he'd gotten used to that. He no longer feared, quite so much, that the next time the panic would never subside.

"Hey!" David's startled voice brought Jed back. "Jed, look! It's Santa Claus!"

A pudgy, out-of-breath corporal from the Quartermaster's Office was trudging down the hall, dragging a tremendous sack. There had been rumors that the hospital staff planned to distribute presents to the lonely, homesick men who were still awaiting discharge.

"Hey, Corporal," David called out. "Make sure my scarf is brown, to match my hair!"

The corporal grunted. "I've got something better, Warshinsky. Mail. Months and months of it. Merry Christmas. Or should I say Happy Hanukkah?"

"Shit, I don't care what you say; just give us our letters!"

"Here you go, guys." The corporal upended the sack, spilling hundreds and hundreds of bundled letters onto the floor. "Looks like a mess, but it's all organized; trust me."

Jed's bundle was huge; there must have been fifteen letters banded together. He pretended not to see that David received only two thin envelopes. Jed shuffled through his stack, placed the envelopes in chronological order by postmark, then lost himself in news of home. He didn't notice when David slid off his bed, letters in his hand, and disappeared down the corridor.

Dear David,

I pray that this letter finds you. A terrible tragedy has happened in your family and I'm afraid that no one is going to tell you, no one will write to you. I don't know how to even say this to you . . . your mother died last month. She fell on the street and hit her head. So, so horrible, because she had gotten better and was out that day to get a job. David, your father, he is out of his mind; I don't think he will ever recover. Ben and Naomi have taken him and Sarah to live with them. Such another horrible thing to have to tell you, but David, don't come home now. Ben has said kaddish for you, and your sister will not talk about you at all. Maybe in time, but not now, it wouldn't be good; they don't want to see you. I know you loved your mother and she loved you, always, so I tell you that she is buried in Mount Judah Cemetery, in Brooklyn. I'm sorry. So, so sorry.

Sadie

Alone in the solarium, David stood with his back to the room, gazing out the enormous window. The letter from Sadie Krinski lay crumpled on the floor behind him; the letter from Rachel lay unopened and forgotten on the window ledge.

The vista before him was beautiful, even in the dead of winter, under a leaden sky. His eyes followed the gentle undulations of the long, well-kept dirt road bordered on both sides by majestic rows of plane trees, their bare branches reaching toward heaven, their trunks thick and grey-barked. It was the road that led off the hospital grounds, the first leg of the journey back home. David looked down that road and bitterness welled up in him like a poisonous sap. It had taken no more than two minutes for him to read his neighbor's letter and learn that he no longer had home or family to go back to. The foolish fantasies he had allowed himself during the long months of recuperation were utterly shattered.

In the pain and solitude of the first weeks, when his burns and fractures and concussion wracked him and Jed was too sedated to talk to, David had missed Anna with all the need of a sick child. He had read and reread her letter a hundred times. He had written to her as soon as he was able, in September, another one-line letter, to let her know, after a silence of three months, that he was still alive. He even thought of his father with affection, for the first time since he'd been a little boy. The fleeting vision he'd had at the moment of his injury of Viktor tossing him in the air gnawed at him. Had that ever happened? Had Viktor ever been so loving and loved a father to him?

He didn't know what he was going to do when he got back to New York beyond knowing he wasn't going back to the Lower East Side. The thought of his old friends, even of Rachel, whose letters had been full of nothing but love, held no attraction for him. What he'd always known was true: he had been an alien in that environment, and as soon as he'd left the irritation caused by his wrong presence had healed over, shutting him out forever. Even so, as the months went by, he let himself believe that Anna, revived and strong, would keep her promise and make peace within the family. That he might someday see them again.

He'd been here, missing them and thinking of reconciliation, while at home death and the need to blame had torn them all apart for good. It was finished now. So be it. Anna was the sun around whom they had all orbited, the gravity that had pulled them together to stand on the same spot. Without her, there was nothing in the world to bind them. Nothing to draw David and his weak-minded, self-righteous brother and sister to one another. David knew now that nothing had changed for them since the night he'd left. They had pushed him out, bolted the door, and manned the barricades. No understanding or forgiveness could get through to them. Fine. Let them hold him responsible for Anna's death. Let them delude themselves into thanking their ridiculous God for His blessings and let them go to hell.

As he'd read Sadie's letter, all the reasons he had had for leaving came raging back into his heart, fueled by an explosion of grief that he refused to own. The firestorm incinerated the fledgling feelings of tenderness he had nurtured over the past months and left him more certain than ever that his choice had been justified. He wasn't responsible for his parents' lives. He wasn't to blame for Anna's death. It wasn't his leaving that had killed her. It was his father's pitiful failure as a provider, Ben's lack of ambition, and Anna's own relinquishing of her strength to years of despair.

David did not know how long he had been at the window, his dry-eyed stare tracking the path to his unknowable future. The torrent inside him subsided, leaving in its wake a determination that ran like a fever through his veins. At the same moment, he sensed that he was no longer alone. Without needing to turn around, he knew that Jed had come to find him. Since the day they'd met, Jed had somehow always been there when David had needed someone. But when they got back to New York, they would say good-bye. David had no illusions that their friendship could last beyond this time-out-of-time experience they had shared. As much as David might dream of dwelling in a world like Jed's, he didn't and probably never would. They would go home, and Jed would rise and David would sink and they'd never see each other again.

He shifted his eyes from the view through the window to the glass itself and saw Jed reflected there, standing quietly a little distance behind him, waiting. Suddenly David felt as alone and frightened as he'd been that night in Pennsylvania Station. A sob rose in his throat and his mind spun back fifteen months to the memory of Jed coming toward him down the aisle of the train. The relief he'd felt at seeing him that morning was nothing compared to what David felt now. He didn't want Jed's friendship to have been nothing more than a passing fascination with something new and different, a temporary convenience during a difficult time.

"David, are you all right?"

David turned around and smiled. "What news from home?"

Jed cast a darting look at the letter crumpled on the floor between them. "Everything is good, except that my cousin, Elizabeth—my father's half sister Zoe's daughter?—she died of the Spanish flu in September. My brother got it, too, but he recovered, and so did one of my grandparents' servants. But poor Libby. She was only nine. She was Zoe and Monty's only child. I feel so bad for them; it's so terribly sad."

"I'm sorry. It's very hard to lose a child. My mother lost two and she never got over it. I'm glad that everything else is good. Any news of Lucy?"

David's voice and eyes were unnaturally bright. Jed began to fear what news was in that crumpled paper, but he knew better than to ask. "Yes. She's browbeaten my mother into letting her go to college after she graduates from Chapin." He smiled. "And she says hello to you."

David continued to look at Jed with a smile fixed on his face, but nothing more would come out of his mouth, no more polite questions about Jed's family while the question he needed to ask and couldn't: *Jed, are we really friends?* blocked his throat.

"David, what's wrong? You're scaring me. That flu was everywhere. Did someone in your family die, too?"

David kicked Sadie's letter toward Jed. "Here, read for yourself."

Cautiously, Jed picked up the letter, smoothed the paper, and read.

"Oh God. David. Your mother. How could . . ." Jed felt as though someone had punched him in the stomach. Tears filled his eyes, but when he looked up to see David staring at him ferociously, daring him to utter some inane bit of sympathy, he fought them back. "What does this mean, that your brother said this . . . *kaddish*? . . . for you?"

"*Kaddish* is the prayer of mourning. It's the prayer for the dead. It means I am dead to him."

"How could he do that? He's your brother." Jed let the letter fall back to the floor.

"Not anymore. He never thought I was good enough for our family anyway. And my sister . . ." David barked out a mirthless laugh. "So, Jed, what do you think? Was this worth it? Did we do the right thing?" David's voice was bitter and mocking, taking them back to the day they'd enlisted, eager and ignorant, convincing each other that they knew what they were doing.

"No, David. It wasn't worth it. But don't worry. You're going to come home with me."

"No, I'm not. I don't want your charity," David said angrily. His blazing eyes held every conflicted emotion he couldn't express in words, but his voice trembled and a sheen of moisture threatened to subdue the flames. "Jed. I already owe you a debt I can never repay. If you hadn't pulled me out of there, I'd have—"

"Shut up, David," Jed interrupted him.

David winced in frustration. In all the months in the hospital, Jed had never once let him express his gratitude. Every time David brought up the subject of what had happened on the battlefield, Jed curtly said that there was nothing to talk about. Maybe he was right. What happened, happened. What happened here, what happened at home, what difference did it make? You ended up where life threw you, and you had to deal with it. "Jed, I—"

"Shut . . . up."

Jed felt himself falling into the swirling core of David's eyes. He was immediately possessed of an aching strangeness, familiar only because it had possessed him so often since knowing David: a sensation of being most vividly, painfully alive and yet shamefully diminished all at once. From the first instant he had laid eyes on him, Jed had seen David as unshakable as an ancient tree, the roots of his being snaked deep into the secret meaning of life, his very person the rich, warm colors of earth and wood and fire. And in comparison, skin to skin, soul to soul, Jed saw himself as a ghost, a *thing* comprised of the elusive color of water, of ice and a pale sun, the color of nothing, with limbs loose and awkward and a core that meandered like an uncharted river searching for a resting place. Without David's ceaseless, purposeful energy to anchor him, Jed would float away, lost forever in the vast chilly ocean of his own fears, his own disgrace. He had to believe that, in return, fire needed water, lest it consume itself and everything it touched.

"There's an old Chinese proverb that says if you save someone's life you are responsible for it. So I'm responsible for you; you don't owe me anything. I owe you." *I owe you. I owe you everything as atonement for my sins.* Jed put his hands on David's shoulders and leaned in until their foreheads were touching. "It wasn't worth it, any of it. Except for this. You were worth it. You're *my* brother now. You're coming home with me."

David nodded silently and brought his hands up to rest on Jed's fair head. The silkiness of the hair under his fingers and the grounding pressure of Jed's hands on his shoulders—the very corporeal reality of him—calmed him, the way Jed always calmed him. He wanted this. Jed would not betray him the way his own flesh and blood had. "All right, Jed. I won't argue. I need you to be my friend. If you want to be responsible for me, I'm yours."

They were received back into the regiment with all the pomp due a conquering army. Within a week of their return, the regiment received the news that they were scheduled to ship home in just over a month. The men went wild. A marauding group of celebrants came upon Jed and David in their tent and gleefully dragged them out. They hoisted Jed, their hero, into the air and carried him all around the camp. Jed smiled and waved, eating up the attention, the adulation, his mind blissfully quiet.

At one point, he glanced down and saw David smiling up at him in pleasure, a knowing look on his face. Jed smiled back, giddy with happiness. Their eyes locked and for a split second everything turned upside down. What was that look? What did David know? Nausea took root in Jed's belly. Then he saw David silently mouth, *Thank you,* and the nausea vanished. David didn't know anything.

David watched Jed being borne off to the mess tent for a dousing of champagne. As he began walking after the crowd, Captain Hummel appeared at his side. "David, it's so good to have you and Jed back safe and sound."

"Thanks, Captain. I don't have to tell you how happy we are to be out of that hospital."

Hummel ruffled David's hair with paternal affection. "No, you certainly don't."

"Do you know what ship they've found to take us home?"

"I heard it's a converted cargo ship from the Spanish-American War. I hope it can still float."

"Captain, I don't care if the damn ship is from the Revolutionary War. I'll row if I have to." David saw Jed twisting around atop someone's shoulders, trying to look back toward him. He waved. He was eager to get back now, to change his name and start his new life as the wartime friend of Jed Gates, under the patronage of the influential Gates family. He should be grateful to his pitiable siblings for not wanting anything to do with him. They would only weigh him down.

Hummel laughed. "I'll help."

They walked a few paces in silence and then the captain took David's arm, pulled him gently some distance from the stream of men heading toward the mess tent. "David. Jed told me about your mother. Don't be upset, I forced it out of him. I could tell you weren't right. No one else knows. We've all missed so much in the lives of our families while we've been here, having our own lives changed forever. I can imagine how hard it's been not being able to mourn her properly, being separated from the rest of your family and your friends. I'm so sorry."

David looked into the captain's searching eyes and felt an explosion in his brain that knocked him to his knees. Hummel squatted down and put an arm around him, supporting him.

"David, David, it's all right. Let go; just let it all go."

David was so dizzy he couldn't keep his eyes open. His head fell heavily onto Hummel's shoulder as he gasped for breath and only then realized he was choking on his tears, bleating, "*Mama, mama*," like a dying calf. He would never see her again, his brave and beautiful mother who had loved him more than anyone in the world would ever love him, whom he had loved more than he had ever let anyone know. She was dead and he hadn't been there with her; he had been precisely where she didn't ever want him to be, and she had died not knowing that he was safe.

Using his body to shield David from the sight of the other men, Hummel stayed kneeling on the cold, packed ground a long time, letting David cry until he was all wrung out.

"I'm sorry, Captain." David stumbled to his feet, wiping at his eyes and nose.

"Don't be. It's a terrible loss you've suffered. You have nothing to be sorry for. Besides, Sergeant, I'm here to look after you, whatever it takes." Hummel smiled. David produced a wan smile in return.

"David, I don't want to upset you all over again, but I have something here that I know you'd want to keep. It was in my camera; I've been holding it for you."

Hummel placed the photograph in David's hands. It was the picture Vern Cooper had taken of David and Jed in the far-away spring of 1918, before they'd gone into battle. David closed his eyes and swallowed hard.

"My God," he breathed, "look at us. We look ten years older now."

"No," Hummel said gently, "you look the same. You just feel older. It will pass. You'll feel young again before another year rolls around; I guarantee it."

David carefully put the photo away, in his pocket next to the picture he still carried of Lucy. He reached out and shook his captain's hand, man to man, survivor to survivor, then walked on to the mess tent. A few glasses of champagne would be good right about now. David needed to celebrate the future, not cry over the past. And getting drunk might just help him forget that no matter what Captain Hummel said, no matter that he was just twenty years old, he knew he would never feel young again.

~ PART TWO ~

August 1923–July 1926

11

"Well, there's a sight I never thought I'd live to see. A Jew playing croquet on Joseph Gates's lawn."

Sally sat in an Adirondack chair under the shade of a towering maple tree, Monty in a chair next to her. From beneath the wide brim of her summer hat, she watched the younger generation cavorting on the lawn in the brutal sun of early August. She couldn't imagine how they were not fainting dead away from the heat. The wind itself seemed defeated by it, coming in as a hot breeze off Long Island Sound, losing promise as it crossed Oyster Bay, and dying completely by the time it reached the grounds of Hidden Cove Farm, Joseph and Evelyn's sixty-acre estate on the bay shore.

"I thought we weren't supposed to mention that our greedy little interloper, Mr. *Shaw,* is a Jew in disguise." Monty swung a crossed leg in a steady, hypnotic motion, creating tiny eddies of air that puffed in Sally's direction, minutely disturbing the fabric of her dress. He wasn't at all hot. The creases in his white linen slacks were perfectly crisp and the skin of his arms and upper chest, bared to the elements in a white open-throated short-sleeved shirt, was dry beneath its modest covering of fine jet-black hair. His eyes were hidden behind tinted glasses.

"I may say whatever I wish in private, to you, mightn't I? I don't care what David calls himself, he will always be a Jew, and I will never understand why this family is so besotted by him. What is he but another pushy pauper trying to be something he's not."

"I'm surprised you've allowed Jed to maintain such a close friendship with him. Bad enough he's a Jew, but he's without acceptable boundaries of any kind. Everything he wants is perfectly obvious in him, including his desire for women." Monty clucked his tongue like a disapproving hen. "He's vulgar; he has no sense of proper behavior."

"How could he have? He has no values. He comes from the dregs of society and brings his lower-class depravity into our midst with all its avarice and excess. You know what those people are like. But really, Monty, what *can* I do? Jed is devoted to him, with this nonsense about saving his life in France." Sally lifted a wayward tendril of damp hair off her neck.

Monty laughed to himself. Sally didn't care a whit about David's lack of values or how many women he slept with. What angered her was that David had made her a beggar for her precious son's time and affection and had from the start been quite beyond the reach of her manipulative skills. To counter his influence, she was forced to dedicate those skills to Jed with increased rigor.

"Jed's first loyalty should be to his family and its reputation. Surely, Sally, if you were adamant with him . . ."

Sally gave Monty a chilly look. "I don't like David, but I'm no fool, Monty. It's too late to try to dislodge him. And I would advise you to remember that. Joseph is devoted to David, too. I know he's a threat to your ambitions at the store, but you will never succeed in turning Joseph or Harry Selkirk against him. Oh, he's weasely, like every Jew that ever lived, but he is undeniably intelligent. Be content with the success you've had since you stopped drinking and started applying yourself. You've made a remarkable turnaround, dear boy. Director of Sales for Women's Wear for goodness' sake."

In fact, Monty was content. The actual work required to fulfill his fine title and highly respectable position was far from difficult and rewarded him with a large salary and easy access to an ever-changing array of wealthy, discreet, unhappily married women, the best and safest targets for seduction, his favorite pastime. The eager young salesgirls would have been even easier targets, but Monty knew better than to foul his own nest. Besides, poor single girls, no matter how physically lovely, were of no use and therefore no interest to him. He didn't particularly want anyone to know how content he was, however, since the Gateses considered ambition to be a heavenly virtue. The occasional sigh of frustration, sent in Sally's direction and thus sure to find its way to Joseph from a palatable source, could do Monty no harm. And his dislike of David was genuine.

"Yes, I could be content. Or I could push him down the store's grand staircase."

"A lovely thought." Sally sighed wistfully. "However, all I care about is Jed's future, and that is quite secure. He was brought up too well to be corrupted by some wild animal. Jed was given proper values, the only thing that will save our embattled society from this modern vulgarity. If anything, Jed will have a civilizing influence on David. Assuming he's even capable of being civilized." Sally leaned back in her chair and attempted to cool herself with an ornately painted silk fan. "Oh, dear God, I am positively *damp*!"

"If you could bring yourself to give in to the fashions of the day you wouldn't be sitting in ninety-degree heat with quite so much between you and what little air there is." Monty trailed a teasing finger over the thin silk that covered Sally's arm. He felt the gratifying involuntary shiver of her flesh at his touch. There were other pleasures to be had on a hot day than giving vent to his distaste for David.

She pulled her arm away and swatted at Monty's hand with her fan. "Don't be insolent, you beast. You know perfectly well what I think of modern fashions. I'm wearing my skirts at my ankles; that's as far as I'm willing to go."

Monty's eyes slid slowly over his sister-in-law, his unbrotherly probing safely obscured by his dark glasses. He often forgot that she was only three years older than he, she was such a staunch upholder of the previous generation's way of thinking. Beads of sweat stood out on her upper lip, at her hairline and her exposed throat. Spots of dampness were visible on her dress beneath her breasts, at the back of her neck, under her arms. Wisps of platinum hair, darkened with sweat, clung to her cheeks and nape. Her face was flushed with excess warmth; her body was limp. She was a beautiful woman and she'd hardly ever looked more desirable. Completely unknowingly, of course, despite her coquettish flirting. That was a mere social habit, no teeth behind it at all. Poor repressed Sally. Freud would have a heyday with her. Sexual freedom running wild all around her and, Monty would bet his life, she didn't even know what an orgasm was. She didn't know that the right man could make her scream with pleasure. He was certain that Philip had never made her scream. He had managed to plant three children in her, but without doubt she had not enjoyed the act that created them. She was so well protected, all gruff and scratchy on the outside, creamy white and pure on the inside, an unplucked coconut. Monty had often thought what delicious fun it would be to crack her. To open her up, suck her virgin juices, scrape her raw, leave her exposed and dry. A small smile pulled at the corners of his graceful lips.

"What are you smiling at, you Cheshire cat? Are you enjoying the sight of the girls with their bare flesh on parade? Oh, look at that!" Sally fanned herself harder as Cissy leaned over to strike at her ball, the hem of an overlarge white shirt riding up the backs of her thighs.

Monty was indeed enjoying the sight of Cissy Harriman, defying the heat in a racy one-piece lavender woolen bathing costume that left her legs bare from the tops of her high socks to the costume's end at midthigh. She had covered herself with one of David's shirts but left it unbuttoned. Monty imagined snaking a hand up under that shirt. Cissy was a ripe tomato if ever he'd seen one, tight and tasty, a real sheba with her shingled hair, provocative clothing, cigarettes, loud, uninhibited laugh. She was a college friend of Jed's who had been hanging on David's arm for the past six months. Monty had to give David credit for having good taste in women. He had admired each successive girl David had charmed and abandoned over the past four years, but Cissy, who had survived the longest so far, was undoubtedly the best. She and David had been running all over town with Jed and his demure girl, Abigail, who was dressed, to Sally's delight, in an ankle-length crepe lawn dress. It did have short sleeves, however, and the turn of her wrist and her slim forearm were quite lovely.

"Come now, Sally. I may be a happily married man, but I'm not blind. It's nice to look, but of course that's all. For goodness' sake, one of those girls is my niece and all of them are half my age. The truth is, sweet Sally, I'd much rather look at you." He put just the perfect amount of jocularity into his voice, reassuring her that his confession was innocent of intent while leaving her uncertain as to the reality of a longtime helpless desire for her. He was rewarded with the sight of her lovely bosom flushing as rosily as her face and heaving, decorously of course, in shock and, he had no doubt, secret excitement. He nearly laughed. God, she'd be easy. As with every one of the numerous fine-born women he'd had, he knew he both repulsed and attracted Sally. After a life with a limp dick like Philip, how could she not entertain wordless wonderings of the forbidden pleasures that might be had with a rogue such as he?

Sally's fan moved at a furious speed as she stared fixedly out toward the lawn and completely ignored his inappropriate flattery. "Please, Monty. Don't remind me that my own daughter is as shameless as that Cissy. Look at her!"

Monty happily did as Sally asked. Lucy was on the eve of her twenty-first birthday and had matured into a striking young woman. She had inherited her mother's flawless pale skin, her father's piercing green eyes, and, so her grandfather loved to tell her, the headstrong personality of Lucy Stoner Gates, Philip's mother, after whom she had been named. Her fiery red hair, bobbed now and lying like a fox's pelt on her shapely head, seemed a gleaming manifestation of her temperament. Her body was petite, perfectly formed, vibrating with energy. The pleasing contours of her arms and legs, the set of her collarbones, the sweet knobs of her upper spine, were all revealed by her simple sleeveless blue linen sheath. Monty slowly shifted his hidden gaze back to Cissy. It was, after all, beyond the bounds of propriety to ogle one's own niece.

"As an objective observer, let me say that Lucy looks

perfectly lovely, and no more or less scandalous than anyone of her generation. You may not approve of her, but you should feel fortunate to have a daughter to watch grow up." Monty's voice dropped to a tearful whisper.

Sally was immediately galvanized to sympathy. She took hold of Monty's hand, dangling sadly off the arm of his chair, and squeezed it tightly. "Monty, my darling man, I'm so sorry. I know Libby would have grown up to be a wonderful, proper girl."

Monty hung his head and returned an infinitesimal pressure to Sally's fingers. Their hands disengaged as Brook, hurling his croquet mallet in anger, came running toward them.

"What's wrong, sport?" Monty called out. "Too tough a game for you?"

"David cheats! I hate him. Why does he have to be here?" Brook fell into a chair on the other side of his mother, arms and legs splayed, and glared out toward the lawn, a petulant scowl on his red face.

Sally drew away from him, from the sweat that clung to every inch of his uncovered skin and his grass-flecked clothing. "Well, what can one expect." She turned her head. "Monty, what time is it?"

Monty consulted his sleek gold-cased Elgin wristwatch. "Five forty-five."

"Oh my. Brook, run and tell your brother he must take the Packard and pick up your father at the railroad station."

"He'll want to take the Duesenberg." Brook jumped to his feet, clearly hoping to get a ride in the grand car.

"The Packard," Sally commanded. "He is not driving your grandfather's fifteen-thousand-dollar automobile. And tell him I don't want him driving over twenty miles an hour!"

"The war is over, Sally. He's not going to get killed between here and the station. Let the boy have some fun," Monty said laconically.

She cut her eyes at him and then called after Brook. "And you, put yourself in a bath this instant! I can smell you from here." Sally pulled herself to her feet. "Don't you presume to tell me what I should or should not allow my son to do. I'm going in to get ready for dinner. I've had enough fresh air."

Monty stayed where he was. Cocktail hour wasn't until seven, and there was nothing else of interest inside that mausoleum of a house. Best to relax in the shade as the evening breeze picked up, enjoy a few cigarettes, and contemplate the evening ahead. All that lovely female flesh had roused him; he would have to do something to Zoe tonight. He didn't beat her anymore. That thrill hadn't lasted long and, besides, it was too dangerous. Evelyn had been suspicious, he could tell, and sooner or later she might have found a way past her fear of the truth and confronted Zoe about it. In any case, it was much more effective and pleasurable to torture his wife by manipulating her still-feverish passion for him: ignoring her for weeks on end, rejecting her beggarly overtures, and then, without warning, taking her to bed and spending painstaking hours playing her touch-starved body like the virtuoso he was, practicing and perfecting the techniques he had learned from or used on his revolving stable of grateful mistresses. He never failed to drive her wild, to pull the leash that bound her to him a little tighter. It bound him, too, he had to admit, her willingness to dwell in the stark, cruel isolation of their marriage now that Libby was gone and leave him free to be a man of decency, diligence, and virtue in the eyes of the world.

"Why couldn't you just let him win?" Lucy rooted herself in front of David, hands on her hips, head tilted, green eyes narrowed to accusatory slits.

"What, is he five years old?" David pushed past her, dragging the croquet cart back to the lawn shed. It was loaded with eight wooden mallets, each with its identifying colored stripe, and eight matching wooden balls. It was hard work pulling the heavy cart across the thick grass and he was hot and tired, in no mood for another bout of Lucy's criticism.

She danced around to stand in front of him again. "You know he's sensitive. Why do you have to be so aggressive all the time?"

David stopped, annoyance etching a line between his dark brows. From the corner of his eye, he saw Cissy and Abigail crossing the lawn toward them. "Because I like to win. He left me the perfect shot. What should I have done, missed it on purpose and let him think he'd played well?"

"It's just a silly game. Would that have been such a terrible thing to do?"

"Yes," David snarled. "Brook isn't *sensitive;* he's a fourteen-year-old baby. Because everyone treats him like one. Your mother tells him what to think and how to behave and you and your father tell him it doesn't matter how well or badly he does at anything. How is he ever going to learn to be responsible for himself? He's going to end up an inept dewdropper who drains other people's money and sits home all day with his nose buried in some stupid book."

"My family can afford for him to read his life away if that's what makes him happy!"

"You're missing the point, Lucy," David said in an irritatingly pedantic tone, and gave her a look of contempt. "He'd be useless. No one should be allowed to be useless."

"Oh, and you're so useful! At least he won't end up heartless and selfish!" Lucy yelled, and stomped away toward the house.

"Oh, go to hell!" David yelled after her, his face contorted with anger. "What a pain in the ass!" he mumbled as he watched her move away from him, watched the soft sway of her hips and the firework lights glinting off her hair in the late-afternoon sun.

"She's got a permanent bees' nest in her bonnet." Cissy laughed and wound both her arms around David's free arm, snuggling up close to him. "That's what happens when you're all work and no play. Lucy really needs a fella." She reached up and kissed David's cheek, licked at his ear. "Hmm, you taste salty."

"Cissy, stop. It's too hot." David shrugged her off. "Why don't you two go back to the house. I'm going to take a swim before dinner."

Cissy threw her arms around his neck, melted against him, her brown eyes muzzy with adoration. "I want to go swimming again, too."

David looked over Cissy's shoulder at Abigail standing quietly a few paces away, staring down at her patent mary jane pumps in acute discomfort. He gently took Cissy's arms from around his neck, kissed her lightly on the lips. "No, baby girl, go back to the house. I want to be alone for a little while. Take Abigail and go have a nice cool bath."

David stowed the croquet cart and grabbed an old towel out of the shed. He raced down to the water's edge and stripped to his undershorts. No one would see him; everyone was safely elsewhere. He waded out until the gentle waves of Oyster Bay Cove swirled around his thighs, then slipped fully under, letting the cool salty water sluice away his sweat and his lingering irritation. He surfaced, shook his head, and sent water flying from his hair like a dog shaking water from its fur. With sure, strong strokes he swam the fifty yards out to the Gateses' private float, a twenty-foot-square wooden raft with chairs and a sun umbrella bolted to it. He unfurled the umbrella and lay down in its shade, the wood warm against his back. The raft bobbed lightly on the water; the air smelled of salt and seaweed; a slight breeze lifted off the surface of the bay and tickled at David's drying skin. His eyes closed. He fell asleep.

He dreamed he was stalking the teeming streets of his childhood, looking for his mother. Every few steps, he stopped and asked men in long black coats and black hats, *Have you seen Anna Warshinsky?* but no one so much as looked at him or spoke to him. Up ahead, he saw Papa, Ben, Rose, Sarah, holding hands and laughing together on a street corner. He rushed up to them, to tell them to wait. He ran right through them as though he had no substance. He looked down at himself and saw that he was glowing like the sun and knew that no one could possibly see him. Then he saw her, standing in an open doorway smiling at him. She could see him. She beckoned. He ran toward her and suddenly his rifle was in his hands. The point of his bayonet pierced her throat and she disappeared.

David woke up staring into the faded underside of the umbrella, his heart pounding. He'd had that same dream several times during the past few years, and each time he'd awoken feeling violated, invaded during the defenseless-ness of sleep by people and thoughts he wanted no part of. He rolled over, reached down, and splashed handfuls of water into his face. He sat up, hugged his knees to his chest, and looked back to the estate grounds, his covetous eyes sweeping across the vast acreage of Hidden Cove Farm and the turreted twenty-five-room house shining like a castle keep in the slanting rays of the setting sun. He banished the last remnants of the dream from his mind. David Warshinsky, one of a million Jews from the slums of the Lower East Side, a boy with no future, was dead; his own brother had said *kaddish* for him. He was David Shaw now, known to the world as the orphaned distant cousin of Eve-lyn Crawford Gates from somewhere outside Cincinnati, miraculously found recuperating in the same hospital out-side Paris as his never-before-met cousin Jed and brought by the family to New York to start a new life. It had ceased amazing David that no one ever questioned his fictional provenance the moment he realized that the world simply didn't question Joseph Gates.

David stood up and closed the umbrella, dove off the raft, and swam back to shore. As he bent to retrieve the towel he had left at the water's edge, he heard the sound of pounding hooves and suddenly Zoe was towering over him from atop her panting horse, Sirocco. Mortified to be standing before her wearing nothing but a sheen of water and a pair of wet undershorts that clung to his body like a second skin, David grabbed for the towel and quickly wrapped it around his waist.

"God, Zoe!"

She laughed delightedly. "Don't be so bashful, David. I've seen a naked man before. But, here, let me turn away while you put on some clothes." She skillfully guided Sirocco into a smooth turn, rode him over the lawn a little ways, and let him prance there a moment while David, wincing in disgust at the feel of his sweat-soaked clothes on his clean skin, drew on his pants and shirt.

"You ride so beautifully, Zoe," David said, watching her in wonder. "You look like some goddess on her mythical steed."

"That's so sweet. I've ridden since I was a child. Alice Roosevelt and I used to lose ourselves for hours in the woods of Sagamore Hill and Hidden Cove."

"Jed talked about Lucy riding, but he never mentioned you."

"He might not remember. I stopped when I got married. But I decided it was time to start again. Maybe I'll teach you the next time you're here. You'd like it. It's very liberating."

"I gather that Monty doesn't ride with you?"

"No," she said, offering no further explanation. "I noticed Lucy breathing fire as she came in before. What did you two fight about this time?"

David glanced up at her in surprise. "How do you know we fought?"

Zoe shrugged. "You're the only one who can get such a rise out of her."

"Well, it's mutual. She is such an annoying, opinionated brat. She finds fault with everything I do. I wish she would just leave me alone."

Zoe looked down at him for a long moment without saying anything. She held her horse perfectly still. "Are you going to marry Cissy?"

David nearly choked. "Jesus, Zoe! You're in a shy mood tonight!"

"I didn't think I needed to be shy with you, David. I thought we were friends."

"Of course we're friends. But if we're going to have a serious talk, would you please get down off that horse? I feel about two feet tall."

Zoe swung down and took Sirocco's reins in her hand. "All right, I'm down. Walk with me to the stables. Now, are you going to marry Cissy?" She headed for the far side of the house.

David followed alongside her. "I've been thinking about it, yes. I'm nearly twenty-five, Uncle Joe says I should have a wife, a family. Good for my career."

"Do you love her?"

"I like her," David said slowly. "We have a good time together. There's more to her than the party girl everyone sees. She's got a good heart. Her family is well respected and—"

"She never argues with you and she thinks you're perfect. You didn't answer me."

"I don't know. How the hell do I even know what love is? Do you have to be in love to have a good marriage?"

"I used to think so. Now I'm not so sure. Sometimes, love can be disastrous." Zoe gave him a quick kiss on his damp cheek. "You'll make the right decision, David, I'm sure. I was just curious about how serious things were getting. I'm a little in love with you, you know. I wanted to know if I should be jealous," she teased. "Six months is a record for you, after all."

David laughed. "Ah, you know I'll always love you, Zoe."

"Thank you, kind sir." Zoe dropped a mock curtsey. "There's a caring and decent person beneath that determined, self-absorbed ambition of yours, David. You're not all that good at hiding it, although God knows you try hard enough. It's easy to make mistakes when it comes to matters of the heart. Please, think things through carefully."

"I think you need spectacles. But I promise, I'll be careful. I don't intend to make mistakes. Speaking of marriage, do you think Jed will marry Abigail?"

"Probably. Sally picked her, just like she picks Jed's clothes. I never realized that finding the right girl could be no more complicated than finding the right Fair Isle sweater."

David shook his head. "Well, you know what I think of Sally, but in this case I think she did a good thing. Abby is sweet and she certainly loves Jed. Do you see the way she looks at him? They're comfortable together. They're pals. I think he'd be happy with her."

"I don't know what makes anyone happy, but yes, they seem a good couple." Zoe abruptly remounted Sirocco. "I've changed my mind. I'm going to take one last ride through the woods." She patted the horse's long brown neck. "If you do decide to marry Cissy, she'll be a lucky girl." Zoe kicked the horse lightly in the flanks and took off across the lawn.

Joseph looked down the length of the candlelit table, anchored on its far end by his wife, the one indispensable person in his life, and filled on either side by all there was of his family—the children he had produced, the people they had married, what remained of the children they had produced. And one who had neither been born to the family nor married into it. David, dropped into their placid pond with the force of a violently thrown stone, the ripples caused by his presence flowing still into the furthest corners, disturbing everyone's desires and expectations.

Joseph indulged himself in a moment of possessive pride as his eyes rested on the boy, engrossed in flirtatious conversation with his pretty little girlfriend. He thought back four and a half years, to Jed's triumphant return from the war with his unlikely friend in tow. Joseph would have helped David simply because Jed asked him to, would have found an insignificant position for him where he could do no harm. But David had insisted on thanking Joseph for his help face-to-face. A ten-minute meeting was sufficient for Joseph to be exhilarated by David's sharp intellect and palpable hunger to succeed. Ten minutes for Joseph to conclude that this boy from nowhere could fulfill all the expectations normally reserved for an heir of one's blood, expectations he never had of his own children and perhaps, despite what he'd always believed, not even of Jed.

Joseph relaxed into his chair, sated and content after a cool, comforting summer dinner and many glasses of chilled Dom Perignon. That first impression of David's potential had been confirmed to him over and over. It was time to think about what the boy's next challenge should be. Joseph was happily contemplating the possibilities when Walter appeared at his side and bent to whisper in his ear that he had an urgent telephone call from Andrew Mellon, secretary of the treasury.

Joseph rose, his mind clear, and followed Walter from the room. He returned a few moments later and knocked his spoon against his champagne flute until he had everyone's attention. "Forgive me for interrupting our evening, but I have some sad news to share. President Harding died this afternoon, while campaigning in San Francisco."

A collective gasp of shock followed by an uncertain silence replaced the sounds of light conversation and the merry tinkling of crystal and silver.

"Oh, that's terrible," Abby murmured. She decorously lowered her dessert spoon, leaving a half-eaten mound of vanilla ice cream abandoned in its chilled silver bowl. "He was such a nice man."

A whispery assent blew around the table like rustling leaves caught in an eddy of wind.

"Old Uncle Warren was looking like a beached whale. I'm surprised he didn't drop dead years ago." Monty drained his wineglass. He had long since perfected the dual arts of appearing abstemious while clandestinely imbibing copious amounts of alcohol and giving a flawless impersonation of sobriety when he was in fact quite drunk.

"Show some respect, Monty, please!" Evelyn said curtly. "Warren was an eminently fair, moderate, hardworking president. He rather worked himself to death, I think."

"Yes. I quite admired him. He understood that we, the wealthy, are the country's leaders and the necessary bedrock of its prosperity. Yet he remained mindful of the needs of the poor." Jed's voice held the conviction of his own opinions, yet his look, directed toward Joseph, sought his grandfather's agreement.

"Well put, my boy." Joseph flashed Jed a smile of approval. "He perhaps went a little too far at times—thank goodness Congress soundly disabused him of the idea of a Department of Welfare—but on balance he avoided partisanship and held things together well. He was smart enough to take Mellon's advice on relieving the tax burden on the wealthy after the war. Without that, there would have been no economic recovery possible."

David nodded at Jed from across the table. "It's ironic, isn't it, Jed, that he died today, the same day the federal courts ruled against U.S. Steel and their twelve-hour workday? A pity he didn't live to savor his victory over such outright greed."

"Ah, David, David. How altruistic of you to care about steelworkers. Twelve-hour workdays are not something any of us ever need worry about, though, are they?" Monty looked at David with a subtly malevolent grin.

David held Monty's eyes briefly and then looked away without responding. "Uncle Joe, who called to tell you?"

"It was Mellon. He's asked me to come down to Washington immediately to help him and the cabinet get Coolidge ready to take the reins. I don't think Calvin even knows yet. He's off at his father's farm somewhere in the wilds of Vermont."

"I'm sure Coolidge will be quite able, but I wish Herbert Hoover was going to be president."

Joseph snorted. "Really, Lucy. The man is an unrepentant progressive. One *can* have too much democracy and too much efficiency, despite what Herbert declaims. He's too aggressive in his poaching on other departments' jurisdictions. No, let him stay at Commerce."

"How can you say that, Grandfather? Hoover is a great humanitarian and not afraid of—ouch, Mother!"

Sally pinched Lucy's arm a second time, leaned over, and whispered harshly in her ear, "Lucy, don't argue politics with the men. It's quite unbecoming."

"Well, at least we know Coolidge won't raise taxes on us rich folk, but the important question is, will he repeal this ridiculous Prohibition amendment?"

"What's the matter, Monty? Aren't you making enough extra money supplying liquor to *us rich folk* from your offshore rum-running friend Bill McCoy?" David said sarcastically.

Monty nonchalantly threw his arm over the back of his chair. "It's actually hardly worth it. I do it as a favor to my friends. And I see you are happy to drink what I bring."

Zoe quickly intervened. "Well, I hope Coolidge does do away with it."

"Don't anyone hold your breath," Joseph said. "Calvin likes his booze just as much as Warren did, but he, too, knows better than to go against the sanctimonious sentiment still prevalent in the country. Righteous idiots intent on saving the workingman from drink while those with means can buy anything they like! Thank God it's not being enforced too energetically in the city."

"Energetically enough to do plenty of harm, make rich men out of petty criminals like that Larry Fay, opening nightclubs, paying off the police while legitimate places go out of business." Philip was indignant. "Have you seen what's happening to Broadway? All the great restaurants and bars in the area that relied on their liquor sales have closed and the entire neighborhood is turning into a cheap, ugly cesspool."

"Well, I think it's a small price to pay for a sober society," Sally chimed in. "I'm delighted those awful saloons have disappeared. What's wrong with a man having to think twice about breaking the law before he takes a drink?"

"Actually, Sally, it's not against the law to have a drink, or to buy one. It's only illegal to make or sell alcohol. I certainly don't understand the rationale of it. Strong support for Temperance would have been so much smarter, it seems to me." Zoe pushed her own wineglass away from her, as though to prove her point.

"Evelyn, find Ralph and then come upstairs and help me prepare. The rest of you, carry on. And don't worry. This will be a smooth transition." Joseph made to leave the room, stopped before he reached the doorway. "Oh, by the way. Mellon reminded me about the Dempsey-Tunney fight scheduled for early next month, in Philadelphia. He and Rockefeller will be there. Think he said Willie Hearst and Pulitzer were coming, too. Thought I'd go down. Who here wants to join me and Evelyn?"

Sally made a face appropriate to having a bowl of excrement waved under her nose and glared a clear warning at Philip. "Ugh! Not us, certainly. Barbaric sport!"

"Ah, Sally, boxers are our modern-day gladiators. These two are great athletes and educated men. You don't find them manly and heroic?" David goaded her.

"Hardly," she said contemptuously. "Intelligent, educated men with athletic ability should find something better to do than beat each other up. But it's no surprise to me that you enjoy such a gross blood sport."

David laughed. "No, I'm sure it's not." He turned to Joseph. "Dempsey hasn't been in the ring in three years. Tunney may be the underdog, but I predict he'll walk away with the title. It ought to be some spectacle. Jed, Cissy, and I have already made plans to go."

"Excellent. I'll make sure we have the best seats. Evelyn, are you coming?" Without waiting for an answer, Joseph walked through the door.

Evelyn stood up, placed her napkin neatly on the table. "Joe and I are sorry to miss this *spirited, hard-hitting* debate," she quipped, pleased at her own pun, "but duty calls. We'll see you all in the morning."

At one o'clock, silence all around her save for the gentle soughing of the wind in the linden trees beyond her window, Lucy finally resigned herself to sleeplessness. She drew on her robe, donned her slippers, and stealthily slipped out into the bedroom-wing hallway. As she started down the stairs, she heard a sound behind her. She glanced back over her shoulder and saw Cissy at David's door. The door opened; David's hand reached out to pull her in; the door closed.

Lucy crept down the stairs, thinking to walk out into the gardens. The silver moonlight would have bleached away all the hot, vibrant colors of the day. She would wander the night-cooled grounds, a shadowy creature at one with the cicadas and crickets, and put her feverish thoughts out of her head. The dew, settling now onto the grass, would soak into her slippers and the hem of her robe.

She crossed the wide main hallway, heading for a back door on the far side of the kitchens that led out directly onto the kitchen garden. Before she had gone very far, she heard a rustling at her right and saw a glimmer of light coming from the library. She tiptoed to the half-open door and carefully peeked in, not wanting to be seen until she knew who was there. It was Jed, fully dressed still in his dinner clothes, bent over a pile of papers in disarray on his lap.

Lucy came into the room and sat down across from her brother. He looked up and they smiled at each other, small sympathetic smiles. Lucy motioned with her chin toward the papers. "Nervous about starting work next month?" He was poring over financial reports, budgets, operating plans that Joseph had given him at the beginning of the summer.

"No, no, not at all. I'm looking forward to it." Jed stretched his arms over his head, brushed his hair off his forehead, and made a show of neatening the papers, putting them aside. "There is a lot to learn, though, and I want to get off to a fast start."

"I can't believe you're really looking forward to it." She leaned over and picked up one of the reports. She made a face. "How boring."

Annoyed, Jed snatched the pages out of her hand. "Well, it may not be interesting to you, but it is vitally important to the running of our businesses."

"Oh, bushwa. Don't be a priss. You don't find it interesting, either. You hated all your economics classes at Columbia. The only time I ever noticed you happy was after art class. Why are you even doing this?"

"There you go again, tarring everyone with your own rebellious brush. It's what expected of me, and I put great value on living up to the expectations people have of me. Don't make that monkey face at me!" Jed reached out and took a playful swipe at her nose, which was scrunched up in disapproval. "You like flying in the face of convention, Lucy; you thrive on it. I don't. Mother and Grandfather have confidence in me, and I don't want—or intend—to let them down."

Before he'd gone off to the war, Lucy had thought that the future the family foresaw for Jed suited him perfectly. He'd been a bright-eyed, eager student, an excited little shadow trailing behind Grandfather at the office, the department store, the stock exchange, the Club, an easygoing, content vehicle for their mother's unfulfilled desires. But since he'd been back Lucy had begun to doubt her assumptions. Jed had come home with the first close friend she could actually ever remember him having, and he was someone from another world. If Jed could do that, then perhaps he was more than the obedient brother Lucy had always known.

"Fine. You know what you don't want. What about what you *do* want? I think all you really want is to go to art school and be left alone to draw and paint. You know you're good. You could be a successful artist, like Father."

"You are not listening to me, Lucy. That's the last thing I want, to be successful like Father. He doesn't command the respect of people who matter. Art is a fine hobby, but it's not an appropriate career for a man with the responsibilities of our economic and social class."

"Mother and Grandfather may not respect Father, but they are *not* the only people who matter, Jed!" Lucy said hotly. "I hope that isn't how you feel about him."

"Of course not," he said, a little too quickly. "Look, I appreciate your concern, Luce, but believe me, I'm happy with what I'm doing. And you are altogether too serious for the middle of the night. Why are you even awake? Why aren't you fast asleep, dreaming up a new way to appall everyone? Surely the shock of your trotting off to college and then going to live on your own in the wilds of upper Manhattan has worn off by now. You scandalous thing, you."

She smiled at his teasing. "Oh, no one was scandalized except Mother."

Jed arched his brows in disagreement. "Not true. Your moving out did cause quite the stir. Grandfather and Grandmother would have been much happier if you'd moved in with Zoe and Monty to be nearer to Barnard. Abby was certainly a little put off until she got to know you, and even Cissy, for all her louche habits, will never leave home until she's married."

"Well, you, David, and Father were fine with it and no one but Mother has ever said a word to me."

"Of course not. Everyone is afraid of you."

Lucy laughed. "I am a little terror, aren't I?"

"Yes, you are, and I for one am glad of it."

"Good, because I have already dreamed up a new way to shock everyone and I'll tell you what it is if you promise you won't breathe a word. I'm not in the mood to defend myself."

Jed made a solemn face and drew a cross over his heart. "Tell, O little terror."

"I've applied to the Presbyterian Hospital School of Nursing for next spring. You know, up near Columbia Hospital? With my sociology degree and a nursing degree, I can really *do* something, Jed. I even thought about applying to Columbia's medical college—they've been accepting women for the past six years—but I don't really want to be a doctor; I'm too impatient. Still, I want to do something to help people. Particularly to help women take control of their lives. I'm hoping to get a position at Margaret Sanger's new Clinical Research Bureau." Lucy was giddy with fervor and fatigue and her words tumbled over one another.

Jed's mouth fell open. "What are you talking about?"

"You wouldn't believe how people live in the great, wide world outside the gilded cage of Gramercy Park, Jed. Have you ever read *The Woman Rebel,* Sanger's original monthly, the one that got her indicted back before the war? Or her pamphlet *Family Limitation,* or her new publication, *Birth Control Review*? The feminists are wrong to think women should be freed from the burden of sex. We need to be free *for* it, without worrying about getting pregnant."

Jed's mouth snapped shut and he squirmed in his chair. "God. Mother will have a stroke."

"Oh, Mother. Let her." Lucy peered at her brother. "You look like *you're* going to have a stroke." Lucy had always found Jed's discomfort with anything that had to do with sex or reproduction ridiculous, a piece of Sally's prudish influence that he should simply discard. But he was Lucy's big brother and she loved him, so she left his delicate feelings unassailed.

"Jed, something has to matter. I swear, all the smart girls I knew in school have just given up. They're either getting married to the richest men they can find and having babies or out dancing and drinking and behaving as though just because that horrendous war shattered our faith in the rightness of the world nothing matters anymore. I don't believe that. Things have to be done; people need help. One still has to live a decent, meaningful life."

"There are different ways to live a meaningful life. What's wrong with getting married and having babies? You're not saying that you don't want that, are you?"

Lucy turned her head so Jed wouldn't see the sudden

tremor in her lips. She studied the library's damask-draped French doors, their windowpanes opaque against the darkness outside. "I don't know that I'll ever get married, Jed. I don't know if there's a man alive who could stand me!" She turned back to him with a self-mocking grin.

"Ha! Very funny." He nodded in teasing agreement. "You are undoubtedly correct, however. All that time in France, I think David had this silly fantasy that you and he would fall in love and get married. Of course, that was before he met you. What a pity you've ended up hating each other. You two fight worse than you and I ever did when we were kids." He laughed as he bent over and began gathering up his papers and putting them back into their thick folders.

A heavy ache radiated painfully through Lucy's chest. "I don't hate David, Jed."

Jed's head snapped up. "What? I couldn't hear you."

"I said, I don't hate David."

Jed stood up with his folders tucked under one arm. "Oh, so it's because you love him that you criticize everything he does." He laughed again.

"He's your friend. Don't you worry sometimes that he's moving a little too fast, leaving too many things behind?"

"He's not leaving behind anything that he wants or needs. Honestly, sometimes I have no idea what goes on in your head. David deserves to have everything. He's the most . . . he deserves it, that's all. But hey, since you don't hate him, why don't you come with us to Yankee Stadium next week? We're going to see the Babe hit a few home runs in the new ballpark!" He made a sweeping motion with his free arm and a *thonk*ing sound with his tongue against the roof of his mouth. "It will be great fun. Me, Abby, David, and Cissy, we're all going. Why don't you bring someone?"

The mere thought depleted her, even though she loved baseball. "I'll think about it."

Jed paused at the doors and turned back to her. "Lucy, about nursing and the Sanger clinic. You're sure? It's what you really want to do?"

She gave him a grateful look. "Yes, Jed, I'm sure."

"We're going to have a bona fide activist in our familial midst. That should be interesting." Jed shook his head. "I won't tell anyone; I promise."

"Thank you. Once I get in, *if* I get in, there won't be any room for arguments."

"You got straight A's at Barnard. You'll get in. Don't sit here too long; you need your beauty sleep." Jed gave her a lingering look. "I love you, Luce. I'm proud of you," he said, and then stepped out into the dark, deserted hallway.

Lucy shut off the lamp. Her too-heavy head lolled against the chair back. Slowly, her eyes adjusted to the gloom until she could see through the French doors out onto the side lawn. Glowing slightly against the blackness of the grass, a silvered river of flowers flowed past the stables, reaching out toward the far woods. She had been given such a fortunate life; why did it feel so hard? She wished she could walk through the doors, step into the silver stream, and be borne away into the silence and coolness of the forest.

Zoe lifted the deadweight of Monty's arm off her belly. He was sound asleep. He always slept after sex, instantly and deeply. Leaving him to his sated dreams, she padded across the warm, pliant parquet floor into the bathroom and turned on the night-light. She needed to see herself. Something had changed, had unnerved her. For the first time since the moment Monty had first put his hands on her, a swooning caress stolen in a shadowed alcove nearly twenty years ago, his touch had not caused the earth to open beneath her and swallow her whole. She had felt intense pleasure; her body still throbbed with it. But she had remained in her bed, in the house of her childhood, in the world.

She scrutinized herself in the mirror of the dimly lit bathroom, touched her love-bruised lips and swollen nipples. If she wasn't the woman who disappeared into submission and ecstasy when Monty touched her, who was she? She stared hard at her reflection but found no answer there. She turned out the night-light and went back into the bedroom. She hesitated at the side of the bed, reached out, and picked up a piece of fraying string with twenty knots tied in it. Zoe stretched out on the chaise under the open window, naked to the soft summer air, and closed her eyes. She fingered the knots, one by one, while she repeated the mantra in her mind, *Every day, in every respect, I am getting better and better.* She fell asleep before she had completed her twenty repetitions, the moonlight a ghostly wash upon her face.

12

Joseph stood at the full-length mirror, trying to adjust the knot in his bow tie. Evelyn sat at her vanity table applying her makeup.

"I cannot believe our beloved Delmonico's is closed. Where am I going to get my Baked Alaska? Philip was so right about Prohibition killing perfectly fine businesses. And it's only gotten worse since the summer." Translucent foundation, a blush of no-color painted on with a damp sponge. Now rouge, the thick dark paste smoothed over her cheekbones up toward the hairline, transformed into a pale pink glow on her creamy skin.

"There's nothing wrong with Gage and Tollner. Just as elegant. Great place for the family to have Christmas dinner. Best steaks in the city, even if it is in Brooklyn." Joseph yanked at his tie, grunted with exasperation. "I had an interesting conversation with David a few weeks back. He came to me with several new ideas for the store that I want your opinion on."

"All right." Black mascara, the cake moistened just enough to make a thin paste, lashes coated with a fine brush.

"Not too much of that, Evie!" Joseph warned, his eyes on her in the mirror. "You know I don't like your lashes looking stiff." He turned his attention back to his struggles. "He suggested that we add more cosmetic counters to the ground floor space, open a beauty salon inside the store, and start selling our own line of cosmetic and beauty products. He wants us to greatly expand our private label ready-to-wear, high-end only. And—and here's my absolute favorite—he wants us to look into conditioning the air in the store with that Carrier contraption that we're using in the mills upstate." The tie was still askew. He ripped it from his neck in frustration, let it dangle from his fingers.

Evelyn gazed into the gilt-framed oval mirror, thinking through David's ideas. After a moment, she nodded in approval. "That boy has a truly remarkable mind and an amazing grasp of what is happening in the marketplace. Young women don't want to be feminists anymore, darling; they want to be feminine. The cosmetics business is nearing five hundred million a year, I've read."

"Would you and your friends patronize a salon inside the store?"

"Most certainly. There are salons everywhere you look now. Who wouldn't prefer the assured quality of a private salon inside the finest department store in the city?" Evelyn rose from her chair, satisfied with her face. "Hard to imagine now, in the dead of winter, but do you know how many people would come flocking into the store all through the summer months if the air was cooled? Could we do it by June? Would we be the only store in the city to have this?"

"For the moment. David found out that J. L. Hudson in Detroit is planning to install one of these centrifugal chillers next year. He wants us to be the first in New York."

Evelyn glided to their bed, where a tight-pleated silk-satin dress awaited her, laid out hours ago by Mary.

"Ah, good. You're wearing your Delphos gown." It was Fortuny's most spectacular design, taken from the linen *chitons* worn by Greek maidens centuries ago. With its unforgiving straight lines, the cling of the light garnet-red fabric, and the cinching of the silver-stenciled belt, it was a dress meant only for women with the most perfect of figures. Joseph watched her slip into it, the Venetian beading on its shoulders, around the armholes, and down its sides sparkling in the light of the chandelier. "My God, Evie, look at you. Sixty years old and you put women half your age to shame."

"Thank you, my love. Should I wear the Fortuny velvet cape or that metallic brocade one with the Deco design?"

"Wear the velvet. You'll be warmer in it. Could you help me with this?" He held the tie out toward her. "Oh, I forgot David's other idea, it's so outrageous. He suggests we open a café in the store! So the ladies can lunch!"

Evelyn's hands ceased their deft motions at his neck, and her eyes opened wide in wonderment. "What a fantastic idea! They don't have to leave the store to eat; they can stay and shop more! He's extraordinary. Why isn't Harry coming up with ideas like this? Did David talk to him before presenting all this to you?"

"Harry is the best manager and implementer the store could want, but I've never relied on him for innovative ideas. He and David are a perfect team. Harry liked the ideas and told David to talk to me directly."

"There." Evelyn finished tying a perfect knot. "Well, good for Harry. I thought he had no use for anyone under the age of thirty or with less than a decade of experience."

"David has made a convert out of him. The boy is too damned smart to ignore. Not a single flaw in any of his proposals. I expect to give the go-ahead for them all. Evelyn, I haven't run across someone like David since, well. . . ."

"Since yourself when you were his age," Evelyn finished his thought. She crossed to the closet and found her cape. "He *is* special, isn't he, our adopted cousin? Joe, why does it seem so much easier to be generous of heart with him than with our own children and grandchildren? Is there something wrong with us?"

Joseph pulled on his tuxedo jacket and looked around the bedroom. "What the hell did Ralph do with my hat?" He leaned out the bedroom door and yelled into the apartment's hallway, "Ralph? Ralph!"

"He's bringing the car around, dear. I'm sure your hat is on the stand in the entryway."

"Ah." He used his palms to smooth his pale blond hair, beginning now to be threaded with silver. "Don't be ludicrous, Evelyn. We have always been generous with our children and grandchildren. What the hell else do they need from us? I even did what Zoe asked after Libby died—I gave Monty a job."

"He's doing well, isn't he?"

"He hasn't shot himself in the foot yet, if that's what you mean," Joseph said begrudgingly. "He's well suited for charming the ladies. In fact, I've heard rumors that he's a little *too* charming with some of the customers. He's still an oily bastard and I don't trust him. I've told David to keep an eye on him."

"Joe! David and Monty already dislike one another intensely. Why do you want to pit them against one another like that!"

Joseph said nothing, just gave her an amused smile.

"Really, Joe! You are so mean." Evelyn came close to him and put her arms around his neck. "Not to mention handsome. That's why I love you."

"I'm not mean. I'm practical. And as for David, it's easy to be generous with him precisely because he is *not* ours and we have no obligation to him other than what we choose. And it's more rewarding to be generous when the person actually earns what you give him."

13

Jed sat staring bleakly at the daunting pile of papers that had accumulated on his desk. His sketch pad beckoned to him from the windowsill. He shoved it into a drawer; out of sight, out of mind. He was supposed to have spent this first six months under the tutelage of John McDonald, J. E. Gates & Companies's longtime shrewd chief financial officer, learning everything he could about the myriad entities that comprised his grandfather's holding company, one of the largest in the country. Jed had been given anywhere from one to a dozen folders for each of the hundred-odd subsidiaries. For the textile mills; for the manufacturers of oil-drilling equipment, electricity generators, farming and mining equipment, logging machinery, household goods, and foodstuffs; for the refineries and the smelting plants; for the retail stores and the commercial real estate; for the advertising companies, the financial companies. . . . The list was endless, the documentation mountainous, the detail mind-numbing. Mind-numbing and duller than the March sky outside his window. He knew that if he applied a monumental effort, as he had done during his excruciating years at Columbia, he could absorb all the information he needed. It wasn't that he didn't have the intellect for it. It was easy enough if you could bear paying attention. Unfortunately, he hated it. He hated the numbers, the formulas, the ratios, the ugliness of the language of making money.

Jed had never had a problem accepting that it wasn't necessary for him to enjoy what he was being asked to do. What he believed to be necessary was that he *do* what he was being asked to do, and do it well. His grandfather's admiration and his mother's personal happiness depended on Jed rising above the greater mass of humanity. He was grateful for the clear, safe road their expectations provided him. Left to his own devices, he wouldn't know where to go. Giving Joseph and Sally what they wanted was a small thing, considering what they were willing to give him. His grandfather was prepared to entrust his life's work to Jed, the extraordinary success of over half a century of toil given without question into his hands. His mother had given him life itself. She had sacrificed her own future to marry well—though not for love, as Jed was made abundantly aware—and devote herself to the needs of her firstborn child.

He had to concentrate. In another few weeks, McDonald would want to know which outposts of the empire interested Jed most and why. He had to be ready to talk intelligently about future growth, ways to increase productivity, patterns of sales, businesses to sell or buy, stocks to invest in, God knows what else. And he had to do it in a way that left no doubt about his passion or ability. He picked a clipped bundle of papers off the top of one of the many piles. He swiveled his chair toward the window and put his feet up on the wide ledge, assuming the executive position he had seen his grandfather take many times. Instead of reading, however, Jed found himself looking out, across William Street into Hanover Square, where loomed the majestic Italianate brownstone building that had once held the Cotton Exchange. He looked at the enormous clock nestled between the building's scrolled columns. It wasn't even four o'clock yet! It was starting to snow. He watched the big wet flakes settle onto the warm rails of the Third Avenue El and melt away. It was deliciously hypnotic, watching the white crystal shapes slowly tumble from the sky, light, and fade from sight. His eyes began to close.

"Jed! Wake up!"

Jed whirled around, startled, momentarily terrified that McDonald was at his back, peering into his empty mind. "David!" Jed leaped out of his chair. David's cashmere coat was dewy with melting snow, and there were drops of moisture clinging to his chestnut curls. His eyes were shining, and his cheeks and nose were red from the cold. "What are you doing here?"

"I'm not sure yet. I have an appointment with Uncle Joe. I'm hoping he's ready to go ahead with my other ideas for the store now that the installation of the air-chilling units is going so smoothly. Harry's been great, letting me work with Hirschorn on the project although it's hardly within my jurisdiction."

"He's a good fellow. But your other ideas need more creativity, don't they? And you're their creator. I'm sure Grandfather will let you have a significant role."

"I hope you're right." David was jumpy with anticipation. He pulled off his leather gloves and crammed them into his pockets. "What are you working on?" He came close to Jed's desk and leaned over, peering down at the mass of papers.

"Just finishing up getting intimate with all the company's assets. By next month, McDonald and I will decide where I'll concentrate my attentions."

"That's so exciting. Your grandfather's holdings are incredible. I've tried to familiarize myself with most of them." He pawed through the piles of paper, flipping pages, running his fingers down columns of numbers, mumbling to himself, shaking his head. "He's made brilliant decisions. Knows just when and what to buy and sell. I'll bet the next divestiture will be those textile mills upstate. What do you think? Am I right?"

David was looking at him with eager eyes, waiting to be told that he'd hit the mark. The problem was, Jed had no idea if David was right or not. What did David know about the mills, anyway? It was Jed who had been reading these damned papers for six months, and he hadn't gleaned anything like that. He smiled slyly. "Maybe. Tell me why you think that."

"Well, the entire textile industry in New England is entering a depression that I think is going to be permanent. I'd get rid of the mills now, while they're still making some money. The industry is being wooed by the South, and it's going to go."

"So, would you buy or invest in mills down south?"

David smirked and dropped the papers back onto the desk. "Very clever, Jed, very nice. Trying to trip up your best friend! No, you know these new mass production techniques will lead to major labor problems in the mills and factories. Real estate, energy, services. Innovative companies like Carrier. That's the way to go. Am I right?"

Real estate, energy, services, new, inventive companies. Jed had his list of interests to impress McDonald with. "Perfect! Hey, you want a job down here? I think I have some influence with the boss."

They laughed together; then David grabbed Jed in an impulsive, crushing hug. "Jed, I don't know where I'd be without you. I owe you so much."

Jed held up a warning hand. "What did I tell you about that?" For the first time in a long while, he felt that hideous crawling feeling in his gut. Like those moments in France when he had loathed himself for the sham he was. But David had been there to save him, and David was here now. Everything would be fine.

"Okay. Calm down. But I swear, Jed, one of these days

I'm going to find a way to pay you back, whether you like it or not."

"Just don't let me know about it," he joked. "I have a thought. Since you're so interested in all this, why don't I sort of tutor you on what I'm up to. That way you can learn, you can share your ideas with me, I'll let you know if you're on track. . . . What do you think?" Jed was inordinately pleased with himself. He would be helping David, David would be helping him—unknowingly, of course—and best of all, they would be alone together more often. Lately, he saw David only at family gatherings or when they doubled with Cissy and Abigail.

"That would be great! We could have a monthly evening, just the two of us, talk business, have a few drinks, dinner. Let's start next week." David turned to go. "I'll let you get back to work. Oh, say"—he turned back—"what are you doing tonight? Cissy and I are going to take in the new Valentino at the Rivoli, late dinner at Sardi's afterward. Want to join us?"

"I'd love to, but I can't. Mother invited Abigail for dinner."

"That sounds fun. But let's plan another evening. The Paul Whiteman Orchestra is coming to Carnegie Hall. Maybe they'll play the new piece Gershwin wrote for them—'Rhapsody in Blue?' I missed it last month when they premiered it at the Aeolian. It got raves."

"Wonderful. I'll have my secretary get us tickets. And, David, call me tomorrow. Let me know what happened with Grandfather."

"Uncle Joe? Miss Steele said I should come in." David walked into the spacious corner office carrying the tea-service tray that Joseph's secretary had handed him. He was amused to see that, like Jed, Joseph was sitting with his back to his desk, his feet up on the window ledge. Unlike Jed, however, Joseph was completely engrossed in the work he held in his hands. David could never seem to hold in his head just how old Joseph was. Everyone he had ever known who had lived to the age of seventy-nine was ancient and doddering. Joseph was still youthful, his face smooth, his greying hair thick, his gait steady, his mind razor-sharp.

Joseph didn't turn around. He stood up and waved for David to join him at the large windows. "I never get tired of this view. Put that down and come look."

Joseph's office was on the Gates Building's uppermost floor, the tenth. It faced southwest, overlooking Battery Park. In the fading light David could just make out the shadowy form of historic Castle Clinton, the Aquarium now housed within its thick, circular red sandstone walls. He really should take Cissy there one day, he thought; she was such a little girl, she'd love it. Off to the left, out where the Hudson River spilled into the Upper Bay, the Statue of Liberty rose out of the water, a beckoning blur almost lost in the steadily thickening snowfall.

"I stood at this window and watched that beautiful lady being dedicated back in the fall of 1886."

David tried to picture what Joseph must have witnessed. But what came into his mind instead was a vivid scene from ten years later: 1896, a ship carrying Anna, Viktor, Ben, and Rose Warshinsky sailing past the welcoming statue, perhaps under the hawklike eyes of Joseph Gates standing at this very window. David's heart seemed to lurch in his chest as he saw the outlines of ships pushing through the snow-clotted air like ghosts from the past. Anna would have been at the rail, even if she'd had to push a hundred people aside to get there. Rose would have been in her arms, Viktor huddled behind her in fear, and Ben clutching at her skirt. Anna would have looked up as they sailed into the harbor, impatient for her dreams to come true. Did she perhaps see a flash of sunlight glinting off a high window in a rich man's building? Did she pray that an as-yet-unconceived son would one day stand where she looked, having surpassed all her dreams and left her behind? If she could look up and see him now, would she be happy? Sudden tears veiled David's vision. He moved away from the window and swiped at his eyes.

"That's an impressive cashmere coat you're sporting." Joseph finally turned and came around his inlaid cherry-wood desk.

"You've seen it before. I got it at Brooks Brothers a few seasons back." David pulled off the still-damp coat and hung it over the back of an oversized burgundy-leather chair.

"Are ours not as good?" Joseph wasn't teasing. He wanted to know why David had preferred a Brooks to a Gates.

"The imported British and Italian ones that we sell are, but they're more expensive. Our own label isn't as good, but it could be"—he fingered the camel-color sleeve, the wool as soft as velvet—"and we can underprice anyone with the right suppliers and manufacturers. Coats, suits, waists, gowns—anything we want. We can sell quality clothing and make a fortune doing it."

Joseph held up a hand. "You've made your case. Sit. We're going to talk." He peered at David intently. "Your eyes are red. Are you feeling all right?"

"I'm fine. It's just the cold. It's getting really nasty out there."

Joseph nodded. "Some tea will warm you up." He sat down opposite David and rubbed his hands together. "Let's get to it. No point in beating around the bush. I want to go ahead with your other schemes, but you can't possibly expect—"

At that moment, Miss Steele poked her head through the door to make sure they had everything they needed. The brief interruption was time enough for David's imagination to complete Joseph's unfinished sentence: *but you can't possibly expect to be given control of such complex innovations.* Disappointment squeezed David's chest like a vise, although he knew he had no right to expect anything more. "You were saying that you want to go ahead with my ideas, but . . ."

"Right. But . . . you can't possibly expect to handle such far-reaching projects while you are running the dry goods division. It's time for a change. Jerome Hirschorn wants to retire by the end of this year. You'll begin working with him immediately, go over every detail of your proposals and let him advise you in the early stages of implementation. In addition, he will familiarize you with the responsibilities of his position. You'll have more than nine months to prepare yourself, although I doubt you'll need it. Starting January, you'll replace him as director of operations and report to Harry Selkirk. And me, of course."

David's mind went momentarily blank as he struggled to absorb the magnitude of what Joseph had just dropped in his lap. His gaze swept toward the window and fixed on the darkened glass as if seeking someone there. She'd be happy.

Something scraped across the table. "Your tea, David." Joseph had poured for them both, a robust English blend perfect for a late-afternoon infusion of energy. His with two slices of lemon floated on the top, David's with three spoons of sugar, sweet and milky.

David filled his lungs with tea-scented air, and a small smile tugged at his mouth. Astonishment gave way to exaltation.

"You look like the cat that's swallowed the canary. Don't get too cocky, young man. You've got a lot of work to do. Where do you plan to start?"

David came to earth. As always, Joseph was all business. No time wasted on niceties. "With everything but the café; that can wait. But the private label line, the cosmetics, the salon, the products. The time is now." He took a long sip of the tea, savoring the flavor, so much more complex than the brew he'd grown up drinking.

"How confident are you in the salon idea?" Joseph squinted at David over his teacup.

"Very, why? Do you disagree?"

He ignored David's question. "Confident enough to put up your own money?"

David crossed his legs and leaned back in his chair. "What's on your mind?"

"Less risk for me if you're wrong, more reward for you if you're right. I'm proposing a fifty-fifty partnership between you and the store. We contribute equally to all start-up costs and a maximum of one year of operation. Whenever the enterprise begins to turn a profit, we share equally in it. If, however, there are no profits after one year, you assume responsibility for all continuing expenses. You will have complete control over the creation and running of the salon, including any decision to shut it down. What do you say?"

Opportunity. That's what Joseph had always offered him—no outright gifts of any kind. Opportunity, with its risk of failure and promise of reward. David had not failed yet. He had taken every opportunity Joseph had offered, every opening and scrap of information, every loan with its stiff interest rate and repayment deadline, and turned it to his advantage. He had learned to play the stock market, to buy and sell real estate, to understand the workings of the economy and the changing directions in which wealth was flowing in this prosperous new world. Now he would be the half owner of an incredibly lucrative business, a moneymaking machine fueled by a new generation of women aggressively pursuing their freedom to earn and spend money on themselves, to be paid attention to.

"I say yes. Although I don't know why you're willing to give away something that could be so valuable." David would never accept some craftily conceived act of charity.

"I'm not so sanguine about the inevitability of success as you, despite Evelyn's positive reaction. It's a huge departure from what a department store traditionally provides. I will feel better knowing that you have a major personal stake in it. You'll work that much harder. Frankly, I wouldn't do it otherwise."

David was satisfied. "We have a deal." He put down his empty cup.

Joseph stood up. "Anything else? No? Then we're done here. Take the rest of the day off. Go celebrate."

By the time David reached the office door, Joseph was at his desk savagely scribbling comments on the top of a memorandum.

"Uncle Joe. Thank you."

Joseph nodded without looking up. He waved his pen toward the door, shooing David away. As the door closed, Joseph's head came up and an affectionate smile curved his lips. He was a content man.

David needed to share the news of his promotion with the one person who would understand what Joseph's trust meant to him. He raced down three flights of stairs, but Jed had already gone. His office was dark. Impossibly neat stacks of paper covered the desk. Disappointed, David stood for a moment, wondering where to go. Cissy, of course. His girlfriend who loved him, who would be delighted for him.

He emerged onto William Street into a white and chastened world. Dancing snowflakes saturated the air and tumbled silently through the light from the street lamps. Sound was muffled and movement slowed. It was glorious. David lifted his head and let the soft flakes fall onto his flushed face. He couldn't remember ever feeling happier in his life.

He headed west through the warren of narrow streets. Beaver to Broadway, up Broadway to Rector. He would take the Ninth Avenue El to 72nd Street, then walk to the Harrimans' river-view apartment on Riverside Drive. When the train reached the 72nd Street station David didn't move. He remained in his seat and watched the doors open, imagined himself walking onto the platform and down the stairs, watched the doors close again.

He left the El at 118th Street and dream-walked four blocks downtown, then west toward the river until he woke up standing in front of the brownstone where Lucy lived. He had seen almost nothing of her since the summer. She had graduated from Barnard the previous June but seemed to still be buried in work, emerging for birthday celebrations and holiday meals like a creature from the deep rising to the surface for an infusion of air and sun. The last occasion had been Joseph's birthday dinner over a month ago. David remembered what she'd been wearing that night. A dress of emerald-green jersey. Her throat revealed by its V-neck. The soft fabric molded itself to her body and hinted at the perfect curves beneath the fashionable dropped waist and calf-length hem. She'd been light and happy that night, floating in a bubble of some secret pleasure. She'd been excited by his proposals for the store, kissed his cheek and laughingly promised that come summer she would bring all her Barnard friends downtown to stay cool. David had wondered if perhaps she'd finally found a boyfriend, and told himself he was happy for her.

Tonight she was wearing a pair of loose cotton trousers, a man's white shirt with the sleeves rolled up over her forearms, and a stunned look. The shirt was too big for her small frame and made her seem waiflike. It was one of Philip's discards, rainbowed with paint stains. David stood in the doorway and smiled down at her like a fool. He didn't know what to say; he didn't know why he was there when he should have been at Cissy's.

"You're soaking wet. It's blizzarding out there. What are you doing here?" Lucy grabbed his hand and pulled him inside. "Take off your coat. There's a clean towel in the bathroom—the blue one. Go dry your hair and your face. I'll make some tea. Or would you prefer a drink?"

She was nervous, he realized. It occurred to him that in the two and a half years she had lived here he had never visited her without Jed or others along. Perhaps, for all her independent ways, she was uncomfortable being alone in her apartment with a man. He wondered if he should leave but knew he wouldn't. He always liked being here, in the warm and sheltering environment she had created. Her four simple rooms could have fit inside her grandparents' grand drawing room, but their high ceilings gave the illusion of greater space. The living room barely accommodated the sofa and two armchairs, the polished wood table with a single dinner service set at one end, an explosion of books at the other, and four wooden chairs tucked beneath its apron. An unusual Persian rug in deep shades of gold and orange covered the floor, bordered by a swath of dark, gleaming wood. In the bedroom, shelves filled with more books covered one wall, leaving room for nothing more than her bed with its beautifully carved headboard, a mahogany highboy, and a small, velvet-covered chair. With Philip's help, Lucy had painted the walls in rich earth tones: ocher and terra-cotta with touches of cinnamon and burnished gold. One wall of the living room was hung with paintings in gilded frames and drawings in plain wood frames. The work of her father and brother.

"This is a great apartment." David carefully eased out of

his wet coat. "It's so friendly. I don't know where to start with furnishing my new place. Want to help me?"

Lucy laughed. "Thanks for the compliment, but no. A four-story brownstone is a little more than I have the knack or time for. I'm sure Cissy would be more useful."

"Yeah, I'm sure you're right. She's already got lots of ideas." He hung his coat on the wooden rack by the door. "I would love a drink, if you have a brandy or some Scotch. And I'd like you to join me. I have something to tell you."

"You're in luck. I have a case of Armagnac that Uncle Monty gave me at Christmas. I don't know what he was thinking. He knows I'm not a drinker."

"He probably gave himself a thrill thinking about you getting drunk and losing your inhibitions," David said sardonically.

"David! That's my uncle you're talking about!"

"Well, your uncle Monty is one strange, unpleasant character. In all the years I've been around him I've never seen evidence of one natural human emotion. He's all pretense and charm, like some clever predatory animal."

Lucy rolled her eyes. "You should hear what he says about you! You two just don't like one another. You're both too busy jockeying for the top outsider position in the family hierarchy."

David groaned in annoyance. "Don't be ridiculous. Where do you come up with these theories, anyway? And I can well imagine what he says about me." He moved toward the bathroom. "I'm going to dry off. No more talk about Monty, all right?"

Lucy scurried into the kitchen. Her hands were shaking as she got down two snifters, dusted off and opened the brandy bottle. She willed herself to calm down. Why did she always say the wrong thing to David? And what was he doing here? What could he possibly have to tell her that required him to show up unannounced at her door? She had a telephone. He could have called. The bottle almost slid out of her suddenly numb fingers; he had come to tell her that he was going to marry Cissy.

By the time David returned from the bathroom, his hair mussed but dry, Lucy was sitting on the sofa holding her snifter in both hands. A second glass and the open bottle were on the coffee table. She had banished her earlier chirpy nervousness and sat quite still, her back straight, her attention riveted on the table as though fascinated by the pattern of the maple burl wood. She didn't look up as David settled himself a little distance away.

"I didn't know how much you wanted. Help yourself." She couldn't look at his face. Instead, she watched his hands as he poured himself a generous drink, watched the movement of his fingers, the perfect planes of his wrist bones where they emerged from the starched white cuffs of his shirt. She looked down into her glass. Her heart was in her throat. "So, what's your news? It must be important for you to come all the way up here in a snowstorm." She took a sip of the brandy, managing to swallow without gagging. She forced herself to look at him, careful to put no expression into her eyes.

He gave her a guarded smile. "What happened while I was in the bathroom?" He gazed warily around the room. "You seemed happy to see me; now you look like you wish I'd leave."

"I'm sorry. Of course I don't want you to leave. I get so few visitors, my social skills are a little rusty." She smiled with what she hoped passed for encouragement. "Tell me your news."

Still he hesitated. He took a mouthful of the Armagnac, held it on his tongue before letting it slide down his throat. "It's really not all that important, I guess." He put down his glass. "I just came from seeing your grandfather. He said yes to all of the proposals for the store that I submitted in the fall." He gave a self-deprecating laugh. "He thinks I'm a genius."

It took a long second for David's words to work their way into Lucy's brain. A long second to realize that Cissy's name had not figured anywhere in what he had said. He was not marrying her; this was about work. Mindless elation erupted inside her.

"Oh! You *are* a genius!" She lunged forward and threw

her arms around his neck, forgetting that she held a glass in her hand, forgetting everything. The brandy flew out onto the sofa, onto the shoulder of David's jacket, into his hair. She burst out laughing and hugged him, drew her head back to kiss his cheek. "I'm sorry! I'm just so happy for you!"

She meant to pull away. But through every place where their bodies touched a trembling weakness seeped into her. Struggle though she did to stay afloat, she was drowning in her desire for him. Helplessly she pressed herself against him. She wore nothing beneath her shirt, and David's heat blasted into her through the layers of cloth that separated them. She felt him pull minutely away from her and then push urgently into her, meeting the pressure of her body with his own. Her breasts swelled against the shirt's velvety smooth cotton, straining for the feel of him. Then her hands were clutching at his hair, the thick drops of liquor sticky on her fingers, and his hands were sliding around her back. His lips were at her neck, then at her ear, her jaw, her cheek. He found her lips and he kissed her and she opened her mouth to him. She tasted the sweet sharp brandy on his tongue.

She wrenched violently away, a terrible icy fear overwhelming the heat of her desire. She wanted his hands to find their way under her shirt, to find their way into the depths of her and never let her go. But she didn't want to die, to be so submerged in him that she would never see the surface of her own life again. It was too soon. She wasn't ready. If she gave herself to him now, she would lose herself in him, ecstatically abandon who she was, wake up one day in misery knowing she had betrayed them both. She had to stay strong enough to resist him, to fight him; he needed someone to fight him.

David released her. He leaped up off the sofa like a cat unexpectedly landed on a hot stove. He shook his head, hard; drops of brandy fell from his hair. He stalked around the living room, trying to steady his breathing, clawing his hands through his hair, his eyes ranging everywhere but toward the sofa where she sat, immobile, watching him. He collapsed into a chair and put his head in his hands. After a moment, he raised his head and looked at her with baleful eyes. Guilt and confusion smeared all over his face like the remains of a messy meal.

She watched him, her body burning, her heart pounding, unable to move yet terrified that this aborted moment was all she would ever get of him. She watched him struggle to compose himself and waited for him to deny what had just happened between them.

"Lucy, I'm sorry. You know I didn't mean to . . . I would never . . . I'm a little out of my mind; I got carried away. You're like my sister, for God's sake. Please, let's just forget that ever happened. You know it didn't mean anything."

He was such a coward. A lying, selfish coward. Doing what he always did, grabbing for what he wanted without thinking about the consequences. Moving so fast he didn't see who lay trampled, reaching for him, in the dust of his passage.

"Don't give it another thought, David. These things happen. The excitement of the moment. Of course it meant nothing." Her voice was flat; her eyes met his and showed him nothing. She refilled her glass.

"Right. Okay." His breathing slowed. He picked up his snifter and swirled the dark liquid around and around. "I didn't tell you everything. Hirschorn is retiring at the end of the year. You're looking at the store's new director of operations, as of January first." He raised his glass in an awkward salute to himself.

Lucy didn't utter a word. It was his own fault that she was cruel to him. It had taken him no more than a second to retreat from the tumult of his emotions to a place of safe, uncomplicated pride in himself, while she remained feeling skinned alive. No wonder she yearned to see him deflate, to glimpse the shadow of uncertainty falling across his confident features, the fear of failure swimming like a shark in the bright waters of his eyes.

David lowered his glass and gave her a tentative look. "Can't you find something nice to say to me?" he cajoled.

She took a sip of brandy. "No, not really," she said coolly. "Don't you think you're a little young for such a position? You've been at the store barely five years; do you really think you deserve it? I think things are coming too easily to you."

David slammed his glass down. Armagnac spilled onto the table. "What the hell did I do now? One minute you're hugging me and now you're . . . Who are you to decide what I deserve, to say that things are coming too easily to me? Your entire life has come easily to you. When are you going to grow up and learn how the real world works?"

"I am growing up," she said, her voice rising. "And I'm thinking about what's right and what's wrong, about having a purpose and a goal. What's your goal, David? To be rich? That's an empty, empty goal. You may not believe in God, but you can still lose your soul! You have responsibilities!"

David stood up, his arms rigid, his hands balled into fists. "Why do I try to talk to you at all? Getting rich is the only meaningful goal to have when you're so poor you have no choices in life. But you couldn't know anything about that. You think it's noble and romantic to be poor? Give up your inheritance and go live on Ludlow Street. You'll come running back with your tail between your legs." He glared down at her. "I'm leaving." He grabbed his coat and yanked open the door.

Lucy leaped to her feet and yelled at his retreating back, "Run away, you coward! You're so good at it! You ran away from your family just because they were poor! You're a horrible person!"

David disappeared into the hallway. She heard his heavy footsteps as he raced down the stairs; he couldn't get away from her fast enough. He hadn't even had the courtesy to close the door behind him. Lucy slammed it shut, opened it, and slammed it again and again. She whirled and ran into the bedroom, catapulted herself onto the bed. She clutched a pillow tight to her breast and curled her body around it, buried her face in it, and screamed into the soft down.

She rocked back and forth, the pillow locked in her arms, sobbing. Her tears ran in a flood onto the crisp white linen of the pillow cover. On her night table lay a letter welcoming her to the spring term of Presbyterian Hospital School of Nursing. She had told no one. It had lain there for two months, secret evidence of her worthy future.

David burst from Lucy's building, furious and dazed. All he had wanted was to hear her say, *I'm happy for you, congratulations.* He should have known better than to have stayed long enough for her to transform into the argumentative shrew who had to pick apart every good thing he did, every success he had. God knows he'd had enough experience of her trying to eat him alive. Why did he keep coming back for more? From the very first, he'd felt exposed by her scrutiny, pinned by green searchlights crawling over him looking for his soft spots, threatening to splay him open like a miserable, trapped rabbit. She was nothing but a coddled snob. A coddled snob with the keenest brain, the sharpest eyes, the most scathing tongue of any girl he had ever met, who made him feel like an infant, squalling and inarticulate, defenseless.

He took a breath and tried to gather his thoughts. What had happened made no sense. This was Lucy, for God's sake, not the sort of manageable girl to whom he was attracted. And she had always made it clear that she was anything but attracted to him. Why had he pounced on her like an animal? Somehow, she'd made him feel like an animal, primitive instinct sending him running after prey only to feel himself plunging over the rim of a cleverly disguised pit. He'd apologized. What more did she want?

He began running toward the El, moving much too quickly on the slippery snow-covered sidewalk, and skidded into a parked car. His side slammed into the frigid metal; a rain of snow cascaded onto his pant legs and shoes. He bent over, breathing hard from exertion and pain. When he could straighten up, he began walking carefully along the nearly deserted streets. The snow was coming down so hard that he was barely able to see a half block ahead of him. Flakes were finding their way down the back of his neck. He shivered and flipped up his collar, hunched his shoulders toward his bare, freezing ears. What a total fiasco. He must have been out of his mind. Now he would go see Cissy, tell her his news, take her out to celebrate. He would drown the bitter taste in his mouth with the sweetness of the most expensive champagne he could buy and the feel of Cissy's willing lips.

By the time the train came, he was so cold he couldn't feel his face. He huddled in the first car, grateful for the warmth, and eagerly awaited the 72nd Street stop, berating himself for not having gotten off there when he should have. He watched the station appear and once again stayed where he was and watched it recede. As it disappeared from view he leaned his head against the shaking wall of the car and searched the ceiling in bewilderment. He gave himself over to the lullaby sound of the metal wheels on the rails, the rocking of the train as it wended its way downtown, and waited.

An hour later, the train expelled him a short walk from Mount Judah Cemetery in Brooklyn. He'd visited her grave only once before, a month after he'd returned from France. Five years later, he knew exactly where it was, even in the dark, even in a snowstorm. It was after hours; the main gate was closed and locked. He climbed over the high iron fence, ignoring the pain in his side as he slid awkwardly to the ground. He was alone in the land of the dead. He felt cold and insubstantial enough, moving through the eerie white night, to be one of them. He walked the maze of narrow lanes, through sections of elegant, widely spaced grave sites with shining marble monuments, until he reached the section where the poor were buried, plain stone markers at their closely packed graves.

Anna Hertzig Warshinsky, born December 13, 1868, died August 10, 1918. Beloved wife and mother. No matter that the stone was covered with snow, David knew what it said. He saw two higher mounds in the snow atop the marker. Sarah and Ben had been there recently, David thought, and left rocks upon the gravestone as a sign of their visit. He looked around him as though their spirits might be hovering somewhere nearby.

He stood like a statue at the foot of his mother's grave and then lowered himself to his knees. He reached out with his gloved hand and brushed away the snow, revealing the meaningless jumble of letters and numbers carved into the small stone. They evoked nothing, captured nothing about her; where was her beauty, her strength, her generosity, in this paltry place where she'd been laid to rest? After all her years of struggle and hard work, this was the best Viktor and Ben could do for her? A spasm of anger shook David. His head turned and he noticed the corner of another stone, one he didn't remember seeing five years before. He leaned forward and slowly cleared the snow, his heart hammering in his chest. *Viktor Warshinsky, born March 24, 1864, died August 10, 1919. Beloved husband and father.*

David rocked back on his heels in shock, numb to the chill creeping through his coat and trouser legs. He stared at the stone. A vision of his father came to him, a hollow-eyed and silent Viktor huddled for warmth in a corner by a stove, gradually fading from life the way light faded from the evening sky until there was nothing but blackness. David knew that there had been no illness, no accident, just a slow, inexorable letting go of what tied Viktor to the living until, on the very anniversary of the day that she passed from this world, he was finally free to join her. In an unbidden flash of compassion, David felt his father's despair, imagined the slipping away of any sense of himself once Anna wasn't there to see him. Who else had ever known and loved the man Viktor Warshinsky, given him a reason to remain in a world that overwhelmed all his sensibilities? David tasted bile in his mouth, and a wave of self-loathing washed over him. He had dared to pass judgment on his own father, weighed his own worth against his contempt for Viktor's fallibilities. So easily forgotten the trusting feel of his big hand holding tightly to David's own small hand as they walked together to *shul*.

A terrible pain spread through David's chest, guilt and anguish fighting to escape the prison of his locked-up heart. His mouth opened and a sound emerged, the cry of a wounded animal who has no words to speak his agony. He collapsed forward, his face smothered in cold, wet gloves. He sobbed like a child, like the orphan he suddenly was. His tears etched hot trails into the freezing skin of his cheeks. He cried for his father, who had died without ever knowing that the little boy he had tossed into the air so long ago harbored deep within him a tiny flame of love. He cried as that flame, burning uselessly for so many years, flickered and went out. Loneliness and desolation engulfed him. What if Ben and Sarah were right? What if, as Anna felt her life draining out of her with her flowing blood, she had wondered why David wasn't there to save her, to save them all?

The silence surrounding him was leaden with the burden of his family's history. It pressed down on him with a tangible weight that he couldn't tolerate. His sobs stopped. The last remnants of his tears no longer hot but frigid now, scoring his skin with cold. He levered himself upright, and in the white mist swirling before him he saw Lucy's accusing eyes boring into him, chasing him from the warmth of her apartment, denying him the right to the rewards he had earned. Like a witch working a wicked spell, she had cast him cruelly back into a dead past. Rage swept through him, at her, at the misery of this place he had run to, at the lingering, clutching spirits of his family, at himself for allowing even a moment of self-doubt to intrude into his life. Feelings of guilt and loneliness were for children. Not for him. He was not responsible for his parents' deaths. He didn't care what his brother and sister thought of him. What Lucy thought of him. He would not kneel at Anna's and Viktor's graves and cry for a loss that was none of his doing.

He knew what was true. Anna would never have blamed him for anything. She would be happy for him, for everything he had traveled into the depths of Brooklyn in a blinding storm to tell her. Why else had she come to this country? He began to whisper into the night air. He told her about everything: his money, his promotions, his new house, his pretty girlfriend, his adopted family. He imagined sitting with Anna at the kitchen table, the room warmed from the stove and a shared glass of tea steaming between them. He didn't tell her that he hadn't seen Ben and Sarah since he'd been back. He told her only the things she'd want to know. He could see her face so clearly. She reached out and squeezed his hand. Tears of pride filled her eyes, and her moist gaze sent him a wordless message. He knew what else she wanted for him, the thing that would calm him and nurture him: his own warm kitchen and someone who loved him unconditionally. He needed to make a family. Uncle Joe was right; it was time.

When the train reached 72nd Street, David got off. It was just eight o'clock when he rang the Harrimans' bell. He heard Cissy's voice calling out, "It's David; I'll get it!" and the sound of her heels tapping toward the door. He would tell her his news and she would be dumbly happy for him, the way she was happy to wear her minks and eat her caviar and drive her Cadillac without a thought to how they'd arrived in her life. And that would be fine; it would be a relief.

The door swung open and she was there in front of him, clean and warm and scrubbed and shining, her brown eyes filled with love and nothing else. "Look at you! You're a snowman!" She laughed and hugged him, kissed him hard on the mouth. "You're freezing, poor sweetheart. Come sit by the fire."

David took a step inside. He hooked a foot around the door and kicked it shut behind him. The reverberations rumbled through the apartment, down the hallway. He grabbed Cissy around the waist with both hands and lifted her off the ground. "Cissy, how would you like to marry me?"

Philip's studio was in the famous Tenth Street Studio Building, where artists had created and shown their work for over half a century. For years Philip had been renting a space that had once been used by Winslow Homer, whose inspirational presence he thought he could sometimes sense. He was on the telephone when he saw Jed push through the door. Philip's face lit up with happiness. He mouthed, *I'll just be a moment,* and quickly finished up the call.

"Jed! What a lovely surprise!" He took his son's outstretched hand and noticed that his coat and hat were wet. "Is it raining out?"

Jed laughed. "Father. It's been snowing volumes for the past two hours. Don't you ever look out the window?" They both knew the answer to that. Philip was notorious for falling into oblivion when he was painting. "I thought I'd come pick you up and we could walk home together. I hope I didn't interrupt an important call."

"No. That was just an old client, Dorothy Woolbright. They've had a leak in their apartment and her portrait sustained some damage. She asked me to come look at it. I was just about to clean up here. I actually remembered that we have company coming for dinner tonight." Philip sounded pleased with himself.

Jed waited in comfortable silence while his father scraped his palette, cleaned his brushes, studied the canvas on his easel, and repositioned some items lying on a table beyond, background for the painting he was working on. Philip's suit jacket was draped over the arm of an old sofa, its cushions sprung and lumpy. His vest was unbuttoned and the sleeves of his shirt were rolled up. As he bent over the table, a hank of light brown hair fell from his neat middle part and hung down over his forehead, reaching for the bowl of the pipe that was locked between his teeth. Jed felt his whole being sink toward serenity as he watched his father's competent, sure movements. Philip was so at ease, so in harmony with his environment and everything in it. He was the master of his art, and that was enough for him. He had never exhibited the need to be the master of anything or anyone else.

With a pang, Jed thought back to the afternoons he had spent here as a boy, nestled into a corner of the sofa drawing childish scenes while his father painted beneath a permanent wreath of aromatic smoke. They never spoke much except for Philip praising Jed's drawings, pointing out a technique he might want to try to get that shadow just so, bringing him over to the easel to show him a particular use of color. Jed smiled now to realize how Philip had made him feel talented, had taught him so subtly that he believed every improvement in his sketches had sprung from his own divine gifts. He glanced over at the sofa and remembered how unshakably safe he had felt hugged by its armrest, how solidly tethered to something real and loving. He had stopped coming here after his school day ended the year Sally insisted that he join the Knickerbocker Greys. Since he most certainly did not wish to be an artist when he grew up, he would no longer want to indulge in a wasteful pastime. He had been ten years old and had not set foot in his father's world more than a dozen times since.

Jed hadn't been in the studio in well over a year. As his father got ready to leave, Jed wandered around, looking at Philip's work. There were studies for portraits he'd sold; finished portraits he must have done for his own pleasure. There were still lifes and landscapes, charcoals and gouaches and even some watercolors, the most difficult of all media. How had he not seen before today that most of the pictures were mesmerizingly beautiful, the rest merely wonderful? His father was an enormous talent. His skill at portraiture had earned him his well-deserved commercial success, but as Jed studied his paintings, he concluded that the greatest expression of Philip's artistry resided in his landscapes. Jed stood transfixed before a painting of a brittle wintry meadow ringed by stark woods, the cold and lifeless elements somehow animated by the vivid orange glow of a winter sunset. Philip did not paint precisely rendered landscapes that attempted to re-create reality; rather, he created the illusion of reality in paintings that were shadowy and richly colored. They were suffused with an unmistakable personal spirituality, the depicted landscape an allegory for the internal experience of the painter. Something twisted in Jed's gut, a hot stab of disappointment. Lucy was wrong; even if he had a lifetime to devote to his own art, he would never be as good an artist as Philip. His own landscapes, though expertly executed, were as precise as photographs; no matter how hard he tried to make them something more, he could not find that deeper dimension within himself with which to enliven them.

"I'm ready, Jed. Shall we go brave the elements?" Philip appeared at Jed's side, buttoned up, coated and hatted, his pipe tamped out and slid into a pocket. The weight of his portfolio case brought his left shoulder down inches below his right.

Jed turned away from the painting and from the pointless comparison between his and his father's abilities. His destiny lay elsewhere. "Let me carry that, Father." Jed took the case from Philip's hand before he could protest. "I love this painting. It should be in a museum."

Philip patted Jed's shoulder. "I'm so glad you like it. It's one of my favorites, too. And, in fact, the National Gallery of Design wants to add it to their permanent collection. It's an honor, but I have to think about it. I would rather hate to part with it."

They left the studio building and strolled east on 10th Street, in awe of the white and silent world. Privately savoring the strangeness of being alone together, neither said a word until they reached Fifth Avenue. While waiting to cross, they looked down the avenue several blocks to the arch at Washington Square and the park beyond. Just half an hour earlier, Jed had stopped in front of David's new house on the north side of the square. The still-uncurtained windows were dark. His meeting with Joseph must have been a long one. Jed wondered if David was home now, getting ready for his evening with Cissy.

Philip's thoughts soared into a more spiritual realm. His chest swelled with happiness. He was walking with his son, and beauty was everywhere around him. "My goodness. Is this not a most wonderful world!" he cried. "I am so pleased that you came by the studio. So pleased. Stand still a moment. Let me look at you." He frowned. "When did you grow taller than me?"

"When I was seventeen!"

Philip's face softened into a playful smile. "I knew that. I remember the very day I realized I was looking up at you while we spoke." His smile became wistful. "Jed, are you happy? Is everything going well with Abigail, with work? Are you finding time to paint or draw at all?"

Philip had crossed the invisible line, the one neither of them could acknowledge but both knew was there. He had invaded territory that was strictly under Sally's control. Jed tried to look away, but his father's gentle eyes grabbed and held him. The whiteness of the air seemed to metamorphose from snow to fog, and Jed was in the back of an army truck, bouncing toward hell, with the image of his father's eyes boring right through him, looking at him as no one had ever looked at him, the way he was looking at him now. Jed wanted to give in and join Philip in the forbidden territory. They could build a mile-high barbed-wire fence and keep her out . . . Two huge flakes hit Jed in the face and brought him chillingly back to earth. He would never breach the boundaries his mother had set for him. If he colluded with his father he would be slaying her. He would be unforgivable.

"Come on, Father. The world won't be so wonderful if we're late for dinner." Jed grabbed Philip and started dragging him across the avenue. "Work is terrific; I swear I'm a born businessman. Ask me anything about the company's fiscal matters and I'll bore you to death! And Abby. We're doing very well; I like her tremendously. I'm happy, Father, truly. Don't worry about me. There'll be time for drawing later, once I've got my bearings at the office."

Philip didn't know if he believed a word of what Jed had said. Why would Jed have shown up at the studio if he were happy? Philip understood that the dusty clutter of canvases and paints had provided his son with a needed escape from the glaring orderliness of his young life. Had that changed just because he was an adult now? But what could Philip do? Beg Jed to let him be what he yearned to be: the father who would teach him and help him and love him no matter who he was? Of course not. Although the possibility had shimmered in front of him for the briefest second before slipping through his fingers like the falling snow. No, he had to respect the choices Jed made. To do otherwise could only cause the boy worse grief.

"Good, I'm glad. You know I love you, Jed. All I want is for you to be happy." At least he was allowed to say that much.

Sally used her handkerchief to clear a porthole-sized circle on the inside of the foggy parlor window. She watched intently as Jed handed Abigail into the waiting taxi. She saw the girl eagerly lift her face toward him, offering her mouth for a good-night kiss. Sally held her breath as Jed's lips slid away and he delivered a chaste kiss to Abigail's cheek. She would have to talk to Abigail. The poor thing had lost her parents at a young age and didn't have a proper mother, a fact that made her all the more appealing to Sally as a potential daughter-in-law. The elderly maiden aunt with whom Abigail lived was without question incapable of providing her with guidance concerning matters of men, marital duties, and the like.

Abigail needed to be told that it was unseemly for a well-bred woman to have, no less express, overt sexual desires. Just because it seemed like an entire society of weak-minded degenerates had chosen to throw away the conventions that upheld a moral civilization did not make such behavior right. People could justify their disgraceful antics all they wanted, spewing forth the "repression" theories of that beast Sigmund Freud, but they would all end up roasting in hell, and that perverted Austrian Jew with them.

Jed and Abigail were going to marry—Sally had tonight made her decision—and the girl had to be reminded that Jed was too sensitive to be exposed to such unpalatable pressure, either before marriage or afterward. Sally felt glorified by her son's purity, of which she had no doubt, and allowed herself the great hope that within his marriage he would continue to shun carnality and approach Abigail only for the purposes of creating a family, as God intended. Abigail simply needed to understand that a man like Jed would not welcome advances; they would displease him and ultimately cause him to lose respect for her, as they would any true gentleman.

Sally was in the vestibule when Jed came back in, stamping the snow off his shoes. She reached up and brushed at his damp hair, trailed her fingers across the smooth, cool skin of his perfect face. She linked her arm through his and leaned against him as she guided them back into the parlor. Philip was sitting in a corner, reading his newspaper, his pipe in his mouth, smoke purling around his head. Brook had been sent to his room. Sally let Jed settle her onto the love seat by the fireplace and then patted the cushion, inviting him to sit with her.

"Did you enjoy the evening, darling?"

"Of course, Mother. Dinner was delicious. Abby seems to be very comfortable here, don't you think?"

"Indeed. And I'm glad of it. I know how much you care for her, and she for you."

"Well, yes, I suppose. We do get on well."

"I should hope so. You've been keeping company for over a year. Jed, let me be direct with you, although you know I would never pressure you into anything." She put a hand on his knee. "It's time for you and Abigail to marry. To be the most successful man you can be, you will need a helpmate, someone to make a home for you, to entertain your business associates, give you children. Dear, you need a wife."

In the periphery of his frozen vision Jed saw Philip lift his head from his newspaper, rise from his chair, and come toward the fireplace. For a ridiculous moment, relief surged into Jed's pounding heart; his father would save him, swoop down like an eagle and carry him away to safety. He turned his eyes away from Philip's approach and trained them on Sally's hot, heavy hand, wishing she would lift it from his leg. The pressure pinned him to the love seat as irresistibly as he was now pinned to a life with Abigail.

Now that this moment had come, he didn't understand why he should feel anything but pleasurable expectancy. He liked Abigail and knew that he would marry her. He had known it for months. He had merely been waiting on Sally's instructions. Being with Abigail was as easy and familiar as being with Lucy. Except when she wanted him to kiss her. He didn't want to kiss her. He had never wanted to kiss anyone. Sally had raised him with a mandate to save himself for the sanctity of marriage, and he believed that was what he had done. His mandate was his protection against the evils of lust, against disease, against being trapped into a shameful marriage by having impregnated some sly, venal girl. It was his shield against ever wondering too deeply why his understanding of the lustful urge was limited to a description in the Bible, a definition in the dictionary. As he had listened to school friends and army colleagues boast of their conquests, as he had watched David perform his impassioned, graceful dance of seduction with one fevered partner after another, all that would rise up in Jed was something ugly and unacceptable, a seething in his blood, something to be squelched quickly. Not a thing that could ever impel him to kiss Abigail, to touch her, to take her to bed and do . . . he wasn't even sure what. When he married, the protection of his mandate would disappear. He would be expected then to become lustful, at least occasionally. How was that supposed to happen? Did the very taking of the wedding vows, the benediction of God, release something in the man who had been virtuous, something different from what squirmed inside him from time to time?

"Do I hear talk of marriage?" Philip sat down across from his wife and son.

Sally gave him a warning look. *Don't interfere, Philip. You promised me.* "Yes. Don't you agree that Abigail would make a very suitable wife for our son?"

Philip looked at his son and considered Sally's question. Marriage might be a blessing for Jed. Abigail clearly loved him, and she was a kind, yielding woman. They could create a life together, one that Jed would have some control over. "Yes, I do. Shall we plan a wedding?"

Sally's hand squeezed Jed's leg. "Yes. A beautiful, blazing September wedding. You won't want to wait any longer than that. I know exactly what we want!"

There was nothing left but to say yes. And in the face of his parents' joy, Jed found that he wanted to say yes. He wanted to marry Abigail. He wanted his own home. He yearned for the freedom to decide what he would eat and off what dishes; to choose the color of the curtains in his living room; to perhaps set up an easel in some high, north-facing room and be allowed to go there. He wanted a friend to sit and talk to at the end of the day, a pretty wife to accompany him to dinners and parties. He wanted children. He wanted a normal life.

"Yes, let's plan a wedding!" Jed beamed at his parents and was instantly smothered in Sally's exuberant embrace. As his mouth and nose filled with the feminine scent of her rose perfume, he reassured himself that marriage would be the liberating key to his dormant sexuality. Although, for the briefest second, he wished there was someone who could confirm to him that it was natural to be twenty-five years old and without desire of any kind.

Brook hovered silently at the top of the stairs. As always, he was excluded from anything of significance that happened in his house. He'd been sent to his room to study his mathematics so that he would not fail his exams for the second time. It was hopeless. He would fail no matter how many chances he was given. He was stupid; he couldn't learn anything. He knew that the only reason he hadn't been expelled from Browning was because his family gave the school a great deal of endowment money. If he had failing grades again this term, he would be shipped off to some stifling prep school in the hope that through rigor he might somehow be made capable of attending college. It wouldn't work, but maybe it would be the best thing. No one cared about him. No one wanted him here anymore. Lucy was gone; Jed would be leaving. Lucy had asked permission for Brook to visit her, but Mother had refused. She said he was too young to be under Lucy's dubious supervision, but Brook knew her refusal was punishment for his disobedience and laziness. Most of the time, though, Lucy and Jed were too busy with their grown-up lives, and when they had any time at all they chose to spend it with David, not with him. His parents had no use for him. He was invisible. He couldn't be any lonelier no matter where he was. He crept back to his room. There was no point in studying. He burrowed his hand under his mattress and came away with a dog-eared copy of *War of the Worlds*. He patted the cover lovingly and then slipped it back in its hiding place, not quite ready to read it again. He groped farther afield, down toward the foot of the bed, until he found his notebook. He settled himself in the window seat and started scribbling furiously, spinning out the next installment of *The Amazing Adventures of Borden Gray, First Man on Mars*. Within minutes, he was lost completely to a world of his imagination.

Essex, Grand, Ludlow, Delancey, Clinton. Once, these streets had defined the totality of David's existence. Once, when he was just a foolish child, he had believed these streets to contain everything he needed. Every single bit of knowledge, every experience or thing or person that he wanted. He kept what was useful or pleasurable and let the rest go, to float away downstream as he struggled against the tide in search of more. It wasn't possible to hide from life in such an exuberant, uninhibited place. But at some point his eyes opened and he saw that his playground was embedded in a sly prison, his family, his friends, his lovers all in their cells, locked down and not even comprehending the fact or nature of their entrapment. By the time he returned from the war, this place and everything in it had disappeared downstream of his new life. Even the war itself, what he had done there and what had been done to him, became debris in the relentless current. David moved on, as he had done since childhood, determined to let no trace of anything useless or unpleasant cling to him.

Now, after an absence of over seven years, he walked these streets once so dear to him and felt nothing. The throngs and the noise and the bustle had no resonance; he couldn't remember how they had ever had anything to do with him. He passed the stores he had worked in, shopped in, stolen from, their wares spilling out on the streets under awnings to protect them from the summer sun. He saw people he thought he knew, but they didn't even raise their eyes to him. He was not one of them and they took no interest in him. It pleased him inordinately that he passed through this realm unrecognized; no one would ever see the discontented eighteen-year-old boy they held in their memories in the composed, impeccably dressed twenty-five-year-old man striding up Delancey Street.

He held the address of RW Fashions in his hand as he scanned the building numbers along Clinton Street. He had done his research and chosen RW to be the supplier of men's outerwear and ladies' dresses for the store's private line. They were relatively new and small but produced an excellent product for an excellent price. They could copy any design he gave them or provide good designs of their own. The owner promised he could deliver whatever quantities David needed. He was eager to meet him. He had sounded on the phone like a straightforward man, someone David could enjoy working with, an enterprising fellow who had already figured the magnitude of the profits they might both reap. David pushed through a scarred metal door and climbed up to the third floor of a double-width factory building.

"Mr. Shaw, I'm so pleased to finally meet you." A tall, lanky young man awaited him at the landing. He smiled and held out his hand. "I'm Reuben Winokur. Come, let me show you around my factory, and then we'll talk."

David liked him immediately. One look and David knew he didn't have to worry about Winokur's honesty. His grip was firm and his gaze direct. He didn't try to hide his excitement about making such a lucrative deal. He was clearly an immigrant, David could pick up the faintest trace of an accent and guessed him to be Lithuanian, but he had obviously done well for himself to be the owner of his own company.

With poorly suppressed pride, Reuben led David through the factory. It was oppressively hot in the big, open spaces despite the constant whirring of large floor fans. The June sun streaming through the west-facing windows gave wonderful light, but it warmed the air beyond any fan's capacity to cool. Aside from the heat, conditions in the factory were impressive. One of the things that had helped decide David on RW was its reputation as a stable union shop and a good employer. David could have saved a few dollars by going with other suppliers, but it wasn't worth the risk of strikes, work slowdowns, employee unrest. One problem like that could kill an entire season's profits.

In a large corner room, a half-dozen women were bent over enormous tables, cutting patterns. As Winokur explained what they were doing, David's gaze fell on the woman closest to the door, a pretty blonde with a sure hand with the scissors. Three months from his wedding, he shouldn't be noticing other women, but nonetheless his eyes roved over her voluptuous figure before returning to her face. With a shock, he recognized her. Rachel Cohen. He immediately turned away so she wouldn't see him. She would know him. From far away or close up, she would know him. She would know him no matter how fine a suit he wore or how fashionable the hat that covered his once-wild hair. She had spent too many breathless hours in the year before he left with her eyes and hands and lips all over him to have forgotten what he looked like. David began walking down the hall, a bemused Winokur trailing after him.

"I thought you'd want to see some of our patterns. We can do anything you want. Our best cutter, you saw there in the front, Rachel Weinstein, she can cut a pattern out of thin air."

Weinstein! Poor Rachel, she must have married pious and devoted Shlomo Weinstein of the sweaty palms and soft body, he whom Rachel's parents preferred over David to an incalculable degree. "I'm sure she can. I've seen all I need to. I'm very impressed, Mr. Winokur."

"Please. Call me Reuben. If we're going to have a partnership, let's not be formal with one another."

"Reuben." David nodded. "Come, let's go to your office and work up our first order. Let's see how much money we can make together."

Reuben beamed. "With pleasure, David."

15

"Sarah, darling. Go home; it's late." Sol Leyrowitz positioned his bulk in the narrow doorway of the tailors' room and watched Sarah Warshinsky maneuver a needle through a piece of expensive silk with the speed, grace, and confidence of a ballerina swooping across the floor in a flawless

series of pirouettes. His aging heart lurched sweetly in his chest as she glanced up at him with her mother's eyes and smiled.

"I promised Mrs. Schwartz that I would have this blouse for her tomorrow. But if you're ready to leave, Uncle Sollie, I'll close up; don't worry. I won't be too much longer."

Sol nodded but made no move to back out of the door frame. He allowed himself the simple yet extraordinary pleasure of looking at Sarah and thinking of Anna, his mind comfortably empty of words and filled with dumb happiness. An uncomplicated man, he had no words for what Anna's death had done to him. All he knew was that from one day to the next he became an old man. How was he to understand that another Sol, slim and fine looking and bold, had existed inside his middle-aged, corpulent body, kept forever young and hopeful by unrequited love? When Anna died, the impossible dreams of that love died with her.

The months after had been a terrible time. The Spanish influenza had raged through the packed tenements and taken many lives. Sol suffered the loss of his wife, whom he had thought mean and bloodless enough to send Death running for cover. He lost old friends like Frank Corelli, Fay Zizkin, Yoshi Krinski. And Sol missed them all; but it was Anna, and the dream of the love he'd had for her, that he missed the most. For months, Sol had stumbled around his store with damp eyes, tortured by thoughts of how close he had come to having her near him for hours each week, of how it would have been his money that would have changed her life, of how it was because she had come to see him that day that she had been out on the dangerous streets. Then one day, out of the blue, the idea came to him. Anna was gone, but he could still be close to her, still help her. Through the daughter, that skinny blank-eyed little thing sitting stunned at the funeral, pale and worn from working slave hours in an attic sweatshop. The obedient, loving daughter whose face and eyes and hair were so much like Anna's that foolish yearnings rose up in him such as he had never felt and he couldn't stop wishing that the little girl was his. His and Anna's.

Sol would have been happy to have simply given Sarah money, so she could go back to school and wear nice clothes and eat candy and put some meat on her fragile bones, but she was as proud and stubborn as her brother Ben and they would not accept his charity. So he decided he would give her a job. Sol ran a good, union shop. When he got his thunderbolt of an idea, Sarah was still shy of fifteen. He couldn't hire her for another year, at least, and with his stable of tailors he couldn't spare her enough piecework to equal the money she made at Pankin's. So he waited. And on the day she turned sixteen, without telling the brother, without telling the girl herself, Sol marched into Pankin's shop and marched out dragging a confused Sarah behind him. He added her to his tailoring staff, where everyone fussed over her as though she were a baby bird fallen out of its nest. Within months, the "new girl," Anna Warshinsky's daughter, was every customer's favorite seamstress, and by the time she was eighteen she had earned the position that Sol had offered Anna the day she died. No one in the shop was jealous; no one thought for a moment that Sol gave Sarah things she didn't deserve because he had been in love with her mother. Everyone knew that Sarah was special. Any fool could see that Anna, so beloved and so missed, would live again in the woman Sarah would become. The girl was the embodiment of her mother's vitality and beauty and sweetness. And Sarah could sew clothing fit for a queen.

Sarah again raised her eyes from her work, realizing that Sol hadn't moved. "Uncle Sol, really, go home."

"Yes, yes. Is the adoring Reuben coming to pick you up?" Sol teased, inexplicably moved by the sight of a soft blush rising to Sarah's cheeks. He began to chuckle. "Maybe I should stay and chaperone you two lovebirds!" His shoulders shook with laughter.

Sarah felt a flicker of annoyance, but it was quickly dispelled. She couldn't find it in her to fault Sol for mocking Reuben's prudish behavior. Not only had there been no marriage proposal, although she was already twenty years old and had long been champing to leave her brother's house—which Ben would only allow when she married; living on her own or with a female friend was unacceptable for an unmarried Jewish girl—but Reuben hadn't yet given her anything more than a chaste kiss on the lips, a careful hug, or a promising squeeze of the hand. She couldn't even say exactly when their friendship had blossomed into a youthful romance, so gradual were the changes in their relationship. But sometime after Sarah's sixteenth birthday, and always under Ben's watchful, patriarchal eye, Reuben had begun a slow, proper courtship. Before Sarah had time to ever wonder about other boys or to consider how she might shape her own life, she understood that she and Reuben would marry one day. Everyone understood. Reuben was not just the young man delivered from God Himself to the suffering Warshinskys to soften the blow of David's disappearance and to take on the role of Sarah's entertainer and protector. Sarah was no longer the eternal little girl who could take the place in Reuben's heart of Ada, the sister he had lost in Lithuania. They were young sweethearts, meant for each other. Providence had brought them together.

"No. My adoring Reuben is not coming to pick me up. He'll be at the factory late again tonight. His business is really starting to do well, Uncle Sol. He has a lot of orders to fill, including yours. You do want your spring clothes here on time, don't you?" Sarah teased back. "And you can joke all you want about how proper he is, but his restraint shows respect, doesn't it? Naomi says that's how Papa always treated Mama and Ben treated her and that it's what a woman should want. Not some selfish boy groping at you all the time. And I agree!"

"Ah, respect. . . ." Sol's head bobbed back and forth with ambivalence. "Respect he can show you after you're married. You're young; you're in love; respect isn't exactly what he should be showing you right now, if you take my meaning. It's not normal."

"Uncle Sol!" Sarah blushed furiously and covered her ears with her hands, leaving Sol to think her as shy and prim as Reuben. She wondered just how shocked he'd be if he knew the secret, impure thoughts that his words conjured in her head, how impatient she was for Reuben to stop treating her like something to be kept safe behind protective glass. She wanted to know what it would feel like if he kissed and touched her like a lover and not like a man afraid of his own urges, of his future brother-in-law's unspoken rules. Sarah might pretend to find Reuben's shyness endearing, but her body shamed her with its truth.

Sol shook his head and patted Sarah's flaming cheek. "Ah, don't be upset with your uncle Sol. I'm a silly old man; what do I know? But I can't help from wondering why he isn't running to marry you. What is he waiting for, until your sister-in-law has so many children there is no more room for you in your brother's house?"

"With four little ones and another on the way, there is already no room for me," Sarah laughed. "No, he says he needs to have enough money to support me properly. I think we already have more than enough, what with the first payments from that big department store order coming in soon, and with you so generous to me."

"Bah." He waved a pudgy hand. "You earn what you get. And when it comes to that, I probably should keep my mouth shut. After all, I don't care if he never proposes," he said, only half-joking. "Once you're married and not working anymore, I will miss you." He patted her cheek again and turned away. "Now I go home. Don't forget to turn the radiators to half before you go. I don't need to keep the boiler running all night to keep the clothes warm."

Sarah looked up, speechless with confusion. She wanted to ask Sol why he thought she wouldn't work once she was married, but his massive back was to her and he was already squeezing himself through the doorway leading back into the main shopping floor. She put the entire conversation out of her mind and concentrated on finishing the alterations on Mrs. Schwartz's blouse.

By seven o'clock Sarah was done. She turned down the radiators, as Sol had asked, and made sure everything was ready for the next day's work, clothing due tomorrow clearly marked, the wall of spools of thread, the drawers of needles, thimbles, pins, measuring tapes, all neatly organized. She was ready to go home, but, as often happened when she was alone in the shop after hours, found that she didn't want to leave. She loved the quiet that descended after everyone had gone, the unfamiliar absence of human energy vibrating all around her. Instead of packing up her bag and putting on her coat, she sat at her table and breathed in the overwarmed air, smelling of new cloth and old tea. She sank into the silence, feeling her mind go still, and, like a bear gorging on berries in preparation for a long winter's trance, tried to suck all available joy from a fleeting moment of pure, calm privacy. A moment was all she would have, for it was at times like these, when the universe caught her safely alone, that she was besieged by thoughts of someone she would never see again and could never talk about. David, the loved, reviled, secret obsession of her life.

She reached into her bag and pulled out a bundle of papers and folded dollar bills secured with string. Hidden inside was a yellowing letter from the War Department informing her that David Warshinsky had been returned to New York Harbor in February of 1919, but no further information as to his whereabouts was available. And inside that was the one photo of him that she possessed, rescued from Anna's shoe box of family mementos before Ben had found and destroyed all traces of David's existence. Sarah laid the photograph on her table, in the bright circle of light cast by her small lamp, and smoothed it carefully as she had done a thousand times before. She stared at his face, vibrant with life even in the utter stillness of the black-and-white image. His resemblance to herself and to Anna was so obvious that it had taken Sarah years of scrutiny to see the subtle ways in which he also looked like Viktor and to realize how handsome her father must have been when he was young. Her eyes moved over David's features as though the intensity of her searching might explain how he could have left them. How he could have knowingly condemned her, at her fragile age, to the inevitable trauma of a sweatshop boss's unrelenting torture.

Her time at Pankin's shop had left its mark. Even after four years at Leyrowitz's, she awoke every morning at an ungodly hour with her heart in her throat, for one sleepy second dreading the day, hungering for the comfort of Anna's love and cursing David for his unforgivable selfishness. He had brought such pain and loss to his family and he didn't even care. He didn't care that Sarah had had to rely on strangers for her future, on Reuben and Uncle Sol, people who weren't her blood but were kinder and more generous to her than her own brother. That she and Papa had had to live in a tiny corner of a room shared with Ben and Naomi's ever-increasing brood, in a stultifying atmosphere of such intense old-world tradition that sometimes Sarah forgot that she lived in America and it was the 1920s. David didn't care that he'd stolen her childhood and his mother's life and his father's only happiness, heartless thief that he was, as glibly as he used to steal pickles from Eckstein's barrel.

Sarah had spent years nursing her bitterness, unable to share a single thought or mention of David with anyone, never having the opportunity to have someone explain to her why, if she hated him so much, she still missed him so terribly. Why she had kept this photo and why she cried when she looked at it. When his features began finally to blur beneath her watery gaze, Sarah replaced the re-wrapped bundle in her purse, her purse in her bag, gathered up her coat, scarf, and gloves, and left the shop.

She walked home in the chill January darkness, working her way slowly through the crowded streets. She was reminded of him by every impatient dark-haired boy who rushed by her, illuminated for an instant by a street lamp, curious eyes snatching at her face.

She walked down Orchard Street and saw that the windows of Rothstein's Dry Goods were dark. A block farther on, Ben was waiting, undoubtedly overhungry and cranky, for her to come home for dinner. Naomi and the children would already have eaten, and while Sarah and Ben had their meal, respectfully served to them by Rose and little Nell, Naomi, four months pregnant with their fifth child, would put Chaim and Wolf to bed. Sarah climbed the three flights to the apartment, and with each step she attempted to quell her discontent and try to remember that her family awaited her, the family whom she loved and who loved her and who would never abandon her. There would be no talk of David, ever, in this house. Sarah and Ben would sit in comfortable silence, a devoted brother and sister who barely knew each other. Ben would eat and wonder whether to put the towels on sale in March or in April. Sarah would eat and wonder how it was possible that the years would pass, that she would marry and have children and grow old and die, all without ever seeing David again.

As she reached the landing, Sarah heard the clamorous sounds of the six humans, four of them under the age of nine, with whom she shared four hundred square feet of living space broken up into two tiny bedrooms, a living room, and a kitchen with tub. She swore to herself that she and Reuben would be married by June, even if she had to be the one to get down on her knees and propose.

16

Joseph and Evelyn's wedding present to Jed and Abigail had been their new home, a converted carriage house in the hidden-away alley of Washington Mews, one of an elegant row of similar houses that, in the nineteenth century, had been stables for the wealthy residents of 8th Street and Washington Square. It felt a world removed from the fast-changing city, cozily tucked between Fifth Avenue and University Place, with Washington Square just around the corner. The couple had been offered an apartment uptown, but Abby had wanted a house and Jed had wanted to live near David. They had furnished and decorated it together. They had eschewed the cool, modern Art Deco furniture with which Cissy had filled David's brownstone in favor of a graceful and refined look reminiscent of the Queen Anne style of a century past. The furniture was appropriately scaled to the small, low-ceilinged rooms and upholstered in warming velvet, chintz, and needlepoint. On the topmost floor, in a small room with north-facing windows, Abby, secretly consulting with Philip, had created a studio for Jed as a wedding gift to her beloved. She never complained about the hours he spent there, nor about anything else.

Jed was grateful that she hadn't complained about celebrating her birthday at home with David, Cissy, and Lucy, although certainly she would have preferred to have been alone with him. A romantic dinner, hours of dancing entwined in each other's arms, a slow carriage ride through the park bundled together in blankets against the early-spring chill—Jed thought he might have managed all that. It was what she would be hoping for when they shut their door to the world after such an evening, and were alone, that he couldn't contemplate.

There had been no transformation in him after the minister had pronounced them man and wife. He had stood on the lawn at Hidden Cove waiting for the thunderbolt of sexual longing to strike him. He had so thoroughly convinced himself that those words of godly permission, *You may now kiss your bride,* were the magic incantation that would release him from his desireless spell that when the sight of Abby's lips, moist and slightly parted, eager to receive his first husbandly kiss, failed to move him in the slightest he had fallen into such a state of shock and agitation that even now, nearly eight months after the wedding, he could not remember a single thing about the party that had followed. The next clear memory he had was of waking up the next morning in the cabana by the water's edge, fully dressed, under a pile of dewy beach towels, aware that he had not spent the night with his new wife.

The day had been resplendent up until that fatal moment. He had had the wedding he wanted, expansive but refined and, best of all, shared with his closest friend. Jed couldn't imagine anything more perfect than standing next to David on their mutual wedding day, acting as each other's best men, side by side in front of the minister, magnificent in their tuxedos, their brides-to-be on either side of them, two angels in white satin and lace. Jed had defied Sally's wishes for a lavish church wedding—as Joseph had predicted, Sally had abandoned her devotion to Christian Science the moment Jed came home—a wedding that would be the talk of the '24 season. And he had insisted on sharing his wedding day with David and Cissy although he knew perfectly well how his mother felt about David. She had protested vehemently against Jed's day being sullied by what she considered the blasphemous union of a mongrel Jew passing himself off as an Anglo-Saxon to a girl barely better than a flapper. But Jed had stood firm, and Sally conceded the battle she couldn't win. She had joined Evelyn in planning the weddings, and the double ceremony on the baronial grounds of the Gateses' Oyster Bay estate was nothing short of glorious, a rite of royalty witnessed by four hundred guests and a brilliant September sky.

Those wondrous hours before the ceremony, when everything he hoped for hung before him like a rosy red apple from Hidden Cove's orchard, were revealed in a single second as a terrible lie perpetrated on him by a cruel cosmos. Still, Jed did his duty. He bent down and kissed his wife in feeble imitation of David's possessive passion as he kissed Cissy. Right up to that last second, Jed continued to hope, but when something repulsive passed from Abby's mouth to his, Jed knew that God had let him down. He would be a failure as a husband. And for eight strained months he had been. He couldn't tell Abby that he simply didn't desire her, that would be too hurtful, so he told her he was frightened, which was true, and then he lied and said that he'd had bad experiences when he was younger. He asked her to be patient with him, and she had been, never pushing him, never asking directly for what he knew she wanted. She didn't have to: he saw her yearning for him in her eyes every time she looked at him; he felt it in her touch every time she laid a caressing hand on his arm.

There was, therefore, no romantic birthday night for Abby; Jed couldn't risk the outcome. Instead, he had bought her a ruby pendant from Tiffany and invited David, Cissy, and Lucy for dinner and an evening of innocent fun, playing fast, noisy games of mah-jongg and howling over the foolishness of a Ouija board.

"Lucy, don't hide by the window; come help me beat these three awful cheaters." Abby laughed as she discarded a mah-jongg tile and beckoned for Lucy to sit beside her.

Lucy reluctantly turned away from the view out the parlor window: the cobblestoned alley lit by early-spring moonlight, rows of coolly glowing trees, their limbs fuzzy with the beginnings of buds, the shapes of their trunks and twining branches still visible. The clacking of the ivory tiles and the hum of the couples' conversation and laughter soothed Lucy's jagged feeling of being with them yet of necessity apart. It was difficult for her to be in David's presence. She knew full well what would have happened a year ago if she hadn't pushed him away. Believing she had done the right thing didn't make it easier to be near him, to see him with his wife, to feel the guarded distance he kept from her beneath the seemingly open charm of his friendship. Believing she had done the right thing didn't make her heart beat any more normally when she saw him. Nonetheless, she never turned down an opportunity to be with the four of them. Painful though it was, she would rather see him than not. She had gradually taught herself how to be near him without falling to pieces. The main defense in her arsenal of self-protection was hostility. Just enough to keep him at bay, not enough to make him an enemy. They were good friends now. Friends who argued and sparred constantly, but friends nonetheless.

"Come on, Lucy; Abby needs your help. She hasn't won a game yet!" Jed gave his wife a peck on the cheek.

"No, I haven't, and it's not fair. You could at least have let me win one hand!" Abby pretended to pout. "Lucy, come. You've been so quiet all evening. We hardly ever see you anymore. Aren't you almost finished with the nursing program?"

Lucy turned from the window. "Yes, by June."

David unceremoniously dumped all the tiles on his rack into the middle of the table. "I'm through with this." He looked up at Lucy. "What are you going to do after you graduate?"

"I've applied to the Clinical Research Bureau, Margaret Sanger's birth control center. There are nearly a dozen nurses working there and I'm hoping to get a position by the fall. But in the meantime, I'm working two evenings and every other Sunday at the Henry Street Settlement House on the Lower East Side."

Jed looked over at David, who had gone completely still. As a child David had spent memorable Saturday afternoons at Henry Street, teaching himself to play the piano or lying on the building's quiet back porch reading from their vast library, learning a thousand things he never learned at school or at home. Their fleet of visiting nurses had tended to every member of his family at one time or another. David stared at Lucy with unnerving fixedness until a flush painted her throat pale red.

"Oooh, how brave to go into that neighborhood at night! I don't think I've ever been below Houston Street!" Cissy said blithely. "What do you do there? What is a settlement house, anyway?" she asked as she and Abby, both oblivious to the charged interplay among the other three, packed the tiles and racks into their leather case.

"I provide nursing care to walk-in patients, or make house calls. Mostly to mothers and children. Sometimes, if I'm not needed for that, I teach English or drawing. The settlement house offers a tremendous array of services to the community. It's a wonderful place. And there's nothing wrong with the neighborhood. It's just poor, Cissy, not dangerous." Lucy couldn't suppress the judgmental edge in her voice.

"Well, I wouldn't be comfortable there, I can tell you that!" Cissy proclaimed.

David pushed his chair away from the game table.

"You stay right where you are, David," Abby cried. "We're going to play with the Ouija board. That way we can all join in."

"Lucy can take my place. That thing is too silly for me." David made to get up.

"Oh no! You have to play. It's good for you to be frivolous every so often. It's my birthday; I order you to ask the first question!"

David smiled and sat back down. "All right, birthday girl. Let's see; what do I want to know?" He tried to come up with something entertaining, but all he could think of was Lucy with her quick brain and sharp eyes wandering through the secret storehouse of his past. He said the first idiotic thing that came into his head. "Okay. Ouija, will the store's new beauty salon be a success?"

The other four shrieked with laughter. "God, David!

Could you not be so serious for once?" Cissy tried to shove him off his chair. "Why don't you ask something like . . . How many children am I going to have, O great Ouija?" Her tone was fanciful, but she gave him a meaningful stare.

David didn't look at her. "You can ask that if you want, Cissy. I've already asked my question. Let's see whether I'm going to lose my shirt or not."

The sudden tension between them momentarily over-rode the gay atmosphere of the party. Lucy immediately jumped in and pulled everyone's attention back to the lighthearted game. "Is David going to lose his shirt?" She put her hands on the moving indicator and Abby covered them with her own, mockingly fighting Lucy for control. In a second, Cissy had recovered her good mood and she lunged in and the three of them giggled wildly as they tried to steer the planchette around the board.

Jed leaned back in his chair. The women had things firmly in hand. "The spring line of the private label looked good, looks like it sold well. Are you happy with it?"

David watched the zigzagging indicator career from letter to letter under the girls' battling hands. He moved his chair away from the table, closer to Jed. "Not entirely. I have very good suppliers, and the men's line is where I want it, but I can't find anyone to design the kind of women's clothing I have in mind."

"I thought RW Fashions had a good designer."

"Yes, I've seen her work. She is good, I took some designs, but nothing was quite what I'm picturing. I can't seem to describe what I want well enough," David said in frustration. "Abby, ask that useless board where I can find a great dress designer."

Abby laughed without looking up from the game. "I don't have to. Remember the dress I wore to Christmas dinner, the midnight-blue crepe de chine with the ivory chiffon collar that you admired so much? And the beaded violet tulle I wore last week to the theater?"

"Abby!" Jed sat up straight.

"Oh, Jed. Don't be silly. The girls already know. Jed designed them for me." She beamed at him, her smile full of pride. "He can sketch out the most fabulous things just like that. He knows all about materials and styles. He's so creative!"

David cocked his head and gave Jed an amused look. "Stop glaring; your wife is paying you a lovely compliment. And you told me you weren't sketching costumes anymore, you rotten liar. All right, that's it. I want to see what you've got."

"David, I'm not going to design dresses for you. Forget it. That's the last thing I need to be doing with my time."

"Just let me bring some pictures and ideas over, see what you think, see what you've already got. No expectations. Okay? One night next week? Please, I need some help."

Jed smiled. "Well, if you put it that way. Wednesday would be good. Maybe I can at least help you articulate what you're looking for."

"Thanks. I have considerably more confidence in you than I do in the Ouija," David said sarcastically.

Jed laughed. "I don't think you need to worry about the salon. It was smart to push to be ready for Easter. You should have a spectacular opening. The place looks beautiful. It must have cost a fortune. Where did you get the money for your share, if you don't mind my asking?"

"I sold my landholdings in Florida. It's a circus down there. Miami, Boca Raton, Coral Gables. People are going crazy for a scrap of land and speculators are buying and selling the same piece three times in one day. In four years my investment increased more than seven times over. You should have put money in when I did."

"Maybe I will now."

"No, no. Don't, not now. When Cissy and I were down there this winter I got the feeling things were going out of control. I'll find something else to recommend for you."

"I *loved* it there!" Cissy gushed. "We stayed at the Biltmore, in Coral Gables. It was like being back in Europe! And Miami Beach is huge and white and the water is so warm. Oooh, it was paradise!" She got up and came to sit on David's lap. "Let's go back, sweetie."

"Maybe next winter, if it's still there. We'll see." David hadn't enjoyed Florida. It was too hot for him, even in the middle of winter. It was seething with crass and greedy people. He had particularly disliked Miami Beach. It reminded him too much of the streets of his childhood. Flocks of black-clad Jewish men, sweating profusely beneath their unkempt beards and heavy, head-to-toe garb, were everywhere. One day on the boardwalk, David passed a man who bore an uncanny resemblance to his father, beard and waist both a bit thicker perhaps. He was so unnerved that he rudely hustled Cissy off the beach and insisted on going back to their hotel, where no Jews were to be seen. "So, what was the answer? Am I going to go broke?"

"No, Ouija says the salon will be a huge success," Abby pronounced.

"Thank you. That's all I care about. If you morons want to continue playing with that thing, I'm going to read." David lifted Cissy off his lap and walked over to the coffee table. He picked up the recent April edition of Henry Mencken's *American Mercury* magazine and started thumbing through it.

"You're a spoilsport," Cissy pouted. "I can't believe you'd rather read that deadly thing than have fun with your friends."

David ignored her. He spoke without raising his eyes. "Did anyone see the article a few months ago about the resurgence of the Klan? It was frightening."

"Yes," Jed said. "It's incredible to me that they have so many followers here, in the New York area. I can't conceive of it."

"They're preying on the fears of uneducated people who blame Jews and immigrants for all the country's woes," Lucy responded. "People have to have someone to hate."

"Well, that's all rubbish. What is there to complain about? The country is in fine shape. And you may not want a foreigner or a Jew for your friend, but unless he's a criminal or something, who cares what he is? And I mean really, how much damage can a bunch of stupid men in white hoods do, anyway? You all take everything too seriously." Cissy waved her hand, dismissing the entire subject. "It's time for birthday cake!"

David dropped the magazine onto the sofa and walked out of the room.

Lucy was the only one who saw the rigidity of his retreating back, the tightness in his jaw, the coldness in his hot eyes. Cissy certainly could be irritatingly brainless, and David usually found her lack of intellect either adorable or ignorable. But he could not ignore the consequences of being married to a woman who didn't know who he was, who didn't know that in glibly talking about being uncomfortable on the streets of the Lower East Side, of Jews not being worthy of her friendship, she was demeaning and insulting her own husband.

Lucy left the others to put away the games and set the parlor table for dessert. She followed David into the kitchen. His back was to her; he was pouring himself a huge glass of Scotch. "David."

He turned around. "Lucy, leave me alone."

They both knew that was something she had never been able to do. "David. How can you be married to someone who doesn't know who you are?"

"She knows who I am. *This* is who I am. This is who she loves. There is nothing more to know." David's face was flushed and the muscles in his jaw bunched under his skin.

"Then why are you in here drinking half a bottle of Chivas Regal?"

"I'm thirsty." They stared at each other. "You think because you know my real name you know anything more about me than Cissy does?"

"I know more than your name, you idiot. I know where you come from, who your parents were, that you have a sister and a brother you never see. I know their names. I know *why* you are who you are now. All Cissy knows is this, this creature you've made yourself into. It's a sham. It's not fair to her. It's not fair to you, David. What do you tell her when she asks you questions about yourself, about your life before the war?"

"I had no life before the war. That's what I tell her and she doesn't ask questions." He began moving toward the door. "Listen to me carefully." He spoke slowly, deliberately. "This is who I am. Why can't you ever just accept that? What do you think you're going to find down at Henry Street?" He turned from the door and took a step in her direction. "What the hell do you want from me?"

The enormity of the answer to his question rendered Lucy mute. She squeezed her eyes shut so she wouldn't have to look at him. She felt him grab her arm, felt a splash of cold liquid hit her foot as his drink sloshed over the rim of the too-full glass he clutched in his free hand.

"Look at me, Lucy."

With a tremendous effort of will, she opened her eyes. For a horrible, rapturous moment, she thought he was going to back her against the wall and kiss her. Her knees went weak and her arm burned where he held her.

He leaned his face close to hers. "Don't you ever say a word to her about me, do you understand?"

She shook her head. "I would never. David. You have to know I would never do that."

"Lucy, David, it's time for cake! Where are you?" Jed called out from across the hallway.

David nodded, let out his breath, and released her arm. "All right. Let's go help Abby blow out her candles."

Lucy had been tucked into a taxi; David and Cissy were waving good-bye from up the street. Abby closed the door and turned back to Jed, hoping that the one birthday gift she wanted might still be hers. Before she had a chance to advance one step in his direction, he smiled at her a little too brightly and reached over to kiss her cheek.

"Happy birthday, Abby. That was a wonderful evening, wasn't it? You must be tired. I'm going to go up to the studio for a little while. You don't mind, do you?"

Abby did mind and she wanted to scream it out at the top of her lungs. She looked into Jed's frightened face and remembered what Sally had told her. She swallowed and smiled at him. "No, my love, I don't mind. I can't wait to see what you've been spending so much time on." She gave him one more chance. "Should I wait up for you?"

"Oh, I don't think so. I'll be a while. You go to sleep. I'll see you in the morning and we'll finish cleaning up then."

He left her standing in the hallway and climbed the stairs. He had a half-finished landscape on his easel, but he wouldn't paint tonight. He had done quite a bit of painting and sketching in the past months, but he spent many hours in his studio doing other things: reading, sleeping, listening to music, hiding. Tonight he'd have to stay a long time. But he'd make sure he was in their bed when Abby woke up so he could kiss her good morning and they could begin the new day properly.

Cissy put her arm through David's as they walked the two blocks home. With a sense of dread, David felt a fiery, stabbing headache begin behind his eyes. The headaches came to him every few months, a debilitating reminder of how close he had come to death on a French battlefield. He never got used to the pain. The first piercing thrust stopped him cold as they turned onto Fifth Avenue. His hand shot up to his face and he grabbed at his forehead.

"David, what is it? Are you having one of your headaches?" Cissy peered up at him from beneath the low helmet of her cloche hat. She put a gentle hand on the back of his neck. "I know what will make it feel better," she said coyly.

David didn't know if it was the sexual release that was responsible—the changes in heart rate, blood pressure, the complex physical cascade that accompanied orgasm—or if it was simply that the pleasure temporarily obliterated the pain, but sex always gave him at least a small amount of relief. He leaned into Cissy's body and kissed her throat. "Yes, you do."

She wound her arms around his neck and held him. "David," she whispered, "let's not use a rubber tonight, please. It's a good time of the month. I want to have a baby with you."

A plume of flame flared in David's head. "No. I told you, I'm not ready. Stop asking me. We have plenty of time; why are you in such a rush? Let's just enjoy ourselves."

Cissy sagged against him, but he was unmoved. He didn't want a child. He didn't want to be a father. He didn't want his wife swollen and graceless and unavailable to him. He wanted his marriage the way it was, fun and easy, a ready source of relaxation to balance the increasing complexities of his career. He wouldn't give in to her disappointment, but he could give her a little hope. "Maybe soon. I'll let you know."

17

Philip took one last look around the studio. Everything was in order, clean, in its place, ready for tomorrow's work. Nothing more to do. Nothing else that needed his attention so that he could put off just a little longer going home to his silent and empty house. Brook was gone since September, sent off to Ridgewood Academy. Philip never realized how sweet and comforting Brook's presence had been until it was no longer there. It wasn't until several months had passed that Philip realized he missed Brook himself, not just the fact of having one last child in the house, one remaining talking, breathing entity to buffer his and Sally's stony existence. Brook had always been so completely overshadowed by his older siblings that the pleasure to be taken from his quiet, endearing nature had gone quite unrecognized by Philip. Sally, clearly, did not find Brook endearing and would not be talked out of her decision to shunt him off to prep school. It was painfully obvious that the boy didn't want to go, but when Sally demanded to know what Philip suggest they do with Brook, failing another year at Browning as he was, he'd had no answer for her.

Sally was out for the evening, keeping Abigail company while Jed had his monthly night with David. Philip hated to go home when she was absent. That long-ago moment after Libby's funeral, when he had dared to hope that their shared sorrow and their shared joy at Jed's return might forge a new relationship between them, had come to seem like the pipe dream of a deluded opium addict. She no longer even bothered to rouse herself to anger at him. Her life was wholly devoted to Jed and now to her hopes of a grandchild. She had no need of faith, of God, of her other children, or of a husband anymore, beyond giving her her identity in the world: Mrs. Philip Gates, wife of the famous portraitist. It had been nearly two years since she had come to his room at night and crawled into his bed.

Philip pulled on his stretched-out cashmere sweater, noting with detached interest that an enterprising moth had eaten a neat hole in the soft brown sleeve. He switched off the lights and opened the studio door. He turned back a moment to admire the early-evening May sunshine washing into his cherished space through the high windows. He loved these long spring days, when the light was every hour a new and exquisite element in his intensely visual world. Finally, he stepped into the hallway and began pulling the door closed behind him, preparing himself for a beautiful walk home, an unsatisfying reheated dinner, and a solitary evening. Before the door clicked shut, he heard the telephone in the studio ring. He debated whether to answer it and then, hopeful that it might be Lucy, he hurried back inside.

"Philip? . . . Hello. It's Dorothy Woolbright. I'm hope I'm not disturbing you."

Philip had finished the restoration of her portrait the previous summer, and since then they had kept in touch from time to time. Seeing Dorothy again after five years had reminded Philip of how much he had enjoyed painting her portrait, more, perhaps, than any other he had ever done. She was a complex woman, an exhilarating subject to capture on his canvas, elegant and poised yet possessed of an unmistakable mischievous streak, a playful zest for life. The hours spent while she posed for him, chatting about everything under the sun, had always passed too quickly. The resumption of their friendship had been a surprising delight for them both, although it had turned bittersweet in recent months. Her husband, Edgar, was dying of cancer, a once-vigorous man slowly wasting away before her anguished eyes. Since he had been stricken, Dorothy had occasionally turned to Philip for friendly comfort, and it pleased him that he could be of use to her.

"No, Dorothy, not at all. I was just preparing to leave for the day. How is Edgar?"

"Not good. He is suffering terrible pain. I never thought I could think or say such a thing, but I hope he goes quickly."

"I'm so sorry."

"Thank you, Philip. I know you mean it when you say that."

"Dorothy. You sound so sad. Is there anything I can do for you? It happens that I am on my own tonight. Would you let me take your mind off your sorrows for a few hours? We could go to the Plaza, have a quiet dinner, talk. I would welcome your company."

There was a moment of silence before she answered. "Yes, Philip, I would love that. There's nothing I can do for Edgar. Nurses are with him around the clock now. I, too, would greatly welcome your company tonight. I'll meet you at the Palm Court at, say, eight?"

And just like that, the long evening ahead didn't seem so bleak.

18

Zoe and Lorena were making an outing of it. Two leisurely days to get there, an evening appointment with the medium, two leisurely days to get back. It was a long trip, almost all the way to Buffalo, but it was a hot week in August and the two women were glad to be out of the stifling city. It had been Zoe's idea to visit Lily Dale. Since the late 1800s, the small town on the shores of Cassadaga Lake had been a Spiritualists' retreat and the permanent residence of a host of mediums, all proclaimed legitimate and competent by the governing Lily Dale Assembly. For the past six months, Zoe had felt compelled to make a trip here, to consult with a real medium, to find out why, suddenly, after so many years of comfort, Libby's spirit seemed to be deserting her.

Zoe had long since drifted away from Christian Science. Unlike Sally, who had let go of her devotion to Mary Baker Eddy's teachings as easily as a distracted child letting go of a deflating balloon, releasing her fledging friendship with Zoe at the same time, Zoe had struggled to accept the religion's tenets. She wanted to believe in a Divinity whose loving power could transform all harsh reality into something bearable, into the benign nothingness of eternal spirit. But no matter how many prayer meetings she attended, how many times she read the books, how often she sat with Lorena in prayer over an ill parishioner, Zoe's rational mind could never accept that the cruel world she inhabited was anything but deadly real. After several years of trying to bend her perception of reality to fit Eddy's philosophy, to reject the pain of her losses as phantoms of her spiritual weakness, Zoe finally resigned herself to the truth: that her parents' love was fatally tainted by their disappointment in her, her husband was incapable of feeling love for her, her only child was dead, and she was in agony every minute of her life. That she felt Libby's presence in the very air she dragged herself through was surely a blessing but did not render her grief any less profound. She didn't think she could stand to lose her daughter a second time. She needed to contact Libby; she needed to know why after seven years of staying close she was moving away.

"Ah, we're almost there!" Zoe swiveled her head to take in the arrow-shaped sign on the side of the road pointing the way to *Lily Dale, N.Y., The Largest Spiritualist Camp in the World.* "I'm so glad you've come with me." Despite having abandoned the religion, Zoe had kept the one precious thing it had given her: Lorena's friendship.

Lorena reached over and patted Zoe's hand, clutched on the Packard's steering wheel. "My dear, wherever your spiritual search takes you, I am willing to go. Christian Science isn't for everyone; I appreciate that. Despite your awareness of Libby's spirit near you, you are simply too attached to this world, Zoe. You tried your hardest, I know, but it wasn't right for you."

"Neither I think was my infatuation with Emile Coué and his knots and mantras."

"Don't belittle yourself. It probably did you good. Coué is just trying to get people to think more positively about themselves and their lives. I approve of that, as far as it goes. It's when we demand profound transformational power from what is merely a vehicle that we run into trouble. No matter what you choose to help cope with life's struggles, it's still *you* that has to do the coping at the end of the day."

Zoe turned briefly toward Lorena with a questioning look. "But you believe in the transformational power of your faith."

"Yes. But it is my relationship to that faith, my constant work at it, that creates the good that comes of it. It does not simply devolve on me without my active participation."

They drove in silence for a few moments. "You know, Lorena, I think the reason why I can't accept any vehicle, as you put it, for myself is because in my heart I consider it a sign of weakness that I should need anything at all." She reached out and put a hand on Lorena's arm. "I speak only for myself; please don't take offense."

Lorena smiled. "I could never, not from you. It's not surprising that you should feel that way, from what you've told me of your family. They judge weakness very harshly, and what they perceive to be weakness encompasses what I consider to be natural human behavior, such as admitting to neediness, to mistakes, asking for help."

Zoe's breath caught in her throat. "I can never do any of those things, not even with my mother." Angry tears sprang to her eyes. "She and my father expect everyone to take care of themselves. They don't want to see any mess, any pain. It would disturb their perfect world."

"How lonely for you, Zoe. How unfair." Lorena brushed the back of her fingers lovingly across Zoe's cheek. "But you know, my dear, there has been a change in you in the last couple of years. Like the gradual accumulation of clouds before a storm, I see you gathering your strength."

Zoe's eyes widened. "I don't feel strong."

"Don't you, not even a little? Well, I could of course be wrong." Her tone made it clear that she was not.

Zoe kept her eyes fixed on the road as they pulled into Lily Dale, its narrow streets lined with storybook gingerbread Victorian houses. She wondered if Lorena could be right. Perhaps it was newfound strength and not, as she'd assumed, habitual, clawing need that was slowly deadening her to Monty's loveless attentions, that made her crave David's uncomplicated, freely given affection. Even now he was married, David insisted on taking her to lunch every month as had long been their practice. There was nothing romantic between them; there never could be; the age difference was too great, and she knew, even if he didn't, to whom his heart belonged. But that didn't prevent the deep affection she felt for him, for the wild and passionate chaos that ruled him, from irrevocably altering her dreams.

"On the right, Zoe! Pay attention. The Grand Hotel. Isn't that where we're staying?"

In a hushed, darkened room, Zoe sweated from the summer heat and her own fear. The medium was a cheerful, chubby woman named Ann. There was no strange paraphernalia, no table from below which eerie knocking noises would come. Just the two of them, sitting across from each other in an ordinary living room, one nervous, one calm, both ready to embark on an unknowable journey.

"Zoe. Tell me a little about your daughter, with whom you wish to speak." Ann's voice was as gentle as the warm breeze that stirred the curtains at the far end of the room.

Zoe's hands were in her lap, clutching at a damp handkerchief. "I don't know what to say. She was my only child and she died when she was just nine years old, of the influenza. She was such a good girl. She . . . she . . ." Zoe's shoulders shook and tears fell onto her hands.

"She what? What, Zoe? Tell me. It's all right." Ann leaned over and laid a soft, warm hand over Zoe's clenched fingers.

"She knew I needed her and she stayed with me. But now, weeks go by and I can't feel her. I don't know what I'll do if she leaves me!"

"It's very unusual for a spirit to stay connected to this world for so long. She must have loved you very much."

Zoe grabbed at Ann's comforting hand and began to sob.

"Let's find out what Libby wants, Zoe, shall we?" Leaving her hand locked with Zoe's, Ann closed her eyes and let her head drop until her chin rested on her ample chest.

Zoe stopped crying, stopped breathing. All was silent except for the sound of Ann's breath, slow and deep, as she moved into trance, searching the spirit world for the essence of Elizabeth, a loving little girl who had hovered in the realm of the living too long.

"Libby says it is time for her soul to finish its journey." Eyes closed, head cocked slightly to one side as though listening. *"I need to go now, Mommy. If I wait any longer I will never find my way home."* Ann's voice was unrecognizable, a gossamer, ethereal filament spun from the eddies of the spirit world with which she was now linked. *"I know it's time because you have released me. You don't need me anymore. I've been so lonely since you turned toward life, leaving me here caught between life and death. I want to go, Mommy. Let me go."*

In a moment, Ann's eyes opened and with several quick blinks she was back in her living room, staring into Zoe's terrified face. She smiled. "Don't be frightened, Zoe. Your daughter's spirit can only tell the truth. She isn't leaving you; you have been letting her go. You are ready. Oh, how wonderful!" Ann's eyes were moist and shining with joy.

Lorena drove the entire way back to Manhattan. Zoe was lost inside her own head. She tried to find Libby there, but the girl was gone, disappeared without a trace. The first day of the drive home passed without a single word spoken between Zoe and Lorena, Zoe curled into the passenger seat, a punctured ball leaking endless tears. By the second morning, she was cried dry, her brain washed clean as though after a thunderstorm. She was able to think about what Libby had said, that she didn't need her anymore, that she had turned toward life. Was that the change Lorena saw in her? Was that what lay at the heart of what she no longer felt for Monty, of what she imagined when she was with David? A pure and simple desire to live.

"Lorena."

Lorena started, nearly swerved off the road. "I thought you were asleep. My dear, are you back with us? How are you feeling?"

"I'm wonderful. What a beautiful day it is!" Zoe leaned her head out the car window. Heavy August air swept across the delicate skin of her face and neck, rushed into her eyes and ears. The hot wind grabbed at her hair and she reached up, pulled out all the pins, and shook free the long, dark waves, letting them billow out behind her. She closed her eyes and turned her face toward the sun, let out an ecstatic sigh as her nose and mouth filled with the delicious, living perfume of sun-baked earth, mown grass, flowers going to seed, a hint of moisture moving up from the south, heat rising off the roadway, gasoline fumes. Drawing back inside, she turned and kissed Lorena on the cheek. "I'm wonderful. Libby has gone where she needs to go and it's time for me to do the same. It's over, finally. I know what I must do. Lorena, I'm going to leave Monty."

19

They were on their way to Connecticut to visit Brook, Jed driving his grandfather's expensive Duesenberg, Abby next to him with maps spread out across her knees, David and Lucy like bookends at the backseat windows, Cissy squirming uncomfortably between them. Lucy thought she and Jed would go for the day—she couldn't bring to mind a time when they had spent a day alone together, all three children, with no parents or friends wedged in among them—but Jed immediately organized a weekend for the inseparable five of them. They would see Brook and then drive to Newport, stay at a Victorian mansion along Cliff Walk overlooking the ocean. A couple of days to swim if the water was still warm enough, play a round of golf, relax, forget about the bustle of the city, school, and work. A last burst of vacation before another winter settled over them. Jed suggested to Lucy that she bring someone. She evaded any discussion of who he thought that might conceivably be by reminding him that even five would be a tight squeeze in the Duesenberg. Everyone knew she had no boyfriend. No one knew that she was sleeping with someone she'd met at the Henry Street Settlement House, a darkly attractive young teacher, affectionate and energetic and happy to satisfy her sexual needs whenever she asked. Her interest in him rose with the tide of her libido and disappeared on the receding waves of her orgasms. She liked him well enough, but it never occurred to her to bring him anywhere except to bed.

"Aren't we there yet?" Cissy whined.

David shot her a look of annoyance. "Almost." He grabbed her roughly around the waist, dragged her over his knees, and deposited her by the window. "See all the pretty colors on the trees?" He shifted closer to Lucy. "God, she has the attention span of a five-year-old."

Lucy pressed herself against the car door. She had to bite her tongue to not say something cutting about Cissy's childishness or David's ill temper. Lucy wished she could dislike Cissy, but it was hard to dislike an animated, sweet-natured little girl, hard to wish her ill, pray for the failure of her marriage, be happy when the husband she adored was mean to her.

Cissy drew in a hurt breath. "I heard that, David! I can't help it; I'm bored. What are we going to do when we get there?"

"We're going to see Brook, why do you think we're here?"

"You promised I could do something fun! Brook won't care if he doesn't see me before dinner and I don't want to spend the whole afternoon at his stupid, dull school."

"Fine. Go shopping. The school is right outside the town

we're staying in tonight. It's a famous, historic place. I'm sure you can find something to spend my money on."

"Well, that sounds more like it. Abs, what do you say?" Mollified, Cissy giggled and dug around in David's jacket pocket, ferreting for his wallet.

"Yes, let's. You all should have time alone with Brook. Jed, darling, why don't you drop us in town and we'll meet at the inn later?"

"Can do. So, little sister, I'm honored that you agreed to take time away from your nursing pursuits to spend the weekend with us. I feel as if we haven't seen you all summer." Jed directed his words to the backseat but, ever cautious, kept his eyes on the road.

"Oh, get that petulant tone out of your voice and don't make me feel bad, Jed. I'm working two jobs now. Days at the Clinical Research Bureau and three evenings at Henry Street. I have very little free time. Be happy I'm here now."

"Why are you still living way uptown, Lucy? Isn't the Bureau down on Fifth Avenue, near Eighteenth Street? You must spend a ridiculous amount of time traveling. Why don't you move back home, or somewhere near all of us?" Abby twisted around in her seat.

The hours Lucy wasted on the subway each day were, indeed, ridiculous. But she had needed to stay where she was. She had needed to be able to sleep at night and wake in the morning as far from David as possible after days spent so close to his home and evenings spent so close to his soul, as close as she could get. She knew, however, that she couldn't continue much longer; she was exhausted all the time. "I still love my apartment, but you're right. I am going to move; I just have to figure out where."

Jed's eyes wandered briefly to the rearview mirror. "So what exactly do you do at the Sanger clinic? I've never been clear about that. What kind of nursing care do the women who visit there need?"

"I don't do the same kind of nursing as at the settlement house. That's why I love having both jobs. At the CRB, I help with contraception and birth control research and I advise women on all the latest birth control techniques. It's so important that they understand that they can choose when they want to have a baby and not be frightened that every time they have sex they might get pregnant. Do you have any idea how many illegal abortions are performed in this country every year? A million! A million! It's horrible. And at least fifty thousand of those women die." Lucy's voice rose with the passion of her outrage.

"I can't imagine why someone would not want a baby," Cissy said softly.

"Oh, honestly, Cissy! There are a thousand reasons why a woman might not want a baby and it's criminal that so many women end up in the position of having to go to some butcher who's paying the police to look the other way while he aborts women with a coat hanger because they don't have access to decent birth control! Obviously you both know what to do to protect yourselves. You're lucky that there was an epidemic of venereal disease before the war or selling condoms would probably still be illegal. Or are you using the diaphragm yet? I don't see either of you getting pregnant so fast."

Abby jerked around and began studying the map lying on her lap; Cissy turned her face to the window. The sudden silence in the car was stunning. Lucy looked about in confusion. "What did I say? You can't tell me you don't believe in birth control. Abby, you joined the American Birth Control League with me last year."

After a moment, Abby lifted her head. "Yes, of course I believe in birth control. We all do, I'm sure. We just weren't prepared for talk about death and coat hangers on a pleasant drive to Connecticut."

"I'm sorry. I didn't mean to upset anyone," Lucy stumbled. "Cissy, I'm sorry. I didn't mean to snap at you."

Cissy rewarded her apology with a bright smile. "That's all right, Lucy. We all know how dedicated you are to what you're doing and, really, I do think it's important. But," she said mischievously, "the *truly* important thing is, is there a cute doctor in that clinic of yours?"

Lucy laughed. "Only women doctors there. But there's a cute someone from Henry Street who I take home with me every once in a while." She tossed it out teasingly, leaving it unclear whether she was serious or just playing with them.

"Lucy! How madly modern of you!" Abby cried.

David slowly turned toward her. Lucy pivoted on the seat and stared at him unblinking, her mouth set in a defiant line.

"And are you using a condom or the diaphragm?" he said, his tone droll and his mouth curved slightly in mockery. He held her stare for what seemed an eternity and then abruptly let her go, lowered his eyes, and swung his head away.

Her heart was racing. She turned back to the window and looked out at the pretty colors on the trees. She needed no urging from David. Unlike Cissy, Lucy could appreciate autumn's poignant beauty all on her own.

Brook stood fidgeting outside his dormitory with the impatience of an inmate awaiting his first visiting day. He was already struggling, only two months into his second year at Ridgewood. He had squeaked by the previous year with marginally passing grades in everything but Literature, in which he'd received an A. He was rewarded for that by having Literature excised from his second-year curriculum, since Sally deemed it a useless and seditious subject that would not help him advance in the world of business. He was now well on the way to failing his economics and mathematics classes and was thoroughly miserable. When the Duesenberg pulled into the gravel driveway, he fairly lunged at the rear door and dragged Lucy out.

"Lucy!" he cried. "You're here!" He threw his arms around her and hugged her with all the exuberance of a little child, despite the fact that he now towered over her by half a head.

"Hey! Not happy to see me, too?" Jed stepped up, offered Brook his hand to shake.

Brook blushed. He pumped his brother's hand in a boy's imitation of what he took to be manly behavior. "I am very happy to see you, Jed. Thank you for coming."

"Brook." David stood a pace behind Jed and nodded politely in greeting.

Brook nodded back, his supercilious expression making it apparent that he wished David were not there.

"Come show us your room, sweetheart," Lucy said. "We've brought some presents for you. You'll open them, and then you can give us a tour, show us what's new since last year."

Brook shrugged as he led them inside. "There's nothing new." His voice dropped. "Lucy, can't you please ask Father to ask Mother to let me come home? I hate it here and I'm doing terribly and I'm never going to get into college. The two of you went; isn't that enough?"

Jed clapped Brook on the shoulder. "Don't whine, sport. You'll do fine here if you just apply yourself. Of course you're going to go to college. I mean, really, you don't want to disappoint Mother, do you?"

Brook's eyes grew huge and his posture came to attention. "No, of course I don't, Jed," he said vehemently. "You're right. I have to stop daydreaming and get to work. And I will. Thanks for the advice."

Lucy glared at Jed as she put her hand on Brook's bony back and rubbed between his shoulder blades. "Just try your best, sweetheart, and don't worry."

In his small, neat room on the second floor, Brook pulled Lucy onto the bed beside him while Jed lounged by the window and David took a chair at a scarred wooden desk. Brook opened his gifts—a thick cashmere cable-knit sweater with matching scarf from Lucy for the cold Connecticut winter and a perplexing box of golf balls from Jed—and then started in surprise as David leaned over and handed him a small package wrapped in paper and twine.

"Here, Brook. I brought you something, too."

With a rude feigning of disinterest and averted eyes, Brook took David's gift. He knew from Mother all about David's phony generosity, although what David would gain by being generous to him he couldn't imagine. Nonchalantly he untied the string and loosened the paper. Nestled in the plain wrapping was a leather-bound first edition of H. G. Wells's *War of the Worlds*. Brook stared down at it, silent with disbelief.

Lucy jabbed his leg. "Brook," she hissed under her breath. "Say thank you!"

Brook raised his head and met David's expectant gaze.

A hateful, all-too-familiar haze of confusion washed through his brain. Was this some kind of trick? He wished Mother was there to tell him what to think. In a dismissive tone he managed to say, "Thank you, David. Of course, I read this years ago . . . ," and then placed the book aside.

"You're welcome." Disgust gleamed briefly in David's catlike eyes. He turned away and thus missed the appearance of two bright red circles on Brook's pale cheeks.

With the siblings chattering about nothing of interest to him, David occupied himself by surreptitiously snooping through the books and papers on Brook's desk, curious to know whether what one learned in prep school was the least bit useful in life. Lying half-buried under a frighteningly large history text was an open notebook, its exposed page filled with Brook's cramped writing. David scanned a few lines and frowned. What he read did not seem to be about any school subject he had ever come across. Intrigued, he carefully excavated the notebook and began to read. He had read some dozen pages by the time Lucy announced that it was too beautiful a day to stay inside and they should take a walk.

David slipped the notebook back into its hiding place. He stood up and stared at Brook, who was slumped on the bed like an old rag doll. David studied the boy, trying to find inside the worthless imbecile he had always assumed Brook to be, the source of the clever tale he'd just read. Brook's right hand rested on the valuable edition of *War of the Worlds*. Aware of David's scrutiny, Brook slowly looked up, his green eyes revealing his shame at his previous behavior. David's eyes drifted to the boy's hand, unconsciously stroking the book's soft, worn leather, then back to his face. David's mouth curved up in a questioning smile.

"Maybe you'll enjoy reading that again. It's an awfully good story, isn't it?"

Brook smiled back, a tiny smile of unmistakable gratitude, and nodded.

As the others readied themselves to go outside, David turned his back to them. He quickly ripped a corner from a piece of blank paper, scribbled a short message, and slid it into Brook's notebook.

Abigail had grabbed at the opportunity to go off with Cissy. She was desperate to get Cissy alone, to talk to her about Jed. It might be humiliating, but Abby didn't care anymore. If there was one thing Cissy knew about, it was sex. Her uninhibited stream of opinion and information, given with a solemn promise to keep secret everything Abby had confided in her, had been eye-opening. If Jed was shy unto paralysis, then Abigail would shake him loose with her boldness. She could no longer trust Sally's assessment of Jed's delicate sexual nature. Abigail was beginning to believe that Sally simply couldn't bear the thought of Jed making love to anyone. She professed to want grandchildren, but it seemed she was counting on divine intervention to produce them.

Abby had been reading Freud. She thought Jed had been taught to repress his sexual feelings by a smothering mother. It was up to her, his wife, to lovingly seduce him and make him see that desire was no sin and sex was a natural expression of the love between a man and a woman. Cissy had given her a thrilling primer on what men liked in bed, including being talked to during sex. Apparently, according to Cissy, they liked to hear how excited they made you, how much you wanted to give yourself to them. It seemed silly to Abby, not something she could ever do, but the thought of it stayed with her. If she let herself, she could almost imagine the things she might say to Jed.

Abby stood naked in the middle of their luxurious room, shaking with nervousness in the cool, wet air wafting through the open window. The hypnotic growl of the surf filled the room, or was that the sound of her blood rushing through her veins? She had asked Jed to stay at the bar for fifteen minutes, to give her time to do her toilet in private. While he remained downstairs, dutifully nursing his brandy, she would set the stage. When he came through the door, she would raise the curtain on their first act of intimacy.

Cissy had helped her find all the necessary props. Abby unfolded the flimsy lingerie that Cissy had picked out for her and slid it on, gasping at its feel and at the sight of herself in the full-length mirror that covered the back of the bathroom door. As she stared at her reflection, she heard David and Cissy crashing into the room next door, Cissy giggling and David murmuring inaudibly. She froze, her mind suddenly filled with thoughts of what Cissy and David were going to do, right there behind the wall the bed was set against. Her heart beat heavily and the untouched place between her legs began to throb. She wanted to love Jed the way Cissy loved David. She wanted to put her hands on his long, pale body, slide her tongue into his mouth, know what it felt like to hold him inside her.

She took from her suitcase a small bag holding scented candles and preserved rose petals. She placed two candles on each of the bedside tables and lit them, sprinkled the petals across the white pillowcases and turned-down sheets. She switched on the radio and heard Graham Mac-Namee's velvet voice, hosting a classical music concert on WEAF from New York. Violins swelled, and she turned the volume down low. Her legs were so weak she nearly fell onto the bed. She arranged herself, one arm flung over her head, one leg slightly bent. Her heart was pounding so hard she was sure David and Cissy could hear it just as she could hear their small noises coming from beyond the adjoining wall. She was ready.

Jed sauntered up the hallway. It had been a perfect day. A bracing swim in the ocean, a bask in the still-warm sun, a good round of golf with David, a fine dinner, a mellowing brandy. He was contentedly tired and relieved that Abby had asked to go upstairs before him. She would be all washed and nightgowned and tucked into bed. He would give her a big yawn, a good-night kiss, and they would get a good night's sleep.

When he opened the door to their room he nearly leaped backward into the hallway, so sure was he that he'd somehow stumbled into the wrong room. Cautiously, he stepped inside and, like a man examining the face of his own doom, took in the elaborate scene that Abby had created. He saw her lying on the bed, smiling up at him, more blatantly sexual in the skimpy, translucent silk camisole and panties than if she had been stark naked. He felt the brandy burning its way back up into his throat.

"Jed, darling. Why don't you come lie down next to me? It's so comfortable and the rose petals smell so good."

Abby's voice was trembling. Jed saw the rapid rise and fall of her breasts, her distended nipples pushing at the weightless fabric that covered them. He should be driven wild by the sight of her; he knew it. What was wrong with him? He couldn't bear to look at her. "I have to wash up." He headed for the bathroom door.

"No! Jed!" Only her head moved. The desperation in her voice stopped him cold. "Please, my love, just come here." Her words were a whispered plea. "Come lie down next to me. Jed, I love you. I want you to touch me. Let me touch you. We'll go slowly; it will be all right. It will be wonderful." She was practically sobbing.

Jed tried to calm his panic. He had to do this. Abby was his wife. He was fond of her, and she had been so patient with him; it had been four months since he had so much as attempted to touch her. He had to find some way to make love to her. How were they going to have a marriage if he couldn't? He took off his jacket and his shirt. Barechested, he lay gingerly on the bed, on his back, staring up at the ceiling. "I'll try, Abby. But I'm really quite tired, so I don't know if—"

Abby rolled over and put a finger on his lips. "Don't speak. Let me do everything."

Jed closed his eyes as her hands and mouth began their exploration of his tense, unyielding body. He could feel the reverence in the kisses she bestowed on his forehead, his eyelids, his cheekbones, the sides of his mouth, his lips. Involuntarily he jerked his face aside as their mouths made contact. She pulled away, buried her face in his neck with a whimper. Jed squeezed his eyes shut; self-loathing coursed through him. He directed himself to touch her arm, giving her permission to continue. After a moment, she raised her head and he felt her mouth on his throat. She was breathing hard, breathing in the scent of him, tasting the texture of his skin with her tongue.

"Oh God, you're so beautiful." Ecstasy in her clotted voice.

The palm of her hand fell lightly onto his chest and swept across the contours of his ribs and sides, the length of his arms. She brushed at his nipples and then leaned over to lick at them. Jed lay unmoving, aware that his body was being worshiped, that Abby was delirious with desire for him, and that he felt nothing in return. When her hand reached down and began to undo the buttons of his pants, every muscle in his body contracted in a spasm of revulsion, but he didn't try to push her away. He had to accept that there was something wrong with him, something he must overcome. He was being made love to by a woman he cared for deeply and yet he wasn't aroused, couldn't imagine becoming aroused. Perhaps he needed more stimulation than other men. If he let Abby touch him and kiss him long enough, perhaps something would happen. He didn't know what else to do, he had disappointed her so often. So he lay still and prayed for something, anything, to make his penis swell, just this once.

Abby sat up and used both hands to get at the buttons. She pulled at his pants and Jed obligingly lifted his hips slightly off the bed so she could slide them down. At the exact instant that his back arched and his hips rose, the sound of a deep, male groan came through the wall. David, making love to Cissy. And an answering cry, *"David! David! Oh, that feels so good!"* Jed's heart crashed to a stop, then leaped to life, its beat now a frantic gallop. His hips jerked violently upward and a delicious throbbing heat spread from his groin into his belly.

The bulge in his undershorts drove Abby to a frenzy. She stripped Jed's body bare and tore off her lingerie, throwing it carelessly to the floor. She insinuated her arms around him and pulled him toward her. "Jed." Her mouth was to his ear. "Come lie on top of me." Her body arched up to him, and her hands grabbed at his hair.

As soon as he was on her, he went limp against her stomach. His length and weight pressed inertly against her. Abby moaned and began to caress him slowly from neck to buttocks, her fingers brushing against his balls, seeking the magic spot that would ignite him again. Jed flogged his rebelling body to not wrench itself away from her ministrations, to stay and respond, to welcome her lascivious touch. What had she done to cause that small, temporary arousal? Why was it gone now? He heard her panting and then suddenly all sound and feel of her disappeared as David's breathy voice came through the wall like a gun blast: *"Oh Jesus, Cissy, yeah, like that, like that."* An earthquake rocked Jed's body and his penis jumped. His blood began to seethe and he thrashed, trying to free himself from Abby's encircling arms.

Abby felt Jed harden. She held him close and began to whisper, words pouring out of her in a passionate torrent. "I want you so much. I love you. I love you. I love the feel of your skin under my hands. Love me, Jed. I belong to you. I'm yours to take. I'm yours. I'm yours. I'm yours." She breathed it into his ear over and over and over.

I'm yours. A bomb detonated in Jed's head. Abby's arms tightened around him. *I'm yours.* David's voice boomed in his brain: *"If you want to be responsible for me, I'm yours." Jed's hands were on David's shoulders, their foreheads were touching; David's hands were in his hair.* David's moans were coming faster now, seeping through the wall and obliterating every other sound in the world. Jed's brain was exploding, deadly shards ripping through everything in their path, and David was lying under him, *I'm yours,* his hard, powerful body writhing, his stiff cock pushing into Jed's belly. Jed was out of his mind. His penis was as rigid as a bar of steel. David's moans filled his universe. A hand was snaking down to reach for him, David's long brown fingers wrapping themselves around him. They were trying to guide him somewhere hot and wet. Jesus! No! Frantically he tried to rear up, but an urgent voice in his head told him to get this disgusting act done once and for all. With a yell, he pushed himself into Abby's body, heedless of her cry of pain, and began to pump his hips in rhythm with David's panting, animal noises that were growing wilder, turning into a mindless chant. *"Oh my God. Oh my God. Oh my God."* Jed cried out with him, "Oh my God! Oh God!" And with a shrill scream he burst inside his bruised and unsatisfied wife.

His chest heaved, his heart thudded, and his mind shrieked in wordless horror. Jed pushed himself off her, scrabbling away from her hands clawing at his back, at his chest. He fell off the side of the bed in a daze, landed on his feet. His body was slick with sweat, his penis stiff and pulsing. He heard Abby calling his name imploringly. He heard David murmuring, *"Baby, oh, baby."* Jed lurched into the bathroom, slammed and locked the door, and vomited into the sink.

Jed crouched on the room's small balcony, wrapped in a spare blanket he had found in the closet, his arms clutched tight around himself. He stared without seeing out over the railing, beyond the steep cliffs to the churning ocean. The sun was just rising over the horizon. A line of fire crossed the water and found him where he huddled, shaking like a leaf in a windstorm. He had lain awake all night in a state of demonic terror, periodically crawling on hands and knees into the bathroom to hang his head over the toilet bowl as his stomach tried to turn itself inside out. He hadn't been able to close his eyes without being assaulted by the memory of his horrific perversion, of how he had succeeded in making love to his wife only by imagining he was making love to his best friend. He had managed the first sustained erection and orgasm of his depraved life by imagining himself with a man. And not just any man. David.

Jed covered his face with his hands and a groan of agony escaped from between his chilled fingers. He was a monster. He was unfit to exist in the company of normal human beings. Nothing he did on his own could be trusted anymore. What if even his innocent-seeming suggestion that they come to Newport was impure? Was he secretly titillated by the knowledge of the shocking scandal of rampant homosexual activity among sailors stationed here after the war? Men had engaged in perverted sex of all kinds along Cliff Walk, undoubtedly right below where he now stood. And not just fairies but normal men who had been hired by the navy to entrap the sailors into homosexual acts and found themselves enjoying it. Did the thought of that excite him? Was that why he wanted to be here?

If he were any kind of a man at all, he would follow the sun's beckoning path, walk over the cliff, and let his vile body be washed out to sea to become carrion for the fish. But he was no man; he knew that now. He was a deviant, soulless coward. He had approached David not just because he yearned to be like him—fearless, independent, and raging with life—but out of base, secret lust. He was a failure and a liar. A hollow, untrustworthy man made of straw who would blow away in a breeze.

He was too craven to kill himself, so he would have to continue to find a way to live. There was only one way he knew to do that. He had done it before; he could do it again. He would devote himself with a frenzy born of hopelessness to his work, to his wife, to the total suppression of his fears and of any aberrant sexual thoughts that might ever arise in him again. He would erase every vestige of the image of David's nakedness that had invaded his mind. He wanted to experience that flesh-melting heat in his loins again, but it had to be with his wife. It could only be with his wife. Abby loved him. He would find a way to let that comfort him. He would do everything a normal husband did to show that he loved her as well. He would find a way to do it all. He had no choice.

He stood up and let the blanket slide to his waist. The first rays of the morning sun washed his chest in their golden glow. He had stopped shaking. Light chased away the demons of the night. He tiptoed back into the room, gratified to see that Abby still slept. Once she had ceased trying to coax him out of the bathroom, she had crawled into bed and fallen into a sound sleep. What he had done to her last night had been cruel. He lifted the covers and lay down next to her. He adjusted the pillow beneath his head.

His hand brushed against the wall and froze there. Like the searing afterimage left by the shock of a photographer's flash, a picture of David's dark unruly curls on a white pillow imprinted itself behind Jed's eyes. He thrust his hand under the covers, savagely pushed the image out of his head. He rolled onto his side, toward Abby, and her eyes opened. Jed's heart jolted in panic; had he buried the image fast enough or had she seen it leeching out of his brain? Was his depravity curled like a snake in his eyes, leering out at her?

"Jed. Darling." Her voice was husky with sleep. Her brown almond-shaped eyes smiled at him adoringly.

"Abby," he whispered. He was so pitifully grateful to her. "I'm sorry. I'll do better next time." She shook her head and stroked his face. He pressed his lips against her palm. "Hold me. Please, just hold me."

She put her arms around him and drew his head to her breast. In a moment, his breathing became slow and deep. He had fallen asleep. Abby lay with Jed in her arms, one hand twined in his hair, the other caressing the hand that had fallen across her hip. Her eyes were damp; her lips trembled. Exultation swelled inside her. Her love had broken Sally's wicked spell. Everything would be all right from now on.

20

"Mr. Shaw? There's someone here asking to speak to you for a moment."

Janet Thorne, David's secretary, as close a replica of Uncle Joe's flawless Lillian Steele as he could find, stood with her back against his closed office door as if to protect him from a possibly unwanted intrusion.

David, deep in concentration over preliminary plans for the store's tea parlor, foggily raised his head. "What? Am I expecting anyone?"

Mrs. Thorne lifted her hands and shook her head apologetically. "It's a Mrs. Winokur. She said she's come to thank you? For the interview? Should I send her away?"

David blinked several times, trying to bring her words into focus. "I don't know any Mrs.—oh, of course. Reuben's wife."

Mrs. Thorne looked at him in bewilderment.

"Reuben Winokur, RW Fashions. One of our suppliers. His wife's a seamstress in some shop downtown. The best in the world, he says." David smiled to himself. "He's a nice fellow. I arranged an interview for her with Kathleen Raymond. A small favor, no promises."

"That was very sweet of you. Do you wish to see her?"

"Why not? Give me another ten minutes here and then send her in." The smile lingered on David's face as he returned his attention to the blueprints covering his desk, remembering how he had gone to thank Joseph in person for giving him his first job. He liked this girl already.

Ten minutes later, David was once again totally immersed in the drawings in front of him, his head down, his hands shielding his eyes like a visor, shutting out his surroundings. Little by little, a small voice, timidly saying his name, insinuated itself into his consciousness. He looked up and saw a young woman standing in the middle of the room, smiling at him like a supplicant before a shrine. A young woman who looked exactly like his mother.

In his confusion, his mind still captured by work, he stared at her as though she were an apparition and whispered, "Mama?"

Sarah's smile dropped away. Her breath stopped in her throat as everything around her ceased to exist except for the man now standing behind the desk that separated them. Her hands flew to her open mouth. The small bag of cosmetics she had bought fell unheeded to the floor.

"Oh my God, David!" She swayed on her feet as a rush of blood surged into her head. Without thinking, she began to move toward him, reaching out for him. Then she stopped, halted by the triumph of her intellect over her instinct and by the deadly coldness that radiated from every inch of his unnaturally still frame.

"Hello, Sarah." David had backed away from his desk and now leaned against the windowsill. He crossed his arms over his chest. "So, you're Reuben's wife." He shook his head and gave a mirthless laugh. "What a stroke of bad luck." His gaze wandered over her features, his face completely still except for his probing eyes. "You look just like Mama," he said softly. "It's amazing." He continued to stare at her but said nothing more.

Sarah stared back at him, paralyzed with shock. This wasn't how she had imagined their reunion. She was meant to have located him in secret, had time to prepare herself, to sort out her emotions. At this fragile moment of reconnecting she should have already known exactly where he'd been and who he'd become. She was supposed to know what she felt and what she needed to do and say that would vent her bitter anger and yet still succeed at bringing her brother back to her. She was meant to have had the time and the skill to fix everything for everyone for all time. This stark encounter with no warning, no foreknowledge of what she would find, was all wrong. Her scalp begin to crawl. She wanted to throw herself at his feet and beg his forgiveness; she wanted to scream at him until he was reduced to rubble before her.

Fearfully she peered into his eyes and tried to find something to anchor her. She knew those eyes so well and yet there was nothing familiar about the person inhabiting them. This wasn't the boy in the photo. This cool and polished man was not the brother who had played with her, teased her, loved and protected her. The fantasy of a reunion that washed away years of confusion and assuaged the pain of other losses turned to dust. The pendulum of her emotions swept toward anger.

"Nothing to say to me?" Now his eyes bored into her.

Sarah's lips began to tremble. "Why didn't you come back? Why didn't you come to see me?" His eyes tore the question from her mouth.

An incredulous look spread across his face. "Oh, did you write to tell me that you wanted to see me again? Funny, I don't remember getting that letter. I don't remember getting a single letter from you, not even one telling me Mama had died. I believe it was Sadie Krinski who had the courtesy to write to me about that."

As a child, Sarah had been frightened by his sarcasm, his clever, vicious shield against anything that made him uncomfortable. Now it infuriated her. She set her lips and raised her chin. "I was fourteen years old. You were gone and Mama was dead—"

"Because of me, right?" he interrupted harshly, simultaneously accusing her of holding him responsible and challenging her to deny it.

She averted her eyes, lowered her voice as though to say something he wasn't quite meant to hear. "You said it; I didn't."

When she looked up again, his eyes had gone dead and he seemed to be looking straight through her. She felt an eely panic claw at her stomach. Sheer stubbornness drove her on. "What do you even care? I'm surprised you bothered to tell us you were leaving. How generous you were to give us an evening's warning." It felt good to fling his sarcasm back at him. "You couldn't wait to get away. Ben was right. You were always selfish. You *left* us. You left me. You knew the money you'd saved that summer wouldn't be enough. You knew I'd have to go to work. And I *hated* it and I blamed you, every day. You knew Mama would have to cope somehow. And it killed her and, yes, I blamed you for that, too!"

"What a disappointment you are. Poor little Sarah," he said mockingly. "Had a tough few years, did you? But then it was Reuben to the rescue, was it? So what are you angry about? You didn't need me."

A child's voice mewled inside Sarah's head. *I did need you. You were my hero. I didn't mean it; I don't blame you anymore.* "No, you're right. I didn't need you. We've managed fine without you."

"That's good for us both. I certainly don't need you."

Unwanted tears sprang to her eyes. "Why are you making this so hard?"

"I'm sorry. Is this too hard for you? Let me make things as clear as possible so it will be easier." David propelled himself away from the window and took a step toward her, perversely gratified to see her moist eyes, to watch her recoil from him, retreat a step back.

"How do you think it felt, lying in a hospital in France, to find out from a next-door neighbor that my mother was dead and my brother and sister didn't want any part of me anymore? Do you think that made me want to rush home and tell you how much I'd missed you? You all tore at me like vultures every day of my life. Ben pecking at me constantly to be a hardworking, pious Jew, you expecting me to entertain you and protect you from having to grow up. Even Mama, clinging to me instead of fighting to get better, expecting me to somehow bring home more and more money. I wanted my own life, Sarah, a life I could stand living. Out of the ghetto. If you think that makes me selfish, I don't give a damn. You all wrung your frightened hands the minute I was gone and slammed the door behind me. So, who betrayed who, Sarah? Did you think Mama's death didn't tear me apart? Where the hell were you when I needed you?"

The deluge of accusation had lain inside David's head for years, coiled and ready to strike, waiting for its day of release. These precise words honed to perfection so as to inflict the most damage. Now, his victim finally before him, David let the words out with all the vicious righteousness of a man who has held a horrible grievance in his heart for too long.

David's unbounded rage battered at Sarah. It beat her back to her childhood, to years lived in a constant state of terror that her smoldering force of a brother would leave her alone with the stultifying remains of her family. She drew in a shuddering, sobbing breath. She blinked furiously, trying to stop the rising flood of tears threatening to inundate her.

"Don't. Don't you dare cry in front of me. I don't want to see your tears again. I can't have you in my life, Sarah. I'm not your brother anymore. I'm not a Jew anymore. You can go home and tell Ben this discard got married to a *shiksa,* by a Protestant minister, no Jews within a hundred miles. Maybe he'll get dispensation to say *kaddish* for me a second time. Am I making myself clear enough? I have a new life and there's no place in it for any of you."

"Stop it!" she screamed, clapping her hands over her ears. "How can you talk to me like that? You're my brother! I'm your sister! You used to love me! Can't you remember how young and frightened I was? All that was left of our family was Ben. I had to believe that he knew what was best."

"No, you didn't. You could have at least tried to remember that you loved me, too." For just a second, though his expression revealed nothing, David lost control of his voice. He took a ragged breath. "I don't think that would have been too much to ask of you."

"I *did* remember! I tried to find you!" Sarah cried. "You didn't even try to find me!"

David's eyebrows arched up. "Why, were you lost? I knew where to find you, Sarah. Obviously, I didn't want to."

Sarah felt herself driven into a corner by David's unyielding sarcasm and by the hostility that throbbed beneath its surface. Like a trapped animal, she struck back. "What happened to you, David? You used to be a nice person. What happened to your heart?"

"You broke it," he jibed, as though that were the last thing on earth that might have happened to his heart. He turned his back to her, looked out his office window down onto the busy intersection of Fifth Avenue and 38th Street. A thousand Jews he could have done business with, and he had to find the one married to his sister. He gave a hard laugh and faced her again. "Get out of here, Sarah. I'm making your husband a rich man. And I'm willing to overlook the likelihood that some of that money, *my* money, will end up in Ben's mean, miserable hands. You're not going to get anything else from me."

"What could we possibly need from someone like you? Tell me, David, what would Mama think of you now?"

David took a step toward her, his face blazing with fury. She stepped back, sickened by the realization that her once-beloved brother had become a pitiless stranger who elicited appalling meanness from her.

"Get the hell out of here." He stalked past her and threw open his office door.

"David." It came out a weak, horrified sound. "No, please."

"I have work to do. Pick up your package and go home."

Sarah couldn't move. Her thoughts careened around inside her mind, trying to find a place where what had just happened had not happened. It was not possible that she had found him only to lose him again. They would be cut off from each other forever and it was all her fault. She should not have lost her temper. She should not have let his hurt and anger fuel hers. A sudden wave of nausea hit her and the room began to spin. She flailed a hand toward the back of a chair, reaching for support. Her hand missed the chair and she fell.

David quickly shut the door again and stared down at her, huddled on the floor, crying. He felt nothing but a pure adamantine anger, lodged like a pearl in a shell-like chamber of his heart, a solid immutable thing. He loved that anger; it comforted him and sustained him. It propelled him. Nothing and no one could touch it, not even a young woman with his mother's face who used to be his little sister.

He strode across the floor, bent down, and hoisted her up. "Breathe." He dug into his suit jacket pocket and pulled out a white handkerchief. He pushed it into her hand. "Dry your eyes." He picked up her package, his detached, pragmatic mind noticing with satisfaction that she had bought store-brand cosmetics. He put one hand under her chin and turned her face up to his. He tucked a loose strand of hair behind her ear. "I don't want you in my life, Sarah. Do you understand? It's too late. Go home and forget that you ever saw me."

"How can I do that!" Sarah wailed. "I can't pretend I didn't see you!"

"Yes, you can. You can finally do one thing I ask of you." He thrust her package into her hands. "Don't give me a reason to cancel the contracts I have with Reuben. I really don't want to have to do that."

He took her by the elbow and steered her toward the office door. "By the way, did Mrs. Raymond offer you a job?"

Sarah looked at him dumbly and mumbled, "Yes."

He escorted her past Mrs. Thorne's desk, into the hallway. "Good day, Mrs. Winokur. It's too bad you can't accept the position. I'm sure you're an expert seamstress. Give my regards to your husband." He didn't wait to watch her stumble toward the elevator, leaning against the wall, pressing the handkerchief to her eyes.

"I don't want to be disturbed for the rest of the day, Janet."

Mrs. Thorne kept her eyes riveted on her desk. "You know you are scheduled to lead the Christmas tree lighting ceremony on the ground floor at five o'clock."

"Find someone else to do it."

"But it's your—"

"Find someone else to do it," David said, just the slightest edge of menace in his voice.

"Yes, sir."

David went back into his office and closed the door. He crossed to the wet bar, poured three fingers of Scotch into a glass, and drank it down, neat. He turned around and hurled the glass against the far wall. It shattered against the hard plaster, sending miniature daggers flying out in all directions. He grabbed the bottle by the neck and took it with him back to his desk. He sat and stared at his closed office door without moving a muscle except to raise the bottle and swallow mouthfuls of the stinging hot liquor. After fifteen minutes, his mind was calm. He put the bottle aside and went back to work.

"Sarah, sweetheart!" Reuben looked up from his cloth-covered desk. "So, *nu*? How was the interview with Mrs. Kathleen Raymond? She offered you a job, yes?" Reuben beamed at Sarah with certain pride.

Sarah smiled at him with an unusual tenderness. "It was fine. She's lovely and yes, she offered me a job, but I'm not going to take it."

"But why not? You would meet such people there! And work on such clothes!"

"I didn't like it there, Reuben. It's too big and cold a place. I don't ever want to work there. I belong at Uncle Sol's, with the people I know and love. I only took the interview because you wanted me to; you know that. You thank Mr. Shaw for me the next time you talk to him, but I'm staying right here."

"Sarah, I only want the best for you."

Sarah came behind the desk and put her arms around her husband's neck. "I already have the best. Let's not talk about it anymore. I need to get back to the shop now."

But she didn't leave. She lowered her head to his shoulder and began to cry.

"Sarah! What is wrong?"

"Nothing. Nothing's wrong. I just love you very much, Reuben, that's all."

Her tears left a damp circle on Reuben's shirtfront. He held her and thanked God for all the blessings of his life, but most of all for the love of Sarah Warshinsky.

21

January 17. David's twenty-seventh birthday. Jed knew he could offer no believable excuse for canceling their monthly get-together for a third month in a row. In the nearly two years since they had begun these meetings, they had missed only one, when David had taken Cissy to Europe for their honeymoon. Then Jed had managed to get out of the November meeting claiming illness; the December meeting, where they would have celebrated *his* twenty-seventh birthday, by confiding, against Abby's wishes, that Abby was pregnant and wanted him home with her. He had avoided being alone with David since the nightmare of Newport, relying on the buffering presence of their friends or family to protect him from what he might not be able to control. Since that night, he had done everything possible to convince himself that what had happened had been a harmless incident brought on by an untimely confluence of brandy, the intrusion of David's and Cissy's sexual noises, and a nascent desire for Abby, come alive finally under her loving hands. But just as Jed had been unable to reorder his knowledge of reality to align itself with everyone's belief in his wartime heroism, so was he unable to configure those three dubious elements into a believable lie. No matter what he did, he was helpless to control the insistent desire that fired his brain and washed over his body with the inexorableness of the ocean's tides. He had no defenses. This previously unknown hunger for the feel and taste and heat of another human being consumed him.

The one thing he was able to do, and he did it very well, was accommodate himself to the unacceptable. After a three-month battle, he and his lust had reached a truce. He would privately acknowledge its existence in return for it not interfering in any way with his life. It would be there, with all the unpleasant physical properties of a nasty itch, but it was understood that there would be no scratching, ever, of any kind. There was no alternative. He could never excise David from his life, and so a way had to be found to live with him. To see him. To resume a normal friendship. And tonight Jed would do just that.

He missed David desperately and knew that David must miss him. Since the earliest days of their friendship, they had been able to talk to each other with an openness that was impossible with anyone else. That Jed now lied constantly to David about almost everything of genuine significance did not contradict Jed's belief in the honesty of their friendship. For one thing, what he told David was often what he desired to be true and therefore not an actual lie; and when he was aware of bending reality, he considered it to be for David's sake, so David wouldn't worry about him. Jed was, after all, still and forever responsible for David's life.

Jed arrived purposely early at the exclusive, muffled rich-men's club, tucked discreetly into the bottom floor of a baroque limestone mansion on lower Fifth Avenue. He chose a table at a long crimson-velvet-draped window overlooking the avenue, sat facing the direction from which David would appear, and ordered a double martini with two olives. Jed normally drank very little, discomfited by alcohol's effects: the fogging of consciousness and the loosening of the internal restraints he held so carefully in place. But tonight he needed something to quell his nervousness. Normal men used liquor to relax, and he was determined to be a normal man. By the time he saw David striding toward the table, a huge smile on his face, Jed had finished his first drink, was starting on his second, and believed himself to be as relaxed as a man could possibly be. He wobbled upright, happily limp, his mind slightly numb.

"Looks like you've started the party without me. Give your rapidly aging friend a hug." David put his arms around Jed with unconcealed pleasure at the prospect of their overdue evening together.

The feel of David's body against his caused Jed's gin-induced serenity to tatter like morning mist under a hot sun. His lolling mind scrambled for control, found enough to guide him back to his chair, put a stiff smile on his face and an unsteady hand on his glass.

A waiter brought David his usual drink, Scotch on the rocks. He took an appreciative sip, let out a sigh of contentment. He unbuttoned his jacket and loosened his tie. He stretched his long legs out in front of him, crossed one ankle over the other. "I'm working too hard."

David leaned his head against the high chair back and closed his eyes. Rendered momentarily invisible, Jed plummeted into inebriated thrall to David's face, to the hollows under the high cheekbones, the taut line of the jaw, the lush mouth falling slightly open as tension drained out of him. To the pale, erotic, razor-thin scar that cut across the smooth skin and heightened, rather than diminished, his handsomeness. To the upslanting eyes, golden and open and staring at Jed. Staring at him. Startled to panic, Jed's eyes immediately skittered away. He clumsily brought his drink to his lips.

"Jed, are you angry at me for some reason?"

"No! Why should I be?" Jed was struggling to stay afloat in deep water.

David shrugged. "I don't know. I realize you had reasons for canceling our last two meetings, but still, it almost seems as though you've been avoiding me recently. And you're already half-drunk and you're not looking at me."

"I'm sorry. I'm not angry with you. I've just been very distracted lately. I'd rather be with you than anyone; you know that. I could never be angry with you."

"Distracted by what? That capital consolidation deal with J. P. Morgan? You're doing a good job, Jed. It's not your fault it's taking so long. Morgan is the most conservative bank in the country. You're too hard on yourself. You don't have to be perfect all the time."

Jed smiled, a natural smile. His eyes were able to meet David's. Suddenly everything shifted back to the familiar. They were having a normal conversation, just like always. Nothing had changed. "Look who's talking."

"Yeah, well." David shook his head and stared down at his drink. "No, it's different with me. I'm not trying to be perfect. I gave that up when I left home—the perfect Jew, the perfect son, the perfect brother, the perfect sacrificial lamb." He made circles on the table with his glass, rattling the melting ice against its water-beaded sides. "I'm not interested in being perfect, as your sister and my wife are always happy to remind me. I'm interested in getting what I want. I've never pretended otherwise. Don't think I'm trying to please anyone but myself, Jed, and maybe you and your grandfather. I don't owe anything to anyone else."

"At least you know what you want. I've always admired that in you. And that you aren't afraid to do what you have to to get it." Calm again, a convert to the rewards of sufficient drink, Jed flagged down the waiter and ordered a third double martini.

"I don't know how admirable I am. It's good to know what you want, but you might rethink your envy of my fearless pursuit of my goals. Sometimes it feels like nothing more than selfishness. Not so nice." David's mouth twisted into something that was not quite a smile. His eyes were fixed on the liquid swirling in his glass. "I saw my sister a few weeks ago."

"What?"

"She came to the store. An unpleasant coincidence. She's Winokur's wife."

"My God! What happened? Are you all right? What does this mean?" It had been so long since they had made any reference to David's past that Jed had nearly been able to forget that he'd ever had one, that there existed in the world people who, by virtue of shared blood and history, were closer to David than Jed could ever be. Jed felt fear rise like bile into his throat.

David smiled and looked at Jed with unreadable eyes. "It means nothing. She's meant nothing to me for eight years and she means nothing to me now. We're strangers. I sent her away. She was quite upset. I suppose I could try to forgive her, but I have no desire to and we both know that David Shaw doesn't do anything he doesn't want to do." He drained half his glass in one swallow. "So much for my being perfect. Don't tell anyone, all right?"

"No, I won't." Relief washed away his fear. David wasn't going back there. He was staying where he belonged. There was nothing more to say.

"Actually, one of the things I admire most in you, Jed, is that you are so unselfish. That you always find a way to simply want what you have rather than fighting everyone and everything for something else. I can't imagine what it must feel like to find life so . . . acceptable."

Jed couldn't respond. A battalion of his unacceptable desires, emboldened by a shakerful of illegal, ninety-proof alcohol, pounded on the heavy hatch covering their prison hold. As soon as the waiter set the drink down, Jed lifted it, took a huge gulp, choked, and coughed.

"Slow down there." David reached over and put his hand on Jed's arm. "Jed, what's got you all—oh, what an idiot I am! The baby! You're worried about becoming a father, worried you won't be perfect at that, either." He gave Jed's arm a reassuring squeeze. "You shouldn't be. You'll be a great father."

"What makes you think that?" Jed's slowly glazing-over

eyes were corralled by the sensuous movement of David's fingers methodically tracing the perfect roundness of the rim of his Scotch glass.

"Because you're such a good and generous man. You're like your father, always trying to accommodate yourself to what people want of you. You care more about other people's happiness than your own. Unlike me, once again," David said wryly. "Cissy wants a baby desperately, but I don't, so I won't let her have one."

Jed's brain came to attention. "You won't let her? How do you stop her?"

David gave Jed a quizzical look. "I use a condom."

Jed blushed hotly. He watched David's hand moving over the smooth edge of the thick crystal. He knew he shouldn't plumb this vein of conversation any further, but he couldn't help himself. "Every time?"

"Either that or I don't come inside her. I pull out at the last second." David's hand stopped moving. His fingers tightened around the glass. "She really hates when I do that."

Jed's lungs stopped working as the image of David aroused to orgasm, ejaculating viscous white fluid onto a flat white belly, appeared on the granite table between them as though etched into the shining stone.

"You know what to do, Jed. Abby didn't get pregnant for over a year."

The liquor singing in Jed's bloodstream was a demon playing mischief with his brain. It stoked his secret excitement and liberated his tongue. "Well, yes, but that was because we didn't have sex until three months ago." He sat in bemused silence, wondering with an impersonal curiosity how that sentence had gotten spoken aloud. His eyes were beginning to lose the ability to focus. He could look at David more easily now that he was unable to see him clearly. It seemed that David was regarding him with tender affection, which would be so very sweet, but it was hard to be sure because there was tender affection inside him, too, and he couldn't tell what was behind his eyes and what was in front of his eyes.

David drew in a hissing breath. "I'm sorry, Jed. Abby doesn't enjoy making love?"

Jed nearly laughed out loud. He managed to shrug and reassemble his face into an expression of acknowledgment.

David slowly exhaled. His eyebrows rose and he grimaced as though in pain. "Well, that could certainly drive a man to drink. Abby loves you, though; there's no question of that. Be patient with her; I'm sure she'll come around in time. Some women have to be taught to like sex; they think they shouldn't."

Jed knew something about women who didn't believe in enjoying sex; he might not have married one, but he had, after all, been raised by one. Through the protective haze of his drunkenness Jed considered, for the first time in his life, his parents' sexuality. He wondered if Philip suffered from Sally's unresponsiveness the way Abby did from his. The answer was immediately obvious. Philip suffered and he wore his suffering in the form of a quiet, pervasive sadness. It wasn't, as Jed had been told and believed for as long as he could remember, that his father was emotionally detached and artistically self-absorbed. He was protecting himself from the torment of wanting someone who didn't want him. A shock of enlightened empathy for him caused an involuntary, "Oh my goodness," to escape Jed's mouth.

David, having no idea what was going through his friend's mind, smiled reassuringly. "Don't worry. I can tell you, bringing someone along . . . that can be fun in itself. Something to look forward to after the baby's born. And, you know, if worse comes to worst . . ."

"What do you mean?" Jed stared at David uncomprehendingly. The worst had already come.

David flushed slightly. "I mean . . . look, if you have to, you can find satisfaction outside your marriage. It's not natural to do without sex, and you don't have to if it comes to it; that's all I'm saying."

Jed's brain gave up trying to make sense of anything. He couldn't feel his hands or feet, only the stiffness of the mask plastered onto his face.

David laughed. "Jed, I think you're drunk." He took Jed's half-full glass and moved it to his side of the table. "You've had enough. I'm going to order us some food, you're going to eat, drink some coffee, and then I'm going to take you home and deliver you to your wife. Definitely do not try to make love to her tonight."

Jed's head gradually cleared while they ate and talked about nothing important. After a plate of meat and potatoes and several cups of black coffee to focus his addled brain, he knew he'd been a fool to have had even one single martini. He couldn't risk Cerberus rolling over and exposing his stomach for a friendly scratch; the gates of hell needed to be guarded at all times. No more liquor when he was near David. By the time they left the club to walk the short distance home, Jed was in control of himself again. They turned downtown on Fifth Avenue, into the teeth of a chill wind swirling up from the open space of Washington Square Park.

"I see you're limping a little tonight," David said with concern, his eyes on Jed's right leg. "Is the leg bothering you lately?"

"It's the cold. It makes the muscles stiffen up. I don't think the three martinis helped any, either. I can barely feel my foot."

"Be careful. Take my arm if you need to."

"No, no. I'm fine. I'm used to it."

David pulled his scarf from around his neck and began to stuff it into his pocket. "I'm sorry the cold isn't good for your leg. I love this weather. I'm always too hot."

"Give me that." Shivering, Jed appropriated David's scarf, threw it around the upturned collar of his coat. "You're crazy."

David grinned into the cold, black night sky. "Who isn't. Say, Jed, I notice that you haven't given me a birthday present," he joked. "So I'm going to demand one from you."

"Oh really." Jed turned to him and laughed. "I thought we had a no-gifts policy on the books. What makes you think I'll give you anything?"

"Because it's something that only you can give me and I know you want me to have everything I need." David smiled at Jed teasingly.

David's words fell on Jed's ears as though shot directly from his own heart. An agony of longing ballooned in his chest. David would flee in disgust and horror if he had any idea of the thing Jed needed that only David could give him. But Jed would give David whatever he wanted no matter what he ever got in return. It was so obvious now. He was in love with David. He had always been in love with David.

Jed's equilibrium deserted him. His right leg was a block of unbending wood. His numb foot lost contact with the cement sidewalk and he pitched forward. David quickly reached out and locked his arms around him, held him steady.

"Jed! What happened?"

Jed closed his eyes and clung to David, giving himself this tiny gift, the duration of one endless, fleeting heartbeat before pushing himself upright against David's straining muscles. He balanced himself carefully; the ground stayed solidly beneath his two feet. "My foot went numb for a moment. It must be the liquor. Remind me never to drink like that again." He resumed walking. "Tell me what you need."

"I need you to create the designs for my women's dress line. You're better at it than anyone I've seen, and despite your protestations to the contrary, I know how much you enjoy doing it. I don't want to hear anymore that you couldn't possibly."

Jed gave in. The pull of the pleasure and the pain of it was too strong. Time stolen from work he hated spent doing something he loved, time spent locked alone in his studio with David. "Well, then I won't say it. But no one can know that I'm doing this for you."

"Why the hell not? You shouldn't hide your talents; you should be proud of them."

"It's frivolous and self-indulgent. I don't want Mother and Grandfather to be concerned that I'm not completely devoted to my career."

David looked over at Jed, at the red blotches staining his pale cheeks, high color that had nothing to do with the biting wind. "Are you?"

"Of course I am!" Jed snapped. "My family didn't invest in my upbringing and education so I could end up being a women's dress designer. I'm the heir to Joseph Gates's empire, for God's sake!"

They walked two blocks in silence, heads turned away from each other. When they reached the entrance to Washington Mews, David stepped in front of Jed, reached out, and tied his dangling scarf snugly around Jed's exposed, goosefleshed neck. "It will be our secret. We don't need to talk about business; we've got all that under control. Let's meet in your studio from now on and have some fun. We'll let our softer sides come up for air where no one else can see them and we'll create clothes that make women look and feel beautiful." David gave a faint smile. "Maybe we'll let Abby help us from time to time. My guess is we'll need actual female input, and I think we can trust her."

Jed caught David's smile in the corner of his eye but could not yet look at him. "Wouldn't Cissy be better? She's so stylish."

"She's a blabbermouth. And she's stylish, but she's too caught up by fads. This flapper look she loves now, it will be out by the time I'm selling what you design for me. It's too unfeminine. Women aren't going to want to look like fifteen-year-old boys for long, with no breasts, no waist, no hips. The only thing I like about it is that I get to see her knees in public." David laughed. "You know, she has to bind her breasts with one of those ridiculous Symington Side Lacer bras to flatten herself out. Aha! I knew I could make you blush."

"Anyone can make me blush; don't be so proud of yourself." Then Jed looked up at him and smiled.

"That's better. I like the way Abby dresses. She's stylish, too, and she always looks like a woman." David put out a hand to stop Jed removing the scarf from around his neck. "You can give that back to me tomorrow. I don't want you to freeze on your way to your front door."

Their gazes locked and there, in the depths of David's eyes, was an ocean of tender affection. This time, Jed saw it clearly.

Jed crept up the stairs and peered into the darkened bedroom. Abby was fast asleep on her back, a pillow hugged against her body. She was suffering terrible morning sickness and was exhausted, in bed by nine o'clock every evening. Jed walked cautiously into the room and looked down at her. His wife, carrying his child. A miraculous conception accomplished during the one and only act of love he'd been able to perform. He bent down and kissed her lightly on the forehead.

He wandered up to his studio, wide awake, sober, aroused, mortified, resigned. He didn't turn on the lamp. The shutters were open and the ambient light in the low room was a spectral grey miasma filled with moving shadows. The air was cold. He unbuttoned his coat but didn't take it off. He lowered himself onto the sofa and, like a fallen leaf spiraling downward toward the bottom of a pond, sank into the cushions, every inch of him weighted down by surrender. His head fell back. He stared up at the whorled design of the pressed-tin ceiling as his fingers closed around the skin-soft silk of David's scarf and he pulled it slowly from around his neck. He brought it to his face and inhaled the memory of David's scent. He let the scarf pool across the stretched skin of his throat while his hands worked at the buttons of his trousers. His eyes fluttered closed and behind his trembling lids arose the image of himself in David's arms, their bodies twined together, a conflagration of desire that could not be tamed, his starving lips on David's skin. Shaking fingers grasped his erect penis and began to move, every urgent stroke accompanied by the fantasy of David's hands pleasuring him. A wounded sound emerged from deep within his belly and his breath came in labored gasps. The length of silk slithered like a serpent down his chest, settled over the tip of his penis. His body convulsed and he came, his semen spurting into the caress of David's scarf.

Jed's eyes opened. His head rolled against the sofa back and came to rest facing the window. He lay unmoving except for the rapid rise and fall of his chest as he panted, releasing the hot, tortured sounds of orgasm's aftermath into the cold room. He stared dully in the direction of the window, his sight turned inward. He would have to amend slightly the accommodation he had made with his perverted desires. One last small adjustment. A rider to the truce that would allow him release at his own hand and leave his mind, his darkest hidden mind, free to do with David every unimaginable thing he could imagine. With Abby three months pregnant, he hoped he had a year before he would be expected to make love to her again. Maybe by then he would have found a way to pretend that Abby's body was David's. He would only need to do it often enough to get her pregnant a second time. Then he could be alone with David again.

22

Rain beat against the dining room windows, driven nearly horizontal by the March winds. Philip and Sally sat across the impeccably set table from each other, eating their dinner in polite silence. Everything was perfect. The crisp-skinned roasted chicken and its accompanying apple compote, the parsleyed potatoes, the buttery green beans, the hot rolls. A bottle of fine French wine decanted into crystal. For dessert, lemon meringue pie, Philip's favorite. Philip ate slowly, chewing his food thoroughly, mashing it to tasteless paste so that it might more easily slip past the lump that had taken up permanent residence in his throat.

At the age of fifty-eight, with an enviable wife, three fine children, success at his chosen profession, good health, social standing, and plentiful wealth, he should have been a happy man. And he might have been but for the loneliness and the conviction that he had failed at the most important thing in his life. He had failed to bring joy and contentment to the woman sitting across from him, whose ethereal beauty and restive soul stirred him as no other ever had or ever could. He had failed to give his wife sufficient reason to love him or to allow him to express his love for her. So that now, alone with her at last, he had no way to bring her close to him.

The children were gone, but the obsessive attention she had always lavished on them, good and bad, had not diminished. The children were gone, but her love, worry, jealousy, impatience, censure, were still there. The physical emptiness of the house magnified her emotions, all directed away from him, and pushed them further apart, she into her corner, he into his. His hopes that Sally would turn to him after Brook had been banished, even if only out of desperation, had been quickly dashed. She now treated Philip with the vacant civility, at times bordering on kindness, that she might have shown a maiden aunt who had come to live in their home, someone she didn't know well yet felt responsible for. Enough solicitous attention to let the beggar know he needn't leave but never enough to make him feel wanted. She saw to all his physical needs, save one, accompanied him everywhere a wife should her husband, and engaged him in her inner life not at all, nor herself in his.

Sally put down her knife and fork, the food on her plate barely eaten, dabbed decorously at her mouth with her napkin. "I'm not joining you for dessert, Philip. I hope you don't mind. I'm going to spend the evening with Abby."

"Well, perhaps I can go with you," Philip suggested, attempting to stave off another evening spent in crushing solitude. "We can take the pie."

"No, Philip, really. Abby is five months pregnant and still having morning sickness. She is terribly uncomfortable. That baby is draining all her energy. Just like me when I was carrying Jed." An unmistakable touch of pride in her voice. "The last thing she would welcome is you and a mountain of sweet pie."

"Well, of course, no pie then. But I could visit with Jed while you tend to Abby. It's been weeks since I've seen him."

"He won't be there. Abby said he has a late meeting of some kind. Jed would never blow his own horn, but I hear that he is doing just marvelously, taking to everything like a duck to water. But, of course, that surprises no one."

Philip sat bemused, wondering from whom Sally was hearing such heartening news. The only response Jed or Joseph ever gave to questions of Jed's progress was an unelaborated-upon *Fine. Doing fine.*

"Besides, they are coming for lunch on Saturday; you

can see him then." Sally rose. "I'm going to call a taxi and collect my things. Stay." She waved him back to his chair as he made to rise with her, perhaps walk with her to the telephone. "Finish your dinner. Enjoy your pie."

Philip pushed his plate away, his appetite quite gone. He stayed at the table, staring off into space, listening to the sounds of her moving through the house, her muffled voice, her light footsteps. As the taxi pulled up in front of the brownstone, she reappeared at the entrance to the dining room draped in a peacock-blue silk rain cape, its hood surrounding her milky skin and platinum hair. Philip glimpsed an angel limned by the bowl of heaven.

"I'm off, Philip. I've left your pipe and tobacco pouch with the newspaper in the parlor for you. Have a pleasant evening. At least you'll stay dry. Don't concern yourself with waiting up for me; I don't know how late I'll be."

Philip remained seated until he heard the taxi pull away. Then he pushed himself from the table, opened the door to the kitchen a crack. "Edna," he called out, "you may clear whenever you wish." He crossed the vestibule, took several reluctant steps into the parlor. As he stood, forlorn and indecisive, he saw the hours that lay ahead of him flowing like heated molasses, cooling as it went, thickening, hardening, slowing, stopping. The house was so empty when she wasn't in it. There was nothing to measure anything against. Even if she didn't say a word to him, merely sat by the fire reading, at least he could see her, hear her breathe. Even if she spent the evening in her room, at least he could watch her glide up the stairs, listen to the rustle of her skirts, feel her presence above him. But if she was not here, he could do nothing.

He returned to the vestibule, stood on the black-and-white marble floor, a pawn waiting for the guiding hand to move him. He could call Dorothy. Since Edgar had died they had seen quite a bit of each other. Philip knew himself to be no fool, despite how he appeared to the world. Dorothy liked him. She was an attractive, lonely woman and she liked him, very much. He pleased her by merely being himself. With her he was released from the uncertainty that bound and gagged him. He talked. He laughed.

He was witty. He liked himself. And he liked her. Very much. He could definitely call her. He heard Edna bustling between the kitchen and dining room. He heard the hard rain beating against the dormant earth outside the front door. He picked up the telephone receiver and toggled for the operator.

"Evelyn! You're making me dizzy. Would you please stop pacing or at least do it out in the hallway!" Joseph snapped shut his book in exasperation. "I am trying to read a little before David and Zoe get here."

"I'm sorry. It's just such an awful night . . ." Evelyn left her thought unfinished as she went to the window and peered out into the tumultuous darkness. Rain was pelting down onto the sidewalk, onto the dark asphalt of Fifth Avenue and beyond, onto the gleaming cobbles at the base of the low stone wall that contained Central Park. Trees swayed ominously in the wind. "Perhaps I should have told her to come tomorrow."

"For Christ's sake, she won't melt! Why in the world are you always so nervous when Zoe calls or comes to visit? She may not be anyone's idea of a competent woman, but she usually manages to find her way here without mishap. Besides, David is picking her up in a hired car after he drops Cissy at her parents'. I'm sure he's clever enough to have brought a nice big umbrella."

Evelyn turned away from the window and her uneasy contemplation of the storm raging outside, seeking the comfort she always took in Joseph's confidence. She put the rain and darkness behind her, but the storm raged on. There was no comfort in the familiar sight of her husband sitting languidly in his favorite armchair, one long elegant leg crossed over the other, his book open on his lap. His bone-deep calm was like a sudden slap across her face.

"Why do you take that tone when you speak of your daughter? Have you any idea how disrespectful you sound? Don't you have any feelings for her?"

Joseph looked up over the rim of his reading glasses. "She's my daughter. Of course I have feelings for her. But I can't honestly say that respect is one of them. We've had this conversation before, Evelyn; I don't relish having it again. She's a grown woman, living the life she chose. Why don't you just stop worrying about her."

She could have answered him. Now, or on any number of occasions in the past, she could have said, *Because I am waiting for something terrible to happen to her, something I could have prevented if I'd ever had the courage to open my heart wholly to her, to insist that you allow me to give her the same love I give you.*

But she never did. Joseph was not asking a question to which he wanted an honest answer. He was giving an order. He was warning her not to disturb the most intimate core of their relationship, which he relied on above all else, by putting someone else's welfare before his own. Her unbreachable devotion to him, and his to her, was the heart and soul of their unwritten marriage contract. She had understood it from the moment he had proposed. It was precisely what she had wanted: to be the one and only person he would ever truly need in his life and for him to be that for her. At the age of eighteen she had learned that she had a female problem and would never have children. She accepted the sympathies of her physicians and her family with grace but privately felt nothing but relief. She had already fallen in love with Joseph Gates, a widower with an absent son for whom he had only the vaguest concern. She knew intuitively what he was looking for in a second wife, and it wasn't a woman to give him more children. He needed a woman who was passionate, poised, intelligent, selfish, adoring, and barren. He needed her and no one else.

When, five years into their idyllic marriage, she inexplicably became pregnant for the first and only time in her life he was, of course, willing to let her have the child. He was no murderer, merely a miserable, unwilling parent. But there was no renegotiating their contract. Whatever paternal instinct he might have possessed was overshadowed by his long-lived and lovingly groomed need to control his world, to maintain his physical and emotional comfort. He was a responsible man, without doubt, and unhesitatingly sheltered, fed, clothed, educated, and criticized his children, thus believing himself to be a far better parent than his own father had been to him. That children might require more never occurred to him, and while he felt fondness for and occasional amusement at the struggles of both his children, there was nothing about either of them sharp enough to pierce his fundamental lack of interest in them as people.

Whereas Evelyn had found herself hostage to an immediate and desperate love for the tiny bundle lying placid in a hand-carved walnut cradle, staring up at her with huge, dark, unseeing eyes. It was unacceptable, that love; it was dangerous. It could disrupt the perfect symbiosis of her relationship with Joseph, and that could not be allowed to happen. How fortunate, then, that Zoe was a docile, eager-to-please, delicate beauty of a girl, a perfect child who never asked for more than she received, as though from birth she'd understood the terrible burden that would have placed on her mother and the rejection it would have engendered from her father. She made it possible for Evelyn to temper her love and dole out her attention from what was left after Joseph took his share. How fortunate that it hadn't been David who had emerged from her womb, a fiery hellion of a boy who would have demanded all the love they possessed and made them rivals for his devotion.

Evelyn consciously drew her thoughts away from the past. She had always believed in living aggressively in the present, even before Joseph had come into her life. She had never seen the benefit in allowing one's sight to remain turned backward overlong. What was done was done and could not be changed; the world of *if only* was comprised of quicksand. Her anger at Joseph dissipated as quickly as it had formed.

Zoe had sounded strong on the phone when she had called to ask if she could come for dinner; there was undoubtedly nothing to worry about. Evelyn walked toward the hall, stopping to stand idly by Joseph's chair. She ran her fingers through his hair, thoughtlessly playing with the shining strands of silver that were becoming more abundant now among the gold.

"Go back to your book, Joe. What is it? The new title by that Fitzgerald fellow?"

Joe turned the book over and looked at the cover as though for confirmation. "Yes. *The Great Gatsby*. The critics love it. What is it they say here? 'Fitzgerald understands the moral malaise of the Jazz Age better than any writer alive.'" He shrugged. "I'm not sure I know what the hell they're talking about, but the story is entertaining enough. Although I can't say I understand what this Gatsby wants, and why . . ." He was talking to empty air. Evelyn had wandered out of the room. He went back to reading.

In the hallway, Evelyn stood with her back against the wall. Out of sight of him, Joe's imperturbability radiated through the plaster and paint, pushed at her from the other side with a tangible pressure. She leaned into it and allowed it to calm her. What *was* she worried about, after all? It had been a long time since she had noticed even the smallest bruise on Zoe. And the shifting shadow of fear behind her eyes, the only emotion visible in eyes gone dull after Libby's death, had leached away over time. The dullness had persisted for much longer, Zoe trapped beneath it. But surely that was only natural; if something were to happen to Zoe, Evelyn could not imagine how the world would look to her through her pain, what her own eyes would show to the world.

"The doorman has rung, ma'am. Miss Zoe and Mr. David are on their way up. Would you like to let them in, or shall I?"

"Oh, Walter! I will get the door, thank you." Evelyn drew herself away from the wall. "Is everything ready for dinner?"

"Yes, ma'am. I'm sure it is. The smells coming from the kitchen are quite delicious." Walter gave her a conspiratorial smile. "But perhaps I should sample a thing or two, just to make sure everything is up to your high standards?"

"Oh, I definitely think you should." She smiled in response and, hearing the elevator doors slide open, the buoyant murmur of two beloved voices echoing in the vestibule, she hurried down the hall and flung open the door.

There, dripping water all over the floor, stood Zoe and David, with dark windblown hair and bright wind-rouged cheeks. Evelyn's heart leaped with joy at the sight of them and hope flooded her breast. Zoe turned to her, laughing at something David had said, and Evelyn saw life sparking in the black depths of her daughter's eyes, something deeply buried waking up and working its way to the surface, into the light. Whatever it was that Zoe wanted to tell them, Evelyn knew it was something that would finally put all worries to rest.

"My classes are finished and the population of the Lower East Side doesn't seem to need you tonight. It's been so cold and wet I think even the germs are running for cover." Jacob Weiss leaned over Lucy's shoulder as she sat at her desk, reading. "There is someone who needs you, though. Why don't you take pity on me and let me take you home early, keep you nice and warm and dry," he whispered into her ear, his voice tremulous with the expectation of rejection.

Lucy giggled softly and turned her head, reached up a hand, and patted his cheek. She looked at him with affection, at his hopeful face with its fine, strong features, clear, pale skin set off by a mop of black hair and near-black eyes. "No, Jake, not tonight. Someone might still come in. Besides, I have to catch up on these articles about birth control techniques being used now in Europe. We are so puritanical and backward here, you'd think that—"

She stopped as she saw his eyes turn muddy with disappointment. "Maybe Sunday. I'll make you dinner." She gave a look around, ascertained that no one was watching them, and gave him a quick kiss. "Go away."

He sighed and straightened up. "I'll be in the classroom, doing some paperwork." He trailed his fingers lightly across the back of her neck. "If you change your mind . . ."

The sound of his footsteps faded, but the tingle left by his touch lingered on her skin. Lucy squirmed in her chair, unable to sit still. She rose and walked into the entryway. As she watched the rain beat against the front windows, the memory of another March storm and the devastating feel of another touch assaulted her with such immediacy it might have been yesterday and not two years ago that she had been in his arms. She pirouetted away from the window, suddenly tempted to find Jake and let him do as he wanted. Why not? She liked him; she liked the way he made love to her. The problem was that he wasn't the one she wanted. And on nights like this, when that knowledge resonated inside every cell of her body, it was not possible for her to lie with Jake. She could only want him when that resonance inside her went dormant again. And it always did, eventually.

Hot tears stung her eyes. She knew she should go back to her desk and keep reading. There were stacks of articles and research reports on the effectiveness of condoms, spermicides and vaginal sponges, diaphragms and the rhythm method she had yet to get to. But her brain refused to focus. She dragged herself over to the rain-streaked window by the front door and leaned against it, pressing her nose to the cold glass like a child. Henry Street was deserted but for a well-dressed man, hunched over and walking slowly, peering at the numbers on the buildings from beneath a dripping hat brim and finally heading toward the door to the settlement house. Astonished, Lucy ran and flung open the door. Accompanied by a gust of cold, wet air, Philip stepped into the entry with a lost look on his face, an unopened umbrella hooked over his arm and a beribboned cake box in his hand.

Zoe placed her news, offered with a mix of pride and deference, into a lull in the dinner conversation much in the way Angelina had placed onto their plates thick slices of rosy roasted lamb bathed in herbs and natural juices.

"So," she said in a clear voice, looking down at her plate as she cut her meat, "what I came to tell you was that I have made some decisions about my life. I am going to divorce Monty, sell the apartment, move to Hidden Cove, and open a girls' equestrian academy."

Someone's Polhemus sterling silver fork clattered against an expensive Christofle porcelain plate, the sound shocking in the sudden silence. Without looking up, Zoe knew it had to be her mother whose fingers had gone nerveless at her pronouncement; neither David nor her father would ever lose their grip on a utensil as a result of anything she might say. She felt the pressure of three expectant stares, her judge and jury waiting for her to meet their eyes so they could gauge the strength of her courage and ascertain the truth of her words.

She raised her gaze from her plate and slowly looked at each of them in turn. The easiest first. David, a small but unmistakable smile of delight on his lips. Then Evelyn, hands pressed against her breast, her face flooded with evident relief and flushed with an emotion Zoe could not interpret. As their eyes met, Evelyn reached across the table and clutched hard at Zoe's fingers.

Then Joseph cleared his throat and all eyes turned to him. "That's quite an announcement, Zoe," he said around a mouthful of lamb. Not only had he not dropped his fork; he continued to eat with gusto. "Let's take a look at it, one item at a time, shall we? We don't need to discuss how stupid you were to marry him in the first place. Frankly, I thought you'd never have the gumption to leave him if you hadn't done it by now. I'd prefer not to give you the chance to change your mind, so let's agree that I will call our lawyer tomorrow and have him draw up papers."

"No." Zoe drew her hands into her lap, pressed them hard between her thighs.

"I beg your pardon?"

"I do not want you to call Mr. Sullivan. When I am ready, *I* will speak to him. I will decide the terms, have the papers drawn and delivered."

"What terms? You are not giving that weasel one penny of my money!"

"What you and Mother have given me is mine. My inheritance is mine. And this marriage, however hideous, is mine as well, and I will decide how it ends."

Displeasure twisted Joseph's features. His eyes turned brittle. He froze Zoe in their blue glare, but she did not look away. After a moment, Joseph grimaced, turned back to his dinner, and popped another piece of meat into his mouth. "Surprise. You have a backbone after all."

"Don't sound so disappointed, Father. I come by it naturally, after all." Zoe released her hands, steady now, and raised her untouched wineglass toward Joseph in a silent toast.

"Fine. Be impertinent. Give him your entire fortune for all I care; you've never listened to my advice. But don't come whining to me for money for your *girls' equestrian academy*," he mocked. "What do you know about creating and managing a business? Is this something to which you have actually given a moment's thought? Enterprises do not run themselves while you are off galloping along the beach."

"Joe, that's a little harsh," David said calmly. "I'm sure Zoe has—"

"Excuse me, but I suspect I know my daughter better than you do, David. She tends to latch onto people and ideas a little too easily, without an appreciation of the details, of costs and consequences, liabilities and benefits. We don't want to see her make another mistake, do we?" Joseph spoke as though Zoe were not present, yet his eyes were on her.

Zoe stared back. "My entire life has been a mistake in your estimation, Father; I know that quite well. And I have no grounds upon which to argue against your opinion, do I? The man I married, against your wishes and your warnings, is indeed unfit for civilized society, more so even than you know." From the corner of her eye Zoe saw her mother blanch and bring a hand up to cover her mouth. Zoe could not look at her.

Joseph grunted. "Don't exaggerate, Zoe." But his tone was considerably more gentle. "You have made mistakes, yes, but your life is not anyone's mistake. It is a gift, one which I would see you use more wisely than you have in the past."

"And so you shall. I actually learned a great deal from you, Father, and in recent years from my hardheaded yet generous friend here." She turned to smile at David. He was watching Joseph, his eyes wary, yellow and glowing like a lion poised to defend his pride.

"And what did you learn, Zoe?"

She turned back to Joseph. "How to first know what I want and then go about getting it. Let me assure you that I will not change my mind about divorcing Monty. And that I have given my plan a great deal of thought. I have spent the past seven months thinking about little else. I have been in touch with horse breeders in Virginia and Kentucky. I have spoken with the two boarding stables in the Oyster Bay area, neither of which offer instruction. Both have asked me to base my school with them. Apparently, my reputation has remained undiminished from my years of competitive riding."

"Petty flattery won't fund or run a business, Zoe. This is a complex undertaking. I don't care how many months you've been *thinking* about this. Thinking isn't enough." Commerce and life being one and the same to him, Joseph began his interrogation, doing what he did to every venture put before him in business, as he had done to every eager idea Zoe had ever offered for his approval. He tore it to pieces to see if the person who had brought it to him could succeed at putting it back together again. "Where are your numbers? What kind of deal are the stable owners willing to make with you? What are your staff and equipment needs? What is the real potential for clients? Forget the nice words of your horsey friends. Anything to do with horses is a monster of an expense; look at the cost of maintaining our own stable. And why haven't you considered expanding it, running the school from Hidden Cove? Come on, Zoe; where is your business plan, your figures, your projections, your—"

"Everything is waiting on your desk," Zoe interrupted. "I had it delivered to your office late this afternoon. And knowing how you value David's opinions, as do I, I have had a copy sent to him as well."

Joseph's mouth gaped open. David's deliciously amused laugh filled the air.

"What the hell are you laughing about? Did you know about this?" Joseph glared at David.

David raised his hands in mock surrender. "Not a whisper. I think we've all underestimated your lovely daughter. I can't wait to see what she's come up with."

"I had the company's own financial director, your trusted John McDonald, recommend the best financial adviser and business manager and we have spent months researching and working out a complete plan for the business, with one-, three-, and five-year projections. I *will* need help. I am not whining, Father, but I am asking you to look over the prospectus and, if it meets your standards, grant me a loan to start the academy. The request and proposed terms are all in what I've sent you."

"Do it!" Evelyn, silent and seemingly forgotten in the battle between father and daughter, struggled to her feet, sending her chair crashing to the floor behind her. Her face was white. For the first time in anyone's knowledge, she yelled at Joseph. "Why do you always have to torture her? Isn't this what you've always wanted her to do? Give her whatever she needs. Just do it! Do you hear me? Do it, or else . . . or else . . ." Her hands plucked spastically at the tablecloth as she stopped short of articulating some unimaginable threat to her husband of forty-three years. She ran from the room.

Zoe buried her face in her hands. She was sure now that Evelyn had known everything, had known and done nothing. And yet love for her mother overwhelmed all other emotions. Evelyn had actually yelled at Joseph. For her. Zoe lowered her hands but kept her eyes from her father's stricken face, from the dismaying sight of his pale skin turned beet red, the steel in his eyes melted with fright and incomprehension. She pushed his wineglass toward him and he reached for it with a shaking hand.

"Take some wine, Father."

David rose and righted Evelyn's chair. He picked her fallen napkin from the floor, folded it, and placed it on the table. He took his seat and stared down at his plate, played with the stem of his wineglass.

Joseph drank some wine. Several slow sips. Then several more.

Zoe looked at him then and put her hand over his. "I

don't want you to support my project because Mother told you to. I want you to believe in it. McDonald thinks it's sound, but if you find something amiss in my thinking, I want you to tell me. I intend to prove to you that I know what I'm doing and I can make this work. But, Father, I need your help."

Joseph withdrew his hand. His color had returned to normal. "I will look at the prospectus first thing in the morning. David, please do the same and then we'll confer. Once we agree that it's sound, Zoe, you'll get your funds. Of course I will help you. I had every intention of doing so. Your mother really didn't need to bark at me."

Zoe returned her hand to her lap. She looked in the direction of Evelyn's exodus, then nodded. "Yes. That's acceptable."

"I have a suggestion, Joe." David pushed his plate away and leaned his arms on the table. "Something I wanted to tell you in any case. Sell that Florida property you've been sitting on since before the war. What do you have, a half-mile stretch of oceanfront in Palm Beach? Do you have any idea what one oceanfront foot is selling for? Over three thousand dollars. What did you pay twenty years ago, five, six dollars a foot?"

"I should hold it. The boom down there isn't over."

"I think it is. It's been built on air for the past year, but no one will admit it. And I can't explain why, but I have a bad feeling that one morning we'll wake up and it will all have washed away. Sell now, Joe. Eight million is enough profit, even for you. You can give Zoe whatever she needs out of that and never miss it."

Zoe stood up. Nausea roiled in her to think that tomorrow her father could be richer by $8 million and yet he fought her over the paltry thousands she would need to rebuild her life. "Are we done here? This has been a stressful evening and I'm tired. Father, please tell Mother I'll lunch with her tomorrow. David, if you don't mind, I'd like to go home."

"Father! What in the world are you doing here?"

Philip looked around him. "What a lovely old building.

Federal style, 1830s, I'd say? Marvelous columns out front." As though startled to see her there, his eyes opened wide as his gaze settled on Lucy. "Hello, darling. Do you have a moment or have I come at a bad time?"

Lucy laughed in delight. "No, it's a fine time. It's been a slow night."

She relieved Philip of his umbrella, put it into a battered stand by the door. "These things do work, I hear. You might have actually used it." She smiled indulgently. "I'm amazed that you remembered I was here Thursday nights. Even so, with this weather I might not have stayed so late. Why didn't you call first?"

Philip looked sheepish and somewhat triumphant all at once. "Well, I didn't actually remember, quite. I did call, and a lovely woman informed me that you were here."

"There you are. Lucy, I'm leaving. Are you sure you don't want to—" Jake Weiss came toward the door, pulling on a long raincoat. He stopped short when he saw Lucy talking with a middle-aged man clearly not of the neighborhood. "Oh, I'm sorry. I didn't realize you were with someone." The slightest speck of jealousy in his voice.

"Jake, come meet my father. Father, this is Jacob Weiss. Jake is in graduate school at NYU, but he's here evenings and Sundays, teaching English and music."

Philip noticed how Weiss's eyes longingly tracked Lucy, even as he politely shook Philip's hand, as he said his good nights, backed away, and disappeared out into the rain.

"A nice young man."

"Yes, he is." She took Philip's arm and led him to her desk. "Hang your coat on that stand there. What's in that soggy box?"

"Ah." Philip lifted the box to eye level and scrutinized it as though it had just appeared in his hand by magic. "Yes. I brought dessert. Lemon meringue pie. I thought perhaps you'd have some with me."

They looked into each other's eyes, identical orbs of green, steady and observant. Lucy laid a soft kiss on her father's cheek. "I'd love some. I didn't have a chance to eat dinner. Wait here while I get some plates."

Philip sat patiently at Lucy's desk. He could have called

Dorothy, but he hadn't. Not because he didn't want to see her but because, condemnably, he did. He could no longer spend time with her and pretend it was only friendship that drew them to each other. They both craved something more, the full flowering of what had been blossoming between them ever since Edgar had fallen gravely ill. They had never spoken of it; they didn't need to. Philip knew what would happen between them if they allowed it. That he might consider turning to another woman for the comforts that his wife denied him magnified his sense of failure to an unbearable degree. He did not believe that Sally's inability to love him entitled him to betray her. And yet, tortured by aloneness, he considered it. More and more often, more and more urgently.

Lucy reappeared, awkwardly juggling plates, forks, napkins, a large knife, and two cups of hot tea. Philip quickly reached out to help her, relieved to be pulled from under the burden of his unsettling thoughts. He set neat little places for each of them as she took the pie out of the box and cut two enormous pieces.

"Mother left you alone again tonight, didn't she? What was it this time? Abby? Or one of her fatuous ladies do-good meetings?"

Philip winced at the derision in Lucy's voice. "Lucy, no. You don't understand her."

"Oh, honestly, Father! After all this time, what is there to understand?" Lucy licked lemon curd off her fingers. "Mmmm, good!" She put a big forkful of pie in her mouth with a show of great contentment.

"Your mother is unhappy. It's her unhappiness that you're seeing."

"Please!" Lucy abandoned any pretense of equanimity and slammed down her fork in anger. "What right or reason does she have to be unhappy? She has everything!"

"No, not everything. She doesn't have the love she needs."

"She has all the love she needs! She just won't take it! It's her own fault that she's not happy." Lucy shoved another piece of pie into her mouth and chewed viciously. "She should never have married you, or she should divorce you so that you can both find someone else. Divorce is all the rage these days. It wouldn't even be a scandal!"

Philip was dismayed by Lucy's distress. He reached out to take her hands, to try to reassure her, untrue though it might be, that his plight was not so dire. She pulled away, not wanting to be placated. "You judge her too harshly; you always have."

"How can you say that?" Lucy cried. "She's not the only one who's unhappy. She's not the only one who doesn't have what she wants. It doesn't give her the right to act like a cold-blooded queen, treat her children like subjects and her husband like the court eunuch!"

Philip stared at Lucy, shocked to silence. Not by her vulgar depiction of his marital situation, since it was, after all, merely the truth. He was stunned by the depth of his daughter's bitterness. It obliterated any thoughts of sharing his own misery with her or of confiding in her his feelings for Dorothy, of obliquely seeking her loving permission to sin.

"No, she's not the only one," Philip said quietly. He assessed the high flush on Lucy's cheeks, the quiver of her lips; his heart trembled to see how beautiful she looked in her rage. He took away her fork and held her hands tightly so she could not pull away. He captured her eyes as he had her hands and turned all his thoughts to her.

"Why are you so angry, Lucy? Is it possible that you understand your mother better than you'd like to admit?" He withstood her belligerent glare. "Your mother is married to a man she believes she doesn't love. What do you think she should do about it? What would you do?" He lifted one of her hands and tenderly kissed her clenched fingers. "Tell me, what are you going to do about David?"

As though she'd been given a sudden, stinging slap, Lucy recoiled and her eyes flew open. She blinked rapidly and fought for composure. "I don't know what you're talking about."

Philip said nothing. He looked at her and waited.

She set her jaw. "David is married."

"To someone he doesn't love."

"He knew what he was doing." Lucy gave a strangled laugh. "What are you saying, that he loves me? He doesn't."

"How do you know that? Just because he has never said so? Just as you've never told him that you love him."

"I *don't* love him!"

"Lucy," Philip admonished, and remembered a day when he'd found her in his studio gripping a brush dripping red paint. Evidence in hand, yet she'd denied that she'd had anything to do with the wet smear of red across his new canvas. Five years old and no less stubborn than she was now. "You can lie to yourself if you wish, but you can't fool me. You love him. You've loved him since the first day he walked into our house. I still remember how haughtily you behaved, how uncomfortable you tried to make him. I remember how frightened you were. Someday you will have to take the chance and risk yourself. If you can't tell him that you love him, there is no hope for you."

Lucy yanked her hands from her father's grasp. "Just like you've told Mother you love her, and look at the good it's done you. Anyway, you're wrong, Father. I don't love him, nor am I afraid of him. All David wants is money and the meaningless things he can buy with it. And a pretty stupid woman to hang on his arm in public and crawl all over him in private."

Philip raised his brows and pretended to take seriously Lucy's dismissal of David's character. "Really? I think you're wrong. I think there is more to him than that. David was poor and he aspires to be rich, yes, that's true. He also wants to be the best at what he does. For him it's not just about the money; it's about being good enough to deserve it. But that's not the important thing about him. I believe that what he really wants is what we all want. To be truly seen and to be loved by the person in whose eyes he sees his reflection. I believe that person is you. Just as I believe, despite everything, that I am that person for your mother. We are the stronger ones, Lucy. We have to help them."

Lucy's eyes filled with tears. She brought her hands up to her throat. "Do you? Do you really think it's me?" The stubborn five-year-old who had denied her culpability and yet cried with relief when Philip told her it didn't matter, he could fix it easily.

"Yes, I do."

"But he's married to Cissy."

"Then you have to have courage and be patient. Wait for your opportunity. I have no doubt that it will come. Or you could give up and marry your lovelorn Jacob Weiss"— Philip gestured toward the street, as though Jake were there waiting for her—"and find a way to make do with something that will never be enough. And hope you're better at it than your mother."

Lucy rose from her chair and went to sit in his lap as she had when she was a child and needed comfort. He put his arms around her and she nestled herself against him, plucked at the lapel of his jacket, inhaled the reassuring scent of pipe tobacco that lingered in the wool. "Did Edna really make that pie? It's awfully good."

"Oh my, no. It's from that Automat place, you know, that David likes so much? Quite the best I've ever tasted. Come, let's finish our pieces and then have seconds." He pulled her plate across the desk, handed her her fork, picked up his. "We both just have to keep trying. What else can we do."

Zoe stood under the shelter of the grand iron and glass marquee above the building's 81st Street entrance while David summoned the hired car waiting halfway down the block. He ushered her into the backseat, careful to hold the umbrella so that not a drop of rain fell on her, then slid in beside her.

"This is fabulous news, Zoe. I'm so glad you're leaving Monty. You deserve so much better. There will be a mad stampede to your door as soon as word is out, you know."

She laughed. "I'll have to build a strong fence. I'm not going to be trampled again. You can man the gate for me."

"I never would have let Monty through, I can tell you that."

"No, of course you wouldn't. You have much too fine a

filter against danger." Although she had had no wine at dinner, Zoe was drunk. Drunk with relief, her mind, body, and tongue gone loose and light in the aftermath of the evening's tensions. She rested her head against the soft leather seat back, then turned toward David and sighed. "I should have done this years ago. It feels so right, so wonderful. Why did I wait so long?"

"You were sidetracked by love," David crooned in jest. "But now that you've come to your senses, you can't fail."

Zoe gave him a long, considered look. "You haven't let that happen to you, have you, David?"

"Oh, nothing sidetracks me; you know that." David glanced away from her, something of sudden fascination grabbing his attention through the water-streaked window. "Let's not talk about me, all right? I was just joking." He took hold of her hand and brought it to his lips for a chivalrous kiss. "I promise to be your first and most devoted student."

"Well, my dear, now you'll have to pay. I've offered to teach you for years—for free—but you've always turned me down." She tweaked his cheek. "You won't ever make time to come riding, David; don't give me false hope. I'll need more reliable students than you."

"You'll get them. You'll be beating people away with your riding crop."

"David." She sighed again, suddenly depleted of energy, and let her gaze wander dreamily through the shadows and light playing over his face in profile. "You are such a good friend to me."

"You make it easy. You always have. Right from the beginning, you were so . . . *nice* to me." He took her hand again. "You have a wonderful warmth about you, Zoe. Quite unlike most members of your family," he said with a light laugh. "I've never understood why you let—"

She cut him off with a hard squeeze of the fingers and a meaningful look. "Let's not go down that road, David. We all make mistakes, don't we? Look at you. You find it easy to be good to me, but you don't know how to be good to yourself."

David withdrew his hand. "Come on, Zoe. I'm nothing but good to myself."

"Really."

He grunted in exasperation. "If you have something to say, just say it, would you?"

Zoe rolled her head away from him. "No. Just ignore me. I'm so giddy after this awful evening I don't even know what I'm saying." How ridiculous of her to imagine she might give another human being advice about who to love or how to love. Whatever mistakes David was making would reveal themselves to him sooner or later.

David rubbed at his eyes with his palms. "Yes. That was definitely a dinner to remember. You were absolutely amazing. You made your father quite proud."

Zoe gave a sour laugh. "How do you know that?"

"He told me so, as we were leaving."

"God forbid he should say it to me." Her voice sank and she closed her eyes.

"He thinks he doesn't have to. That you shouldn't need to hear it. You know how he is."

"Yes. And he's wrong," Zoe muttered as the cab pulled up in front of her building.

David, bending to gather up the umbrella, didn't hear her. He helped her out of the car and walked her to her front door. "Do me a favor, would you? Call over to the Harrimans' and let Cissy know I'm on my way. Tell her to wait for me in the entryway."

"Certainly. And David. Thank you for being there tonight."

He kissed her cheek. "You don't have to thank me. Whenever you need me, Zoe, I'll be there. You know that."

She let herself into her darkened apartment and waited quietly in the entry until she heard the sound of Monty's drunken snores coming from their bedroom. She exhaled in relief. He wouldn't wake until morning. Despite the confidence with which she had announced her decision tonight and the assurances she had given about not changing her mind, she was frightened. It was fear, not practicality, that cautioned her to wait until all her plans and arrangements had been made before telling Monty. To wait until her bags were packed, the car was loaded, her hat pinned to her hair, before she looked him in the face and told him she was leaving him. She would need protection, people behind her who would help her escape. That was why she had told her parents and David now. It had been a long time since Monty had laid a violent hand on her, but she never understood why he had stopped any more than she'd understood why he had started. A part of her, buried deep in that place that Monty had controlled for so long, lived still in a state of fearful anticipation. He wouldn't want her to leave. It would make him angry. He would try to stop her. He would try to find a way to trap her once again in his maze and force her to stay. She was afraid he might yet have the power to succeed, and so she would wait and plan and sneak away like a thief in the night.

She went into the parlor, made the promised call to the Harrimans, then went directly into the room that she now used as her own, the room that had once been Libby's. She locked the door behind her and sat in the dark in a chair by the window. The rain had nearly stopped, but the trees in the inner courtyard continued to drip copiously, their branches buffeted by the wind. She shuddered, suddenly chilled and damp, wrapped her arms around herself. She wondered how long she would have to wait before she knew true happiness again.

The rain had finally stopped. Lucy and Philip, bundled against the cold, wet wind, walked west on Grand Street, heading for the Third Avenue El. By sheer force of will they had finished the entire pie, and a brisk stroll to aid in its digestion seemed in order.

Lucy walked Grand Street, in both directions, three times a week, in sun, in rain, in snow. Often she veered one block north on Ludlow to Broome and then back down to Grand again. The slight detour took her to the building where David had lived for seven years of his life. In what rat-infested hovel on what squalid street he had spent the first eleven years she had no idea. All that anyone in the family knew of David Warshinsky they had learned from Jed in those first weeks after he had walked off the ship with David at his side. Information to be clearly heard and then forever forgotten. Some dates, some names, some small history about a sad and difficult past that David wished only to put behind him. That he had been born a Jew, grown up in poverty on the Lower East Side, had two dead siblings and a dead mother; that a living father, sister, and brother had disowned him. From David himself no one but Jed had ever learned anything.

Although, in part, Lucy had chosen to work on the Lower East Side as a way to worry at her love for him the way one would a toothache, she had never asked a soul about David or anyone else named Warshinsky. Whether anyone of David's family still lived in the building on Broome and Ludlow, Lucy didn't know. For all she knew they were all dead or moved to the Bronx or Florida. When she needed to, she would stop on the corner and look up, wondering which window had been his. Tonight, her father with her, she wouldn't dare. He might know all about her secret love for David, but she wouldn't act like a heartsick schoolgirl in front of him.

"So tell me again? How are we getting home?" Philip slid his hand under Lucy's arm.

"We're taking the El at Grand Street and the Bowery. I'll get off at Ninth Street and you'll get off at Eighteenth."

"You'll have a hearty walk home. Is it safe? Shall I come with you? I can call a cab from your apartment."

Lucy hugged his hand to her side. "It's fine, Father. I do it all the time. It's just ten minutes pretty much straight across Ninth Street, and it's perfectly safe, with NYU, Cooper Union, and all the new residential streets."

Six months before, Lucy had finally moved downtown, to an apartment on Perry Street near West 4th, in Greenwich Village, into one of the districts zoned for residential use during the previous decade. She loved the small-town feel of the irregular tree-lined streets and the big-city stimulation of the resident artists, writers, intellectuals, and bohemians who were transforming the neighborhood. It was perfect. Convenient enough for work, far across town from her parents, and far enough from David. She made a point to avoid Washington Square Park. Although sometimes, coming home at night, she would be pulled helplessly southward and instead of remaining safely anchored to 9th Street, she would find herself adrift on his block.

"If you say so. So then I'll go straight home." Philip ducked his head against a gust of wind and chuckled.

"What?" Lucy asked, her own head down, ready to be amused by one of her father's flights of fancy.

"We are like two charging mountain goats in human form. Bulling forward, heads down, shoulders hunched—"

And Lucy walked smack into another goat coming in the other direction.

"Oh! I'm so sorry!" Lucy instinctively reached out a steadying hand.

A young woman, sodden red kerchief plastered to her dark hair, wet tendrils slipping loose to frame the perfect oval of her face. Startled dark eyes with slightly puffy lids, filling with curiosity, darting between Lucy and Philip. Protective hands over her slightly swelling stomach. A shy smile, a deferential dip of the head in apology although she was not to blame for the small collision. With a mumbled, "It's all right," and one long, wondering look, she scurried on into the moonless, wind-whipped night.

Lucy and Philip stood side by side, watching her disappear into the thick darkness.

"Well, that was a magical moment, wasn't it? Like the appearance of a unicorn in the deepest forest. She had an aura about her, don't you think?" Philip stared on down the block although the girl was no longer in sight.

"I think she's pregnant. And I think she'd been crying." Lucy began to move on. "I wonder why," she said, looking back over her shoulder.

Philip took her arm again. "A lovely face. Something familiar about it. Did she remind you of anyone?"

"No, not really." But she did; Lucy just couldn't think who. And so she assumed it was herself, because the girl had been crying and there had been love and loss in her eyes.

Sarah hurried on. Reuben was waiting for her, keeping dinner warm, probably worried sick. She should have been home by now. She should not have allowed herself to wallow in useless emotions and waste fifteen minutes sobbing under the entryway stairs of the building next door to the shop. But her heart had given her no choice. For the past three months she had been wracked by the aftershocks of her meeting with David. Like a melody running amok in her brain, the wish that she had never seen him plagued her constantly.

She missed her mother. Once Sarah realized she was pregnant, her longing for the comfort and security of Anna's presence was so urgent she thought she would curl up and die. Anna had been her confidante, her teacher. Now Sarah was alone with her fears and her secrets; there was no one she could talk to. She loved her husband and her brother and sister-in-law, but she could never ask them the questions that echoed constantly in her head. Why did she get pregnant in January and not in October or December? Why did Reuben make love to her always in the dark, under the sheets, insisting on keeping their nakedness hidden from each other's eyes? Was it shameful that she wanted to see him, wanted to be seen, that she liked what they did so much? Did she sin against her dead parents, against herself, her brother, her nieces and nephews, her quickening child, by telling no one about David, letting him remain cast out of his family? Or was the sin against David himself, her lost and unrepentant brother?

The need to ask her questions of someone had been rising in her like steam in a pressure cooker. Soon she would start to leak. Little hissing bursts of the confusion in her heart that no one would understand. Her unhappiness would frighten the people she loved and they would be angry with her. Sarah found herself yearning to talk to a stranger, perhaps to that pretty, smartly dressed woman on the street. Sarah had seen her before, on other late Thursday evenings, an anomalous creature walking along Grand Street. She looked so smart and so sympathetic, and tonight it seemed she saw down into Sarah's soul and knew what frightened her. Childish wishful thinking. No one could read her mind and solve her problems. Once Anna had been able to do it. And David. But they were gone.

What Sarah had to do now was dry her eyes, climb the four flights of stairs, and be happy for everything that remained.

Philip sat in front of the fire smoking his pipe and reading the paper. The house was as still as a tomb. Sally had not come home yet; Edna had retired to her room. He was for the moment content, grateful that Fate had steered him away from talking to Lucy about Dorothy. He realized how wrong it would have been. Although he cherished her friendship, Lucy was first his daughter; she was not his intimate, not an equal. He had no right to seek her advice or ask her to shoulder responsibility in the personal matters of his life. He should do that for her, not the other way around. In any case, he had gotten the answers he sought. In talking to Lucy about David, his own patience and courage had been renewed. It was still possible that Sally could love him, that his opportunity awaited him even after all these years. For now, at least, he would not seek to be unfaithful to the woman he loved.

23

David strolled south on Clinton Street, the portfolio containing Jed's first batch of sketches tucked securely under his arm. He hadn't been back here for nearly two years, since his initial meeting with Reuben in July of '24, when they'd begun doing business together. The few times they had needed to meet face-to-face in the interim, Winokur always insisted on coming to Gates & Co., sparing David the waste of his precious time. It was possible that he didn't need to be here now, either. If Rachel was as good as Winokur said she was, she could be trusted to understand the essential nature of the designs without his guidance. He was here because he wanted to be sure and because he wanted to do it this way. He wanted Rachel to see him, the way Sarah had seen him, and know that he could fly that close to the flame without getting singed.

All these years he'd believed he wanted nothing from his past. But he'd been wrong. He wanted something. He wanted his past to tender what was due him. He even wanted the frisson of danger he felt as he walked the streets and anticipated revealing himself to Rachel. Why play at all if not for high stakes? If there was motivation beyond commercial profit and the tightrope thrill of personal risk pulling at him, something deep and needful, he wasn't aware of it.

He walked slowly, savoring the freshness of a rare April afternoon and the almost erotic pleasure of the powerful satisfaction that suffused him. He was fulfilling his destiny, the destiny that Anna insisted would be his, the destiny he had always seen for himself. He had rejected the inevitability of his birthright and gone in search of the key that would open the door to the life he wanted. He had found it, he had grabbed it, and in the space of seven years had forged from his own mettle a success even he had not dared dream of. Young David Shaw was quietly acknowledged by the city's ever-watchful, predatory business leaders as Joseph Gates's lucky find, the uncannily brilliant golden boy who would be king. It was his genius and unflagging effort that had made Gates & Co. the city's most popular and profitable department store; he had already earned more money than seemed reasonable for any one person to have; he boasted a grand home at one of the finest addresses in the city and a pretty, vivacious wife. And it was just the beginning. For the past eight months he had been splitting his time between the store and the company offices downtown, attending meetings of division heads and company officers with Joseph and Jed, completing his education about the company's affairs, offering input on all aspects of the business. Although he and Joe had not yet spoken of it specifically, David's unerring intuition was telling him that by the end of the year he would be gone from the store altogether and installed in the Gates Building, beginning his ascent to heaven itself.

Short blocks away, his contemptuous and contemptible

brother, Ben, with the blessings of the nonexistent God in whom he put his faith, was living his ordinary life, an ignorant man of no consequence, while his reviled little brother, with the blessings of the flesh-and-blood rulers of the real world, was living as an equal among giants. Today he felt there was nothing he couldn't do. The world bent to his will. Lesser people bent to his will. He had never worried that Sarah would disobey him and tell someone that she had found him. A confusion of love, loyalty, guilt, and self-denial would paralyze her. She would fear displeasing him even further and agonize over her choices, opting finally to do nothing. He had no worries about Rachel, either. He knew that the power he had wielded over her nine years ago was still potent.

Reuben was not happy to be excluded from any part of such an important conference, but David had convinced him over the phone to let him meet first with Rachel alone, for artistic reasons, and then together they would hammer out the production details. Now he waited for her, his back to the door of Reuben's office, Jed's sketches laid out on the desk. David heard her footsteps coming down the hall. For a second, now that it was too late to leave without her seeing him, he felt a disturbing breach in his implacable confidence. What if he couldn't control everything, after all? What if Rachel told Reuben, and Reuben told Sarah, and Sarah confessed that she already knew, and they came looking for him and soon everyone on the Lower East Side knew who he was and then everyone in the city knew who he was? An impostor, an uneducated Jew living among the privileged under false pretenses. What would happen if the taint of this life began to ooze into the life of David Shaw, corroding the seams he had soldered so securely? Not even Joseph would be able to protect him.

He heard the office door open and close. A familiar voice behind him. "Mr. Shaw? Mr. Winokur said you wanted to show me some design sketches?" David didn't turn. He kept his back to her, breathed deeply, calmed himself. He was being foolish. There would be no problem. Nothing from here could hurt him anymore. "Mr. Shaw?"

David turned around then and faced her. "Hello, Rachel."

He let her look at him, gave her the time she needed to understand who it was standing before her. He wondered if she might cry, as Sarah had, but he saw immediately that she wouldn't, that she had done her crying years ago. She held herself straight and still, but he could see her distress in the flare of her nostrils and the sudden straining of her breast as her breath ran away from her. Shock widened melting brown eyes that he knew so well, and in them David saw a mix of love and loathing. He wanted to look away, but he didn't. It would have been too cruel and, suddenly, cruel was the last thing he wanted to be. She was still beautiful and David remembered what she'd been like when they'd both been seventeen and in heat.

"Oh no. It can't be you." Her voice was barely more than a whisper. Her eyes raked over his face, traveled up and down the length of him, examining every inch.

"No, it's not me. It's David Shaw." His tone was light, but not light enough to hide the clear warning that his identity was to remain a secret. "Someone quite different." He smiled with sudden pleasure, surprised at how moved he was to see her. "You look wonderful, Rachel. It's good to see you again."

He kept his eyes on her. He saw her pale, thought he saw a shimmer of color around her head, a riotous aura of emotion reaching out into the ether. He waited for her to sort it through, know her feelings, decide what it was she needed to say. He had no right to ask it of her, but he didn't want her to hate him.

"We have to get past this moment, Rachel. We need to be able to work together." He gestured toward the sketches on the desk. "Say what you want to say to me. Get it over with."

She drew in her breath and gave him a venomous look. "It was over with when you didn't come back, when you never wrote, when I married Shlomo. I have nothing to say to you."

Whatever softness David had felt toward her hardened

instantly. "Good. Then we can get down to business. But before we do let me make it clear that you are not to talk to anyone about me, about who I was. Not to anyone. I wouldn't have exposed myself to you if I hadn't thought it was necessary and that I could trust you. Don't prove me wrong."

"Don't worry, David. Why would I want to tell anyone? Who would I tell, anyway? No one cares about you anymore, not even Sarah. And I care too much about her and Reuben and Ben and Naomi and your nieces and nephews to wish you back into their lives. You do know that your sister is married to Reuben, don't you? And that she's pregnant, did you know that, too? You're going to be an uncle again. Another human being you can pretend doesn't exist."

David exhaled sharply, as though he'd been hit in the stomach. Knowing that he had earned the worst she could throw at him did nothing to mitigate his fury at having his current state of grace so harshly attacked. He refused to think about Ben and Naomi's children, about a pregnant Sarah. "Thank you," he said coldly.

He moved toward her and grabbed her roughly by the arm. He pulled her to the desk. "Let me show you what I want done with next winter's women's line."

They stood side by side, eyes anchored on Jed's sketches. They began a terse, professional discussion about folds, draping, material, proportions. This was his vision of clothing that didn't look like anyone else's, clothing that enhanced and flattered women's bodies while maintaining fashion's long, straight silhouette. She quickly grasped what he was after, suggesting a lace bodice here, the addition of beads there. More gathering at the low waist, a shorter sleeve. He saw that she could execute what he wanted. The tension between them began to dissipate as they concentrated on the work, turned their focus away from each other to something safe and manageable.

He reached out to trace the lines of a dress, to clarify a point he was making about an unusual mix of fabrics he had in mind. His hand brushed against hers where it held the sketch flat against the desktop. An electric charge leaped from her to him and suddenly her hand was lying atop his, light as a cloud, hot as a poker. Neither moved. Their eyes stayed on the fine black and white lines that no longer seemed to have any meaning. Slowly, David turned his hand so that their palms touched. He twined his fingers through hers and she gripped him tightly, held on with all her strength.

"I loved you so much. How could you have left me like that?" Her words were barely audible and there was no more venom in her voice, only sorrow.

"I don't know. I'm sorry, Rachel. I just couldn't come back here." David knew he should remove his hand. This tender feeling was nothing more than a ghostly relic of an innocent time when actions had no consequences. In his peripheral vision he saw a tear drop onto the white paper. "Rachel, don't. Please, don't cry. I never meant to hurt you. You knew I was never coming back."

There was a knock at the office door. Rachel tore her hand away and wiped her eyes with her sleeve, blotted the sketch where her tear had smudged one of Jed's meticulous lines.

"*Nu?* Enough time already, the two of you." Reuben came into the room, impatient and tired of being exiled to the factory floor.

A wave of vertigo hit David like a hammer blow. He stumbled, bracing himself against the desk with rigid arms. He was locked in a lie with a man he respected, who believed him to be an astute businessman named David Shaw, the scion of a wealthy high-society family. Reuben had not a clue that this sham *goy* was his wife's vanished brother, his own brother-in-law. He would never dream of joyfully confiding in David Shaw that his young wife was pregnant; it would be wholly inappropriate to be so personal and familiar with a business colleague so above him in social standing. And David could not tell Reuben that he knew and was happy for him. Because how would he have come to know what Reuben would never tell him? To reveal that Rachel had told him was to reveal that she knew him, knew that the child Sarah was carrying was David's own niece or nephew. And poor Rachel, who had once known everything about him, now knew just enough to have to pretend she knew nothing.

"David, are you all right?" Reuben took a step closer and placed a hand on his shoulder.

His head ached from the pressure of the secrets crowding the air of the confined, windowless room. He was so close to his past he could feel its gravity pulling at him. This was no good. He couldn't ever come down here again. He had enough lies to keep straight in his real world; he couldn't juggle his life in this precarious shadow world as well.

"No. I suddenly don't feel too well. Rachel understands exactly what needs to be done. I'll let her go over it all with you. We'll speak tomorrow. Call my office in the morning."

Reuben looked at him in astonishment, then at Rachel. "Yes, you can do this?" he said to her.

"Yes, she can do this, Reuben," David said. "You've got quite an asset in Mrs. Weinstein." He managed a smile, happy to see the look of gratitude on Rachel's ashen face. "Rachel, why don't you show me out. There's one last thing I want to go over with you."

"Of course, Mr. Shaw."

They left Reuben poring over the sketches and walked through the shop's front room, out into the empty hallway. David made sure the door was securely closed behind them before he turned to her.

"Rachel—"

Before David could say another word, Rachel placed a gentle finger on his lips and shook her head. "I won't say a word, David. I don't understand how you live like this, cut off from your family and everything you knew, but then I never did understand you, did I? In any case, I know it's not my place to tell them. That's a decision only you can make."

He kissed her fingertip, then took her hand and drew it away from him, let it go. "Thank you. And thank you for not despising me completely. I know this was hard, Rachel, but believe me, it was hard for both of us. Don't ever think that I've forgotten the times we had together."

Rachel stared up at him with luminous eyes. That intimate moment in the office had trapped her. He had to release her, release them both from any possibility of misunderstanding. Kiss her cheek, like the secret old friend he was, and say good-bye. He leaned toward her. A kiss on the cheek. He meant to turn his head to the side, but her arms were around his neck, pulling him down, she was kissing him, and his head began to buzz with an old, fiery desire. Fully aware of how wrong it was, David gave in to his excitement at the feel of another woman after three years with only Cissy. He kissed Rachel, let her lean her full body against him, listened for the little whimpering sound she always made when they kissed, a sound that never failed to make the blood race through his veins. He heard it; the blood raced through his veins and he knew he had to stop. He pulled away, held her at arm's length.

"You don't want this, Rachel," he whispered, knowing full well that she did.

"You never cared about what I wanted before. Why do you care now?" There were tears in her eyes.

"I don't want to hurt you again. I don't." He shook his head. "You're still so beautiful, it would be so easy to . . ." He lifted his hands from her shoulders and took a step back. "I don't need another regret in my life, Rachel. Don't tempt me." He waited until she lowered her lids, shutting out the sight of him as acknowledgment that she would, again, do as he asked. "I'm going to leave now. I'm not coming back here. I'm not going to see you again."

Rachel nodded without opening her eyes. She didn't see him struggle with himself to stay where he was. She didn't see him mouth one last silent, *I'm sorry.* She didn't see him turn and head for the stairs. She only heard his footsteps moving away from her and she stayed where she was, her eyes closed, until she couldn't hear them anymore.

David pushed open the building's metal door. It swung shut behind him and he fell back heavily against it. He stared up into the pale blue spring sky and willed his head to clear. He would not tolerate another headache on such a beautiful day. He breathed deeply, dragging air into his throat and lungs. The ache behind his eyes began to fade and he sighed, nearly moaned, in relief. He'd been right about Rachel, about the power he still had over her, but he felt no satisfaction in the knowledge. He had been excited by her, by the young girl's love for him still burning in her woman's eyes, and his response to her disturbed and confused him. He needed to get away from here, go back uptown where he was safe. No more visits to the ghosts that stalked these crude streets. He wouldn't come back again, not ever.

He began walking north up Clinton, just two and a half blocks until he'd cross Houston Street and leave this neighborhood behind. But his feet turned west on Rivington and he plunged into the heart of it, his instinct for self-torment rising to the fore. A few more automobiles, a few less pushcarts than he remembered, but the same mass of humanity, the same babble of voices. He negotiated the crowds with the same deft grace he'd had as a boy, barely aware of his own movements. He was heading toward the Bowery and then he'd be out. It wasn't until someone crashed into him, almost knocking him over, that he realized he had stopped moving. *Leyrowitz's.* A huge sign, hanging in front of him. Sarah was in there, nothing but a wall made by the hands of man separating her from him. That and the perfect pearl in his heart. The pearl of anger and solitariness that he had had to repolish and force back into its shell after Sarah had left his office that awful day. Sarah, working over someone else's fine piece of clothing that she could never afford for herself, her belly tight and rounded. She was carrying Anna's grandchild, his niece or nephew, a child of his family's precious bloodline. While he deprived his wife of the child she wanted. His child.

Like an evanescent image from a dream—vivid in the mind's eye for a fleeting instant before being lost forever to wakefulness—he saw Sarah's child firmly placed in its world, its reason for being born undeniable, and he saw his child floating in the emptiness of space without purpose or place. Then the vision and any understanding of it was gone and David was filled with a sense of danger. Something stalking him with fearsome menace, disguised in the sad and seductive forms of his former lover, his own sister. They wanted to plant their guilt and loneliness in his heart.

They wanted to destroy what he had become and reduce him to the nothing he had been. They wanted him to believe that all their misery had been his fault. That Anna had died because of him.

Someone jostled him in annoyance as he stood blocking the flow of human traffic, lost in the workings of his mind and unconscious for the moment of his surroundings. The movement brought him back and his first thought was that he had to escape. He began walking again, faster and faster, then he was running through the crowds, and he ran until he was gasping for air and the stabbing pain in his side forced him to fall onto a bench that had appeared in front of him. But it was all right. He was in Washington Square Park. He was home.

24

Zoe's Packard was parked and idling at the curb, crammed to its limit with trunks and suitcases. Ralph, on loan from her parents for the day, sat patiently in the driver's seat, waiting to take her to Oyster Bay. Mary and Walter were at the apartment, arranging to ship the things Zoe wanted that could not fit into the car. Nothing of real value was to be left behind for Monty to abuse. No artwork or jewelry or china or sterling. Nothing for him to destroy out of spite or sell out of greed. And nothing that had once belonged to Elizabeth for him to pretend to cry over.

Zoe had exploded into a blur of action the moment Monty had left the apartment that morning, every step of her escape carefully choreographed. Like an enraptured dervish, she was driven on by her own manic energy. Now she found herself hesitating on the pavement outside the Fifth Avenue entrance to Gates & Co., the last vestiges of the old Zoe rooting her in fear, telling her that she didn't have the courage to face him, to go through with it to the end.

A gust of unseasonably hot May wind snatched at her

dress and swirled it around her legs. The fabric felt like a live thing tickling at the muscles of her calves, urging them forward. Zoe ceded herself to the heavy revolving door and let it discharge her into the store's square-block ground floor. The repetitive *whoosh* of the door thumped at her back as she moved through the high-ceilinged space filled with gargantuan arrangements of spring boughs and blooms, pussy willow, crab apple, cherry, forsythia. Intoxicating scents of lilac and lilies rode the gently stirring eddies of cooled air.

In the seven years that Monty had worked here, she had dropped in to see him unexpectedly only once before. He had asked her never to do it again. He claimed it had embarrassed him and diminished his authority over his staff by reminding them that he was married to the owner's daughter. Even then, Zoe had known Monty was lying. He simply didn't want his wife coming upon him as he worked his seductive charms on another rich, lonely client.

And, not surprisingly, that was precisely what she did.

Her last, most tenacious fears and doubts, the ones that had hung on through her long reawakening, were dispelled once and for all by the sight of her husband enjoying an unmistakably intimate moment with another woman. Zoe stopped just beyond the range of Monty's awareness and watched him. He was so very good at what he did, she almost had to admire him. The way he stood, so thrillingly close behind the flushed woman, and ran his hands over her hips, pretending to help smooth the fabric of the costly dress she was without question going to purchase. The way he leaned over her shoulder, his cheek next to hers, and let his eyes caress her reflection in the full-length mirror. The honey in his voice as he murmured, "This dress was made for you. Look at yourself!"

Zoe stealthily placed herself next to the oblivious couple and suddenly there was a crowd of three in the mirror. She smoothed her hands over her own curves. "Darling, don't you think I would look good in that dress?"

"Zoe!" Monty quickly took his hands off the woman's

bony tulle-swathed hips. "Jesus Christ, what are you doing here?"

The customer's startled eyes met Zoe's in the mirror. Zoe smiled, a bright, false smile. "No offense my dear, but you need some flesh on those bones to wear that. Don't let my husband sweet-talk you into buying it."

The woman blushed bright red. Her eyes sought out Monty in the mirror.

He put a reassuring hand on her arm. "Don't listen to her, Mrs. Carrington. She's—"

"Oh, let her go, Monty. I'm sure you'll find other prey before the day is out."

Mrs. Carrington, beyond mortified, gathered up the too-long skirt and scurried away toward the changing rooms, nearly colliding with a saleswoman.

Monty turned to Zoe with a steely look. "You just lost me a very good sale. I've told you not to disturb me at work. Why are you here?"

"I suspect I lost you more than a sale." Zoe matched his obdurate stare and was coldly thrilled when Monty dropped his gaze first. "I'm here to give you something." She reached into her purse and held out a thick envelope.

Monty made no move to take it. He looked her severely up and down. "You only wear that outfit when you're making an automobile journey. I don't remember you telling me you were going somewhere. What's gotten into you? This is all totally unacceptable, Zoe."

"Yes, it is. I quite agree." Zoe dropped the envelope at Monty's feet. "I'm divorcing you, Monty. No negotiation. My lawyer, Mr. Sullivan, will be taking the papers directly to Judge Hartley, an old friend of my father's, who will grant the divorce without trial. We don't really need to prove in public that you have fulfilled New York State's requirements for divorce by being unfaithful to me, do we? We don't wish to embarrass ourselves or the many Mrs. Carringtons in your life."

Monty glanced down at the envelope and then back at Zoe, a chiding, quizzical look on his face. "*You* are embarrassing us, my dear. Coming here like this and misinterpreting my behavior. If this is your idea of a joke, it's not funny, I assure you. Are you still angry that I forgot our anniversary? I thought I'd more than made up for that lapse." He smiled, a suggestive reminder of how much she'd appreciated his apology.

Zoe stared back at him without saying a word, until his smarmy smile wobbled and wilted. "The terms of the divorce are clearly spelled out. It should take no more than three months to become final. I've been unnecessarily generous to you. I'm going to live at Oyster Bay. You can stay in the apartment through the summer, but it will be sold in the fall, so I suggest you find a new home for yourself. Perhaps Mrs. Carrington can help you."

Zoe watched Monty's skin turn ashen beneath the faint blue blush of his closely shaved beard. His lips tightened to a slash. A shiver of exultation rose from her toes up into her head. Her scalp tingled and her ears filled with the sound of rushing blood. A burst of joy erupted from the top of her skull and cascaded down all around her like fireworks. It was done. She was free. Libby could rest in peace.

Zoe turned and began walking back to the elevators. Her heart was thudding heavily, but she felt as though she were floating six inches above the carpeted floor. Although she couldn't see or hear him, she knew that he was coming after her. She kept walking.

Monty grabbed Zoe's arm and swung her around to face him. "You can't do this."

"I can and I am. Take your hand off me."

"Zoe." Monty crooned her name, softly stroked her arm and cheek. "You don't want to leave me. Someone's been filling your head with nonsense. We understand one another, darling. You won't be happy without me."

Zoe forcefully pushed his hand away from her face. "I couldn't possibly be less happy without you than I am with you. Even loneliness will feel like a godsend. Whatever you think you understand about me may have been true once, but not anymore. I can't live with you another second."

She scrutinized him long enough to see his mask collapse and his handsome face grow ugly with anger and panic. She didn't say good-bye. She just turned and walked away. This time, he didn't follow.

There was a commotion outside his office, Mrs. Thorne's voice raised in alarm. David rose from his desk. He had not closed half the distance to the door when it flew open and Monty crashed through. Before David had time to react, Monty, snarling like a rabid dog, grabbed him by the throat and slammed him against the wall. David's head hit unforgiving plaster with an audible smack. Through the ringing in his ears and his instantly blurred vision he heard Mrs. Thorne yell, "Mr. Glennon! Mr. Shaw!" and saw her fly down the hall.

"You put her up to this, you conniving kike. What did you do to her? Did you fuck her?" Monty's saliva sprayed all over David's face. "Are you fucking my wife? Is that what you do when you take her to *lunch* every month?"

David brought his knee sharply up into Monty's groin, his body intuitively responding with the dormant but intact muscle memory of a hundred youthful street fights. Monty screamed with pain and released David's throat to clutch at his genitals. David pushed himself away from the wall and roughly shouldered Monty aside, nearly knocking him to the ground. He reached the office door just as Mrs. Thorne reappeared with a store security guard at her heels.

"I'll take care of this." David closed the door in their faces.

He turned back to Monty, who, though wincing still, was standing upright. David forced himself to stay at the door, gripping the knob, fighting the urge to rush across the floor and beat this man he loathed to a bloody pulp.

"You are some piece of work." David stared at Monty with a look as deadly sharp as the point of his wartime bayonet. "You fuck everything in sight and then have the nerve to accuse me of sleeping with your wife? I don't do that."

Monty smiled, a huge mocking smile. "No, you're such a goddamned saint. You'd never take advantage of an unhappy woman who adores you. All right, so let's say I believe that you didn't get to her through her cunt . . ."

David lurched away from the door, a guttural growl of disgust in his throat, took a step toward Monty.

". . . but you got to her somehow." Monty didn't move. The mocking smile remained. "I notice you aren't asking me what the hell I'm talking about. You know. You put the idea in her head. It's the only way it could ever have gotten there."

"*You* put the idea in her head, Monty, not me. But I surely did encourage her."

Monty wagged a threatening finger. "Screw you. This is your fault. If she doesn't change her mind, you're going to pay."

David shook his head and smirked. "She's not going to change her mind and I won't have a thing to do with it. But, what the hell, I'll give you something to blame me for. I'm going to get you fired."

"You don't have the power, you son of a kike bitch. Harry Selkirk makes those decisions, and he knows how much money I bring into this store."

"He might not care when he learns just how you do it. I'm going to make it my personal mission to flush your life into the sewer with the rats, where you belong."

Monty's smile turned to an ugly rictus. "You might want to rethink that, David. I'm sure you wouldn't want your lovely wife to somehow learn *your* secrets, would you? What *would* the Harrimans think if they knew their pure and precious only daughter was being ravished nightly by a filthy Jew?"

David's breath hissed from his nose. The muscles of his jaw clenched. He fixed Monty with a look of hatred so strong Monty stumbled backward.

"Don't threaten me, Monty. I have many allies, but no one in the world gives a damn about you. Before you could do anything to hurt me, I'd crush you like a cockroach."

David strode to the office door and yanked it open. Mrs. Thorne and the guard stood where he had left them on the other side, frozen in shock and indecision.

"Go back to work; everything is fine here. Mr. Glennon was just leaving."

Monty strolled calmly toward the door, the veteran performer reclaiming his audience, soldiering on after a slight slip in character. "Consider what I said, David. Maybe you'll want to talk to Zoe after all. You know, you help me and I'll help you?"

David smiled amiably. "I don't think so."

25

*If Jed could have done it without moving and thus disturb-*ing the sublime tranquillity of the moment, he would have wished to paint the scene. Abby, his radiant wife, one month shy of giving birth, sat in a corner of the sofa, her dainty slipper-shod feet upon a tapestried ottoman. Jed sat beside her, one arm around her back, the other under her stomach. His open hand, its fingers stretched wide and long, rested protectively along the bulging side of the sacred vessel, waiting patiently for the exhilarating feel of a kick from within. Jed's head lay against Abby's full breast. She stroked his face over and over with a slow, loving caress. It was Sunday morning and the world had stopped, just for them, at a rare and immaculate juncture in the universe, leaving Jed adrift on a calm sea, safely alone and in love with his wife and unborn child.

June sunlight gushed through the alley outside, a river of melted gold that spread into the parlor through the open windows, bathing everything in glorious honeyed luminescence. The delicate trilling songs of distant birds floated into the room on waves of light and echoed gently off the walls and ceiling. All else was silence save for the hollow thump of Abby's heart and the airy hum of Jed's own breath. Somnolent as a bee sated on pollen, unwilling to move, Jed made the light his canvas. In his mind's eye he painted the scene, watched it dry, framed it, and hung it on the wall; then he crawled through the frame and took his place on the canvas where he could remain in this crystalline moment of peace for all eternity. No messy encounters with flesh-and-blood life. No sex. No demands. No yearning. No shame. Nothing but the perfection of limbo.

From his place of safety, Jed rested his drowsy gaze on the mound that contained his son. He knew the child was a boy. The certainty of that fact came from a source inside himself that he neither recognized nor understood. He simply accepted what it told him. For the past months he had been possessed of a strange, exalted sensation of being able to see into Abby's womb and observe the miracle of the tiny being that he had created. He had watched him grow and been happier than he could ever remember being. Abby's pregnancy had allowed him to languish in a state of suspension where he could believe in the possibility of contentment. In four weeks, the gears of life would ratchet up and begin to turn once more and once more he would be dragged somewhere beyond his knowing or his control. As his eyelids began to droop, he clung to his wife's beautiful, ungainly body as to the precious moments that remained to him.

Abby's caresses had stopped. Her breathing was deep and even and her hand had drifted from his face to rest on the arm that cradled her stomach. Jed's eyelids grew heavier and heavier as the rise and fall of Abby's breast beneath his head lulled him to join her in sleep. His eyes closed fully and he breathed in the light, the birdsong, the perfumed air. From inside the frame of his idyllic painting, he breathed it all in and let it all out, the creator varnishing his creation with the breath of life. As he sank the last distance into sweet unconsciousness, voices, harsh and unwelcome, brought him back to wakefulness. There came the rasp of a key in the door and the voices became a piercing babble moving into the room, slashing across his pastel canvas in lurid chrome tones. In total confusion and helpless outrage, he lifted his head and opened his eyes to see his world utterly violated.

"Darling! How sweet you two look, curled up like little puppies! You missed a lovely service today. Father

Franklin sends his regards." Sally sailed toward the parlor table like the devilishly animated masthead of a great pirate ship, rapacious and overbearing. "It's after noon, you sleepyheads. I've brought some lunch. Philip." She gestured behind her.

"They're napping, Sally," Philip whispered as he edged toward the table. "Perhaps we should just leave the basket and go."

Jed's vision slowly came into focus and he saw his father, holding a large, heavy-seeming picnic basket, glancing toward the sofa with a desperately apologetic look. He saw his mother's face close down as she turned and grabbed for the basket's handle. Suddenly there was no breathable air in the room.

"I want to have Sunday lunch with my son. What is wrong with that!" She took the basket from Philip's hand and swung it up onto the table. "Jed, don't lie on Abby like that. It can't be good for the baby. Come, dears. It's time for something to eat."

Jed levered himself up and began to untangle his arms from around Abby. She grabbed at his hand as it rose from her belly and her eyes grabbed at his face, beseeching him to resist.

"Mother . . ."

"Yes, darling?" Sally whirled toward him, her eyes two cobalt beams scouring his face, the intensity of her love for him shining with the purity and heat of an equatorial sun. She gave a gay laugh. "Oh, I'm bad, I know! I should have called. Your father said I should. But you forgive me, darling, don't you?"

Jed felt the pressure of Abby's need on his fingers, the pressure of his mother's need on his heart. His own need he couldn't feel at all. But his duty was as clear to him as the blue of Sally's eyes. "Of course we forgive you. And we're starving, aren't we, Abs?"

He rose, helped Abby to her feet without meeting her eyes. As they walked sleepily toward the table, Abby laid her hand lightly on the small of his back. At her absolving touch, a tidal wave of grief crashed over Jed. He put a hand to his face to hide a shocking gout of tears and pretended to politely cover a long, enormous yawn. One day, all his betrayals and his lies and his failures and his secrets were going to coalesce into a massive ball, black and heavy as a starless, moonless night, and chase him right off the edge of the world.

26

Janet Thorne was startled by the sound of a quiet cough. She turned from her filing to see a sweet-faced, rangy young man standing by her desk. She had not heard him approach, nor sensed his presence behind her. He stood before her now with his back straight and his head tilted at a haughty angle, but his wide-open, frightened green eyes gave him the appearance of a hare caught in the glare of an automobile's headlights. Above his upper lip the endearing fuzz of an adolescent mustache bloomed, and on his rebellious teenage chin a pimple threatened to erupt. He wore a formal suit, too heavy for the July heat. Sweat stood out on his forehead.

Mrs. Thorne resisted a maternal urge to reach out and smooth the boy's sandy hair off his damp brow. She smiled at him encouragingly. "Hello. Can I help you? Are you perhaps looking for the men's department?"

Brook cleared his throat. "No. I'm looking for Mr. David Shaw. Would you be so kind as to tell him that Mr. Brook Gates is here to see him?" His attempt to address David's secretary in the same imperious tone he had so often heard his grandfather use might have succeeded but for the way in which his voice cracked, twice, from nervousness.

Mrs. Thorne's lips quivered imperceptibly. "I'm so sorry, Mr. Gates. Mr. Shaw isn't in the building at present. Was he expecting you?"

"Ah. No. That is, well, I, no . . ." Brook turned bright red and his eyes skittered all around Mrs. Thorne's work space before settling down to a careful study of the ceiling above her desk. His shoulders sagged and he looked as if he might bolt at any second. "Ah."

"Mr. Brook Gates. Are you by any chance *the* Brook Gates, grandson of Mr. Joseph Gates, owner of this store?"

Brook lowered his eyes and looked into Mrs. Thorne's kind face. He drew in a proud breath and squared his shoulders. "Why, yes, I am. How nice of you to recognize my name."

"Well, indeed. It's an honor to meet you, Mr. Gates. Mr. Shaw will be sorry to have missed you, I'm sure. Is there anything you would like me to tell him on your behalf?"

Brook swallowed, licked his lips, visibly summoned his courage. "No message, no. But if you would be so kind as to give him this"—he handed her a letter-sized manila envelope of some thickness—"I would be most appreciative."

"He will have it immediately upon his return."

"Thank you, Mrs. Thorne."

"You're most welcome, Mr. Gates."

Brook walked back to the elevators, his pulse pounding in his ears. As he rode down to the ground floor, he pulled a ratty piece of paper out of his pocket and reread the note for what must have been the hundredth time since he'd found it sticking out of his notebook: *Brook, forgive me for reading this without your permission. I think now we know where your talents lie. Please let me see the story when it's done. By the way,* War of the Worlds *is one of my favorite books, too. David.*

27

Monty left the store early, claiming that he was unwell and needed to go home and lie down. He apologized abjectly to his staff for leaving them to cope with the summer sale rush of business. The women gathered around him, a covey of fluttering birds cooing with sympathy, and herded him to the elevators. He tried so hard, but they could see that he was indeed ill, ill with confusion and despair, shell-shocked by the rupture of his marriage to a woman he adored. "*How cruel of her to leave him like that . . .*" If he occasionally, uncharacteristically, exhibited the aftereffects of strong drink, that was only to be expected and forgiven. "*How heartless of her to refuse his calls . . .*" The outraged flock twittered among themselves as they glided across the carpeted floor back to their duties. "*Everyone deserves a second chance . . .*" "*I wouldn't turn him away. . . .*" "*And his only child dead years ago . . .*"

It was not the first time since the day Zoe departed for Hidden Cove that Monty had allowed the extent of his manly suffering to be observed by his coterie of sympathetic, clucking women. That their whispered accounts of poor Mr. Glennon's undeserved humiliation, his bravery in the face of such rending personal pain, his determination to win his wife back, found their way into the ears of nine floors' worth of Gates & Co. employees certainly did his cause no harm. And on those other occasions when he had feigned illness he had in fact gone home. And he did at some point lie down, but not before he had drunk enough, sitting alone at the dining room table in a dark and silent apartment, to club into submission the anxiety that had been crawling over his skin and clawing at his stomach since he had realized that Zoe was not coming back.

With every passing week, the strange and unsettling conviction that he was somehow becoming visibly *fuzzy* around the edges grew. As though without the molding and defining pressure of her presence the lines that drew him simply could not sustain their exactness. Just that morning, while he was looking in the mirror as he shaved, his features had suddenly pulsed and bulged in front of his bleary eyes. He had spasmed in shock, given himself a nasty cut on the chin. There was too much space around him now she was gone; little by little he was oozing into it, unable to contain himself without Zoe there as the guardian of his essence. He needed her back. He needed to be her husband, with all that accrued to the title: the social status, the financial security, the protection of his warty soul.

This day, Monty did not go home. He walked to Pennsylvania Station, bought a roundtrip ticket, and less than an hour later arrived at the Oyster Bay station. While the train made the short, pleasant trip out of the scorching city, Monty's mind took a separate journey. It traveled to a place of certainty where what Zoe wanted was for him to come after her. He wasn't fooled by weeks of unreturned telephone calls and unanswered messages sent through Sally. Zoe wanted what she had always wanted, for him to seduce her and tell her what to do. What else did she know? No matter what David, that manipulative fraud, whispered into her ear, it was he, Monty, who had what Zoe needed. He had to see her alone; that was all. Stroke her. Melt her. Remind her of how well they fit. Mollify that laughable female pride of hers.

He stepped onto the platform. He stood for a moment, arrested by the entangled aromas of bitter sun-scorched metal and sweet newly mown grass. All his senses were heightened and he was sweating profusely, not so much from the gathering heat of the summer afternoon as from a tenacious hangover. He hadn't needed to feign symptoms today; another long night of solitary drinking and unnatural sleep had left his eyes bloodshot and heavy lidded, his tongue furry, his muscles aching. He began walking toward the quaint, half-timbered station house. The stationmaster could call a taxi to take Monty the five miles to Hidden Cove. As he reached out to turn the knob on the stationhouse door, he noticed that he was alone on the platform. A sun-bludgeoned July weekday. No one was out and moving if they didn't absolutely have to be. Inarticulable caution stayed his hand. The stationmaster and all the taxi drivers knew Monty, just as they knew everyone who came and went from this station to the grand homes around the bay. They were all gawping cretins with wagging tongues and it was none of their business that he had come to Oyster Bay in the middle of a workday in a state of dishevelment to talk his estranged wife into coming home. Better they didn't see him at all.

He went around the eastern end of the building. As usual, there were several bicycles leaning against a vine-covered fence. Monty swiftly removed his jacket and tie, bundled them into the wicker basket that hung from the handlebars of the finest of the bicycles, then rolled up his sleeves and his trouser legs. From his pants pocket he removed a silver whiskey flask and placed it carefully atop his clothing. His head hurt at the thought of the sweltering ride, but it would be quicker than walking. And wouldn't Zoe be roused by such evidence of his strength and masculinity. He tied his handkerchief around his neck and pedaled off.

The last ten minutes were torture, despite the bounty of shade afforded by the towering horse chestnut trees that bordered the interminable winding gravel drive leading to the house. He was covered in dust and sticky with sweat. As soon as the house came into view, he all but fell off the bicycle and wheeled it between the trees, into the dense woods beyond, and hid it where no one would see it. The staff didn't need to know he was here, either, not until he and Zoe had settled their business. He retrieved the flask and started walking, careful to stay off the driveway. His throbbing head felt swollen and his leg muscles were cramping, but despite the physical discomfort, it was smug satisfaction that he felt most keenly. Satisfaction with the raptorlike instincts that had brought him everything he'd ever wanted in life. He had left the city today with no clear plan, but he wasn't worried. With his instinct and his irresistible charm, he would find Zoe, chase her up the familiar tree, and keep her captive there until she'd agreed to come home.

A suggestion of a breeze descended from the treetops, bringing with it the small noises of insects and birds, along with the sudden acrid whiff of something gone rancid. Monty realized that the fetid odor was coming from him, from his saturated clothing and oozing pores. Hugging the edge of the woods, he headed for the water. He passed the house unseen by the ubiquitous groundskeepers working over the kitchen garden and the adjacent rose garden. Women's laughter and the clink of dishes and silver drifted through the wide-flung doors and windows. The staff hard at work, exactingly tending to the mansion's every need. It had always seemed to Monty that they were Hidden Cove's true owners, the ones who knew and loved the place profoundly. The family were nothing but a brainless flock of ducks, dropping occasionally to the surface, bobbing with their asses in the air and having no idea what lay in the depths beneath the range of their puny vision. They were idiots. And they wanted to peck him out of the flock, back to the scummed-over pond from which he had risen. That was not going to happen.

Monty skirted the house and made for the stables. A plan took shape in his mind when, from a safe distance, he saw that Sirocco was not in his stall. As Monty had hoped, Zoe, the only family member in residence until the weekend, was not in the house but out riding, alone. He looked at his watch. If she was true to her habits, Zoe would finish her ride within the hour and return to the stable through the heavily wooded trail leading from the bay shore. He sneaked furtively down to the water for a cooling, cleansing plunge and then positioned himself along the trail, out of sight of the stable, and waited for her. One hour later, practically to the minute, he heard the sound of hooves biting at hard dirt. He returned the nearly empty flask to the pocket of his pants, dry now but stiff with salt water. He rose up from the large, flat, sun-warmed rock upon which he'd been sitting and moved onto the trail.

Zoe had woken at dawn from a portentous dream in which she had been a bird, a powerful, untamable sharp-eyed bird, perhaps an eagle or a great owl, soaring in silence and solitude, back and forth, high, high above the heartbreakingly perfect curve of Hidden Cove's white beach. She had come awake and lain unmoving in her bed, sunken still into the rapturous sensation of having been released, finally, to inhabit her true form. For the first time since childhood, Zoe was purely, innocently happy. Safely alone at Hidden Cove, she had gradually shed the confining skin of the past. Leathery layers, stealthily deposited while she had sleep-walked through life, loosened and fell away from her. As she rode daily through the pristine paradise of the woods with the sun warm and nurturing on her new, infant's skin, her mind had run as free as her horse. She had come to know herself, to feel as powerful and untamable as the bird of her dream. She had come to understand that happiness was not what she had thought it was: an eternally elusive reward denied her, hiding in some vainly sought-after object or belief or person. Rather, it was an ever-present part of her, alongside sorrow and self-hatred and abnegation. It was up to her to choose it.

Today, her happiness was boundless. She had risen from her bed while the rest of the household was asleep and slipped down to the water. She'd swum, naked as the fish that swam with her, the dawn-kissed water like liquid pearl on her skin. She'd eaten a huge breakfast, spent the morning working on a brochure for her business. But the afternoon, when her father's estate was at its most beautiful, was reserved for riding. She and Sirocco had been out for hours, first galloping recklessly fast on the narrow, winding trails through the woods with the sun flickering all around them, now bursting out of the trees onto the beach. She wore loose white cotton pants rolled up over her calves and a sleeveless blouse the color of beaten brass. Her burnished skin was beaded with glistening droplets of water kicked up from the bay. Her hair was unbound. She was barefoot and rode without the encumbrance of a saddle. A light rubber bit and leather bridle were mere adornment for Sirocco's mouth and head; reins lay ignored on his neck. She commanded him with the pressure of her thighs and the touch of her hands and he responded instantly, with brute devotion. Zoe slowed him to a trot and hugged his neck, laid her cheek against his hard, warm flesh. She turned him, steered him back along the shoreline, onto the final trail of the day, the one that wound through the broad clump of woods on the stable side of the house. Cook was making fresh trout for dinner. Zoe was ravenous.

She came around the last bend in the trail before the long, straight run that let out to the lawn and the stable beyond, leaning low over Sirocco's neck, ready to give him his head for one final gallop. A man was standing in the middle of the trail, some twenty yards ahead of her. With dismay, she realized who it was. She pulled up sharply in a cloud of dust.

"What in God's name are you doing here, Monty?" She made no attempt to conceal her annoyance.

Monty smiled ingratiatingly. "My goodness, Zoe. I barely recognized you. You look like an Amazon, galloping out of the mists of some primeval forest."

With his lids provocatively at half-mast and his intent unambiguously sexual, Monty let his eyes travel slowly from her bare head down to her bare toes. He walked toward her and reached out his hand. Slowly, he caressed the silky skin of her leg. His fingers traced the curve of her calf, then moved downward to encircle her slim ankle in a possessive, erotic embrace.

"Darling, don't you think it's time for you to come home?" He tugged gently at her foot.

She stared down at him from her imperious height with the astounded curiosity of a scientist who has discovered that his laboratory chimpanzee had overnight turned into a mouse. She exploded with laughter. "My God. To think, that used to move me." Her laughter echoed off the dirt path, laid waste to the muffled din of the sleepy woods.

The smile faded from Monty's face and his eyes grew hard. "You're coming home with me. Now." He tightened his grip on her ankle.

She kicked out at him. "Don't be ridiculous. You're disgusting." She looked him up and down. "What did you do? Try to bathe in the bay? You stink of sweat and liquor. You couldn't even pay a whore to go home with you."

"I'm warning you, Zoe."

"Let go of me. You are ruining a perfectly wonderful day." She twisted and squirmed with unexpected strength.

He grabbed at her with both hands. "You're still my wife and I'm ordering you to come home."

"You can go to hell!" she cried. She kicked out again. Her heel cracked against his jaw.

"If I go, you go with me, you miserable twat!"

One hand had Zoe's ankle in an iron grip; the other shot

up to capture her wrist. She pulled away from him, scrabbled for the reins, and spurred Sirocco forward. Monty's hand slid along her arm until he found purchase at the crook of her elbow. He dug his fingers into the tender flesh there and she screamed.

"Let go of me! Monty! Let go!" Zoe flailed at him with her free arm, slapping at his face with the stinging ends of the leather reins.

Spooked by his mistress's agitation, Sirocco lurched to a snorting halt and began to rear. Zoe screamed again and grabbed for his mane.

"Monty, stop! I'm going to fall!"

"Beg me, Zoe. Beg me not to pull you off that fucking horse!"

"Never, never again, you loathsome bastard!" Zoe shrieked, and, enraged beyond reason, dropped the reins so that she could smack the side of Monty's head with her fist. She tried to hold her seat, using her legs against the horse's flank, but with no saddle and stirrups, it was impossible. She tilted precariously to the side, started to slide off Sirocco's broad back.

Monty snarled. "Down you go."

He yanked as hard as he could and then released her. She sailed off the horse, her body twisted to one side. Time stopped and she was flying, like in her dream, but without the majesty and power she was meant to have. Her eyes widened with astonishment. A terrible stab of disappointment lanced her heart; it had been just a dream, after all.

Monty tracked her trajectory as she fell to the side of the beaten-earth trail. Her upper back hit the dirt; her head snapped backward as though in response to a sound in the trees above her. Her skull smashed against the edge of the flat rock on which he had sat, just moments before, drinking and waiting. Her body convulsed once, arms and legs thrashing, back arching, then collapsed into the ground. The dreadful disturbance caused the dust to roil; it coated her skin and clothing with a dry brown film. Her eyes stared upward into the sun, their pupils eerily dilated even as a bright, slanting ray of light fell across her face. She had gone from wild, writhing motion to deathly stillness in the time it took him to let out his angry breath.

He calmly knelt beside her, his narcissistic rage quite gone, and contemplated her. She was so beautiful lying quietly, gently tinted like a sepia photograph, her deep dark eyes open, her hair fanning out beneath her head, her lovely body stretched out like a pagan offering to the gods of lust. He'd only meant to stop her riding away; it was not his fault that she'd fallen onto the rock and cracked her skull. Still, it was rather convenient. A week shy of a final divorce decree, he'd be the grieving widower. Everyone knew how much he'd wanted her back. David could not get him fired now. The family would have to keep him in the flock or be revealed as heartless devils.

Good old Zoe. He knew she'd give him what he wanted; she had never been able to refuse him. He plucked his flask from his pocket and finished the whiskey, basking for a moment in its sour bite like a lizard warming in the sun. His tongue came out and he licked the final drop off the warm metal; he was an upright reptile, lacking the internal mechanism that regulated feelings of human warmth just as the real reptile lacked the internal ability to control its body temperature. Alcohol was what he used instead of sunlight and shade to support his natural cold-bloodedness. He put the flask away and smiled down at her.

As if in ghoulish response, she twitched and blinked; her chest heaved. He jumped. That wouldn't do. Not at all. He cocked his head to one side and shook it, a regretful moue on his lips. He leaned forward and cradled her face in his hands, lifted her head, took a deep breath, and drove her head down onto the rock again. His hands vibrated with the shock of the contact. He waited a few seconds, then pressed the tips of his fingers against the side of her throat. Nothing. He closed her eyes. Blood leaked from her left ear. He was careful not to get any on him.

He stood up and glanced around. The horse was a statue in the middle of the trail. Soon, the groom would realize the time, know something was wrong, and come looking for Zoe. He had to leave. He took one last look at her and frowned. He put the toe of his caked shoe against her hip and pushed. Her body rocked minutely. This wasn't actually what was supposed to have happened. A touch of anger spiked through him again. Now he was going to have to learn how to hold himself together on his own. She really shouldn't have laughed at him. She shouldn't have looked down on him as though waiting for him to kneel before her. The haughty bitch had expected him to beg. Well, Montgomery Glennon did not beg any woman. Women begged him. He shrugged. It didn't matter, anyway. As long as he had money he'd be fine.

A red-winged blackbird, glossy and fat, landed on Zoe's stomach. It hopped there several times, plucked at her shirt with its beak, then settled onto the warm, nubbly fabric and began grooming itself. Sirocco came close. He neighed repeatedly, tossing his huge head in distress. The bird lifted its tiny head from beneath its wing and looked at the beast with beady eyes. Sirocco bent his head, nuzzled Zoe's neck with his nose. He pushed and pushed at her, but she didn't move. He waited for her hand to reach up for his mane. He gently lipped at her face, smearing the blood that trickled down the side of her neck. She didn't move. He turned and cantered down the trail, toward the stable. The bird watched him go, then went back to examining its wing. There was nothing to disturb it. The body beneath it was more still than the earth itself.

~ PART THREE ~

July 1926–March 1927

28

The hearse was a mournful locomotive, pulling three reluc-
tant black cars in its steady, sturdy wake, moving at a
snail's pace. The small procession crept through the sum-
mertime mayhem of the Manhattan streets, its grief-
deadened occupants deaf and blind to the ongoing tumult
of life. It worked its way uptown to West 155th Street,
crossed the Harlem River into the Bronx over the Ma-
combs Dam Bridge, continued northward on Jerome Avenue. Evelyn had, quite hysterically, insisted on taking this
laborious route, but no matter how slowly they were forced
to travel, inevitably they arrived. The hearse turned right,
through the gates of the Jerome Avenue entrance to Woodlawn Cemetery. The cars swung to the left, one after the
other, the great weeping linden and the towering white pine
standing somber guard to their passing, swung right again
onto Pine Avenue, and came to a stop.

There had been many mourners at the funeral. Lorena
and others from the Church of Christ, Scientist, enduring
friends from Zoe's school days, from Oyster Bay, from the
equestrian world. But out of respect for Evelyn's fragile
sensibilities, only the family had come to witness Zoe's
burial. Momentarily immobilized by the end of the long
journey, unwilling to exit their vehicles and acknowledge
the reality of this place they had come to, they sat docilely,
as though in a stalled train, and waited. In the first car were
Evelyn, Joseph, and Philip; in the second, Monty, Sally,
and Brook; in the third, Jed, Lucy, David, and Cissy. Abi-

gail, nine months pregnant, had been taken home after the church service.

"We could have been here an hour ago. Why the hell did they open the damned Bronx River Parkway if no one is going to use it?" Joseph snapped the cuffs of his black suit.

"Oh, do forgive me!" Evelyn shrilled, a frightening sound wrenched from a throat raw with crying. "I didn't realize you were in such a hurry to bury your daughter!" Her mouth filled with tears and she hid her face in her handkerchief, turned her shoulders away from him.

"Jesus Christ!" he muttered. Without looking at her, he reached out and took her hand, holding it almost punitively tight.

She tore herself from his grasp. "Let us not waste another moment of your precious time!" She fumbled with the door handle and all but fell from the car.

Joseph closed his eyes and hung his head.

Woodlawn Cemetery was a four-hundred-acre park of such bucolic beauty and celestial architecture that the dead could not help but rest in peace. Because of its trees, shrubs, and flowers, the cemetery had become a bird sanctuary and birdsong and the soft susurrus of flight filled the air. Not long after his marriage to Evelyn, Joseph had bought a large plot in the northern Pine section of the cemetery, deeming Woodlawn the only resting ground fine enough for his family. At that time, such famous men as R. H. Macy, Herman Melville, and Jay Gould were already interred there. In the decades since, they had been joined by a bevy of appropriate neighbors with whom to spend eternity, among them Joseph Pulitzer; Thomas Nast; that other Gates, John, of Texaco and U.S. Steel fame; and fellow merchant prince F. W. Woolworth, whose family mausoleum was directly across from Joseph's. Joseph had commissioned Daniel Chester French—the sculptor who had created the powerful statue of Abraham Lincoln that inhabited the Lincoln Memorial—to create for him a memorial structure equal to anything that might ever be erected in the cemetery. For eight long years Libby had lain alone, under a grave-sized brass plaque, in the shadow of the massive, soaring monument, with nothing but cold, stone angels for company. Now, someone had come to join her in eternal rest.

David, Jed, Brook, Philip, Joseph, and the hearse driver, enlisted to stand in for a nearly fainting Monty, took their places on either side of Zoe's coffin. They hefted the mahogany box and carefully made their way with it to the newly dug grave at the base of the memorial. Monty leaned heavily against Sally as she took his arm and gently, carefully, guided him. The coffin was lowered into the grave and the minister, who had accompanied Zoe in the hearse, blessed the family and spoke the traditional words of consolation, assuring them of the newly deceased's deliverance unto the kingdom of heaven.

With the final drop of the coffin into its snug, deep hole, Zoe's death became true and absolute in a way it had not been before. When the minister asked them to take a last moment to think of her life, Evelyn began to wail. Joseph gingerly placed an arm around her. She collapsed against his chest and allowed him to hold her in a sheltering embrace. He looked out over her bent head, his sharp gaze making clear his impatience to be gone from there. He led Evelyn toward the car, gesturing with his head for everyone to follow. They began to stagger away from the grave site, huddled close like a lost and decimated herd, each sunken into their private, unimaginable thoughts. How could it have happened? How could the girl who had not fallen off her horse since she was eleven years old have fallen now, and to such inconceivable harm? How could Zoe, so happy and so alive just days ago, be gone?

Only David did not move. As Lucy, Philip, and Brook limped by him, Brook looked at David's face, at his pain-filled eyes staring off into the distance and the slight trembling of his mouth, and his own heart filled with fear. Using the alchemical abilities of his young mind, Brook had transmuted a dangerous enemy into his personal savior. He did not want David to show weakness. Brook disengaged himself from his sister and cautiously put a hand on David's arm, which was hard and muscled beneath his own soft palm. Startled, David glanced at him and said, "Oh, Brook. I'm sorry, I haven't had a chance to read your story yet."

"No, I don't care; that's not why I . . ." Brook began to cry. He pulled at David's arm. "Come on; you have to come."

David smiled distractedly and lifted a hand to Brook's head, brushed a wayward lock of hair back into place. "You're a good boy, Brook. Go with your father." He pushed him in Philip's direction.

David walked to the grave and halted at its precisely dug edge. He looked down into the mini-abyss that fell vertically away from the emerald lawn. Suddenly he bent and scooped a handful of dirt from the excavated mound. He held it, studied it, then stood up and slowly, deliberately, turned his hand and released the dirt to fall onto the lustrous wood of Zoe's coffin. He had reverted to a ritual of his heritage. He didn't know how else to dull the sharp prick of guilt that stuck him, as it so often did; rightly or wrongly, he could never believe himself fully innocent of another's misfortune, no matter that he claimed responsibility for so little. The need to be good secretly consumed him, as it did Jed. They had always had that in common, though they might not know it. The dirt hit the coffin with a hollow thud and everyone turned at the sound.

David put his back to the grave. He walked quickly, and when he came abreast of Monty and Sally he veered and positioned himself in front of them, forcing them to stop. Monty kept his eyes down while David, silent and expressionless, stared at him. He stared so long and so hard that Sally grew red in the face and muttered, "Really, David, that's quite enough." He dropped his eyes and continued on in step behind Joseph and Evelyn, Jed and Cissy reappearing on either side of him.

As Joseph reached to open the car door, something made Evelyn put out a hand to stop him. A faint brush of warm air over her head that lifted her veil ever so slightly. With just that small sensation, she felt their passage before she saw or heard them: she raised her head from Joseph's shoulder and looked up to see two red-tailed hawks soaring away toward the treetops side by side, one large and one small. As she watched them loft ever upward, an exquisite lightness of spirit permeated her. She watched them until they disappeared into the horizon. When she could no longer see them, she took Joseph's hand in hers, kissed him, and said, "I'm ready to go home, my love. Let's take the Parkway."

29

It was the middle of the night. The hour of the wolf. The time when the uneasy dead rose from their graves to haunt the living; or perhaps it was when the uneasy living rose from their beds to haunt themselves.

Joseph stood alone just outside the door to the bedroom he and Evelyn shared, happily still after so many years. He peered dazedly into the dimness of the hallway. From the single lamp that had been left burning in the entryway an anemic illumination diffused like plasma into the air.

He took several shuffling steps and stopped before the shadowed hallway mirror. He examined his face and did not know himself. Not even the flattering darkness could hide the fact that he was old. Very old. Somehow he had aged fifteen years in the month since Zoe died. No one else noticed, not even Evelyn. To the world he looked the same. Only he saw the change in him, the doubt. He was suffering a kind of thinking hitherto alien to his mind. He feared he had overlooked something crucial in life.

He stared into the eyes of the man in the mirror and did as the image bade: he thought about his dead daughter. He pictured her as he'd last seen her alive, the Sunday before her death, waving good-bye to him and Evelyn from the head of the driveway at Hidden Cove. It had been a limp and humid evening. He'd climbed into the car in an irritable mood, uncomfortably hot and clammy with sweat. When he'd turned back to look at Zoe standing on the crushed gravel in her cool silver dress, sparkling like a distant star emerging into the purple-grey dusk, ebullient and unfazed by the elements, his irritability had vanished. He had thought, *Next weekend I will come back and she will be right there, standing in the driveway waving hello to me.* And for the first time that he could ever remember, he had wished he could stay a little longer.

He let the moment go, as he had to. The next weekend had never come and that was the end of it. He couldn't even be sure that his last memory of her was a true one. That strong, confident woman was certainly not the daughter he had known for nearly four decades. He would not clutch at a romanticized memory like some hysterical woman in love with her own breast-beating loneliness, as Zoe had done when Libby died, obsessively nurturing her bereavement instead of pulling herself up and getting on with things. One didn't have to behave that way. After all, Evelyn was a woman, a mother, and she was not giving in to the temptation to disintegrate under the weight of her grief. She had been weeping lavishly, of course, but inside—Joseph was relieved to perceive—she was fine; she was solid. As for himself, he had not cried. He was not going to cry. He was going to stand just where he was until he once again recognized the face in the mirror.

He stared at himself. Never before had it bothered him that Zoe had inherited nothing from him, that she had been a replica of Evelyn, dark, regal, and utterly female. Never before had he looked into a mirror and hoped to see in the cast of his face something reminiscent of hers. *Don't despair, Father. Remember all the things I learned from you. Qualities more valuable than my appearance.* He half-expected to see her reflection in the mirror, so clear was her voice inside his head. So odd, yet not odd, to hear it there. His unblinking eyes filled with tears. Foolish old man. It wasn't her. What imbecility. He snorted in self-derision and glared at himself. Yes, that man he knew! And that voice he knew as well. It was his own, pragmatic and unemotional, reminding him of the obvious. That those qualities she seemed to have possessed at the end—stubbornness, determination, spirit—were the essential qualities in himself that he must never lose. They defined who he had always been and who he would always be. He had to remain strong and calm; the world relied on him. He tightened the belt of his dressing gown and turned from the mirror.

Evelyn emerged from her restless sleep into a hushed, airless room, immediately fully awake. She had stopped taking the narcotic potion that Dr. Barre had given her; it hadn't helped her fall asleep or stay asleep, merely muddled her head and made her feel even more tenuously connected to anything real. Nothing but the warmth of Joseph's body next to hers was of any comfort to her at all. It was the gradual chill that spread toward her from his empty place on the bed that had woken her. She shivered and reached her hand out in a momentary panic, feeling for him. The bathroom door was closed and she thought that perhaps he had had to urinate; he needed to void more frequently these days. She listened for movement, for any sound from behind the door, waited for the telltale flush. All was silence.

She lay on her back, her hands folded over her breast. Alone in the darkness she allowed free rein to the wild, unreasoning relief that had shoved its way to dominance over all her other emotions in the aftermath of Zoe's death. The catastrophe that Evelyn knew would one day descend on Zoe had finally revealed its form. Evelyn had thought it would look quite different. But in the end, it didn't matter what it was that harmed her daughter. The only thing that mattered was that now nothing and no one could ever hurt Zoe. She was safe and Evelyn was freed from the tyranny of her dreadful anticipation. One always had to pay a high price for freedom. That was the way of the world. Zoe fell off a horse and died, and Evelyn continued to live. How would that equation have been altered had Evelyn done even one infinitesimal thing differently? It wouldn't. And yet how tenaciously she held to her memory of that moment at the cemetery when she had looked up and seen the heaven-bound birds and had, absurdly, felt the purifying balm of Zoe's forgiveness. Without that memory, relief would not be possible. Her life, sustained by her love for Joseph, would not be possible.

Joseph. Evelyn looked at the clock on her night table. It wasn't even four o'clock; why wasn't he in bed? She got up, drew her robe around her, and opened the bedroom door. The hallway was empty. On bare feet, she glided toward the salon, trailing white satin across the polished parquet. He was in his chair, a pile of ledgers at his feet, a document on his lap. She pulled her chair close to his and perched, her upper body inclined toward him. As she placed her hands on his knees, he set his work aside, then slid his hands up under the loose sleeves of her robe and caressed her arms. He kissed her.

"I thought I'd left you sound asleep."

"Your absence woke me." She smiled at him. "What is all this that can't wait your attention until morning?"

He glanced at the mess on the floor. "The usual. Everything seems to need my attention."

She cocked her head. "That's the way you've always wanted it, Joe. You have people capable of making decisions, but you never let them. Perhaps you should let go a little. I could probably tolerate having to spend more time with you," she teased. "It's been almost three years; isn't Jed ready? He has you and John McDonald and Drew Douglass behind him."

He kicked at one of the ledgers. "I'm going to bring David downtown."

Evelyn dropped her head as though a weight had landed on her neck. She closed her eyes. After a moment, she looked up. "Must you? Give him the store. Isn't that enough?"

"He's already wasted there; you know that." He shook his head. "You should be a fly on the wall at an officers' meeting. Hear the way he and Drew argue and how everyone waits on his opinions." He shrugged. "I know what you're thinking, Evie. But Jed can't do it."

"Can't do what? He can run the company. He's more than smart enough. It just won't be the way you would do it."

"He won't make it better. At best he'll hold it together. I

don't want my company to stagnate or, worse, to fall apart if the economy goes bad, which it may. Smart is not enough."

Desperation flared in Evelyn's eyes. "He's your grandson."

"Jesus, Evie, I'm not tossing the boy out!" Joseph attempted to rise, but Evelyn's hands on his legs had grown impossibly heavy. "There will be plenty for him to do. He'll be fine."

Joseph heard his thoughts clearly inside his head, but something was wrong with the way the words sounded as they came out of his mouth. Evelyn was gaping at him. He saw her mouth move and through the fog before his face he read his name in the shape of her lips. He couldn't hear. He tried to speak, to tell her not to worry, but his face was numb and his lips felt like putty. His head was floating light as a balloon and yet it fell like a stone to the side, his ear nearly hitting his slumping shoulder.

"Joe! Joe! Oh my God!" Evelyn screamed. The right side of Joseph's face had collapsed and his body sagged to the right. His twisted mouth flopped open and out of it came eerie, inarticulate sounds. His eyes were fixed and staring.

Terrified, she ran down the hallway. She pounded on Mary and Walter's door, screaming for help. She didn't wait for a response but flew back down the hall and into the kitchen, took the telephone in her shaking hand, and called Dr. Barre.

30

Fucking inhuman Joseph. Still recovering from that little stroke—Christ, why couldn't he have just dropped dead—*but he had enough venom left to lean on his friend the judge and get the divorce decree made official as of the day* before Zoe died. As if he'd seen the angel of death and it had said to him, *Hey, Joe, you hard-nosed bastard, I don't want you yet. Go back and have some fun; go bust your son-in-law's balls.* "*I've been unnecessarily generous to you,*" the lying bitch had said. Ten thousand dollars she'd promised him, but Joseph had somehow gotten the judge to reduce even that niggardly sum to five. Now Monty was being kicked out of the apartment. How was he supposed to finance a comfortable lifestyle on that shitty little amount of money and without anyplace to live? He still had his salary, but he knew better than to count on it for much longer. David was watching him with the pre-strike avidity of a starving falcon. Monty knew he'd be unwise to underestimate David. The wily kike would either unearth a true soft underbelly—a Mrs. Carrington or those so-far-unfound small discrepancies in the sales figures for his department—or manufacture something. Either way, he would rip Monty's guts out and leave them steaming on the pavement of Fifth Avenue. He was sure it was David who had convinced Joseph to lever him out of the apartment so it could be sold before the end of the year, good for tax purposes or some other bullshit. David seemed intent on ruining Monty's life as a way of coping with Zoe's death. Almost as though he knew what had happened.

Monty had been drinking steadily all day, as he had been for the past six weeks, but he was singularly clearheaded with purpose. It was, in fact, the alcohol that made it possible for him to keep a clear head. It was the glue that held him together now that Zoe was gone. Only when he pissed more out of his system than he put in did his brain grow lax; only then did he have trouble maintaining his carefully scripted public persona. As long as he was sufficiently fueled, he could still conjure the man he was meant to be. He could high-step his manipulative dance with as much grace as ever. Maybe Joseph was ready to leave the ball, but Sally, the repressed romantic, had yet to have her first gavotte. It was time to call in his chips with her, to see what she might really be worth to him if he backed her against the wall. He had no choice. She could get him the money he'd need and, besides, he'd been looking forward to this for years.

"How can they make me leave here, Sally? All I have left of her are my memories of our life in this apartment." Monty rotated unsteadily in the center of the living room, his arms spread imploringly, a look of disbelief in his dark blue eyes. A thick wedge of shining black hair fell over his pale forehead. "Have they no hearts at all?"

"It does seem cruel, to turn you out so quickly," Sally ventured. "Anyone can see how you suffer."

"You see it. You see the real me, Sally. You and Zoe. You're the only ones who ever did. Joseph sees only my faults. And I have them, I admit readily. I wasn't a perfect husband, no, but I loved her. I think I've been punished enough." His voice rose and he pulled violently at his hair.

"Monty," Sally murmured in alarm, and took a hesitant step into the room.

He held up his hand. Apparently humiliated to have her see him struggling with his emotions, he composed himself. "Sally. I am so sorry to pull you away from your own comfort. I just so needed to see a friendly face. To have someone to talk to who understands my grief." A wan smile flickered bravely across his face.

Sally stood just inside the French doors and glanced at the mess Monty had somehow managed to make of the sparsely furnished room. She wondered what of Zoe he could possibly sense in this impersonal space that had been thoroughly denuded of anything that spoke of her. "I didn't realize that Zoe had taken so much with her. My dear, do you really still believe she was going to come back to you? That she would not have gone through with the divorce?"

Monty's rotations slowed and he came to a gradual stop, like a creaky carousel horse. He faced her and fixed her with a heartbreaking look, his eyes glittery with suppressed tears. "I don't know anymore, Sally," he whispered. "She knew how much I needed her. I thought she needed me. I can't bear to think that . . . But what's the use!" he cried, and collapsed upon the sofa, burying his face in his hands. "She's gone and I'll never know if she still loved me."

Sally moved a little farther into the room.

He raised his head and leaned slightly toward her, every aspect of his posture beseeching her to understand his misery. "You can't imagine how lonely I've been these past months, Sally. And I have no one I can confide in. No one but you, and I haven't wanted to burden you. Can you forgive my weakness today?"

Her heart was pumping her blood too rapidly through her veins. The apartment was too quiet, too empty with just the two of them in it. Monty's hair was all mussed like a boy's, his sleeves rolled up and collar unbuttoned, the insides of his wrists and his soft throat exposed. For the past several months he had looked terribly unwell. He had lost weight, become bony, his skin and the whites of his eyes stained an unnatural yellow. But today he looked beautiful, his translucent skin and swimming eyes and his delicate thinness making him seem something from the spirit world, his sharp shoulder blades like wings inside his baggy white shirt. Sally knew that she ought to back away, into the hall, busy herself in the kitchen, make them a cup of tea. Anything but remain standing in front of him bewitched by a seeming vulnerability that revealed his unquenchable passion for his dead wife and by his dark angularity, so different from Philip's bland roundness.

"Sally, will you sit next to me, hold my hand?" He reached out an arm, stretched his pale fingers. "I'm so starved for simple human contact."

She pressed a palm beneath her breasts, attempting to tame her heart's runaway beat. She made a show of smoothing the bodice of her dress. She felt light-headed. Why was she afraid to sit next to him, to let him touch her? They had touched before, held hands, entwined arms. He was lunatic with grief and what he asked of her was so innocent. She could not refuse him such a small measure of comfort. "Yes, I will sit with you for a little while. I really shouldn't stay too long, though."

"No, of course not. I wouldn't want you to put yourself out on my account. Even a moment will mean so much."

She sat down. Monty took her hand, laced his fingers in hers, let their twined arms fall gently onto her leg. Somehow, without seeming to have moved anything other than his hand, he eradicated the small space that she had carefully left between them so that from ankle to shoulder they were in contact. She felt the sharpness of his hip bone against hers. She felt the hardness of his body pushing against the softness of hers along every inch of her side. Her breath trembled in her throat as pricking, tingling currents ran like ants up and down her skin beneath her dress.

"This is so nice, isn't it?" His voice was low and terribly sad, wistful almost. He kept his head down. His fingers moved, stroking her palm with his thumb.

A jolt of electricity shot from her hand to her breast, spread through her belly and to the place between her legs that had always been carefully guarded against sensation, no matter how Philip had tried to arouse her. It had been so long since she had allowed her husband anywhere near any part of her that she had forgotten that she could feel anything at all.

Monty lifted her hand, dipped his head farther, and kissed her fingers. His lips were hot and dry. While his head was down, she dared to look at him. His hair falling in disarray around his face, the elegant arch of his neck. His wide, square shoulders and long, tapering back. He turned his head and his face came fully into her sight. How handsome he was, how intensely blue and stormy his eyes, how fine his nose, how compelling the contrast between his black hair and white skin. This was what Zoe saw. This was what Zoe wanted. Monty was a villain: Sally had always understood that without ever knowing the truth of what made him one, and now she understood, not with her confused mind but with her inflamed body, the powerful lure of his seductive brand of villainy.

He slowly raised a hand to cup her chin. His fingers trailed along her throat. "Sally. You are so beautiful." He breathed the words, a look of desperation and longing in his eyes.

His hand was as hot as his lips, as if his grief and loneliness raged inside him like a fever. Her lips parted. He leaned forward. His hand moved insistently to the back of her neck and he pulled her toward him. His touch felt nothing like Philip's. No tentativeness, no asking permission. His spell-casting eyes swam out of focus as he came closer, closer, and his mouth was so near she could feel the damp heat of his breath on her. The hand that had held hers moved upward. His demanding fingers enveloped her breast and she swooned.

His lips hovered over hers. "Sally. It's all right. You know you can trust me. We both need this, don't we? Let me make you happy."

He kissed her and leaned his weight on her, pressed her into the sofa. Her nipple was a little bullet boring into the palm of his hand while the rest of her body melted into him, her hands gripping his shoulders with surprising strength. He felt the conqueror's thrill of victory in his gut and a corresponding sexual thrill in his groin. Oh, this was going to be more than fun. This was going to be better than he could have possibly imagined. She was a luscious volcano finally ready to erupt. He'd been right. Her screams were going to reach to the heavens, rip apart the clouds, and Joseph's gold would rain down upon him. Hallelujah.

31

"It's good to see you again, Mr. Shaw. Everyone at the Club was so sorry to hear about the terrible loss in your family."

"Thank you, Edward. That's very kind." David sat in the same chair at the same table looking out the same window as he had the night of his birthday nearly ten months earlier. But now, instead of January's bleakness outside the window, pellucid September light shimmered and gleamed on the granite tabletop. And, instead of Jed's grinning, drunken, blond, blue-eyed majesty across from him, there was Brook's somber, sandy-haired, green-eyed adolescent awkwardness. "I'll have my usual, please."

"Certainly, sir. And for the young gentleman?"

David gave Brook a questioning smile. "What would you like?"

"What are you having?" Brook asked timidly.

"Scotch on the rocks."

Brook took a moment to give visibly serious thought to what he might want for himself and finally said, "I'll try that."

David was quite sure that Brook had never so much as sniffed a glass of Scotch, or anything else alcoholic, in all his young life. Sally had forbidden him to drink before he was twenty-one, four long years away. David had to suppress a chuckle at the thought of escorting this particular Gates scion home to his mother in a shocking state of inebriation. "Edward, make that two Scotch on the rocks. And bring something for us to munch on."

Brook perched as though the seat were made of sharp stones instead of cushy leather. He played with the cuffs of his shirt. He tried to keep his gaze politely on David, but his attention wandered around the room and out the window.

"Relax, Brook. I won't tell your mother you've made peace with the enemy; I promise." David immediately regretted his taunt as a look of intense discomfort splashed across the boy's features.

The merest suggestion that he might displease his unpleasant mother threw Brook still into a paroxym of guilt, a habitual response of truly Pavlovian proportions, and yet here he was, ordering a Scotch. A nice bit of boyhood rebellion. But even more significant was that he'd had the courage to separate himself from Sally's influence and establish an independent opinion of someone she had commanded him to dislike. That act promised a higher order of maturity than David had ever thought Brook possessed.

"I'm sorry. That was uncalled for, even as a joke."

Brook acknowledged David's apology by picking up his glass in a gesture of a toast. "Here's to peace among friends and enemies alike." He drained off a very decent amount of the Scotch, held it in his mouth for a moment to get its flavor, and then swallowed, without choking. He gave David a wide-eyed look of delight. "My first Scotch. Very good. Very good indeed."

David stared at Brook in amazement. He let out a laugh, but his amusement betrayed him by turning instantly melancholy. His nose and eyes stung with sudden tears and his laugh ended as a pained sigh.

"What's the matter, David? Did I say something wrong?"

"No. No, of course not," David reassured him. "You're a little bundle of surprises these days, and you just reminded me of your aunt Zoe. I don't know why."

"Maybe because she surprised everyone at the end."

"Yes. She certainly did." David turned a blind stare toward the window. "I promised her I would always be there if she needed me, and I wasn't. I still can't believe this happened to her."

Brook turned to the window as well, as if trying on a grown-up emotional response to see if he were man enough yet for it to fit him. "You couldn't have done anything. It was an accident. People can fall and hit their heads and they can die and there's nothing anyone can do about it. But I understand how you feel. I was playing with my cousin Libby the day she got sick, and somehow I always thought it was my fault. That I already had it and I gave it to her, that if she hadn't come to see me, she would have lived."

David was unprepared for a conversation with Brook, of all people, about accidental falls and dying children. Zoe's death, and especially the manner of it, had breached a vulnerable spot in his defenses, and since her funeral his thoughts had refused to stay neatly confined to the present. Now, memories of his past insinuated themselves into his mind, no matter how he tried to push them away. "You were wrong. There was nothing to be done. Children die. They get sick; they get hurt; they get killed."

Brook knew that David wasn't talking about Libby and Zoe anymore. Brook didn't want David to drift somewhere he couldn't follow. "I still miss Libby. Sometimes I think I see her. It's weird." He leaned across the table. "Does that ever happen to you, David? That for a second, before you realize it's impossible, you think you see someone who died? Do you ever see Aunt Zoe? Or your mother, do you ever see your mother? You must miss her."

David fell back into his chair as though pushed by an unseen hand. Brook's eyes were on him and David's mind instinctively retreated from the risk of exposing anything of his private self. But those eyes were so innocently questioning, so like Jed's when they'd first met. There was no threat here. Brook didn't want to know any secrets from David's past; for him it was purely a matter of the moment. He hoped that he and David might share a special kind of experience. And that this man whom he had chosen, wholly unexpectedly, to trust, trusted him in return. He wanted an honest response.

"I used to see my mother," David admitted finally. "I'd see her getting on a bus, or shopping at a fruit stand. It hasn't happened for a long time. I still dream about her, though. It's not weird. People remain alive in your heart long after you've lost them in the flesh."

"I'll never forget Libby. I think maybe I had a little crush on her. Well, as much as a nine-year-old can have." Brook looked down in embarrassment.

David took advantage of Brook's momentarily dropped gaze and allowed himself to express the surprising tenderness he felt for the boy with an enormous smile. He gave Brook's arm a fatherly pat. "Ah. Never too young for a crush. Don't apologize for it. I think I had a little crush on your aunt." David raised his glass. "Here's to crushes and to lost people. Here's to Libby and Zoe."

"To Libby and Zoe," Brook agreed. He took a sip and put his glass down. "I am a little nervous, actually, meeting with you."

"I know." It was time to stop tormenting the boy. David reached into his briefcase. He placed onto the tabletop the manila envelope Brook had left in his office three months before. "Do you think I invited you to share a drink with me at my favorite club only to tell you that I didn't like your stories?"

Brook pushed his glass away from him. "No. I think you invited me here to tell me that you do like them and that you think I should keep writing and not stay in business school."

"Now I'm a little confused. Are you not happy that I liked the stories?"

"No. I'm not. Because you've been so kind to me, bringing me that wonderful book, and snooping in my notebook"—a glare of mock anger and David responded with a mock-apologetic dip of his head—"and then writing me that note, which I still have, and taking time to read these"—he put his hand on the envelope—"and I'm going to disappoint you and I don't want to disappoint you."

David said nothing for a moment, just sat quietly and took note of the raw regret that darkened the boy's pale green eyes. He relaxed back into his chair and crossed his arms over his chest. "Then don't disappoint me."

"I can't keep writing, David."

"Why not?"

"I don't have the energy for it. When I write I can't do anything else. I don't have room in my head." Brook's voice shook slightly, but he had the fortitude to not look away from David's critical stare.

"Then maybe you shouldn't be doing anything else."

Brook's jaw clenched.

"I guess that means you're really enjoying NYU's business school."

Brook made no response.

"Sorry, Brook. You can't convince me that you don't want to write."

"I didn't say I didn't want to. I said I couldn't."

"Remind me again why you can't do both?" David refused to relent.

"If I write my stories, I'll fail at school."

"I think you're making the wrong choice, Brook," David said. "Why do you want to struggle through business school and become an office drone or marginally honest stockbroker when there is something worthwhile that you love and are good at right in front of you?"

Brook's mouth began to tremble. "You know why."

"Yes, but I want to hear you say it. I want you to hear your own stupidity as the words come out of your mouth."

Tears began to crawl down Brook's cheeks.

"Oh God, don't cry." David leaned his elbows on the table and put his head in his hands. He felt like crying himself. "Brook, this is your life. The only one you're going to get. What you do or don't do is not going to save your mother from her own unhappiness. You can try to make her happy, but believe me it won't work."

"Maybe I can't make her happy, but I won't do something I know will make her unhappy." Brook wiped at his cheeks with his cocktail napkin. "I just can't. I'd hate myself."

A picture of Viktor appeared behind David's eyes and a hard, angry voice inside his head urged him to tell the boy the truth. *You're going to fail. You're going to end up like my father, a beaten-down nothing man, cut off from what you love. Your mother will never be happy and you will end up hating yourself after all.* Then Viktor disappeared and David saw himself sitting alone in the lifeless kitchen of his huge, fancy house drinking a glass of sweet, milky tea while Cissy went to church with her parents. He pressed his palms into his eyes until the image went away and then he lifted his head. He wouldn't say such terrible things, not to this boy.

"Christ, why do I even give a fuck what you do? Go; go please your mommy. I'm sure the world needs another clerk more than it needs a storyteller." That was cruel enough.

Brook sat up straight, stiff backed and dry-eyed. "I'm sorry, David. I just can't do what both of you want. I have to make a choice."

"All right. Let's say you do. But the choice isn't between me and your mother. It's between your mother and yourself." Watching, he saw that the boy had done all the rebelling he was going to do for now. In any case, if there was one thing David had taken home from France, it was the knowledge that one botched battle didn't necessarily lose the war.

Brook took another sip of his Scotch. "This is wonderfully good. But it's awfully bitter, isn't it?"

David shook his head and sighed. He raised his glass again and touched it lightly to Brook's. "Yes. It is. Delicious and bitter all at once. Just like life." He pushed the manila envelope firmly to Brook's side of the table. "Drink up."

32

Sarah lumbered and sweated her way up the block, a clumsy tugboat forcing sleeker models out of her way. At eight months pregnant she was still unusually small and slim, but she felt like an elephant. The baby was a hundred-pound weight in her belly. A weight that kicked. Her back ached all the time. She put down the shopping bag and stretched.

At Reuben's insistence, she had stopped working at the end of July. He wanted her to rest, to protect the baby from all the commotion and strain of her job. Six weeks later and it was still disorienting to be out on the street in the middle of the day. After eight years she didn't know what to do with herself if she wasn't working. She knew she'd have her hands full soon enough, but that didn't reassure her at all. Despite Naomi extolling the joys of motherhood and everyone telling Sarah how fortunate she was not to have to work, the truth was that she was unhappy without her job.

She loved everything about being the head seamstress at Leyrowitz's. She loved leaving the apartment with Reuben early in the morning, even during the winter months when it was cold and dark. She loved walking up Ludlow Street with him as far as Rivington, kissing him good-bye on the corner before turning west as he turned east. She loved letting herself into the shop with her own key and greeting Uncle Sol, who was always there before her no matter how early she arrived. She loved entering the dark and quiet tailors' room, *her* room, and readying it for the day ahead. She loved feeling the room come to life as it filled with *her* staff. She loved sitting at her table letting out a seam so that Mrs. Kravitt could say she took a size 12 instead of a 14. She loved the respect and admiration she received from her customers and fellow workers, who after so many years had become her extended family. And she loved the paycheck she took home every week.

She didn't know how to tell Reuben that he, her wonderful, adoring husband, and their coming child weren't enough for her. It wasn't that she didn't want this baby. She did. So frighteningly much that she often sat up at night, alone at the dining room table, hands on her belly, sobbing with worry and grief as she imagined every terrible thing that could happen to this yet-unborn child. Despite Judaism's insistence on the finality of death, Sarah found herself secretly believing that the soul of either Anna or Viktor would be returned to her through her child. She wanted the baby. She just didn't want to have to give up her life for it, and she knew there must be something wrong with her for feeling that way. What else could possibly be more important? What else could she want?

She picked up her bag and kept walking. She had wanted to bring something special to Reuben for lunch today. She'd decided on a nice cold thermos of borscht with a generous dollop of sour cream stirred into it. Sweet and cool. As she trudged up the stairs to the factory, she admitted to herself that it was really in the hope of talking to Rachel that she had come. Rachel had two children and she still worked. True, she had to, since Shlomo, the butcher's assistant, didn't earn much money, but Sarah was sure that Rachel enjoyed her job. Of course, she had her mother and mother-in-law to take care of Leah and Sam. Who could Sarah ask to take care of her child? Naomi had five of her own, two not yet in school. It would be scandalous to pay a stranger to perform the duties of motherhood while Sarah went to work for her own pleasure.

Sarah found her husband and Rachel in his office, examining dresses hanging on a rack against the wall. As soon as she walked in, she realized what a fool's errand she'd come on. There was nothing Rachel could tell her. The problem wasn't who she might ask or hire to watch her baby; the problem was that she had no possible justification for not doing it herself. This is what Uncle Sol had meant when he'd said he wasn't in a hurry for her to marry; even he, who knew better than anyone how much she cherished her job, expected her to stay home. It was shameful that she wished she could continue working, even a few days a week. Best not to tell anyone or they would know how abnormal a woman she was.

"Sarahle, sweetheart, what are you doing here?" Reuben hurried over, took the bag out of her hand, and gave her a careful hug. "You should be home, resting, not shlepping around in this heat."

"Hello, my love," she said, in as bright a voice as she could muster. "I hope I'm not interrupting your work. I wanted to bring you some cold borscht. Hello, Rachel."

Rachel smiled. "She's not going to break, Reuben. It's all right for pregnant women to walk, you know." She kissed Sarah on both cheeks. "How are you, Sarah? You must be ready for this little one to make its appearance, I would think." She patted Sarah's stomach.

"I guess so," Sarah said hesitantly.

"You guess?" Reuben joked. "What, you want to carry it around in there forever?"

Sarah laughed. "No! I guess I'm a little scared. About the birth, about afterward, everything actually." She looked at Rachel, willing the older woman the ability to read the silent questions in her eyes.

Rachel put an arm around Sarah's shoulder and hugged her. "Of course you're scared, but try not to be. Giving birth may not be the most pleasant experience you'll ever have, but once it's over you forget about the hard part and only remember the miracle. I envy you. The first baby is so special and you'll be there for every moment. You're a lucky girl."

Sarah's heart dropped into her shoes. "So, you would stay home if you could?"

"Hey, no ideas in her head, please!" Reuben teased.

"Your husband knows I love my job, but yes, I would stay home if I could. At least until they were both in school. They grow and change so fast and I miss too much. My mother and *shviger* spoil them terribly, Shlomo is too soft, and I end up being the disciplinarian. Don't worry, Sarah; you will love being a mother. You're young; you can go back to work later. Sol will always find a place for you; you know that."

"What nonsense is that? What am I working so hard for? No, we want more children, and I will make sure Sarah won't ever need to work. That's the way it should be in this country. Mothers free to stay home with their children. If I could afford it, I would pay you *not* to work, Rachel," Reuben said earnestly.

"I like the sound of that. I think you should seriously consider it." Rachel gave Reuben an affectionate smile. "Let Sarah have this one first before you go planning for more."

Sarah suddenly felt calmer. Rachel had given her a glimmer of something hopeful. Perhaps she wouldn't have five children in nine years like Naomi and end up trapped in her house. Maybe she could have one or two quickly and go back to work when the children went to school. Could a woman actually plan something like that?

"Sarah, as long as you are here, come look at these dresses. Aren't they beautiful?" Reuben, filled with pride, took her arm and pulled her over to the rack.

Indeed they were beautiful, quite the most beautiful dresses Sarah had ever seen. "My goodness. These are gorgeous! What are they? Who are they for?"

"This is how our wonderful Mr. Shaw is making it so I can afford for you to stay home! They're Gates's new winter line and they're going to make everybody rich."

Rachel turned away and busied herself at Reuben's desk.

"Oh." Sarah dropped the sleeve of the dress she'd been fondling.

"Aren't they something? They are so important to Mr. Shaw that he brought the drawings here himself, to show to Rachel exactly what he wanted. Right, Rachel?"

"Yes, that's right." Rachel continued shuffling through a pile of invoices, although she didn't seem to find what she was looking for.

Sarah thought she would vomit. She clutched at the bar of the rack to steady herself and took several deep breaths. "You met Mr. Shaw, Rachel?"

Rachel lifted her head. "Yes."

"And what is he like, our mysterious benefactor?"

"You didn't meet him when you had your interview at the store last year?" Rachel asked.

"No. Why would I have? He didn't interview me. I've never met him. And all Reuben tells me is that he's shrewd but honest. Malka, at the front desk, practically faints every time she says his name, so I think maybe there's more to him than that?" Sarah managed to keep her voice light and playful.

Rachel matched Sarah's frivolous tone. "Malka is seventeen and ready to burst over any rich, good-looking man. To me, Mr. Shaw appeared very driven, overly ambitious. I didn't think I'd like him, but he was really very sympathetic."

"So, he didn't make you faint," Sarah said, her eyes plumbing Rachel's expression.

Rachel flashed a quick smile. "No. I'm not seventeen anymore." She kissed Sarah good-bye. "I have to get back to the cutting room. Everything will be all right; you'll see. Please, don't worry."

Sarah's thoughts were spinning out of control. Rachel had seen David and was pretending that she hadn't. Of course, she didn't know that Sarah also had seen Mr. *Shaw*. No one knew. What was she to think? Was Rachel lying to protect Sarah? Or was she protecting David? He must have told her to keep his identity a secret. But it seemed as though Rachel was trying to tell her something important, that David was unhappy. But if Rachel didn't know that Sarah knew . . . her head began to hurt.

"Sarahle, you don't look so good. Come, sit for a little while and then you go home and lie down. I'll get you something to drink." Reuben led her to his chair and stroked her hair. "I'll come home early tonight, all right?" He left in search of a glass of water.

Sarah put her head down on the desk. Shockingly inappropriate though she knew it was, she couldn't stop herself from laughing. Life was so hopelessly ridiculous. Secrets crowding out truth and love like toxic weeds, new ones sprouting up this very day.

Sarah had a new secret of her own now: she knew she was just the same as David. She wanted for herself, in her heart of hearts, the same freedom to live her own life that he had left home to find. It was not possible for her to remain angry with him. This bitter estrangement, due to her own ignoble cowardice, should never have existed. She had to find a way to end it. Somehow, she had to take her life in her hands and reach for what she wanted. Not yet, however. Right now, she had to survive having this baby.

33

"How did you know it was going to happen, David?" Joseph closed the office door and made his way to his chair, his right foot dragging reluctantly along the carpet. He had been back at work for three weeks, ignoring Dr. Barre's admonition that he needed at least another month to regain his strength.

"What do you mean? I didn't know. The real estate market was going to collapse; that much I figured out. I meant washed away in the figurative sense, for crying out loud. I didn't know all of southern Florida was going to get blown away by a hurricane. Four hundred dead, thirty million in property damage." David shook his head. "What a mess. Did you sell in time?"

"Of course. I take your advice seriously. And for this little piece, you deserve a reward."

David grinned. "What's my reward? You're going to make me pay the capital gains tax on your eight-million profit? Your initial investment was less than twenty thousand dollars. Maybe you'd have been better off kissing that good-bye."

"I'm not even chuckling, you notice. It's a ridiculous, counterproductive tax, but I still have plenty left." Joseph held out a check. "Enough to give you this. Here."

"I haven't earned it, whatever it is, and really, I don't want it."

David forced himself not to look away from the piece of paper flapping in Joseph's hand. It was painful to see his indomitable mentor and patron weakened, with trembling hand, limping gait, and drooping face. Joseph wasn't the same man he had been before the stroke, although his mind was sharp as ever. He had been humbled, tumbled from his godlike pedestal. Uncertainty tainted the rarefied air in the corner office. David didn't want to think of the day when Joseph would falter and come to a halt. This was a man who deserved to go to his grave believing in himself and in what he'd accomplished, strong and effective to the end. David owed it to Joseph to help him do that. But it was hard to pretend that nothing had changed. There had been a subtle shift in the balance of power between mentor and student, and David knew it would be foolish and irresponsible of him to ignore it.

"You earned it." Joseph's hand shook harder from the effort of holding the check aloft. "Think of it as a commission. My goddamned broker didn't advise me to sell; you did. I've never known you to turn down money. What's wrong with you, are you sick?" He thrust the furiously fluttering rectangle of paper toward the younger man.

"A momentary aberration. Ignore it." David took the check. Anything so that Joseph's hand could fall peacefully back onto his lap.

The check was for six hundred thousand dollars. David did a quick, unconscious calculation. Approximately 10 percent of the after-tax profit. The amount of all his earnings combined from the first three years after the war. A hundred thousand times what his mother slaved and suffered to earn in her entire lifetime; the equivalent to what Reuben might hope to make from forty years of a successful business sustained by long, hard six-day workweeks. Twelve times what Zoe might have needed to get her academy going. Inexplicably insufficient to buy his own happiness. He folded the check and slid it into the inside pocket of his suit jacket. He would take the money, but that didn't mean he had to keep it.

"Speechless!" Joseph gloated. "I can still surprise you, I see." He rubbed his hands together in glee. "All right. Take a breath. We need to have a talk about business."

David's mouth twisted in a cynical grimace. "Business is great. The times have bred a nation of greedy, suggestible consumers, eager to overspend and overextend themselves to support the country's overproduction. It should hold for a while longer and allow us to profit nicely."

Joseph sighed. "Ah yes. Before the war, the only debt people carried was a mortgage."

"I don't even consider that a debt. At least a house begins to appreciate from the moment you buy it, unlike a car or furniture. Credit is now the tenth largest business in the country. Personal debt is growing two and a half times faster than personal income."

"How times have changed. What's become of our Puritan belief in waste not, want not?"

"All gone. Now it's wait not, want not." David waved his hand in a parody of a royal flourish. "And thus do revenues from the advertising and credit sectors grow and grow."

"That advertising *goniff* from Chicago, Albert Lasker, is he angry with you for hiring away his best man to start up our firm?"

"I doubt it. He single-handedly created the industry—"

"With the invaluable help of radio." Joseph held up a warning finger. "You must admit, if advertisers couldn't get their little lies directly into the homes and ears of the masses, Lasker's hard-sell messages would not be earning the industry two billion dollars a year."

David dipped his head in agreement. "Quite true. How could any wife and mother, the protector of her family and keeper of the home, resist running out for a bottle of Listerine after hearing a poignant testimonial about how it will defend her loved ones from germs and the indignities of halitosis?" He laughed. "No. Lasker has lost good employees before. The industry's growth is good for everyone. I'm sure he's satisfied with the million a year he pays himself from Lord and Thomas's earnings."

Joseph cackled. "Ha! A million a year and he doesn't produce a goddamned thing that anyone can use! It's a new age, my boy!" Steadying his quaking right hand with his left, Joseph attempted to pour a glass of water from the heavy crystal pitcher on the table between them. As much as got into the glass splashed all over the polished wood, and the glass began to slide on the slick surface.

"Let me help you." David leaned forward and reached out to hold the glass.

Joseph put the pitcher down and slapped at David's hand. "I don't need your help."

David withdrew. As Joseph awkwardly mopped up the water with a napkin, David smoothly returned the conversation to matters of business. "I have a new idea for us to consider."

"Only one today?" Joseph balled the wet linen in his left hand. "You're getting lazy."

"Only one, but it's a good one," David promised. "I want to look into buying either Kelvinator or Frigidaire. In-home refrigerators are going to be the next telephone or electricity. Everyone is going to have to have one."

Joseph shook his head. "They're expensive, David. When the economy falters, they'll go the way of all luxuries."

"I don't agree. Like a car or a telephone or electricity, a refrigerator is already considered a necessity, not a luxury. It's a life-transforming possession. The prices will likely come down with greater production, but as we discussed a moment ago, the population has gotten used to being in debt. One-fifth of everything people buy is bought on credit. Why shouldn't we make money from the sale of the product as well as its purchase? Just let me look into it, all right? Neither company may even be available."

Joseph settled back into his chair. He contemplated David with an uncharacteristic sedate thoughtfulness. "Yes, look into it." He smiled. "David, it's time. I want you down here with me before the end of the year, while I still have the strength to teach you the last bits you need to learn. You're going to take over the company when I'm done."

David felt no surprise. In his heart he knew this was his ultimate destiny. To be at the helm of this vast ship of commerce, to be the one to steer it over the coming decades into the new world being created out of the fragmented pieces of the past. He could see his future gleaming before him. Just as he had two and a half years before, he turned his head to stare out the window and thought about what Anna would want for him. She would want, more than anything, for him to be happy. And just like that he felt his destiny veering off course, his future slipping through his fingers.

Quietly he said, "Jed is your heir, Joseph, not me."

"Why? Because he carries my name? That means nothing. This company is my legacy, and it will forever have my name on it. J. E. Gates. You could occupy this office for the next fifty years, eclipse my accomplishments, and yet no one will ever think of it as David Shaw's company."

"He carries your blood. Doesn't that mean anything?"

Joseph squinted, as if trying to bring something that had gone blurry back into focus. "Since when do you care about blood? Sentimentality doesn't become you, David. Jed's heart isn't in it; that's the bottom line."

"It is. His heart and his soul. All for you." A feathery sensation brushed the back of David's neck, like loving fingers trailing across his skin. His head dropped and his eyes closed for a barely noticeable second. Behind the lids, his eyes were hot.

"You know what I mean, David. He doesn't love it, the competition, the winning, the accruing of power and money. Despite Sally's best attempts, the boy is more like his father than like her. Don't get me wrong; I know he applies prodigious effort and intellect to his work. He could do a serviceable job keeping what I've built intact. But that's not enough for me. The conversation we had a moment ago, can you imagine me having that with him? You know what I want done with this company and we both know you're the one to do it."

David felt a pain in his stomach, the twist of an invisible knife forged from an alloy of regret and responsibility. An ironic smile played across his face as he met Joseph's impatient stare. "I'm afraid I'm not as hardheaded as you after all, Joe. I can't do that to Jed."

Joseph's eyes were blue ice. There was no sympathy in them. The drooping lid gave his granite face a malevolent cast. "Don't be a fool, David. You'd be doing him a favor."

"No. You don't understand." He leaned forward; he had to make Joseph see. "You're right. Jed isn't made the way you and I are. He doesn't have the natural instinct, the cold-blooded drive that pushes sons of bitches like us to the top. But he is a good and loyal man. He's turned himself inside out to do what you and Sally expect of him. He's lived up to his end of the bargain, Joe, and you have to live up to yours. If you let him know that he's disappointed you, he'll be devastated. You'll be doing terrible harm to someone who has done nothing but try to give you what you wanted."

Joseph evinced no reaction to what David had said except to distance himself by leaning back in his chair and crossing his legs, using both hands to hoist his right leg up and over the left. "So, have we at last found the limits of your courage, my boy, or are you truly noble unto stupidity? In either case, what exactly are you suggesting I do? Sacrifice my company to spare my insufficient grandson's feelings?"

For the first time, David saw, truly and with frightening clarity, the inescapability of the web that Joseph and Sally had spun out of their own callous ambition to bind Jed to them. Jed hadn't been born with the resources to do combat with people like them; he hadn't had a chance. Like a dumb animal caught in a cruel trap, he would have had to gnaw off his own limb in order to free himself, but he didn't possess even such rudimentary instincts for survival. He had emerged from the womb directly into the web and never realized he was snared. Dismay flashed through David and in its wake a lightning bolt of an idea.

"No, you don't have to sacrifice either your company or your grandson," he said, his tone matching the coldness in Joe's eyes. "Bring me in to work with him, but leave no doubt that Jed is the man in charge. I promise I'll stay with the company, with him, no matter what. You can die in peace, knowing your empire will be well taken care of, and Jed can live with his pride and belief in who he is intact."

Joseph sneered. "What are you going to do, whisper in his ear and let him take credit for your ideas? No one will believe it."

"I'll make it work, somehow. People respect Jed and expect you to honor your bloodline, despite my impressive performance," David replied. "They will be tolerant."

"And what do you get out of this, David?"

This was it. The secret payback he had promised Jed he would make someday. "I get to do work I love, for which I will no doubt be overly well compensated. And I get to live with myself. I think it's a fair deal."

Uncomfortable moments passed in silence.

"Joe. Please."

Little by little, the ice in Joseph's eyes melted away. "That's a word I have rarely heard you use." He smiled faintly. "Evelyn asked me not to place you over Jed as well. I must indeed be getting old, letting myself be influenced by a woman and a boy." He looked down at his lap, at his disobedient hand, twitching along his leg without permission. His head hung as though it weighed more than his spine could support. "I am. I am getting old."

"It's not the worst thing that can happen to a person." David stood up and put a firm hand on Joseph's shoulder. "I'll go get Jed. We should tell him the good news together."

Hours later, David climbed the steps to his front door. Before he needed to reach for his keys, the door opened and Cissy was there, waiting for him. It happened like that most nights. He would kiss her good-bye in the entryway in the morning and she would be there when he got home at night. He knew she did things on her own during the day, but in his mind she was permanently in the vestibule, waiting for his return like a faithful pet.

"How do you always know when I'm coming home?" He took her face in his hands and kissed her.

"I watch for you, silly." Cissy followed David into their parlor, her hands fluttering at his sides as she helped him out of his suit jacket. She dropped the jacket onto a chair and sat down on the settee. He sat down next to her. Surprised, she moved close and ran her fingers along his arm, her touch vibrating with need. "Don't you want a drink, love?"

He grabbed at her roving hand and held it still. "No. Let's just . . . talk for a moment."

She stiffened. "Is something wrong? Did I do something?"

He squeezed her hand. He couldn't fail to notice how tense she was much of the time. How distrustful and frightened she had become. They never talked about it. It was safer to ignore it. To spread reassurance over her fears like ointment on a cut and leave it alone to heal itself. "No, Cissy. Nothing's wrong. Something happened at work."

She relaxed and brightened, snuggled against him. "Tell me. I probably won't understand, but I'll listen." She laughed at herself. "Unless you got another promotion. That I'd understand!"

"Well, I did, actually. Joseph wants me out of the store and downtown permanently."

"What? What are you going to do downtown? Work for Joseph? How is that a promotion?" She was indignant. "I thought you'd be taking over the store."

"Cissy!" he exclaimed in frustration. "The store is just a tiny piece of the whole company. Don't you realize at least that much about the business?"

"Well, of course, David! I'm not a total idiot. So, what are you saying, that you're going to run the whole company?" She gasped and pulled back. "Oh my God. You're going to run the whole company!" She clapped her hands to her cheeks.

"Not exactly."

"Why not! You're the smartest person in the world!"

He laughed and kissed her again. A gentle, grateful kiss that left them both a little breathless.

"Well, you are," she mewed.

"But I'm not Joseph's grandson." David took a breath. "Jed will run the business and I'll be his right-hand man." He paused, waiting. Would she see the wrongness of it, ask him why uncharitable and unemotional Joseph would give his company into the hands of the less capable of two candidates?

"Silly me. Of course Jed's going to run things. I mean, the business was always meant for him, way before you came along. And he's almost as smart as you!" She giggled and patted his knee. "Oooh, you're going to be so important. I'm so happy! Oh, I don't mean I'm glad that Joseph is getting old and sick, but Jed and you running the company together . . ." She leaped up, fairly jabbering with excitement. "I'm going to call Abby. We should go out and celebrate."

He stood and caught at her arm. "No. Don't. I'm tired. We'll celebrate over the weekend. We'll go up to the Cotton Club. You like it, don't you?"

"I love it! But let's go to the Paradise. It's even hotter than the Cotton Club. It's the hottest spot in Harlem!"

"Whatever you want. And tomorrow, go buy that Lanvin dress you liked so much."

"Oh, David! The ivory tulle one with the gold sequins and silver beads?"

"All I remember of it is that I could see your beautiful legs. And that it matches those gold leather Perugia shoes you bought."

"You're so wonderful! I'm going to make you dance with me. Ooh, the blues is so sexy!" She sashayed around the room in a suggestive tango and stopped in front of him. "We can celebrate now, all by ourselves. That kiss put some naughty ideas into my head."

David ran his hands through her short, straight, dark-blond hair, then brought them to her narrow waist, over the flare of her hips and the swell of her buttocks. Sex was what they were best at, after all. It never failed them. It was the bandage over her insecurity and the balm to his agitation and disappointment. Although, as time went on, it became more difficult to balance the pleasure they gave each other in bed with the pain he caused her by refusing, still, to have children. When the balance tipped, he didn't know what would happen to their marriage.

"How naughty?" he said, pulling her to him.

"Take me upstairs and I'll show you."

And so he took her upstairs. He shut down his mind and let the movement of his hands and body make irrelevant, for the moment, the growing lack of intimacy between them. He took his time with her, enjoying the comforting, familiar feel of her beneath him. He appreciated how incredibly well she knew his body, knew all the ways to excite him. But even as she caressed and kissed him, coiled her limbs around him, even as he grew more and more aroused, he remained empty and unmoved inside. It was merely his skin she knew, his facade. Nothing more. She didn't know what tarnished secrets lay beneath the shiny veneer. Into his mind came a memory of Lucy's penetrating eyes staring through him as she demanded to know how he could live with someone who didn't know who he was. And of himself, full of denial and hostility, lying in response. Despair tugged at his heart. He refused it, applied himself to Cissy with a single-minded attentiveness that left no room for his own dissatisfaction. But the more tenderness and passion he lavished on her to cover over the shallowness of his connection, the more he fooled her into believing he had even more to give.

He rocked in and out of her with slow, rhythmic strokes, nearing his own completion. He heard her labored breath in his ear, her sharp cry as she came, felt her contract around him. She would know he was on the brink; she always did. And he prayed that she would not ask for what he couldn't give. But she couldn't help herself. She pulled him in deeper and panted out her desire.

"David, stay inside me. I want you to come inside me. Please."

For a second he thought he might do it, that maybe it was, after all, what they really needed. A baby to be the cement that held them together. A bond imposed from the outside as a substitute for the bond missing from within. But as he felt himself begin to spurt, he panicked and pulled free, spilling his seed on her leg.

Cissy cried out again, this time without joy, and twisted in his arms. He tried to hold her, but she squirmed viciously and turned her back to him, curled up like a child, and began to cry. David wanted to leap from the bed and run, to be anywhere but here. There was no point in apologizing. The words had been said too many times before. He pulled the sheet up over them and pressed himself against her back, held her now unresistant, shaking body. He held her, his hand at her breast and his lips in her hair, until her sobs subsided and she fell into sleep.

34

The baby was napping. The nanny was out. Abby and Jed lay on their bed, tentative and delicate. They gazed at each other through the air's melancholy gloom, spun from the light of an overcast November afternoon filtering through the bedroom window. They gazed at each other and waited. For him to move. For him to touch her. For him to be ready to make love again, as Abby had been ready for months.

Jed thought he could do it. He had used the nine months of her pregnancy and the four months since Henry had been born to perfect the art of pleasuring himself. He had abandoned his shame in his unnaturalness and given himself over to loving and needing the response of his body to his own hand. He had created an array of elaborate fantasies to accompany his actions, most involving David but some about men, one in particular, he had seen on his several skulking forays into the immoral streets of the West Village. He was still determined that any actual sexual contact be with Abby only; anything else remained unthinkable. Now that he knew how to arouse himself, where to put his head while his body followed its own wishes, he believed he could make it happen in concert with Abby's body. He just had to keep his eyes closed and his mind focused and she would never know that he wasn't really there. He produced a hopeful smile and reached for her.

He found the strength to pull his pants on but then had to sit back down onto the edge of the bed. At least he hadn't rushed into the bathroom to vomit after it was over, and he tried to tell himself that that made it better than the last time and he should consider it a victory. But he didn't feel victorious. He felt vile. He sat and stared at the floor and swallowed convulsively as he fought back the urge to weep. He had done it, but it had been horrible. The fantasy that served him so well when he was alone had failed him. Worse, it had turned on him, become an intrusive entity in their bed, reminding him every second how intractably dissociated he was from Abby's femaleness, despite the love he felt for her as a person, as a friend, as a mate. He didn't know how it would be possible for him to ever do this again. The thought of it made him want to jump out the window.

Abby was in the kitchen heating a bottle for Henry's afternoon feeding. She was humming. The sound of her happiness crept up the stairs and into his consciousness. Jed wanted her to be happy, but realizing that she had found something to feel good about in this awful thing they had done together only made her seem more alien to him. He forced himself to stand up and walk out of the room. He stood in the hallway. He should go downstairs and be with Abby, do something more with her in a normal aftermath of their encounter—it was out of the question to call it lovemaking—as though he had any idea of what was normal between a man and his wife. But he couldn't.

Jed walked into the nursery just as the infant came awake, gurgling and cooing with contentment. Henry, named after Abby's long-dead father. Henry, the redeemer of all pain. Jed bent over the cradle and picked the boy up. All thoughts of the past hour were swept from Jed's mind by the feel of the small body in his arms, the smell of innocence that rose off the top of the fair head. He stroked Henry's hair and kissed him repeatedly. The love he felt for his son was like the love he felt for David in its completeness and sensuousness. Jed's love for Henry overfilled him. It tortured him with a physical rapture indistinguishable from pain. It left him floating free of himself, without need of any kind save for the need to cherish and protect. He held the infant close to him. Henry's head, too big for his body, lolled against his father's shoulder, and his chubby fingers grabbed at Jed's shirt. Jed took the little hand in his and kissed it, then succumbed to the desire to put the entire perfect appendage in his mouth and lick and taste his child the way he might an ice-cream cone.

"Babies are absolutely edible, aren't they?" Abby stood smiling in the doorway. "Look at my two boys. Look how much they love each other."

Jed reached out an arm for her. "He's perfect. And we made him. You and I. Sometimes, I just can't believe it."

She nestled inside Jed's embrace, but her eyes were on Henry. "I know." She took one of the sparse blond curls in her fingers. "He's going to look just like you. I'm so glad." She leaned her nose into Henry's pudgy neck and inhaled. "Bring him down to the kitchen. His bottle is ready."

Jed tightened his arm around her. "Abby. You know this is what I want, don't you, us all together like this? No matter what, even if we don't . . . well, you know. You know that I love you, don't you?"

Abby removed her gaze from the baby and brought it to Jed's face. "Yes. I know you love me, Jed. And you know that I love you. And today I let myself hope that maybe, after we—" Her eyes filled with tears. "But it's hopeless, isn't it? I wish I understood what kind of love it is you feel for me, because I can't think anymore that it's ever going to be the same as what I feel for you." She put a hand on his arm, stretched up onto her toes, and kissed him lightly on the mouth. "Is it?"

Her love for him was so pure and clear it pulled at him like an open door. He took a terrified, oblique step in the direction of the truth. "What if it's not?"

Abby bit down on her lower lip and clutched at his arm. Tears spilled down her face. "Is it enough to keep you here? To make us a family? Give Henry a sister or a brother someday?"

The baby began to mewl. Jed was holding him too tightly. "Yes. I swear. It's enough for all of that. I do love you, Abby. I meant what I said. This *is* what I want. Just don't expect . . . I don't think I can—"

She nodded and wiped her tears away with the burping cloth she had thrown over her shoulder. She smiled gamely. "Then we'll be all right. We'll do the best we can and we'll be all right. And I won't expect anything, but I won't stop hoping, either. And if you keep trying, maybe someday you'll come to like it. Cissy says that can happen." Cissy also said it wouldn't happen until Sally died, but Abby wasn't about to repeat that. "Just tell me that you'll try from time to time. If it's no good we can stop. And promise me that you won't go somewhere else."

He felt such relief that he didn't care that Abby had talked to Cissy about their intimate life. In fact, it was good because together the women had come up with a wonderfully safe explanation for his lack of sexual passion, just as David had wrongly assumed Abby to be at fault when Jed had confided that they had had no sex for over a year. With Cissy's help, Abby now believed he simply didn't like sex. They probably put the blame on Sally, somehow, since blaming mothers for everything wrong was in vogue these days. The amazing thing was that Abby was willing to accept him that way. He didn't want to think about trying, ever again, but if she had no expectations, then as long as he made some effort once in a while, he couldn't really fail. And perhaps it would be worth the skin-crawling, bone-chilling repugnance if it meant he could have another Henry, or a daughter.

"I promise."

Abby took the crying baby from Jed. "Let's go feed our hungry little boy."

35

Monty knew it was all over. Yesterday two humorless cadavers from the accounting department had been snooping around, asking to see the past weeks' receipts. And this morning that stupid girl ran crying from the sales floor, just because he'd put his hand on her ass; she flirted with him like a whore, but let him react and she screams rape. He wasn't going to wait for David to send the guards to throw him out. He'd be damned if he would let that smug, righteous parvenu humiliate him in public. He'd been given his cue; it was time to exit the stage.

He took his overcoat, checked to see that the cash he'd removed from the sales drawer was snugly in the pocket, slung it over his shoulders, and without fuss walked down the wide marble staircase at the center of the store. He stopped on the second floor, in the men's department, where he collected three excellent suits he'd had his eye on, some matching shirts, ties, and hose, and, at the last moment, a fine wool coat for good measure. He bundled it all into a Gates garment bag, saying he was taking it on speculation for the husband of a good client—something he legitimately did from time to time—and left the store.

He took a taxi to Central Park West. He had vacated the apartment two weeks before but left all his lightweight clothing behind. No one had asked him to remove any of it, so he surmised that nothing had been done with the apartment yet. They were quick to force him out, but no one in the family seemed to want to touch the place. Which was good, because something had been nagging at him. He needed to make one more careful assay before he disappeared from sight. He didn't want to leave anything behind that might cause anyone to come looking for him. What he'd taken from the store wouldn't be a problem. David would consider the loss of a few hundred dollars' worth of clothing an acceptable price to pay to be through with him; David probably expected a bit of thievery from him anyway, and Monty certainly didn't want to disappoint dear David.

Monty gave the building's venal daytime doorman five dollars to let him up and then forget that he'd ever seen him. He wandered through the apartment, not sure what he was looking for. He considered pilfering a few small silver knickknacks that he knew he could hock but thought better of it. He thought about taking the rest of the booze—it made him shiver with dread to picture that bitch Lorena or poor Sally pouring it all down the drain—but he knew it was foolish and unnecessary; he could get plenty more. He could, however, enjoy some while he was here. He grabbed a nearly full bottle of whiskey and carried it with him as he went into the bedroom. He opened the closet where his summer wardrobe hung, untouched. He had lost enough weight that he would likely need to buy new summer clothes, but he picked out a few of his favorite things and added them to the contents of the garment bag. As he re-arranged the remaining items hanging on the closet's wooden rod to make it look as though nothing had been disturbed, he saw it. The suit he'd worn the day Zoe died, crumpled into a sweat-and-dirt-stained ball of seersucker on the floor, shoved into a corner of the closet. He would never wear it again, but he couldn't leave it there. Gingerly, without looking at it too closely, he gathered it up and crammed it into the bag. He didn't notice the flecks of dirt that fell out of the wide cuff of one trouser leg, nor the small rectangular piece of paper that tumbled from the pocket of the upended jacket. He left the whiskey bottle, now more than half-empty, on the kitchen counter.

He went back to his hotel, a decent midtown residence hotel where he had been keeping up appearances while allegedly looking for a suitable home for his sad new bachelor existence. He packed quickly, and by the time the daylight had faded from the early-winter sky he was resettled across town—temporarily, of course, just until he got his new life organized—in a tiny suite of shabby rooms in a disreputable hotel owned by an old buddy. It was a lucrative establishment in the Tenderloin district of the west thirties, where sexual assignations of all kinds took place all hours of the day and night and where Monty could disappear into the mass of pimps, whores, johns, and wide-eyed tourists as completely as if he'd crossed the ocean and not merely the teeming, narrow island of Manhattan.

The five thousand dollars from the divorce settlement was secure in a safe-deposit box, but he was owed more and he had one last shot at getting it—one bit of business to attend to before he closed the book on his life as Zoe Gates's husband and resumed his long-interrupted residency in the underworld that had birthed and suckled him and reared him to adulthood.

He walked to Gramercy Park. A fifteen-minute stroll from the scarred wooden and glass door of a whorehouse hotel to the gleaming black-lacquered door of a wealthy woman's town house. A cluster of hearty chrysanthemums still bloomed cheerily in Philip's garden, unaware that winter was fast bearing down on them. Monty plucked one and stuck it in a buttonhole. He knew it was Philip's habit to remain at his studio until well into cocktail hour, but just to make sure that the meticulous artist and gardener had not chosen today to exhibit spontaneity, Monty had called the studio, hanging up when Philip answered.

"Ah, something smells good, Edna." Monty sniffed appreciatively as Edna closed the front door behind him.

"I've got a nice roast beef in the oven. Are you staying for dinner, Mr. Glennon? Mrs. Gates said nothing to me." Edna hooked his coat on the stand in the corner of the vestibule.

"No, no. Don't worry. I've just come to speak with her for a moment."

"Right, then. She's in the parlor. I'll let her know you're here."

"Don't bother; she's expecting me."

Monty stole into the parlor, closed the double doors behind him without making a sound. He crept across the carpet to where Sally sat at her desk, head bent in concentration over a note she was writing. He leaned down and kissed the back of her neck.

Sally dropped her pen with a small shriek and whipped her head around. "My God! Monty! I thought you were Brook come home from school." She stood up and backed away from him. "How dare you come here like this!"

They had not seen each other since the day he had bedded her. He had called her several times, whimpering contritely that he blamed himself for what had happened, that he had taken advantage of her sweetness and generosity at a time of great need. He confessed how very desperately he wanted her, although he knew the experience was one that could never be repeated. Actually, he would have happily screwed her again, anytime. She'd been quite a wild ride. But she'd never allow it. He'd caught her with her guard down once; it wouldn't happen a second time. However, his calls served their purpose well enough, leaving her titillated and mortified all at once. She was gently reminded of her sin and led to believe that mutual atonement was called for. His atonement was to never have her again, and hers was to get him money. She could atone for her sin of giving herself to a man other than her husband by helping Monty disappear from her life. Not by paying him to leave, oh no, nothing so crude. Just to help him a little. To concur that after twenty years he should have been better treated by his wife's family.

"I dared because I must. Because I am leaving."

"Leaving?"

Monty smiled indulgently. "No one wants me around anymore. Not even you. I'll take my small settlement and make a new life elsewhere. After today, the family will be rid of me. But I needed to see you one last time. You and I have a special friendship, after all . . ."

Sally stood rigid, her arms locked around her midriff. "Yes, of course we do." Her voice was weak. "But you're right. It's best for you to move on."

He bowed his head in acknowledgment and then looked up at her from beneath his long lashes, shamed and apologetic. "Sally, I hate to bring it up, but . . . were you able at all . . . did you . . . ?" He fumbled over his words.

Sally flushed bright red and shook her head vehemently. "I tried, once, but Joseph cut me off before I could even make a case for you. There's nothing more I can do, Monty. He doesn't even want to hear your name. He won't give you anything."

"Well, perhaps you can give me something yourself. Because of our special friendship." Monty tried to stay in character as the wronged widower, the obsequious lover. But even as he spoke the cajoling words he felt his mask slip, just for a moment, pushed aside by loathing and greed.

In that instant, Sally saw the flash of cruelty and avarice in his eyes. Cold dread and humiliation broke over her like a mammoth ocean wave and she clutched harder at herself so as not to be tossed and tumbled. She had given herself in total abandonment to this seductive, horrid man and realized that she had done so *because* he was horrid and so there was no danger of her ever feeling anything for him.

"I have nothing of my own to give you. You know that." She moved toward the closed door. "You have to go now."

He stepped in front of her. "Don't tax yourself. I'll let myself out." Pretense unnecessary now, Monty leered at her. He seized her face and kissed her, harshly and with malice, holding her head tightly as she tried to pull away. Keeping his mouth on hers and using his body forcefully against her, he pushed her backward until she crumpled into her chair. "Don't forget me, my little ice queen. I certainly won't forget you."

He left her there and went swiftly into the vestibule, shutting the parlor doors behind him. He reclaimed his coat, then opened and shut the front door with an audible impact, but he didn't leave the house. Instead, he ran nimbly up the stairs into Sally's bedroom, pawed through the large jewelry box on her vanity table, and helped himself to her most valuable possession: the blue-white-diamond and emerald earrings and matching necklace that had been Philip's wedding present to her. Worth a small fortune; precious jewels whose loss she could not possibly hide or explain. Monty didn't give a damn how she managed it, but she would have to buy them back from him somehow. Booty in his pants pocket, he tiptoed down the stairs and out the door and disappeared into the night, disturbing nothing, not even Philip's mums.

36

"I wish Joseph hadn't asked me to do this."

The apartment was as dauntingly silent and airless as a tomb. David stood forlornly in the entryway, reluctant to move. He could feel the lingering accretion of unhappiness pushing at the walls and ceiling and floor. He couldn't bear to think of Zoe living in this place, buried in the dark, alone with Monty.

"Why didn't you refuse?" Lorena asked as she snapped on the lights in the entry and kitchen and then moved into the parlor. She opened a window, letting in a blast of clear, cold air.

David followed her from room to room like a little boy

afraid of the dark. "Because I'm the only one he trusts to clean up the place. I really appreciate you coming to help me."

She took his hand. "I'm glad you called me, David. And as hard as it is to be here and be reminded of the tragedies in Zoe's life, I think we two are the right people to do this. We were the ones who knew her best and cared for her the most, don't you think?"

"Maybe. But we couldn't save her, so what good were we to her?"

"Saving her wasn't our responsibility, David. And you know perfectly well what good we were to her."

He grunted and glanced around. "I don't know what Joseph expects us to do here."

"I noticed that Monty left quite a bit of clothing. I'll go pack it up. Why don't you make a list of anything that the family might want to keep? Then you can send someone to take those things back to Oyster Bay, and I'll send someone to come pick up the rest for the church to give to our needy."

A short while later, David appeared in the bedroom doorway. "I'm done. There isn't much here that has any personal significance. Zoe took all the things she really loved. You can have almost everything." He sat down on the bed and looked idly around the room as Lorena folded Monty's clothing and packed it into a carton; two already-filled boxes sat on the floor. The closet was empty, the door standing open. David's gaze swept past it, then back. He got up from the bed and picked up something from the closet floor.

"Lorena. Look what I found."

She took from him the torn stub of a Long Island Railroad ticket to Oyster Bay. She stared at it, then slowly handed it back to David.

"He was there."

"David, you don't know that. There's no date on this and it's stained. It could be years old. They both took the train to Oyster Bay, innumerable times." Lorena's words were reasonable, but her voice revealed her unreasoned distress.

David crumpled the stub in his hand. "He was there. You suspect him; I can tell. You were close to her, Lorena. She confided in you. Tell me what you know."

Lorena hesitated. She didn't know *what* she knew, not really. She had never found a way to talk to Zoe about the horrible secret that Libby had given up before she'd died. It had not been possible to ask Zoe if her husband beat her or whether her dead daughter had been so frightened by her parents' fighting and her mother's misery that she imagined something violent and extreme. Lorena had no evidence to confirm Libby's story, though Zoe was far from shy in confiding the depth of her unhappiness with her marriage, Monty's drinking, his emotional coldness. If Lorena had seen anything, perhaps she might have taken the risk of so profoundly invading Zoe's privacy. Instead, unwilling to believe that it was true, Lorena never said a word to anyone. But now a vast chasm of doubt opened in front of her.

"Tell me, Lorena."

She sat heavily on the bed. "I was alone with Libby when she died. She told me something in confidence. David, I don't even know if it's true," she cried.

David waited.

Lorena wrung her hands. "Libby told me that her father hit her mother. That he beat her." She turned away from the accusation in his eyes. "Don't look at me like that, David. Zoe never said anything to me."

"He killed her. She didn't just fall off her horse. He killed her. I have to find him."

"David, don't. You can never know what really happened. What I just told you proves nothing. Libby was a child, a frightened child of a terrible marriage. She could easily have imagined violence that wasn't actually there. Don't take this on yourself; it will destroy you. If Monty did it, he'll get what he deserves in the end. The Lord will see to it."

"I don't live in your world of sure faith, Lorena. And in my world *I'm* the one who will see to it."

Christmas decorations were strung all up and down Central Park West. It was a beautiful sight, but David was in no mood for beauty. He knew he should go home, Cissy was waiting dinner for him, but he was in no mood for her, either. The atmosphere in his house was becoming disturbingly similar to the empty misery of the apartment he'd just left. He decided to walk downtown, through the park and down Fifth Avenue. He wanted to be alone, an anonymous man on the crowded holiday streets, admiring the displays in the store windows like any other stroller. He wanted time to clear his head, to think of what to do.

By the time he got to 14th Street, he was hungry but he still didn't want to go home. He went into the Automat, fed his nickels into the slots, chose chicken pot pie and a cup of coffee. As he sat down, he saw a familiar figure working the room. A young waitress, with curly red hair, freckled skin, and blue eyes. A nice body. Trim ankles. Cute. David had noticed her several times before. They had noticed each other. He waved her over to his table and watched with open appreciation as she sauntered up to him.

"Is there something you need?" She stood close to the table edge, her hip jutting out provocatively.

"Can I get some cream for my coffee?"

"You can get anything you like." She held his eye just long enough for there to be no mistaking her meaning, then grinned and flounced away.

Cute and bold. It had been a very long time since he had flirted with anyone. It felt good.

She returned before his smile faded, leaned over the table, and put down the creamer. Her hand remained wrapped around the sparkling white ceramic pitcher. "Is there anything else I can get for you?"

He reached for the creamer and let his fingers brush against hers, all the while keeping his eyes on her face. A pretty blush threw her freckles into stark relief, and her eyelids flickered. He could have her for dessert if he wanted. He withdrew his hand. "No, thanks. Not tonight. Just the cream."

He returned his attention to his coffee. As she slowly wandered away, his thoughts returned to Monty. Lorena was right; he had no proof of anything. She was a smart woman and her advice was sound. He knew he should heed it. Even if he could find the slimy rat, what could he do to him? He wondered if perhaps he should tell Joseph what he'd found; would he want to know or would it be a burden too great to bear? David did not know what to do, a state of mind he did not enjoy. He resolved to think about it some other time. Right now, he would drink his coffee and eat his chicken pie and in due time he would wander home.

37

It wasn't destined to be a festive New Year's Eve for the ex-tended Gates clan. Joseph and Evelyn were at home; he tired too easily now to face a long night out. Philip and Sally were with them, Sally having declined Philip's offer of dinner and dancing. By ten o'clock, Joseph was nodding in his chair, Philip was browsing through an art journal, and the women were sitting close to the fireplace, talking quietly about this and that. Evelyn cast constant nervous glances at Joseph; Sally cast constant nervous glances at Philip. The women were oblivious to each other's unease, and the men were oblivious to the women. Although Philip had noticed that Sally seemed to watch him more often lately, and differently, with an indescribable, intense sort of curiosity that lacked her usual critical rigor. As though she were a recovering amnesiac trying to find a person she remembered in this man she'd been told was her husband. To Philip, the eternal optimist, it was a hopeful kind of watching, and he liked it. And Joseph had noticed that Evelyn seemed to watch him more often lately, and differently, with a sidelong scrutiny that lacked her usual confidence. As though she were a cowering hyena waiting for the lion to move off the kill so she could feed. To Joseph, the eternal autocrat, it was a demeaning kind of watching, and he didn't like it.

Downtown, the younger generation was gathered at Jed and Abby's. There was a conspicuous chill between David and Cissy and a subtle sadness between Jed and Abby. Brook was positively morose and Lucy was simply exhausted. The only happy person was Henry, and he was sound asleep.

Sometime close to midnight, David and Lucy found themselves alone in the parlor. Abby and Cissy had gone into the kitchen an hour before to make coffee and never returned. Jed, amazingly, had ten minutes before taken Brook up to his studio; with Henry unavailable for the remainder of the night, Jed's eager fatherly attention spilled over onto his young brother. The two left-behinds sat across from each other, one on the sofa, the other in an armchair. They had not spoken since the men had left the room. They sat and breathed in concert with each other. They did not take their eyes off each other. Eventually, David closed his eyes and leaned his head against the back of the chair.

"You look tired." Lucy shifted position on the sofa, tucking her legs under her.

"I am." He opened his eyes. "So do you."

"I am."

They both laughed.

"Are you still enjoying your work?"

"More than ever. I meet the most wonderful women. The clinic and the settlement house are so vital. And someone out there agrees. Henry Street received an anonymous gift for some absurdly large amount of money last week."

"That's good. A rich, guilty Jew, no doubt."

"Or a grateful, generous Jew who doesn't crave recognition."

"Either way. *Mazel tov.*"

Lucy goggled at him. "I never heard you speak Yiddish before."

David shrugged. "It's Hebrew, actually. It seemed appropriate. And we're alone. It's nice, sometimes, to remember that you know things about me."

Lucy dared not assume that David's small disclosure was an invitation to greater intimacy. She played with her glass of eggnog. "So, how are you and Jed getting on in your new positions?"

"Very well." He turned to rummage through a pile of magazines on the end table beside his chair, picked up a copy of *Harper's Magazine*, and started thumbing through it.

She watched him. "Why aren't you the one moving into Grandfather's office? You're the better man for the job."

David's eyebrows rose in exaggerated astonishment. "Well, that's one of the more generous things you've ever said to me."

Lucy blushed. "It's just the truth."

"No. I'm not the better man. Jed is. He'll do fine. And I know he'll never fire me." It was meant as a joke, but neither of them laughed.

They looked at each other and in the awkward silence Lucy came to her own conclusion. She knew that Joseph wanted David to run his empire when he no longer could; there was no one else he trusted or admired as much. And one of the *things* she knew about David was that whatever unthinking or even conscious harm he was capable of inflicting on the weaker, the less intelligent, the merely human, he would never knowingly do anything to hurt Jed.

"Grandfather asked you to take over, to step over Jed. And you refused."

He didn't answer. The desire to open up to her nearly choked him, but how could he tell her what he had done and trust that she wouldn't take his confession and twist it and mock him for his false, self-serving nobility? He didn't want her approval or her sympathy; he merely wanted to be able to tell someone the truth. And even as he backed away from the risk of another scene like the one in her apartment years before, he admitted to himself that she knew him better than anyone and that it was her he wanted to tell. He put a carefully neutral expression on his face and changed the subject. "I want to talk to you about Brook."

Lucy knew then that she was right. She wanted to hit him. She wanted to pound on him until she split him open and forced him to tell her the truth so that she could solace him, tell him that she loved him. But he had shut her out. And Cissy was in the kitchen. "Oh? What about Brook?"

"He's wasting his time in business school. Did you know that he writes stories?"

Lucy frowned. "No."

"Well, he does. And very good ones. Fantasy adventure and some more serious things, too. He should be a writer, but he won't listen to me. He still needs to please your mother."

"What do you mean, he won't listen to you?" She sounded annoyed, jealous that David knew something about her baby brother that she didn't. "You've talked to him?"

"Aren't you listening to me, either? What the hell is wrong with your family? Yes, I've talked to him. I've read his stories. I told him to write. He could probably get into the writing program at NYU, but he won't do it. Can't you do something? You got a chance to do what you love; he should have the same chance."

Her petty annoyance vanished. Like a sleepwalker unaware of her own movements, she got up, walked to him, reached down, and put her palm against his cheek.

David jerked his head and stood up, took a quick step away from her. "Don't do that. I'm not turning into the compassionate, responsible person you keep telling me I should be. The world doesn't need another leech, that's all. If the boy can do something, anything, he should goddamned well do it. Talk to your father. He helped you; he should help his son, too." He threw up his hands and pivoted on his heel. "I need some coffee."

As if on cue, Abby emerged from the kitchen, emptyhanded and white-faced. "Where is Jed?"

"Upstairs, with Brook." Lucy moved to Abby's side. "What's wrong?"

"I think you'd better go get him. Your mother just called. Joseph has had another stroke and it looks like a bad one."

38

On January 1, 1927, twenty-eight-year-old Joseph Edward
Gates II inherited the day-to-day running of J. E. Gates &
Companies from his permanently invalided grandfather.
Along with the position came the corner office with its in-
spiring view and the stalwart assistance of Miss Lillian
Steele. When one morning several weeks later Miss Steele
announced the arrival of his mother, Jed was sitting in
Joseph's chair behind the massive desk, its usually neat
surface cluttered with papers, and David was sitting next to
him, in an armchair dragged from the center of the room.
Their jackets were off, their sleeves rolled up, their heads
bent together, nearly touching, light to dark. David was
talking and Jed was scribbling.

"I'm sure you boys are terribly busy, but I need to talk
with Jed. David, would you mind giving me a few moments alone with my son?" Sally pulled off her gloves but
kept her coat on and remained standing just inside the office doorway.

David looked at Jed. Jed nodded. "I'll let you know
when I'm done."

David rolled down his sleeves and put on his jacket. He
gave Sally a kiss on the cheek as he went by. "Nice to see
you, too, Sally."

She surprised him with a small smile of apology and
said, "Don't be fresh."

Sally closed the door on David's retreating back and felt
an immediate change in the atmosphere of the room. The
assertive energy it had always had when Joseph occupied
the space had disappeared. David had taken it with him.
Resentment and anxiety roiled in her stomach. This was
Jed's inheritance and no one else's.

"I should have come to visit you sooner. Don't you look
perfect behind that desk."

Jed played with his pen. "You really think I do?"

"Of course. How could you even ask your proud mother
such a ridiculous question?"

But he didn't look perfect at all. Sally imagined she could see right through his flesh, through the window to the river behind him. He had Joseph's imposing height and faultless classic face, the older man's blond hair and intelligent blue eyes, but the substance was missing. The dark power had left the room with David. It wasn't fair. Now she would have to be grateful for David. She would have to be nice to him. It was infuriating. But what choice was there? Jed would succeed, he would retain his authority and his place, even if it meant enslaving the mind and soul of that son of an immigrant.

Jed put down his pen. "I'm glad you're proud of me, Mother. But if you're to stay proud, I'm going to have to get back to work. What do you need to talk to me about?"

Sally sat in David's chair and placed her gloves on the desk. She put her hand on Jed's arm. "I need a favor from you, dear. I need you to give me five thousand dollars."

Jed recoiled. "What do you need five thousand dollars for? And why are you asking me? Why can't Father give it to you?"

She pressed hard on his arm and with her other hand cupped his chin and held his face still so that he was forced to look into her eyes. "Jed," she said firmly, in the tone she had used with him since he'd been a little boy, the tone that allowed for no argument, "I need you to be a good boy and give me five thousand dollars and not question me. Just trust me when I tell you that I cannot go to your father and you cannot breathe a word about this to him." She had to get the jewelry back from Monty before February. She always wore the diamond and emerald set for Joseph's birthday. Always. "And I need it in cash."

Jed struggled out of her grip and pushed his chair away from hers. He rubbed his hands on his thighs and glanced desperately toward the closed door. "All right. Calm down; don't get angry." He looked back at her. "Of course I'll give you the money. If you tell me you need it, that's enough. I don't need to know why. And I won't say anything to anyone."

"Thank you, darling." Sally took a deep breath and rose from her chair. "I knew I could count on you. A mother could not have a better son." She reached for her gloves. "One last thing. I need it by the end of the week."

Jed nodded mutely.

She pulled her gloves on. "I won't keep you any longer. I know you and David have a great deal to do. Now, walk me to the door."

He did, and just before she passed through it she turned and said, as softly as silk on skin, "Jed . . . ," and nothing more. What was next on her lips could not be said out loud. *I'm sorry.*

When she'd gone, Jed found his chair and sat. When finally he could move, he went and stood at Miss Steele's desk.

"Mr. Gates?"

"Lillian. Let David know that I'm ready to go back to work. And please get me some tea and biscuits. I'm suddenly feeling a little sick to my stomach."

Sally rode down the ten floors to the lobby in the building's executive elevator. For once, the opulence of its marble mosaic floor and burnished hardwood-paneled walls with their inset plaques of gold, each one depicting a different view of the downtown skyline, did nothing to satisfy her greedy soul. A heavy, dull pulse throbbed in her stomach; she was nauseous and her face was hot. On the street, she gulped down mouthfuls of cold air, shook her head from side to side so the coldness could wash over her flaming cheeks. There was a cab stand in front of the building, but she turned her back on it and walked north, then west and north again, until she came to Trinity Church. She slipped inside and stood by the door, in the silence and dimness, and closed her eyes.

She had just done a monstrous thing and her relationship with her son would never be the same. She had forfeited her right to his devotion by using him to provide to her the things she could not provide to herself. Just as her mother had used her, in the aftermath of her father's death and their sudden impoverishment, by forcing her to choose a husband without first allowing her to find love. So young and so bitter, unable to blame the mother who had always smothered her with love, she had blamed Philip and refused to recognize the love she felt for him. Instead, she had forced her love on Jed, forced her will on him. She had done it all his life, but never as blatantly as she had today. And never before had she been so aware of the consequences. Today, she had literally forced him to pay for her sins. She deserved to lose him, although she knew she wouldn't. He would never stop loving her; she was his mother. But he had Abby now, and David, for support. He had his own son, his own life. She would step back from him, as he would undoubtedly step back from her now, and allow him to live it.

39

David was in his large and peaceful kitchen, the only room in his house where, he could honestly say, he felt comfortable. Not that anyone had ever asked him. He hadn't shaved or bothered to get fully dressed, just thrown on a pair of old flannel trousers and padded downstairs, barefoot and bare chested, as soon as Cissy left the house. If he lived alone, he would have spent seven twelve-hour days a week at the office instead of just six. But he had a wife, and so he reserved his Sunday afternoons for Cissy and his Sunday mornings for himself.

It was twenty degrees outside, but it was warm in the kitchen. Surrounded by silence, accompanied by the sunlight coming through the kitchen windows, a happily disheveled David methodically conducted his weekly ritual: he made the special breakfast of his childhood, the one Anna had made for him when he was sick or unhappy or when she was simply overwhelmed with love for him. He took two pieces of soft bread, buttered on both sides, and fried them to a beautiful brown in a cast-iron skillet. He made little round hole in the center of each piece and popped the bread circles into his mouth while he fried eggs. Into the waiting holes went the perfectly done yolks, ready to run over the crisp whites that flowed out over the brown bread. And to drink, a pot of strong, dark Russian Caravan tea, poured into a tall glass, sweetened and paled with a large splash of milk. Too hot to hold except by hands that were accustomed to it.

David ate slowly, savoring the textures, the tastes, and the solitude. When he was done, he would clean the kitchen and then sit at the table and read until Cissy got home. He would get at least another hundred pages further into Theodore Dreiser's latest, *An American Tragedy*, and try not to think of the irony of himself enjoying a book about a lower-class young man's deadly pursuit of fame and wealth. Lately David tried not to think about much of anything. Save for his work, there didn't seem to be anywhere satisfying to send his thoughts, and he couldn't think about work all the time.

He was on his way to the sink with his dirty dishes when the sound of the front door knocker invaded his tranquillity. It was so unexpected a sound on a Sunday morning that David wasn't certain he had even heard it. But then it came again. When he opened the door, a wave of frigid air hit his bare chest and right behind it was the startling sight of Rachel standing on his front stoop, shivering from more than the chill wind.

David blinked like a sleepy bat confronted by a beam of light.

"It's cold, David. Invite me in before we both freeze."

He didn't say anything, but he stepped back and let her enter, closed the door behind her.

"I know this is a terrible intrusion, but I couldn't think what else to do. This is the only free time I have, Reuben doesn't open the factory until noon on Sundays, but I often go in early, so I told Shlomo—" She stopped her babbling and drew in a deep breath. Her hands shook a little as she held up a large flat brown envelope. Her voice fell to a whisper. "I brought some dress sketches so you can tell your wife—"

"She's not here. She goes to church every Sunday morning with her parents. I'm alone."

"You don't go with her? She knows you're Jewish?"

"She knows I'm an atheist."

The unmitigated strangeness of the moment, of Rachel materializing into David's world, standing with him in the hallway of his grand home, reduced them to a pained and poignant silence. The seconds passed, counted off by the grandfather clock ticking sedately in the parlor. David didn't offer to take her coat.

When he could take the silence no longer, David said, "You shouldn't be here. Why have you come?"

"It's not what you think. I'm not here because of you, or anything I might still feel for you. I'm here because I need to talk to you about Sarah."

David shook his head. "I have nothing to say about her."

"You don't have to say anything. Just listen. Three months ago, your sister gave birth to a little girl after a horrible twenty-hour labor. The baby died the next day."

"Oh God, no." David covered his eyes.

Rachel reached up and pulled his hands away from his face. "David. She's a wreck. She's so depressed she won't leave the house. She won't talk to anyone. Reuben is frantic with worry, and Ben and Naomi—" She stopped when she saw the hostility in his eyes. She raised her hands. "All right. All right," She took another breath and began again. "She needs you."

He gave a strangled laugh. "I am indisputably the last thing she needs."

"David, she's in trouble. She needs *you*. Anna is gone and there was never anyone else but you that she loved as much. You have to go see her."

"Believe me, she has no reason to love me anymore. It wouldn't do her any good to see me. It would only do her harm."

"I've never known you to be a coward."

David's body went rigid. "You have no right to talk to me like that."

She touched a finger to his close stubble, trailed it lightly down the center of his chest. "My God. You look just like the boy I remember."

He didn't move. "Don't delude yourself, Rachel. I'm not."

"No, you're not. You're hard and calculating. Every action considered and weighed for its benefit to you. Where is the David who cheated at poker with Irish thugs to buy a doll for his sister's birthday, who climbed two floors up a filthy air shaft to get to me through my bedroom window?"

"What difference does it make? That's not who I am anymore."

"I know." She dropped her hand and smiled at him with sadness. "And I'm not the girl who loved you. But I know you, David, and I know that you love your sister."

"Who and what you know comes from another life, Rachel. You don't know anything about me now, or about what's become of my love for my sister, or hers for me."

"Maybe you don't know yourself. One of the most wonderful things about you, always, was how contradictory you were. You could be incredibly selfish and then turn around and be astoundingly kind. Is there no kindness left in you, David? Not even for your own sister?"

"The kindest thing I can do for Sarah is stay away from her. I'm sorry about the baby, and I appreciate you telling me, but I'm not going to go see her. She has good reason to be depressed. She'll get over it in time. She does not want or need me to help her."

"You're wrong." But she could see she had no hope of convincing him. She glanced bleakly at the door. "I have to get to work."

David reached into his pants pocket and produced a five-dollar bill. He tried to give it to her. "Here. There's a cab stand on Fifth Avenue."

She stiffened. "No, thank you. The El is fine for me."

After the door closed solidly behind Rachel, David returned to the kitchen. He washed and dried the dishes and put them away. He brewed another pot of tea. He sat at the table, picked up his book, and stared at the ink marks on the page. He put the book down. His sister's baby had died, that baby whose place on earth David had seen so clearly in his fevered vision on the streets of the Lower East Side. There was nothing he could do to change it and nothing he could do to help her. They lived in separate worlds. They had convinced each other of their mutual distrust and enmity. Blame and unforgiveness were all they'd offered each other. For all he knew, she'd find a way to blame him for this death, too; she had always been a match for his own stubbornness. And so, stubbornly, there he sat, huddled in his lonely kitchen. He lived in a house he didn't like; he was married to a woman he didn't love. He confided in no one. Rachel's words echoed in his head. He was a coward who didn't know himself anymore.

40

Lucy passed between the scrolled stone columns on either side of the stone steps and pushed through the double doors of the white-brick building on Hester Street. She looked down at the assignment slip in her hand: *Mrs. Reuben Winokur, infant death, severe depression. The settlement asked by a concerned friend to send someone to talk with her.* Reuben Winokur. The name seemed so familiar. Maybe they had used the settlement's nursing services before. Fifth floor. Apartment #503. Lucy knocked firmly on the apartment door. This was a decent building, much nicer than many she'd visited. The Winokurs were doing well for themselves. Except for this terrible tragedy.

"Who's there?" A timid voice from the other side.

"Mrs. Winokur? My name is Lucy Stoner. I'm from the Henry Street Settlement House. Your friend Rachel Weinstein asked me to come talk with you a little. Will you let me?" Lucy Stoner was the name she used here. She didn't want the people to whom she ministered to discover that she came from one of the wealthiest families in the city.

The door opened and Lucy smiled into the beautiful tear-streaked face of the unicorn girl, the mysterious girl she and Philip had bumped into on Grand Street on that miserable rainy night in March. Lucy had been right; the girl had been pregnant. And the baby had died. Lucy felt herself grow physically weak from the unbearable sadness of it. She leaned against the doorjamb.

The girl's flecked brown eyes widened in recognition. "Oh! I know you! I've seen you!" She grabbed Lucy's hand. "Come in; come in." Sarah pulled her through the door. "Please don't call me Mrs. Winokur. I'm Sarah. Sarah."

Lucy held firmly to Sarah's hand. "Hello, Sarah. I'm Lucy. I've seen you, too. The last time, you were crying in the rain. And look, you're still crying." With her other hand, she brushed Sarah's cheek. "That's not right. It's too long a time. I'm going to help you stop."

Sarah's tears flooded down her face. Lucy put her arms around her and held her. "Yes, that's good. One last cry. And then we'll talk."

Tea with lemon in a fine china cup for Lucy, Sarah's in a glass with sugar and milk. Steam rose from the two surfaces and merged in a warm, wet cloud that hovered above their hands, clasped and resting easily on the kitchen table.

"Sarah, do you believe me now? You must give up this superstitious guilt you've been torturing yourself with. It was a heart defect that killed your little girl, not your mixed feelings about motherhood. So many women are afraid of how their lives will change. It's normal. And it's normal not to want to try again for a while after such a terrible experience. You lost a baby, Sarah. You need time to recover."

Sarah was afloat inside a fantasy. She had dreamed of this woman appearing in her life, and here she was: Lucy Stoner. She was real. And she was everything Sarah had wanted her to be. "Yes, I believe you. But being able to say what I was feeling to you . . . it's like a weight has been lifted from my heart."

"I'm so glad. And you'll bring your husband to see me and we'll talk about planning the family you want to have? And first thing tomorrow you'll march yourself over to . . . what is it, Lebowitz's?"

"Leyrowitz's," Sarah corrected with a laugh.

Lucy rolled her eyes. "Leyrowitz's . . . and you'll tell your uncle Sol—who sounds like quite a character—that you want to come back to work."

Sarah's eyes filled with tears, but there was a smile of

pure happiness on her face. "Lucy, you are a gift from heaven. I feel as though I've known you forever."

Lucy felt an almost embarrassing rush of pleasure flood her brain. Her work was often ridiculously satisfying, but this girl, this Sarah . . . there was something special about her. Philip, with his penetrating eye, had seen it in a single glance. Something special and familiar. Lucy felt as though she knew Sarah, too, but was loath to say it. It wasn't always wise to get too fond of one's clients.

"Sometimes it's easier to talk to a stranger than it is to your own family," Lucy said. She gave Sarah's hand a last squeeze and stood up, signaling that the visit was over.

"Perhaps. But easier still to talk to a new friend."

Lucy relented. "Yes. I'd like us to be friends, Sarah."

"Then we will be."

Lucy linked her arm in Sarah's as they walked to the apartment's small entryway. "Did you make the dress you're wearing?" Lucy asked. "It's lovely."

Like many immigrant women of the neighborhood, Sarah dressed modestly, in the style of the decade past. But Lucy could see that her dull-colored, high-collared shirtwaist and long skirt were well made and of an above-average-quality wool.

"Thank you. Yes, I did. But I look so old-fashioned compared to you."

Lucy was careful to wear her older, simpler pieces when she worked, but she didn't own anything dull and no matter what she wore, it was clear she was not from the Lower East Side.

As she put on her coat, she admired a grouping of antique accessories on a small, wooden table. A brass samovar, an enamel and inlay music box. A woman's silver hairbrush.

"These are beautiful." Lucy picked up the brush. Ornately engraved on the shining silver back were the initials A W H. The same initials were engraved on the samovar and spelled out in lapis on the music box. "The 'W' is for 'Winokur'? Did these belong to your husband's family?"

"No. They were my mother's. Anna Hertzig Warshinsky." Sarah stroked the elegant curving side of the samovar as though it were a living thing.

The brush fell from Lucy's hand. She teetered precipitously against the fragile table.

"Lucy!" Sarah gripped Lucy's elbow. "Are you all right?"

"I'm sorry." She managed a hoarse whisper. "Standing in my coat, it's warm . . . I'm sorry; let me—" She tried to bend down.

"No. No. I'll get it. It *is* warm in here. It's hard to control the radiators." Sarah bent to pick up the brush.

Lucy shoved her hands into her pockets to stop herself from falling to her knees and caressing Sarah's bowed head. This beautiful young woman, her special new friend, was the alienated, abandoned sister of the man she secretly loved. Everything that had felt inexplicably familiar about Sarah now came into blazing focus. The high cheekbones, the brown eyes with their odd, light centers, the abundant dark curling hair. The sadness and feeling of loss that radiated from her. She was David's sister and Lucy didn't know how she was going to find the strength to love them both and hide herself from them both and keep all of their secrets safe.

Sarah straightened and placed the brush back on the table. "You need some fresh air. I'll see you Sunday morning, with Reuben in tow!" She laughed and hugged Lucy tightly. "Lucy, thank you so much. Thank you; thank you."

Lucy could not resist. Her hands came out of her pockets, her stiff back relaxed, and she wrapped her arms around Sarah and hugged her with all the strength she had. As the two women rocked gently from side to side, Lucy lulled herself into a dream where she had the courage to bring them all together and no one would have to keep secrets anymore.

41

David's mind was churning over a problem with one of the company's subsidiaries that he and Jed had failed to resolve after an entire day of effort. Thus he came nose to knocker with his shut tight front door before he realized that he would actually need to find and use his key. Cissy had not opened it as he climbed the stairs, nor was she waiting for him in the vestibule as he let himself in. The moment he entered the house, he wished he had not given in to Jed's insistence that he go home and relax. The air was laden with a tension he could almost see, a misty, swirling agitation reaching out for him, squeezing his head like a vise. A hot pain throbbed instantly in his right temple. He wanted to crawl under the bed like a frightened dog sensing the shift in atmospheric pressure that heralded a tornado. But instead he went into the parlor, pulled there against his will by the palpable emanations of his wife's distress.

Cissy sat on the chic settee, hard and uncomfortable like every other piece of expensive, stylish furniture she had bought with David's money and without his help or interest. She had been crying. Her eyes were puffy and red, but she wasn't crying now and her back was ramrod straight. She watched him walk into the room as though he were a dangerous animal she was tracking in the crosshairs of a rifle.

David warily took off his coat and threw it on a chair. He didn't sit. "What's the matter, Cissy?"

Cissy stared up at him. The muscles in her jaw bunched as she fought to compose herself. A piece of folded white paper lay in her lap. A letter.

He nodded toward it. "Did you get some bad news from someone?"

She rose, walked to the fireplace, and put her back to it. The letter dangled from her hand.

"What did you do with the six hundred thousand dollars Joseph gave you in October?"

David was taken aback. "How did you know about that?"

"Jed talks in his sleep," she said acidly. "Abby asked me what we were planning to do with your big bonus." She stared at him. "Well, David? What are we going to do with it?"

"Nothing. I gave it away."

"Without even talking to me?"

"What did I need to talk to you about? It was my money. I'm already a multimillionaire; we didn't need it. Why? Is there something you want that I haven't bought for you?"

She stood silent and stony faced.

David rubbed his temple and let out an exasperated sigh. "Come on, Cissy. I know you think I have psychic powers when it comes to business, but honestly I can't read your mind. At least not all the time. Tell me what's wrong. What's in that letter?"

She made a show of dropping the letter into the flames dancing gaily behind the metal grate. "What else have you chosen not to tell me, David?" Her mouth was partially open; anger caused her head to shake ever so slightly.

She waited for a reply from him that never came. At length she said, "Are you a lying bastard Jew named David Warshinsky?"

David thought the top of his head was going to detach itself from his body. An inarticulate grunt escaped his throat. He laced his fingers behind his neck to steady himself and said, "What did you just throw into the fire?" although he was quite sure he knew.

"A letter from Monty informing me of your true heritage."

David had done nothing to try to find Monty. The family was well pleased to be rid of him forever, and calm logic cautioned David to just let him disappear. But he was still out there, plying his mischief from the safety of some secret lair. "Where's the envelope? Where was it postmarked?" Cissy's accusatory question faded to insignificance beside David's desire to put his hands around Monty's neck and squeeze the life out of him.

"God, you're horrible! I burned the damned envelope! I'm asking you is this true, and all you care about is where that drunken lecher Monty is? What is the matter with you?" She screamed at him, her words flying like daggers. "Don't you have any feelings for me at all?"

David took a step back, turned his eyes away from her. He had known the answer to her anguished question long before this moment. He had never cared enough about her to reveal himself. He hadn't cared how or if she ever found out or what her reaction might be.

"Look at me, you bastard!" she cried. "Look at me and tell me if this is true. Are you Jewish? Have you been lying to me all these years about who you really are?"

He looked her calmly in the eye and said nothing. Cissy walked to him, drew her arm back, and slapped him across the face as hard as she could. He winced at the pain of the blow but made no sound.

"Is it true?" Her porcelain skin was mottled with rage.

David nodded, no apology in his eyes, on his lips, or in the set of his jaw. If she had truly known him, she would have known that no one had ever gotten what they wanted of David by trying to beat it out of him.

She slapped him again, even harder. "Why didn't you tell me? Do you think I'm so shallow and stupid that I would care? I love you and you treat me like I'm a fool. Do I mean so little to you that I don't deserve to know what everyone else close to you knows about you?"

David put a hand up to rub at his stinging cheek. "It's not something I want the world to know, Cissy. You can understand that."

"I'm not the world! I'm your wife! Don't you trust me?"

He had never considered his not telling her to be a matter of trust. "It wasn't something you needed to know. You didn't fall in love with David Warshinsky."

"But I did! Because that's who you are!" Cissy fairly shrieked. "How could you love me and not—" She stopped in midsentence, her fury collapsing as she realized that there could be only one reason why David had never told her the truth about himself. "You don't love me." Her voice had lost all its strength. Her rifle had missed its mark and the terrible recoil was going to knock her to the ground. "That's why you won't have a baby with me. You don't love me."

"Cissy." David spoke her name softly, the sound mingling with the killing exhalation of his sigh of acquiescence. The pain in her eyes was unbearable to see. He wished he could say something to comfort her, but there was nothing to say.

Cissy lost control and began to cry. Tears streamed down her cheeks. She threw herself at David, clutching at his arms. "David, please. I don't care who you were, who you are. You're right, you're right, I fell in love with *you,* and I love you so much. Let's have a baby. You'll see; it will make you happy. You can love me; I know you can. Please, David, tell me we can have a baby now!"

David felt the vise around his head tighten. A small voice in his head told him to just say yes, give her a baby, try to love her. That was, after all, what he'd thought he wanted: an adoring wife, a home, a family. And Cissy deserved a reward for loving him so generously. But he knew it was impossible. Every time he had ever thought about having a child with her, locking himself into that future, he felt a slow death creeping over him.

This was the end; there was no way to fix things between them; there was no way to go on. Cissy's worst fears were true. He shouldn't have married her; Zoe had urged him to think carefully about his decision, but he'd ignored her, so sure of what he wanted. He had taken advantage of Cissy's blind love for him, gotten what he needed from her, and now he was going to discard her.

He wiped at a trail of her tears with his thumb. "No, Cissy, I can't." He slowly shook his head. "I'm sorry."

She stood stunned and desperate, digging her fingers into his arms, humiliation turning sorrow again to fury. "You're not sorry. You're never sorry about anything. You're a heartless, lying monster! I hate you! I hate you!"

She came at him with balled fists. He let her flail away at him, her fists pounding against his chest in rhythm with her sobs, punctuating her grief like drumbeats. After a moment, he felt the strength of her blows begin to subside and he grabbed at her wrists, holding her hands still.

"Cissy, stop. Stop. Please. Stop."

She wrenched back and forth, trying to free herself, but he was too strong for her. With a keening wail, she stopped struggling. Leaning her head against his chest, she sobbed like a heartbroken child. David rested his still-flaming cheek on her sleek hair and, releasing her wrists, put his arms around her and held her.

"Cissy. I am sorry, believe me. I never meant for things to end like this. I care for you, deeply. I thought we could be happy together. I'll give you a divorce; you can have anything you want. I trust you not to talk about my past, but beyond that I don't care what you tell anyone. We can't go on like this; you know it. We'll end up hating each other."

Cissy clung to him. David let her stay in his arms until the pressure building inside him became too great and he had to push her away. He couldn't stand to see her lovely face contorted by misery, knowing that he was the cause of it. The entire right side of his head was on fire. The pain spread down into his neck and shoulder and forward into his eye, jagged flashes of crystal light blurring his vision. He felt sick to his stomach, from the headache and from his disgust at the mess he'd made of his marriage, at the damage he'd done, yet again, to someone who loved him.

"I have to leave." David crossed the room and grabbed his coat.

"David! Don't leave me here alone!"

"God, Cissy, just let me go! It will only be worse if I stay. I'll come back tomorrow for some clothes. You can stay here as long as you want, or go home to your parents; it doesn't matter. Just tell me when you've made up your mind."

David left the room without looking back at her, left the house without taking the time to put on his coat. He didn't need to look, or use his second sight, to know that Cissy lay crumpled on the settee, its cushions as unyielding as his heart, all her dreams of happiness gone, following him out the front door into the frigid night.

David staggered across the street, through the grand archway into Washington Square Park, pulling his coat on as he went. It was so cold that the air itself seemed a white, solid thing where it hovered in the light of the gas lamps. Frozen tree branches stood silhouetted against the leaden night sky. As he reached the winter-stilled fountain in the park's center, a violent wave of nausea knocked him to his knees. He hung over the wide rim of the huge, circular fountain, a shallow pool of black ice stretching away in front of him, and tried to retch, to expel the sickness and the pain and the ugliness inside him. His stomach heaved and cramped, but nothing came up. He raised his face to the cold, misty air, wrapped his arms around his middle, and took several long, slow breaths. He was aware of people scurrying past him in the dark, their heads, tucked for warmth down into their coat collars, swiveling to observe him, no one stopping to ask if he was ill or needed help.

The nausea subsided, but his headache intensified. One sadistic demon was hitting him in the temple with a dull, heavy hammer and another was stabbing stiletto-sharp pricks at the nerves behind his eye. The pain was so intense he wanted to bang his head against the cold concrete to make it go away. With a moan, he rose and made his way to a bench. He fell onto it, dropped his head into his hands, and hung there, suspended in time and space, his skull bursting, his stomach roiling. He didn't know where he belonged. For a fleeting dishonest second, motivated solely by his terrible discomfort, he pictured himself standing up and walking back into the house, telling Cissy he'd made a mistake. He wanted someone to soothe him and she was so good at it, why couldn't he just let her have what she wanted?

He shook his head, sickened by his self-indulgence, inviting the agony the movement engendered, feeling as though his brain were smacking against the inside of his skull. He hardly needed to remind himself that his greedy mistake had been in marrying her when he didn't love her, not in leaving her. He had done the right thing tonight, despite Cissy begging him to stay.

David heaved himself off the bench. He couldn't sit there all night. He fleetingly considered going no farther than around the corner to Washington Mews. Jed wouldn't be home yet, but Abby, forgiving and sympathetic, would put him to bed in a darkened room with a cold compress over his eyes. Unfortunately, much as he craved it, the golden ring of oblivion was far out of his reach. He would not be able to grab it until he found what he needed to calm his overwrought mind and his vibrating body. Every nerve, not merely the tormented one behind his right eye, was awake and jumping, leaving him at once exhausted and overstimulated. And so he jammed his hands into his pockets and started walking.

Passersby, their faces unrecognizable under scarves wound around upturned collars, hats pulled down over tingling ears, stared suspiciously at his bare head and exposed throat. Not for the first time, David wondered at the identity of the unknown ancestor—probably a marauding Mongol from the northern steppes—who had bequeathed him the constantly stoked furnace that burned inside him, making his skin hot to the touch and his body restless, prodding at his mind to keep moving, keep thinking. Most of the time he loved the clarity and power of his own heat and energy, loved all the things it drew to him. But occasionally he wished the engine would stop, just for a little while, and give him some rest.

He wandered out of the park, moving south down Thompson Street, into the heart of Greenwich Village. He walked past cafés and restaurants, their windows clouded over with steam. The mere thought of their warmth and noise and light descending on his throbbing head made him gag. East on Houston Street and suddenly he was at the edge of the Lower East Side, on the northern end of the little strip of park that ran up Christie Street from Canal to Houston. He stepped off the street to stand just inside the park. He faced southward and a little east, in the direction of his past. He didn't know why he had walked here; there was no comfort for him anywhere in that place that had been his entire world for the first eighteen years of his life.

He closed his eyes and his mind took off, meandering up and down the once-familiar streets. Past friends, lovers, family. They were gone to him. He knew their addresses, the locations of the small, hot, overcrowded apartments they lived in, but it was too late. Too many years had passed; the wall he had built to separate the new from the old was too high. He was mere blocks away from two women who had once loved him and whose love he had callously discarded, blocks that might as well have been oceans. Sarah. Rachel. Two more beautiful tearstained faces turned up to him, dark eyes beseeching him for a crumb of understanding, of affection, of softness.

His eyes flew open. Sharp flashes of blue-white light burst behind his right eye. The traffic rushing by on Houston Street roared, shockingly loud. He could smell, as pungently as though he were standing in the kitchen, the strong odor of frying onions and fatty meats coming from Katz's Delicatessen three blocks away. A new wave of nausea assaulted him. Sarah, who wanted him in her life again. Rachel, who wanted him in her bed again. He had nothing to give either of them. Just as he had nothing to give Cissy. He had nothing to give anyone; he was his own man now. There was only one thing that could make this pain go away, even if just for a little while, and he knew where he could find it. He turned his back on his memories and began walking as quickly as he could uptown.

The Horn & Hardart was bustling, as always, people from all walks of life lined up at the Nickel Thrower's booth, exchanging their dollar bills for twenty nickels—enough for half-a-dozen meals—grabbed and tossed to them by the cashier with unerring speed and precision. People feeding their nickels into the slots, opening the little glass doors, coming away with steaming bowls of clam chowder, slabs of pie, mounds of baked beans, doughnuts. Cups of strong coffee, the famous gilt-edged brew, pouring from nickel-metal dolphin spouts.

David stood by the booth, fighting to keep his eyes open against the brightness, his gorge down. Through half-shut lids he surveyed the room, looking for her. The redhead. After a moment, he saw her come through a door in the wall at the far end of the long row of food slots, a tray in her hand. She began clearing empty dishes off the marble tables, wiping their surfaces with a cloth. He noted the direction of her progress through the room and moved to intercept her, blocking her access to the next empty table.

"Excuse me, sir." She looked up, smiling, already starting to step around him. She stopped, her eyes riveted on his face, her smile fading as she recognized him. She drew in a sharp breath.

"When are you done here?" David said. He hadn't been wrong about her interest in him.

"Not for another twenty minutes." Her quaking voice betrayed her excitement.

David shook his head and saw a small flash of panic cross her face. He took out his wallet, extracted a twenty-dollar bill. "Here, give this to one of your girlfriends and have her cover for you. I'd rather not wait."

She hesitated a second, then folded the bill into her apron pocket. "Five minutes."

David waited outside, leaning against the wall, head back, eyes closed, trying to think of nothing. Gloved hands wrapped themselves around his arm.

"Here I am."

He pushed himself upright, squinted down at her. He was breathing fast through his mouth from the excruciating pain in his head. It was taking more and more effort to not simply sit down where he was, shield his head in his arms, and weep. Answering her was more than he could manage.

The girl looked up at him, concern in her eyes. "Hey, are you all right?"

He struck himself in the temple, hard, with the heel of one hand. "A bad headache. You can make it feel better. Just tell me you live near here; I can't deal with the train."

"No, I'm just five blocks away. Come on." She linked her arm through his and led him across Broadway. After a few minutes of silence, she leaned lightly against him. "Don't you even want to know my name?"

David looked at her uncomprehendingly. He didn't care what her name was but was conscious enough to realize that he could not say that. He laughed a little, pretending to be embarrassed. "Sure, sorry. What's your name?"

"Mary."

"Okay. Hello, Mary."

"That's it? 'Hello, Mary'? Aren't you going to tell me your name, talk to me?"

David winced in frustration, took the girl by the arms, and turned her around to face him. "Listen. Let's be honest. We're only here for one reason, and we both know it. I want to take you to bed. I don't want to hear your life story or tell you mine. You want to know my name, fine, it's David. Beyond that, I'm not interested in talking. Is that all right with you?"

Mary stared at him, slightly shocked and thoroughly aroused. "Yes, it's all right with me."

Once through the door of her cheap, overheated apartment, David stripped off his coat, let it drop to the floor. He swung Mary around and pushed her coat off her shoulders, throwing it behind him. He backed her against the wall and pinned her there, holding her arms over her head, forcing her body to strain against the cloth of her prim waitress's uniform. Her breath shuddered as she responded to the raw look in his eyes, the sureness of his hands, and she arched away from the wall to find him. He held her there for a moment and then bent his head, ran his tongue over her lips until she moaned and grabbed at him with her mouth. He pressed his mouth against hers, his body into her body, feeling her struggle to get closer to him, her breasts and her hips pushing hard against him. He felt himself begin to dissolve, to forget the pain in his head. This was what he needed. A few hours with an eager girl, a stranger who wanted nothing more from him than a good time, and he might even forget what a miserable son of a bitch he was.

The redheaded girl lay sleeping heavily, curled up in a ball, spent and satisfied. David sat up leaning against the headboard, a little calmer, in a little less pain, but still awake, still vibrating. Exhaustion lurked on the fringes of his brain but had not yet gathered enough strength to still the steady buzz of his thoughts. He was grateful for the soporific pleasure of the past hours, but something she had done during their passionate, anonymous lovemaking had disturbed him. At some point, at the moment of one of her numerous climaxes, she had cried out his name, cried out, "I love you." With a sense of uneasy disbelief, it occurred to him as he sat there, watching her sleep, that he had never said those three simple words to any woman he had ever been with. Not to Rachel, to whom he'd made voracious love for a year and who had told him she loved him a thousand times. Not to the dozens of women he'd slept with after her, no matter how much he'd enjoyed them. Not to Cissy, his wife, never even once in four years. With her he had used the word "love" in devious ways, told her he loved the way she looked in a particular dress, the cute upturn of her nose, the way she cried at silly, sentimental movies, the feel of her breast in his hand. He had found innumerable ways to make her believe that he might love her without ever saying the words. Never to any of them. He had always assumed it was because he simply hadn't loved them. Looking down at the sleeping girl, who had so willingly and openly given herself over to loving him—even if the emotion and its expression were no more than an uncontrollable hormonal spasm of the moment—he knew that he hadn't wanted to love any of them. Love was a useless and stifling emotion, far inferior to the galvanizing, productive forces of ambition and finely honed desire.

He got up off the bed, careful not to disturb her. There was no reason for him to be there when she woke up. He retrieved his clothes from where they lay scattered around the room. He dressed quickly, prepared himself to go back out into the cold and dark, to sleep in a borrowed bed in a house that wasn't his own. He picked up the half-empty bottle of lousy whiskey, the best she could afford, and slipped it into his coat pocket. He threw some money on the table so she could buy herself something better. As he pulled the door closed behind him, he thought not of Mary but of Zoe, walking with him across the lawn at Hidden Cove, warning him against the pitfalls of love. He had made sure they would not trap him. He had made love unnecessary. He shivered in the warm hallway and wondered just how bad a mistake that was going to turn out to be.

Jed walked east, away from the sinister streets of the meat-packing district sprawled against the Hudson River, through Greenwich Village, thinking furiously of another alibi for his whereabouts that Abby would believe. It was late and he walked swiftly, impelled by a bone-chilling cold exacerbated by his implacable guilt and his growing terror. This was the sixth time in the past two months that he had spent hours after work trolling through one of the city's most notorious degenerate enclaves. Not as flamboyant as the Bowery or the Tenderloin, the Village was nonetheless a veritable warren of bohemians, free-love advocates, queers, fairies, and lesbians. Jed walked and watched, learning the signs that slowly revealed to him the existence of a parallel universe, a vibrant, throbbing world hidden in plain sight. Like the lost realm of Camelot, this lavender world floated alongside the normal world as in a magical mist. Once one knew how to see through the miasma, one could enter it at will, step into the life, and then step out and let the hidden world sink back into oblivion.

Tonight Jed had seen that young man again. The one with the curly dark hair and olive skin. Seen him briefly as he disappeared around a corner, pulling an anonymous man after him in his strong clasp. Jed had stopped and stared after him and the young man had turned his head with a flash of recognition in his eyes and the beginning of a small smile pulling at his full mouth. He'd boldly met and held Jed's stricken gaze, his gleaming eyes making clear his interest. Jed's pulse was still racing as he hurried toward home.

Two short blocks from the Mews, as he approached Fifth Avenue from Washington Square North, an unmistakable figure appeared before him, walking unsteadily out of the park.

"David!" Jed caught at David's arm as his friend turned toward the sound of his voice and nearly stumbled. David clutched an empty bottle in his ungloved hand and his lids were at half-mast. Jed recognized the manifestations of one of David's terrible headaches.

"Jed." David peered at him out of pain- and liquor-tightened eyes and swayed slightly on his feet. His coat hung open. "It's late. Where the fuck are you coming from?"

"I could ask you the same thing. Where have you been?" He looked down at the bottle.

David shook his head slowly from side to side. "Everywhere I shouldn't have been. Not that you'd know anything about that, thank God." His words were slurred and he was quaking with cold.

"What's wrong?" Jed had never known David to exhibit such obvious signs of drunkenness. David drank, but usually in moderation, one or two Scotches or glasses of wine after work to ease the transition to day's end. But even on the rare occasions when he drank to excess, all one ever noticed was an increased intensity; he became more tightly focused. He never swayed on his feet or slurred his words. He never looked as though he might implode at any second. "You have a headache and you're drunk. You know you shouldn't drink when your head hurts. What's the matter?"

"Yeah. I'm drunk. And I have the mother of all headaches. What's the matter? Well, let's see. Oh yes. I walked out on my wife tonight and I don't know . . . I don't . . ." David's strained voice trailed off into incoherence. He leaned his head against Jed's shoulder and exhaled an agonized breath. The bottle fell out of his hand and shattered on the pavement. "Jed. I don't think I can stand up anymore. Can I sleep on your sofa?"

"No. You can sleep in our guest bedroom."

Jed steadied David with an arm around his waist and led him home, to the small spare room behind the kitchen. The house was quiet. Abby, Henry, the nanny, mercifully all asleep upstairs. Jed helped David out of his coat and sat him in a deep armchair. He opened the radiator knob halfway and began making up the single bed.

"Do you want to tell me what happened?"

David's eyes were closed and his head lay against the chair back. "I came home and we had a fight. Something . . ." He paused. "Something happened that made her realize I don't love her. And I couldn't pretend anymore." He suddenly pitched forward, covered his eyes with his hands. "Christ, I can't stand this pain. I think I'm going to die."

"You're not going to die." Jed came and knelt by the chair, put a hand on David's bent neck. His fingers trembled against David's skin. "You're so hot."

"Your fingers are cool. That feels good. Jed." David raised his head. He looked in the direction of Jed's face, but it was impossible to tell if he could see anything clearly. Every exhalation was accompanied by a sharp grunt of pain, and with each grunt David grew a little more still, dislodged another strand of the tension that wracked him.

"Jed. Do you remember, in the hospital outside Paris, in the solarium? Has anything changed? Has anything been worth any of this, this hell that life can be?" David's body was going slack, his voice sinking lower, the edges of his words blurring one into the other. "I really am a bastard, aren't I?"

The question wasn't meant to be answered. Jed knew well the shape and form of David's dark places. He knew, too, that like his own they were not to be brought into the light and looked at. It was pain, alcohol, and disappointment that was causing David to vomit up this rare brew of self-loathing and self-pity. In the morning, it would all be forgotten; his energy and confidence would return. He'd be bright eyed and sharp minded at the office and he'd deal with divorcing Cissy with the same clarity and precision that he dealt with everything else in his life.

"A real bastard," David continued. "But I had to be, didn't I? Everyone always needed so much of me. They want everything I've got. I have to keep something for myself. Except for you, Jed. You've never asked me for anything. No conditions on your friendship. You've never made me feel that I'm disappointing you, or that I'm going to one day." With a monumental physical effort, David reached out an arm and dropped it across Jed's shoulder, leaned his head against Jed's head. "I love you, Jed. I don't know what I'd be without you."

It took all of Jed's will to stop himself from putting his arms around David in a crushing embrace. "I love you, too, David," he whispered, grateful that David couldn't see his face. "You could never disappoint me; you know that."

"I know. I know." He struggled to rise from the chair. "I need to lie down. I need to go to sleep."

Jed stood and pulled David up with him, maneuvered him the few steps across the room. David sank down on top of the bedcovers and began to fall over onto his side, his eyes closing.

"David, you have to take off your clothes and get under the covers."

"Can't," he mumbled. "Let me sleep." But he dragged himself back to his feet and began fumbling at the buttons of his jacket.

Jed could see that David needed help, but he was paralyzed with the fear of what might happen if he let himself touch him. He remained where he was while David slowly and clumsily undressed, dropping one piece of clothing after another onto the floor until he stood, wholly unaware of himself, in his undershorts. It wasn't the first time that Jed had seen David nearly naked, but here, alone in the darkened bedroom, the sight of him shedding his clothing was catastrophic; it was the stripping away, piece by piece, of all conventions of civilization until the one thing in the world Jed desired above all others stood before him, a purely physical creature, primitive and powerful and forever untouchable.

"Get into bed, David."

David nodded but didn't move except to list slightly to one side, his body no longer capable of following the commands of his brain. His eyes closed and it seemed he would fall to the floor. In two quick strides Jed swallowed the space between them. He took David's deadweight in his arms and lowered him to the bed. He pulled the covers up to David's chest and then, in agony, withdrew his burning hands. David's eyes had not opened; he was passing out, his head rolling on the pillow, moaning in pain still despite his slide into unconsciousness. Jed remained bent over the bed. He couldn't breathe. He could not bring himself to straighten up and move away. How easy it would be to lie down now and mold his body to David's, to be as the helpless tide given shape and purpose by the pull of the moon. In a waking dream, he bent farther and placed his lips against David's mouth. He kissed him gently, one lingering kiss on numb, unknowing lips. From there, so easy to move his mouth along the line of David's scar, from under the chin up toward the ear. The brush of silky, dark curling hair seared Jed's cheek. He let his hand fall, delicate as a snowflake, onto the hard flesh of David's arm and left it there to slowly melt and run on his hot skin. His breath trembled. David's moans changed tenor, grew soft and less pained. Jed stopped. His hand had found its way to David's belly, his mouth to David's throat.

Jed stumbled backward, away from the bed. When his legs hit the edge of the chair he sat. He watched David's restless sleep and made no move to wipe at the tears that spilled from his eyes. After a time, he rose and exiled himself to his studio, bringing David's coat with him. He lay down on the sofa in his clothes, covered himself with the coat. Late in the night he heard David cry out in his sleep, "*Mama*," as though he were the baby in the house and not Henry. He heard David get up from the bed, go to the bathroom. He waited to hear him retrace his steps but, instead, heard footfalls coming up the stairs. Jed's heart began to pound and he prayed for a miracle, that David was coming to him. The footsteps passed on down the hall. Jed snuck to the studio door and saw David enter Henry's room. He saw him stand over the crib, place a careful hand on the baby's head. His heart aching, Jed thought what a perfect world it would be if he, David, and Henry could live together. David running the family empire, Jed working in his studio. Henry growing up in a house full of happiness where love wasn't dangerous. And Abby would be there, taking care of them all. He tiptoed back to his lair. The time was coming, he knew, when he would walk through the mist into that other life. His resolve to stay within the safe confines of his fantasies was no match for what he had felt tonight, for what he had come too close to doing. Soon, he would seek out that young man and begin living shameful lies in two worlds at once. It hardly mattered what he did, really. Whatever he found there, or anywhere, would never be good enough. It would never be David.

~*~ PART FOUR ~*~

March 1927–April 1928

42

"Hello, darling." Evelyn *placed a loving kiss on David's* wind-cooled cheek. "He's in his study. He'll be so happy to see you."

"How is he today?" David dropped his coat onto the hall bench. He put his arm around Evelyn's shoulders as they walked down the hallway.

"Not bad, actually. He's getting a little stronger every day, maneuvering the wheelchair on his own now. And it's amazing how adept he is already with his left hand; it's not even three months. He's very resilient."

"This is a man who loves a challenge. How's his mood?"

Evelyn smiled. "He's horribly cranky. So I would say his mood is quite good." She slowed her step and turned to face David. "I have to thank you, and Jed, for coming every week like this, keeping him up-to-date on the business and asking for his advice. I doubt that either of you need it, but it makes him feel useful."

"He *is* useful, Evelyn," David said emphatically. "And you should know it. Of course we'd come anyway, and yes, Jed and I could manage on our own, but why should we while he's still here? Every time we talk with Joe we come away smarter about something. Today, in fact . . ."—David paused, rubbed at his forehead—". . . today I have a problem I really need help with."

"Well, good. Give him something to sink his teeth into." She took David's hand and looked up at him with concern.

"Darling, are you getting a headache? Do you want some aspirin?"

"No. No headache. The one I had last month should keep me for a while," David said with a wry smile. "How about we have a cup of tea when I'm finished with Joe?"

"Stay for dinner. Angelina will feed you and you will tell me how you are doing."

David waited in the hall while Evelyn disappeared into the drawing room. He didn't know if he should be doing this, talking to Joseph about Monty. He only knew that he was driving himself crazy with vengeful ire. His acceptance of Lorena's sane advice had not been faring well since Monty had sent that letter to Cissy. He needed to talk to someone who thought as he did, who knew Monty for what he was. For one of the few times in David's life, he wanted to be told what to do. And Joseph was one of the rare people he had ever allowed to do that.

"Punctual, as always."

Joseph's querulous voice met David before he was even halfway through the study doorway. The younger man smiled to himself. "I can be late next time, if you would prefer."

"Huh! I'd like to see that. You're constitutionally incapable of it." Joseph's wheelchair was pulled up close to the fireplace. He jockeyed it around a bit so that he was head-on to the low Italian mosaic marble table, mounded with newspapers and folders. With his eyes, the good left one and the dolefully drooping right, determinedly averted, he contrived nonetheless to see when David came abreast of the wheelchair. He reached out his good left hand and grabbed at David's hand, held it fast, and then released it. When David was settled onto the small sofa, Joseph raised his head and scowled at him. "So, what do you novices need help with now?"

"Some small matters. But first, I need to talk to you about something personal."

Joseph abruptly dropped his curmudgeonly guise. "What is it? Are you having a problem with Cissy, with the divorce?"

David shook his head. "No. Cissy has always been a

sweet girl; she can't bring herself to be vindictive. We've worked everything out and her mother is going to take her to Europe." David let out a nervous breath, licked at his lips. "I want to talk to you about Monty."

"Monty? I don't want to hear a goddamned word about him!"

David gave Joseph an imploring look. "Joe. I really need your advice here."

Joseph calmed himself. He took a moment and scrutinized David's face. "I don't like the look in your eye. I thought we were rid of that son of a bitch. Was I wrong?"

"Apparently, we were both wrong." David leaned his elbows on his knees, looked down at his hands, clasped and unclasped them repeatedly. "Last month, he sent a brutal, ugly letter to Cissy telling her the truth about me, about my past. It was the catalyst that destroyed us. Our marriage wouldn't have lasted in any case, but that letter, having her find out that way . . . it robbed her of any faith that I'd ever cared for her, that I'd ever been truthful about anything. He did it to hurt me, which I can accept, but he did it without caring who else might be harmed more. It was cruel. Viciously cruel."

David raised his eyes to Joseph's face and the pain in them made Joseph wince. "I'm sorry, David. Cissy didn't deserve that. But that's water under the bridge, right? Why do I think you wouldn't be bothering to tell me about it if there weren't something else, something worse, something perhaps that you think we need to deal with?"

David almost smiled. "Talking to you is never disappointing, Joe."

"So. What else did that black Irish bastard do?"

The words didn't want to come. Again David wondered if he was making a horrible mistake. He didn't know whether his suspicions were within the bounds of rationality or were, as Lorena had conjectured about Libby's revelation, a chimera cobbled from his own hatred and sorrow. He could end up engendering in Joseph a much worse guilt for not protecting Zoe than David himself could ever imagine, and for nothing.

"David?" Joseph's voice still held its sharp bite of authority. "Tell me, son. What else?"

"Joe, I'm sorry. I don't know if I should even be telling you this." Too agitated to sit, David nearly jumped off the love seat. "I'm going to pour myself a brandy; can I get you one? Yes?"

Joseph took the snifter from David's hand. "David. Sit down and start talking. You're trying my patience. I'm an old man. I might die at any moment."

David made a face and sat. He took a pull of his brandy. "The night Lorena and I cleaned out Zoe's apartment, I found the stub of a train ticket to Oyster Bay on the floor of Monty's closet. No date on it and it was faded and stained, but it was upsetting to see. It hit Lorena hard, and I pushed her into giving up a confidence. Your granddaughter Libby told her that Monty hit Zoe. Lorena doesn't think it's true. But, Joe, I can't get this crazy scenario out of my head: that Monty was at Hidden Cove the day she died, that he did something to her."

Joseph tucked his weak, shaking hand under his leg. His drink was untouched. "And . . . ?"

"And nothing. Lorena convinced me to be rational and let it go. But after that letter arrived, I got wild again. I talked with one of the saleswomen at the store. She remembered the day, of course. She remembered that Monty left early. She swears that he was really sick. The whole thing is absurd. I haven't taken it any further. But it's left me with a bad feeling."

"Your feelings are often uncannily accurate, David," Joseph said cautiously, and reached out his good hand for his brandy.

"Maybe, but I don't trust myself here, Joe. I hate that man. I don't think I've ever disliked another human being as much. I don't necessarily think I'm right. I just know that the thought of it has been eating away at me."

"You know I hate him, too." Joseph grew contemplative. "But I've always seen Monty as the consummate opportunist, not a man of action. His forte is to prey on the vulnerable. Zoe was vulnerable and he seduced and married her for her inheritance. After Zoe's death, he preyed on Sally's inexplicable sympathies—she asked me to consider giving him a larger settlement, can you believe it? Your marriage was vulnerable and he used that to cause you pain."

"*I'm* vulnerable, Joe. What if he exposes me?"

The left side of Joseph's mouth curled up in a humorless smile. "You're not vulnerable, David. He won't ever take you on in the public arena. You're too successful, too important. No one would care anymore that you're a Jew, and anyone who did would never admit it. You are who you've become. There would be no benefit to him in exposing you, only danger. Monty knows that if he ever gave either of us sufficient reason, we would destroy him." Their eyes met above their brandies and held in silent communication.

"But he hasn't given us sufficient reason, has he? We don't know whether or not he's graduated to making his own opportunities."

"No. Not from what you've told me." Joseph drained his glass.

"I could delve a little deeper."

Joseph gave a wry smile. "No. If you really wanted to, you'd have done it already. I think perhaps this is more than you want to deal with. That's why you've come to me. I was her father. I'll deal with this, David."

"You'll call Hillman?"

"I'll consider what you've told me, what your intuition is telling you, and if I think there is anything to it, I'll call Hillman. I don't want you involved. I don't want you distracted. These are challenging times; your mind needs to be clear for business. I will keep you informed of what I decide."

Joseph held out his empty glass. "Here, take this away." He rummaged through the mess on the tabletop and extracted a slim ledger. "Are those oil fields in Oklahoma producing yet, or is our money still being flushed into the ground?"

David rose and put the empty glasses on the green granite surface of the sideboard. He felt better. He didn't want to believe in his own conjecture and he didn't want to deal with Monty. He wanted to put the last eight months behind him, Zoe's death, Sarah's baby, Joseph's debility, Cissy's misery, his own sudden aloneness, and get on with his life.

He sat back down, bent over his briefcase, and found the Oklahoma file. Fat folder in hand, he looked up. Across the low table from him, Joseph was straight backed in his wheelchair, a deep frown of concentration on his lined, asymmetrical face. No sign of distress. David was suddenly breathless. For eight crucial years of his life Joseph had provided the strongest paternal presence David had ever known. He always understood what David needed, what he wanted. He had known exactly why David had come to talk to him tonight, known that he needed to have the burden of his suspicions taken from him by an older and wiser man. The delicate balance of their relationship, so much more than that of mentor and protégé, may have altered, but a boy never ceased to need a father. And a man never ceased needing to be needed.

"Yes. They're gushing all over the place. I have the figures here. You'll like them."

"That's my boy. Right again." Joseph smiled without raising his head. "You'll stay for dinner?"

"Evelyn already invited me. What are we having?"

"I believe I heard something about a duck, with prunes and port."

David's heart gave a little lurch. Everyone knew that was his favorite.

43

At the very moment that David sat down to his duck, the issue of what to do about Monty once again intentionally reduced to a matter of unimportance, the unimportant matter himself was threading his way through the fecund streets of Chelsea. Monty would have been charmed to know that even in absentia, even after the explosion caused by his bomb of a letter had subsided, he had continued to cause David such impotent grief. He had considered helping the world discover that David was a Jew, but that revelation would have had minuscule repercussions on the large scale compared to what it had had on the small. And, since Monty could think of no more ways to torment the family, he contented himself with wishing them ill until a new opportunity might present itself. For the moment he was quite satisfied.

He would need that new opportunity at some point. The money he had now wouldn't last forever, not the way he liked to spend. Just because he had gone to ground in the underbelly of the urban beast didn't mean he would no longer live well. Within a month of the day he left his old life behind, he had reinvented himself as Hugh Montgomery and registered thusly for a long-term stay in a solid three-room apartment in the Hotel Chelsea on West 23rd Street, where there also dwelled a host of dedicated drinkers with whom he could remain drunkenly unimpressed at having O. Henry and Edgar Lee Masters among the hotel's many famous onetime residents. He'd made his rooms more comfortable with several fine pieces of furniture and Persian carpets and, in a display of transparent excess, arranged for a delivery of fresh flowers to his apartment every three days. He'd bought himself a swell new wardrobe, not because he had tired of the old but because he had somehow lost so much weight that even his custom-made hundred-dollar suits hung like rags from his bones. Occasionally the thought flickered through his head that he should eat more, but he had lost his appetite for food. He didn't feel well a lot of the time. His skin had taken on a yellow cast; he was always tired and sometimes nauseous. It was the strain of twenty years of playacting, of pretending to enjoy being treated like a worm. It had taken its toll on him. Now that he was free of it all, he was sure he'd come to feel better. His thirst, however, was never slaked. He replenished his bar regularly with the best his bootleg buddies had to sell.

What was left of the divorce settlement he'd invested with a group of cronies who were buying up brothels and gay bars all around Greenwich Village, the Tenderloin, Pennsylvania Station, and Times Square. A steady but unspectacular return, but safer than the soaring stock market.

What soars eventually falls, but degeneracy lives on forever. Sally's extorted payment for the return of her wedding jewels—which he surmised she could only have gotten from pressing her suffocating motherly love on her pedigreed lapdog of a son until he coughed the cash right out of his creamy windpipe—was safe and fluid in the country's richest bank, New York's own National City Bank. For an emergency, a promising business venture, Monty's future security. And, to cover his daily expenses, to keep his mind sharp and his social skills greased, he had found the perfect job, to which he was now headed.

In the brisk March night air, Monty walked the five blocks from the hotel through the bright, beating pulse of the Tenderloin's theaters, restaurants, resorts, and brothels to 28 West 28th Street, just off Broadway, and let himself in the side door entrance of the infamous Turkish bathhouse the Everard, where he was a night manager. The Everard had been offering its wealthy and middle-class clientele the finest in steaming and bathing amenities since 1888. There was a pool and a gymnasium. There was steam or sauna. There were cooling rooms with cots, private dressing rooms, and a parlor. There were masseurs and manicurists. By the time of the World War, the Everard had become known by queers and fairies throughout the country and as far away as Europe as a refuge for men of their predilections. Here, they could find one another and engage in sexual activity quite openly, often with fascinated heterosexual men looking on, and with little fear of being caught out by the Society for the Suppression of Vice.

This reputation had been a boon to the Everard's bottom line. Regular customers were grateful, and in a busy week, as they almost all were, Monty pocketed as much as a hundred dollars in tips from the perverts who came to do their business quietly in the billowing shadows of the steam room or the privacy of their dressing rooms or brazenly in the hallways or public cooling rooms. At least once a week, instead of cash Monty accepted a tip in the form of getting his cock sucked. The pretty boys liked him, with his masculine contempt and dreamy pallor below his shockingly black hair; a mature piece of rough trade with a big dick was always a thrill. Everyone knew he wasn't a queer. He didn't find other men sexually attractive, he just didn't particularly care who pleasured him, and lately he had no patience or energy to turn on the charm for some stupid, seducible woman or even for a casual fuck with some slut. When your eyes were closed, lips and tongues all felt the same.

All in all, Monty's new life suited him very well. He was happy to coil up for a little while and wait to strike another day.

44

Philip was incapable of feeling resentment, but it didn't make him happy that David knew more about Brook than he did. Of course, he had no one but himself to blame. What effort had he ever made to apply himself differently to Brook's upbringing than he had to Jed's? He had remained passively neglectful because he, too, was desperate to court Sally's favor. And Brook had become, if that was possible, even more needful of his mother's approval, no matter the cost to himself, than Jed had been at his age.

At least Jed had been jovially content to accommodate himself to what Sally wanted of him, except for that period of several years leading up to the time of his engagement to Abby, when Philip thought he had glimpsed a dark blotch beneath Jed's eternally sunny surface. Postwar restlessness, undoubtedly. Jed was well settled now, prospering at work and at home.

Brook, on the other hand, had always been skittish and cringing. Philip didn't want it to take until Brook was nearly sixty, as it had taken him, to realize that Sally's love could not be lured out, no matter what tasty bait was dangled before her. She ruled her emotions from some closed and guarded place, and only when and if she chose to do so would she let the softer ones out. Philip was a grown man and her husband. His decision to wait faithfully for her love was proper, and lately her behavior toward him had given him reason to hope that his patience might actually someday be rewarded. But Brook had no such responsibility.

Philip shifted the heavy box of books to the crook of one arm and knocked on Brook's door. "Brook, can I come in?"

A flurry of activity from the other side and Brook swung open his door. "Father!" His look of astonishment turned to curiosity. "What have you got there?"

"A little present for you." Schoolwork littered the boy's desk. "Can I pull you away from your studying for a moment?"

"Please do."

Philip came into the room and deposited the box on the bed. "Close the door and come over here." He opened the box and began placing books on the dark green chenille bedspread. "You have always loved to read and I don't like that you spend all your time with your texts lately. You need your pleasures, too, Brook. Now I know some of these are a couple of years old, and perhaps you've read them—and if you have that's all right; I can always return them for others—but I did some research and put together a collection I thought you'd enjoy."

Brook walked slowly over to his bed and looked down at the feast of literature that was being laid out on his bedcover like one of Angelina's copious meals on his grandmother's tablecloth. His eyes grew huge.

Philip bent over the bed. "So . . . you're almost eighteen now and have probably outgrown Booth Tarkington, Zane Grey, and the like. Although . . ."—his head bobbed in appreciation—". . . I must say, those westerns really are fun. Ah, but you can find them on your own. And I know you've read all of Wells already." He picked a book out of the box and stared down at its cover. "Now *this* looks absolutely fascinating. Just came out. *Revolt in the Desert* by T. E. Lawrence, fully illustrated. All that recent turmoil with the Arabs and British in the Middle East, great exotic adventure, don't you think? And here's Sinclair Lewis— *Main Street, Babbitt, Arrowsmith.* I'll get you the new one, too, *Elmer Gantry.* Lewis is surely one of the greatest writers of our times. And for something a little lighter, here's Sabatini's latest, *The Sea-Hawk*—you enjoyed *Scaramouche,* didn't you? All that swashbuckling. Oh, and I've gotten you a subscription to that Book-of-the-Month Club that was started last year."

Philip prattled on as he drew volume after volume out of the box like rabbits from a top hat, but Brook wasn't listening. He was all but salivating, ready to throw himself onto the bed and wallow among the treasures there. Authors he recognized, like Edna Ferber and Mary Roberts Rinehart with her spiffy murder mysteries, and people he'd never heard of: Ernest Hemingway with something called *The Sun Also Rises; Soldiers' Pay* by someone named William Faulkner. Mark Twain's autobiography!

"Father." Brook flung his arms around Philip's waist, disengaged himself so quickly Philip had no time to react, and sat down on the edge of his bed.

"Good. Good." Philip sat down next to him. He cleared his throat. "Now. Your birthday is in June and I have an idea for a present. What if you and I spend two weeks up at the Chautauqua Institute this summer? That lake and the northwestern New York landscape always inspire me, and perhaps I could teach an oils class or lecture on art history. And you could take some literature courses and perhaps a writing workshop. . . ."

After a long moment of silence, Brook looked his father in the eye and said, "David spoke with you, didn't he?"

"No. He spoke with Lucy, and she spoke with me. And he was right to do it." Philip put his hand on Brook's knee. "I will never pressure you to do anything you don't want to do. I'm just asking you to consider not disowning your talent. Believe me when I tell you that it can be a great gift to you, to your life, if you accept it. Why don't you come to my studio one afternoon a week, and use that time to write?" He shook Brook's leg to get the boy to look at him again. "I'll find a way to talk to your mother about it."

Brook's head rose swiftly. "No! Don't! She'll feel we're ganging up on her, just like you and Lucy always did. I don't want her to be angry at me for some stupid stories! It's not worth it. School isn't so bad, really."

"I can make it clear that it was wholly my idea to bring the subject up at all. That you even asked me not to."

"No!" But he put his hand over his father's with a mournful sigh.

Philip turned his head away and smiled at the wall. "Well, what about the idea of coming to the studio?"

Brook pouted. "What's the point of writing once a week? Would you want to paint if you could only do it once a week?"

"That's a valid question." Philip's eyes traveled around the unadorned, somewhat sterile room and he thought of how miraculous it was that for him there was something worth looking at in absolutely everything. "The answer is yes. I would accept being able to paint only once a week if the alternative was to not paint at all. But that's me. No one can tell you that you need to write. That is something only you can know. Have the courage to find out, Brook. That's all I ask of you."

45

"What's wrong with this?" Jed stepped back from his easel and looked at his canvas in disgust. "It's awful and I don't know why."

David stopped pacing long enough to stand behind Jed and squint over his shoulder at the luminous watercolor depiction of a family picnic. "What do I know? It looks great to me. You know who your work reminds me of? Those Red Rose Girls, the three women illustrators who do all those magazine covers and children's books. I remember getting my hands on a copy of Robert Louis Stevenson's *A Child's Garden of Verses* at the settlement house when I was about eight. It had amazing drawings by one of them, Jessie Wilcox Smith, I think. I loved it so much I stole the book and kept it at home for years."

Jed gave David a withering look. "It's a little late to tell me that I've befriended a thief."

David grinned and chewed absently on his thumb as he contemplated Jed's drawing. "Seriously, Jed. You could do covers for *Good Housekeeping* or *Ladies' Home Journal*. Or book illustration. You're more than good enough."

"I'm no Norman Rockwell. Surely no Wyeth."

"Stop denigrating yourself," David said in annoyance. "It's absurd to try to compare Rockwell and Wyeth to one another; why compare yourself to either of them? You're you. And just because your primary focus is business doesn't mean you can't use your other abilities to their fullest as well. I, for one, hate that you get no credit for designing our women's dresses, although pretending they're designed for us in France and Italy does makes them irresistible. Why not sell your work openly where you can?"

Jed stood stiffly at his easel. He avoided looking at David and said nothing.

David poked him lightly in the back. "I'm sorry. I shouldn't lecture you. But you really have to learn how to take a compliment," he joked.

Jed turned and smiled faintly. "Thank you, Mr. Shaw," he said with exaggerated formality. "But no. I don't want to try to sell my drawings. It's never been what I wanted and it's even less so now."

Perhaps he did love to paint, but so what. He was a mediocre talent, despite what people said, and as an artist he would have nothing but his suspect ability to prop him up. He'd be a second-rate hack illustrator. At least at the company he had a strong safety net under him and David right beside him. With that bit of help, he was succeeding admirably.

"We've talked about this before, David. Why do you keep thinking I'm not happy where I am?" Jed watched David as he resumed roaming restlessly around the small studio, a sleek, powerful thoroughbred unfairly held back behind the starting line. A rattle of guilt shook Jed's security. "I might begin to wonder if you want to get rid of me."

David spun around. "Don't ever say that, not even in jest.

Don't you ever think that. We're a good team. Your caution tempers my impetuousness, you take more time with things than I'm usually willing to, and you sure as hell are better with people than I am. You're whip smart and you know what you're doing. I don't think you're not happy, Jed. I guess I just have trouble accepting your modesty. If I had a talent like yours I'd want everyone to know it."

Jed burned with pleasure at David's praise, but the conversation about his happiness and modesty had gone quite far enough. He turned his attention to his drawing and the conversation to something less precarious. "How are the redecorating efforts coming along?"

"Fabulously. Your wife is starting to scare me, though, she knows so perfectly what I'm going to like. Did you see that fabric sample she brought? That brown velvet? God, I want to eat it. We're having a lot of fun together. Thanks for letting me borrow her."

"She's enjoying it." A feeble lick of ambiguous jealousy flared up from Jed's bowels. "So, it's almost three months since you and Cissy broke up. Don't you have a new girlfriend yet? I think this is the longest I've known you to be without one." He looked back at David and put a smile on his face. "Just kidding again. Really, how are you doing?"

"I'm doing fine," David said, and laughed in self-amazement. "You may have been kidding, but except for the time in the army, this *is* the longest I've ever gone without a steady girl in my life. I like it. It's actually an incredible relief."

As always, when it came to David, Jed couldn't keep his prurience under control.

"Pardon my French, but, my goaty friend, what are you doing for sex?"

With his usual lack of modesty, David wiggled his eyebrows suggestively and said, "Found me a cute little redheaded waitress. We spend a few hours in bed every once in a while. That's all she wants, all I want. Neither of us will cry when it's over." He leaned against the wall by the window. "I wouldn't have brought it up, Jed, but since you did . . . how are you and Abby doing with that?"

Jed chose his words carefully. "We're doing the best we

can. I'm not . . . unsatisfied." Another perfect half-truth, half-lie. He had gotten so incredibly good at them.

David nodded. "Okay. Good." He turned to look out the window. "April showers bring May flowers," he murmured. "This is a beautiful kind of rain, warm and soft. Your father should be happy; his garden is waking up."

Jed put down his paintbrush. If his life depended on it, he could not have stopped his parched gaze from drinking at the bottomless well of David's profile. Tears stung his eyes and nose and he swallowed to push down the longing that rose into his throat. "David, don't you have to go?"

David checked his watch. "Oh, I do. I have my piano lesson in fifteen minutes." He beamed with childlike excitement.

"It's good to see you happy again. I was worried about you." All trace of the libidinous love that had been etched on Jed's face a mere second before had vanished.

"It's been a hard fall and winter. But it's over now. I'm feeling better than I have in years. I'm enjoying working less—isn't it nice to take the occasional Saturday off like this?—and it feels good to be broadening my horizons. I'm finally going to buy myself a car—"

"Oh? What are you thinking of getting?"

"I'm going to go to hell with myself and get a Stutz. And I'm even thinking about letting Lucy teach me to ride a horse this summer."

Jed snortled. "Maybe you should find a teacher who'll have more patience with you."

David looked dismayed. "Why? Does your sister still find me such a trial? I thought we were getting along pretty well."

"My goodness, all my jibes are falling flat today," Jed laughed. "My sister is inscrutable to me. If you think the two of you can survive her teaching you, I'm sure you're right."

"Well, I think it might be fun. And Zoe would love it." David pushed off the wall. "I'm off to desecrate J.S. Bach," he said jauntily. "I'll see you Monday." When he passed by the easel he stopped and said, "I still think that's a terrific picture, Jed."

Jed stared at his work and picked up his brush again. "Maybe you're right."

When he heard the front door close, Jed went across the hall into Henry's room, but not to see his son; the baby was downstairs with Abby. He went because Henry's room faced south, onto the cobbled alleyway, and from the window he could watch David saunter away. He had fought so hard to keep his balance, but that night in February when he had put David to bed had pushed him off the tightrope. He had tried, several times since, to find a way to make love to Abby. He had called upon every trick, every pretense he could conceive, smuggled his dizzying desire for David into the bed he shared with his wife like a desperate army secreted inside the Trojan horse of his own body, but nothing had made it possible for him to sustain his arousal long enough to complete the deed. He couldn't go on like this anymore. This love inside him had to be released or it would strangle him in his sleep; it would burst him open like rotten fruit; it would cook him alive in his own boiling blood.

46

Jed walked down the shadowed street with the smell of the river and the slightly rancid odor of butchered meat in his nostrils. He walked slowly, stepping in and out of pools of light cast by the widely spaced street lamps. He craved only the darkness, where the person he had once thought himself to be ceased to exist and the person he now knew he was came to life, blood pumping, heart racing. Each second in the light was a brutal exposure of the beast that lived in the darkness inside him, that rose to stalk the darkness of these streets. He moved closer to the warehouse, into the shadow of its massive brick wall. As he reached the middle of the block, an unseen figure detached itself from a small depression and placed itself in front of him, half in shadow, half in light. A young man, in his early twenties, in plain clothes, his shirtsleeves too short for his well-muscled, sculpted arms, curly black hair falling around a strong-featured face, his skin smooth, eyes glinting, the street lamp's rays reflecting off their dark curved surface. A queer but no nancy-boy; as intense and masculine looking as David. The one he'd been dreaming of, had come to this street tonight hoping to find. To be found by. To be taken by. Jed stopped. His arms hung loosely at his sides, his only movement the quick rise and fall of his chest.

"I've seen you here before, walking and watching like this. You've watched me. You've never stayed, though, have you?" Cool fingers trailed along the line of Jed's jaw. "Were you looking for me? Because I've been looking for you." Dark eyes caressed Jed's face. "God, you're so pretty."

Gentle fingers brushed against Jed's lips and his mouth fell open, his desperate breath forging a path to release. A small moan accompanied the puff of air that escaped him; his eyes fluttered shut.

"My name's Tony. What's yours?"

Jed opened his eyes and looked at Tony's disheveled hair lifting slightly in the cool evening breeze, disobedient tendrils swaying against the clear brown skin. He said nothing.

"That's okay. I don't need to know your name." Tony smiled, took firm hold of Jed's hand, and tugged forcefully at him. "Let me do you. I can pay you something. You'll like me."

Jed couldn't speak. He couldn't take his eyes off Tony's face. The rapid beat of his heart filled his throat. He let Tony lead him to the small recess in the wall and position him with his back against the damp bricks. There was no resistance possible anymore, nothing left inside him strong enough to overcome his need for human contact, a need that was daily eating away at him like a slowly progressing cancer. Tonight, his will weakened irrevocably, he was finally ready to be found by the man who would take advantage of his vulnerability and infect him with the fatal pleasure that would be his downfall. He took no comfort in contemplating his own passivity. Whatever happened to him tonight would still be of his own doing; he could blame no one else. He leaned against the wall and waited for the thing to happen. The pounding in his chest and head deafened him. He was in agony, excruciatingly aware of the young man on his knees before him, head tilted back, dark eyes searching his face.

A twisting line of heat moved down Jed's body as Tony's gaze left his face and traveled the length of his torso, coming to rest just below his waist. He didn't move or utter a sound as Tony slowly unbuttoned his pants and took him in his mouth. Warm wet lips on virgin flesh; Jed stiffened instantly and nearly lost consciousness. A long sigh escaped from somewhere deep within him and he sagged against the bricks, all feeling gone from his legs. He braced himself with one hand against the wall and the other on Tony's bowed head, his fingers gripping tightly at the thick dark hair. Too heavy now for his neck, Jed's head lolled back against the wall. His eyes fell closed as he abandoned himself completely to his descent.

Tony stopped for a moment, compelled to look up once more. An unfamiliar tremor shook him to see what was so starkly revealed on the man's face and to feel long, avid fingers clutching at his hair. There was something imperfect in the man's devastating beauty that made Tony's jaded heart twitch wildly in his chest, a transparent mask of misery and hopelessness that lay over the exquisite features, profound and tragic. The image of a fallen god brought to his end by his lust for a mortal being seared itself into Tony's mind. A burning desire to be that mortal, to burrow deep beneath this man's surface, flared up in him. He was invaded by the utter wantonness suggested by the stretched length of the man's throat, by the blue line pulsing in the white skin, and that wantonness took possession of him.

Brazen hands pulled at Jed's pants and undershorts until they were down around his knees. Impatient fingers insinuated themselves under his shirt, pushing it out of the way. Moist lips and tongue kissed and licked at his stomach, his hip bones, while the fingers traveled up his chest, caressed his nipples, hard now as little diamonds. Jed's knees began to buckle, his head fell forward, and he leaned all his weight on Tony's sturdy shoulders. Cool hands slid around Jed's hips, cupped the round, tight muscles of his buttocks, and pulled him forward to be engulfed again by hard, wet heat. A delirious peacefulness rocketed inside him along with his orgasm, a relief and a rightness beyond imagining.

Jed cried out and slithered down the wall like a snake, boneless, mindless. He came to a halt in a tight crouch, back jammed against the wall, knees tucked under his shoulders, trousers pooled around his ankles. He panted as he stared into Tony's face, his eyes barely able to focus. He shoved his fingers roughly into Tony's hair. Ignoring the jolt of shock in the dark eyes, Jed clasped the boy's head firmly, drew him close, and kissed him passionately, his mouth open wide and his tongue moving, burning from the bitter taste of his own fluid in Tony's mouth. Tony struggled to draw back, but Jed kept his grip tight and felt the other suddenly yield, press forward, and return Jed's kiss with a strong, unfeigned passion of his own. Tony's hands slid over Jed's arms and neck and came to rest on his head, soft as a feather.

No longer innocent or ignorant, Jed understood the horrible significance of that simple kiss. It exposed him to his deepest, perverted core. It revealed him to be something other than what Tony had taken him for. Jed had come here wrapped in the protection of his wedding ring and his overt masculinity. He had presented himself, and Tony had accepted him, as a piece of trade—a wholly masculine man who nonetheless would allow a queer like Tony to give him money for the privilege of giving him sexual pleasure. But trade did not kiss the man who pleasured him. Trade did not take another man in his mouth. In the spontaneous expression of the simplest of his repressed desires, Jed had proved once and for all that he was not normal. He was a queer, a degenerate. He could pretend to the world that he was nothing more or less than the man it saw, but on these streets the mask came off. This was where he belonged. And he would return, soon, and seek out this Tony who looked so much like David. Who, like David, had never been a child and could take Jed where Jed wanted a man to take him. And next time Jed would be the one on his knees and he would do the next feverishly dreamed-of thing, and the next, and there would be no opportunity ever again in his life to step back into safety.

He didn't care. If he was going to sin, he wanted it all. He wanted it all right now but was afraid if he allowed himself to take it he would never go home again. Here he could live the way he wanted, his pleasures spread out before him like a row of exotic hothouse flowers. He was going to Hell in any case, for so many transgressions; why not have a moment in heaven before he fell?

Jed drew back, his hands still cradling Tony's head. They both knew that no money would change hands, not tonight, not ever. Between gasps he said, "My name is Jed. When can we meet again?"

Jed sat on a bench in Washington Square Park and waited for the blood tide surging through him to subside. He didn't know how to calm it; what swept through his heart and lungs and fed every cell of his sparking body was not the same stuff that had flowed through him mere hours earlier. Tonight the mists had parted for him and he had died and been reborn as a different creature in a different world. Everything he had ever been before had been burned away in the inferno ignited by Tony's mouth and hands; he was nothing now but a pile of ashes smoldering inside a familiar-looking husk. Just as his helpless infant son needed his father's protection from the dangerous world, Jed's newborn life needed to be kept safe. That smoking husk, what was left of the Jed Gates everyone knew, was his shield against discovery. He had to shelter it and wear it like a cloak woven of shadows. No one must be allowed to see what was huddled under his shell: the lust-drunk queer living in secret, fearful exile from everything that might ground him to a normal life.

Minute by minute, breath by breath, heartbeat by heartbeat, Jed laid the cloak over him. When he felt himself fully encased, he rose off the bench and headed for home. The harsh clack of his shoes on the quaint cobbles echoed loudly off the low, close-in buildings of the Mews. He stood before the door to his house and pictured himself walking in, looking Abby in the eye, and telling her that, yes, he'd had a very pleasant after-dinner stroll in the damp, balmy spring night. He could visualize it but didn't see how it would be possible for him to actually do it. Jed knew that there were men who were able to live fully in both worlds, but he was not one of them. He loved Abby, but he would never attempt to make love to her again. He would tell her a deeper lie about his sexuality, something so outrageous and unarguable that she would believe it. He would give her permission to take a lover. There would be no divorce. His only regret was that there would be no more children, and he had so wanted a houseful of children. But there would be Henry, his precious innocent son conceived in deceit and shame, who must never know the truth about his father.

He couldn't stand outside all night. The sooner he collected himself and got this over with, the better. Abby might even be relieved, to finally know where things stood between them. He went into the house and found her curled in a corner of the parlor sofa, dozing over a book. As he approached, she woke with a sleepy smile.

She closed her book and stretched. "Did you have a nice walk?"

He perched on the edge of the sofa and stared at her.

"Jed? Darling?" Her smile wavered. "You look flushed. Are you all right?" She reached a flat palm toward his forehead as if to feel for fever.

Jed flinched away from her. Misery bloomed in her eyes and he felt a rush of blood swamp his chest. He opened his mouth to begin to explain how their lives would be from now on, and his craven mind squirmed into some remote hidey-hole, leaving him numb and idiotic. Words tumbled from him, running all over one another like rats fleeing a sinking ship.

"I'm never going to make love to you again. I can't."

The color drained from Abby's face and her eyes grew frantic. Jed plunged on. "I swear there's no other woman. There's something wrong with me, since the war; we have to face it; I can't perform like a normal man. But you should have sex. You should. You should take a lover. I won't mind. But I won't divorce you, ever. You're my wife and I love you.

And Henry." He jumped up and began stalking about the room. With every giddy word he spoke, he sailed further away from rationality into a sea of delusion. A perverse light illuminating his wildest fantasies went on in his head. "You can sleep with David!" He whirled on her, his eyes wide with the brilliance of his solution. "I know you like him. He's alone. And he's so beautiful."

Moving as though under a mesmerist's spell, Abby rose slowly off the sofa, abject horror distorting her features. She backed away from him. When she spoke, her voice trembled and broke. "Are you drunk or are you just insane? What's the matter with you?" She swallowed and drew in a shaking breath. "Jed, you're frightening me!"

"No! Can't you see it? It's perfect!" Jed looked at her with blazing eyes, amazed at his own ingenuity. "You and David. My wife and my best friend. Wasn't Cissy always telling you what an accomplished lover he is?" He twirled around, tilted his head up to the ceiling, found yet more inspiration there. He went on, red-faced and wild-eyed, completely out of control. "You could have his baby. We could raise it. Don't we want more children? We could have David's baby."

Abby screamed and ran from the room in an eruption of tears. The instant she was gone, the spell Jed had fallen under disintegrated and he was left standing in the middle of his parlor in a state of shock. Her footsteps reverberated on the stairs and down the hall. The door to their bedroom slammed shut. He staggered across the floor and fell onto the sofa. He would fix things with her in the morning. He had just lost his mind for a moment. Tomorrow they would have a reasonable conversation and work out an arrangement for the continuance of their loving, sexless marriage. All marriages had arrangements of one kind or another. They were adults; they knew the way things were. They loved each other; they had a child; they would stay together. Neither had to know what the other did, in private, to make the arrangement livable.

For tonight, he was done. He didn't even have the energy to take off the suit he had donned in the far distant past of the morning, before everything had changed. He lowered himself onto his side, his back pressed into the soft cushions, his arms dangling over the sofa's edge. He stirred briefly, to take the crocheted cotton throw from the back of the sofa and pull it over him. Then, in the midst of thinking that he would surely be awake all night, he fell sound asleep.

47

It was just shy of an hour's walk from the Gates Building on William Street to Washington Square. When he could spare the time and if the weather was not totally abysmal, David walked home from work. On those occasions, by the time he'd reached the corner of West Broadway and Vesey Street and was unlikely to run into any business colleagues he would have abandoned the sartorial strictures of his wealth and position and reverted to the less formal, considerably more comfortable requirements of his lower-class beginnings. Tonight being unusually sultry for early June, he strolled slowly with his double-breasted suit jacket slung over his shoulder, his shirtsleeves rolled up above his forearms, his tie stuffed in his pants pocket, and his wide starched collar unbuttoned. His fedora dangled loosely from his left hand.

When he had set out at eight o'clock, it was still light and he was happy. By nine, when he climbed the steps of his brownstone, darkness had descended on the city and a pensive mood had settled over him, another reversion, he thought, this time to the time-honored Slavic affinity for melancholy. If he was any kind of Russian at all, he would be drinking bootleg vodka and not Scotch. But he felt himself no more a Russian than he did a Jew, and Scotch was what he liked. He unlocked the door. He had thought of selling the house after Cissy left. It had been too big even for the two of them. Once he and Abby had refurnished the place, however, he realized how much he loved it, not just the house itself but all that space, four floors for him to roam around in undisturbed, enough space to house half the population of the Ludlow Street building he'd grown up in. As an indigent boy he had dreamed of living among the monied denizens of hushed Gramercy Park. But when he became a rich man, he found that the wide-open urban beauty of Washington Square, the diversity and vitality of the surrounding streets of Greenwich Village, held more appeal for him. And he didn't expect to live alone forever.

Not forever, but for a while longer. He wasn't ready to relinquish his solitude, although for the first time since his marriage ended he felt a twinge of real loneliness as he walked into the empty house. He picked the mail up off the floor of the entry, turned on lights, opened windows. He settled into the parlor with a Scotch, a roast chicken sandwich, and the mail. His melancholy deepened when he saw Cissy's flowery handwriting scrawled across the face of a pink envelope. She was still in Paris; the letter was postmarked May 22nd and had been sent from the Ritz Hotel. He withdrew the sheet of expensive stationery. It was liberally perfumed with the sweet smell of *Romance*, the scent she'd worn for as long as he'd known her. For an unsettling moment David saw her standing in front of him, in her little black Chanel dress, her pearls and her perfume, just as she had on the night of their last wedding anniversary. His body ached, remembering what they'd done when they'd come home from their romantic dinner at the Café des Artistes. His body ached, but his heart didn't. He didn't miss her, not in any profound way, although he looked forward to hearing from her. It pleased him that they'd remained friends.

Dear David,

We had the most extraordinary experience last night. And it's still you I think of when I want to share something, so here goes. Maman and I were having tea at the Café de la Paix yesterday and all around us people were talking about how The Spirit of St. Louis had been spotted off the coast of Ireland and was expected to land at Le Bourget that night. So, we rounded up Tucker Corwith (I told you about Tuck, didn't I?) and his cousins and we all tromped out there after dinner. What a scene! There were people ten deep pressed up all along a high iron fence, but we found a spot on the steps of a building. We waited what seemed like forever. No one knew anything. It got dark and we were just about to leave when all these searchlights came on and rockets went off. It was so amusing! And then . . . David, it was so exciting . . . a little after ten Lindbergh's plane came flying out of the night like some great shiny bird and landed right in front of us. Everyone went crazy. They were screaming and yelling and they pushed the fence to the ground and swarmed all around the plane. I was a little scared, but Tuck grabbed me and we ran along with the crowd and got up close. People were tearing at the fabric of the wings—poor Lindbergh, he'll have to buy new ones!

Anyway, I'm sure you've read all about it by now, but I thought you'd appreciate a firsthand account! The only thing that would have made it more thrilling was if you'd been there with me. I know I shouldn't say things like that, but I still miss you. I can't help it. I'm trying to get worked up over Tucker, he's really so sweet and he's all goofy about me, but it's hard.

We're going to go to the Riviera for the summer, but we'll be home, finally, in September. I'm sure I'll be over you by then, so plan to take me to lunch!

Love, Cissy

David put the letter back in its envelope. She might still miss him, she might even still love him, but the increasingly buoyant tone of her letters was definitive proof of how happy she was to be free of him. Her love had brought her nothing but pain in the end. Let her marry damned Tucker and have six kids. David eyed the rest of his sandwich, but his appetite had disappeared. Suddenly he didn't want to spend the evening alone. He didn't want sex; he didn't even particularly want to talk to anyone. He just wanted to sit quietly, with a good book, in the presence of another human being who knew him and valued him and would be glad he was there. He wanted to be with Jed.

Leaving the lights on and the back windows open, David locked up the brownstone and walked the couple of blocks to the Mews house. Jed had left the office before him; he and Abby would be through with dinner; Henry would be asleep. Maybe Jed would be in his studio. David loved watching him paint, inhaling the tangy smell of turpentine and oil, listening to the radio, falling asleep on the couch. But when he got there he found only Abby.

"David! What a surprise!" She stepped back from the door to let him in, a too-bright smile on her face. "Jed's not home, you know. Or did you forget? This is his night at the Club. He doesn't usually get in before midnight."

David's hesitation was infinitesimal. He blinked twice and said, "Right. I forgot." He peered beyond her into the cozy parlor. "I got a letter from Cissy today, and I'm feeling a little blue. Do you mind if I stay here with you for a while, or would you rather be alone?"

"No, I don't want to be alone."

There was something off in her manner that made David uneasy. For the past several months the soft, smooth fabric of Abby's personality had been compromised by a scratchy edge. She wasn't happy. Tonight she was all but vibrating with veiled distress and with something else, something David had never felt from her before. It took him a moment to recognize what it was as they stood, uncharacteristically self-conscious with each other, and when he did it nearly sent him reeling. A heady sexual current was flowing from her and it was directed at him. She was staring at him the way a stupid *goy* might upon learning he was a Jew, looking for the horns that were supposed to be growing out of the top of his head. He could feel her prying at him with her gaze as though she were looking at him for the first time, looking to see if he might be something other than what she had always taken him for. And behind the gaze was an intense blast of sexual desire. He felt it like a startling burst of invisible energy gently and teasingly pricking at his skin.

A dull curtain fell over Abby's eyes and she turned away. The sensation was gone. David followed her into the parlor with not a little trepidation; his confusion was enormous. She'd been reading; a book was lying, spine up, on the sofa. She resettled herself and smiled at him as he claimed the armchair.

"I'm finally getting around to reading *Diet and Health*. It's only been three years on the bestseller list," she said lightly, holding up her book. "For all I know, I've been poisoning my husband and son all this time." She adjusted a pillow behind her back and gestured toward the coffee table between them. "There's today's *Herald Tribune* and *The Sun*. I think the new *Reader's Digest* is there somewhere. Stay as long as you like. This library never closes."

David watched Abby's bowed, dark head for a minute, then took up the *Tribune*. He stared without reading at the front page, his mind caught by what he had seen and felt from her. Jed had led him to believe that Abby was frigid, but this was not a frigid woman. This was not even a sexually reticent woman. Abby was clearly dying to be touched, and David knew full well that she wouldn't have looked at him the way she had if Jed were touching her. Where the hell was he tonight? He wasn't at any club that David knew of. Was he having an affair? If he were, it would be like him to respect David's affection for Abby and not burden his friend with the knowledge of his betrayal. But why would Jed have an affair? He had a lovely, willing wife, whom he adored. Why would he want to screw some other woman?

Jed had always been a little strange about women, about sex. Terminally shy and prissy. And with that icy, alabaster mother. It was one of two things, David concluded. Either Jed didn't like sex and his solitary evenings out were just that, a way to get away from all responsibilities for a few hours, or, more likely, he was one of those puritanical men who were appalled at the thought of their wives as sexual beings. He wanted his wife, the mother of his children, to remain saintly and virginal, like his own mother, unsullied by the sex act unless to procreate. David had known men like that, mostly but not only repressed, Hell-threatened Italian and Irish Catholics. So Jed put Abby on a lonely pedestal and found himself a flesh-and-blood woman to have his fun with. David felt bad for Abby, for both of them really, but he would not get in the middle of it. If Jed chose to talk to him about it someday, that was one thing, but otherwise, it was none of his business. With some effort, he put it firmly out of his mind and set about reading the newspaper from front to back.

By eleven thirty, Abby was yawning. David thanked her for the company, kissed the top of her drooping head, and went home. He stood on his stoop for a moment, looking out over the park. It was late, but people were still out, enjoying the night's warmth. David wondered whether if he stood there long enough, he might see Lucy walking home from the El, but no, coming past the park was out of her way. He went inside, to his piano. He was getting quite good, but then a monkey would sound good on a Steinway grand. If he'd stayed out a moment longer and looked harder, he might have seen Jed, limp on a deeply shadowed bench on the park's far perimeter. And ten minutes later Jed, if he'd been able to open his eyes, might have seen Lucy stop in front of David's house to listen to the moody, lyrical sounds of Mendelssohn floating into the summer air from the open window.

48

Although he was on his knees, his back to the house, hunched over a patch of earth, Philip sensed Sally watching him through the window. Something was shifting inside her, a tectonic plate of emotion dormant for a lifetime. He'd felt it in the fall but most markedly since the new year, when the combined pull of all of Jed's adult responsibilities grew strong enough to tear open a shallow yet implacable gulf between mother and son. Jed was still dutiful; Sally was still doting. But from across a divide. There was coolness between them now. The focus of Sally's life was moving further and further out of range. Philip could only imagine how frightened she must be. He wouldn't push her. He was the rock in her landscape.

From the corner of his eye he saw her move away from the window, and felt for a moment that the sun had gone behind a cloud. Perhaps he still expected too much. He busied himself with his geraniums. He wasn't aware that she had come out of the house until she spoke.

"The garden looks beautiful this year, Philip. I love it; I love that it's all red and gold."

He looked up at her over his shoulder. "Yes, well, they say it's going to be a hot summer. I thought, why fight it, let's have a garden to capture the heat."

"No," she said vaguely, "why fight it." She stepped off the stone walkway onto the dirt. "Will it disturb you if I sit on the bench while you work?"

Philip stood. "Of course not. But you should change your shoes and dress. The ground is wet; they'll get ruined."

She took another step into the small patch of earth. "I have other shoes and dresses. It doesn't matter." She smoothed a stray lock of his hair back into place. "Your hair is windblown. Most men your age don't even have hair anymore. Yours is still thick and there's hardly any grey. Like your father's."

He guided her to the little stone bench along the iron fence. She sat. He went back to his gardening.

"What is that you're planting?"

"Coreopsis. It has a pretty yellow flower and the feathery leaves are a nice contrast to the salvia, don't you think?" He kept his eyes on his digging. "Sally, what would you say to my taking Brook up to Chautauqua for two weeks in August?"

"Why? So our son can get away from me and write his stories? Which everyone knows about except, supposedly, his ogre of a mother."

Philip nearly impaled himself with his spade.

"Brook is no better at hiding things from me than Jed was. Why do boys think their mattresses are invisible forts?" She brushed a clot of dark, rich dirt off the bench. "You can take him to Chautauqua. But he stays in school. I'm not ready for that."

"He stays in school."

Sally sat with her back straight, her face turned up to the

sun. Philip puttered around at her feet, watering, planting, weeding. Minutes passed in comfortable silence. He waited.

"What do you hear from Dorothy?"

Ah, yes, finally. Dorothy. "Nothing for a while. She's settled in Rome. It seems she will live there now." Philip raised his head then and he and his wife gazed at each other through a patch of sun-excited air.

"She liked you," Sally said softly, sadly.

"Yes. She did."

"Did you like her?"

Philip smiled. "Not as much as she would have wished, perhaps. But I was a good friend to her when she needed one."

"Of course you were. You're a good man." Sally's hands were folded neatly in her lap. "Do you miss her?"

He squatted on his haunches before her. The sunlight turned her eyes the color of sapphire. "No. I miss you."

Her knuckles turned white. She inhaled once, a long, deep breath, then exhaled and rose from the bench. Philip remained where he was. As she went by him, she placed her hand on the back of his neck and let it gently fall away. At the door she hesitated, then said, "I miss you, too," before she disappeared indoors.

Philip picked up his watering can. His hand shook. He was sick with happiness.

49

With the ineffable permission of a sympathetic universe, the Gates family was allowed to recognize the turning of their new year at the coming of summer. The solstice arrived, peaked, and receded and swept them from the lingering depths of a dreary and difficult winter. The long, warm days eased their pains, and the inevitable passing of time brought with it the sweet, necessary relief of acceptance.

When Evelyn suggested that the entire family spend the weekend of Henry's first birthday at Oyster Bay everyone was eager to say yes. One and all, they were ready to celebrate the joys of life and try to forget its sorrows. And so, several weeks past the year's longest, most hopeful day, the family gathered at Hidden Cove for the first time since Zoe's fatal accident. Their shared world had been turned upside down by tragedy and the aftershocks of Joseph's strokes, David and Cissy's divorce, Monty's abrupt disappearance; their private worlds by a host of unspeakable thoughts and emotions. But with one more timely spin of the planet everyone had settled back to earth in a reordered existence. There may have been only a smattering of genuine happiness, but there was everywhere the appearance of happiness and much willingness to remain hopeful despite uncertainty. In all cases, the need for calm reigned supreme.

The July afternoon was glorious. Evelyn and Joseph sat on the great lawn of their majestic estate, side by side within the dense shadow of a large umbrella, his metal wheelchair pushed as close to her wooden chaise as its bulk would allow. Unread copies of *Vogue, Collier's, The Saturday Evening Post,* and *Harper's Magazine* littered a small wrought-iron table to Evelyn's left. An unread *Wall Street Journal* was folded across Joseph's thin legs. A light cotton shawl lay across his no-longer-square shoulders. Evelyn held his hand snugly in hers. Despite the commotion on the lawn, they both dozed, snoring lightly in harmony, Evelyn with her head falling back, Joseph with his head hanging down.

Philip and Sally sat nearby on a blanket spread under an immense European beech tree. She was bent in concentration over an intricate needlepoint. Sunlight filtered unevenly through the swaying pale-green leaves and glinted off her smooth, platinum head. Every so often, Philip lifted his eyes from his sketch pad and looked at her, his charcoal-stained fingers hovering delicately in the air. Once she caught his eye, then smiled and turned her gaze to the antic display on the lawn in front of them.

Jed, Abby, and Brook cavorted on the grass, in happy

worship of the sun and of Henry. Three giddy buffoons, they pranced in an incomplete circle with the baby as its inconstant center. Henry, dumbly unaware that it was his birthday yet seeming to sense the need to do something extraordinary, was trying to master the impossible art of walking. Lurching like Frankenstein's monster, he made futile attempts to escape through one of the changing openings in the human fence around him.

Jed stood still for a moment and peered off toward the woods behind the mansion. "David's lesson must be finished. I think I see him and Lucy."

"Oh, good. Reinforcements!" Abby cried gleefully. "You'll never get away now, Henry!"

Upon hearing his name, Henry let out a piercing shriek and careened toward a space between his parents, chubby arms waving in the air, torso beginning to pitch forward ahead of his stumbling legs. Abby caught him up before he crashed headlong to the ground. When Jed moved close behind her, she stepped back and leaned into his chest with the baby hugged to her breast. Jed put his arms around them.

"Abby, look." Jed laughed and pointed at his grandparents. "That's going to be us in thirty years. Nodding in our chairs while Henry and his children play on this very lawn."

She bent her head to the side and pressed her lips to Jed's bare forearm. Modest physical affection between them outside the bedroom was possible now that the specter of sex had been banished. "Yes. I will look forward to it." She lifted her head and craned her neck so that she could see his face. "I love you, Jed. I will love you always."

Everything between them was fine now. Early in the morning after the night of his little fit, Abby had come downstairs, red eyed but calm, and had assured him that she could live without sex as long as she had his love. That he could have one night a week for himself as long as the other nights were spent with her and Henry. The subject of her one day finding a lover was never raised. David's name was never mentioned. They had not spoken about any of it since. They had accommodated themselves to their arrangement without fuss. Jed didn't see why it shouldn't last forever. "I love you, too."

"You really did incredibly well for your first time on a horse," Lucy called out to David as he walked ahead of her along the narrow trail leading away from the stables. She meant to be nothing but complimentary. Unfortunately, she was so habituated to being annoyed at the careless ease with which David took to everything that she could not keep a distinct edge of antagonism from her voice. It didn't help any that she was also furious with him for not having discerned her feelings for him without her having to say anything. That was, after all, safer than being furious at herself for letting five months of his bachelorhood slip by with her still mute and prim with fear of rejection.

"I can't tell whether that pleases you or not," David said wryly, without looking back at her. "What a shock."

When the trail gave out onto the edge of the lawn, David stopped and waited for her to catch up to him. He used the moment to appraise his torn and bloodied shirtsleeve and the ugly, oozing scrape on his upper arm. "I fell off, for crying out loud!"

"Oh, don't be a baby. Falling off at least once is mandatory. Let me see."

David was unconcerned with his injury—he was disgusted with himself for not having controlled Sirocco perfectly; it was irrelevant that he'd never even sat on a horse before—but stood still as Lucy stepped close and gently pulled the sticky material away from his abraded skin. With her full attention riveted on his arm, she couldn't know that he stopped breathing for the duration of her examination, or that his eyes lingered on her bent head and his lips parted just a fraction. When she looked up at him and said, "You'll live," all she saw on his face was a distant expression that matched her own sardonic assessment of his condition.

"Thank you, Nurse. Do all your patients get treated with such a warm bedside manner?"

Her mouth twitched. "You're a big boy. You don't need my sympathy." She walked out onto the perfectly cut emerald-green grass, then stopped and looked over her shoulder. "You really did do well. You're going to be an excellent horseman. Zoe would be proud to have you riding Sirocco."

His expression softened. "Thank you. That was a lovely thing to say."

"You're welcome." She slowly turned back to face him. "It's hard, being here all together again. I felt Aunt Zoe's absence so painfully while we were riding. And Uncle Monty's. And Cissy's, too. The family is so diminished."

David looked past her. Some three hundred feet away, up the gently sloping lawn, the rest of the family could be seen, arrayed between sun and shade, enjoying the afternoon. He thought he saw Jed looking in their direction. "Nothing stays the same, Lucy. We've lost Zoe, but now we have Henry." He waved. "I don't miss Monty. You shouldn't, either. But, surprisingly, I miss Cissy. She loved it here."

Lucy watched him, safely unobserved as he continued to gaze into the distance. "She's coming home soon."

He nodded. "In a couple of months."

"Are you thinking you might get back together?"

He looked at her in surprise. "No. Never. We were a bad fit. You know that. I'm just beginning to appreciate what a terrible husband I was to her. I'm not going to inflict myself on any woman for a while. Not until I'm sure of what I really want."

Lucy's mouth turned up in a hard smile and she blinked several times, rapidly. "How decent of you. You're a real gentleman." He stood no more than six feet from her but he might as well have been on the far side of the moon.

"Ah. Here come David and Lucy." Philip watched them stride across the lawn. Instead of walking by David's side, Lucy forged ahead, moving quickly. Even from this distance, Philip could see the angry set of her jaw. And he could see David's eyes on her straight back as he followed, making no attempt to overtake her. Philip's heart ached. He watched them drop down onto the grass with the others to play with Henry, who had quite exhausted himself.

"David is a good friend to our sons, isn't he?" Sally put the needlepoint down and squinted thoughtfully out into the sun. "He and Jed are doing an excellent job together." She smiled as Henry laughed hysterically at something David whispered into his ear. "He's so good with Henry. He should have had children. He'd have gorgeous children, don't you think? He really is a striking-looking young man."

Every day now, it seemed, Sally found another way to astonish him. Philip had become expert at showing no reaction. "David will have children one day, I'm sure. When he's ready. Everything in its time, Sally, isn't that true?"

She didn't answer him or turn to look at him, but the smile lingered on her face. "We have a beautiful family, Philip. Look at Lucy. She's so lovely. And so smart. Should we be worried about her? She's nearly twenty-five. When is she going to find someone to love?"

Philip was worried, but not about Lucy. He was worried that his own chest might explode. "I wouldn't worry too much, my dear." He watched as David tossed the baby in the air while Lucy stared at his face, her anger forced aside by a far more honest, less conscious emotion. Philip composed himself and turned back to look at his wife as she, too, observed her children and grandson. Philip was beginning to believe in miracles. "I have a feeling that Lucy's heart will open very soon now. Very soon."

Evelyn woke from her afternoon nap but did not open her eyes right away. She lay still and let her other senses bring the world to her. She felt the complex caress of summer air on her face and arms, hot air drifting in under the umbrella and mingling with the cooler air trapped there. She felt the weight of Joseph's hand and arm on her leg, the dryness of his skin under her fingers. She smelled the grass as it baked in the sun, the spicy perfume of the marigolds that bordered the rose garden, the intoxicating sweetness of the fifty different roses planted there. Oh so subtly, beneath the heady scent of the roses, she could smell the bay, the salt and seaweed, the moisture. She heard birds cawing, trilling, chirping. She heard insects whizzing and whining. But most wonderfully she heard her family. Little by little, she discerned the sound of each and every one of them as they talked, cooed, snored, yelled, laughed. They were all there. In another moment she would open her eyes and look at them, but for now she kept them closed in secret supplication. The past year had been full of loss, hardship, and decline. Let this year be full of life and growth. Of course, Henry would grow; he would learn to walk and talk. But there had to be more. Let Abby get pregnant again. Let David find a new love, Lucy a first love. Let Brook become a swan and leave his ugly duckling days behind. Let Sally and Philip rediscover each other now that their children were grown up. And let Joseph live to see it all. She smiled to herself as she enjoyed her moment of utter contentment and her romantic dreams. She smiled and couldn't help but wonder why they shouldn't come true.

50

Anthony Rafael DeMarco, the bright and loving son of strict Catholic Italian immigrants, had been renounced by his family and thrown out of their home at the age of sixteen, when his father discovered him in an act of sodomy with a neighbor boy in the dark, dusty basement of their Mulberry Street tenement. Tony had lived on his own for the five years since, by day excelling as an eager clerk for a brokerage house and by night as a tight young body for hire on the streets of the Village and Chelsea. When Tony met Jed, he gave up his night job.

Immediately after their fateful sexual collision in April, Jed and Tony began meeting weekly. Most of their trysts took place in Tony's room, a square, spare space in a simple, clean rooming house, owned by a tolerant landlady, on way west 26th Street, in the grimy heart of the Chelsea docks. On evenings when the privacy of Tony's bed was too confining for their growing adventurousness, Tony chose from among the gay bars he knew and they made love in a back room or—furtively and bursting with insatiable lust—in a shadowed booth. Jed was terrified to wander the streets with Tony in hand, even streets traveled almost exclusively by men like themselves, but his terror only added to the depths of his desire and the potency of his response. There was nothing he wouldn't eventually try. He frightened himself and he thrilled to his own fear.

On this hot, frisky night in July, when Tony's room was sweltering and the bars were crowded and stinking of beer and male sweat, Tony suggested an evening at the nearby Everard Baths. It would be hushed and cool there. For a dollar apiece admission, they could soak and steam the city grit off their skin, then find a place to make love. Jed balked at first; it was too public, too many people there. He couldn't possibly do it. But Tony only smiled. He had quickly learned what Jed really meant when he said he couldn't possibly do something. By nine o'clock they had finished bathing and were in the steam room, half-hidden from view in the thick, white mist.

Tony sprawled on the tile bench below Jed's with his dark head resting on Jed's lightly tanned right thigh. He ignored the scars on his lover's leg although they scraped roughly at his cheek; he had asked Jed about them once, and once was all that was needed for Tony to understand that he was not to ask again. He moved his head languorously to the left, allowing his heavy hair to brush against Jed's genitals. Instantly Jed's hips moved upward and his penis stiffened against Tony's skull. Tony let his head fall back onto Jed's belly. Jed's eyes were already glazed with desire; he slipped two fingers into Tony's mouth and breathed hard as Tony swirled his tongue around them, then closed his lips over them and sucked. Jed leaned down, slowly pulled his fingers free, and put both hands on Tony's chest. His thumbs traced perfect circles around the hardening brown nipples.

Tony exhaled with pleasure. "Let's go back to our dressing room."

"I thought you said there were cots in the cooling room. That would be more comfortable, wouldn't it?" Jed said quietly.

"It's not private. It's for the exhibitionists, not us. We'll make our own comfort." He took Jed's hands and pulled him off the bench. "Come on. And take this beauty with you." He closed his fingers briefly around Jed's erect phallus.

Wrapped at the waist in damp towels, oblivious to everything but each other, they stumbled down the long hallway to their dressing room. They put their towels, one overlapping the other, over the bare bench.

"Lie down, on your back," Tony ordered in a low voice.

Jed did as he was told. Tony stood a moment and ravished Jed with his eyes, his breath coming fast and his own penis thickening and rising. He climbed onto the bench, straddled Jed at the hips. He bent down and kissed his way slowly from the tip of Jed's quivering cock to the tip of his aquiline nose. Then he stretched his legs and arms and settled himself over Jed like a human blanket.

At the simplest sensation of Tony's ardent breath on his cheek, Jed was lost to the world. He lay supine, awash in ecstasy, reveling in the weight of the protective, knowing body atop him. He stroked and caressed Tony greedily, exploring everywhere, possessing everything he found as Tony's hands took possession of him in turn. Their hearts pounded in rhythm through the flimsy divide of muscle, bone, and skin. The wet tip of Tony's tongue gently entered Jed's ear and brought forth from his open, waiting mouth a moan of the most luscious pain. The tongue withdrew, replaced by a whisper. *"I've never been with anyone like you, Jed. I've never felt anything like this before. I'm in love with you."* Jed didn't answer, just turned his head and sought out Tony's mouth. He knew it was true. He recognized Tony's love in every stark and unmasked glance from the boy's dark eyes. It was the look Jed longed to give to David, and did sometimes in utter secret, with all his adoration, covetousness, and thirst nakedly revealed. Jed would never look at Tony quite that way; he would never feel for Tony what he felt for David, at least not in his heart. But his body was something else entirely; David didn't want it, and so now it belonged to Tony. "*Jed, lift your legs.*" Jed did, arched his hips up off the bench, and let Tony take what was his.

Long minutes after they were done and Tony lay panting with his leg thrown over Jed's hip, Jed continued to shake with little convulsions and his heart still beat so hard that he thought the bench would collapse from it. With every tremor of his body, another tear fell from his half-closed eyes onto the towel. He loved this so desperately and he was so ashamed of himself for loving it. He lay loose limbed, nearly insensate, and looked blearily around the small, dimly lit room. He might have been an addict in an opium den for all the awareness or concern he'd had for his surroundings. Muffled noises and whispers floated into the air from the hallway.

He would have lain with Tony on a cot in a cooling room. He would have let Tony fuck him in full view of strangers and not cared who saw him. He was too far gone to care. But he should have cared. Cared very much who had come by on his night off for some quick fun and had been leaning against the hallway wall, his pants unbuttoned and his penis in some man's mouth, watching with wicked delight as Jed and Tony staggered down the hall toward their forbidden union.

The rest of the summer was so brutally hot that even a walk to the baths required more effort than they could muster. They languished away their weekly evenings in the darkened interior of Tony's room, the single window flung wide to catch whatever little breeze might be coming in off the Hudson River. Their bodies sweated and slid on each other, in and out of each other, as though they'd been greased. Jed had thought the heat would surely rob him of his energy and dull his passion. But it didn't. It engulfed him and infused him and made him wilder than ever. It made everything inside him open as wide as an ocean to take Tony in. Fleetingly, agonizingly, he realized this was what Abby yearned for from him, to feel him filling her up where she was empty. His sadness for her made him weep. When he was with Tony he wanted to never leave; he wanted to fuse himself to Tony's body forever. Every week, he had to forcibly extricate himself from the web spun from their coupling, and every week the web grew stronger and tighter and he had to struggle more and more desperately to free himself. He pictured the clock in his dining room, in the house where he lived his visible life, striking midnight. He threatened himself that if he was not there to hear it a cataclysmic upheaval would occur: like a blighted Cinderella at a ball held on the lowest level of hell, if he did not leave this magical realm in time, he would turn into a ravening beast who would devour and destroy everyone he loved.

Jed stayed later than he should have this night. He had fallen into a narcotic slumber that even his own fear could not pierce and probably would not have woken until morning if Tony hadn't roused him. He dragged himself up off the wet sheets. With the tepid water from the washbasin and a scratchy cloth he washed Tony off his skin. Then he dressed. With each piece of clothing he donned, he camouflaged himself so expertly that when he was done he resembled Joseph Edward Gates II, husband, father, scion, corporate executive, so uncannily that Tony wondered where his Jed had gone and if he would really return the following week. When he was done, no one could have known that as he stood upright and reserved by the foot of the bed saying good-bye, he was imagining himself ripping off his accursed clothes, crawling onto the bed on his hands and knees, and licking every glistening bead of sweat off Tony's naked, spread-eagled body. Or that as he walked out the door the devil on his shoulder was exhorting him to abandon everything and give in to his reckless, flaming desire to be with Tony constantly; to install him in a bachelor apartment hotel, steal an hour every night after work to be with him, sneak away on weekends, pretend they might live together one day.

Although it was nearly midnight, he sat for a few moments in a postcoital stupor in Washington Square Park as he always did until his pulse calmed and his wits gathered. He needed those transitional minutes to blunt the shock of returning to his house and to ensure that Abby would be protected from ever discovering him in an erotically charged state should she be awake when he walked in the door. There was, in fact, no chance of that ever happening. He never saw Abby when he came home. She made sure of it. They lived their life now as though a week was comprised of only six days. The seventh had no substance. It had become empty air, a joint deep inhalation and held breath. Decent people both, they honored their commitment to their mutual pretense: Abby pretended to believe that Jed spent one evening a week in restorative solitude at an unnamed businessmen's club. Jed pretended to believe that Abby believed his lie. She was always asleep when he got home, or at least abed with the door closed, and he made his bed in the downstairs guest room. He did not sleep well, beset as he was by guilt, but it was no worse than the other six nights when his hyperawareness of Abby's body and her repressed desire for him tortured him like snakes crawling on his skin. In the morning, they exhaled and everything returned to normal for another week.

Jed eased the door shut behind him. The clock in the dining room chimed the twelfth and final stroke of midnight and fell silent. Imperfect darkness spilled down the narrow staircase from the second floor of the carriage house, carrying with it the imagined sounds of his wife and son tossing in their sleep, gripped by bad dreams in which he was the causative figure. This was the worst time, coming home, his brain booming with guilt and fear, his body already hungering for Tony. From the moment he opened the front door until he fell asleep, Jed felt himself cleaved in two, his disparate parts rubbing each other raw.

He went into the parlor. On the small table there Abby had left the lamp burning and the day's mail for him to see. He picked up the small pile of envelopes and shuffled through it uninterestedly. All familiar and unimportant. Except for one. He turned it over in his hand and frowned with curiosity. His name and address were neatly typed in capital letters in the center of the envelope. There was no return address. He tore it open and removed a single sheet of paper folded around a grainy photograph.

My dear nephew,

Well, well. Imagine my surprise at seeing you at the Everard last month. I'm so sorry I didn't have the chance to chat with you and your pretty little friend, but my duties as night manager keep me rather busy of an evening. Your friend—Tony, isn't it?—seems a most lovable boy, with a very nice ass, if you like that sort of thing, which obviously you do, but somehow I doubt you'd want the family to know of your relationship with him. I can't imagine him and your mother getting along—can you?— although it might be interesting to bring them together and see what happened. We really should talk about that. And about what you think The Wall Street Journal *might make of the enclosed photo. Although now I think about it, the New York* Daily News *would probably find it much more useful. Why don't you come by the Everard one evening, sometime before the end of September would be advisable, and let's see what we can work out.*

Your loving uncle Monty

A black veil fell over Jed's sight, but not before he had seen the clumsily taken yet clear black-and-white image of himself and Tony kissing on the street outside Tony's rooming house. He went blind and deaf. The room spun. His bad leg collapsed under him and he was on the floor, shaking and whimpering like a dying animal. He tried to stand, but his leg wouldn't hold him. He commanded himself to not lie there like that. Abby might have heard him fall. She might come downstairs to see what had happened to him. He commanded himself to stop making those horrid noises and to move. With the letter and photo in his hand, he crawled across the hall into the kitchen. Grasping at the edge of the sink, he pulled himself up, keeping his weight on his left leg. He struck long wooden kitchen matches one after the other and burned the letter, envelope, and photo in the sink. He fought the urge to vomit but lost, as he had lost all his other battles. The contents of his stomach spewed from his mouth and chased the ashes down the drain. He hung over the sink for an eternity, eyes closed, throat burning, until he was sure he could move without falling or throwing up again. He splashed cold water on his face, made sure the sink was clean, and then walked carefully upstairs, past the closed door to the bedroom, into Henry's room.

He carried the rocking chair from the corner and placed it at the side of the crib. The lamplight was soft and dim, just enough to cover Henry in an ivory glow. Jed sat. He leaned his forehead against the top bar of the crib, wrapped his fingers around the vertical slats, and looked down between them at the sleeping baby. He could have been looking at himself at a year old, so exactly did Henry resemble him. He stared at Henry's perfect face and died inside to think that he might have passed on to his son the taint of his perversion along with his blond hair, blue eyes, and long limbs.

"Don't grow up to be like me." Jed began to rock. "Oh, please God, don't grow up to be like me."

He didn't know whom he was asking this favor of. He didn't know who or what he believed in anymore. His whole life was a delusion. How had he ever believed that he could balance his responsibilities with his desires, his darkness with his light? On each side of the scale there was a fatal flaw, a missing piece. When he prostituted himself to be what his mother and grandfather had raised him to be, he betrayed his father's legacy and his own calling to create beauty for an ugly world. When he secluded himself in his studio and painted things no one but his family ever saw, he denied his need to be recognized as a successful man. When he lay with Tony, he violated every moral belief he held and endangered the love, trust, and safety of his family. Within the purity of that sin, he sinned even more deeply: when he made love to Tony and dreamed of David, he was unfaithful to all the love being given him and to the love he had to give. And when he posed as a normal man he ripped his own heart to shreds.

The treads of the rocking chair creaked rhythmically against the uneven wooden floor. The sound went on and on and on. When the household exhaled the next morning, Jed was still in the chair, watching Henry.

51

On the evening Jed spent with Tony during the first week in September, Jed did not go home by midnight. When, at eleven thirty, Tony stirred and sighed and began to roll out of bed, Jed pulled him back down.

"I want to stay the night."

Tony didn't ask for an explanation. He merely ran his brown fingers through Jed's yellow hair. "You can stay forever. You know that."

"And you know that I can't." Jed closed his eyes.

The air coming in the open window was dry and cool. The heat wave had broken. As they drifted into unconsciousness, Tony shivered and pulled his thin blanket over them.

At four o'clock in the morning, a small miracle occurred: Jed awoke from a purely peaceful sleep sheltered in his lover's embrace. Missing were the fear and grinding tension that gripped him nightly in his own bed. Nearly unhinged by gratitude, he rolled delicately within Tony's arms and took Tony's quiescent member in his mouth. With every last speck of yet-untapped feeling in him, Jed slowly brought Tony out of a sound sleep to a shuddering climax. He didn't stop until he'd made Tony scream; then he painstakingly worked his way up the length of the heaving body.

"You make me so happy." Jed's bright eyes burned like blue flame in the dark room. "I love you."

In a reprise of the spontaneous passion of their first meeting, Jed grasped Tony's face between his hands and kissed him with wild abandon, Tony's hot, salty fluid mingling on their entangled tongues. And, as he had that first time, Jed saw the jolt of shock in the limpid brown eyes melt and yield to helplessness, to love.

"Jed." A choked cry.

"It's all right. It's all right," Jed murmured, and covered Tony's face with kisses. "Turn over. Let me hold you." He kissed the back of Tony's neck. "Go to sleep. I'm going to leave before it gets light."

Jed didn't sleep any more that night. He lay with Tony in his arms, listening to him breathe, inhaling the smell of him, warming himself with his heat, trying in vain to imprint Tony's deliriously loved shape onto his own skin. When the first glimmer of daylight appeared at the window, he rose off the bed like an evaporating mist. A minute later he was dressed and standing at the open door. He looked back at Tony, curled in sated sleep and unaware of his lover's leaving, and wondered how it was that his heart still beat.

At six o'clock on the following Friday evening, Jed let himself into David's house. He had left his friend at the office, where, Jed knew, he would remain for several more hours. In a few moments Jed would go home, help Abby pack up the car, and then he would chauffeur his wife and son to Hidden Cove for the weekend. By nine, David would be finished with work. He would come home, change his clothes, pick up Lucy and Brook, and drive out to join them. It would be late when the threesome got there. Abby and Henry would be asleep. Jed would be awake, lying stiffly in bed with his wife.

Jed walked slowly through the downstairs rooms: the parlor, the dining room, the music room, the kitchen, the pantry. He climbed the stairs; the bedrooms, the den, the library. Nothing remained of Cissy's fastidious and stylish interior decoration. Abby had helped David create a home for himself, one that suited his true nature. Now, the house looked to Jed like an extension of the wild, untamable David he had first seen on the enlistment line at the Armory, on that fateful day ten long years and a lifetime ago. Beautiful, earthy, and slightly messy, despite the signs of sophistication and wealth and the skills of a five-day-a-week housekeeper. Brown and cream walls; oversized sofas and chairs covered in caramel-colored velvet; dazzling Persian and Chinese Deco carpets over polished parquet floors; tables, dressers, sideboards, and desks of warm wood, granite, and marble. The pantry stocked, food in the stainless-steel and porcelain Frigidaire, dishes in the sink. Lalique glass panels, gilt-framed mirrors and paintings on the walls. A Steinway grand piano, sheet music strewn on the floor and bench. Everywhere a profusion of books and magazines. A black sweater crumpled carelessly on the floor at the side of the bed, where Jed stood in a shaft of waning daylight.

He shook himself as though from a dream, walked across the floor to the carved-walnut armoire along the west wall of David's bedroom. He pulled it open and found the garment bag with David's Brooks Brothers cashmere winter coat stored snugly inside. As Jed unbuttoned the bag, the smell of camphor rose into his nostrils. From the inside pocket of his linen suit jacket he removed a slim sealed envelope. Neatly scripted on the face of it in blue-black ink was David's name. Jed traced the curving letters with one slow finger. He slid the envelope into the left-hand outer pocket of David's coat, rebuttoned the garment bag, retraced his steps through the house, let himself out, relocked the door, and walked the two blocks home.

The sun was not yet over the horizon, but the sky was growing light. Through the window across from the bed, Jed beheld the ceiling of the world change from misty grey, to rosy pink, to the palest blue, paler and more perfect than any color that could ever be placed upon a canvas. He lay still and marveled. He had lain unsleeping all through the night. He had heard David, Lucy, and Brook arrive, later than he'd expected, and quickly go to their rooms. He had heard the crickets of autumn singing to one another in the thick lawn. He had heard owls hooting, bats swooping, and nocturnal mammals rustling in the woods. He had heard birds twittering and calling as the darkness faded, their cacophony swelling with the coming day.

He eased himself from under the sheet that was all the cover they'd needed during the mild night. Abby was turned on her side, her back to him, breathing evenly. The strap of her pink silk nightgown had slipped from her shoulder. He reached out and drew it up, watched it come to rest on the knob of her collarbone. He took his thin cotton robe from the hook on the back of the bedroom door and put it on, the belt loosely tied around his waist. He slid his feet into a pair of open-back slippers. Moving quietly, he went to Abby's side of the bed and squatted down in front of her. Her breath was warm and sweet, and when he kissed her on the temple her eyes opened in sleepy confusion.

"What time is it?" Her eyes wanted to flutter closed again; she was only acting at being awake.

"It's early," he whispered. "Go back to sleep. I'm going for a swim." He kissed her again. "Thank you for loving me, Abby."

But she was already asleep.

Jed sidled through the half-open door that connected their room to the small chamber where Henry slept. Henry lay on his back, the love-mangled paw of his teddy bear clutched in his hand. His blond hair was damp with baby sweat; the sonorous hum of his hungry baby breath filled the room. If he had awakened and opened his innocent baby eyes, he would have screamed with fright to see his father standing over his crib staring down at him with a look of soul-robbing intensity; he would have known, even in his infant's word-deaf ignorance, that his father was never going to look at him again. But mercifully, Henry didn't wake. He slept on in an unchanged world and didn't see his father leave the room and step into the hall.

The first rays of dawn lanced through the large octagonal stained-glass window at the hallway's far east end, bathing everything in a kaleidoscope of riotous color. The pale walls, the oaken floor, the white cotton of Jed's robe, all were surfaces for the world to paint its glory upon. The glorious end of the world. Jed floated lightly down the swirling corridor, letting his fingers brush against the walls, imagining he was dipping into melted jewels, dipping his stained fingers in smears of ruby, emerald, sapphire, topaz. Colors rich and hot. He was in the heart of a prism, turning and turning, colors washing all over him. He floated to the door to David's room and hovered there. He placed both palms against the thick wood and drew out David's magnetic hues, feeling them seep into him through his hands. Red fire, brown wood, black earth, golden sun, searing colors rousing him to hateful life, igniting the dead wick inside him. The burning wick that had to be extinguished.

He went down the stairs, left the spinning kaleidoscope world behind for the gently turning world outside. He picked his way across the wet lawn, his slippers quickly sodden and clinging to his cold feet. He came to the water's edge. The bay was calm; inviting little fingers lapped at the white sand. The sun was rising now. A delicate mist drifted up from the sheening pink-gold of the water's surface. Jed took off his robe and dropped it next to the discarded slippers. He stood for a moment dazzled by the light, then pulled off his pajamas and undershorts and left them on the sand. Naked, he walked into the water and kept walking until his feet could no longer touch bottom. Then he pushed off and swam out until there was nothing but water and sunlight all around him. He dove under several times, disturbing schools of minnows making their way toward the shallows. Each time he broke through the surface and stretched his arms above him, he tilted his face up to the sky and breathed deeply of the damp morning air.

He dove under again, knowing that this time he would not surface. He kicked down deep, his leg strong and obedient. With the indolent grace of a porpoise, he rolled onto his back and looked up. He smiled. All was stillness; nothing could find him here. He hung, suspended in liquid, awaiting the moment of his release. From one second to the next, the oddly pleasurable tightness in his chest gathered into a thunderous pressure and with it came an instinctive panic. But despite its urgency Jed knew it to be false. He had not come to this realm to continue struggling. Thoughts of Henry came to him as the pressure ballooned to fill his entire body. He closed his eyes to the unutterable beauty above him, to the golden sunlight streaking through clear, blue-green water, to all the things that would never be his. Jed opened his mouth and inhaled, let his lungs slowly fill with cool water. He began to sink as bubbles rose from his mouth and nose. Serenity enveloped him, a silken net woven of blue and green and gold. It was exquisite. More exhilarating than lying with Tony. More wonderful than kissing David. Terribly, more amazing even than his love for Henry. It was perfection, immutable and final. He fell silently through the unresisting water, arms spread wide, and as thoughts of life faded from his mind he realized, in awe, that after all of his sins, after even the most heinous sin he was committing by this very act, he was being allowed to die in peace. A beneficent warmth infused him; when his body settled onto the bay floor, he was no longer there to receive its sandy embrace.

David started awake once, just after dawn, as though from a bad dream. He couldn't capture the source of the disturbance and soon the dimness of his heavily curtained room soothed him back to sleep. He woke several hours later, groggy and uncomfortable in the stifling air, the sun well up and beating against the curtains. He stumbled to the bathroom, relieved the pressure in his bladder, splashed cold water on his face, and with wet hands attempted to reorder his untidy hair. He put on a pair of bathing trunks, drew on baggy cotton trousers and a white cotton shirt, left unbuttoned. He realized he had forgotten his slippers and so he left his room and went downstairs unshod. No one of the older, more decorous generation was here to glance at him askance.

It was quiet in the bedroom hallway; a faint rosy-gold glow filled the air and dyed the walls. All the doors were closed and there was no sign that anyone was yet awake. As he made his way down the stairs, however, the stimulating aroma of coffee wafted up to him, along with the lilting of Abby's voice and the disarming babble of Henry's meaningless utterances.

Abby looked up as David walked into the dining room, an engraved silver baby spoon full of cereal in her hand, poised in front of Henry's mouth. "Ah, the first sleepyhead arises."

"Good morning. Henry Henry Henry, why is there more cereal on your face than in your tummy?" David came over to the high chair, bent down, and licked playfully at his godson's cereal-crusted cheek. The baby grabbed at David's hair and screeched with delight. "Henry, you smell terrible," David said in the same teasing, adoring tone. The baby yanked hard at David's hair and screeched louder.

Abby snorted. "You may smell better, but you look worse."

David laughed and rubbed his eyes. "I can't seem to wake up. I'm going to go for a swim. Jed's still asleep?"

Abby glanced at the pendulum clock on the far wall. "Actually, no. He went out for a swim, too, hours ago. He must have fallen asleep on the float."

"I'll bring him back with me." He breathed in the smell of bacon coming from the kitchen. "We won't be long. Hunger calls."

David walked down to the beach. From a distance away he saw the faint disruption where Jed's discarded clothing broke the flat plane of the shore. As he came a little closer, he scanned the wooden float for the outline of a reclining body. There was nothing there; Jed must have gone for a walk. And yet David's heart began to race. He broke into a trot. At the water's edge he stood staring down at Jed's things, in particular at his undershorts, and at the footprints in the soft sand: one set only, leading into the water. None coming out. David peered out over the placid bay, and the vague unease he had woken with earlier burgeoned into a pure panic that grabbed him by the throat.

"Jed! Jed!" David yelled, his gaze darting about. He told himself to calm down, the footprints meant nothing. Jed could have emerged somewhere down the beach and walked into the woods. But David knew he hadn't; it was the undershorts, lying there indifferently, encrusted with sand, Jed's modesty abandoned.

Wild with fear, David tore his clothes off and ran into

the water. He raced to the float, kicking and stroking furiously, hauled himself onto it. He searched the horizon line as far as he could see in every direction for a long body floating on the surface. Nothing. Sky, water, both empty of anything save a few seagulls.

"Oh God. Oh my God." The words escaped him in a frantic, terrified whisper. He couldn't drag enough air into his lungs. He put his hands over his eyes and panted in near-hallucinatory hysteria. Then he gulped down a huge breath and dove off the raft. He barely knew what he was doing, but he dove over and over again, moving farther and farther away from the wooden float, from the shore, pushing himself deeper under the water the farther out he went. Finally, he saw it. A lumpen shadow on the bay bottom. An involuntary scream forced open his mouth and water filled it. He kicked up again, choking and sobbing.

He broke the surface thrashing. He shrieked, an endless, "No!" that ricocheted off the heavens and chased the gulls away. One more breath and he dove again, all the way down, until he reached Jed's lifeless form. He took one of Jed's arms and wound it around his own neck, holding fast to the limp hand. He slipped his other arm under Jed's back to raise him, then bent his knees and pushed with all his strength off the sand. The weight of Jed's body against his neck and shoulder threatened to carry them both to the bottom again, but David fought his way upward, inch by inch, scissoring his legs and flailing his free arm. Just when he thought his lungs would burst, his head came out of the water. He turned quickly onto his back, hooked Jed under the chin, and paddled with him to the shore.

David dragged Jed out of the water and laid him on the sand. He put his hands, one atop the other, over Jed's heart and reared up, positioning himself to pump his chest, but when he looked down into Jed's face he froze. Jed's eyes were open, staring sightlessly into David's; a fine film already shrouded their startling blue clarity. His lips were parted and tinged grey. Streams of clear liquid gushed from the sides of his mouth over his ghostly pallid skin. His thick blond hair was heavy and dark, saturated with water that now soaked into the sand beneath his head. He was dead. He'd been dead for hours.

David's eyes locked onto Jed's face as he knelt beside the body; he was immobilized with shock, like a bird that had flown headlong into a windowpane and plummeted like a stone to the ground. The earth turned and the sun rose higher in the sky and flowers opened to its light, but David could not move.

His gaze slowly traveled the length of Jed's naked body, his lean, ivory-toned, perfectly formed body, and came to rest on his right thigh, on the scars that covered the damaged nerves and muscles beneath the skin. David lowered one hand onto Jed's maimed leg. With his other arm he gathered Jed around the shoulders and lifted him slightly off the ground. He bent over until their cold foreheads touched, then whispered, "Why did you go out alone? Why couldn't you have waited for me?" At last he began to sob, bitter, bitter tears, as he rocked Jed in his arms. Wavelets of warm water tickled his feet. The hot sun bathed his back. He felt nothing. After an endless time, he heard the sound of someone approaching at a run and Brook collapsed at his side with a strangled cry.

David laid Jed down. It was the hardest thing he'd ever done. He forced himself to turn from the dead and acknowledge the living boy next to him. He put his arms around Brook, felt the boy crumple and cling to him with desperation, as though even the bay's puny waves might wash him out to sea. David hugged Brook tight, his ferocious grip annihilating any possibility of reserve or inhibition between them. They cried against each other's shoulders. Gradually, David was able to harness enough self-control to release Brook and pull away.

"Go back to the house." In response to the horrified look in the boy's eyes, David put a comforting hand on his cheek. "Do what I tell you. Find the gardener and send him to help me. Then go to the house and tell Abby to come." The comforting hand became a vise clamped tightly on Brook's shoulder. "Don't let her bring Henry."

Brook scrambled away and after another moment David was able to stand up without fearing that he would drop to the ground again. He retrieved Jed's cotton robe and care-fully covered the body with it as best he could. Then he stood by Jed and waited and prepared himself to do what had to be done. Whatever had to be done.

52

Joseph had called Hillman eight months before, after his talk with David about the ticket stub in Monty's closet. He respected David's feelings, but it had come as no surprise that the detective had been unable to find evidence that put Monty at Hidden Cove the day of Zoe's death. Yes, he had left the store early, but no one at the Oyster Bay station or at the house had seen any trace of him. On the other hand, the doorman of the building on Central Park West thought he had seen him that afternoon, remembered definitely that he'd been quite ill that entire week, but of course it was so long ago now and Mr. Glennon had often been home of an afternoon after Mrs. Glennon had moved out, so he couldn't be sure. There was no one left on earth who knew whether Monty had been abusive to Zoe. And the telltale stub that had no tale at all to tell had been discarded by David early on in a fit of rationality. No evidence, and no peep out of Monty since the letter to Cissy. Just the intu-itive blame of two strong-minded and frustrated men.

Not nearly enough, not for someone whose ruthlessness was balanced by a fierce personal integrity, as Joseph's had always been. His success, the influence he wielded, and the respect he enjoyed had all been earned as much by his hon-esty and ethics as by his piercing intellect and his willing-ness to work harder and longer than most other human beings. People had at times suffered as a result of his deci-sions, but those decisions were always made on the basis of facts and figures, never out of petty greed or because of personal likes or dislikes. Neither animosity nor sympathy compelled him. And so, with some reluctance, he had told

Hillman to go no further. Monty seemed to have finally disappeared. David was the only one with a secret, and he was too big a target; no one else in the family presented any kind of target at all. The detective, a man as ethical as Joseph, had concurred. But yesterday Joseph had set aside his deference to the real and tangible and called Hillman again.

From the recesses of the room where he now spent most of his life, Joseph held himself very still and listened to the sounds of Leonard Hillman's arrival. Joseph had to work harder and harder every day to maintain the integrity of his being, to be recognizable to himself and to others as the man who had long inhabited this failing body. Since a time soon after the optimistic occasion of his great-grandson's birthday—the last optimistic occasion Joseph expected to experience in what little time remained to him—he had begun to suffer a series of small seizures. They did not have any noticeable effect on his physical condition, poor though it was, but they played havoc with his mind. They released in him emotions he had never known he possessed and magnified others to a size his shrunken form could barely contain. For several months he had done heroic battle with the storms inside him, believing that he could best them and recover his iron-willed equilibrium. On the day he received the news that his twenty-eight-year-old grandson—whose presence, devotion, and future he had taken for granted and whom he had, like his daughter, unknowingly loved with all his heart and soul—had drowned in the warm, kind waters of Hidden Cove, leaving his promise unfulfilled and his son without a father, Joseph finally admitted that no recovery was possible.

And yet, over the course of the two months since Jed's death, the tenacious animal inside Joseph had found something to sink its claws into and keep it alive. Too many calamities had befallen his family with too little explanation, and now Joseph sniffed the same lingering spoor everywhere, too strongly to ignore. With an animal's atavistic hunger for survival and supremacy, Joseph had decided it was past time to go hunting. If he couldn't protect, at least he could avenge.

"Joe, Leonard Hillman is here."

Evelyn appeared at the side of his chair. She had not asked why the investigator was here again, but sooner or later she might. Joseph felt compelled to offer an allaying explanation. "I thought I'd try to get him to reconsider taking a position at the company. We still need a crack personnel manager and recruiter. David asked me to talk to him." The lie came easily. It could even have been the truth. He had offered Hillman a job more than once. "Evelyn." His voice clutched at her with greater strength than the hand with which he reached for her as she turned to go.

She caught his hand in hers, pressed it against her breast. "We'll all survive this, Joe. We must." Her voice broke, but she quickly collected herself. "And I'm going to insist that everyone be here for Thanksgiving. Life has to go on," she said, though it sounded more like a plea than a statement. She squeezed his hand. "I'm glad that you can focus on work and that you can still help David. I know it comforts you. Don't forget to thank Leonard for his card and the flowers."

Joseph knew that it comforted her to think of him applying himself to a problem of business. It would not have comforted her at all to know what he was actually going to ask Hillman to do. Joseph had been one of Leonard Hillman's first clients after he'd retired early from the New York City police force. The men had known each other a long time and Joseph trusted him. The investigations he had conducted for Joseph had all been in the corporate realm, straightforward information gathering, aboveground, in the light of day. What Joseph had asked of him eight months ago, what he was going to ask of him today, was different.

"Help yourself to some brandy if you want, then sit down. We can make this brief and to the point."

Hillman, used to Joseph's bluntness, declined the brandy and sat. "Tell me what I can do for you, Joseph. I didn't realize you were actively involved in company affairs again."

"I'm not. I want you to find out what my ex-son-in-law had to do with my grandson's death."

Leonard Hillman was not an easy man to shock, but Joseph had managed it. "What? Joseph, Jesus. We went that route with Zoe; there was nothing there. What possible connection could Monty have to Jed's drowning? Joe, the boy's injured leg failed him. What on earth could Monty have had to do with that?"

"That's what you will discover."

"Joe. The only thing we know for certain is that Monty played some hateful mischief with David and his wife." He shook his head. "It's been nearly a year since he disappeared. Joe, Jed drowned. It's understandable that you crave an explanation for why such a tragedy had to happen, but I don't think—"

"I'm not hiring you to think, Leonard."

"What are you hiring me to do, Joseph? Manufacture evidence that doesn't exist?"

Even with only one fully open eye, Joseph's glare could still silence the most confident of men. "Track him down. Find the shithole he's climbed into. Find out if there is any conceivable link between him and Jed. He's a vile snake and he's responsible; I know it. I want retribution for what has befallen my family." Joseph's voice rose, his calm rationality displaced by a strangling, impotent fury. His eyes began to leak and his head shook. Hillman politely looked away. Joseph took several deep breaths. "And I want you to do it without disturbing or talking to anyone in the family. Or revealing yourself to Monty."

Hillman looked back at him in total exasperation. "Joe, you're completely tying my hands. I really must advise against going ahead."

Fully composed again, Joseph stared at the investigator. "Is this the way you maintain your clients' loyalty, Leonard, by arguing with them? Don't you like to eat?"

At that, Hillman had to laugh. "Yes, I like to eat. And even though you are rude and cantankerous and delusional, I still like you. All right. Give me a few weeks. I'll see what I can find out. But don't expect anything and don't bite my head off when I come back empty-handed. You're clutching at straws, Joe; you're letting your grief and your hatred get tangled up together."

Joseph continued to stare at him. "If it's all the same to you, I'll keep my expectations intact for the moment. Did I offer you a brandy already? And by the way, thank you for your card and flowers. They were very much appreciated."

53

Sarah gathered her courage and headed for Henry Street instead of going straight home from work. Reuben would be at the factory for at least another hour or two; there was leftover *cholent* ready to be reheated for dinner. Sarah had time for a visit and Lucy always worked on Thursday evenings. She had no excuse not to go, only her own fear of being unwelcome stopping her. She had not seen Lucy for over two months, having last visited the settlement house in August. She wanted badly to believe that Lucy's warmth was genuine and not just a sympathetic professional veneer, but she couldn't be sure. It was obvious that Lucy was an educated, cultured woman from a well-to-do background. That she might find anything worthy of her affection in someone like Sarah, who had so little to offer, seemed unlikely. Even after a half-dozen encounters over the spring and summer, all initiated by Lucy, it was hard for Sarah to accept that Lucy might actually feel the same special kinship that Sarah felt for her. Lucy had drawn her out of despondency and given her the knowledge, tools, and support she needed to control her life in a way she had never thought possible. And she had done it with such care and generosity of spirit that Sarah had come to love her like a sister. And that was dangerous, because Sarah knew that you could lose sisters, just like you could lose mothers and brothers. A sister could die or disappear before you were old or wise enough to survive on your own.

Since August, weeks had gone by with no call, no message, no embarrassingly thrilling surprise of Lucy suddenly showing up at Leyrowitz's. But today, bursting with the wonderful, terrifying knowledge that she was newly pregnant, Sarah couldn't wait any longer for Lucy to contact her. Her desire to share her news finally overrode her insecurity. Despite her expectation of loss, Sarah's heart told her that Lucy would never abandon her; Lucy would never abandon any patient, and certainly not a friend.

There was no one manning the desk in the entry hall.

Sarah knew the way to Lucy's cubicle, but before she had taken two steps in that direction, someone appeared from out of a back room.

"Mr. Weiss!" Sarah recognized him immediately. At some point during every visit she had made here, he had materialized. Sarah was charmed by him, by the adorable lovesickness he clearly suffered over Lucy. He was very sweet and quite attractive, but Sarah didn't think that Lucy loved him, although they seemed more than friends.

He peered at her for a moment, then said, "Sarah, isn't it?" He beamed. "You look wonderful! How are you? We haven't seen you here for a while. Is everything all right?"

Sarah blushed. "I'm fine. I was looking for Lucy. Is she here?"

Jake's smile wilted. "No. She's not."

A hard knot formed in Sarah's stomach. "But she'll be here Sunday?"

"No. She may not be back for a while. Maybe not until the end of the year."

"Why? What's wrong? Oh, Mr. Weiss, please tell me she's all right."

"Please, Sarah, call me Jake," he said gently. "Lucy is fine; don't worry. But there was a death in her family. Her older brother drowned in September. They were very close. She needs to spend more time with her family now."

Sarah had never thought about Lucy having a family, although now she remembered seeing an older man with her on the street, that night in the rain. Perhaps that had been her father. But Sarah had had no idea that Lucy had an older brother. An older brother she loved and had now lost.

"If I speak with her, I'll tell her you were looking for her. That you're sorry for her loss. Shall I?" Jake asked, tactfully saying what Sarah could not find the words to express.

She nodded dumbly and, nodding still, backed away from him and, out the door. She walked home in a daze and sat at her kitchen table in the dark. Lucy had an older brother and she loved him and he died. The thought repeated itself over and over in her mind and then suddenly changed: Sarah had an older brother and she loved him and he died. Wrenching sobs tore at her. She pressed her hands against her belly. But her brother hadn't died. He lived. He lived and had seen her and sent her away. She had to pray to God to give her the strength to face him again. Because he could die, too. He could get hit by a car or catch pneumonia or be trapped in a burning building or be pushed onto the tracks of the El by a maniac . . . the world was so dangerous and he'd always been so reckless. He could die and if he did before he knew that she loved him, she would die, too.

54

There were no more eggs in the Frigidaire, no milk for his tea. There was no more bread in the pantry drawer. David stood, half paralyzed, in the middle of his kitchen. He could no longer bear the devastating loneliness that had been his constant companion since Jed died.

It was early on Thanksgiving morning and David was alone in his vast, echoing house. The family was gathering at Joseph and Evelyn's for dinner later that night; there would be no pretense at thankfulness, but at least they would be together. David just needed a way to get through the day. He had spent much of his time these past months at the brownstone on Gramercy Park or the apartment on Fifth Avenue or, more recently, the carriage house around the corner, now that Abby was ready to try living there without Jed, but he didn't think he could face any of those difficult places this morning.

It was unsettling being alone with Abby. A tension that he knew must not be eased had risen between them. David once again felt her looking to him for the answer to the unanswerable question of why Jed hadn't been able to love her in bed. She and David cared for each other, and she was desirable, and the need for physical comfort had always been strong in him; he knew how easily they might fall into each other without thought or real love, how their friendship and his relationship with Henry could change forever if they did. The tension would dissipate in time along with the grief and confusion; for now it was best to avoid temptation.

Being alone with Joseph and Evelyn was so sad it made David want to lie down, close his eyes, and go to sleep forever. They were outliving their children and grandchildren and now the imminence of Joseph's own death seemed to haunt their apartment.

It was most comforting, oddly, to be with Philip and Sally and Brook, whose grief, though terrible, did not reach out for him. So he thought, briefly, of going to Gramercy Park. But he remembered that there was a Thanksgiving service at Sally's church and Lucy, who had as yet been unable to move back to her own apartment and would certainly not be going to church with them, would be home by herself. And being alone with Lucy was torture.

He needed to get out of the house and find something to eat. He needed to stop thinking about how stupid he had been to believe that money could buy the safety of the people one loved. He needed to stop thinking about Jed and about why he felt responsible for what had happened to him, why he felt responsible for the fate of everyone whom he had ever loved or who had loved him. It was a responsibility he didn't want to own but had never figured out how to unload. So he punished himself with guilt and loneliness.

The Automat. Coffee. Eggs. Toast. Chocolate cupcakes, in mute honor of Jed. But no thinking of any kind. No redheaded waitress, either; no stranger masquerading as a lover. David grabbed his sweater from the back of a kitchen chair, he opened the front door, and was immediately knocked back inside by the arctic chill that had descended over the city during the night.

He slammed the door shut and sprinted upstairs to his bedroom for his cashmere coat. Even in his unhappy state, he took pleasure in slipping on the coat for the first wearing of the season. It meant that the clean, cold weather of winter had arrived. As he ran back downstairs, he felt a stiffness in the supple fabric, on the left side. At the bottom of the stairs he stopped and put his hand in the pocket. He didn't remember leaving anything there when he'd packed the coat away in the spring. He pulled out the envelope and his blood turned to ice when he saw his name written in Jed's hand across the vellum. His stomach twisted as he forced himself to slit open the envelope and extract two sheets of paper covered with Jed's meticulous writing. The grandfather clock in the parlor chimed, nine times, and that was how long it took David, the elapse of nine slow, deep chimes, to unfold the paper, step into the light coming through the window by the front door, and bring his eyes to focus upon the first page. Against his will, he read:

My dearest David,

So it is winter again and today you are wearing your favorite cashmere coat for the first time. I can see you in it, so elegant and handsome. I hope it has been long enough since I died. That you are ready for confirmation of what, in your deepest heart, you must already know. My death was not an accident. Please try not to be upset, because what I did was the best and only thing I could do. Monty, my uncle who once I thought I loved, stumbled upon my shameful secret and threatened to expose me to the family, to the world. I could not ever let that happen. But I need you, and only you, to know the truth.

I am a sexual degenerate, a queer. And though I tried, I was too weak to conquer my unnatural desires. In the last months I succumbed to the hellish fever of a relationship with a young man named Tony DeMarco. And it was in the depths of that exquisite hell that Monty found me. You understand that I could not risk him following through on his threat. Nor could I trust that he wouldn't expose me one day out of malice, no matter what I gave him to keep silent. David, I know you will want to, but don't blame Monty overmuch. He can't help what he is any more than I can. Even without his assistance, I would have come to this end eventually. I could not have gone on forever living such a horribly fragmented existence. Monty brought me to the inevitable sooner than I might have wished, yet it is almost a relief to have it over.

Since the first moment I became aware of myself in this world, I have been a coward and a fraud. There is no aspect of my life that I have lived honestly or with my full, willing participation. The only things in my life that are not a lie are my love for Henry and my love for you. Now that I am safely beyond any possibility of your contempt or rejection I have the courage to tell you that it is you I have loved and desired more than any other person. I have loved you with unfailing passion since the day we met, and I used whatever means necessary to keep you close to me, believing that I was helping you achieve your heart's desires when really I was selfishly pursuing my own.

I never saved your life, David. That was another lie. But you have saved mine countless times without ever knowing that it was your friendship, your strength, your love—which I realize now I have always had—pulling me forward. You owe me nothing, but I know you will never believe that and so, selfish to the end, I am going to ask more of you.

Please, do everything you can to make sure my family never learns the truth about me, about what I was or what I did. Take care of Abby and Henry. Live honestly, know what your heart wants, and be good to the people you love. Promise me that you will be happy, for I couldn't bear to think of you otherwise. Above all, forgive me.

The letter fluttered to the floor. David tremored with chill inside the warmth of his coat. His stomach was attempting to devour itself. He needed to get something to eat. He didn't need to deal with this now. He would deal with it later. He was all right; he was fine. He pushed at the letter with the toe of his shoe as though it were harboring a venomous snake, his movement careful and slow. He pushed it away and left it on the floor, a dead-white patch on the glowing brown wood. He walked calmly out the door and locked it behind him. He crossed the stoop. As he put out a foot at the top of the steep stone stairs, his body failed him utterly. His head swam; dark spots appeared before his eyes. His knees buckled and he fell, an instinctive grab at the wrought-iron railing all that prevented him from tumbling to the sidewalk. He crawled back to the door, fumbled it open, crawled inside, pushed it closed with his shoulder, and then could go no farther. He lay curled, tangled in his coat, blood roaring in his ears, arms wound around his head. After an eternity, he managed to drag himself to the wall. He propped himself against it with his knees drawn up to his chest and his arms wrapped around his shins. The plaster was solid and unforgiving beneath his skull, and he methodically and repeatedly banged his head against the wall until the black spots coalesced into one huge black mass and his brain emptied. His forehead fell onto his knees and he wept as he had not wept even when Jed's body lay cold and stiff in his arms. He wept as he had not wept since that long-ago day in France when Captain Hummel's kindness had forced him to face Anna's death and the agony of it had bludgeoned him to the ground.

The clock chimed ten. His forehead still rested on his knees, but his tears had stopped. He raised his head and stared at the letter. The words Jed had written echoed in his mind in Jed's voice, frightened and without hope. At some point, he would read the letter again, though he didn't need to. Anguish consumed him. All these years he thought he had been a good friend to Jed, but now he knew he was mistaken. Somehow, he had done something horribly wrong. Otherwise, why would Jed not have known that he could have trusted David with any truth, with his life? David was overtaken by the conviction that if he sat there, alone, for another second he would lose his mind. He mopped at his eyes and face with the sleeve of his coat, ran his fingers through his hair. He got up. He retrieved the letter and folded it into a small square, buried it in his coat pocket. He left the house and this time made it down the stairs and onto the street. He turned east and began to walk, letting Jed's excoriating confession chart his course.

When the knock came at the door, Lucy ignored it. Although she still needed to be in her childhood home, close to her parents and surviving brother, she cherished her hours alone when Sally dragged the others to church or to Jed's grave. She refused to accompany them and, for once, Sally did not admonish her. The shocking, relentless pain of Jed's death scored them all equally. They shared their agony but left one another alone to mourn as they needed.

She sat on a sofa by the parlor fireplace, staying warm in a skirt and sweater of fine merino wool the color of rich Burgundy wine, a dark-green cotton shawl thrown over her bare legs and feet. A second knock came. It could only be another well-meaning, caring, intrusive Park neighbor at the door, coming with yet more flowers or another cake. She mouthed a silent, *Go away, go away, go away,* and didn't move.

A hard banging on the door. "Lucy? Lucy? Are you there?"

She leaped up, David's voice like a hot wire running through her limbs. She tripped on the shawl, banged her ankle against the leg of the couch. She skittered to the door.

"David!"

His brilliant cat's eyes were dulled, red rimmed, and swollen. He looked as though he'd been beaten, though there wasn't a mark on him. He stood at the threshold, succeeding at looking at her and away from her at the same time.

"You look terrible. Come in; don't stand out there in the cold." She backed away and let him walk past her, through the narrow vestibule into the parlor.

"I couldn't . . . I—" He stopped and, with an enormous effort, inhaled. His left hand seemed to be trapped in his coat pocket. With a wincing exhalation, he drew it out and let his empty fist fall open. "I just didn't want to be alone. I've been thinking about Jed all morning."

"Me, too."

He seemed not to hear her. She could see his restless mind working behind his eyes, behind the rigid mask of his face.

"David, take off your coat. Sit down."

He let his coat fall onto a chair but remained standing.

"Lucy, there's something wrong with me. I suddenly feel as though I don't know anything, I've misunderstood everything important. Why didn't I help him?"

"What are you talking about? You were a wonderful friend to him, always."

"No, I wasn't. If I had been . . ." His agitation was fearsome, and yet he looked and sounded drugged. "Oh God, I can't stand it. I'm every horrible, selfish thing you have ever accused me of being. I can't stand myself. I don't know who I am anymore." An uprising of tears threatened, and he sank into a chair and buried his face in his hands.

Lucy was terrified. He had come here, to her, knowing she'd be by herself. He was in pain, he didn't want to be alone, and he'd come to her. She could help him; she could give him everything he would ever need, if he would just give her a sign she could be absolutely sure of. The opening through which she could finally show herself.

"David, why are you here?" As soon as the words left her lips, she knew it was the wrong thing to say; he would misunderstand, think she was chastising him for some mistake only she could see.

His hands came away from his face. He looked like a lost boy. "I don't know. Lucy . . . I'm sorry. I'll be all right. You don't need this. I'll leave." He fumbled for his coat and rose.

She screamed, "No!" She clapped a hand to her mouth, let it drop away. "No." Now a whisper. "I don't want you to leave. David. Look at me."

He did, and she saw on his exposed face, in his moist eyes, all the emotions she had so furiously wanted to see him tortured by and had foolishly convinced herself that he was incapable of feeling: pain, doubt, need, remorse, fear, helplessness, love, and sorrow. She had long awaited the thrill this moment would bring, but the sight of his suffering brought her no joy, no satisfaction. It was devastating. She felt as if her heart was about to shatter.

She knew that this was her one and final chance. Her father's long-ago words reverberated in her head. *What are you going to do about David? . . . If you can't tell him that you love him, there is no hope for you.* She needed courage and she stood there a coward, afraid to lose even the tenuous, dishonest connection she had with him. . . . *there is no hope for you.* She realized that she had nothing to lose because she had nothing. And so she stepped off the edge of the high cliff, nothing but empty air beneath her, life or death awaiting her below, an eternity of loneliness pushing at her back.

"David," she whispered. "I know who you are. I know everything that you are. And I love you."

He looked at her with clouded eyes, a man trying to wake from a dream. "No, you don't. You think I'm a monster. You've told me so so often and you're right."

"I lied. I wanted to hurt you for not understanding how frightened I was of you, for not loving me when I loved you so desperately."

"I don't understand." His voice was crazed with bewilderment and disbelief. "You don't love me; you couldn't."

"But I do. I love you. I have never loved anyone but you."

She tumbled off the precipice and fell and fell and fell as she waited for his answer, waited for him to catch her before she hit the rocky floor below and broke into a million pieces. But he said nothing. Just stood there, immobile and mute, his dulled eyes on her.

Philip had been wrong. She wasn't the one he needed. She wasn't the one in whose eyes he wanted to see himself. He didn't love her. The rocky floor swooped up to meet her. She began to cry, standing there before him, her tears falling uncontrollably.

"Lucy. Don't. Please, don't cry." He came toward her. "I need you. I need you to help me. I need you to forgive me." He touched her cheek, drew his finger slowly through the wetness glistening there, let his hand fall away.

Her heart beat against the wall of her chest like an animal throwing itself against the bars of a cage. "You don't have to be forgiven, not for anything. David, please. Don't leave me like this."

The banked fire in his eyes flared to life as he looked at her, really looked at her for the first time since setting foot in the house. "No. I've done that too many times. To too many people." His hands came up and he buried his fingers in the thick fall of her hair. "Never again. And never, never to you." He pushed her hair back from her face and gazed at her as though planning to devour her. "I love you. I have loved you since the moment Jed gave me that photograph you sent for me. I carried it with me all through the war and I swear it kept me alive. The thought of you kept me alive." His voice shook as he finally uttered the words, the dangerous, liberating truth he could no longer deny. "I love you." He tilted her face up to him. "Lucy, do you hear me? I love you. Only you, ever in my entire life."

He bent his head and kissed her softly, his lips barely brushing hers.

"David, why did we do this to each other? Why did we waste so much time?"

"It doesn't matter. We'll make it up. We'll make it all up, now, today."

A wild pulse beat in the space between his collarbones, in the perfect hollow of his throat where she had dreamed of burying herself since the first day she had ever seen him. She leaned toward him until her lips touched that perfect place and at the moment her mouth made contact with his skin she turned to liquid, every sharp edge and angle and pointed corner inside her melting down to smoothness, running in a torrent to pool between her legs. Her knees went weak and she fell against him.

He gathered her in his arms and lifted her off the floor. She flung her arms around his neck and clung to him as he carried her up the stairs, along the dark and silent hallway, to her old bedroom. She wasn't aware of anything but him. The energy that ran through him without surcease flowed like a river beneath her, taking her where he wanted her to go. To her bed, where he laid her down and held her in his arms, his eyes drinking her in.

She wanted to tell him of the rapture that was rising inside her, the rapture that was her love for him. But she had no more words. Her arms tightened around his neck. His hands came away from around her back and the absence of his touch was a cold stab in her heart. Her gasp of pain filled the small space between them. Then his hands were on her face; his thumb lingered lightly on her lips and her mouth opened, wanting to take him in. But his hands kept moving, to her throat, her neck, her shoulders. When she felt him at the curve of her breasts, she moaned. The thrill of his touch washed through her body, riding the wave of her pounding blood. He kept moving, deliberate and searching, his hand resting for a moment over her heart, feeling its heavy beat, and then sweeping slowly down across her ribs. Then lower, the flat of his hand on her stomach. With slow, circular motions he traced the contours of the soft, vulnerable center of her, between her rib cage and her mound. A gesture of such intense possessiveness that Lucy began to cry anew, silently, her tears bubbling up from deep beneath the very spot he touched. David's hand inched ever downward, came to rest on the high mound of her sex, and molded itself to the shape of her and held her there, and she cried out as her hips came off the bed to press against him.

Lucy's lids fell over her eyes; were she to die at this very moment she would die in ecstasy. She heard David say her name and her eyes opened, immediately captured by his. Their eyes locked, green into gold. Lucy put a hand on his face and felt the beauty of him under her fingers. She moved her body until she felt him everywhere against her; she drew him down to her and opened her mouth to him. This time he came to her and everything that ever existed before was swept away; all that remained in the world was the two of them.

Lucy watched David sleep. She had seen him asleep many times, on the beach at Hidden Cove, on a couch in Jed's house, but never before had she seen him at rest. Always before, true repose eluded him. At moments of even the deepest sleep, his mind and body struggled against his own unconsciousness. He was impatient to wake up, to open his eyes to the world, inhale his surroundings, move. There was no struggle visible in him now. He lay on his back, sunk into the bed like an ages-old rock half-buried in the earth. One arm was crooked over his head and the other reached out to her where she sat, cross-legged and hypnotized, on the bed beside him. His fingers fetched up against her shin. His face was turned toward her; serenity blanketed his features. He looked as vulnerable as a child. The bedcovers were pushed down to his waist and she could see the minute movement of his stomach as he breathed, slowly and silently. Every other part of him, even the searching eyes behind their lids, was immobile. He was at peace.

Lucy watched David sleep. Her mind could barely accept the reality of him lying in front of her. His skin glowed in the oblique rays of afternoon sunlight slanting low from west to east, searching him out through the south-facing windows of his bedroom. Not wanting to be found by Philip and Sally and Brook, not wanting to be found by anyone, they had retreated to David's house. Had hastily dressed, crept down the stairs, out the door, through Philip's dying garden, taken a cab to Washington Square. Twenty torturous minutes not touching. Barely through his front door they had turned on each other, tearing at each other's clothes, leaving discarded layers wherever they fell, a line of crumbs from entry to bed to help them make their way back to the world if ever they found the will to rise from the bliss they had fallen into. They had been making love for hours, the heat of each explosive ending gradually subsiding to fuel the next beginning. Her entire body ached, her lips were swollen, she was sore and battered, and as she sat and looked at him she felt herself grow wet and wanted him inside her again. She stretched out a hand to touch him and hesitated. She so wanted to let him remain in this state of tranquillity and obliviousness, as though if he stayed there long enough he could make up for a lifetime of deprivation. And so she caressed him without contact, her eyes closed, her hand hovering an inch above his skin, feeling the shape of him in the solid warmth radiating from his flesh. Cautiously, she curled up against his side, coiled both her arms around his, and fell asleep.

David bolted awake, his heart hammering with dread, his peace withering to grief in the aftermath of his nightmare.

He had dreamed again of that horrific moment when he had looked down into Jed's face and known that he had lost his best friend forever. He squeezed his eyes shut, brought his arm down to cover his face, tried to press from his mind the image of Jed lying on the warm, tawny sand, grey-lipped and glassy-eyed. A new surge of guilt rolled through him. He opened his eyes and stared up through the dimness at the ceiling. The last vestige of daylight stained the room with gold. He concentrated on the motes of dust floating in the weakening rays, tried in vain to calm himself. The image wouldn't leave him.

Lucy was next to him, warm and still, holding his arm, anchoring him to her. He turned onto his side, ran his hand along her back, buried his face in her neck, breathed in her scent, felt her pulse throbbing against his lips. She stirred and, still groggy, sighed out his name. His mouth at her ear, he whispered, "Wrap yourself around me." Not fully awake, she loosely twined her arms and legs around him. He whispered again, "Tighter." She tightened her grip. "Tighter." Urgency and pain in his voice. Where her body touched his, he was warm. Everywhere else, an unfamiliar cold assaulted his skin. He wanted to cry but didn't. Not anymore, not in front of her. A small shift of his body and he was deep inside her and she held him tightly there as well. She began to move under him, but he stopped her, using his weight to press her down. He kept them there, merged and unmoving, for an eternity, forcing an awareness of each other's bodies that was almost intolerable. He wanted to burrow beneath her skin, to open his veins and have his blood flow into her and course through her body, to dissolve inside her. When he could no longer stand the waiting and the fear that no matter how fully and tightly she enveloped him he would never be close enough to her, he whispered once more into her ear, "I love you," then he released them to slowly, slowly tumble again into the abyss.

David stood at the window, naked, his back to the room, silhouetted by the cold, eerie light of the wavering gas street lamp outside his house. The blackness of a dense winter night had stolen over the city while they'd loved and slept the day away. Lucy rose from the rumpled nest of sheets. In the near-total darkness, she padded to the bureau and lit four of the large candles arrayed there. She left two where they were, set one on the table by the bed, and carried the last to the window, placing it on the wide sill before coming to stand behind him. Pools and tendrils of flickering yellow light pushed back the shadows. The candle on the windowsill burned brightest, reflecting off the glass, illuminating the right side of David's body. In the candle's glow, the network of shrapnel scars, white and squirmy like a mass of worms, looked nearly a thing of beauty: a chorus of white snowflakes dancing on a pale brown background. A terrible flaw on his otherwise flawless skin, writhing along his hip bone and waist, down the outside of his thigh. During the past hours, Lucy had explored the complex pattern with her hands and her tongue, yearning for the power to heal him, wanting to kiss and stroke away all the damage he'd ever suffered. Now she put her right hand on his leg, feeling the unnatural smoothness of the scars beneath her palm. She leaned into his back, pressed her lips between his shoulder blades.

David put his hand over hers and held it still against his marred flesh.

"You're so cold. How long have you been standing here like this, while I slept?" She spoke into his skin, her voice soft and muffled.

"Awhile. I didn't want to wake you. I needed to think."

Something sharp in his voice pierced cleanly through the heavy fog of satiation and happiness that enveloped her. Suddenly she remembered the terrible state David had been in when he'd arrived at her door. "What did you need to think about?"

"This." David held something in his left hand. He turned and offered it to her. "I need you to read this. I'm sorry, Lucy, but I can't handle it by myself. I thought I could, but I can't. I need help."

She took the folded papers, elated at the surrender of his strength to her love but frightened of what could have caused such a capitulation, so antithetical to his pride and fierce independence. She unfolded the paper, and immediately recognized Jed's handwriting. A chill settled into her limbs, which, just a moment before, had been so warm and languid. She moved closer to the candle's light. David stepped behind her, held her lightly around the waist as though ready to catch her if she faltered. She read; a string of quivering cries served as punctuation. When she was done, she refolded the pages into the same square that David had made of them and placed it on the windowsill. David's arms tightened around her.

"Oh. My poor brother," she moaned. "My poor brother. That he should have hated himself so much." She covered her mouth with her hands. Sobs shook her small frame.

David turned her in his arms and held her. "Lucy, forgive me. And I hope Jed can forgive me. He asked me to keep his secret. But I can't do it. It's too hard and it isn't right." He stroked her hair, then put his hand under her chin and forced her to look at him. "He asked me to be honest and happy and how can I do that if I keep this from you? Not just his secret but what knowing it means to me? I don't want to live that way with you. It's too lonely."

She shook her head. "No. I want your secrets. I don't want you to ever hide your feelings from me. You're not alone anymore, David. I'm with you now. You were right to show me Jed's letter. We will find a way to bear this, together." She began to sob again and leaned heavily against him.

"You may have to bear it for both of us, because I don't know if I can." He bent to kiss her, and their lips trembled as they touched. "Lucy, why didn't he tell me he was a homosexual? He knew I had no problem with any man's sexual preferences."

"Jed wasn't any man, David. He was your best friend, your closest friend."

"Then why didn't he trust me enough to tell me the truth?"

"Oh my God, how can you ask that? Because he was in love with you! If he had told you he was a homosexual, you would have known that he loved you that way. You would have seen it. How could he trust that that knowledge would not destroy your friendship? It took me nine years to tell you I loved you. Jed would never have been able to tell you, never. But why didn't he trust *me*?" she cried. "I was his rebellious terror of a sister. He had to know I would love him no matter! There are homosexuals in my neighborhood. There are some in my building, I know them; I like them. I've treated homosexual men at Henry Street." She took a deep breath, striving for calm. "There are men who look normal and live normal lives, but the signs of the conflict are there if you look closely enough. I knew he and Abby had terrible problems. Why didn't I see the truth?"

"Because he was your brother and you weren't looking. No one was looking."

"No," she whispered, "I wasn't looking. My beautiful brother. He wanted me to believe he was happy, even though I knew he wasn't, so I didn't look. This is so horrible, so sad. But it makes so much sense; it explains everything, everything I've felt about him all my life. I'm glad to know who he really was," she said fervidly. "I am. I'm glad."

"Then I'm glad for you." He picked his undershirt off the floor and wiped her wet face with it. "You think that I wouldn't have loved him, too, no matter what?"

She took his hands in hers. "David, I know you would have loved him no matter what. But working side by side every day, spending evenings and weekends together . . . if you'd been aware all the time that he wanted *this* with you, the kind of love we have now, would it have been possible for things to stay the same?"

David shuddered as he asked himself the same questions. Would their ten-year friendship have been poisoned by the tension that would surely be constant between them, a million times deadlier than the transient discomfort he felt now with Abby, for it would have been real and never-ending? Would his love for Jed have been enough to overcome David's despair at knowing that he was disappointing the one person he believed he could and would never disappoint? Worse, what if Lucy was wrong? What if he couldn't hold on to his love for Jed once he knew that Jed had been lying to him for ten years? Once his belief that Jed had been the one person who had never wanted anything from him that he couldn't give was revealed as another lie, nothing but an illusion? Once Jed himself, the one friend David had ever allowed himself to have, was revealed to be an illusion?

Would it have been possible for things to stay the same? He wanted to answer, *Yes. Our friendship would not have eroded. I would not have let it.* He wanted it to be true. He needed it to be true. He had relied on their perfect friendship for too long for his heart to do without it. And so he said what they both needed to hear: "Yes. It would have been possible. I loved him. I would have protected him. He should have trusted me."

"I'm so happy you feel that way, David. But we shouldn't blame ourselves that he couldn't confide in us. The problem wasn't with you or with me; it was something in Jed. You and I, we believe in the right to our lives. But Jed didn't. You know that. You know it was his weakness, his fatal flaw, that he didn't believe in himself."

David firmly put aside his doubts. He would have loved Jed, no matter what, and everything would have been fine. Lucy was always right about him; she had to be right about this, too. He would have loved Jed. "How did you get to be so smart?"

"I was born that way. And you're a smart man to recognize it," she said in quiet jest, trying to lead them back to each other. "I love you." She put her arms around his back and held him close. "At least Jed found his own way to peace. Let's try to be happy for that and try to find our own peace in accepting the choices he made." She felt him relax, then suddenly go rigid in her arms. She stepped back and looked at his utterly changed face.

"Monty. I want to kill him." David's voice was made brutish and ugly by the depth of his hatred. In sudden fear for him, Lucy put a steadying hand over his heart.

"I understand how you feel. But you aren't like him. You could never hurt anyone like that. You could never kill anyone; you know that."

"Really?" He took her hand and dragged it down over his hip and leg. "Have you forgotten where I got this? I've killed people, Lucy, men I didn't know and had no personal reason to hate. I don't even know how many I killed, and it wasn't that hard. I was trained for it and I was good at it. Rifle, bayonet, a rock, my bare hands, whatever it took. What makes you think I couldn't do it again?"

"That was war, David. Listen to yourself, the horror in your own voice. You were expected to kill and you were in danger every day of being killed. This is different. You could never kill anyone in cold blood."

He started to shake. "I want to put my hands around the throat of that piece of filth and stare into his eyes while I strangle him to death. I should have done it the last time."

Lucy's stomach gave another fearful lurch. "What last time?"

"Oh, shit," he moaned. "Why did I say that?"

"Because you want to tell me. What last time?"

He lifted her hand to his mouth and kissed the inside of her wrist. "There is no proof, but I'm convinced that he killed Zoe, especially now, knowing what he did to Jed." He told her everything, told her about the letter Monty had written to Cissy, and then said, "He should be dead, your charming, loving, sociopathic monster of an uncle. Zoe and Jed should be alive and he should be dead."

Lucy was silent for a long time. "Yes," she said finally. "That's the way it should be. But it's not. And nothing can change that. Killing him won't set it right, David. It won't liberate you. It will only drag you down. It will kill you, too. And me."

David ceased trying to hold back his tears. "Then tell me, what the hell am I going to do? I have to do something."

Lucy put her arms around him again. "David. David. You're freezing."

She half-pushed him until he was sitting on the bed. She grabbed a fallen blanket off the floor and draped it around his shoulders, arranged it over his bare legs. She knelt on the floor in front of him, her hands on his swathed thighs.

"Jed asked you to protect him and protect the family. And he asked you to know yourself and to be happy."

David nodded.

"Then that's what you'll do. That's what you're already doing. You're honoring his requests according to what *you* know is right. Take some time to think about Jed, about what he really meant and wanted, David, and you'll know what to do." She reached up a hand and wiped the wetness off his face. Her eyes searched his and she said, "Try to put it all out of your mind for now. It will come clear to you; I promise."

"There's something that is already clear to me. Jed asked me to take care of Abby; but keeping this from her won't do that. She doesn't need to know how Jed felt about me, but she does need to know that it wasn't her fault that Jed didn't want her. It's going to be horrible, but I have to tell her. But no one else."

Without hesitation Lucy said, "Yes, I agree." She glanced toward his armoire. "It's cold. Can I have something warm of yours to wear?"

"No. Come here. I'll keep you warm." David held open the blanket and she instantly straddled his thighs, put her legs around his waist and her arms around his neck. He closed the blanket around her back, tenting them together in a cocoon of buttery wool. They kissed, a rain of soft kisses falling onto each other's lips.

Lucy gently ran her fingers through his hair. "Jed would have been so happy for us. He loved us both so much." She caressed the back of his neck.

"Do you think he loved that young man? Why did he tell me his name? Why do I need to know that?"

"I don't know," she said, surprised at the question but not at the anguish in his voice.

"Why? Does he want me to go find him, that . . . Tony? To explain . . . ? What if Jed just left and never said good-bye, never told him he wasn't coming back?" He groaned and pulled the blanket more snugly around them. "I can't think about Tony. I can't think about Monty. I just want to think about us. I want you to come live with me, right now. I want to marry you."

"As long as we're together, we can work everything out. You'll see."

David let go of the blanket and cradled her face in his hands. "You are so beautiful. And so brave. I want to believe you, that we can do anything."

She smiled at him. "Well, very soon we're supposed to be at my grandparents' for dinner. Do you think we can do that?"

David laughed. "I don't know. It won't be easy."

"I'll tell you one thing I won't be able to do. I won't be able to keep my hands off you."

"I'm offended that you would even want to," he said. "I don't intend to try. I'd be dooming myself to abject failure."

Lucy sighed. "We're going to make fools of ourselves in front of the family."

"Yes." David nuzzled at her throat. "We're going to make fools of ourselves. Happy fools. I think everyone but us knew we were meant for one another. They're going to know what's happened the moment we walk in the door. There's no shame in it, Lucy; let them see."

Lucy closed her eyes for a moment, as if the sight of him were more than she could bear. She leaned her forehead against his chest, then brought her mouth up for a kiss. "I adore you. David. Make love to me, one more time; then maybe I'll be ready to face the world again."

"We're going to be late," he warned. "And you know how your grandmother feels about people being late." But he slid carefully to the floor with her in his arms, the blanket falling beneath them, and faithfully did as she asked.

55

David had been right. They had all been rescued from an oppressive Thanksgiving dinner by the infectious happiness that burst upon them the moment David and Lucy arrived, quite late, arm in arm, unable to hide, even for a decorous second, the wild joy of their love. As soon as Evelyn saw them, her admonishment for their tardiness died on her lips. The world had spun again, and where there had been a void there was now a promise. And with that small alteration the family was given at least one thing to be thankful for. The possibility of a livable future was returned to them. In the face of David and Lucy finding each other at last, in this darkest of times, it suddenly became permissible to hope for, even expect, more. It wasn't a cure for what ailed them, but it was a start. While the new couple suffered impatiently the need to be alone again, their display of tenuously harnessed passion brought silly smiles and a beneficent calm to everyone else.

By the end of the evening, Brook at least had had quite enough of the sight of his sister and David mooning over each other, despite the inexpressible comfort it gave him to see it. He was an immature eighteen; no Jane had as yet been permitted into his private Tarzan dreams. As soon as he and his parents arrived home he excused himself and went to bed. Philip wanted to prolong the evening's hopefulness for at least a few more hours.

"Well, Sally, I think we can assume that David is going to be our son-in-law. How do you feel about that? It's no secret that you never liked him."

She didn't answer immediately. She was standing in the hallway, gazing up the stairs. "That was the past. I've grown quite . . . appreciative of David this past year. I imagine I'll become fond of him in time. I admit that I was wrong about him. And how churlish would I have to be to not want for my daughter such happiness as she so obviously feels with him." She looked back. "Philip. If you don't mind, I'm very tired. We can talk about this to your heart's content in the morning, all right?"

And she went to her room, and soon Philip, abruptly alone, with no one to share his excitement and feeling like an insensitive oaf, succumbed to sadness again and went to his.

She stood on a high ledge with nothing but a solid wall of rock behind her. It was a shallow ledge, and short, and she was quite alone on it. Up so high, the air was thin and cold. She was dressed in her favorite summer frock, a long swath of gauzy turquoise silk. She was warm, and she could breathe, but she didn't belong on the ledge and didn't know how she had gotten there. She was the only thing of color, the only thing alive. Nothing grew on the rocky surfaces, not even moss or lichen, and there were no birds in the sky. Before her, the world fell away to a magnificent vista where, far below, she could see miniature towns and emerald countryside and cobalt rivers, an artist's fantasy of heaven on earth. In the air before her there suddenly arose from the land below a plume of warm air. It had been sent for her. She had only to leap out and it would carry her down to the ground. Excited as a child, she lifted her skirts to jump, and something grabbed at her ankle. She turned and Jed was sitting on the ledge, his grey hand clamped on her pink flesh. His eyes were no longer blue, his hair no longer gold. But still he was beautiful to her, as beautiful as what lay below, and she could not take her eyes from him. The plume began to fall away.

Sally woke sobbing. Before her was life and behind her was Jed. There was no place where life and Jed existed together anymore. And though it was clear that her dream was her own mind, telling her to choose, she felt incapable and unwilling.

Her sobs eased as the dream grew fuzzy and her thoughts drifted. David and Lucy. She would indeed grow fond of David. She would, in fact, grow to love him almost as much as she had loved Jed, for how could she go on resisting a man who had loved and taken care of her son so well? And she had no illusions about the care David had taken of Jed. It had been better than her own. He took better care of all her children than she had.

Her mind continued to drift and, in time, so did her body. She rose from her bed. In the dark, she went to her husband's room and stood in the doorway until her presence woke him, as she knew it would. When she saw him raise himself off his pillow, she spoke.

"Philip. I want Brook to transfer to the writing program. Do you think we can do that in the middle of the semester?"

He made no comment on her coming to talk to him about Brook's schooling at four in the morning. "I'll find out. If not, he can start in the spring. I'm sure that will be just as good."

"I'll tell him in the morning." She walked partway into the room. "I just realized that David's gorgeous children will be our grandchildren."

Philip sat up and swung his legs off the bed. "Indeed they will. But I hope some of them will look like our gorgeous daughter."

"Yes. The way Henry looks like Jed." She began to cry. "Oh, Philip."

He rose and came to her. "Would you like to stay here with me tonight?"

She didn't answer, just slowly put her arms around his neck and pressed herself into the living, breathing warmth of him. "I'd like to stay here with you tonight," she whispered. "Is it too late for that? Have I made you wait too long?"

His arms closed around her. "I would have waited until hell froze over."

She peered past his shoulder. Outside the frost-encrusted bedroom window, the branches of the trees were robed in ice. "Look, Philip. I think it just has."

56

Joseph rarely slept more than two or three hours a night now, which was why he slept alone. Since the summer, his nocturnal restlessness had become so extreme that it had dragged Evelyn into a state of constant sleep deprivation. After forty-five years of sharing a bed, they had finally had to admit that it wasn't for the best anymore. On the Monday night after Thanksgiving, having received Hillman's report earlier that day, Joseph hadn't slept at all.

He had lain awake all night, his emotions seesawing

from the zenith of jubilant vindication to the nadir of horrified disbelief, only gradually reaching an acceptable balance. Sometime past midnight he heard Evelyn tiptoe past his door and he'd given out a few peaceful-sounding snores so she would think he was asleep. She'd gone on into the kitchen. In the deafening stillness of the dead of night, every sound carried and found its way to his ears. He heard her make tea, could almost smell the camomile; he heard her shuffle into the drawing room, heard the click of the lamp switch, the clink of her cup as it landed on the glass coffee table, the slow swoosh of the turning of pages in the photo album. The sounds were soothing to him because he knew that she was calm. Sad but calm. They had talked openly about many things yesterday afternoon, difficult things like pain, death, and sorrow, and about many people. Monty had not been one of them. The one easy decision Joseph had made immediately had been to spare her and the rest of the family knowledge and suspicion that would prolong their suffering. It didn't matter if his went on. He wouldn't be here that much longer.

It was now six o'clock on Tuesday morning and Joseph was wide awake.

The sky was lightening. He thought how different the stillness of early morning was from that of the dark of night. A man could breathe and think in that anticipatory stillness before the day broke upon him; all a man could do in the dark of night, with all his fears pressing in on him and shadows taking the form of his mistakes, was pray that day would come.

Rather than ring for his nurse to help him, he struggled into his dressing gown and pulled himself into his wheelchair, carefully positioned next to the narrow bed. The fire was banked, but the radiators were hissing and the room was warm. He reached under his mattress and withdrew Hillman's report. He put it in his lap and wheeled himself across the room. He opened the shutters. He settled his hands over the envelope and stared out the window. Before him Central Park sparkled and shimmered in the early sunlight. It was covered with ice and deserted of people, and emerged from the darkness like an alien, cold-planet paradise spun of diamonds and white gold. It made him ache to look at such heart-stopping beauty while something so ugly lay beneath his hands.

Joseph,

Montgomery Glennon is living at the Hotel Chelsea under the name Hugh Montgomery. Until last month, he worked as a night manager at the Everard Baths on West 28th Street. After decades as a highly functioning alcoholic, he is now incapacitated with symptoms of advanced cirrhosis of the liver. Like many failing addicts, he managed his recent life by maintaining a circumscribed existence, comprised of the baths and the bottle. Unless Jed also inhabited one of those milieus, he and Monty would have had no way of intersecting.

We know that Jed did not drink and the only salient and pursuable characteristic of the Everard is that it is a bathhouse well-known for hosting male deviants. While this at first seemed to have no likely relevance to Jed, a husband and a father, my inquiries revealed that since at least last spring your grandson was engaged in a relationship with a young queer named Anthony DeMarco. Their liaison was ongoing, occasionally indiscreet, and clearly sexual, often blatantly so. DeMarco, who was aware that Jed had drowned and seemed genuinely shattered by his death, admitted that they had visited the Everard once, on a Wednesday night in mid-July, but did not see anyone known to either of them. Monty did not work Wednesdays. He was known to sometimes drop by on his nights off, but no one remembers him there that particular night. There is no evidence of any subsequent contact between him and Jed.

These disturbing findings raise suspicions of a circumstantial connection which you will no doubt be quick to make, but as before they prove nothing. Joseph, I strongly advise that you nurture the love and compassion I know you have for Jed and let him rest in peace. Please call me when you are ready to discuss this.

Leonard

The detective owed him a goddamned apology, because there it was. The connection he knew in his gut had to exist between Monty and Jed's death. Monty saw Jed having sex with a man at the Everard and had tried to blackmail him.

Love and compassion. Joseph knew what Hillman was trying to tell him. That he hadn't had enough love and compassion for Jed while he was alive, but here was an opportunity to make up for his hard-heartedness. A noble sentiment, but Joseph knew himself too well. If he had come into possession of this information while Jed were still alive, whatever love or compassion he had for the boy would have been as nothing in the face of Joseph's revulsion and anger. There would have been no forgiveness possible. He would have come down on Jed like the wrath of God and commanded him to abandon all perverted thoughts and perverted behavior forever, or live the remainder of his life in exile. There was no forgiveness possible now, either, not for what Jed was or for what he had done. Joseph's revulsion at the thought of his grandson being a faggot had not faded during the long night. Nor had his fury at the revelation that his namesake was made of such weakness of the flesh and the spirit that he wantonly risked not only his own disgrace but also the disgrace of the Gates family and the business for the momentary satisfying of his deviant lusts.

And yet, horribly ironic though it was, Joseph had never felt prouder of Jed than he did this morning. As with Zoe, Joseph no longer needed to be his grandson's fearsome judge now that death had obviated the danger that came when one softened to another's imperfections. When one allowed love and compassion to find their way from one's heart to one's head. In the end, Jed had done the right thing. He had removed himself so that his family would not suffer the consequences of his gross indiscretion. Joseph had no doubt of it. And it was the bravest thing the boy had ever done, braver than anything he might have been asked to do on the battlefield.

Joseph crushed the envelope in his good hand. Love and compassion *had* found their way from his heart to his head these past months; he could not pretend that wasn't so. He could not pretend that there was no love beneath the rage and disgust. He had loved his grandson and would move heaven and earth to bring down the man who had caused his death. And who had perhaps caused Joseph's daughter's death as well. He was glad to know that Monty was dying of cirrhosis, but it wasn't nearly enough; he had to answer for the things he had done.

Joseph wheeled his chair to the side of the fireplace. He smoothed the envelope against his leg and hid it inside a dusty old company ledger on one of the low shelves there. He wheeled himself a little farther and pulled on the cord above his bed. In two minutes, his nurse arrived, fully dressed and ready for him.

"You're up so early, Mr. Gates. And look, you're in your chair! That's wonderful."

He smiled at her. He really had to stop giving her a hard time; she was quite competent and not bad to look at, either. "Yes, I feel strong today. I want to bathe and dress. And tell Angelina to make me a good breakfast. But first, I want you to call Mr. Shaw at home—"

"At this hour?"

"He'll be awake. Tell him I need to see him after work tonight."

Someone had to inflict pain on Monty, make him aware of the judgment that had been leveled against him. Joseph couldn't do it. There was only one man Joseph could trust to share his need for vengeance: his fellow warrior, the man in whose hands he was leaving everything. David would take care of it. When he knew what Joseph knew, he would want to.

57

David was awake when Joseph's nurse called. He normally left the house by seven and at six thirty would have been eating breakfast, perfectly able to get to the phone after one ring. But for the past five days he had been running a little late in the mornings. Happily, lustfully late. Fortunately, Joseph's nurse was a very patient woman and she allowed the phone to ring until David picked up.

For five days David had not thought about Monty. He had had to force himself to think about work, about anything other than Lucy. His mind was swollen with an adolescent fever of love and desire. It seared him when he was with her and tormented him when he was apart from her. He was absurdly happy. But all thoughts of Lucy and love and happiness were sent into temporary exile the moment Joseph handed him Hillman's report.

It never occurred to David that Joseph might take such a step. Sharing what Jed had confided in him with Lucy was a matter of David's own emotional survival and a symbol of the binding intimacy he craved with her. Telling Abby had been the right thing to do, though it was as if she had known all along. Abby, demure, unworldly Abby, had thoroughly shocked him with her response. She had not flinched or gasped. She had not cried. She had simply looked at David for a long painful moment and then said, "Of course. It was you he loved, wasn't it, David? It was you."

David had spent the past five days shoring up his determination to keep the truth from everyone else. No matter from what angle he looked at it, he could see much harm and no benefit in anyone else ever knowing. Even now, with the damning facts in his hands and Joseph's eyes on him, for a fleeting moment he considered protecting an old and spent man, lying to him, trying to talk him out of the astute conclusion he had come to. But as Joseph talked, David realized that Joseph might indeed be old, sometimes weak and weepy, but he was far from spent. No matter what it took, he would remain master of his universe until the moment he died.

Between the two of them they had all the information they needed: the truth of what Monty had done and the facts of his condition and where he could be found. And together, as with so many endeavors over the previous decade, they brought their intellect and resolve to the plotting of a strategy and then applied their strength to its execution. All that remained for Joseph to do was to call Hillman and tell him to meet David at the Hotel Chelsea in an hour. It was up to David to focus his besotted brain and curb his rage long enough to do the rest.

Security was a cheap commodity at the Chelsea. Three dollars bought David unannounced visitation rights to Monty's apartment and assurance that Mr. Montgomery would be allowed no other guests that night except for Mr. Leonard Hillman, who would be arriving within the hour.

The hall was spottily lit; several of its bulbs were burned out or missing. David stopped in front of Monty's door and stood there in the gloom, dizzy with the knowledge that he was about to face the man he held responsible for the deaths of two people he had loved. He took time to steady himself, and when he was sure he was in control of his intent and his actions he knocked, hard and persistently. There came scrambling on the other side of the door, a slurred voice calling, "Eddie, you lazy fuck, you'd better be bringing the good stuff this time," locks being thrown. The door was flung wide and Monty loomed out of the oozing darkness of his apartment, blinking in the feeble hallway light.

"What the fuck?!" His eyes popped open. They glinted with bald guilt.

"I thought we'd have a little talk about Jed," David said with eerie calm.

Monty's face assumed a placating expression, but his eyes radiated terror. "Oh, David, I was so sorry to hear about the kid's death. What a terrible shame." His voice was oily with false sympathy.

And at the sound of it, David's self-control could not hold. He lunged at Monty with the speed and ferociousness of an enraged animal, slammed him against the nearest wall and wrapped his fingers around his throat, pressed his thumbs into its soft, vulnerable center. All conscious thought had vanished. He was a creature of pure instinct: the instinct to protect and avenge the innocent, to destroy the guilty. To salve his own pain and guilt through the actions of his own hands. For a long moment—while

Monty's face contorted and he began to choke and thrash against the wall, his hands flailing vainly at David's arms—David hung suspended in a conscienceless place, where what was horrific and forbidden was rendered necessary and redemptive, a place he had never known existed until he'd gone to war. From that place he saw himself choking Monty and believed that he could kill without remorse, heedless of the consequences. Lucy was wrong about him. She would be so disappointed; she would not love him anymore.

David's hands released their grip. He raised his arms in the air as if in surrender and stepped back, leaving Monty to crumple to his knees. David's entire body shook violently and his breath came rapid and rasping. He was aware of Monty's bent head nodding grotesquely, fingers clutching at his neck. David took another step back as his arms dropped to his sides and the terror over what he had almost done rose into his throat like acid. His chest heaved. He groped along the wall by the door until he found a light switch. Sickly yellow light flooded the entry. He slammed the door shut and leaned his back against it.

Monty raised his head. He struggled to rise, but David pinned him with a stare like lightning bolts thrown by an angry god.

Monty scuttled backward, wrapped his arms protectively around his legs, rested his head against the wall. "Why did you stop? I know you want to kill me." His voice was a harsh croak.

David scrubbed at his face with his hands. His breathing slowly returned to normal as the boil of emotion that had overwhelmed him subsided. He looked down at Monty, his horribly sallow skin mottled purple and his fear-filled blue irises glowing bizarrely against the yellowed whites of his eyes. Livid red marks striped his neck.

"Because you are nothing." David spat out the words. "You are less than nothing. You are dirt. I'm not going to ruin my life for the pleasure of killing you. You may have had that kind of power over Zoe and Jed, but you don't over me. And now here I stand, between you and everyone I care about. Do you understand me?"

David pushed himself away from the door and stepped closer. He glared down in disgust. "God. You look like shit." He hadn't seen Monty in a year. Even having read Hillman's report, David was unprepared for the sight of the wreck cowering in front of him. Monty's neck was bruised from David's attack. There were worse bruises on his bare arms and ankles. His belly was swollen, his eyes the color of pus. His once-athletic body was skeletal. David had seen dozens of men dying of cirrhosis when he was young; he knew what it looked like.

Monty whined, "I feel like shit. I need a drink."

David smiled cruelly. "Well, that's a pity, Monty, because you can't have one. Not now, not ever again. You have to pay for your sins somehow. Really, you know you do."

A different kind of fear appeared in Monty's eyes, along with suspicion and abhorrence. He stared at David. "What sins? What are you talking about?"

The cruel smile lingered. "Jed killed himself because of you, you loathsome fuck." David saw surprise flicker across Monty's face. "No. Of course you wouldn't think his drowning had anything to do with you. Nothing is ever your fault. Tell me, Monty, what did you think he would do when you threatened him?"

Monty didn't make any attempt to deny David's accusation or even ask how he knew. There was no point anymore. "I thought maybe he'd give me some money. And I wanted to have a little fun with him. He was always such a good boy. Finding out he was a queer . . . You can see how it was hard to resist. I didn't think he'd kill himself."

The color drained from David's face. "Just like you didn't think Zoe would die when she fell off her horse? How did you manage that, Monty? How did you get her to fall?"

It was a long while before Monty responded. The atmosphere grew leaden as he and David stared at each other in hate-filled silence. "You don't understand anything. I loved Zoe. I never meant to hurt her, or Jed."

David dropped into a crouch and grabbed Monty's throat again with one strong hand, pushed his head back until it hit the wall with a fearsome crack. "You lying prick," he hissed. "Don't you ever say their names again, do you hear me? Do you hear me?"

Monty jerked his head away, wrenching against David's grasp. "I hear you," he whispered.

David released him and returned to lean against the door. "Come on, Monty. It's all over now; you can tell me the truth. Did you kill her?"

"Go to hell."

"Maybe I will, but you're going to get there before me. And it won't be a pleasant journey. Did you ever have the D.T.'s Monty? I've heard that men beg to be allowed to die, that's how terrible they can be, especially for someone who's been drinking as much and for as long as you have."

Monty's eyes grew wild. "Come on, David. Look at me. I'm dying. You don't have to do this. I'm finished. Just leave me to drink myself to death."

"No, I don't think so," David said thoughtfully. "You can't really expect me to trust you, and, as I said, you have to pay for your sins. Dying of cirrhosis is bad, but it's far from sufficient punishment for what you've done. So, this is what's going to happen. I'm going to stay here with you until a private detective named Leonard Hillman arrives with one of his able henchmen. They will escort you to the psychiatric hospital at Bellevue, where you will remain, under guard, without alcohol, without visitors, without access to a telephone or pen and paper, until you die."

"Jesus!" Monty breathed. "Please, David."

"Oh, how ugly that word sounds in your mouth. Don't waste your breath asking me for leniency. You're not going to get any. You will get good medical care. We don't want you to go too quickly, after all." At his back, the door shook with the announcement of Hillman's arrival. "Ah. Your fate has found you, Monty."

Hillman and an associate came quietly into the apartment. "Everything is arranged. I have someone waiting downstairs with a car. Go home, David. You're done here."

David was indeed done. The muscles in his arm trembled under Hillman's hand. He couldn't speak another word. He took one last look at Monty, then turned and walked away, but not quickly enough. A gob of bloody spittle flew from Monty's mouth and landed on his shoe.

David went home and went directly upstairs. Lucy was waiting for him in the parlor, but he couldn't face her. He went into the bathroom, stripped off his clothes, and stepped into the shower. He turned the water on as full as it would go and as hot as he could stand and he scrubbed every inch of his polluted body with a brush.

He would never believe in the existence of God. He knew that there was no almighty creator who rewarded good and punished evil. The universe was chaos, and life was without reason or fairness. But sometimes a man got what he deserved. Monty was going to die an agonizing, miserable death, unloved and unmourned. David and Joseph would have to find a way to be satisfied with that.

He stood under the scalding downpour and let the water wash away the tears that would not stop coming. He stood there until the water turned cold. Until Lucy came to find him and took him, numb and shivering, from the shower, wrapped him in a soft towel, led him by the hand to bed, curled her body around him, and warmed him to sleep.

58

It took a few weeks, but now if they did not sleep through the night it was because they couldn't wait until morning for each other and not because he'd woken, agitated and refusing to be consoled, from a bad dream. The dark circles were fading from under his eyes; their golden fire burned steadily once more, spreading incandescent heat all through her whenever his gaze so much as flickered her way. He was arriving late at the office so often that Lillian Steele had ceased to schedule any appointments for him before ten o'clock.

Lucy bided her time and watched carefully as David's battered psyche began to mend. There was one more thing that had to be done before he could truly be whole again. If she'd had any doubt of it, if she'd allowed herself to ever be uncertain that it was what David wanted, losing Jed had convinced her otherwise with a finality as powerful as her love for both of them. It had to be done and it was up to her to do it.

"Where did you really get this?" She touched the scar on his face. It glowed faintly against his tawny skin in the pale predawn light. "And tell me the truth. I don't believe what Jed said, that it was over a girl you tried to kiss. That sounds like you being a big tease."

David laughed softly. "You're right. Jed would have believed any piece of nonsense I told him. I'm sure he got a charge out of that, he was always so fascinated with my sex life—" His laughter gave way to a moan. "Oh my God."

She put a finger over his lips. "David. It doesn't matter anymore; don't think about it. Please, just stay here with me." She touched his face again. "Tell me how you got this. What really happened?"

He removed his hand from where it lay lightly on her breast and brought it to the thin raised line along his jaw. "What really happened is that my dear brother Ben gave this to me." His gaze drifted off into the bedroom's shadowy interior.

Lucy raised herself up on her elbow and stared down at him. "What? He cut you? Your brother?"

Almost reluctantly he turned his eyes to her again. "No. He didn't cut me. It was an accident." His voice was full of acid.

"I don't understand. If it was an accident, why do you sound so angry?"

"Because it wouldn't have happened if he'd just left me alone. But he could never do that. None of them could ever leave me alone even though that's all I ever asked them to do."

David's extreme discomfort with the conversation was a palpable presence in the bed with them.

"That's what you've always said about me," she said

playfully, knowing she had to go on. "And look how things turned out." She smiled at him, but he didn't smile back. She stroked his arm, which was lying inert between them. "Should Ben have left you alone then, the time that this happened?" She watched the rapid rise and fall of his chest. They looked at each other and she could see the strength of his desire to turn away to put an end to the discussion. She held his eyes and held her breath, and after a minute she said, "David? Should he have?"

"I don't know," he admitted, his eyes and voice gone flat. "I was sure of everything then, but now . . . I don't know. . . . I was so young. Eleven. Two friends and I stole a bottle of Passover wine and snuck off to the school yard to drink it. When I didn't come home for dinner, my mother sent Ben to find me. He was always being sent to find me." David caught and held her hand as it traveled down to his wrist. "I saw him coming and tried to climb the school-yard fence to get away. He pulled at me and I slipped and a piece of twisted metal sticking out of the fence slashed my face. It was good that I was drunk and floundering around, because I just slid off the fence. If I'd been sober, I would have struggled and tried to hold on and the metal probably would have gone straight into my throat. As it was, I was bleeding like a pig and Ben panicked. He thought he'd killed me, and he ran with me in his arms to Henry Street, to one of the nurses there. Then he dragged me home, furious, yelling at me the whole way. He hauled me upstairs, yanked me so hard he nearly dislocated my shoulder." He stopped, lost in memory. When he resumed, Lucy could barely hear him; he seemed to be talking to himself, as though he'd forgotten she was there. "Everyone yelled at me that night. Even Sarah. She was only six and for the first time in her life I terrified her, her savior, her hero, with my bandaged and bloody face."

Lucy willed herself not to cry, not to throw herself on him.

He let go of her hand and got up off the bed. He didn't kiss her. He didn't even look at her. "I'm going to the office. I have a lot to do."

She didn't try to stop him.

———

Lucy stood in the doorway to the tailors' room, her heart beating fast. She was sure of the rightness of what she was about to do, but still she was afraid. She looked across the room at Sarah, rapt in concentration over an expensive velvet dress and a delicate lace collar she was attaching to it with perfect, invisible stitches. Lucy was rapt as well, at the sight of Sarah's bent head, her chestnut hair gleaming in the lamplight just like David's. Love as well as fear made Lucy's heart beat fast. Love for David. Love for Sarah. Fear of failure. Even if Sarah had not been David's sister, Lucy would have loved her. It was impossible not to. But she was David's sister and Lucy wanted so much more than to simply care for her and be her friend. Dedicated nurse that she was, she wanted to heal her, as she wanted to heal David, for from the moment they'd met Lucy had seen the damage that Sarah's losses had done her.

"Sarah."

Sarah lifted her head. "Lucy!" She rose up out of her chair. She cast aside her work and paid no mind as the fine dress landed on the dusty floor. "Lucy."

Sarah ran across the room and Lucy's arms opened of their own volition and gathered Sarah in. The women hugged each other like sisters who had suffered a long and painful separation.

"You're back. You're back. I've missed you so much."

Lucy smiled. "I won't actually be back to work until next week, but I couldn't wait to see you. Oh, Sarah, I've missed you, too." Lucy held Sarah at arm's length so she could look at her. "And look what I've missed—you're pregnant!"

"Yes." Sarah's eyes lit up with a shy, apologetic joy. She glanced down at the tiny swell that Lucy's trained eye had seen immediately. "And I wanted so much for you to know. I went to Henry Street weeks ago, but you weren't there— oh, Lucy. Mr. Weiss told me about . . ." Her joy dissipated. "Lucy, I've been thinking about you so much. I'm so sorry about your brother." Her eyes welled with tears. "It's such a terrible thing. I haven't been able to stop thinking about it. I feel so bad for you; I really do."

Eight sets of fingers had stopped sewing and eight pairs

of eyes had turned toward the women. Lucy took Sarah's hand and led her from the room into the quiet hallway.

"I know you do, Sarah. I know how well you understand the pain of it. You have a brother who you think is lost to you, don't you?"

Sarah's moist eyes widened. She couldn't speak, but she nodded. *Yes. I have a brother who is lost to me.*

"That's why I'm here. To talk to you about your brother. About David."

"How do you know about David?" Sarah cried. "My God, who are you that you know so much about me?" She began to sob. Tears rolled down her cheeks.

Lucy put an arm around Sarah's shoulders and guided her to the back of the shop. "Come. Sol said we could use his office." She closed the office door and sat Sarah down in Sol's oversized chair.

Lucy knelt on the floor at Sarah's feet and took both her hands in her own. "Sarah, this is going to be difficult, so please, just try to listen to me." She clutched Sarah's hands tightly, lifted one, and pressed it to her cheek. "My real last name is Gates, as in the department store Gateses. I don't use it at Henry Street because I don't want clients to know I come from such a wealthy family." She shook her head; it was so unimportant now. "My brother, who died . . ." She fought to remain composed. It would not help Sarah to see her cry as well. "My brother's name was Jed. He was David's best friend. They met during the war and became inseparable. Sarah, I've known David for nine years. The world knows him as David Shaw, but I've always known his real name. The first day you and I met, in your apartment, when you told me what the initials on the brush stood for . . . that's why I nearly fainted, not because it was too warm. You want to know who I am? I'm someone who has loved your brother for nine years and never told him and nearly threw her life away."

"What!?"

Shock impelled Sarah to try to rise from the chair, but Lucy held her hands fast. "After Jed died, everything changed. I took a chance. I told David how I feel about him. And what a miracle, he loves me, too. I'm going to be your sister-in-law, and I don't intend to get married without you there." She smiled gamely. "David needs to be reconciled with his past and what's left of his family. He won't talk about it, but I know him. I can see how lonely he is for you, for what was precious to him before. Even for Ben. Believe what I'm telling you, Sarah. He needs you, just like you need him. You all need to forgive one another."

"I want to. You can't imagine how much," Sarah said. "There hasn't been a single day since he left that I don't think about him and wonder how it's possible that he's gone. And since I heard about your . . . about Jed . . ." She bit at her trembling lip and squeezed Lucy's hand. "He must have been beautiful, like you," she whispered.

Lucy's breath caught in her throat. "He was. He was beautiful. The exact opposite of David. Pale, blond, and blue-eyed. When they were together, you didn't know who to look at first." She disengaged her hands and smiled tremulously. "Our brothers. And, thank God, yours is still alive."

Sarah looked away from her, down at her lap. "He doesn't want to see me, Lucy. Two years ago, I interviewed for a job at the store, and I went to thank this man I knew as Mr. Shaw for setting it up . . . He threw me out of his office." She looked up; her tears fell unchecked. "He threw me out! I don't know if I can face him again."

"I can imagine what might have happened two years ago. David can be quite merciless when he's angry or hurt or feels that he's being attacked. But whatever he did or said, Sarah, it wasn't the truth. And he's not the same person he was then. He's come to understand what's important in ways he never did before. You have to take a chance, like I did. You owe it to yourself, and to him."

"I've been telling myself that forever. I just have no idea what to do."

"Well, I *do* have an idea. You don't think I'd come here without a plan, do you?" Lucy stood up. She pulled Sarah to her feet and kissed her on the cheek. "I assume that you follow the traditions of your religion?"

"Yes, of course. Reuben and I are more modern than Ben and Naomi, but we're very observant. Why?"

"So, on Fridays you observe Shabbat?"

"Yes. Naomi and I alternate, dinner one week at my house, one week at hers."

"And where will you all be this coming Friday?"

Sarah paled. "My house."

Lucy took a deep breath. "Why don't David and I bring the *challah*. Will three loaves be enough?"

By the time David came home to Washington Square, he was tranquil, their morning's conversation and the emotions it had engendered in him seemingly forgotten. He changed into old, comfortable clothes and together they made dinner and ate it at the kitchen table. When they were done, he washed the dishes and she dried them. He brewed tea, a delicate Darjeeling, in the pot of a Wedgwood china tea service and placed everything they needed on a silver tray and carried it into the parlor; he had yet to drink sweet, strong, milky Russian Caravan tea out of a glass in front of her. While they had been in the kitchen, the fire had burned down to a bed of red-hot embers. He artfully constructed a tower of logs on top of them and stoked the embers until the tower was ablaze. He wiped his hands on his pants legs.

"Perfect, David. That should keep us warm for a while. Come; sit with me."

While David had been resuscitating the fire, Lucy had settled herself on the sofa, David's favorite of the half dozen scattered throughout the house, a fruitwood Biedermeier with cushions covered in rep the color of caramel. A second tray, holding a white cake box tied with red string, a knife, two plates, and two forks, had materialized on the table next to the tea service.

"Where did that come from?"

"A bakery I walked by today."

"What is it?" David eyed the box suspiciously, then reached out a slow hand. Lucy slapped it away.

"It's for later; it's a surprise."

"Ow! You're so strict. Do I have your permission to have tea?"

"Yes. You may have tea. And you can pour some for me."

He poured their tea, but he didn't drink his. He took her

hand. "Are you looking forward to going back to work next week?"

"Yes, very much. It's time for me to be doing something useful again."

He played with her fingers. "Lucy. Do you remember telling me about a large, anonymous gift to Henry Street, back last winter?"

"Of course. We talked about it at New Year's Eve. The same night you told me about Brook's writing, and lied to me about what you'd done for Jed."

"I didn't actually lie to you. I just didn't choose to confirm your theory at the time."

"No. Because you didn't trust me not to find a way to turn what you'd done back on you, which I was so good at doing."

"I forgive you. And we don't need to talk about how terribly nasty you used to be to me." He caressed her palm. "I do want to talk to you about that gift, however."

"Why?"

"Because it was from me, and I . . . You really have to stop looking at me like that," he said with false annoyance.

"I'll stop looking at you like this when you stop being amazing and wonderful."

"Then I guess I'd better get used to it." He smiled and kissed her. "The gift. Joseph gave me a lot of money that I didn't need. I wanted to give it away. I set up a foundation and distributed the money to a few organizations whose work I admire. I want to continue being able to do that. People are going to need a lot of help in the coming years."

She gave him a puzzled look. "What do you mean? The economy is booming; people are making money hand over fist. The stock market—"

"This economy is going to collapse, Lucy. I give it another year, maybe two. The booming stock market is built on corruption, lies, manipulation, and the avarice of ignorant people. Banks are failing all around the country every day. Coolidge is an idiot when it comes to the economy and the Federal Reserve doesn't have a clue how to protect the money supply. I'm happy to take advantage of what's happening now, but I'm spending most of my time positioning the company to prosper after the bubble bursts. You don't really have to be a genius to know how to protect yourself. But when it does all come crashing down, a lot of people are going to suffer, and not just people with money in the market. I've been endowing the foundation since last year, managing it for quick growth. In six months it will reach five million. We could do a lot of good with that. I was thinking that maybe, if you get bored with what you're doing, or for some reason you can't work the way you do now, maybe you'd want to administer the foundation. You and Abby. Your mouth is hanging open."

She closed her mouth.

"Think about it, all right?"

She nodded. "I will. I most definitely will."

"Good. Enough about that then." He let go her hand and leaned back into the sofa, his body limp and relaxed. "I love this. Being with you this way. With Cissy everything was uncomfortable, not just the damned furniture." He shook his head in pained disbelief, remembering. "We always had to be dressed properly. I never wore things like this except when I was alone. We never cooked for ourselves. She found it unsettling that I actually knew how. Men weren't supposed to do that. She'd have the cook make us fancy, tasteless meals. . . . I was playacting all the time with her. I didn't realize it until I stopped."

"How could you not playact with her, David? She didn't know you. But I do and I love being with you this way, too. As soon as I moved out of my parents' house I discovered the joys of taking care of myself, and having an environment where I could be myself." She fondled the open collar of his worn shirt. Her fingers brushed across his throat. "I love you in these old clothes. I love who you are when you wear them."

He put his arm around her waist, drew her close to him. "I'm glad you let your hair grow again. I love the way it frames your face, like a helmet made from polished copper. You look like Clara Bow. But more beautiful. You've got a hell of a lot more It than she does." His hand slid up her back until it reached the blunt-cut line of her hair at the base of her neck. "Lucy. You let me breathe. I love you so much."

"Will you let me do something else for you?"

He laughed at her coy tone. "Anything you want."

"I want you to let me take you somewhere for dinner on Friday night."

She smiled at his delighted reaction and then she put her arms around his neck and she kissed him, so tenderly and for so long that his charmed expression faded and he became very still. She drew away from him. She picked up the knife, cut the red string, and opened the white cake box. She lifted out a cinnamon *babka,* cut two pieces, put them on plates, and placed one in front of him.

"David, you trust me now, don't you?"

He stared down at the cake. "I trust you. Where are you going to take me?"

She reached out and took his face in her hands, turned it toward her. "Somewhere I know you've wanted to go for a very long time but don't know how to get to on your own."

The look in his eyes nearly undid her. "David, don't be afraid," she whispered. "It's going to be all right."

"My God, how did I ever live without you?"

"Don't. Don't look back. There's nothing there. We're going to go forward together. Everything is waiting for us. Everything."

"Lucy. How did you do this? How did you know . . . ?"

"Shhh." She caressed his face, toyed with his hair, wound the chestnut waves around and around her fingers. Not for one second did she take her eyes from his. Not until she saw the fear in them subside. "I'll tell you, later. Right now, I think you should eat your cake. It's from Gottbaum's. Sarah said it's the best in the entire city."

59

Sarah and David stood on the landing outside the Winokurs' fifth-floor apartment. Sarah had been waiting there when he and Lucy came up the stairs. She had been waiting since half an hour before sundown. Lucy had quickly kissed her and then slipped through the door with her armload of bread, leaving them alone, a brother and sister, separated for a decade by willful misunderstanding and destructive pride, standing two yards from each other, listening to the muted sounds of laughter and greeting coming from within, not knowing how to begin the rapprochement they both so achingly desired.

"I promised myself I wouldn't cry."

"Well, you're not doing a very good job of it."

"I don't notice you doing any better. You're supposed to be my role model, remember?"

"That was always your mistake, Sarah, looking to me for clues to proper behavior."

"I looked to you for much more than that. And it wasn't a mistake."

Fearful and uncertain, they fell back on the safety of their barbed wit and the Warshinsky family tradition of sniping and teasing as prologue to the honest expression of love. They were following the same script, and they both knew the prologue would be a long one, a delicate minuet of coming together and backing away.

"So, Ben is in there."

"Yes, of course."

"Do you think he's planning to hit me?"

"I doubt it. But he probably should." She pulled her shawl more tightly around her. "Try not to hate him, David. He didn't know what else to do with you."

"I don't hate him. I know I wasn't . . . easy. We bore the burdens of our responsibilities in very different ways."

"He and Naomi have five children now; did you know that?"

"Yes. Rachel mentioned it. Tell me about them."

"They're all adorable. You'll see. A few of them are blonds, like Naomi's sisters. The three youngest are boys; Avram is eighteen months, Wolf five, and Chaim seven. Nell is nine and Rosie is eleven."

"Unbelievable. In my mind Rosie is still a baby." David's face darkened. "Sarah. I knew that you lost a baby last year. I should have come to see you then."

"It would have been wonderful if you had." She

shrugged, accepting of what they had both been unable to do. "And I should have come to see you so many times."

His expression eased. "Lucy said you're pregnant again. I can't tell," he said, looking her up and down. "Are you?"

"Yes," she said.

"This one will be all right. It will be perfect."

She gave him an amusedly skeptical look. "Tell me, great Svengali, how do you know that?"

"A big brother knows these things."

Her graceful aplomb wavered slightly and she was, for an instant, just a little sister wanting to believe in the magical abilities of her older and wiser brother. She tossed her head and laughed. "Rosie claims she remembers you."

He smiled. "She couldn't possibly."

"Well, she says she does. Maybe she's got you confused with Edward Israel Iskowitz."

"Enlighten me?"

"Eddie Cantor to you *goyim*. Naomi swoons over him; she has a framed publicity photo on her kitchen wall!" They both laughed at that.

"Levelheaded Naomi a romantic?"

"People change." Sarah's laughter died. "Or maybe they just reveal themselves little by little." The expression on her face could have melted a heart of steel. "Look at you." Her full mouth trembled. "Just in from the freezing cold with your coat open, no scarf, no gloves, your cheeks glowing. While I stand in the warm hall, shivering. Some things don't change."

"No, they don't. It's still the same blood in my veins, Mama and Papa's blood. The same as yours." He took off his coat and draped it around her shoulders. He drew the collar close around her neck and pulled her gently toward him. "Sarah. I'm sorry. For everything. You know I didn't mean the things I said to you in my office that day. Please forgive me. I want to come back. I want to be your brother again."

"You never stopped being my brother. Even if I'd never seen you again, you would always be my brother. David. I've missed you more than you'll ever know. Please, promise me you'll never leave us again. Please."

"I promise."

The last little space between them disappeared. They fell into each other's arms. The minuet was over.

"We should go in. Rosie helped make the chicken soup, just for you. She'll kill me if it gets cold."

He nodded. "In a second." He stroked her dusky cheek. "I want to go visit Mama's and Papa's graves with you. Can we go tomorrow? I can pick you up."

"David. Tomorrow is Saturday. I can't go anywhere, remember? Are you a total *goy* now?"

He laughed with embarrassment. "I guess so. I'm sorry. Sunday then?"

"Sunday will be good."

Sarah gave him back his coat. When he took it from her, she put her hand over his and smiled up at him. "I'm so happy you're here. We'll make a Jew out of you again; don't worry."

He shook his head. "Well, you can try." He stopped her from taking her hand away. "I lost Mama's Star of David."

"Oh no. Where?"

"In France. I was wearing it when we went into battle. I must have pulled it off my neck when I was hit. It's buried in that field now, where such terrible things happened."

"But it did its job, David. It kept you safe."

"I was injured, Sarah."

"But you weren't killed."

"God, you're stubborn." He smiled. "Come on. Let's see if Rosie really remembers me."

She was waiting in the entry, prancing impatiently from one foot to the other. With the uncomplicated selfishness of a child, Rosie flung herself at David the moment he walked through the door, wrapped her arms around his waist. "Uncle David! I remember you! I remember you!"

He kissed the top of her head and chuckled. "No, you don't. You were this big"—he held his thumb and forefinger an inch apart—"the last time I saw you. Oh, and you were ugly, like a little monkey. Are you sure you're really Rosie? You're all blond and beautiful!"

"I was never that small," she said indignantly. "And you never thought I was ugly!" She blushed and batted her eyes at him, a smitten little coquette. "I do remember you. I look at your picture all the time and I know it's you."

"What picture?" David smiled and looked over her head at Sarah.

"The one Papa keeps in his drawer, under his handkerchiefs."

David's smile faltered; his breath stopped and his eyes closed for a second. He turned his head and there was Ben, emerging timidly from the kitchen doorway, forty and already going grey, his body round and soft. David looked at him and knew that Ben had never raised a hand to his children. He looked kind and a little bewildered. He looked like Viktor. David felt the truth then of how he had tormented Ben with his disobedience. How he had gone far beyond the need to express his independence. He had pushed and pushed and tested Ben's endurance, because Ben was the only one who would or could come after him when he strayed. He was the only one who fought back, and David had always needed someone to fight with.

Suddenly Lucy was at his side, her hand at his back. David's faltering smile steadied. "Don't let go of me, please," he said quietly as Ben came up to him, his hand outstretched.

David put out his own hand and it was immediately crushed in Ben's calloused paw.

"We start from here, yes? We forget before. I am wanting only to . . . When Sarah told me—"

David rescued him. "Ben. You're my brother. The only one I have. We have to try again. For Mama and Papa."

"For Mama and Papa, yes. But for us, too. Duvid. I never meant that I should chase you away."

Lucy's hand was firm and warm. David drew in a shaking breath. "Ben. You didn't. It wasn't you. I couldn't live here."

Ben reached out and touched David's face, touched his scar. "Look what I did to you." His face collapsed. He put a strong arm around David's neck and hugged him, his big hand clasped to the back of David's head. He let David go, stepped back. "But you're still so beautiful. Enough that this wonderful woman is loving you."

David stood, stunned and speechless, and groped for Lucy's hand. Suddenly he was engulfed by wild commotion, energetic little bodies spilling out of the kitchen, Naomi, plump and smiling, her eyes huge behind thick glasses, trailing after them. Reuben, lanky as ever, hazel eyes shining, materializing with a steaming tureen in his hands.

"David! For three years, I think to myself, that Shaw, he's really quite brilliant, generous and ethical for a *goy*, and look, not only do you turn out to be a Jew, but you're my brother-in-law. It's so good to have you in my house, and to see my wife so happy! Come, everyone; it's time for Shabbat dinner."

Rosie finished lighting her *Shabbat* candle and scurried back to David. She dragged him to the table, beautifully set with the china Anna and Viktor had brought from Russia over thirty years before, which had become part of Sarah's dowry. Rosie placed David next to her, with Lucy on his other side. He began to sit, but she tugged at his hand. "We stand for *kiddush*, Uncle David," she whispered. In a daze, he let her direct him through a ritual that had once been as familiar to him as breathing. *Kiddush*, the joyful prayer of sanctification recited over a full glass of wine. She tugged on his hand again. "You can sit now. I made the cover for the challah; do you like it?" He nodded. The bread, broken into pieces, the delicious yeasty chunks distributed around the table, quickly devoured. Then the soup, carefully ladled into eleven waiting bowls, even one for little Avram, although he didn't get the good china yet. Rosie, nervous as a cat, couldn't sit. She hovered over David, waiting for him to taste it. "I made it. I asked Aunt Sarah if I could. I hope you like it." She vibrated with anticipation.

He lifted his spoon, dipped it into the rich yellow broth, brought it to his lips, and swallowed. The taste of it, so well remembered and so long missed, swamped his mouth and his brain all at once, rushed to fill his stomach, his limbs; like a raging river, it found its way everywhere. He moaned in what sounded like pain but wasn't. His spoon clattered to the table as his head dropped into his hands.

"Uncle David." Rosie placed her bony arm protectively

around his shoulders. "Did you burn your tongue? Is it too hot? You don't like it?"

He laughed through his tears and lifted his head, put his arm around her tiny waist. "Rosie. I like it. I love it. It's perfect. It's the most delicious thing I've ever tasted in my life. Thank you."

Sarah's eyes, yellow flecked and wet, just like his, were on him. "Mama's recipe," she said. "There's nothing like it in the world, is there? I'll make it for you, David, anytime."

David picked up his spoon again, finished his bowl, and asked for more. He didn't speak much as he ate. Later would come hours of talking, but for now he was too euphoric to be coherent. Lucy to his left, Rosie to his right, Sarah across from him, his mother's chicken soup in front of him. He grew weak with gratitude for the love that surrounded him, and with a release in his heart like a dam bursting open he knew, for the first time since he'd left home ten years before, that he could finally stop pretending. He was really and truly safe.

David and Lucy didn't get home until after midnight, exhausted and emotionally drained but too exhilarated to sleep. Too overwrought, for the moment, to make love. Although as they lay in each other's arms, talking quietly, their hands were far from still. A low, fat, steady candle set on David's nightstand provided just enough light for them to see each other within a cocoon of darkness. An unexpected flurry of snow hissed softly past the bedroom window, a soothing backdrop to their hushed voices.

"If you never did anything else for me in my entire life, I would love you forever for what you did tonight."

"Since the day I met Sarah, and discovered who she was, I have dreamed of this, David. I knew how much you loved one another, but you were both so helpless. And I wanted to be the one to bring you together. I had loved you for so long, and been unable to show it. So I dreamed of something I could do that would make you see—"

"Lucy. Don't cry." He tucked a shining strand of her deep red hair behind her ear, kissed her moist cheek.

"You can't imagine what I felt tonight, seeing you and Sarah together."

"I can. I saw your face."

There was a period of silence and in the absence of adequate words there were kisses and caresses and then a drawing back. It was too soon.

"Your family is so funny. Even the little ones have such sharp wit."

"Ah, yes. The famous Jewish humor. Useful for many things, including verbal torture. It can be a very effective weapon, like an icicle: you can stab someone with it and then when it melts you can look around and say, 'What! I didn't do anything!' " He laughed. "Sarah and I were particularly adept at that."

"There was no weaponry tonight. Everyone was happy and the humor was joyous."

"Yes, I know. It was lovely. I forgot how entertaining we can be."

"Indeed. It will be very interesting to have everyone together for Passover. My family is not known for their wit."

"Ah, you're wrong. Pay more attention. Your parents are both rather droll, and Joseph has a great acerbic wit. And Brook . . . he can be a riot in his writing, quite wacky. I think they'll all get along quite well, actually, our two families."

"And Henry will have more aunts and uncles, and cousins. I can just see Nell dragging him everywhere, like one of her dolls." She smiled at the thought.

"Yes, it will be quite a merger. How the world is changing, Lucy, that we can imagine all being together like that. It's so powerful."

Lucy's eyes filled with fresh tears. "I love you. I love you I love you I love you. I have to know everything. Tell me everything, from the day you were born until the day I met you. And before, where you come from, who made you."

His brows rose. "That's a lot of everything. I'll have to dole it out to you little by little, so you won't lose interest in me."

"I will never lose interest in you." Her hands were moving on him, stroking him, feeling for him.

"Lucy." His voice was thick. "If you expect me to talk, you have to stop that."

But she couldn't stop, and he couldn't talk, and once they began, the fire spread quickly. Soon he was gently pushing at her lips, seeking entrance. She shifted, seemed to struggle beneath him.

"What is it? Am I hurting you?"

"No. I . . . I didn't put in my diaphragm. I should get up and—" She looked over at her nightstand, but she didn't move.

He waited, poised and ready. "Are you vulnerable?"

"Yes. It's not a good time of the month."

He didn't withdraw. Instead, he pressed a little closer to her. "Maybe it is." His breath quickened. "Lucy, let's make a baby."

"David! We've hardly had any time together. Are you sure it's what you want?"

"Do you want to wait? Lucy, look at me. Don't tell me what you think I want to hear. Tell me what you want. Do you want to wait? Because we can. It would be all right."

"I want to have a baby with you," she said. "But I want you to be sure. You never wanted one—"

"I never wanted one with Cissy."

"I just want you to be sure," she pleaded.

"I see that my words are not convincing. So let me show you how sure I am."

Their bodies merged, and in the rapturous mindlessness of their union, in their intent to fuse themselves together so completely that a new life might be created from their joining, David felt as close to her as he could or would ever be to another human being, and he knew it was enough. It was, and would always be, enough.

When they were done, they needed to talk again.

"I think I would like to run your foundation. When you said if I couldn't work the way I do now? Is this what you meant, if I got pregnant?"

"Yes. I knew I wanted us to start a family right away. There'll be time for everything."

"I hope you don't intend us to fill this house with children. There must be eight bedrooms! You do remember what I've been doing for a living for the past three years?"

"We can negotiate the number," he teased. "You know, tomorrow is my people's day of rest. Which my sister had to remind me of, infidel that I've become. I'm going to stay home from work. I think we should stay right here"—he patted the mattress—"and make sure we get this baby thing right. Even if it takes all day."

"An excellent idea. It might indeed take all day. Maybe even all night."

He smiled. "Lucy." He lost himself in the bottomless green of her eyes, gleaming in the candlelight. "Lucy. I love you in ways I never knew it was possible to love anyone."

"I know. Lie still now. It's late and we're going to have a busy day tomorrow."

He turned, blew out the candle, and then rested his head on her breast. Her arms came around him and her fingers grabbed and released his hair, over and over, until suddenly her hand was still and he knew she had fallen asleep. He lay awake. The snow had stopped and a white winter moon had emerged from behind the clouds. He lifted an arm from the warm bed of Lucy's body and reached up into the column of moonlight coming through the window. His bare flesh turned ghostly. Lucy lived and breathed beside him, but in the silvered silence his eyes and ears filled with the spectral emanations of other presences. He saw their faces. He heard their whispers. Jed, Zoe, Anna, Viktor, Rose. Wolf, the brother he'd never met but knew nonetheless. So tempting to hold on to them, to the pain of their absence. He stared at his arm. He had to let them go. He could keep his love for them alive forever, let his memories of them sustain him and become the fuel for the new fire that burned in his heart. But it was time to let them go and to accept, finally, that all any of them had wanted or expected of him was nothing more or less than this: his life, honestly and generously lived, shared with someone he loved.

He watched his arm fall through the moonlight. His open hand settled onto the soft, natural swell of Lucy's stomach and he prayed, fiercely and with every fiber of his being, to a God he did not believe in, to whatever forces might possibly exist in the universe to help him, that at this very instant a baby was beginning its life beneath the palm of his hand. He let go of every other thought and with that prayer on his lips he fell asleep and he slept, an innocent, dreamless sleep, until the dawn of the new day.

Epilogue

APRIL 1928

Everyone agreed. The day of Joseph Gates's funeral was the most brilliant spring day to be visited upon New York City in anyone's memory, and there were many very long memories among the hundreds of people who came to bid him farewell. It was a day of astonishing clarity, a day when one could imagine seeing forever and beyond, to a limitless future. A fitting day to rejoice in such a life as Joseph had lived. There were tears, of course, especially among the family, but even theirs were tears shed easily for a natural and timely death. After a decade punctuated by three premature and unjust deaths, they were free to mourn this departure without the added misery of incomprehension. Joseph's death was truly a passage, a smooth gliding off the far edge of the universe into whatever lay beyond. Not, as the others had been, a wrenching tear in the fabric of their lives.

Like the day itself, the company gathered at Trinity Church on Wall Street, mere blocks from the eponymous building from where Joseph had ruled his empire, was vast and brilliant. In the pews directly behind the family were the country's luminaries, among them President Coolidge himself, along with Andrew Mellon, Herbert Hoover, and other members of the administration; Senators Copeland and Wagner; James J. Walker, mayor of New York City; business giants John D. Rockefeller, Samuel Insull, J.P. Morgan, Jr. Farther back were people with names less well-known but no less important to those in the very first pews, among them Sarah and Reuben Winokur, Benjamin Warshinsky and his daughter Rose, Rachel and Shlomo Weinstein, Cissy Shaw Corwith, née Harriman, and her new husband, Tucker. The crowd spilled out onto the street. People had come from far and wide to pay their respects. Many came to express their condolences personally, to firmly shake the hand of, to have their respectful presences noted by, David Shaw, who had recently married the deceased's visibly pregnant and radiant granddaughter and on whose shoulders so much now rested. They came to look at him and take his measure and lay their odds on whether, now that Joseph was gone, his charismatic young prodigy had the steel inside to survive the burdens of empire and the enmity of those who believed his replacing the barely acceptable grandson to be unjust and ill-considered.

The timing of Joseph's death was not something to which the majority of the mourners gave any thought. But it had mattered very much to Joseph. He might have gone sooner, after he and David had put Monty in his private prison, where the villain had died of liver failure on a moonless night in March. But there was a burgeoning fullness to Joseph's life that he wanted to savor before he left. The emotional earthquakes had stopped with the onset of the new year, but they had opened his head and his heart for good. He wanted to attend his first Passover seder at the home of David's sister; he wanted to raise a toast at the wedding of his cherished granddaughter to his adopted heir; mostly, he wanted more time to share with Evelyn this new, unfettered configuration of their intimacy. As the world inched its way from winter into spring, Joseph grew more and more content, more eager to stay and yet more ready to leave. In the end, it was his tired heart that made the decision and not his formidable mind. One April morning, when the world awoke, Joseph simply did not.

The massive gates of Woodlawn opened to receive them once again. This time the line of cars stretched back to Jerome Avenue.

David took his place at the head of the coffin. As he and his fellow pallbearers hefted the coffin and began the slow, uphill walk, the family close behind and everyone else trailing after them, his thoughts were not on this Joseph, who'd had the tremendous good fortune to die when he was ready, but on Jed, the Joseph Edward Gates who had died too soon. As they came abreast of the Gates monument and grave sites, David glimpsed something at the periphery of his vision. He turned his head. A bouquet of flowers lay on Jed's grave. Blue hyacinths; lavender blue, the color of Jed's eyes. David's throat tightened and he wished more than anything that Lucy were beside him. Fresh flowers, left today by someone who had come and perhaps already gone. Or perhaps not. David turned his head farther so that he could look back across Pine Avenue. There, under a tree. A good-looking dark-haired young man standing by a bicycle. No hat, no jacket, inexpensive clothes. Seen from this distance, he could have been David stepping off the boat from France ten years before.

David and Tony looked at each other across the meaningless space between them. David thought he might choke from sadness and remorse. Jed had been loved. He was loved still. Even if it had been for too brief a time, he had found what he needed. David's heart grew lighter; he knew he would have wanted that for Jed, no matter what else he doubted. David let the weight of the coffin rest on his shoulder and raised a hand, palm out, in silent greeting. After a moment's hesitation, Tony's mouth turned up and he lifted one hand in response. Then he mounted his bicycle and rode off. As David helped lower Joseph's coffin into the deeply dug grave, redolent with the life-sustaining smell of moisture and newly turned earth, he was smiling.

HIDDEN
by VICTORIA LUSTBADER

ABOUT THE AUTHOR

Victoria Lustbader was for many years a fiction editor at Harper & Row and The Putnam Publishing Group. Following that, she enjoyed a second career with The Nature Conservancy on Long Island and New York State. She is now a full-time writer, living in New York City and on Long Island, and is married to novelist Eric Van Lustbader. *Hidden* is Victoria Lustbader's first novel.

ABOUT THE BOOK

Both panoramic and intimate, *Hidden* marvelously recreates New York City in the 1920s, from the hustle and bustle of the Lower East Side to the hushed hallways of the homes of the rich and powerful. And it is here, concealing their passions and innermost thoughts even from those they love most dearly, that the Warshinskys and Gateses love, lust, seize power, do battle, and strive to rule themselves and their city during a decade of turmoil at home and abroad.

The battlefield traumas of the Great War cement an improbable friendship between Jed Gates, scion of the wealthy Gates family, and David Warshinsky, first-generation American from New York's poverty-ridden Lower East Side. David sacrifices his family and his Jewish heritage in pursuit of his untamable ambition while in eerie parallel, Jed sacrifices his private desires to assume the burdens of familial expectations.

Brilliantly evoking time, place, and person, *Hidden*

draws readers deep into the past to illuminate the present. For nothing is more eternal than human feeling, and nothing more important to the human heart.

QUESTIONS FOR DISCUSSION

1. *Hidden* begins and ends with David Warshinsky/Shaw, the character who most obviously hides in plain sight, living an entirely new life only blocks from his estranged family. Jed and Zoe also harbor secrets around which their lives are structured. Who do you think is the most "hidden" in this story? What secrets do other members of the families hide, and what, if anything, ultimately reveals those truths? Is it a relief or a catastrophe when that happens?

2. The family relationships in *Hidden* are rife with reversal of the relationships between parents and children, as seen in Libby's desire to protect her mother from her father's violence. What are the boundaries between parents and children in the Gates and Warshinsky families? Do you think that the qualities of these relationships are primarily a function of the era in which the book takes place, or are they more determined by the personalities of the characters? What obligations do you think children have to their parents, realistically? Who in *Hidden* fulfills some or most of those obligations, and what cost, if any, does that person pay?

3. Sexuality and sexual desire play an enormous role in the lives of most of the adult characters in *Hidden*, sometimes with disastrous results. How does sex influence the choices that these characters make? What are the forms their urges take, and what are the different ways they find to express, tame, or otherwise cope with them? Do you think that sexuality exerts as powerful an influence on human behavior as it does in this story? How might these characters' struggles with sex and sexuality be different if the story took place today?

4. Monty seems to be the serpent in the garden of the wealthy and privileged Gates family. But does he have another role in the arc of the story? Is he a truth-teller? A foil for other characters' arrogance? How do you feel about the punishment that Joseph and David ultimately mete out to him? Is it sufficient to his crimes?

5. David vanishes from the world in which he grew up and transforms himself into a new person. Yet he never leaves the city of his birth and ultimately lives in splendor within walking distance of his discarded and impoverished past. What does this say about the stratification of New York in the 1920s? Does that stratification still exist in American cities and towns today? Where in the story do people of different classes and different cultures intersect? What happens when they do?

6. Redemption is a major theme in *Hidden*. Many characters look to other family members to save them from unhappiness or painful experiences, to redeem their terrible losses or shattered dreams. Which characters seek redemption, and to whom do they look for it? Are human beings ultimately responsible for their own happiness? What responsibilities do family members have in securing happiness for one another?

7. David and Jed are best friends, devoted to one another as to no one else. What binds them? How much of that bond is honest and altruistic and how much unacknowledged or selfish? How do you think the love between friends differs from the love between family members or partners? Despite their devotion, David and Jed ultimately cannot help one another deal with the most difficult issues in their lives. Why not? What are the responsibilities of friendship? What do you believe would have happened to this friendship if David had learned the truth about Jed while Jed was still alive?

8. How are different religions portrayed in *Hidden*? Are Judaism, Christianity, and Christian Science helpful and strengthening to the characters who practice them, or are they oppressive or misleading? Does anyone disavow religion and, if so, why? Does religion function differently for the Gateses than for the Warshinskys? Are the various religions in the story portrayed in sufficient depth to allow you to understand their beliefs and precepts? Anti-Semitism is a subtext throughout the book. At what points does it come to the forefront of the story, and who displays it? What sort of a Jewish life, if any, do you think David will go on to have after the story's end?

9. David's presence in the Gates family creates, as the author says, enormous ripples of consequence. How does David influence the lives of various family members? What roles does he play within the Gates family? Do you think that he, more than other characters, is a catalyst for change? What do you think would have happened to the Gateses if David had not become part of their lives? Do members of the Gates family find him easier to relate to precisely because he isn't a blood relative, and does David feel the same way about them? Which characters in the story do you think are most truly kin?

10. Family expectations play a huge part in how both the Gateses and the Warshinskys raise their children. Do you think that parents' expectations can be helpful in guiding children? Are they ever helpful in *Hidden*? Who flouts family expectations most consistently, and, conversely, who suffers the most from the burden of those expectations? How do expectations differ in the two families, based on socioeconomic class, culture, and religion?

11. *Hidden* takes place at the dawn of feminism. Which female characters are feminists? In what ways do the women in the story try to obtain and assert power? Does their ability to do so change due to the burgeoning of the women's movement during the years in which the book takes place? How do you think that these women's lives would be different if they lived decades later? How many of the issues faced by the women in the story are still faced by women today?

12. Though the book is filled with highly emotional characters and situations, the value of emotions is constantly in question in *Hidden*. What role does emotion play in the Warshinskys' family and community, and how does it differ for the Gateses? Who suppresses emotion most vigilantly, and why? Typically, women are said to be more in touch with and guided by emotional life than men are. Is this true in this book? Does class play a part in determining whether displaying or even feeling emotion is a virtue or a weakness? Which of the book's many emotional moments do you find most affecting?

13. *Hidden* seems to wrangle with the character of Joseph Gates. Is he an admirable and decisive leader and mentor or a rigid, hidebound dictator with unflinching expectations of his family? Or is he both? How much esteem do you think he deserves, and why? Toward the end of the book, we discover that Joseph believes his grandson did the right thing by committing suicide to avoid disgracing the family with the revelation of his homosexuality. How does this affect your opinion of Joseph? What qualities set Joseph apart as a leader, and how do those qualities color his family life? How is David—the heir Joseph believes is most like him and best able to continue his leadership—similar to Joseph, and how is he different?